Now, God Be Thanked

Now, God Be Thanked

a novel by

John Masters

McGRAW-HILL BOOK COMPANY

New York   St. Louis   San Francisco
Düsseldorf   Mexico   Toronto

This book is the first volume of a trilogy entitled

LOSS OF EDEN

It is complete in itself, as will be the other two. Each volume is, or will be, wholly a work of fiction, in which no reference is intended to any person living or dead, except that many historical characters are mentioned, and some occasionally appear on the scene.

J. M.

A limited edition of this book
has been privately printed.

To the victims of the Great War,
among whom were
the survivors

PEACE

Now, God be thanked Who has matched us with His hour,
 And caught our youth, and wakened us from sleeping,
With hand made sure, clear eye, and sharpened power,
 To turn, as swimmers into cleanness leaping,
Glad from a world grown old and cold and weary,
 Leave the sick hearts that honour could not move,
And half-men, and their dirty songs and dreary,
 And all the little emptiness of love!

Oh! we, who have known shame, we have found release there,
 Where there's no ill, no grief, but sleep has mending,
 Naught broken save this body, lost but breath;
Nothing to shake the laughing heart's long peace there
 But only agony, and that has ending;
 And the worst friend and enemy is but Death.

Rupert Brooke (1914)

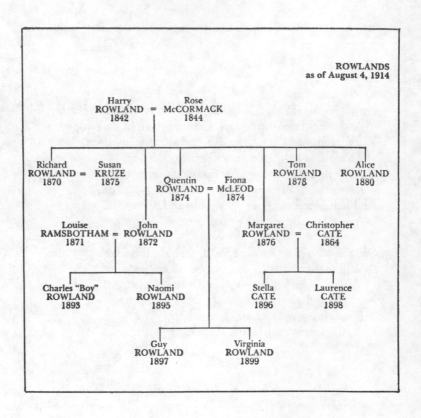

ROWLANDS
as of August 4, 1914

Harry ROWLAND 1842 = Rose McCORMACK 1844

Richard ROWLAND 1870 = Susan KRUZE 1875

Quentin ROWLAND 1874 = Fiona McLEOD 1874

Tom ROWLAND 1878

Alice ROWLAND 1880

Louise RAMSBOTHAM 1871 = John ROWLAND 1872

Margaret ROWLAND 1876 = Christopher CATE 1864

Charles "Boy" ROWLAND 1893

Naomi ROWLAND 1895

Stella CATE 1896

Laurence CATE 1898

Guy ROWLAND 1897

Virginia ROWLAND 1899

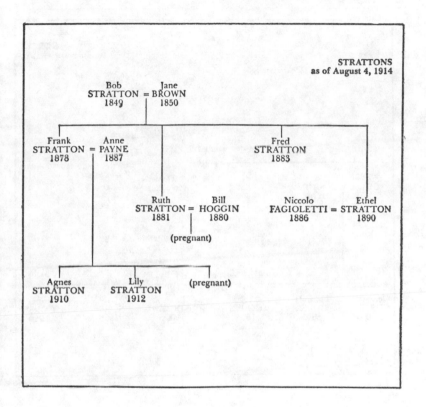

STRATTONS
as of August 4, 1914

Bob STRATTON 1849 = Jane BROWN 1850

Frank STRATTON 1878 = Anne PAYNE 1887

Fred STRATTON 1883

Ruth STRATTON 1881 = Bill HOGGIN 1880

(pregnant)

Niccolo FAGIOLETTI 1886 = Ethel STRATTON 1890

Agnes STRATTON 1910

Lily STRATTON 1912

(pregnant)

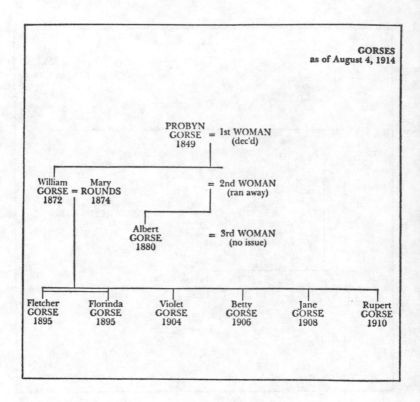

GORSES
as of August 4, 1914

PROBYN
GORSE   = 1st WOMAN
1849   (dec'd)

William   Mary
GORSE   = ROUNDS   = 2nd WOMAN
1872   1874   (ran away)

                    Albert
                    GORSE   = 3rd WOMAN
                    1880   (no issue)

Fletcher   Florinda   Violet   Betty   Jane   Rupert
GORSE   GORSE   GORSE   GORSE   GORSE   GORSE
1895   1895   1904   1906   1908   1910

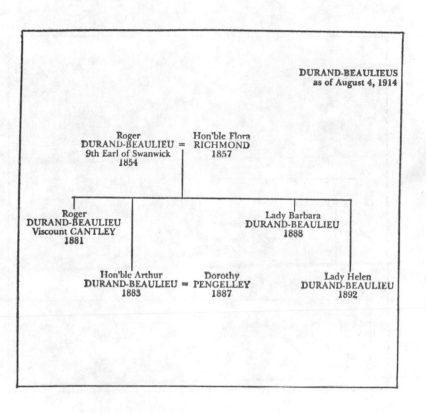

DURAND-BEAULIEUS
as of August 4, 1914

Roger
DURAND-BEAULIEU = Hon'ble Flora
9th Earl of Swanwick   RICHMOND
1854   1857

Roger
DURAND-BEAULIEU
Viscount CANTLEY
1881

Lady Barbara
DURAND-BEAULIEU
1888

Hon'ble Arthur
DURAND-BEAULIEU = Dorothy
1883   PENGELLEY
                  1887

Lady Helen
DURAND-BEAULIEU
1892

Saturday, July 4, 1914

1 As the arc of dawn passes over the steppes of Russian Asia it moves swiftly westward to pour its warmth on a royal and long-established continent—Europe. The sun lightens dark forests of pines, so carefully tended that no fallen branch litters the ground; it sweeps over sandy wastes preserved for hunting birds and beasts; and warms rich soil carefully tilled by husbandmen who had lived in the same cottages, serving the same lords, for centuries; and it illumines smoking factories that speak of vast new wealth and power. Mountains divide this nation from that; but the shining railway lines break through these barriers from the Urals to the Atlantic, to link German factory and Italian vineyard, Dutch port and French Alp, Belgian city and Norwegian meadow. Only England stands apart, aloof behind the grey Channel . . . of Europe but not in it.

The land of Europe is deeply shaped by the industriousness of man, and decorated by the creations of his spirit: cathedrals, aqueducts, bridges, statues, hospitals, museums, ripening wheat, darkening grapes on ordered vines. The men and women who populate it speak a score of languages, but for nearly two thousand years they have shared one history, one religion, one tradition of music, one ideal of beauty. There are sixteen kings, but only three republics—Switzerland, France, and (since 1910) Portugal. Poland, Finland, Lithuania, Latvia, Estonia, Czechoslovakia, and Yugoslavia do not exist: some have been dismembered in past wars, some will be created by a war that many feel must soon come.

Though small in area, Europe draws to it the eyes of the earth, for as in centuries past it proclaims itself the axis of the world, the home of civilisation, the seat of power. In Chancery and Palace, Embassy and Court, men, in golden epaulettes or frock coats, crested helmets or silk hats talk of *'Lebensraum,'* 'spheres of influence,' 'buffer states,' 'national interest,' 'balance of power,' 'a place in the sun,' *'Drang nach Osten,'* *'revanche,'* 'two-power doctrine,' 'interior lines.' Only a divine being could untangle the numberless webs of conflicting desires, fears, and greeds hidden in the webs of oratory; but an intelligent man or woman, and there are many, can see that three sets of opposing forces have created tensions of almost unmanageable proportions. First is the struggle for control of Eastern Europe, pitting Germany and Austria, as the Teuton powers, against Russia, as the protector of all Slavs. Second is the thrust of Germany to escape from its geographical encirclement by creating colonies in Africa and Oceania—a policy which can survive only under the protection of sea power—a sea power which, by becoming reality, must threaten Great Britain. Third is France's burning desire for revenge for her defeat by Germany in 1870, and the recovery of the two provinces then seized from her, a desire countered by Germany's own determination to hold what she has won and, if opportunity offers, to destroy for ever France's power to hinder her grand designs.

All European nations have standing armies; and nearly all have a system of conscription under which all able-bodied young men serve a year or two with the Colours before entering civilian life where they become the reservists who can, within a couple of weeks, by the process of mobilisation, convert the standing armies into nations in arms. From a careful planner's point of view, the best time to mobilise is after the harvest is in and large numbers of men are freed from the land . . . to fight. Railways and modern roads give armies the ability to wage autumn and winter campaigns so that a war can be launched in, say, August, and ended, at the latest, by March—in time to release the men back to the land for spring sowing.

On June 28th, 1914, in the powder keg of Eastern Europe, a Serb schoolboy shot and killed the visiting Archduke Franz Ferdinand, heir presumptive to the Austrian throne. For a time no one seems to notice that the event touches all the tensions needed to produce a great crisis—it pits Austria (which will be backed by Germany) against Serbia (which will be backed by Russia); it enables France to consider seeking her *revanche* while Germany is engaged to the east; it enables England to consider destroying the naval threat against her by acting in concert with France and Russia, rather than alone; and it happens when, after due time has been spent in negotiating, the harvest will be in.

In England, for some weeks, the assassination is not considered an event of great importance. On Saturday, July 4th, 1914, in that island kingdom, the heart of the largest empire the world has yet known, protected by the Channel and a mighty battle fleet, the brilliant 'season' is in full swing. The Derby has been run (and won by Durbar II); the Birthday Parade held at Horse Guards (the Colour trooped was that of the 1st Battalion, the Grenadier Guards); the finals of the Men's and Women's Singles are in progress at Wimbledon. The nation's attention is focused on its beaches, playing fields, and rivers—and in particular on the Thames, and the small riverside town of Henley. It is the last day of Henley Royal Regatta.

The Thames here is three hundred feet wide, flowing evenly under the town bridge toward tidewater, London, and the North Sea. The water is twelve feet deep, not diamond clear, but a sheened translucent green, full of swirling weeds, for the river is born in no mountains, but in the honey rock of the Cotswolds, and in its course has already flowed a hundred miles through farm land scored by the ploughing of centuries, under bridges that have heard the creak of Saxon cart wheels, over fords, once stained with the blood of the Legions. Water meadows and woodland copses line both banks, backed, on the right, by the rising Berkshire hills. On that side, also, stand the clustered buildings of Remenham Farm and Rectory. At Henley Bridge and town, the left bank is in Oxfordshire, but half a mile downstream, nearly opposite Remenham, it passes into Buckinghamshire. The river is unobstructed and nearly straight for that mile and a half; except that near the lower limit an island—Temple Island, decorated by a little Palladian temple of marble—divides the river into two channels.

From a point just below Temple Island to a point below Henley Bridge, upstream, is the Henley course, the water and the distance—1 mile 550 yards—over which all the races of the Regatta are rowed, and have been, with minor modifications, since 1839. The Regatta is held every year at the end of June and the beginning of July, and until recent years ended on a Saturday with the finals of all the events, including the most important, the Grand Challenge Cup, a race for eight-oared boats open to amateur oarsmen from all countries.

The boomed channel is 150 feet wide. Since the oars of a racing eight make eighteen-foot sweeps on either side, two crews abreast take up seventy-two feet of water. At Henley this leaves ample room for manoeuvre—but not for another boat; so all races here are match races. Between the booms and the bank, especially near the finish, mass the canoes and rowing boats and punts of the spectators, so dense that the water can scarcely be seen between them, only the coloured parasols, the women's long pastel dresses, the men's white flannels, coloured blazers and straw hat ribbons. On the banks there are stands for more spectators; and the house that is home of Leander Club, and the marquees for the Stewards, and for the shells, and tall wooden boxes on stilts above the booms, from where the races are judged; and the lawns and rambling buildings and giant trees of Phyllis Court; and the narrow towpath on the Berkshire bank, alive with coaches riding bicycles or horses, and young men running and shouting encouragement to the crews representing their school or college or club.

This day, in 1914, the final of the Grand was to be between Harvard University and the Union Boat Club of Boston. The start was set for 4.15 p.m. Preceding the Grand was the final of the Diamond Challenge Sculls, between Giuseppe Sinigaglia of Italy, and Colin Stuart of Cambridge; and before the Diamonds was the Ladies' Plate, between two Cambridge boats—Pembroke, and First Trinity.

Guy Rowland resettled his left arm more comfortably in the sling and winced as pain stabbed up from the wrist. It wasn't his bowling arm, but even so he wouldn't be able to bowl next Saturday, as he had hoped, and as Quack had half promised. Well, no good crying about it. There'd be other sunny Saturdays, other batsmen to face and outwit. He yawned slightly, and stretched his shoulders. Shouldn't have eaten so much cold salmon at lunch; or had that second glass of white wine.

"Tired, Guy?" the man next to him said, smiling.

"No, Uncle," he answered. "A little sleepy, that's all."

Beyond his uncle a fair-haired sturdy boy of his own age—seventeen —cupped his hands and shouted across to the nearer racing shell, "Go it, Charlie! You'll beat 'em."

No. 5 in the First Trinity boat, its stern held at the start line, raised one hand off his oar in acknowledgement and then settled down as he saw the umpire put his megaphone to his mouth in the motor launch *Enchantress,* its screw churning slowly to hold it in place against the current.

The fair-haired boy cupped his hands to shout again, but another, slightly younger boy in the group muttered audibly, "Silence in the pig market . . ."

Dick Yeoman looked round, frowning; but Guy said, "You'd better be quiet, Dick. They'll be off any moment."

The umpire shouted, "Are you ready? . . . go!" The maroon banged deafeningly, the men in the punts let go of the stern posts, the crews bent to their oars. Water splashed as oars dug deep, riggers and stretchers creaked, rowlocks rumbled, greased slides trundled under straining bodies, coxswains' voices rose in urgent cadence "Oo-one . . . two-oo . . . three-ee . . . !", spectators shouted and cheered. Dick Yeoman began running up the towpath toward the distant tower of Henley Church, yelling, "Trinity! Trinity!"

The boats disappeared behind Temple Island, and the younger boy called to the lone girl in the group, "Come on, Stella, do you good to run."

Stella Cate pouted and waved a hand. "Too hot—besides, I don't have a brother in the race, like Dick. I don't care who wins."

"But you think the Pembroke stroke is very handsome, don't you? You're sweet on him, aren't you, sis?"

"Don't be ridiculous, Laurence. I haven't spoken a word to him. I've never seen him before. And which is stroke?"

"Liar! You . . ."

"Now, now," Tom Rowland said, "let's walk up at a gentlemanly—and ladylike—pace, watch the finish of the Diamonds, perhaps, and then come back here for the Grand."

"Jolly good idea, Uncle," Guy said, slowing his pace. One good thing about rowing was that it usually took place in pleasant surroundings, he thought; but then, so did cricket. And rowing didn't have much finesse: either you were faster than the other fellows, or you weren't . . . His Uncle Tom was striding after Dick Yeoman, several yards ahead. His cousin Stella fell in beside him, a picture of loveliness in a pale green organdie dress and wide-brimmed, flowered straw hat. The crews were far ahead now, the barking of the coxswains growing fainter every moment. Guy slowed still more. The sun was hot, the breeze fresh, and like Stella he didn't really care who won. Besides, you needed to look where you were going, to avoid the swan droppings strewn thick along the towpath.

At the foot of the Phyllis Court lawn, on the Oxfordshire bank, overlooking the river by the wall, Richard Rowland sat in a striped deck chair, his wife Susan beside him on his right and his unmarried sister Alice Rowland on his left. He had been coming to Henley every year since he was a wetbob at Eton, and that was thirty years ago now. A pair of small tables was set before them with teapots, cucumber sandwiches, silver jugs of milk and hot water, cups, spoons, and sugar. Alice was pouring—Susan had been born Susan Kruze, of San Francisco, and no English lady could be persuaded that she knew how to pour tea. They were right, Richard thought, watching his wife put lemon in her tea, with no sugar; barbarous way to treat tea, he thought, though to be honest this wasn't Broken Orange Pekoe. He glanced across the river at the Leander lawn and the Stewards' private Enclosure—a sea of pink or blue rowing caps. He thought that the only pink cap not over there was the one on his own head, for he was a member of Leander, having rowed for Cambridge in his time.

Alice said, "Are you going to have a holiday before September, Richard? You'll be kept quite busy afterwards, will you not?"

He replied, "No, taking over the plant will be holiday enough. And I don't think I'll have to sit there, right on top of everything, for more than a year. By then I'll have made any changes I want, and be sure everything's in order and running the way I want it to. Then I'll take Susan off for a trip—to America, we think. She's been pressing me to go ever since we got married."

"I want to see my father and mother again," Susan said.

Richard took off his thick-lensed glasses and polished them. To him, now, the scene was no more than a tinted blur, as he said, "We'll go to San Francisco, of course, but I really want to see Mr Ford's factory at Detroit, and work out how we can apply his methods at Rowland's . . . if it's possible at all."

"Do you think the Governor will like that?" Alice said.

Richard replied, "I've been waiting nineteen years for Father to retire, and when he does, I must do what I think best, for these days . . . not what he thought best, for those days. How is he, by the way?"

"Resting, with Mother. He thought he'd be down for tea, but he obviously isn't. That was quite a nasty shock for both of them, especially Mother."

"Being thrown out of a cab can be serious for anyone, let alone people of their age."

"They'll be down for the Ball tonight, even if only for an hour or two. Neither of them would miss that for anything . . . Here are the crews!"

Richard jumped to his feet, putting on his glasses, and shouting, "Trinity! Trinity!"

The two shells came on fast, the rhythms of the plunging oars and bow-stringed bodies hypnotic in their strength and speed. The scattered shouts fused into a low roar. The bows flashed by and Richard sank back, a disgusted look on his face. He took off his glasses and polished them crossly. "Pembroke by two and a half lengths. Well, better luck next year . . . where are the others? Tom and the boys went down to the start with Stella, I know, but where are Margaret and Fiona?"

His sister answered, "They had lunch in Leander with Cantley and Arthur, but that should have been over long since. Shall I go and find them? It would be nice if we could all watch the Grand together, and the crews will be going down any time now. I hear they are both very fast. It ought to be a good race."

"If some beastly suffragette doesn't jump into the river in front of them, the way that woman ran out onto the Derby course last year," Richard said. "Downing the King's horse! Women who'd do that are a disgrace to the country."

"That poor woman is also dead," Alice said gently.

Richard muttered, "And no British crew in the final of the Grand, for the first time in history! That's a real disgrace."

Susan looked at her Regatta programme and said, "The Diamonds come before the Grand. The Italian is a giant of a man. Did you see him?"

Alice said, "No, but . . . look, there are the boys, below the Stewards' Enclosure. See?"

Richard put his binoculars to his eyes and stared across the river. The two Grand finalist crews were paddling slowly past. The grassy Berkshire bank was hidden under the feet of thousands of milling spectators brought out by today's perfect weather, even more enticing after yesterday's all-day drizzle. The punts were jammed together along the Oxfordshire bank, mostly containing just one languid young woman and one young man, but sometimes crowded with larger parties . . . A face he recognised sprang into prominence: that school friend of Guy's, Dick Yeoman, disappointment clear on his face. Of course, his brother had been in the losing Trinity boat just now. Tom was there, putting a hand on the boy's shoulder, smiling, consoling; Laurence Cate, hanging close to Guy, looking up at the older boy, eager hero worship as clear in his face as disappointment in young Yeoman's . . . Stella on Guy's other side . . . Guy smiling at something, readjusting his sling; then, somehow, in all the crowd, catching sight of him, his uncle, across the river and cheerily waving his free hand.

Richard waved back and said, "Some of them are over there."

"Signal to them to come across for tea," Alice said.

Richard lowered the binoculars, made motions of raising a teacup, beckoned, and raised the binoculars again. The boys and Stella stopped, all staring. Then Guy signalled back, pointing down river back to the start, and making motions of rowing, then of running. Richard said, "I think he's saying that they're going down to watch the Grand. Yes, they're waving . . . all going down."

"Even Stella? She doesn't like missing her tea."

"All of them. Naomi and Rachel Cowan have just joined them, heaven knows where from."

"They were with friends somewhere . . . in Leander, I think."

"We must keep some tea and sandwiches for all of them," Richard said; and "Yes, Richard," his sister answered; and then, "I must go and find Margaret and Fiona."

The two women, both close to forty years of age, who strolled together off Leander Club lawn seemed to embody the races from which they were sprung. Although, through the centuries, there had been many intermarriages, in these two the genes of Black Celt and Red Celt had run separately true. Margaret Cate (née Rowland), descended through her mother, Rose Rowland (née McCormack), from Cormac, High King of Ireland, was of medium height, with shining thick black hair and deep blue eyes, a high nose and a strong-set big-bosomed body. By her side, an inch or two taller, Fiona Rowland (née McLeod) was long-faced, long-legged, and pale-haired, with a glint of red at the roots. Her still supple body moved with the half-tamed wildness of her clan's wild island, Skye. It was easy to believe that her eyes, grey as the island's mists, could see into the unknowable future. Margaret was wife to Christopher Cate, squire of Walstone, in the county of Kent, whose work with his tenants gave him no time to come to Henley. Fiona was wife to Quentin Rowland, Harry and Rose's third son, a major in the Weald Light Infantry, now stationed at the Curragh, Ireland.

Both women wore long skirts, Margaret's of blue to match her eyes, and Fiona's of pale green; and white blouses with frilled cuffs, and straw hats perched on the front of their hair; and they carried parasols, now folded and swinging in their hands, for something of the power was leaving the sun. They crossed over Henley Bridge and walked down the crowded waterfront on the Oxfordshire bank.

Fiona said, "It's not fair that anyone—let alone two brothers—should be born with so much as Roger Cantley and Arthur . . . titles, money, good looks, and good heavens, what brains! I can not understand why Cantley hasn't married long since."

"He prefers his paintings," Margaret said, "and, perhaps, his freedom . . . And I doubt whether they do have much money. Lord Swanwick tries to keep his financial affairs private, but everything can not be hidden from the servants, who gossip in the village—and the villagers tell Christopher. He knows more than he will tell anyone."

"Even you?"

Margaret laughed, and the laugh was not quite bitter, nor was it light, and certainly not joyful; let us say it was slightly abrasive. She said, "Especially not me. I do not tell Christopher anything of what I do in Ireland, where *my* duty is. So why should he tell me anything about his village, where *his* duty is?"

"But you are husband and wife! Does not that make a difference?"

"We have not been husband and wife since seven months before Laurence was born." She turned suddenly, and looked her sister-in-law straight in the eye—"Nor you and Quentin, I think."

Fiona looked down, avoiding the deep eyes. At length she said, "Not as long as that . . . but yes, you're right."

"I know what I'm fighting for, and I decided long ago that my marriage was nothing compared to it. What have *you* decided?" Then, before Fiona could answer, she said, "There's Alice, coming to look for us. Where are the girls? We're supposed to be in charge of them."

"I don't think anything can happen to them at Henley in broad daylight," Fiona answered, privately excluding Stella, Margaret's daughter, from the remark: Stella Cate was eighteen and gave the impression that something would happen to her if there were any men around, whatever the time, or place, or circumstances. Fiona was sure Stella was still physically untouched, as indeed she should be at her age and class, but for how long would that last? She said, "They said they were going down to the start, to meet Tom and the boys there."

Then Alice Rowland came up, and Margaret said, "Here we are, in good order. Arthur asked us to stay for tea, but we knew the Governor would want us with the family. He always has, hasn't he? Or are they still resting?"

"Yes," Alice said and, turning, walked slowly with them down the street, into the Phyllis Court drive, and at last onto the lawn, to join Richard and Susan.

Johnny Merritt paused to watch the racing scullers pass. The man on the near side was huge: that must be the Italian, Sinigaglia, who seemed to have a good fifty pounds weight advantage over Stuart, the British sculler. Sinigaglia was two lengths back here, about a quarter of a mile after the start. He was having trouble steering . . . going dangerously close to the piles now . . . but with that weight and power, and a good action, he'd be a hard man to beat.

The scullers diminished up the gleaming water, and Johnny strolled on toward Temple Island, hands in pockets, humming under his breath. This was the last day of Henley and he was trying to make time move more slowly. Now he almost dreaded the moment he and his father had come three thousand miles to witness—Harvard's hoped-for triumph in the Grand Challenge Cup; because, after all the yelling and the backslapping and the throwing of the cox into the river, it would mean . . . it's over. For him, not only Henley, but Harvard—over, finished. He was a senior.

He was wearing white shoes, white flannel trousers, a crimson blazer with the Harvard crest on the pocket, and a straw hat with the crimson silk Harvard band. He walked with a slight limp, favouring his left ankle. The towpath was crowded, though less so here than near the finish. Immediately in front of him was a large group which appeared to be all of one family—three youths, three young women, and a man in his late thirties with a sun- and wind-burned face, thick black hair, and a jovial manner, for as he walked he kept turning and talking animatedly to the others. The youth on the man's right carried his left arm in a sling and Johnny wondered idly whether he was in the same boat as himself; or, to be more precise, out of the same boat. Johnny had badly sprained his left ankle a week ago, and had had to give up his place as No. 3 in the Harvard boat; but by then they were already in England, and his father had readily agreed that they should stay at least through the Regatta. Perhaps the tall boy with the sling was in one of the British college crews, and had suffered a similar misfortune, and was unable to take his place in the boat; but he hardly looked more than seventeen, too young to be at a university.

Close in front of him, one of the three young women said, "What's the use of rushing so, Naomi? We can't possibly keep pace with the boats when they do start, so why don't we just stop here? And sit down?"

The tall girl in the middle snapped, "I could keep pace with them, Stella—very nearly—if I could wear trousers, like the men." Johnny thought she must be five foot ten or more, and about nineteen, though she gave the impression as she strode along that she was not yet quite fully formed as a woman. Her movements were a little awkward, like a fifteen-year-old's, and her flesh not rounded, but still angular. She added, "Even Mr Lippincott couldn't keep up with a one-legged man, if he had to wear these skirts . . . Anyway, we said we'd go down to the start with Guy, so we'll do it . . . this year."

Johnny listened idly. The girl on the right, the one who had spoken first, her head now half turned, was a knockout—a bit younger than the tall one, perhaps, but more womanly, rounded, big-bosomed, walking gracefully, the moving skirt showing rather than hiding the curves of her haunches. She said now, "What do you mean, 'this year,' Naomi?"

"This year we'll let them have their silly Regatta. Next year, we'll bore holes in the boats."

"Naomi!"

"If they haven't given women the vote by then."

"You wouldn't!"

"Why not? I was in the window smashing last year . . ."

"You never told me!"

"You never asked. Nor did Daddy or Mummy. They'd never dream I'd do such a thing . . . Guy, Uncle Tom, wait a minute! We can't keep up."

Then the young men stopped, and they all gathered together, the lovely girl fanning her face with a programme, as Johnny walked past. He glanced at the youth with the sling and, a long moment later, pulled his gaze away with a start, realising that his passing glance had become a stare: for the boy, about his own height of six feet, but slimmer, had one bright blue eye—his right, and one soft deep brown—his left. He caught Johnny's stare and held it a moment. His smile was downturned and quizzical, as he turned away. As Johnny passed on, the third youth, the youngest of them, cried, "Look, Guy! A sedge warbler!" and the boy with the sling turned, asking, "Where, Laurence?"

"There, in the reeds, with the creamy eye stripe . . . *Acrocephalus schoenobaenus!*"

"What a mouthful!"

Johnny walked faster, thinking of the British family. Guy something, with one blue eye and one brown; and Laurence, about fifteen, a birdwatcher, or probably he'd call himself an ornithologist; and Uncle Tom, who worked outdoors, with that complexion; and Naomi, the tall girl with the small high breasts—one of these wild suffragettes; and a small young woman who hadn't opened her mouth and looked Jewish, not one of the family; and the lovely one, Stella. Stella what? Sister of Guy? Or Laurence? Cousin?

It was quiet at the start—a tethered horse, bicycles lying in the buttercups, bees droning in the long grass, a large horse-chestnut tree set back from the river, people sprawled in its shade. He went over and sat down at the edge of the shade, his hands clasped round his knees. This, too, was Henley, but a world removed from the bustle of the Regatta— the town bridge, crowded with watchers, groaning with traffic, klaxons bleating, horses neighing, wheels crunching: at Phyllis Court, marquees and spread awnings, sandwiches and chairs and tea and chatter; everywhere bustle, coaches and crews, shouldered boats, cries, warnings . . . Here, the Grand crews were slowly turning their boats. The umpire's launch *Enchantress* was coming back down the course, its engine thudding, the only intrusive sound here under the chestnut tree, under the pale sky dotted with wool-fleeced clouds. A blackbird chortled near the river's edge and a pair of ducks winged fast overhead, circling, looking, heading on upstream. He closed his eyes, and hoped that the singing of the blackbird, and the lap of the Thames, would soothe his sense of impending loss.

Five minutes later he opened his eyes a little as the group of young people he had passed on the towpath arrived, and settled on the grass nearby. The older man, Uncle Tom, looked at his wrist watch and said, "Five past. Ten minutes to go."

Stella said, "They look ready."

Guy said, "They may not be ready up at the finish. Anyway, they won't start before the proper time—four-fifteen." His straw hat was tilted well forward, hiding his eyes. Its ribbon was pale blue and yellow. Johnny wished he could join them, to talk to the lovely Stella with the bee-stung lips and peaches-and-cream complexion; and because he was curious, to find out what Uncle Tom did for a living, and . . .

Guy said, "Did I hear you say something about window smashing, while we were walking down, Naomi?"

The tall girl said, "You did, and we'll do worse next year, if we don't get the vote."

"But everyone knows women are mentally incompetent. They have tiny brains, to make up for their big behinds, and . . ."

Naomi shook her fist at him, "One day we'll get the vote, and then we'll know what to do with men like you, Guy. We'll form women's unions, and . . ."

Guy interrupted—"Hide behind trees in overwhelming numbers, jump out, and . . . what? Debag us? Dear, dear!"

"Don't be disgusting!" She was smiling; and caught Johnny's eye. Was she staring at him? Did they think he was eavesdropping on their family talk? He got up, walked to the bank, cupped his hands and shouted, "Good luck, Meyer . . . wish I were on that oar."

The Harvard No. 3 acknowledged the call with a grin and a wave. Johnny cried, "Let 'em have it, Leverett . . . row 'em out of the water, Charlie—"

Then the umpire put his megaphone to his mouth and the coxswains shouted together, "Eyes in!," and Johnny started up the towpath. The family were close in front of him, walking easily. Perhaps he'd get a chance to introduce himself, though the British were usually pretty stuffy.

Naomi Rowland turned to her uncle, and said, "Who is this race between? I only come to Henley because Grandpa insists, and Daddy and

Uncle Richard want me to see them in their Leander caps and blazers once a year."

Commander Tom Rowland, R.N., answered, "The Union Boat Club of Boston, and Harvard University . . . though I think they call themselves the Harvard Athletic Association Boat Club, or something like that, officially."

His nephew Guy said in a needling tone, "Boston is a city where they threw perfectly good tea into the harbour because they didn't like King George III, which seems a peculiar way of showing dislike . . . but what *is* Harvard?"

The breeze had momentarily died; the sound of their feet was deadened in the trodden earth of the towpath; and the river was silent. Guy's remark hung loud in the air, the question mark at the end almost visible in the thick summer light.

An American voice from close behind them said tartly, "Harvard is the oldest university in America, sir, and the best university in the world, bar none."

The Rowland party turned. The speaker was the young man whom the boys had seen earlier, limping fast to the start. He was about six feet, powerfully built with dark brown hair and grey eyes, and big hands and feet. His face was red and his mouth, when he had finished speaking, shut firm; but Naomi suspected, from a look in his eye, that he was not as put out as he wished them to think.

Guy said politely, "What about Lima, Mr —."

"Merritt," the other answered. "I meant, in the United States."

"Ah!" They all walked on together now. Guy said, "But if Harvard is so good, and I'm sure it is, why does one not hear more about it?"

Johnny Merritt said, "Because the English newspapers are like the *Mechanicsville Gazette* . . . if it doesn't happen in England, it doesn't happen. You're so sure you have the best of everything that you don't bother to find out what other people are doing. One day, you'll be in for an unpleasant surprise, my father says, when you find that others have improved their manufactures, their ships, their tools, to beat yours."

"Surely not the ships," Tom said, smiling. "Britannia rules the waves, eh?"

"I think the song says 'rule,' subjunctive—not 'rules,' indicative, sir," Johnny Merritt said. "And Britannia doesn't. Who holds the clipper ship record?"

"*Cutty Sark,* isn't it?" Stella Cate said, blushing.

"No, miss. It's *Flying Cloud,* designed by Donald McKay of East Boston, Massachusetts." He kept his eyes on Stella now, and Naomi thought, ah, it was just as she had suspected; his intrusion was not solely out of pique. Stella's eyes were wide, her lips parted in excitement and interest, her whole attention focused on the young American. Heavens, she looks gorgeous, Naomi thought—and she really doesn't know it.

Johnny said, "I must apologize. I had no right to butt into your conversation."

Glancing over her shoulder, Naomi saw that men were mounting bicycles, and the coach on horseback gathering his reins. Tom cried, "It's perfectly all right! We should have known about Harvard, and I'm sure my nephew does know more than he pretends. Never take Guy at his face value, Mr Merritt. I'm Tom Rowland. Allow me to introduce you to my nieces—Miss Naomi Rowland, and Miss Stella Cate . . . Miss Rachel Cowan—she's a friend of Naomi's at Girton—a college for women at Cambridge."

"It's just a little place in the fens," Guy said *sotto voce*, "nothing much to look at, but—"

Johnny shot him a sharp look, then started laughing. "You don't catch me again, Guy."

The dark girl said, "I'm at Girton on a Draper's Company Scholarship." Her accent was quite different from the others'.

Tom finished the introductions: "My nephew, Laurence Cate. Guy's friend from school, Dick Yeoman. The young men have been allowed a weekend *exeat* from their public schools."

"Which in England means private. I know," Johnny said.

"Guy and Dick are at Wellington, and Laurence is at Charterhouse."

From downstream the bang of the maroon reached them. Laurence cried, "They've started!"

They all walked faster. Johnny said, "Harvard's on the far side, in the crimson singlets . . . Harvard! Harvard!" he yelled, though the crews were still much too far away to hear him.

"I'll shout for Boston," the dark girl said. "Harvard's a bastion of privilege . . . Boston! Boston!" her treble rang out. She began to run, holding up her skirt.

Johnny said to Tom, as he too broke into a limping run, "I'm the regular No. 3 in our boat, sir . . . sprained my ankle."

"And Guy sprained his wrist or he wouldn't be here. He'd be playing cricket for Wellington . . . Harvard, Harvard!"

"We're striking about thirty-six, Boston thirty-nine," Johnny muttered, stopping and peering back, his hand shading his eyes. "Our boat's very smooth in the water . . . Boston's got a canvas in front, I think."

They ran on. Suddenly Stella stumbled and fell headlong, revealing her legs up to white-stockinged knees. Johnny Merritt was down beside her in a flash. "Are you hurt? Are you all right?"

She sat up, the big eyes wide, lashes fluttering—"Oh, thank you." Her hands pushed down the skirt, the colour coming and going in her cheeks. Naomi watched in amused annoyance; once, she had been sure that all Stella's reactions in such circumstances were carefully calculated, and practised, to attract the opposite sex. Slowly, unwillingly, she had come to believe that Stella could not help herself. Everything that happened to her, everything that she did in relation to men, was without her volition or intent.

Johnny helped her to her feet. She dusted herself down. The boats came on fast. Johnny yelled, "See you at the finish line!" and ran limping on as fast he could, screaming "Harvard, Harvard!"

The racing boats came. Harvard was still striking slower than Boston, but rowing a longer stroke, catching the water farther behind the riggers. The long bows needled past, level. The hunched bodies coiled, uncoiled, the blades made sixteen circles in the river. For a moment there was no sound but the splash of the oars, the creak and slat of the slides, and the barked cadence of the coxswains. Then the coach trotted by on his horse, shouting, and bicycle bells trilled, and they all hurried forward, jostling on the narrow towpath, Johnny Merritt's figure flying ahead. The crews became smaller, until they seemed like mechanical water-boatmen toys.

Guy shouted, "Harvard's in front!" Then the men settled down to a steady trot, and a few minutes later came upon Johnny Merritt standing outside the Stewards' Enclosure, an ecstatic grin splitting his face. He spread his arms wide. "We won! Length and a quarter! They've already thrown Kreger into the river . . . we did it! We won the Grand!"

"Even without you," Guy said gravely.

Johnny said, "Even without me!" He stuck out his hand. "You've got your nerve for a . . . what are you? Senior? Junior?"

Guy said, "I'm seventeen and a bit."

Johnny said, "God help us all when you're twenty-one."

Then they all wrung Johnny's hand, and clapped his back, congratulating him on the victory; and the girls came up, panting, to congratulate him in their turn, even Rachel Cowan. Then Johnny said, "Excuse me . . . I'd like you to meet my father, and I sure would like to meet your people . . . but they're pulling Kreger out of the river, and I have to go for now. I'll look for you afterwards, when I find my father."

He turned to Stella. "Will you all be at the Phyllis Court Ball tonight? My father and I are going . . . and all our crew. The Phyllis Court people have been kind enough to invite us as guests."

"We're members," Guy said, "and some of us will be there, but Stella's really in quarantine for measles, so she——"

"Guy!" she screamed, "I'm not in quarantine for anything! I'm going to the ball. We all are, Mr Merritt."

"We'll meet again there, then, if not sooner?"

"I'm sure we will. We'll look for you and your father."

"And I'll look for you, Miss Cate."

Daily Telegraph, Saturday, July 4, 1914

YACHTING: CLYDE FORTNIGHT
THE KING'S CUTTER BEATEN

The Clyde yachting fortnight opened yesterday in excellent sailing weather. The breeze, which was from the northwest was light at the start, but gathered strength as the racing proceeded, and was fairly steady.

The chief interest centred, naturally, in the appearance of the King's cutter *Britannia*, which returned to the Clyde after an absence of some fifteen years and fortunately four good-class yachts were got together to test the powers of the famous racer. In addition to the *Wendur*, which has been competing with the *Britannia* since the Holyhead Regatta, the Clyde yawls *Rose* and *Harbinger* joined the class, and on the day the winner turned up in *Rose*, which saved her time from the Royal yacht by 4 min 17 sec.

Christopher Cate, sitting in a comfortable chair by the window of his library, office, and music room in Walstone Manor put the *Telegraph* down, yawned, and stretched. It was a hot day, and the bees were making a great humming in the Virginia creeper on the wall outside. A shaft of sunlight illumined the shelf where he kept the philosophers— Spinoza, Kierkegaard, Kant, Socrates, Marcus Aurelius, Santayana— and all their comrades, upright as soldiers and solemn as judges, in their tooled leather bindings. It was time he tackled Spinoza again. The problems of farming in the Scarrow valley in this year of 1914 were by no means few, or small; but from time to time the brain needed to bite into something more chewy, something which demanded total concentration, and that for hours on end . . .

Perhaps he should turn his philosophical eye on himself. Christopher Cate, fifty years of age, squire of Walstone in the county of Kent—only no one but Probyn Gorse called him 'squire'; the position itself, and all that the word had connotated for so many centuries, was slipping away, retreating into the past to a sound of faint music—early Victorian hunting horns across far fallow perhaps, or part songs round an Elizabethan maypole. If Mr Lloyd George had his way with taxes, the landed gentry would soon cease to exist. He ought to consider that possibility as dispassionately as he could. Was it now desirable? . . . disastrous? . . . inevitable? If the last, then he should begin to think how he could prepare Cawthorn, Shearer, Mayhew, and Fleck, his tenants, against the day when they would have no squire—call it 'landlord'— standing between them and the vagaries of the weather, diseases of animals and plants, and other acts of God. He yawned again, and got up.

His father-in-law, Harry Rowland, would be retiring in a month or two. He'd worked hard, and had a good life. But the two statements were connected: he'd worked hard, *ergo* he'd had a good life. Would it be the same for the younger generation—for Stella and Laurence and Guy and Naomi and the rest of them? He must try once more to find a husband for Alice—thirty-four now and as ripe a woman as she would ever be, going to waste. His brother Oswald ought to have married her fifteen years ago when he'd had a crush on her for a month or two; but he'd married that . . . that hard-mouthed mare in skirts instead.

Perhaps he could retire, himself. But how? When? The idea was ridiculous as long as he owned land. But hadn't he just been pointing out to himself that he might soon lose it?

He yawned a third time. The racing would be over at Henley now, or nearly so. Tomorrow he'd better walk over to the Home Farmhouse and talk to Matthew Fleck about what fertilizer was best to use on the farm's 460 acres of arable land . . . and how to pay for it.

And while he was there, he might hint to Matthew that his witness as to Probyn Gorse's sterling character would be appreciated at Probyn's trial, due in ten days' time. Matthew had done some poaching himself, when younger, and certainly held no messianic views on the subject, but what on earth had persuaded Probyn to go out after pheasant in high summer? He should know better than that . . .

And he must say a sharp word to that young rogue Fletcher, Probyn's grandson. It had been easy to find a husband for Mary Maxwell, because the girl was handsome and strong and sensible, and would make anyone a wonderful wife. No one but Fletcher could have turned her head. But, having got the wretched girl pregnant, he should have married her . . . but in truth she'd be a great deal more wretched if he did. Fletcher Gorse was a superb human animal, but would never be a superb husband, surely.

He picked up the paper . . . must read the farm news and stock and grain prices, or he'd never be able to give his tenants sound advice. A small half-buried headline caught his eye: ARSENAL STRIKE . . . strange information to find on the sports page. The piece began: "A serious situation arose yesterday at the Royal Arsenal, Woolwich, resulting in a strike of about 1,500 men."

He read on. All the members of the Engineers' Union had walked out because one of their number, a man called Entwhistle, had been dismissed for refusing to erect some machinery on concrete bedding which had been prepared by non-union labour. Now the Arsenal was practically shut down because without the engineers the rest could do little or nothing.

Cate put down the paper, shaking his head. Heaven knew where the rights and wrongs of the matter lay, at bottom; but it was fortunate indeed that England was at peace . . .

Henley: Saturday, July 4, 1914

2 The orchestra swung into *The Blue Danube* and the level of sound in the ballroom rose in the same lilting rhythm. The women's dresses, white and blue and pink, swung wider, the tails of the young men's black coats whirled faster. Under the myriad lights, their bronzed faces glowed from the days in the sun, on the river. Their white-gloved hands rested on the matt, white backs of the young women dancing in their arms. The floor creaked *one*—*two*—*three*, in rhythm to the pounding of their feet. Rose Rowland settled herself as comfortably as she could on her chair. She still ached all over from yesterday's cab accident, but there was no longer any sharp pain. She was sorry to have missed the day's racing, but resting all day had been a great help. She twirled her fan a shade faster to keep time with the waltz. She liked the waltz. In their time, she and Harry had waltzed as well as any of these youngsters on the floor now—better, for today's young seemed to be more self-conscious than her generation, never able to lose awareness of who and where they were. She remembered times, in Harry's arms, when she had known or cared about neither. Had her feet touched the floor in those magical evenings? How, without her remembrance of any time or place of transition, she had been lying in his arms, no gloved hand on her back, but his fingers digging in, his body thrusting hot nectar into her vitals?

She slowed her fan. Time passes, age comes, and with it, pain. Dullness and aching where the nectar flowed.

She said, "That's the third dance Stella's had with that young American you told me about—Johnny Merritt, isn't it? What cow's eyes she's making at him!"

Alice Rowland, sitting at her mother's side along the wall of the ballroom, said, "She can't help it, Mother. Or perhaps she's flirting to get Margaret's attention. But I don't think she's watching. She doesn't like dancing."

Rose said, "Margaret takes no better care of Stella than Fiona does of Virginia. Louise is the only one who seems to care about her daughter. It's a shame she and John couldn't come this year."

"Louise takes more care of Naomi than Naomi likes, often," Alice said. "She's a very independent young lady."

Her mother said, "It's better when Margaret's away. Then Louise feels free to keep an eye on Stella, too, which she can hardly do when the girl's own mother is present . . . Why are Naomi and that Cowan girl sitting out this dance? Look over there."

"I don't know, Mother. They're not old maids like me."

"You're not an old maid, Alice, you're just too intelligent for these silly men. And that's what Naomi and the Cowan girl think . . . that the young men are too silly for them. I can see it in their faces, from here."

She heard a man's voice beside her—"Mother, you love the waltz. Are you feeling up to dancing this one with me?"

She turned her head, smiling. "Thank you, Richard, but old-fashioned waltzing is for younger legs than mine. Why don't you dance with Alice? You mustn't let your sister be a wall flower."

Richard bowed exaggeratedly. "Will you waltz, Miss Rowland?"

Alice rose, giving a slight curtsey. "I shall be honoured, Mr Rowland."

Her brother laughed. "Come on, Dormouse. You look about twenty-two tonight."

They swept away and Rose changed her position on the satin-covered chair. She could never stay comfortable in one position for more than a few minutes these days. It was nothing to do with the accident, just old age, old age . . . She shook her head, wiping the thought, and the nagging slight pain, from her conscious awareness. She looked about, examining, her fan swishing slowly now—a tall woman now in her seventies, straight backed, dark hair grey-streaked, the face and mouth a little severe, and beginning to be etched with the signs of a permanent physical pain, always suppressed . . . There was her eldest son, Richard, dancing with her youngest daughter, Alice. There was her youngest son, Tom, standing in a doorway with Guy, the boy's arm still in the sling, and his friend Dick Yeoman. They were not dancing, while rows of pretty girls waited, any of whom would be delighted to dance with a commander, Royal Navy, even though they might think the boys too young for them. They were a good-looking trio, Tom mature and square-faced, Guy hawklike, and the friend almost as long-lashed and pretty as a girl in the face, but with a young man's solid body . . . Where were the rest of her family? She knew that her husband Harry was in the lounge, but where were . . . ah, there was Fiona, dancing with a man whom Rose did not recognise. She raised her lorgnette and examined him carefully as they passed. No, she did not know him. She must remember to ask Fiona who he was . . . but Fiona looked bored. She always did, even when Quentin was home.

She turned her head as she heard her husband's voice beside her—"Rose, I'd like to introduce to you the gentleman whom Tom and boys met after the races this afternoon—Johnny Merritt's father. We have been talking in the lounge. Mr Stephen Merritt. . . my wife."

She smiled up. He was a tall man in his fifties, balding, with a monk-like tonsure of grey hair, angular in his motions, a little stooped. She patted the chair beside her. "Sit down, Mr Merritt. I hope you are enjoying yourself in England."

"I certainly am, Mrs Rowland. And Johnny even more so, from the looks of things." He gestured toward the floor, where Johnny was again dancing with Stella Cate. He said, "Your granddaughter is a very lovely young lady, ma'am. I have a girl about her age at home."

"You should have brought her over," Harry said, from the chair on her other side. "Enough young men at Henley to make *any* girl feel she's a beauty . . . though, of course, I'm sure your daughter really is," he added hastily, catching Rose's flicker of warning at his near-gaffe. "Mr Merritt's a banker, Rose."

"A merchant banker, you call them here," Merritt said. "We look for opportunities to invest in businesses that are well managed but need more capital to reach their full potential. Or we buy control of businesses that are not being well managed, and for that reason have depressed earnings—and of course, price—and then put in new and efficient management. Your husband has been telling me about his firm. Of course, we have heard of Rowland automobiles in America. They have a high reputation." He always spoke slowly, Rose noticed, in a deep, rather flat tone. He said, "I can say that it is Mr Rowland's field, automotive, that is our specialty. In fact, our bank—Fairfax, Gottlieb—is looking for suitable opportunities in Europe, including Great Britain . . . Mr Rowland mentioned that one of your daughters-in-law is American."

Rose said, "Susan is. Richard's wife. She was a Miss Kruze. Her father was in the timber business, in San Francisco."

"They have no children," Harry said, as Rose knew he would. Harry hated people to ask about Susan and Richard's family, because then he'd have to tell them that they didn't have any, after sixteen years of marriage.

Stephen Merritt nodded, saying nothing, until he said to Rose, "Do I detect a touch of the Emerald Isle in your voice, ma'am?"

"You do," she said, "I am a McCormack. And you? Many Americans are Irish, I know, though you have no brogue."

"Not I," he said. "Pure English by descent."

"If there is such a thing," Harry cut in.

Merritt said, "My wife's ancestors—she's passed away, God rest her—were originally Huguenots. Both families farmed in Maine for many generations, but my grandfather came to New York, and we have lived there ever since—New York State, specifically Nyack. It's on the west bank of the Hudson River in Rockland County, about thirty miles up from Manhattan."

Rose said, "Is the river as pretty as the Thames?"

Stephen Merritt stroked his long jaw and considered before replying, "I wouldn't call it pretty, Mrs Rowland. I would say that 'grand' or . . . 'imposing' would be better words. From our boathouse it is nearly four miles to the Westchester shore, opposite."

"Goodness gracious! It's like a sea. It must get very rough sometimes."

"It does."

Harry said, "You live in this place but your office is in New York—the city, surely?"

"Yes, sir. Most men in my position would live in the city—on Upper Fifth Avenue, perhaps, but I travel daily by the railroad to New Jersey and then by ferry to Wall Street, and back the same way every evening."

"A long day," Harry said.

"I think it's worth it, sir—for the fresh air, and the view . . . Mr Rowland was telling me that you are planning a trip round the world in September. I would be honoured if you would spend a few days with us in Nyack."

Rose said, "How kind of you, Mr Merritt. We must see if we can fit such a visit into our plans. We are due in California at the end of September—I don't remember the exact date. We go there from New York by train."

"That'll be an all day and night trip, I expect," Harry said, "America's a big country."

"You had perhaps better allow a bit more time than that," Mr Merritt said diplomatically. After a silence, he said, "Would you care to dance, Mrs Rowland? This is a nice slow one, at least."

Rose considered. Why not? She must not give up living just because of a little pain, a few bruises. She rose, holding up her hand.

"Why haven't you been dancing?" Richard Rowland asked his niece, sedately two-stepping round and round the floor in his arms, "I know that you have been introduced to several young men."

Naomi said, "Oh, Uncle, I've *told* you. I can't stand them! They're all so stuck up, so . . . insulting! They think that all women ought to be silly little flibbertigibbets, with rosebud mouths and turned-up noses and big round eyes."

"That's an exaggeration," Richard said. "And anyway, Cantley asked you. He's over thirty, and he's an important banker. Good heavens, girl, he's off to Baghdad soon, he told me, to negotiate some huge loan to an oil company—and you think he's stuck up?"

"Are you trying to marry me off, Uncle?" Naomi said, laughing at him. He was nice, she thought; and, like her parents, he worried so much. She said, "Mummy said it was all Fred Stratton's fault that she and Daddy couldn't come to Henley this year. He wanted these days off, and one of the cowmen is ill, so they had to stay."

He said, "I haven't been down to High Staining for a while, but Fred seemed happy when I last saw him."

"He's not now. And Mummy's come to hate him. Rachel says it's because he won't bow and scrape and touch his cap every moment."

Richard said nothing. Rachel Cowan was too clever for her own good, he thought. Not a lady, of course . . . God knew where she'd come from, what her background was, and his sister-in-law's attempts to find out had met thin air. They only knew that she was Naomi's friend from Girton, where she was on a full scholarship; that her father was in business in London; and that they lived in Stepney. Richard didn't think that anyone in the family had ever before met anyone from Stepney.

The dance ended, his wife Susan joined them, and with one woman on each arm he headed for the supper room. The long tables, loaded with cold salmon, lobster, chicken, salads, trifle, and great silver bowls of white wine cup, were surrounded by men heaping food onto plates. Most of the women stood aside in twos and threes, talking animatedly, or singly, waiting for their partners to serve them, but a few younger girls were at the tables helping themselves.

"I'll get my own food, Uncle," Naomi said firmly, before he could open his mouth. She disengaged her hand from his arm and pushed between two tall young men.

Richard found Guy at his side. "Naomi doesn't like anyone to think she's a poor helpless female, does she, Uncle Richard?" Guy said.

Richard smiled. "No. Well, she's as healthy as any man here, and stronger than some, so I suppose it's all right." They moved toward a table.

Guy said, "What's going to happen to Probyn Gorse, Uncle?"

Richard said, "I don't know him very well, but your Uncle John and Uncle Christopher both say the trouble is that he's obstinate. He thinks he has a right to take a certain amount of game, wherever he can find it. But Lord Swanwick thinks he hasn't. And *he's* just as obstinate . . . and a lot more powerful."

A voice behind his other shoulder said cheerfully, "Are you implying that my noble father is conducting some sort of vendetta against Probyn Gorse?" Richard turned, to meet the smiling face of the Honourable Arthur Durand-Beaulieu, second son of the Earl of Swanwick.

He said, "Hullo, Arthur. How's Dorothy?"

"Fine. She's here somewhere . . . Hullo, Guy. I see you took seven for twenty-eight against Winchester last week."

"And sprained my wrist catching one in the slips—fell on it," Guy said. "What about Probyn, sir?"

"Your uncles are quite right. Pater hates Probyn with a consuming hatred. Foams at the mouth when his name is mentioned. He'd give Walstone Park to anyone who would guarantee putting Probyn in gaol for life."

They reached a table and began to help themselves. Arthur continued, "I've tried to tell Pater that Probyn's family have lived on the land in Walstone several centuries longer than ours—longer even than the Cates—and we ought to give a little, share some things with him, not as a favour but as a right . . . but he won't see it that way. What's Probyn been up to this time?"

"Poaching again," Guy said. "A couple of pheasants, last month, out of season, of course. It was at night, and he had a stick, which the keepers are going to say was a weapon."

"When's the trial?"

"I believe it's on the 14th."

Arthur shook his head. "I'd like to go down and help, but I can't. I'm off to Italy on Monday."

They had all loaded their plates and sat now on scattered chairs in the lounge, eating gingerly, the plates balanced on their knees. Susan said, "Dare we ask what your mission is?"

Arthur said, "It's no secret. *The Times* gave details last Thursday. A strong Foreign Office team is going down to try to pry Italy out of its Triple Alliance, with Germany and Austria."

Richard said, "What are you going to offer the Italians?"

"Ah, now that *is* rather private . . . You'll be playing for Kent when you come home for the holidays, I hear, Guy."

"They've asked me to try out, yes."

"Good luck . . . I'd better find Dorothy, and there's my brother, dying to tell me more than I care to know about some wild Spanish painter called Picasso." He went off, smiling, balancing the half-empty plate.

Richard said, "A great family," adding in a lower tone, "—except for the Earl, I'm afraid."

Naomi joined them, Rachel Cowan at her side. "Where's that American?"

"Johnny Merritt?" Guy answered. "I don't know."

"With Stella, I'll bet," Naomi said.

Rachel said, "Can he be in love, so soon, only meeting her this afternoon?"

Naomi laughed. "Well, Stella's always in love, so why not? As soon as this one sails for America—or even leaves the ballroom—she'll be in love with someone else."

"That's not a very nice way to speak about your cousin," Richard said reproachfully.

"I don't mean it badly, Uncle. That's just the way Stella is. She can't help it."

"We can all help ourselves," Richard said firmly. As he spoke, he wondered whether he really believed his own words, or whether he was speaking for the instruction of the young—who were not listening.

Stella Cate walked slowly along the edge of the Phyllis Court lawn, below the wall that marked the upstream corner. Across the river at the Regatta Fair, a steam organ blared out *Alexander's Ragtime Band,* the merry-go-round swooped and rose, girls screamed with laughter, barkers cried, rifle shots cracked out from the shooting booths. Here the moon-bright Thames flowed soundlessly on her right, Johnny Merritt walked at her other side, his shoes silent on the grass. She felt that another river was flowing inside her, carrying her toward the lip of a fall. She had been to that fall before in her mind, and swooped over, falling dissolving, an imagined, impalpable presence upon her like a weight, her secret body longing, opening like a bud. She had seen the bull with the cow, the dog with the bitch, and once a farm boy with a girl, her outflung legs white, he thrusting, hawthorn's white blossom raining on her closed eyelids, upturned, ecstatic mouth gaping. Was it possible that other girls, well brought up girls, ladies, felt as she did? Or was she alone in her helplessness, and longing, and wickedness? Could she ask her mother? She shuddered involuntarily.

Johnny cleared his throat and she looked at him, the moonlight bright on his starched white shirt, white waistcoat, white tie. He said, "I . . . Stella . . ." His voice was hoarse.

"Yes?"

He cleared his throat again, looked away, and after a while said in a different tone, "I keep being introduced to lords and honourables . . . Honourable Arthur something, Lord Cantley or Bantley . . . and someone said they're sons of another lord. Can you explain, so I don't make a fool of myself?"

Stella was relieved that he had so obviously changed the subject. If he had said something tender—moved to kiss her, taken her in his arms under the giant trees, she knew she would have responded.

She thought about lords. Everyone knew which was which, and why, but explaining it was harder. She said slowly, "There are lots of different kinds of lords. We have one in Walstone called the Earl of Swannick, or Lord Swannick—that's spelled s-w-a-n-w-i-c-k. He's a member of the House of Lords. But before they were made earls, ages ago, they were only Viscounts—Viscount Cantley—and since then, the earl's eldest son always uses that title, by courtesy, and is called Viscount—or Lord—Cantley. But he can't sit in the House of Lords until his father dies and he becomes the earl. Younger sons of earls are Honourable, but all the daughters are Lady, with their christian name, and the family name. The Swannicks' family name is Durand-Beaulieu, so the earl's second son is called the Honourable Arthur Durand-Beaulieu, and his daughters are Lady Barbara and Lady Helen Durand-Beaulieu. None of them can sit in the House of Lords."

Johnny laughed. "And what happens when one of them marries? Does her husband become Lord Barbara?"

"Of course not! When Lady Barbara marries, she'll change her surname, but keep her title—which her husband won't share. They'll be Mr John and Lady Barbara Smith, or whatever."

Johnny said, "Well, I don't suppose it'll be of much concern to me in another week."

They turned and walked back, again silent. Stella felt the constriction, the tension again growing between them, blocking out the raucous blare of the Fair. He wanted to say something to her, as a woman.

"It's beautiful," he said, his voice again hoarse. His gloved hand crept out to touch hers. She felt his grip tighten, then relax. "I've never seen anything so beautiful in my life."

From Phyllis Court's five French windows, light poured out across the green lawns that swept down to the river. Half a hundred men and women strolled on that brilliant grass, their voices, the clink of their glasses, the sparkle of their laughter floating down to Johnny and Stella in the velvet night.

She said, "It's nice," her voice strangled.

She prayed he would not try to kiss her. If he did, she'd scream . . . faint . . . fall back on the grass, spread-eagled. And there was another couple close behind them, the man smoking a cigar. After two endless minutes Johnny said, "I guess we ought to be going back. Your mother will be worrying about you."

"I suppose so," she said, waiting a moment before turning, hoping, deep, that he would not turn, but take her on into the dark. The other couple had already turned, and were now fifty feet away. In a moment her legs would give way and . . .

He said, "What do you think about the assassination of the Archduke?" His voice was unsteady and she thought, he has been fighting the same battle as I. The thought gave her strength. If a man was resisting temptation, she could help him. It was when a man looked at her with confidence in his power, and she saw herself as he saw her, that she began to respond, helplessly, to his emotions and desires. But men were so chivalrous, and helped her even there, just as they might carry her across a difficult place in the path. Men were . . . men.

She gathered her wits and said, "What Archduke?"

"Franz Ferdinand of Austria, at Sarajevo. My dad thinks it could lead to trouble."

"It's nothing to do with us, is it? Or with America?"

"I don't think so, but Dad says we should keep out of it, whatever happens. The future of American youth is on American soil, he says, not under European dirt."

"This is not European dirt," she said, feeling a brush of patriotic resentment. These Americans, coming over here, winning the Grand, and then talking about European dirt! "This is English soil."

"Oh, England's different," Johnny said hurriedly. "Why, Magna Carta was signed not far down this very river. Dad and I went to see Runnymede the day before yesterday. If England were involved, I couldn't feel, well, apart. Nor could Dad really, though he pretends to think all foreigners are alike. But how could this affect England?"

"I don't know," Stella said; adding to herself—'and I don't care.' The young man saw her disinterest and said, "I shouldn't be talking about politics." He stopped, the two of them standing at the foot of the lawn, just on the grass now, the lights bathing them from the windows of Phyllis Court. Fainter from the inside of the club, music streamed out, inseparably mixed with the light and the round moon, and all three with the subtle presence of the moving river. He said slowly, holding both her hands, at arm's length—"I want to say, Miss Cate, that you are the nicest, the most beautiful young lady I have ever met. May I write to you?"

"When are you going back to America?" she asked quickly. Let him not go: they were surrounded by people: she was safe, and he hand-some and strong . . .

"Not just yet. Soon. I'll give you my address. I know yours. I asked that young fellow you say is so good at cricket."

"Guy."

"Yes, Guy—earlier this evening. And we'll dance some more tonight, eh?"

They walked toward the French windows. She said, "I think I have one or two dances left. Here, look at my programme."

He took it, and looked at it, and through it, seeing nothing. This morning he had felt a sense of loss . . . Henley, finished; Harvard finished; his time of youth, going . . . Now there was no past, only the now and a future brilliantly glowing, but seemingly out of his reach. She was the most wonderful girl he had ever met, lovely beyond words, gentle, pure . . . he had felt from the tremor in her voice, by the river, that she was afraid he would take her too far into the darkness: no thought had been farther from him. He had lain with a couple of Bos-ton street girls, but Stella . . . ! Oh God, and he was going home within a week! What to do, how not to lose what had suddenly fallen into his heart from the hot blue skies of this amazing English summer?

Margaret Cate waited till the third woman went out of the ladies' room, leaving her alone with her sister-in-law; then she said, "Fiona, there's something I must talk to you about."

Fiona tensed. Margaret continued, "It's about Archie Campbell, your lover." Fiona stood very stiff, at one of the dressing tables, staring into the mirror, one hand frozen in her back hair.

Margaret said, "More and more people are getting to know. A friend in London mentioned it to me in a letter. Louise knows."

"Mother?" Fiona said, trying to keep her voice steady.

"Not yet, but it's only a question of time, isn't it?"

The music seeped dully to them here. The heavy damask curtains swayed gently in front of the open windows like slow dancers in the heavy earth-scented air.

Margaret said, "She asked me if I knew of any reason why you have not joined Quentin at the Curragh."

"I don't like Ireland—or the Irish. You know that. So does Mother."

"I don't think she accepts it as a sufficient reason. She is wondering, thinking . . . Are you going to see Campbell when you go to Skye to visit your mother?"

Fiona looked across at her sister-in-law then. Margaret was a fanatic, herself. Surely she must understand?

Margaret met her burning eyes. "He's a nice man, from what I hear —and a good painter. His class doesn't matter. But your marriage does. Your children's lives do."

Fiona snapped, "You are in no position to talk about your family's lives. You and your people are doing your best to kill Quentin, who's your brother as well as my husband. You're destroying Christopher, and will destroy Stella and Laurence, by neglect. At least I *try* to be a mother to *my* children."

Margaret's face tightened. "It's a matter of proportion," she said. "The freedom of Ireland is one thing. A sordid love affair is another."

A knot of anger twisted in Fiona's bowels . . . not anger, something more animal, an emotion that would kill, as for a defenceless child or cub: in this case for a love that was as much beyond reason as the instinct of a mother wolf.

She said, almost snarling, "I am seeing Archie on my way to Skye. And that's the last word I shall speak to you on the subject. Or wish to hear from you."

Another woman came into the room, and Fiona went out, leaving her sister-in-law looking after her, her face set. Perhaps she understands now, Fiona thought furiously.

"I'm taking over the control of Rowland's on September 1st, Mr Merritt," Richard said. "My father retires that day. He will not be an easy man to follow."

He raised his champagne glass toward his father. The six men were sitting on chairs at the top of the lawn, not far from the French windows of the Phyllis Court lounge. A pair of champagne bottles stood on a small table in front of them. Couples passed, music lapped them, distance muted the more raucous sounds of the Fair across the river.

Harry Rowland raised his glass and drank, acknowledging the compliment. Then he sighed inwardly. Richard couldn't wait to get his hands on Rowland's. But he wouldn't find it so light a weight on his mind once the responsibility was actually, and all, his. It was easy for him to reckon that he had spent so many years preparing himself for this moment; but when the master—himself, Harry Rowland, founder of the Rowland Motor Car Company—was no longer there to turn to, to carry the untransferrable burden, Richard would find it different. Who knew what crises might arise?

And what changes could Richard have in mind—for he certainly had some? Rowland's made as good motor cars as any in England, and that meant, in the world. It made money for himself and his children; it employed four hundred men of Hedlington and brought a great deal more than their pay packets into the city's economy. What did Richard, who had never created anything of his own, know that he, who had, did not know?

He drank cautiously. Youth would be served. And Richard wasn't really young—forty-four or five, wasn't it? Almost as bad as poor Edward VII, having to wait till he was over sixty before he could be King.

Stephen Merritt was speaking. "We have barely begun to tap the potential of the automobile. The time to come will be known as the Automobile Age . . . and such men as you and your father will be its pioneers, its heroes."

Richard, champagne glass in hand, said, "I would like to agree with you, Mr Merritt, but the manufacture of motor cars is such an expensive business that I sometimes wonder if they can ever be more than the luxuries of the rich. I would dearly like to change that, but can it be done?"

Stephen Merritt waved his cigar energetically. "It must change, sir! Prices must be brought lower, output must be raised! Profit is to be made not from a few expensive machines, but from many, many inexpensive ones. I tell you, Mr Rowland, great opportunities for capital investment in the automotive field now exist all over the world, most particularly where there is already a network of good roads . . . England is such a place and, as I mentioned to your father, the bank of which I have the honour to be chairman of the board is actively studying the situation."

While he had been speaking, two young women joined the group, but remained standing behind Tom Rowland's chair. Harry saw that they were Naomi and her friend Rachel Cowan. Richard said, "What are you looking for, in particular, Mr Merritt?"

"Management," Stephen said emphatically, with another wave of his cigar. "There is plenty of skilled mechanical labour almost everywhere in this country. There are innumerable good sites for factories. Communications, power, water, political situation—all are excellent. But . . . what there is not very much of—excuse my saying so, gentlemen— is a modern outlook on production."

"What do you mean, Mr Merritt?" The girl's voice was clear, the tone sharpened by a cockney accent.

Stephen Merritt rose from his chair, bowing generously. "Oh, do please sit down," Rachel Cowan said, "I don't want to be treated like a queen. I'm interested, that's all. And we like standing."

"But you are a lady, Miss . . . Cowan, isn't it?" Merritt said, while the Englishmen rose more slowly, clearly thinking that Merritt was rather overdoing the chivalry, for such a young and pushy woman.

Harry took the opportunity, while they were all standing, to push himself up from his chair. He was feeling suddenly weary. His bones ached from the accident. He should have retired with Rose. He knew that Merritt and Richard would be talking about methods and ideas which he did not agree with, and he would get grumpy listening to them. He said, "If you will excuse me now, please . . . I'll see you tomorrow at breakfast, Richard." He shook hands with Merritt, then walked slowly into Phyllis Court and up to his room.

When he had gone, the others sat down again. Stephen Merritt said, "A fine gentleman, your father, Mr Rowland . . . Where were we? Ah, modern outlook on production . . . The aim of any productive unit, whatever it be, must be quantity as well as quality. The product must be good . . . but it is axiomatic that the best is the enemy of the good. Once you have a good product, quantity becomes more important than quality. The whole production process must then be looked at with quantity as the goal . . . mass production. Only so can enough goods be turned out to lower the unit price significantly . . . which will sell more goods, and so increase the gross profit, thus enabling the producer to turn out still more . . . which will find still more buyers . . . and . . ."

"What about the workers," Rachel asked, "do they share in the increased profit in any way?"

Merritt said, "The labour force must be paid fairly, more than fairly, they must be paid well, because the end point at which we are aiming is that the labour force shall also be the consuming force . . . but since they do not share in the losses of a producer, they do not share in the profits. Their wages are fixed."

"What about efficiency experts, sir?" Guy Rowland asked. "Do you have them?"

Merritt looked keenly at the youth, whose blue eye caught the light from the club as he moved his head, like a searching flash from a lighthouse, the other eye dark and unlit. He said, "We are interested in time and motion study. We think it is the basis of efficiency inside the factory."

"If our trade unions were as strong as they ought to be, they wouldn't accept that," Rachel said.

Tom Rowland put down his champagne glass and got up from his chair with one hand raised and a smile on his square face—"These waters are too deep for this simple sailor. I suppose the dance will be packing up soon. Want to take a final look at the river, Dick?"

"Love to, sir." Guy's school friend rose quickly.

"Guy?"

"I'll stay, Uncle."

Tom and Dick Yeoman strolled down the grass, the outline of their shapes fading as they moved under the trees.

Richard said, "I wish you could find time to visit our plant in Hedlington, Mr Merritt . . . We have been looking at things differently in England. Here, we've been trying to make the best, down to the smallest detail. Which puts up the cost . . . and cuts down the volume of production. No one could have done better than my father has, but . . . we must look at everything afresh . . . question what we have taken for granted . . ." He took off his glasses and polished them, peering sightlessly at Stephen Merritt, ". . . learn from others, study the new. I have been reading everything I can get hold of about Mr Ford's operations, and will certainly visit Detroit as soon as I can. And even before I take over our factory, I have arranged to visit the Ford works at Trafford Park, Manchester."

Stephen Merritt watched him keenly. He thought, here's a man who sees the future but is shackled by the past; and knows he is . . . shackled also by loyalty to his father . . . nothing wrong with loyalty, in its place—more honour to him, for it—but loyalty should be only to people, not to ideas and ways of thought that have outlived their time.

Richard was saying, "We work with what we know is good, but I think that some of the new processes, the new materials, may be not only cheaper, and more amenable to large volume production, but better in themselves . . . At all events, I can tell you that I am going to look very carefully into the possibilities of directing the Rowland Motor Car Company toward mass production, a simpler motor car, standardised interchangeable parts, ease of maintenance, a good network of dealers for spare assemblies—while keeping up the high standards my father has made synonymous with the name Rowland."

"Good man," Stephen said, drawing on his cigar. "When you're ready with plans, write to me if you think we can help. I assure you that Fairfax, Gottlieb will be interested, and we can provide a great deal more than money . . . know-how, for instance. Management skills: Technical expertise . . . If you were making commercial road vehicles, now, we'd be even more interested."

"I don't think any of us has ever considered that," Richard said. "I know my father has not."

There was a silence, broken after a decent interval by Guy—"What about aircraft, sir?"

Again Merritt shot a glance at the boy. He said, "You think there will be a large market for aeroplanes in the near future?"

"I hope so, sir," Guy said. "I'm going to Handley Page's when I leave Wellington, and fly their aeroplanes until I can design, and make, and fly my own."

Merritt said, "Well, I certainly wish you luck, my boy, but I fear that you're some years ahead of your time as far as mass production goes. I can't see aeroplanes becoming widely used for another half century."

Guy said, "Unless something forces change, and improvement, more quickly."

"Such as what? I can't imagine anything."

"A long war, sir."

"Good heavens, what an idea! But such a war might have the effect you mention, I must agree. Fortunately there's very little chance of a general war . . . unless Germany somehow uses the present crisis over the murder of the Archduke to foment one. She knows that France is looking for an opportunity to avenge herself for the debacle of 1870, and she may decide to strike first."

Rachel broke in quickly, "Oh, I'm sure she won't, Mr Merritt!"

"How can you be so sure, Miss Cowan?" Merritt said, with a tartness that his American courtesy had not allowed him to show before.

"I have German relatives," Rachel said. "I've visited them in Frankfurt. They—not just our relatives, but everyone in Germany—are ordinary people, like people here. They don't want a war."

"I think the ordinary German people will have to do what the Kaiser tells them," Guy said. "And *he* will have to do what his generals tell him."

"Quite right," Merritt said, "and there's the danger . . . But let us not talk about such a gloomy subject any more on this glorious night. I think I'll go in. Perhaps you would be good enough to tell Johnny if . . . Ah, there he is!"

Johnny Merritt came slowly toward them, his white teeth smiling in the moonlight, Stella Cate at his side. Everyone stood up.

Stephen Merritt said, "Johnny . . . ladies and gentlemen, I fear the time has come to say goodbye, and . . ."

Guy Rowland said, "One moment, sir! . . . Naomi, Stella, Uncle Richard . . . everyone. A toast!" He raised his glass. "To a birthday." He looked round the circle, his blue eye gleaming, the brown quiescent, velvet soft.

"What birthday?" Richard said. "It's not mine. Yours?"

"It's not mine," Rachel Cowan said, "or Naomi's."

Guy was looking at the two Americans, father and son. Stephen Merritt said, "Well, I'll be . . . Thank you, thank you, Guy!"

"To the United States of America," Guy said. "A hundred and thirty-eight today."

Rachel said, "Is it? I had no idea . . ."

Stephen Merritt said, "I didn't wish to raise the subject in these surroundings. Not tactful, among so many Britishers."

"You really *were* pulling my leg, this afternoon," Johnny said, "pretending you didn't even know what Harvard was!"

They drank, laughing, glasses clinking, and together walked up the last short slope of lawn, through the doors, through the lounge, and into the music. The Regatta Ball was near its end, but the dancers were oblivious of the moving clock. Silk and satin swirled, diamonds glittered, as a society rich in power and privilege enjoyed the night and the river, secure in the centuries-old peace of the English countryside.

Daily Telegraph, Wednesday, July 8, 1914

SETTLEMENT OF THE WOOLWICH STRIKE
PREMIER'S STATEMENT

In the House of Commons yesterday.

MR CROOKS (Lab. Woolwich) asked the Prime Minister whether he could make any statement regarding the Woolwich Arsenal labour dispute.

MR ASQUITH: . . . it is desirable that two points should be made clear. The first is that the contract under which the labour to which exception has been taken (runs) till 1915. Works of various kinds have been erected under this contract, and during the whole period of the dispute in the London building trade no question of the character of the labour employed was raised until last week.

The second is that the men left work without representing their grievances through the proper channels, and it
would have been only fair to the Government as to any
other employer that this should have been done before
resorting to the ultimate weapon of the strike. If the usual
and reasonable course had been taken, the way would have
been much clearer for a solution. The Government have
decided to appoint a court of inquiry . . .

MR CROOKS: Can Entwhistle return at once?

MR ASQUITH: Pending the inquiry.

The moon, a week past full, shone on Margaret's bed the other side of
the bedside table, her hair spread over the pillow. The little ormolu
clock on the table showed a few minutes past four in the morning.
Cate thought the purring of a nightjar had awakened him, but the bird
was silent now, and no breeze stirred in the warm summer-scented
night.

He turned the pages, the rustling of the big sheets sounding loud in
the silence. He had left the house before the newspaper arrived yesterday, and not returned till late evening; and taken the paper upstairs
with him, meaning to read it before he went to sleep; but had fallen
asleep almost at once, to awaken now, to the nightjar . . . He was glad
the Arsenal strike was over, though it worried him that responsible
English working men, skilled men at that, should have been so eager to
go on strike, without making any attempt to use the channels that
existed to air and settle grievances. There must be a hidden bitterness
there, somewhere.

He saw another headline—IRELAND, and closed his eyes. The very
name made him uneasy. Carson was doing his best to foment a civil
war in the north, and the wild Sinn Feiners the same in the south. He
wondered how many southern Roman Catholics really boiled with
suppressed rage against England and the northern Protestants, and vice
versa—and how many wished there could be some accommodation.
Well, he was in no position to lecture anyone about good will or accommodation. If his ancestors had been more accommodating to the Con-
queror's agents, and later to the Plantagenets, he'd be an earl, or a
duke, and own thousands of acres instead of hundreds.

It was just as well he wasn't. Swanwick was worse off than himself;
taxes hit even harder and he had no real source of strength. He owned
land here, and mines and property elsewhere, but had no deep contact
with any of them. They just produced money for him. On the other
hand he didn't have the power that once accrued automatically to earls

—that had long since been seized by professional politicians and middle-class bureaucrats.

The relations between the races and religions in Ireland were not good; but were the relations between classes here in England as good as they had been, even when he was a boy? The Woolwich affair, and the bitterness hidden behind it, showed that they were not; perhaps not really bad yet, but certainly not as sure on their foundations as they once were. "God bless the squire and his relations, and keep us in our proper stations" was a joke now, not a widely shared principle . . . But why? Because there weren't really many squires left. Because land, and the people who lived on it and worked it, were becoming commodities to be bought and sold—not sacred trusts—joys—proud burdens. Half the land-owners he knew had no feeling for the soil that was legally theirs, still less for the men and women who physically inhabited and tilled it.

But what *about* men and women, then? There one would have thought that nature would ensure harmony, but the suffragettes had shown that was not so. The obstinacy of men had driven them to it. If one went back far enough in time, women had plenty of power, and a strong say in the government of the tribe. They were not then set up on pedestals, to be worshipped and enslaved in the name of chivalry.

He still felt uneasy, and wondered whether he would be able to get back to sleep. It was a time of change, but how many were ready? There would be losses, decays, abandonments—but also chances, opportunities, practical visions of a better England. Just let there be no revolution, here or in Ireland—only change in the English way, an ordered evolution with good will, a careful loosening of old bonds and as careful a refastening, so that the bonds chafed less.

The nightjar sang again, a continuous outpour, reeling from high to low pitch. Cate listened, enthralled, his sadness and unease dispelled until the day.

Hedlington, Kent: Saturday, July 11, 1914

3 From Henley, the Thames flows east and south, in sweeping curves by Eton and Windsor and Runnymede; past Cardinal Wolsey's tower near the mouth of the Mole; by Kingston, where Saxon kings of England took the crown upon their heads; by Richmond on its hill; to tidewater, Westminster, and the City, Bridge, Tower, and Pool of London; by Limehouse Reach and Gallion's Reach, St Clement Reach and Northfleet Hope, to Gravesend, Lower Hope, Sea Reach and the brown estuary. A few miles on, at Sheerness, at the point of the Isle of Sheppey off the south shore, another estuary opens on the right, being the mouth of a lesser river. Where this Kentish river narrows, going upstream, lie Dickens's Rochester, and one of England's three traditional naval bases—Chatham.

Let us call this river the Scarrow, which is not its name, and follow it upstream toward the long chalk line of the North Downs. At once the land begins to rise on either side—in 1914 almost bare of houses—covered with short grass, thorn bushes, scattered small trees tugged by the wind, a few flocks of grazing sheep, their shepherds leaning on their crooks, the sheepdogs lying close, eyes bright and ears cocked for the smallest signal from their masters.

The river valley narrows, squeezing in a railway and two roads, one on each bank. At the narrowest part, navigation ends, even for the long barges which straining horses heave up from Chatham. Smoke rises from three or four factories. On the west a racecourse with a minimal

grandstand is tucked in between the river and the down on that side—
Busby Down. This is North Hedlington.

Continuing south, almost at once the valley becomes residential
rather than industrial. The spire of Hedlington Church pierces the sky,
the houses grow larger and spread up the hillsides. Hedlington Gaol is
a pile of blackened Victorian brick on the lower slope of Beighton
Down; opposite, on Busby Down, another pile of the same brick, built
at the same time, and much like the gaol in outward appearance, is
Minden Barracks, depot of the Weald Light Infantry.

Past the South Eastern railway station, the open space by the Town
Hall, and some rows of small shops and houses, the country soon
changes again, to water meadows by the Scarrow, the county cricket
ground, and Hedlington fairgrounds. Beyond here is real country,
Kent, the garden of England . . . hop fields, oast houses with their
tilted spires, cattle grazing, wheat ripening, orchards and sand-coloured
country roads, the signposts guiding to Cantley, Felstead, Beighton,
Walstone, Taversham—all villages; and to the towns—south-east to Ashford, east to Canterbury, south-west to Tonbridge, west to Sevenoaks
and so back to London.

By authority of a Royal Charter granted by King Richard III in
1484, Hedlington was granted the right to hold a Fair on the second
Saturday of each July, the Fair to start on the Thursday before that second Saturday. This became known, from about 1520, as the Hedlington Sheep Fair.

The third dog of the trials was a Bearded Collie. It stood still at its
master's side until, at a muttered command, it took off across the field,
running easily but fast toward the three sheep waiting at the far end.

"Oh, doesn't he run fast, Bill," Ruth Hoggin cried.

Her husband grunted non-committally and then shouted, "I'll lay
two to one on this one! Quid!"

"Done!" a man a few paces away in the thin crowd called.

The Beardie had reached the sheep and started them toward the first
pair of hurdles, running silent, wide on their outer flank. "That's the secret," Bill Hoggin said. "He's got the buggers running fast, see, but
they're not frightened."

"Don't use that awful language, dear," Ruth muttered. She felt a
flush rising in her neck. Bill was a darling—so strong and sure, but he
hadn't been brought up proper. His mother was a dreadful old woman,
coarse as a pig, and pure cockney. It wasn't Bill's fault.

The sheep trotted between the two hurdles and swung right, heading for the next gate, as the Beardie came far enough forward for them

to see him out of their left eyes. Now, as they came close to the next gate, one of the three broke away and made to pass outside. Bill muttered an imprecation under his breath, and the shepherd, watching intently from the starting position, raised his crook and made as though to shout; but the sheepdog had already seen, and acted, and was on the straying sheep's flank in a flash. With a short low bark he turned it back to join the others as they hurried through the gate.

"Lost a point there," Bill said. "He could 'a done it without barking. He's young."

The Beardie took the sheep through the remaining two gates and into the final pen in fine style, the shepherd dropped the last hurdle into place, and the judges bent their heads together in confabulation.

"That's the best so far," the man who had taken the bet called across to Bill. "But wait till you see this 'un."

The next dog stood waiting, its master a little behind it. Like all the other contestants except the third, it was a Border Collie, but taller than the rest. It stood, shivering a little, one forepaw raised. It dropped that paw and lifted the other.

"This is the best dog in Kent," the other man said, "I seen him on the Downs."

"No good," Bill said, "too nervy."

"Garn!" the other man said. "He just wants to get on with the job."

Bill felt in his pocket, found his pipe and tobacco and began to stuff the bowl of the pipe. Ruth watched the dog with the same breathless interest she had felt from the first time . . . not just the first time this year, the first time she had ever watched the sheepdog trials at the Sheep Fair. The Fair used to be centred on the buying and selling of the sheep—the sheep themselves, their lambs, their wool—that used to graze on the Downs. But since the industrial revolution reached the North Weald, much of the land had been enclosed for the parks of rich manufacturers, the sheep had been dwindling in numbers, and in her own lifetime of thirty-three years the sheep part of the Fair had much lessened in importance. Only last year her father, Bob Stratton, had said, "I don't reckon we'll see many more sheep markets or trials at the Fair . . ."

She had protested, not wanting to believe him, for to her the trials were the best thing about the Fair. What wonderful dogs! But she knew he was right. The rest of the trappings of the Fair went on, increased even—the hurdy-gurdies, the coconut shies and side shows, the stalls loaded with cheap cotton goods and shoes; at night the garish ragtime music from the clanking steam engine, which also provided power for the merry-go-round, and the electric lighting . . . the young people dancing on the soiled grass under the lights strung on wires between tall poles, the smells of gin and beer and tobacco, and at the edge of light, the dark figures on the grass, the heaving and whispering . . .

Three o'clock in the afternoon, and the sun was flaying down as it had all summer. She mopped her face every few minutes and wished there were some shade at the trials, but at the Fair there wasn't much shade anywhere except inside the big tents where the peep shows were, and the food and tea marquee.

The last dog ran its course. A few minutes later, Bill's choice was declared the champion. "That's it," he cried triumphantly. He walked over to the other man, through the dispersing spectators—" 'And over, mate."

The man pulled out a sovereign and slapped it into Bill's hand. "There goes my month's drinking money. I was bloody sure that other tyke, the tall one, would win." His eyes held a begging look that he did not have the courage to put into words: give me back the money, or half of it, anyway, the eyes said, let's pretend there wasn't no bet.

Bill said, "If you can't stand the cold, keep your hand in your pocket, mate."

He turned away, pulling Ruth's arm through his. "Silly bugger," he said. " 'Ow do you feel? No more puking?"

"I'm over that," she said, blushing. "Why, Bill, I'm . . . nearly three months now."

He reached across with his other hand and laid it on her belly. She whispered, "*Bill!* Everyone's looking!"

He growled, "Wot the 'ell's that to me?"

He stood, looking at her, a fat strong man in his mid-thirties, straight black hair brushed carelessly across a big bald spot, black hair dense at the wrists of his shirt, the eyes blue, a little bulged. He stabbed a thick forefinger at her, "We're going down to Lovers' Bank, and if anyone sees us they'll think I'm going to poke you, and they'll be right, see?"

"Oh, Bill!" she cried, in fearful expectation.

He said, "An' if it's your mother she'll yell 'Stop that!'" He broke into a falsetto, " 'What are you doing to my darling daughter?' And I'll say, 'Up yours, Mrs Stratton!'" He raised one middle finger in a short strong gesture, " 'Up your 'igh and mighty Stratton arse 'ole!' They look down their noses at me 'cos I'm a barrow boy, an' my mother doesn't know 'oo the 'ell my dad was, but what are the Strattons, eh? Mechanics! Mechanics what 'ave made a bit of money by being 'ere when Rowland started 'is fucking factory. Come along now."

She said softly, "Wait a minute, Bill. Are you sure that . . . doing that, won't harm the baby now?"

He tossed back his head and laughed. "At three months? Why, the little bugger's about this size—" he held his fingers an inch or two apart. "When he's seven months, perhaps his daddy'll give him a punch in the eye now and then . . . Don't you worry about it."

"Anne's going to have hers in October. Do you think that Frank . . . you know . . . still does it?"

"More fool he if he doesn't. Some other sod will . . . Come on."

Jane Stratton shifted her weight from one leg to the other, and fanned herself restlessly with her big flowered hat. When Bob got the Sheep Fair committee to agree to his running a motor car gymkhana, as Mr Harry called it, four years ago she'd been pleased for his sake. But she had not realised how many hours a gymkhana went on for. There were never enough places to sit down at the Fair, but before the gymkhana came she didn't have to stay and watch anything—she could sit under a tree by the river, or in a tent, and rest for half an hour before going to look at something else. After all, she was not as young as she used to be —sixty-four now . . . Bob ought to get some benches put out, he really ought. She'd speak to him about it, and . . .

"It's too hot," her daughter-in-law muttered beside her. Anne was looking every day of her six and a half months, which was natural as this would be her third; but she was looking well, too, considering the heat. It was the woman on Jane's other side, her own youngest daughter, who was not looking well—and she was not pregnant, as far as Jane knew. She tapped her on the arm. "You're looking peaked, Ethel. I thought so this morning when we met you at the station, but now you're worse. Is anything the matter?"

"Nothing, Mother," Ethel said in a low voice, "I'm just . . . not feeling very well today. I'm all right," she added hastily, as though she expected her mother to press some unwelcome remedy on her.

Jane turned her attention back to the motor cars. They growled and banged through the intricate little course that Bob had set up, backed between coloured flags, stopped on an artificial ramp, started again, raced down the short straight toward her. Goodness, they went fast . . . they must be going thirty, forty miles an hour near the end. What would happen if they couldn't stop? Well, many of them were Rowlands, and that would never happen to a Rowland.

With an effort of will she closed her mind to the cars, and thought of her daughter . . . Something *was* the matter with Ethel. It was that

Italian husband probably. No use beating about the bush, especially with Ethel.

She poked her daughter suddenly in the ribs. "What's Niccolo doing to you? Eh? Come on, Ethel. I'm your mother."

Ethel burst into tears. The men and women huddled near them by the gymkhana course looked curiously at the weeping woman for a moment, then away again. Jane said, "Come, let's go for a little walk. We need to stretch our legs. You come too, Anne, walking's good for the baby." They moved together away from the gymkhana crowd, and across the fairground thronged with people, dogs, children, each following her own personal trajectory, heedless of others.

"He gambles," Ethel sobbed, half leaning on her mother's shoulder, "and he doesn't make enough money as it is."

"Or doesn't bring it home," Jane said grimly. "Them waiters make plenty in tips, but how's the wife to know? Gamblers—pah! I hate them worse than anyone."

Ethel muttered, "An' he beats me when he's had too much wine . . . because I don't have a baby."

"Lots of people don't have babies in the first two years, however hard they try," Jane said firmly, "and who says it's *your* fault?"

"It can't be his," Ethel whispered, "he . . . does it all the time, till it hurts."

"Filthy dago!" Anne said angrily.

"That doesn't prove anything, how often he does it," Jane said, "but it only goes to prove that you shouldn't have married him. None of *us* could see what you saw in him. Well, what can't be cured must be endured, but Dad will have a word with Mister Niccolo and then I don't think he'll beat you any more. I wish he was here now. I'd give him a piece of my mind . . . Calls himself an Englishman just because he got naturalised! He's no more an Englishman than the Pope of Rome!"

"He says he'll divorce me if I don't have a baby soon. A boy, it's got to be, he says."

Her mother stopped, hands on hips, staring at her. They all three stopped. Ethel mopped at her eyes. She was a mousey woman with a small sharp face but big breasts and hips.

Jane Stratton said, "Who does he think he is? *Where* does he think he is? He thinks he's in Timbuktu, not England, that's what! He can't divorce you for not having a baby! He can only divorce you if you have a fancy man."

"I haven't," Ethel sobbed. "Never! I love him, but he says he can get the marriage washed out, made like it never happened."

"We'll see about that," Jane said. "Now, wipe your eyes and let's find Mary Gorse and the children, and have a nice cup of tea."

The brothers Frank and Fred Stratton stood at the edge of the crowd watching the gymkhana. Frank, the elder by five years, was two inches the shorter of the two, and had much the bigger ears; but otherwise there was a strong family resemblance—both men in their thirties, stockily built, hair sandy to ginger, eyes wide set, big work-hardened hands. Frank's expression was open and pleasant, Fred's rather hard.

Their father, in charge of the proceedings, was wearing a blue suit and a bowler hat, clip board and pencil in hand, his steel-rimmed glasses glinting in the sun, sweat trickling down the side of his face into his short, square-cut pepper and salt beard. Frank had seen his mother nearby a few minutes ago, with Anne and Ethel, but they seemed to have gone. Bored, probably. Dad certainly wouldn't have spent any time with them. Nothing and no one else existed when he was dealing with motor cars, except Victoria, the motorcycle he was building at home to break the world's speed record.

Fred said, "How are they doing? I haven't been paying attention."

"All right. It looks as though the Works Ruby's going to win. Smithie from the paint shop's driving it."

"Dad's not judging, is he?"

"No, it wouldn't be fair for him to judge Rowlands . . . Hey, you know what I saw, just before I came over here?" He dug his elbow into his brother's ribs, and his voice dropped, "In the bushes, on Lovers' Bank . . . Hoggin banging our Ruthie!"

Fred laughed shortly, "And she with a bun in the oven!"

"Couldn't wait till bedtime," Frank said.

"I know the feeling," Fred said, "even though I'm not married. But I don't think that's why Hoggin did it here. He does things like that to show us what he thinks of us." He raised a middle finger, the back of his hand toward his brother. "He's a rude bastard."

"That he is. But he loves our Ruthie, I think, in his way. And she worships the ground he treads on."

"Fat sod! Ruthie's much too good for him. Same as Ethel for that wop."

Frank began to say something, then cried, "Hey, look at that!"

A car, its driver hauling ineffectively at the steering wheel, had failed to take a curve, and was mowing down the marker flagpoles. "Brake, brake!" Bob Stratton bellowed. The driver reached for the handbrake and tugged mightily. The blue-and-yellow-painted car slowed sharply, but not before it had struck and knocked sideways a big man in workman's clothes, standing close by one of the flags, who had been looking the other way.

The man stood up groggily, patting himself in a cloud of dust. The driver jumped down from the stopped car, dustcoat flying, and ran toward him, tearing off his goggles.

"Hey, that's Willum," Frank said.

He made a move forward, but Fred said, "He's all right. And Dad's there."

They saw their father take the big man's arm and speak to him; and the man shake his head, feel himself all over, grin, their father clap him on the back, and point. The driver returned to his car, and the big man set to replacing the flags that had been knocked down.

Fred said, "Dad might 'a got someone else to do that, after he's just been knocked down."

"Willum Gorse *likes* being ordered about, that's the truth of it. He likes to do things for people, too—then he knows they need him. If Dad or Mary didn't tell him what to do, he'd just stand about, like a horse, for ever. He's simple, that's all. That's why we can't use him except to sweep out the shop floor, though he's a good enough workman, and he'd work twenty-four hours a day if we'd let him."

"Well, *I* won't," Fred said in a hard voice. "And that's why I'll likely not be staying much longer at High Staining."

"Mr John work you too hard? I thought you liked the farming life."

"Oh, it's all right, and so's John Rowland, I suppose—though Mrs is always looking down her bloody nose at me. I thought I was going to like farming, but it was really anything to escape from Rowland's, and making motor cars, and that's a fact. Farming's not so pretty as it looks. It's hard, boring, same things again and again . . . lonely . . . not enough money . . . tied down . . . the cows have to be milked at five o'clock in the morning and half-past three in the afternoon every bloody day. They don't stop giving milk just because you need a holiday."

"Fred, you ought to get married," his brother said firmly. "Then you won't find yourself one day paying some fast girl seven and six a week . . . or having her dad stick a twelve-bore in your ribs. Seriously, Fred, there's nothing like it . . . if you're lucky. I don't know how I'd live without Anne . . . nor she without me. It's not only what we do in bed, though that's great. It's being together, having her to go back to every night, and her knowing I'm coming back. She needs me, I need her, we have each other, and we're both better for it. I like my work, but there are times when I couldn't stand it, without her."

"I don't want to get married," Fred said shortly. "I want . . . something else."

"What?"

"I don't know, man! Lord, if I knew, I'd be going out and getting it. You know what *you* want—to be Works foreman of Rowland's. And as soon as Mr Harry and Dad retire, you're going to get it. But I don't know what I want. I'm looking . . . Here, let's go and have some tea."

"Sit down, Dad," Fred said, moving up a place on the bench. "Have a cup of tea. You look hot."

"Thanks, Fred. I'll bring another pot."

Fred looked round. The whole family was here, in two long rows at a table in the big marquee, except for Ethel's husband, Fagioletti. Ethel didn't look well; but Ruthie did . . . perhaps because of what Frank had seen on Lovers' Bank. His two sisters were very alike to look at, except that Ruthie had small tits and Ethel big ones; and Ruthie wore glasses and Ethel didn't. And there was Mary Gorse earning a shilling by looking after Agnes and Lily, Frank and Anne's little girls; and that meant that Mary had brought her own four younger ones. And, as Mary was here, so was Willum, sweating, beaming on the world, rushing to do everyone's bidding, bringing tea, buns, milk, mugs. Being knocked down hadn't hurt him a bit. More likely, he'd bent the car's mudguard.

Fred said, "I'm going to have a pint. Shall I be getting you one, Anne?"

She shook her head. "You know I don't touch liquor." Her voice and expression were virtuous, and Fred hid a smile. His sister-in-law was careful not to take any alcohol when Dad would know about it, because their church didn't approve of drinking: but in fact both Frank and Anne took a drop now and then, at home. Time was when Frank, too, pretended never to touch the Demon: but this last year he seemed to be paying less attention to what Dad thought . . . getting more independent at last.

Bill Hoggin came back with a pint of foaming mild-and-bitter in each hand, and sat down beside his wife Ruth. Ignoring his father-in-law's frown he said, "Drink up, Ruthie. It's good for the little 'un." He drank, wiped his lips, and turned to Bob Stratton. "You never told us what you're going to do when you retire, Dad. When is it?"

"September the first," Frank answered for him.

Hoggin continued, "Going to take Mum round the world, Dad, like old Rowland?"

Bob shook his square head and brushed a few drops of fallen tea from his beard. His Kentish accent, when he spoke, was stronger than his wife's or any of his children's: there had been little education when he was growing up in the small market and county town of Hedlington. He said, "No, I'm not. I'm going to stay at home and work on Victoria. I'm going to go a hundred miles an hour on her, before I'm finished."

"A hundred miles an hour!" Ruth gasped. "Why, Dad, that's impossible!"

"It's not impossible, woman. It's only a matter of hard work, and using your head, and your hands."

"Go on, Bob, you're sixty-five; you can't go that fast," his wife said. She drank more tea, and repeated, "You're sixty-five."

Bob said, "Aye, and I'll likely be sixty-eight before I break the record." He turned to his eldest son. "And the way you said 'September the first,' just then, about my retiring, I suppose you've got a calendar all marked out, counting down the days till I go, eh?"

Frank nodded amiably, "That's right, Dad."

"You won't find it easy being Works foreman of Rowland's, I can tell you."

"I reckon I can do it. I've had enough training to get ready, like."

The old man softened his tone a little. "It won't be so bad. Mr Richard'll have to find a better steel for the valves, and another supplier for steering wheels—these handmade things need too much labour . . . and we might look at aluminium for the windscreen frames. It's difficult to solder or weld, though . . . but the worst will be the men. The Union of Skilled Engineers is weak in the motor trade, but they've sent some men into Hedlington, to try to organise the factories here. There's only us and four, five others, so that Union men don't have to spread themselves too thin. Keep an eye on Bert Gorse. He's the sort that would listen to them."

Willum Gorse, leaning over the table nearby to set down another pot of tea, said, "Bert don't like the wages, Mr Stratton, nor the hours, nor the rules. Bert don't like anything. Bert ain't in the Union, but if he had his way we'd all be on strike all the time." He laughed cheerfully.

Anne said, "How can Bert be so different from you, Willum? You're half-brothers, aren't you?"

"Yes, Mrs Stratton . . . but *my* mother was kind. She never hit anyone. She hugged me. Dad would 'a kept her, only she died. Dad's next woman, Bert's mother, was bad. I didn't like her. She beat me and shut me in the cupboard. When Dad found out, he hit her on the nose and threw her in the Scarrow. She ran away after that."

"Proper unreasonable woman," Fred murmured.

Jane turned to her husband. "That reminds me . . . Niccolo's beating our Ethel, Dad. And he says he'll divorce her if she doesn't have a baby, a boy, soon. The very idea! You men must speak to him."

"Oh, Mother," Ethel Fagioletti said, sinking her head into her hands, her elbows on the bare table.

"I'll have a word with him, that I will," Bob said heavily.

"But how, Dad?" Jane said. "When? He works in London. He doesn't come down here. He daren't. You can't go up unless you don't go to chapel one Sunday."

"I'll go," Fred said shortly. "I'll tell him."

"He gambles, too," Jane said, "and loses money so Ethel doesn't have enough to keep body and soul together. Look at her dress!"

"We can't pay the rent," Ethel said, raising her head. She was crying, Fred saw, and thought she had been crying a long time, perhaps all day, perhaps she cried all year round, now. He remembered her laughing in the water, a seven-year-old girl, her dress splashed with mud where they were playing together in the edge of the Scarrow in North Hedlington, near where the barges unloaded. He was fourteen but she'd been fun then, in spite of being a kid, and a girl.

"You can't take a day off from the farm, can you, Fred?" his mother asked anxiously.

"'Course I can! Rowland doesn't own me body and soul, Mum. I'll tell him I have to go. I'll give him two or three days warning and he can damn well . . ."

"Don't swear, Fred."

". . . do the jobs himself that day."

"Shhh! There's Mr Harry and Mrs Rose, and Miss Alice."

"Ask them to come and sit here, Frank. Hurry now!" Jane said, "and Fred, you go and get some tea for them. Make room there, Ethel, and wipe your eyes. You don't want Mr Harry to see you like that. Move along on the bench, Ruth. Mary, clean those children's faces. Agnes, take that bun out of your mouth . . ."

They all stood up as Harry Rowland approached with his wife and daughter, the last leading three dachshunds on a single leash. They wound through the noisy crowded tent, the dogs straining and dodging among people's legs, everyone tinged a strange shade of brown from the sun's rays filtering through the dun canvas.

Jane gave a small, almost invisible bob as she greeted Rose Rowland, and then the two elderly women embraced, briefly enfolding each other in their pleated and starched white-clad arms. Harry put out his hand. "Kind of you to ask us to share your place, Bob."

Bob shook his employer's hand. "Sit down, Mr Harry, sit down."
The two men smiled at each other, hands clasped. Both had short
square-cut beards, Rowland's pure white, Stratton's grey flecked; their
height was nearly the same, about five foot eight; and their manner was
somehow the same; but there the resemblance between the parson's son
from Devonshire and the plumber's son from here in Hedlington
ended. Harry Rowland was strongly built and ruddy of complexion,
with a shock of curly white hair and a beak nose; Bob Stratton was
thin and hunched, snub-nosed, grey skinned, and wore glasses. They
had known each other, and relied on each other, since the year Harry
came to Hedlington and founded his bicycle factory—1876, thirty-eight
years ago.

Then Harry was shaking hands all round, and Rose was sitting
down next to Jane Stratton; and Alice Rowland by Anne, the dachshunds bouncing under the table with Anne's little girls, and everyone
was saying, "You're looking well," and "Here's your tea, m'm," and "I
hope your husband's well, Ethel," as though they had not set eyes on
each other for a year; whereas many of the men saw each other every
day, and the women frequently enough. But this was Hedlington
Sheep Fair and it was only on this day and one or two others that the
families sat down together, and then only briefly, for Mr Harry did not
spend much time at the Fair now. His sons hardly ever came at all, but
Mr Harry was about the most important manufacturer in Hedlington,
and a leading supporter of Hedlington Rovers, the town football team,
and of the town band, and a score of other worthy organisations, and
he felt it his duty to attend—to see, and be seen.

"How did the gymkhana go today, Bob?" he asked.

"Oh pretty good, pretty good. The best on it was that one of ours
won."

"What? One of the new ones? A Sapphire?"

"No, Mr Harry, and this'll surprise you. It was the Ruby, built in
1910—I looked at the serial number. She's easier to start and stop on a
hill. Johnson did all right with the Works Sapphire, but—" he shrugged
"—wouldn't start a couple of times. Valve trouble. Mr Richard's going
to have to design a better one, and that's a fact."

"Bob!" Rose Rowland said, shaking a finger at him across the table.
"Shop, shop! This is a holiday. Do you and Harry never come out of
the factory?"

"Sorry, m'm," Bob said, grinning. "Mr Harry knows there's nothing
else inside my head, except motor cars—and Victoria—eh, Mr Harry?"

Then for a time everyone was asking about babies and children and
whooping cough, and a listener suspended invisible above the long

table where they sat would have thought again that these people had not seen each other for a long time.

Harry Rowland broke the chatter by saying, "Now we're all talking like a Women's Club outing, and that's just as bad as men's shop. Have we nothing else to think about, at the Sheep Fair?"

"Frank Woolley will be playing at the County Ground, August Bank Holiday, Mr Harry," Willum Gorse crowed, "an' I'll be there, watching him make a century!" He swished an imaginary cricket bat through the air, beaming.

Harry Rowland said, "Only the Almighty could guarantee that, Willum . . . but Woolley *is* a god, to you, isn't he?"

Willum beamed wider, but said nothing.

Frank leaned toward Harry Rowland. "What's going to happen about the murder of that Duke at that place, blowed if I can pronounce it?"

"Nor can I," Harry said. "It's a storm in a teapot, Frank. Oh, Austria might invade Serbia, I suppose. They might have a little war down there, even—nothing to do with us."

"I hope not," Jane said fervently. "Those nasty foreigners can't behave themselves for five minutes."

"Thank heaven for the English Channel," Harry said. "Why, if they had a war and we were in it, I could hardly take Mrs Rowland round the world, could I?" Everyone laughed.

Frank said, "How's the major, m'm?"

"He said he was quite well, in his last letter. Though I wish he'd get out of Ireland, for his sake as well as mine. There should not be any British soldiers in Ireland."

There was an awkward silence. Everyone knew of Rose Rowland's views on Ireland, but that did not make them any easier to accept, in such a place and among such people as these.

Ruth Hoggin said in a small voice, "I see Eton College didn't do well at Henley, Mr Harry."

Harry said, "'Fraid so, Ruth . . . but I didn't know you followed rowing."

Ruth said in a still smaller voice, "It's Eton College, Mr Harry. I always remember there was a picture of Master Richard, as he was, in the papers, rowing for the College. I cut it out and kept it till I lost it. I was only a little girl, then."

Harry laughed, "Well, well! Alice, those dogs of yours are jumping all over everybody . . ."

"Down, Bismarck! Down, Freda!" Alice Rowland snapped. "These animals have no patience . . . or too much energy. They've been trying to pull us in here for the past hour—they smelled the food—and now they're trying to pull us out."

Harry said, "I suppose we'd better be going, Rose. I'll take the dogs, Alice . . . Goodbye, Jane. See you on Monday, Bob . . . goodbye, goodbye . . ." They went out of the tent, the dachshunds straining at the leash.

"Miss Alice is looking very nice," Jane announced as soon as the Rowlands had left the tent. "It's a crying shame that some nice gentleman hasn't asked her to marry him long since."

"She's no chicken," Fred said. "Must be thirty-five if she's a day."

"Thirty-four, and a real lady," his mother said firmly, "and it's a shame."

"Perhaps someone has asked her," Ethel Fagioletti said timidly, "and she said 'no'."

A man at the next table got up and came toward them. He was short and slight with a big head, ginger hair, high cheekbones, green eyes and a wide, down-turned angry mouth. It was Willum's younger half-brother, Albert Gorse.

Willum saw him and said, "Hullo, Bert. I didn't know you was in here, or you could 'ave came and sat with the rest of us, couldn't he, Mr Bob?"

Bert ignored him and spoke to Frank. "Frank, I heard you ask old Rowland about the mess in Europe, but couldn't hear what he answered, the woman next to me over there was making such a bloody row. What did he say?"

Frank said coldly, "I'm Mr Stratton to you, Bert Gorse, and don't you forget it . . . Mr Harry said that it was nothing, least, not to England. He said it doesn't concern us."

Bert Gorse's lips readily formed into a sneer; but Fred thought that he didn't always mean it as that, it was just the way his lips were made. Now they went deliberately to that sneer, as he said, "If the bosses and the capitalists think there's money in a war, we'll be in it. Money's the only thing that concerns them, always, anywhere."

"Hey, are you talking about Mr Harry?" Willum burst out. "That's . . . *silly*, Bert!"

Frank said, "You're talking—" he checked an expletive, and ended "—nonsense!"

"It's no nonsense, you'll see," Gorse said, the sneer deepening. "There's money in war for the bosses. For the working man, death." He walked cockily back to the other table. Willum shook his head slowly from side to side, like a puzzled weary ox; then caught Fred's eye and smiled generously and waved a hand. He never had understood Bert, or what he wanted, but he liked Fred.

Fred stood up, saying, "I'm going to take a breath of fresh air."

The ground shook to a heavy thud, soundless, carried through the earth. Almost simultaneously there was a loud explosion—then silence. After a few seconds' hush, the silence was drowned by a roaring hiss, by screams and cries and the crunch of rending wood. Frank and Bill Hoggin were on their feet, Fred running for the exit of the marquee, three long strides ahead of them. Men followed from other tables. The women slowly huddled together. Ruth started after her husband, brushing off her mother's restraining arm.

"Wha' . . . wha' . . . what was that?" Ethel's voice was tremulous.

"I don't know," her mother whispered. " 'Twas like nothing I ever heard on this God's earth."

Fred was among the first half-dozen men out of the crowded marquee and almost as soon as he reached the open air, he stopped dead. Fifty yards away the great merry-go-round was half hidden in a cloud of steam. Shards of metal lay scattered on the grass among seated or prostrate figures, some moaning, some silent. The machine's wooden canopy was shattered, the painted horses and gryphons and giraffes broken and twisted. Half hidden in the steam and drifting smoke, the sun now low in the west, children and a few adults crawled out of the wreckage, some dragging a blood-soaked leg or arm, some holding their stomachs and retching, some scalded an angry scarlet by the steam.

Fred found his sister at his side and pushed her roughly back. "Go back, Ruth, this is no sight for women. Stay inside, all of you."

He didn't wait to see if she would obey him, but ran forward, nausea rising to his throat. He realised that Willum Gorse's wife, Mary, was running at his side and he shouted roughly, "Go back!"

She said, "I'm not afraid, Mr Stratton. I can help."

Then they were among the ruins of the merry-go-round. Fred saw a hand sticking out from under the heavy wood and steel platform that had once carried sedately bobbing riders round and round. He seized the edge of the platform in both hands and grunting like a madman tried to lift it free of the hand and the child—it was a little girl's hand—that lay underneath. Bill Hoggin ran to him, shouting roughly, "You're wasting your time, Fred. We can't lift that—it weighs a ton, the supports are broken and she's dead as a doornail, must be. Come here. Look." He pushed through some smashed hobby horses to a small figure lying among them face down, motionless, in a lake of blood. He lifted a hot, jagged, steel plate off the boy and together they gently turned him over. He was alive, a painted splinter from some wooden animal sticking into his stomach, which was streaming bright blood, part of his entrails hanging out below the splinter. "Christ Almighty," Hoggin muttered, wrenching off his coat. He began to tie it over the boy's wound, by the sleeves, when Mary Gorse joined them, crying, "Wait, sir!" She ripped off her pink blouse, revealing a large white bodice, and knelt beside the boy, who had begun to whimper, clawing helplessly with his one good arm at his belly. She propped him up with her knee and said, "Hold him there, one of you." Fred took over, feeling his gorge rising. He turned his head and vomited, still holding the boy, as Mary Gorse pushed the trailing entrail back into the cavity and tied her blouse round the whole, fastening it at the back. "Carry him out now, both of you. On his back, lest more falls out."

They took him up, and stepped out slowly through the dying steam, over and through the wreckage. When they were well clear, Hoggin said, "Put him down, Fred. We got to go back and see if there's any more. 'Ere, you, look after this kid till a doctor comes. Don't let him move."

They went back together into the carnage, to join a dozen others on the same task. Blood was everywhere, in pools and still-dripping rivulets, slowly congealing. And hair, and skin, and once a hand and wrist, wrenched off the man to whom they had belonged. There were only three more people too severely hurt to move without help—two children and a woman; other rescuers were freeing them and taking them out. No sign of the man without a hand, Fred thought; he's probably somewhere in the crowd, walking about, dazed and shocked, his dangling sleeve ending in a bloody stump.

"What happened?" he said to another man.

"Boiler burst. One of the Fair fellows said it's only happened once before in England—Croydon, 1912, he said. Now we have to get it."

"There weren't too many people here," Fred said.

"I reckon not, not being dark yet and all . . . but there's half a dozen bad from the steam, besides those who got bits of wood or steel into them."

"I saw," Fred said. The taste of vomit was sour in his mouth. There was nothing more he could do. A man was kneeling on the grass beside the boy they'd carried out. He recognised one of the Hedlington doctors. With the doctor were a couple of women, sleeves rolled, blouses stained. A man had lent Mary Gorse his coat, to cover her near nakedness. The two bobbies on duty at the Fair were holding the crowd back, "Stand back there now, stand back, sir . . . stand back . . ."

He walked toward the marquee. Frank joined him, and they went in side by side, heads bent. Frank said, "How many were killed, do you think?"

"Eleven, someone said, counting the scalded. And about fifteen hurt, some of 'em bad."

Frank shook in an uncontrollable fit of shivering. "I reckon we'll never see anything worse however long we live."

"Reckon not."

"Thank God."

Daily Telegraph, Saturday, July 11, 1914

Kent beat Somerset at Gravesend yesterday, with supreme ease, the victory by nine wickets being accomplished shortly before four o'clock. Some such result was made likely by the progress of the game on Thursday, when the champions, with a wicket in hand, had already secured a lead of 134 runs. Kent's innings closed in the first few minutes after resuming for the addition of a solitary run, and then the visitors opened their second attempt so successfully that shortly before luncheon they had only two men out for 118. Then came a complete change. The home team had only 49 to make. Naturally enough, on the improved pitch this task proved an easy one.

Cate glanced down the tabulated score. The Somerset first innings had been a disaster for them, with only Poyntz standing up to the bowling. Hubble had made a century for Kent, and Blythe had taken eleven wickets for 133, and bowled 33 overs against a total of nine wickets and 49 overs for Kent's three other bowlers. The figures would be enough indication of Blythe's genius as a left-hand slow spinner even if you did not know that he was frail of constitution, and suffered from epileptic seizures. Half closing his eyes Cate could see him now, as he had watched him so many times at Hedlington or Canterbury—stuttering, hesitant run to the crease, left arm curving back, the hand almost in his right trouser pocket, then the arm flying over, the ball curving lazily down toward the batsman, hitting the turf, fizzing with spin, darting like a knife clean across the wicket . . . unplayable!

He put down the paper and glanced at the clock on the mantelpiece. Four o'clock. What needed to be done, before tea? Last night the port had been low in the decanter, he remembered. It would be a good time to go down to the cellar and decant another bottle. He got up, found a spare decanter in the dining-room sideboard, and went to the cellar

stairs. At the head he swung open the creaking old door, dating from
the Manor's fourteenth-century predecessor, and switched on the electric light. He went carefully down the uneven stairs—no one knew
when they dated from—moving his head instinctively to dodge the
beam, also from the fourteenth century, that stuck out of one wall half
way down. His father had wanted to have that beam taken out forty
years ago, but Probyn Gorse had sworn the whole house would fall
down if he did . . . Cate doubted that, but it was dangerous to fly
against Probyn's advice, when he chose to offer any; his sources of information were hearsay from centuries back, probably, perhaps occult—
but when they could be tested (which wasn't often) they seldom proved
false.

The port bin was in the far corner, by the piece of exposed flooring
from the Roman villa which had stood on this site before the mediaeval
manor house. It was dusty in there, and the mosaics were quite hard to
see even with the electric light on. It was a pity they weren't in the
open, for the colours were still bright in the woman's face and the edge
of the man's robe, the couple who had lived on this land so long before
him.

July 11th . . . it was his brother-in-law Quentin's birthday, on the
18th—his fortieth, wasn't it? If Quentin and Fiona had been at home in
Hedlington he'd have taken them a bottle of the Cockburn '83 to celebrate. But Quentin wasn't; he was at the Curragh, and Fiona was at
home alone . . . something wrong there, yet Quentin loved Fiona, he
was sure of that. Perhaps Fiona wasn't . . . Quentin was a good soldier, unimaginative, perhaps, but brave, utterly honest, devoted to his
men, the best type of British subaltern. Only, he wasn't a subaltern
now, he was a major. As a major, he should have more—what? Ability
to question? Look round corners? He wondered, frowning slightly, how
many other majors and colonels his description of Quentin fitted? How
many generals? Did it fit the British army as a whole? Possibly. Probably, he admitted with an inward sigh.

What about the navy then? Enormously powerful, dedicated, fiercely
proud of their great tradition . . . too proud, perhaps? Somewhat nar-
row-minded? Undoubtedly, but beloved of the people certainly . . .
Conscription for the army, as all the continental nations had it—enrol-
ment of every able-bodied youth at the age of eighteen or so for two
years with the Colours—was unthinkable here: apart from general dislike of the army, an all-volunteer force was best suited to its peacetime
role of imperial policing . . . but compulsory service for the navy was
quite imaginable, because it might become necessary for survival. It
would just be an extension of the old press gangs, and everyone knew

how essential they had been. But . . . he wished he could think of some great naval hero of the moment: Nelson and his captains were long gone; Lord Charles Beresford—gone; the Royal Navy headed by a German prince and that cocky political opportunist, Churchill—cocky, but brilliant, he couldn't deny that. People talked of Admirals Jellicoe and Beatty, but they hadn't proved their worth yet, and couldn't, except in battle. So, just how effective was the navy whereon—how did the powerful old phrase go?—under the good Providence of God, the wealth, safety, and strength of the kingdom do chiefly depend? No one knew: they only believed.

And now some people were talking of the need for a separate air force. Impossible to imagine! Those frail kites could hardly stay up in the air, let alone destroy anything—except themselves and their riders . . . but they could see, spy, like circling vultures they would be, in a war . . .

But what was he doing, standing motionless in his cellar, thinking of flying machines and war, when he had come down to select and decant a bottle of port for his table? He chose a bottle, opened it with the corkscrew in the bin and, pouring very carefully, decanted it; then climbed slowly back up the stairs, switching off the light and closing the creaky old door behind him.

Hedlington: Sunday, July 12, 1914

4   "Satan lies in wait. Satan does not sleep. The hand of Satan is not seen unless we search for it in every action, by the light of God's Holy Word, as set forth to us in the scriptures. Like the wicked wolf, Satan clothes himself in sheep's clothing. Like the foolish sheep, man is devoured . . . unless he judges not by what he sees with his outward eye, but by what he sees with the inward eye that God gave him, the eye of judgment, informed by the Holy Word as set forth in the scriptures. Satan . . ."

Bob Stratton's thoughts wandered. It was a hot morning and he wished he could have left off his thick serge coat and waistcoat, but that would be unthinkable for chapel. The Reverend Mr Hunnicutt had spoken for twenty minutes already, and looked to be good for twice as much more. The text of his sermon was from *Exodus* 20; 9,10: *Six days shalt thou labour, and do all thy work: but the seventh day is the sabbath of the LORD thy God: in it thou shalt not do any work, thou, nor thy son, nor thy daughter, thy manservant, nor thy maidservant, nor thy cattle, nor the stranger that is within thy gates.* The Reverend Mr Hunnicutt was particularly hot on the subject, even more so than on the evils of drink, which was unusual in a Wesleyan minister. He gave this sermon, or one uncommon like it, at least three times a year.

Jane's elbow digging gently into his ribs made him raise his head. Jane must have thought he was about to doze off. He stroked his beard and kept his head up, gazing at the minister, but in fact looking through him to the bare wall and plain window behind. The Wesleyans did not go in for the pomp and paint of the Established

Church, and quite right, too. Chapel goers were plain people, honest men who mostly worked with their hands, and took an honest week's wage for an honest week's work.

Frank and Anne were here, he knew—they were good chapel people, devout and regular—but neither of his daughters, nor Fred. Ethel was in London, where that Fagioletti was probably trying to turn her to the Whore of Rome . . . Fred was back in Walstone, at Mr John's farm. Or was he? Jane said there was talk of him being entangled with a widow here in Hedlington. Perhaps she'd come late to the Fair, and they'd danced, there on the stained grass, among splinters of wood and sharp bits of steel. And then gone to her home, and stayed all night, and he'd taken the first train back to Walstone this morning . . . or maybe even walked. It wasn't more than twelve miles if you knew the short cuts.

They should have cancelled the dancing, after what happened. But he'd heard, on the way to chapel this morning, that the dance had gone on as usual to the music of a pair of gypsy fiddlers . . . wilder than usual, even, as though the recent passage of violent death, so close, had heightened everyone's lust for life. And lust was the word, by George, his informant had said—the young people going off in couples to Lovers' Bank, holding each other tight, staggering down into darkness, coming back into the flaring lights, the reek of gin and spilled beer, faces glowing, burrs in the girls' hair and on the backs of their dresses. Disgraceful, but women were frail cattle, and when the young men wanted them badly, they gave in.

". . . on the Sabbath thou shalt do no labour. That means *no* labour!" the Reverend Mr Hunnicutt thundered, pointing down. "The Lord God did not say, Thou shalt not do *much* labour . . . or, thou shalt do only a *little* labour. He said, Thou shalt do NO labour. And yet Satan . . ."

Bob wondered, for the hundredth time perhaps, whether Mr Hunnicutt would count his work on Victoria as labour. There was that word 'work,' but it wasn't work really, not to him. He didn't get paid for it, the way he got paid as Works foreman at Rowland's. He didn't do it regularly, the way he went regularly to work at Rowland's . . . but that was a lie. Regular as clockwork, he worked—he *pottered* with Victoria in the shed every Sunday afternoon; and every work day, after he had come home and washed his hands and eaten his dinner, he went down to the shed to look at her, and sometimes do a little more . . . pottering. But wasn't that just what he did when he went to Rowland's—look in at his office, just beyond where the linoleum ended on the passage floor, then to the machine shop, then the storage room, the fitting assembly shop, the adjustment shop, the fabrication shops for steel and wood, then back to the offices and a word with Mr Harry or Mr Richard . . . looking, noting, doing what had to be done? Pottering.

He had never thought it necessary to tell Mr Hunnicutt what he did on the Sabbath and, so to speak, ask his blessing. That would be a mite popish, like confession. Besides, what if Mr Hunnicutt said working on Victoria *was* labour? Most people knew, because it was no secret that Bob Stratton was working on a motor cycle to go faster than any had ever done before. Botheration! Was it or wasn't it 'working'?

Mr Hunnicutt was drawing to a peroration: the sermon wasn't going to last as long as he had thought. He settled himself more comfortably in his pew. He missed Ruth. She had been his favourite daughter and a devout chapel goer. Now she was married to that red-faced Hoggin and she never came. Hoggin was Church of England, he said; but Bob doubted that he ever actually attended. From the look of him, spending the day in pubs or at a cockfight would be more his mark; and he was dragging Ruth down into that ungodliness with him. To tell the truth, she'd gone willingly. He'd never seen anyone so happy, except Frank and Anne, and they were different. Ruthie adored Hoggin—that was the only word for it, the Lord knew; and Ethel, poor snivelling Ethel, had found something to snivel about when she married that dago, and . . .

But hadn't Fred read in a book where it said that the Sabbath was made for man, not man for the Sabbath? He might ask Mr Hunnicutt about that. How would that square with his sermon? Better not. Better let sleeping dogs lie. Just find another word for what he did with Victoria—potter wasn't right. Nor was play. Hobby? He'd have to think of something. *Worship?*

The sermon ended and he knelt to pray. He willed himself, as always in these final moments of the service, to see God. He was tall, English of course, and clean shaven, he was sure of that—nothing like the pictures they painted of Jesus, with a blond beard. No, He was stern, with big hands and feet—powerful, serviceable hands, not dirty in the flesh or under the nails, but marked with the signs of labour in the hardness of the skin, and with skill, in the way they moved. Not a carpenter, like His Son . . . a blacksmith, or a stone mason, perhaps. Women knelt round His feet. There were no other men, no Son or Holy Ghost, only the Father, and the women, silently praying, heads bowed.

"Amen!"

"Amen!"

"And finally let us say a special prayer for the victims of yesterday's terrible accident at the Fair, even though none were of this congregation . . . Oh Lord, in whose sight a sparrow does not fall unseen, take into Thy bosom the souls of those killed in yesterday's disaster at the Fairgrounds, and grant them eternal peace. This we ask in the name of Jesus Christ, Our Lord. Amen!"

"Amen!"

Bob rose heavily to his feet, gathered up his prayer book and Bible, found his hat and stick, and walked down the aisle at Jane's side, their son Frank and his wife close behind.

Outside the chapel, they waited their turn to speak a word of praise to the minister. Mr Hunnicutt stood in the sunshine beside the little yew at the chapel door, the graveyard to his right. Below the tall spiked railings of the churchyard, rows of houses stretched down to the Scarrow.

"An excellent sermon, if I may say so, Mr Hunnicutt," Bob said.

"Thank you, Mr Stratton, thank you. I always value your opinion. You are looking well, Mrs Stratton."

"Yes, Mr Hunnicutt, and feeling it too, praise be."

Frank and Anne spoke to the minister in their turn, then the four of them started down the gravel walk toward the gate to the street.

"Excuse me, sir . . . Mr Bob!"

Bob looked up. "Hullo, Willum. What are you doing here? You're not Wesleyan."

"Oh no, Mr Bob, Church of England we are. I come here to ask if I could have the day off, Tuesday, like."

"What for?"

They were all gathered, watching the big man in the worn work clothes, with the big pleasant face and vacant eyes. His hands were twined together, knotted, not painfully, but as though they could not separate.

"It's my dad," he said, "down to Walstone." He looked embarrassed and fell silent.

"Well, what about Probyn?" Bob said. "Out with it."

Frank cut in—"It's his trial, isn't it?"

"Yes, Mr Frank, that's it," Willum burst out. "It's at the magistrate's court in Walstone, Tuesday. I'm his son."

"I know that, but what can you do?" Bob said. "You're not a lawyer. You can't give any evidence that the magistrates will listen to. I suppose it's poaching?"

Willum nodded and said, "I ought to be there, Mr Bob, that's it. He's my dad."

"Sure you're not going to sneak off to the County Ground and watch Frank Woolley and Colin Blythe now?"

"Oh no, Mr Bob!"

"All right then. But mind, I'll have to nick you a day's wage."

"All right, Mr Bob, thank you." He wrung Bob's hand suddenly, touched his lock, and turned to run off.

Jane called, "Wait there, Willum!" Willum turned, looking alarmed. Jane said, "Tell Mary that I'd like her to make a pair of dresses for Frank's girls. I forgot to tell her yesterday. Let her come to the house tomorrow afternoon, and we'll talk about it."

"That I'll do . . . dresses for Frank's girls . . . I'll tell her."

"Tomorrow afternoon, Willum."

Willum touched his forelock again, and ran off with an ungainly long stride, out of the gate and down the street toward the river.

Jane looked after him with a sigh. "Mary's far too good for him," she said, "but he'd be lost without her, so I suppose it's all for the best."

"And they love each other," Anne said in a small voice, "even if Willum is simple."

Then after a few moments, Frank and Anne said goodbye to their parents, and headed for their own house, holding hands like lovers. Bob and Jane walked sedately on, her hand resting on the serge of his navy-blue sleeve. It was past noon, and the closer they came to the river the louder grew the sounds of the town. They passed what seemed to be a solid row of public houses, sloping steeply down toward the river. Trams passed, steel brakes squealing on steel wheels, bells clanging, the front and back platforms crowded with standing men. Outside the pubs the men basked in the sun, leaning against the pub walls, laughing, quaffing great draughts of bitter. There were women, sitting on benches, pushing each other, giggling, their hair disheveled, glasses of gin beside them; there was a boy of about nine running down the street carrying two foam-topped tankards of ale; there was a man senseless in the gutter, his head in a pool of vomit . . .

Bob and Jane passed on, unswerving, heads high, galleons before a steady following breeze. Bob was aware that he knew some of these men, for they worked in Rowland's. Some were here just for a pint, and then home. Some would be here till stoptap, their week's wages gone, their weeping wives come to support them home. But he never spoke to any of them when they were drinking at a pub, especially on a Sunday. He would not even recognise them, or see them then, lest he be prejudiced against them at work the next day.

Jervis Street was a row of semi-detached houses on the north side of Hedlington, on the west side of the Scarrow valley, barely ten minutes walk from Rowland's factory. A low iron railing separated the two small front gardens—barely more than plots—belonging to the two sides of each house. All the houses were nearly similar, except where here and there minor alterations had been made. Like the rest, No. 85 had two stories and a basement—kitchen, pantry, back parlour, which was also used as the dining-room, front parlour on the ground floor; and three bedrooms on the second, plus one bathroom and water closet. There was a small room, with another water closet, in the basement. There slept and had her being each of the endless succession of girls who had been general maids for the Strattons for the past thirty years— girls who had come at fourteen or fifteen, worked for two or three years, then moved out of the basement and the house, to marriage, or a shop—or, in at least one case, Bob and Jane knew, to the streets, as a harlot.

"You go and read the paper," Jane said. "I'll look at the joint. We'll have our dinner at half-past one sharp . . . Nellie!"

Bob pulled his watch from its fob and checked it against the grandfather clock in the hall. In the kitchen, he heard Nellie washing dishes. Jane had gone up for her usual Sunday afternoon nap. He himself had dozed, as always, in his favourite chair in the parlour. Now he walked down the passage and let himself out of the back door. The back garden was twenty yards long and ten wide. On each side a creosoted wooden fence seven feet high separated it from the neighbouring back gardens, of No. 84 on one side, No. 86 on the other. A narrow gravel path ran down the right hand fence, of No. 84, all the way to the end, where it led to a shed and to a gate in the back fence. Between the path and the fence of No. 86 the ground was covered with grass, not as thick or as well kept as Bob would have liked to see it. Jane's interest lay in the flower bed in front of the house, and his own in the shed. It was in that shed that he was building Victoria. Victoria had been his mother's name. He had worshipped her.

The shed was seventeen feet by ten feet six inches, one long side against the back wall of the garden. The door by which Bob had entered was in two equal parts; when both were open, he could wheel out the machine which, raised a foot off the floor on a steel trestle and supported on either side by wooden props, dominated the room, not by its size but by its sheer presence. It was a motor cycle, but as the sun shone on it through the door as Bob went in, a man with eyes half open could believe it was St George . . . shining, brilliant, burnished steel.

It was lean and low, the saddle set back over the rear wheel, handlebars curved downwards and tucked in close against the front fork—for this was Victoria, which existed only to reach 100 miles an hour over a measured mile in two directions; and to achieve that the rider had to flatten himself along the machine and cheat the wind. None of the metal work was painted, and never would be. The only dark parts of Victoria were the brown leather of the saddle, the grey-black of the tyres, and the matt black of the two cylinder barrels.

She occupied the middle of the floor, crouching, heading for the now-closed doors. Along the back wall was a Drummond precision lathe, and a larger lathe for rougher work, both driven by belt from a 1½ hp electric motor. To one side stood a piece of apparatus, heavy-set bearing brackets supporting a shaft on which ran a flat-faced pulley wheel; shaped wooden blocks pressed against the pulley's edge, and a long steel balance arm projected beyond the upper of the two blocks: this was the Prony brake, used to measure the power output of Victoria's engine. Above the workbench, and all along the other wall, were wooden racks of screwdrivers, spanners, hand drills, and files—bastard, half-round, needle-nose, riffler . . . each with its own part in Bob's great task.

After looking round, breathing deep of the mixed smells of worked steel and clean oil, he removed his coat and waistcoat and hung them on a hook behind the door—the bowler hat never left his head except in chapel, and in private houses. Working carefully, he disconnected the flexible coupling between Victoria's driving shaft and the Prony brake, and refitted the engine sprocket and primary drive chain. Removing the props from either side, he lowered the back wheel onto a broad rubber wheel set in the floor, and connected a thick rubber tube to the exhaust, to carry its fumes to the outside through a hole in the wall.

Then he placed a pair of filled sandbags across the machine's saddle to represent a rider's weight, restored the props, making sure that the machine was now upright and steady, and checked the clamps that gripped the front wheel. He poured a pint of petrol into the fuel tank, gave the plunger of the hand oil pump a couple of hefty shoves, adjusted the setting of the air, magneto, and throttle levers, pulled the half-compression trigger and kicked the engine into life. Gradually he let in the clutch, and ran up through the gears—first, second, top—opening the throttle lever until the back wheel was rotating on the floor wheel at close on twenty miles an hour; then he stood back a pace, listened, and watched. The engine ran smoothly, the machine vibrating slightly but evenly, restrained by the props. Yet, last time he ran her, he was sure the vibration had been uneven. That was after he had fitted the first of the pair of Rudge rear wheels which Collis had tuned for him in Rowland's wheel shop—after working hours, his time paid for by Bob—all with Mr Harry's blessing.

He stepped forward, increased the speed to thirty miles an hour, and stepped back again, watching and listening, his head cocked. Still nothing.

He pulled back the throttle lever a little more, watching the needle of the Stewart speedometer climb to forty . . . fifty . . . sixty . . . ah, now he was getting it—faint but clear. At seventy it became definite to the eye as well as the ear—a rhythmic vibration that coincided with the speed of the rotation of the wheel. At seventy Victoria trembled in short bursts to that periodic rhythm. It would be bad on road or track, really going this fast . . . but at a hundred, what then?

He stopped the machine, detached the driving belt, slipped out the rear wheel and, in its stead, inserted the second of the Rudge pair that Collis had tuned.

Ten minutes later he started the engine again, and again ran the simulated speed up to seventy miles an hour. There was no vibration, no audible thrumming. The driving vee-belt ran true, the motor cycle remaining steady on its mount.

He sat down, staring at Victoria, thinking. Collis had tuned both wheels, and he was a good man, steeped in the art of spoking. He was getting a little old perhaps, but no older than himself. He'd have to take the faulty wheel back and have Collis mount it in his trueing jig, there to adjust each spoke nipple delicately until both belt rim and wheel rim ran in perfect alignment. He could do some balancing himself, by wrapping lead wire round a pair of adjacent spokes, close to the rim, and taping over the wire so that it wouldn't come adrift at speed . . . but the final balancing would have to be done with the tyre in place, the wheel held firm by its three evenly spaced security bolts.

Well, he couldn't do any more there now. He decided to spend the rest of his time working on the inlet tract of a spare cylinder. At everyday touring speeds the internal finish of the passageways for the petrol and air mixture was relatively unimportant, but when an engine was demanding all that the carburetor could supply they had to be smooth as glass, to cause no turbulence in the flow. He held the cylinder up to the shed window. Yes, there was a rough patch just behind the valve guide. He picked out a riffler file—narrow, its point curving upwards like the toe of a Turkish slipper.

He stood a moment, file in hand, thinking. When he began to feel the onset of a slight tremble, he groaned, put down the file, opened a drawer in the workbench and pulled out a battered piece of cardboard some twelve inches long by eight or nine inches high. On the cardboard was pasted an advertisement for Rowland cars, showing specifically the 1910 four-cylinder Ruby tourer, which he had cut out of the magazine where it had appeared. He propped this up in the window that looked out on the lane, the picture side outward, against the glass, then he drew the curtain behind it, set the cylinder on the bench, picked up the riffler file and began to work slowly, carefully, and with love. He was waiting and listening, too, but they were not uppermost in his mind, as long as he was at work.

Jane Stratton awoke, yawning and stretching luxuriously. Warm air blew gently through the open window, stirring the lace curtains, bringing with it the sound of boys playing in Jervis Street outside. She had slept an hour, as she always did, secure in the knowledge that Bob was in his shed, Nellie reading a love story in the basement, and nothing to be done in the kitchen or anywhere else in the house. Later, Bob would come in for his tea, with bread and butter and perhaps a boiled egg or some cold meat left over from dinner, and then they'd walk out of the house and to the chapel for evening service.

She liked to spend this half hour thinking of her house and family. During the week she felt that she never had a minute for *thinking*, because she was always *doing*. As soon as one job was done, the next was there, waiting. So on Sunday afternoons she tried to look a little farther ahead and around. Frank and Anne were the easiest: never anything to worry about there, except perhaps that Anne worked too hard, what with the two little girls and another on the way. She'd be better off when Frank took his father's place. Then she could afford a harder working girl than that useless Clara, or perhaps have Clara work longer hours . . . Fred ought to get married. The widow he was seeing was a hussy—had been a hussy before she ever married, and her husband's drowning hadn't changed her—why should it? The only good thing about her was that she lived here in Hedlington and Walstone was fifteen miles away by road. The foreman of a farm didn't have much spare time to go gallivanting after women. But she ought to find a good woman for Fred . . . not too young, certainly not flighty. She ran pictures of girls and young women of her acquaintance through her mind, like one of those new moving pictures: Mary Dale . . . too young; Jane Moody . . . too old—why she must be four years older than Fred; Annie Kingston . . . a flibbertigibbet—she'd have Fred in the poor house in no time; Jill Parsons . . . ah, there was a nice young woman, twenty-four or five to Fred's thirty-one; good family, well set up, took care of herself, worked hard in her father's drapery shop, always polite to customers . . . the only snag was, Jane had heard that another man was courting her—Michael something . . . And how could Fred be persuaded to come to Hedlington to do *his* courting if he had so little spare time? She'd have to speak to Bob about it . . . Bob . . . she acknowledged that she was dreading the moment when he retired, and she'd have him about the house all the time. He'd spend most of the day in the shed, of course. With luck, he'd just treat the shed as though it was Rowland's; go down there at seven-thirty sharp, with his lunch pail, work till the whistle went—he could hear the whistle at Rowland's if he left the windows open—eat his lunch there, then back to work again till he'd walk up the path and in at five o'clock. The only difference in their lives then would be that he'd leave and return by the back door instead of the front.

She got out of bed and stood up, yawning. She was wearing her chemise and nothing more—a pigeon-like woman with a big bust, blue eyes, and greying brown hair. She washed her face and hands in cold water at the wash-handstand and began to dress, paying no attention to what she was doing, for her thoughts were still elsewhere . . . on Ruth, so proud of that coarse husband, and of the baby she was going to have. Well, that was all right. The world would be a sorry place if women didn't love the babies they carried under their hearts . . . except perhaps if they'd been forced on them, like. Ruthie was so sure it was going to be a boy and would grow up to be just like Bill Hoggin. God save us all from that, and him a bastard into the bargain! Well, a Christian shouldn't hold that against a man, as Frank said. It wasn't his fault that his mother was a slut that drank gin and went with sailors down narrow alleys by the docks—for money, no doubt . . . Ethel ought to stand up more to Niccolo, that was a fact. Fred had said he'd speak to him, and that was good; it had to be done. But someone ought to speak to Ethel, too. It was all right for a husband and wife to make love—though her Bob had never been much of a one for that, to tell the truth—but when it came to a woman being hurt, the way Ethel said Niccolo hurt her, down there, always on her, not caring how she was, all hours of the day and night that he was home, and then talking about divorcing her because she hadn't had a baby! It wasn't always the woman's fault. She should go to the doctor . . . and suppose it turned out that Niccolo was the one who couldn't make a baby? What a disgrace that would be for Niccolo! That's the only thing he had any sense of shame about—he certainly didn't have any about beating Ethel, or spending his wages on gambling, and heaven knew what else. It came of being a foreigner. Bob despised all foreigners. He'd certainly been right about Niccolo . . .

She went downstairs, puffed up a few cushions in the parlour and sat down to read the juicier items of scandal in *The News of the World* . . . *Then he made a certain suggestion to her* . . . *What did he do then? He removed a portion of her clothing, m'lord* . . . *intimacy was committed.* It must have been in the motor car! Disgusting! She read on for twenty minutes, then turned to the society pages. *The Duke of Aviemore had the honour of an audience with His Majesty* . . . *The Right Honourable Sir George Meanwell and his party are sailing to St. Malo in Sir George's yacht* Temptress. A nice gentleman, Sir George, and a pillar of the Conservative party, to which Bob belonged, of course. Though Mr Harry was a Liberal . . . not much to choose between those two parties, to tell the truth, though, gracious, there'd be an uproar if you said so out loud. The Socialists now, they were different . . . *they* ought not to be allowed, the way they tried to upset the working men, and . . .

The front door bell rang and she heard Nellie scurrying up the basement stairs. Then she heard Harry Rowland's voice, "Good afternoon . . . it's Nellie, isn't it? Is Mr Stratton at home?"

"Yes, sir."

Jane went out into the hall, "Come in, Mr Harry. Good afternoon, Miss Alice."

"I'm afraid we've brought the dogs, Mrs Stratton . . . Down, Bismarck!"

"Come into the parlour. Would you care for a cup of tea?"

"Not now, thankee. Alice and I were walking the dogs—Mrs Rowland's not feeling so well today—and I thought we'd come by this way, as I'd like to have a word with Bob."

Jane called, "Nellie! Go and tell Mr Stratton that Mr Harry's here."

Harry Rowland said, "Oh, that won't be necessary. I'll walk down. I know the way."

"All right then, Mr Harry. Miss Alice and I can have a nice chat."

He went out and the women heard his tread down the hall, then the opening and closing of the back door.

The three dachshunds pushed and played, the leads tangling round the legs of the parlour's polished and aspidistra-crowned table. "They're nice dogs," Alice said, "but, oh, they stray! If I let them off the leash for a minute it takes me five minutes running and calling to get them back . . ."

"Oh dear. What a worry that must be."

Alice sighed. "One day we're going to find one in the street, run over by a motor car. They don't realise how fast the motor cars go."

Jane Stratton settled herself more comfortably. Frank's wife, Anne, had told her yesterday that she'd seen Miss Alice on Thursday last, walking in Hedlington High Street with a man—a gentleman. Now would be a good time to find out who the gentleman was, and whether there was any hope of a husband for her in that quarter. Might as well go at it direct. Miss Alice knew how much she, Jane, hoped for her to get married. She said, "Anne—our Anne—saw you with a gentleman . . ."

Bob heard the crunch of boots on the gravel, stopped his work, quickly took the picture out of the window and put it back in its drawer. He felt empty for a moment, but immensely relieved. Going to the door he saw Mr Harry coming down the path, wearing his usual dark Sunday suit and his old square-topped hat, and carrying an ivory-topped gold-banded cane and a pair of kid gloves. Bob rubbed his hands on a piece of waste, and then stepped out.

Harry Rowland stopped and said, "Hope I'm not disturbing you, Bob, but I'd like a few minutes of your time."

"Come in, Mr Harry. There's the chair and it's clean."

"I'd have telephoned, only you don't have one. We'll put one in for you, if you like. At our expense, for the business, of course."

"I'd rather stay as we are," Bob said. "Those telephones are always ringing, interrupting a man when he's thinking . . . And it's not me that should have it, if anyone does, but Frank, now."

"Ah, that's what I wanted to talk to you about, in a manner of speaking, just between ourselves. Not in the office, where those girls always seem to have their ears against the wall . . . and the partitions are too thin. Never thought we'd have women and typing machines when we started there, did we, eh?"

"That we didn't." Bob stood against the workbench, resting one hand on it, waiting for his employer to come to the point.

Harry said slowly, "Our time's coming to an end, Bob."

Bob indicated Victoria on her stand. "I've plenty to keep me busy."

"I was thinking of the factory . . . The Rowland Motor Car Company. Mr Richard has different ideas from mine. Things are going to change."

"I reckon so. Frank thinks different from me, too."

"But I don't know that I approve of what I believe Mr Richard's going to do—follow Ford's example, mass produce, install a moving assembly line perhaps. The cars will not be hand-crafted any more, the responsibility and pride of a particular team. They'll be cheaper. The Rowland name will lose its reputation."

Bob thought, he doesn't want to go. No more do I; but he promised, and if he goes, I go.

Harry said after a long pause, "Do you think we ought to reconsider —stay on another few years, perhaps?"

It was Bob's turn to pause, to weigh his words carefully. At last he said, "Mr Richard would take it hard, very hard, Mr Harry. He's been working and planning a long time to be ready to do what he thinks ought to be done. My Frank's the same. And sometimes I think I don't understand the world any more, nor the people in it. They don't think the way I do, and I don't like the way they do think."

"Nor I."

"So how can I make motor cars for them?"

Harry swung his cane intently, frowning at the floor. "Perhaps you're right," he said. "I promised, and I ought to keep my word . . . But, Bob, it's going to be hard, to stand by, to see what we made, you and I, changed, destroyed perhaps . . . I can't sleep at night, thinking about it."

Bob said nothing. Mr Harry was showing the strain in his face; but it wouldn't last much longer, and after the break had been made, it would soon be all right . . . if the break *was* made, finally. And if it weren't—what would *he* do?

Harry Rowland got up with a decisive movement. "Well, thanks for your opinion, Bob . . . That was a terrible accident at the Fair yesterday."

"So it was. You would have missed it, just?"

"We heard the noise as we were leaving. We drove three injured people to the hospital in our motor car. Wright spent an hour afterwards, washing the blood off the seats and floor. Mrs Rowland took it very well."

"She's a strong lady, Mr Harry."

"Thank you. Jane was good enough to offer us some tea, but we'd better be going. I'll find my own way up, Bob."

"All right then, Mr Harry. I've maybe half an hour's more work here, so . . ."

"See you tomorrow."

Upstairs, in the house, Bob finished washing his hands in the bedroom wash-handstand and carefully dried them. A few minutes talk with Jane about tomorrow's dinner, and then it would be time to walk to chapel for the evening service. And tomorrow, to the factory, to see that it was ready to start, and to sign off the night watchman. Then six days of labour: and the shed. And Sunday, morning and evening, to chapel, respectful greetings in the streets—Good morning, Mr Stratton, good morning, Mrs Stratton—and so round the cycle again: but only till September the first. Then, suddenly, he would no longer be himself. Of course he'd still have the shed, and Victoria, and the house, and Jane, and Nellie the girl, and sons and daughters and grandchildren, but he, the person behind the name, would disappear. The person who had been Bob Stratton, Works foreman of Rowland's, would become Frank Stratton, and Jane would become Anne. It was a strange and frightening prospect, and he understood, suddenly, the suppressed panic that had brought Harry Rowland here this afternoon. But what escape was there? From that, or the other compulsions in a man's life?

He went downstairs, just as Jane came to the foot of them and called up, "Bob! Nearly time to go."

Daily Telegraph, Tuesday, July 14, 1914

FINANCE BILL
SUPER-TAX ON GROSS INCOME PENALISING
AGRICULTURE FOREIGN INVESTMENTS

The House went into Committee on the Finance Bill, Mr Whitely in the chair. This was the first of the four days allotted under the Prime Minister's guillotine motion, to the remainder of the Committee stage of the bill . . . On Clause 5, which prescribes the taxation of income from foreign investments, MR WORTHINGTON EVANS (U., Colchester) moved an amendment exempting income from Colonial investments from the scope of the clause. The amendment was selected by the Chairman in order to give a general discussion, and the mover took the opportunity of warning Mr Lloyd George that he would not, as the clause stood, get at the people he wanted to 'catch.'

MR CASSEL (U., St Pancras) seconding, said the Chancellor was aiming at crows, but owing to his haste a great many would escape, and he would hit a good many pigeons. (Laughter.) He was deliberately handicapping British insurance companies, which were already in severe competition with foreign companies, both here and abroad. It was an old principle that immovable property abroad should not be taxed here, but he was taxing the product of such property, namely, the rent.

Christopher Cate read on, carefully. Economics was not a favourite subject of his, especially when it was liberally mixed, as here, with politics; but it was his duty to know about the taxes, for his own and his tenants' benefits.

"Your coffee's getting cold, Christopher," his wife said.

Cate got up and poured himself some more. Stella took the paper off his chair and read a few lines. She turned to him as he sat down again. "What are invisible exports, Daddy? It says here that Mr Throckmorton made a speech in Manchester yesterday, that without our invisible exports we'd be bankrupt."

"Quite true," Christopher said, sipping his coffee. "Insurance is an invisible export—and one of our biggest. People—businesses, shipping companies, foreign governments, even—insure things in England, usually through Lloyd's. The premiums they pay, less whatever the underwriters have to pay out, is an invisible export. It comes to millions of pounds a year. Shipping's another."

His wife went round to the sideboard and helped herself to grilled kidneys and bacon. Cate continued—"We own half the world's shipping tonnage. People hire British ships to take cargo from one place to another, usually not from port to port inside their own country—in most countries that trade is reserved for its own ships—but anywhere else. We have the ships, and the organisation, and people trust our seamen, even though a lot of them are lascars or Chinamen."

"What's a lascar?"

"An Indian . . . mostly from Bengal, I believe. The money the shippers pay to the shipowners is an invisible export. Another smaller one is expert services. British lawyers and doctors are frequently asked for by foreign princes and kings and multi-millionaires, because we have the best, and they know they can rely on an Englishman's word."

"Not a Scotsman's?" Stella cut in.

Cate shook his finger at her. He said, "Another very big invisible export is dividends from companies we own abroad. We own most of the South American railways, for instance. There's a special sort of stockbroker who deals only in South American rail shares. We own an enormous amount of business in India and the Empire, of course—coal mines, sheep ranches, steel foundries, cotton mills, even though those are in direct competition with our own mills in Lancashire . . . You've read about the great cattle ranches in America?"

"Yes. In Texas, or somewhere."

"Well, most of the really big ranches are owned by British companies, and as long as they make a profit, the money that is sent back to

England is an invisible export. British firms own a great deal of the United States."

"Does that mean America has to do what we want it to do?"

"Not a bit, I'm afraid, but it does mean we have big reserves of their money—dollars. The pound sterling is the strongest currency in the world, and the foundation and medium of all international trade, because it is backed by our holdings in the Empire, and in every trading nation. People know they can trust it. Whatever happens to cruzeiros or marks or dinars, the pound sterling will always be worth twenty shillings."

Stella's attention was wandering, and she had turned to another page of the newspaper. "Oh, what a pretty hat Lady Avondale was wearing at Hurlingham yesterday," she exclaimed. "Look, Daddy!"

Cate glanced at the page his daughter held out for him and said, "H'mmm . . . it's as big as a Burmese coolie's. I suppose you want one like it?"

"Oh, no, it's too old for me. She must be thirty."

Garrod came in silently, put the back of her hand against the coffee pot and the hot milk jug and said, "Will you be wanting any more coffee, sir?"

"No, thank you."

"Madam? Miss Stella?"

"No thanks, Garrod."

The head housemaid said, "Then I won't make any more," and went out.

Cate said, "You and Laurence are lucky children—lucky people—to be born English. Not just because of the invisible exports, of course, but because of people like Garrod, and Probyn Gorse . . . and the King. You can rely on them . . . and they know they can rely on you."

Margaret Cate said, "His Majesty can't rely on *me*."

Christopher said, "That's different."

Walstone, Kent: Tuesday, July 14, 1914

5 "Frank's down at the cowbarn, Mr Cate," Jessie Cawthon said from the open door of Abbas Farm house. "Thank you, Jessie," Christopher Cate answered. He touched the peak of his tweed cap, and went back down the walk toward the barn. John Rowland followed, stepping faster to keep up with Cate's long strides, his golden retriever, Viking, trotting to heel. The sun shone, it was ten o'clock in the morning, dappled clouds sailed high and slow over the Weald of Kent, oast-houses rose like tilted fingers among the heavy trees. To the north, water gleamed here and there, where the Scarrow slid out from under its protective arch of elm and oak, and for a few yards flowed past field and garden.

Frank Cawthon was not much taller than his wife, and the same shape—squat and wide, with big hands and grizzled hair. He was stirring something brown in a feeding trough, and hardly looked up as Cate said, "Morning, Frank."

"Morning, Mr Cate." The farmer stirred the gluey mixture more powerfully. "Morning, Mr Rowland . . . I don't know whether this dratted stuff does any good."

"Molasses and linseed?"

"Aye." The farmer straightened his back slowly, letting the heavy wooden stirring rod rest against the side of the trough. "I've got to buy some young cows, Mr Cate, and a few heifers."

"You told me last month. Mind if Mr Rowland listens?"

"Mr John here? No, sir! He knows as much about our troubles at Abbas Farm as I do, or Jessie—everyone in Walstone knows, come to that. The fact is, I reckon this milk fever we're having at Abbas is because half our cows are too old. There ought to be some way to cure it, but if there is, no one's told us about it. I've nursed this herd along as far as it will go. We've got to buy new young blood, and soon."

Cate leaned over a cow stall, a straw in his mouth, the cap tilted forward on his long head, one leg in a Newmarket boot set up on the stall bar, elbows leaning on the rail. Cawthon returned to stirring the mix. Cate said, "Suppose we forget the rent this year?"

"That'll help," Cawthon said, but as though grudgingly. John Rowland knew him well, and knew that he was moved and appreciative; but Frank Cawthon was not the man to show it. Cawthon added, "It'll need more than that, Mr Cate. It's forty cows we're talking about. About fifteen of them should be heifers in calf."

Again some minutes passed in silence, emphasised by the heavy glugging of the molasses mix. Then Cate said, "Suppose I guarantee a bank loan for you? I'd lend it myself, only I can't this year."

"Aye, 'twould do it," said Cawthon, still grudgingly.

"How much?"

"Three hundred and fifty pounds."

"All right, Frank. I have to go to Hedlington tomorrow. Come with me and we'll talk to Mr Olcott at Barclay's."

"Aye."

"The ten-five train, then we can have a bite at the Crown afterwards, eh?"

Cawthon stood up. "Thankee . . . I'll be paying it back as soon as I can, rent and all."

"I know that, Frank. But pay off the bank first."

Cawthon nodded and Cate slowly uncoiled and, with a wave of his hand, walked out into the sunlight. Cawthon returned to his stirring. Viking barked at a farm cat, which continued to stalk across the yard, coldly ignoring him.

John walked at Cate's side down the bramble-lined lane toward another farm farther along the low rise of land that bordered the Scarrow valley on the south. Cate said, "Cawthon's a good farmer, John. About the best. Abbas Farm has bad soil, old equipment, old cows . . . yet until this outbreak of milk fever he was making it pay."

"I wish I was as good," John said.

"There's no reason you shouldn't be. Why don't you spend some time here, watching Frank, learning from him?"

"He wouldn't mind?"

"Not a bit. You know Frank—the outside of him growls, the inside purrs. You could leave the day to day running of High Staining to Fred Stratton."

"I suppose I could. He would certainly be happier with me out of his way. We just don't get along, never have, though he's a good foreman."

Cate said, "You should learn to be your own foreman. It'll be hard work, but you—you and Louise—could do it, and save Stratton's wages. Of course, you'd have to get an extra boy for milking, but he'd get less money than Stratton."

"I'll think about it . . . What's the problem at Upper Bohun?" John asked, jerking his head at the rambling thatched house they were approaching, surrounded by oast-houses, sheds, and the other accompaniments of a hop yard. "Mayhew's let some of the crop get nettle blight," Cate said briefly. "And he's asking for rent relief. I'm not going to give it to him. He's a Lady Day tenancy and I'll tell him he can expect his notice from me next March, unless he mends his ways. Of course, I'll give him another crop, really, but I want to frighten him."

"What's the matter? Carelessness?"

"Drink," Cate said. "Better not come with me this time, John."

"Of course not. I'll wait here looking at the view. It's a glorious morning."

Cate went on alone toward the house, while John leaned over a five-barred gate and thought about what Cate had said. He was right: if you considered yourself a gentleman farmer, and acted like one, you had to pay the price. You were in the hands of your foreman, of the labourers even, because they knew more about farming than you did, although they were much less well educated. Why? Because your status mattered more to you than your profession . . . wearing a pink coat to hounds, becoming a Justice of the Peace, perhaps, being invited to Walstone Park for balls, having your young accepted as suitable playmates, and mates, to the County. He wished that he had the drive to be a good farmer . . . a good anything. Richard wanted to make good motor cars, very badly; Tom wanted to have his own ship, and be the best post captain in the navy, very badly; and he—nothing—except perhaps to be a good and loving father to Boy and Naomi.

The heavy thud of hooves approaching at a trot stirred him from his thoughts. He looked up to see the 9th Earl of Swanwick, Master of Foxhounds, crowned by a brown bowler hat, posting heavily toward him on a large roan gelding. The earl was wearing a tweed hacking jacket and, like squire Cate, cavalry twill breeches and Newmarket boots, without spurs. He carried a short hunting crop in his left hand.

That arm was slightly but noticeably withered. He reined in the big horse—"Morning, Rowland."

"Good morning, Lord Swanwick," John answered. He knew the earl and countess very well, and their children even better. After the initial meeting of a day, they often came to christian names: but at the outset of an encounter he felt it appropriate not to presume. Swanwick was a nobleman who did not like being presumed upon.

"Taking the air?" the earl asked.

"Visiting some of Cate's farms with him. He's in Upper Bohun now."

"Trying to solve his bloody tenants' problems, eh? Vickers is out doing the same thing for me, but nothing ever does get solved. It's one damn thing after another for a landlord and always it comes to more money. Cate's talking to Mayhew?"

"Yes."

"Their girl's been walking a pair of bitch puppies for me, and I'm taking a look at all our boarders." He stared out over John's head, as though searching for something. Glancing the same way, John saw one of the wings of Walstone Park, the earl's seat, showing above the trees, two miles away across the Scarrow.

The earl said abruptly, "John, I've got too much on my hands this year . . . here, London, the Welsh mines, rising taxes, rising wages . . . How about you taking over the hounds?"

John tried to look astonished, not finding it easy because Lord Swanwick had mentioned the subject once before, nearly a year ago; and after some consideration, and discussion with Louise, John had told him he could not do it. He rode to hounds regularly, and wore the hunt button; but following hounds was one thing, hunting them was another.

Swanwick said, "Wilkinson's an excellent huntsman, y'know. So's Billing. Old Eaves will stay on and he's as good a secretary as any hunt could hope for. He knows every farmer in the bloody district."

John said, "It's very good of you to think of me, but I don't feel up to it."

Swanwick turned his head, the horse easing round, pricking his ears and fidgeting, his head also turning. "Still, blast you!" the earl growled. Cate came down the farm lane toward them. "Hello, Cate," the earl said.

"Morning, Swanwick."

"Been trying to talk John here into taking over the hounds. If he won't, where the hell can I turn?"

Cate said, "I've been thinking about it ever since you mentioned to me that you wanted to give them up. Can't come up with anyone who has the money, and the knowledge . . . and the desire."

"Any English gentleman ought to be willing to give his right hand to be a Master of Foxhounds," the earl growled.

"Ever thought of a committee?"

The earl said, "Don't hold with committees. Like councils of war . . . bloody well sit on their arses, and talk, and talk, but do sweet damn all. Well, I've got to look at those puppies."

"I saw them," Cate said. "They're in good condition."

"Good. That'll save me a quarter of an hour listening to that blasted Mrs Mayhew babbling on about nothing."

Cate put on his cap, which he had been dangling in his hand since he came down from the farmhouse. He looked up and said, "We must be on our way . . . Flora well? And Helen and Barbara?"

"They're all fine—eating me out of house and home," the earl said, "Arthur's in Italy and Cantley's on a train to Baghdad, I believe . . . See you this afternoon?"

Cate looked mystified for a moment, then said, "Oh, the court. Yes, I shall be there."

"Good. We'll put that bugger Gorse where he belongs—behind bars." With a wave of his crop he turned his horse and rode back down the lane the way he had come. Cate and John, also turning, headed toward another of Cate's tenants, Isaiah Shearer at Lower Bohun.

There were only a dozen spectators in court that afternoon, including the bespectacled reporter from the *Courier*, Hedlington's weekly newspaper. Willum and Mary Gorse were there near the back, Willum fidgety and unhappy, Mary sitting tall and straight, firm mouthed. Albert Gorse sat in the front row, paring his dirty fingernails with a small knife. Willum and Mary's eldest children, the twins Fletcher and Florinda, sat in the same back row as their parents, but not close to them. They had always seemed, to Cate, to be undemonstratively fond of their parents, but town life, even such as was offered by Hedlington, was not for them, and since they were twelve they had lived with their grandfather. They looked unconcerned now, lolling back in the insolence of their youth and animal grace, Fletcher's neck rising in a bronzed column from the open collar of his shirt, Florinda's auburn hair cascading free down both sides of her oval face, lit with dust-laden sunbeams.

Four magistrates occupied the bench. Cate, sitting under the royal coat of arms in the dingy room, had Colonel Wadleigh on his right and Terence Edwards, Esquire, on his left. The Earl of Swanwick sat on the far left, but as it was his pheasants that were alleged to have been poached by Probyn Gorse, he had disqualified himself when Probyn's case came up. He had not done it with a good grace, but only after the clerk of the court had pointed out that if he sat as a magistrate in Probyn's case, whatever verdict and sentence were given would most certainly be set aside; and a severe rebuke administered from the Lord Chancellor's office for disregarding the basic principle of common law. Cate wished he could have had the other two J.P.s with him, rather than Wadleigh and Edwards: for Wadleigh, an arthritic retired lieutenant colonel of artillery, was a strict upholder of discipline and punishment; and Edwards, though only a small landholder, was a fanatic believer in the sacred nature of the game laws.

The case had been going on for half an hour already. The clock on the left wall ticked monotonously, as Skagg, Lord Swanwick's head gamekeeper, described how he and Dan and Amos, the other keepers, came upon the accused in the middle of Hayling's Copse on the southern edge of Walstone Park, at 2.35 a.m. on the morning of Tuesday, June 23rd. Gorse was carrying an electric flashlight, and an offensive weapon.

"What sort of weapon?" Colonel Wadleigh asked, perking up.

"A club, your honour, about this long, and . . ."

" 'Twas my walking stick," Probyn Gorse interrupted from the dock. The policeman beside him said, " 'Ush your trap, Probyn."

"We thought we seed him earlier with a little gun, a folding .410 perhaps, but we couldn't find it."

"Then what you thought you saw is not material," Cate said. "Proceed."

The gamekeeper was perspiring in his heather mixture tweed suit, the matching peaked cap twisting in his hands. Lord Swanwick chose the material every September from an outfitter in Hedlington, and had each of his gamekeepers fitted and furnished with one suit and hat, all of the same material, each year.

Skagg continued, describing how they saw pheasants' tail feathers sticking out of Gorse's coat pockets and on examination found them to be one cock and one hen. They had both been shot in the neck and head, and then hit on the skull, to kill them.

"Did Gorse threaten you at any time?" Cate asked.

Skagg hesitated. "Well, sir, he raised his stick when we was coming."

"I didn't know who was coming. And when I raised the stick, they was twenty yards off," Gorse said. He added *sotto voce*, "And if it hadn't been blowing so hard I would have heard their clumping boots a mile away."

The case continued. Corroborating evidence from Dan and Amos. Report from a police constable. Proof that the birds had existed, as described—they had long since been given to the Workhouse in Hedlington and eaten by the inmates.

"What do you have to say?" Cate asked finally.

Probyn Gorse was small and wizened with small bright black eyes, crinkled apple cheeks, and hair that was probably gingerish-grey, but was kept dyed gingerish-black. He had taught Christopher Hengist Cate country lore when Cate was a boy; and regarded the office of squire of Walstone, once Lord of the Manor, with a reverence remarkable in one who had no reverence for anything else created by man, especially pomps and titles. Cate's family claimed descent, in this vale of the Scarrow, from Hengist, Danish King of Kent in the fifth century; and had carried his name in their own ever since; but when he was with Gorse he often thought that the little man's lineage was even older, direct from the Britons who had been here when the Romans came under Caesar; and, later, called themselves Romans when Hengist came.

Gorse looked over at Cate on the bench now, and said, "'Course I took some of his Lordship's pheasants, squire."

"Were you hungry? Was there no food at home?"

"I say, Cate," Colonel Wadleigh said, "that's nothing to do with it, really. I mean . . ."

"Not until the defendant has been found guilty, if he is," the clerk said from below.

Cate said, "Why did you do it?"

"'Tis my right," Gorse said, "an' they shot Prince Albert three days later, out of spite."

"What, what?" Wadleigh said, sitting up with a start.

"His dog," Cate said. "You can't prove that, Probyn. And it's nothing to do with this case, so don't mention it again."

Wadleigh harrumphed and Edwards examined the prisoner through cold eyes.

Gorse added, as though to underline the inalienability of his right, whatever his circumstances, "We had plenty of food. And money. My Woman done some washing. Fletcher earned a few shillings with the scythe. Florinda cut two ladies' hair."

Cate raised his head. Willum Gorse caught his eye, pleading. He heard Wadleigh and Edwards muttering to each other across his back, leaning out of their chairs. Albert Gorse was looking at him with a sneer undisguised on his face. The twins were yawning.

Cate turned to the others and said in a low voice, "What do you think?"

Edwards snapped, "Guilty." Wadleigh said, "He's admitted it."

Cate said, "I agree. There's no doubt."

He looked at Gorse. "This court finds you guilty as charged." Feet shuffled in the room, someone blew his nose.

Cate said, "Any previous convictions?"

The clerk of the court, a Hedlington solicitor, stood up. "Your honour, this man was found guilty of taking and destroying a hare on Lord Swanwick's estate on October 24th, 1908."

"That's the only time he's been caught," the earl growled. "He's been in there a hundred times."

The clerk continued, "He was sentenced to a fine of ten pounds. Sureties against his offending again within one year were found by Gorse himself, and by Mrs Christopher Cate, each in the sum of ten pounds—as required by law. These sums were returned after one year without a further conviction of Mr Gorse for the same offence."

"So this is his second poaching conviction?"

"Yes, your honour."

"There is a character witness, I believe—Matthew Fleck."

"There is, your honour. But if Fleck testifies as to his good character, others are free to testify in the opposite sense."

"I don't want no help from Fleck," Probyn Gorse said belligerently. "He don't know nothing about my character."

"Very well then."

Cate motioned Wadleigh and Edwards to come closer. They leaned in, and he said in a low voice, "You know the law as well as I do . . . Second offence can get up to six months with hard labour, and recognizances for two years—twenty pounds from Gorse and two others of ten pounds each, or one other of twenty. Or prison for another year."

"And the third offence, he has to go to Assizes or Quarter Sessions," Edwards said, "and can get up to seven years."

"What do you think we should give him?"

Edwards said without hesitation, "The maximum—six months. The court let him off very lightly last time—I wasn't on the bench on that occasion, but poaching is, damn it, it's his profession. We've got to show these people they can't break the law with impunity."

Cate turned to the other man. "Colonel?"

"I agree with everything Edwards said."

From beyond, Lord Swanwick said, "Is six months all you can give the swine?"

Cate said, "I think you had better not take part in this discussion at all, Lord Swanwick, or our proceedings will certainly be set aside." He turned back, thinking, why don't I let him rant on, encourage him even? Then we'll get a caning from the Lord Chancellor, the sentence will be set aside, and Probyn will go free . . . but it wasn't his role in life to do such a thing: and Probyn would be disappointed in him if he stooped to it. His duty was to ensure a fair trial and a fair sentence. He spoke quietly to the other two magistrates. "Gorse is guilty, we all agree. I don't think he had any intent to strike any of the keepers, and they certainly haven't proved any such intent. He must have used a gun, and hidden it. He's not a violent man. I don't think it will change him at all, sending him to gaol."

"What will, then?" Edwards said.

"Nothing, I suppose," Cate muttered. "Look, six months is a very long sentence when no violence was committed, or even threatened. We only gave that Sussex tramp six months last year for stealing ten pounds and hitting Mrs Warren in her shop. This is not comparable."

"What do you suggest?" Colonel Wadleigh asked. He looked unhappy and Cate thought, the old boy realises he's going to have to offend either the earl or the squire, both pillars of his world.

Cate knew he could not get Probyn off without a prison term this time; and he was not sure that he wanted to, for Probyn was being foolishly obstinate. He said, "I think two months is enough. Public opinion about poaching is changing. There's been no violence and only two birds taken. It's not like the bulk poaching for the London market."

Lord Swanwick got up, left the bench and walked out of the court room. Edwards said, "You know Gorse better than I do, but I couldn't go below three months in all conscience."

"Nor I," said Wadleigh, seeing a possible compromise.

"All right," Cate said quickly. He faced Gorse and raised his voice. "This court sentences you to three months imprisonment, at hard labour."

"Come on, Probyn," the policeman at the dock said.

Albert Gorse leaped off the bench where he had been sitting, and shouted, "You call this justice?" He stabbed his finger at Cate—"Lord Swanwick was up there telling you all what to do, and you were too afraid of his high and mighty lordship not to do it!"

"'Ere, 'ere," the constable by the dock said. "That's enough of that."

"Lord Swanwick was not a member of the court in this case," Cate said, "and he had no part in our proceedings."

"It's you who ought to go to gaol, the whole fucking lot of you!" Bert yelled.

"Now, mind your language there," the constable said, seizing Bert's arm. Christopher Cate banged his gavel on the table and said, "Take him out, constable."

Probyn watched his son's removal with the hint of a sardonic smile on his face. Willum, his other son, was on his feet, hands twined in entreaty. Struggling and shouting, Bert Gorse was pushed out by the constable.

Cate said, "Sit down, Willum." Mary was pulling at the tail of Willum's jacket, muttering, "Sit down!"

But Willum said, "He doesn't mean it, sir . . . I'm sorry for him using such language . . . he's just put out about Dad going to prison."

Cate said wearily, "We understand. It's not your fault."

The constable returned, tugging at his tunic. "I gave him a piece of my mind," he said. "Told 'im 'e was lucky not to go to gaol with his dad, for contempt."

"Thank you, Fulcher. How are you going to get Probyn to Hedlington?"

"Take him up on the morning train tomorrow, your honour. He'll sleep in our back room tonight. My Mary'll give him his supper."

"All right. Next case."

The clerk said, "The plaintiff didn't show up, your honour. And that was the only other case."

Cate looked at the other magistrates and said, "Then if we sign the committal warrant for Probyn, we can adjourn. Right?"

The clerk of the court said, "Yes, your honour."

"Make out the warrant, then."

At six o'clock in mid-July, it was still broad daylight, the sun low over the Weald. Christopher Cate walked down the lane along the Scarrow's bank toward Probyn's cottage. It was invisible from anywhere except across the stream, for huge growths of brambles, nettles, and hazel bushes hid it until, when you were right up to it, you saw the gap in the brambles, and the worn earth of a path between the nettles. The cottage itself was of brick, very old bricks by their shape and colour, with a tiled roof. It had had a thatched roof thirty years ago, but mice and starlings and rot had got into the thatch, the rain had poured through it, and one of Christopher's first acts, when he succeeded his father as titular squire of Walstone, was to give Probyn a new roof. Typically, Probyn had not said a word of thanks . . . but then he had never expected any for all the hours he had spent showing the boy Christopher the way of weasel and fox, rabbit and pheasant, mole and plover.

A few pink roses grew beside the cottage door, which was of the stable type, the top half open, and along the wall there was a row of tomatoes and another of cabbages. A wooden lean-to housed, as Cate knew, Probyn's ferrets, many snares and nets, traps and gins, and a few elementary gardening tools. A smaller hutch was the kennel, now unoccupied. Twenty yards away in the dense undergrowth, a path beaten to its rickety door, was the out-house, and Cate always felt, when he saw it and, when the wind was in the wrong direction, smelled it, that all Probyn's ancestors back to the woad-painted Britons had used that exact spot for their defecations.

Probyn's Woman was hanging up clothes—a woman's skirt and cotton blouses—on a string hung from a nail in the mortar to a small apple tree.

Cate touched his cap to her, "Good evening, Mrs Gorse."

Probyn had never married her; he never married any of his women, but she might well have been married to someone else before deserting him and her previous life to join Probyn, and Cate always called Probyn's Women 'Mrs Gorse.'

She said, "The twins are inside," and went on hanging up her laundry.

Cate knocked on the upper door and a man's voice from inside called, "Who's there?"

"Cate," he said.

"Oh, come in, Mr Cate." Fletcher Gorse appeared out of the gloom, smiling, a book in his hand. A pile of groceries covered the battered table. His sister Florinda was at the sink, peeling potatoes.

Cate said, "I came along to see whether you had enough to eat, but apparently you have."

Florinda threw over her shoulder, "Your lady brought them. An hour ago."

Cate said, "Mind if I sit down a minute, and light a pipe?"

" 'Course not."

Cate sat in a hard-backed chair, and found his pipe and tobacco. He wished Margaret would tell him where she was going on her errands as the squire's wife; or perhaps he ought to know without being told. She did her best to perform her duties in that field, he had to admit. It was a pity that her acts had no feeling or emotion behind them—for these people were Kentish, not Irish.

Fletcher said, "Old Swanwick was bound and determined to get Granddad sent to clink for the rest of his mortal life." He chuckled.

"I'm sorry he had to go at all," Cate said, "but he really deserved at least that."

"Oh, of course he did! He should know better than to let that flat-foot Skagg catch him. 'Twas the wind and not having a dog. Prince Albert would 'a smelled those keepers a mile away, but he had the colic. Skagg stinks like a badger, and Amos is not much better."

"Do you think they shot him—the dog?"

"'Course they did! Three days after they caught Granddad. A twelve bore in the head that evening, and they left him across the river there. He was a good dog, but when Granddad wasn't here, he'd like to wander off a bit, sniffing things for himself. I think 'twas Amos saw him, and killed him. None of us was here, except her." He jerked his head to the outside. "She told us when we all come home, about the shot, but we didn't see nothing till the morning. Granddad knew though, when Prince Albert wasn't home by his bedtime."

Cate had his pipe drawing, and tried to make himself comfortable on the hard chair. "What about money while Probyn's in gaol?"

"We'll be all right," Florinda said. "I've got a little saved up. And there's a job as lady's maid at the Court, if I want it."

"Lady's maid?" Cate said, astonished. "You?"

She was out of the sink now, facing him, rubbing her wet hands on her dirty skirt. She tossed her heavy auburn hair—"Why not? I can learn quicker than any of those London sluts they have up there. I can learn anything."

"I'm sure you can," Cate said.

"And I can look good, dress right—if I want to," she said.

Probyn's Woman came in and said, "Garth's going to marry that girl Fletcher put in the family way, eh?"

Cate said, "Yes. The wedding's to be next month."

"And the baby four months later."

Cate wanted to change the subject. He said, "We're playing the Light Infantry Depot next Saturday, aren't we?"

Fletcher said, "Yes. I'll be playing. Pity Guy Rowland won't be back from school. He'd show them soldiers something."

"He won't, I know. Besides, Ted England doesn't like playing him for Walstone unless he's staying at High Staining, or with us. He does live in Hedlington, after all, not here, and the other villages grumble if he plays, and say it isn't fair."

There was no clock in the house and he did not want to bring out his half-hunter, because a preoccupation with time seemed inappropriate here. Only wind and calm mattered, light and dark, sun and rain. He said, "I'll visit Probyn as soon as he's settled in."

"He'll be all right," the Woman said. "It'll give him a good rest, and time to think how he can best tweak Swanwick's tail. He won't let Skagg catch him next time."

Cate started to say that Probyn would do better to think of other matters than revenge, or how to improve his poaching skills; but that would be an impossible wish or hope, and for Probyn, an unacceptable life.

He said, "Are you still writing poetry, Fletcher?"

"Trying to," the young man said, grinning.

"Can I see some of your latest?"

Fletcher opened a drawer of the table and pulled out a few sheets of paper. Cate drew on his pipe and read. The papers were smudged and stained, the words misspelled, the poems unformed, some in blank verse, some in simple rhyme, more often in a powerful free form reminiscent of Walt Whitman. The subjects were as formless as the poems: was this about man, or the sky, or a lark ascending? It was difficult to tell. Perhaps it was 'about' all three . . . or none. What was certain was that the poems were alive with a soaring lyric power and beauty akin to Shelley's.

Cate handed them back. "These are very good, Fletcher."

The young man shoved the papers back, and banged the table with his fist. "I can't write proper! I can read . . . but sometimes I don't know whether the words in my head are real, 'cos I don't know words, see? I mind in school, teacher reading poetry. She said 'twas Shakespeare, and the words went into me, not here—" he touched his ear— "but here—" he slapped his chest—"an' they weren't words, that I could use myself, but like waves, big waves, or wind blowing, sometimes soft sometimes hard. Shakespeare made the words do that, see, 'cos he knew words, like Granddad knows pheasants and ferrets—but until I know 'em, the poetry won't be nothing. Stands to reason, don't it?"

Cate stood up and, while thinking, knocked out the dottle from his pipe into the fireplace. Would it help this natural genius to see the shape of others' poetry on the printed page? Or would it frustrate and worry him, from not being able to find those words in his own vocabulary? He made up his mind, and said, "Fletcher, come to the Manor whenever you feel like it, and read in the library. The first time I'll show you where the books of poetry are, and make some suggestions about what you might start with. Most books you can take home, too."

"Blyth won't let me in if you're not there," Fletcher said.

"I'll tell him to," he said. "Well, goodbye for now. Goodbye, Mrs Gorse."

The Woman nodded; the twins said, "Goodbye, Mr Cate," and Cate walked out, down the path, through the gap in the brambles and out of sight.

When he was gone, Florinda said, "He looks thin."

The Woman said, "It's her. She doesn't care nothing for him. Nor her kids. Nor none of us."

Fletcher said, "Laurence is a good kid."

Florinda said, "He'd be happier if he was a Gorse, living here and poaching with you and Granddad."

"Except he doesn't like to kill anything. He can tell any bird there is, sometimes before I've even seen it . . . Think they're going to get Stella married off soon? She's been to Buckingham Palace and all. She likes the men."

Florinda jeered at her brother, "You think she likes *you*? Just because you got Mary Maxwell on her back?"

"And some others . . . I could get her, too, if I wanted to . . ."

Florinda said, "Poor squire."

". . . but I don't, see?"

The sun was setting, across the Scarrow a man was scything hay in a late-growing field, that would be sown to winter wheat. Bees still drowsed through flowers, and the smell of ripening hops sharpened the warm air as Cate walked through the edge of his village, the men touching their caps to him as he passed, toward Walstone Manor.

Daily Telegraph, Wednesday, July 15, 1914

LONDON DAY BY DAY
FORTHCOMING MARRIAGES

The marriage of Captain Anthony Fielden, 10th Royal Hussars, and Miss Phoebe Brand will take place at Glynde on the 27th inst.

The marriage will shortly take place between Major Alexander Houstoun, Royal Field Artillery, of Clerkington, East Lothian, and Evelyn, only daughter of the late Sir George Lauderdale Houstoun-Boswall, Bt., of Blackadder, Berwickshire.

GARDEN PARTIES
HON. MRS WOOD OF HENGRAVE

The Hon. Mrs Wood of Hengrave was 'At Home' to her friends in the garden attached to 52, Grosvenor Gardens, and among the many present were:

The Chilian Minister and Madame Edwards, Lord and Lady Sinclair, Geraldine Marchioness of Bristol, Lady Brownlow Cecil, Lady Hatherton, Lord and Lady Mostyn, Alice Countess Amherst and Lady Enid Vaughan, Sir Edward and Lady Coates, Sir Reginald and Lady Hardy, Lady Beatrice Pretyman, Sir John and Lady Smiley, and Sir Owen and Lady Phillips.

COURT CIRCULAR
BUCKINGHAM PALACE, JULY 14

The King and Queen visited Queen Alexandra, the Empress Marie Feodorovna of Russia, and Queen Olga of Greece at Marlborough House today, and remained to luncheon.

MARLBOROUGH HOUSE, JULY 14

The King and Queen, the Queen of the Hellenes, and Princess Irene of Greece, Princess Frederick Charles of Hesse, Prince Philip of Hesse, Prince Wolfgang of Hesse, and Prince Christopher of Greece visited Queen Alexandra today and remained to luncheon.

Prince and Princess Louis of Battenberg called at Marlborough House this afternoon.

Christopher Cate, reading in the garden, continued browsing, alert for hidden nuances in the announcements. The Court Circular and society columns seemed ridiculous relics to a lot of people, Americans in particular—but they contained a great deal of useful information, if you knew some of the names, and listened to what was being said over the port or at the tea table. And, whether one liked it or not, society was in fact like a layered cake, the Royal Family the icing-sugar statuettes on top. But, far more important than that, they were also the cement holding the nation and empire together. In that role they were much more than mere figureheads. The Sovereign, of course, had real constitutional responsibilities: he had the right to be informed by his ministers; to advise them; to dissolve parliament; to ask anyone he wished to form a new government. Of course the man he selected could not succeed unless he was widely supported by the majority party in the House of Commons, but still, the Sovereign's power was there. And he, and only he, had the power to create peers; indeed it was that power, used as a threat, which had finally persuaded the House of Lords to pass Lloyd George's revolutionary social insurance bills of 1910–1911.

Was the monarchy, then, secure and well loved? He considered, and decided he could not say so with a clear conscience. The old Queen had started the trouble by retiring into almost total seclusion after the death of the Prince Consort—so, until the Golden Jubilee over twenty-five years later, the people were hardly aware they had a Queen. Edward VII had done good things diplomatically in his later years, but by then he had alienated much of the middle class, the chapel goers, by the well-known sexual immorality of his private life, and that of his circle. Then there were the whispers that his eldest son, the Duke of Clarence, was, in secret, Jack the Ripper. Cate couldn't bring himself to believe that such a thing was possible . . . but when both Edward and Clarence were dead, and George V succeeded, he was faced with a new rumour—that he had secretly contracted a morganatic marriage. Denials and denouncements were to no avail . . . more indigestible matter for the Nonconformist Conscience. So, how strong would the monarchy be, if a storm blew up? It would depend on George V, and his somewhat forbidding German wife . . . but she was a descendant of George III, too . . .

He yawned . . . When Greece and Rome had shown the world that the best form of government was a Republic, how was it that Europe was now nearly all monarchies? And none of them very stable. Kaiser Wilhelm II of Germany was a poseur, shallow, and jealous; it was frightening to think that he commanded the mightiest army the world had ever known. Francis Joseph of Austria seemed to be a dear old thing, as *gemütlich* as his people, but they too were an unstable lot, the heir murdering his mistress at Mayerling, and then committing suicide —full of drugs, he'd heard; and the Empress, having her annual flings with Bay Middleton in Leicestershire, in the hunting field and in bed . . . dead now, poor woman, assassinated . . . unstable, *and* unlucky, the Hapsburgs were. The Czar of Russia, another cousin of the King's, and not very intelligent according to rumour, and certainly not well fixed in the affections of his people: look at what happened to his grandfather—another assassination—*and* he had a foolish, stubborn German wife . . . Italy—too newly formed a country to be settled in anything and its King such a funny looking little fellow . . . Alfonso XIII of Spain, quite a ladies' man, and a gay blade, but his people so bigoted, and poor—but was that the king's fault, or the Roman Catholic Church's? Or the fault of both, seen by the people as one? That unity of Church and State could be a source of strength; or it could be very dangerous . . . Turkey, the tottering sick man of Europe. It would really be a kindness to break up the Turkish Empire into its constituent peoples of Kurd, Arab, Syrian, Jew, Egyptian, Bulgar, Circassian, Armenian, and heaven knew what others . . . but the Sultan was also the Caliph of Islam, and what he did and how he acted could have important repercussions in the British Empire, which contained over a hundred million subjects of Islamic faith . . . France, an Empire, and a Republic, both, its governments going in and out of office like spinning tops—corruption rampant, the Dreyfus affair still fouling relations between all parties, religions, and classes! Look at . . .

He awoke with his chair in the shade, a little chilled. He picked up the fallen newspaper and went back into the house, thinking that he might have visited Probyn in gaol this afternoon after his lunch with Frank Cawthon; but perhaps it was too early. Better wait a week, and then make it a special trip.

St Pancras Station, London:
Friday, July 17, 1914

6 Fiona Rowland waited on the platform half a dozen steps beyond the booking office door of St Pancras. The station clock showed 11.45 p.m.—a quarter of an hour to go before the midnight sleeping car express left for Scotland— their train, their magic carpet. It was two months since she had seen him, and then only for a single night in his Chelsea studio. She had been waiting here for over ten minutes. Why did he not come? Her travelling suit was of tan linen, the jacket belted at the waist. A veil hung from her ample hat, half covering her face. Her porter waited with her suitcase, hat box, shoe box, and bag of golf clubs. She wondered for a moment what the porter thought of her—for whom he imagined she was waiting, and what was the nature of their relationship. Not many married couples would set off on a golfing holiday from separate houses, only meeting at the station, though of course a husband might come direct from the office. In that case he'd be wearing city clothes . . . unless he took his sports clothes to the office in the morning . . . but a meeting at midnight? She cut short the speculation. What did it matter what the porter thought? Or the inspector standing at the barrier, examining the tickets held out to him—"Down the train, sir . . . That way, sir . . . Near the front . . . It's the third carriage from the back . . . Good evening, madam. Fifth carriage from this end, and your maid will be in the next carriage forward . . ."

She saw him, wending steadily through the thin crowd toward her, and her heart bumped. He rolled a little still, from his early years at sea —anything rather than follow his father's calling of coal miner; he'd seen what *that* did to a man . . . the nose broken in barroom brawls and cheerful escapades in foreign ports; cleft chin, sloping powerful shoulders, narrow-set deep-sunk blue eyes, searching, non-committal. She waved her hand, standing tiptoe inches above her considerable normal height. He saw her, and he was close enough so that she saw the spark light in the guarded eyes. She flew to his arms, wordless, raising her veil. He engulfed her and said, "There, there, lass! Ye're looking bonnie the nicht."

"Oh, Archie!" She smiled at him, for though he would never speak with the la-di-da southern accent, nor the pure accurate English of Highlanders who had learned it only at school, their native tongue being Gaelic, he had taught himself well enough, as he had taught himself painting; and only used this broad Gorbals speech to tease her.

"Where are your bags and clubs?" she asked.

"The porter's taking them straight to our compartment. Hadn't you better put your veil down again, lass? This place is probably thick with Rowlands and Cates and their friends, all dying to take you in adultery."

"I don't care who sees me," she said, "and you didn't kiss me."

"That can wait . . . not long, though. We only have two minutes. Hurry along, now."

At the barrier the inspector said, "Good evening, sir, good evening, madam. Nearest carriage but one. Compartment D. There's the attendant, sir."

Archie pressed something into his hand, they half walked half ran down the platform. Their porters were handing the bags to the attendant, Archie again reaching in his pocket. The guard stood close by, green flag unfurled, whistle in hand. He put it to his mouth as they stepped up and into the compartment. The attendant said, "I'll get the bags into the compartment first, if you'll wait a moment, sir."

They stood pressed close in the narrow corridor space by the carriage door. Through the open window drifted the smell of coal smoke and the hot presence of the crowded platform. The guard's cheeks puffed as he blew his whistle, the green flag waving imperiously in his other hand. From ahead, one engine whistled back, then another. The train began to move, and the guard stepped aboard. The gigantic iron and glass arch, over a hundred feet above them, echoed to the volleying blasts of the engines' exhausts. The lighted platform slid faster backward, and they passed out into the night.

She closed her eyes, leaning against him, feeling her consciousness slowly concentrate in her body, her loins.

The attendant said, "All ready now, sir. I can serve you a snack in

your compartment, if you wish, sir. Or a bottle of champagne, perhaps?"

"The champagne," she said, wishing him away, "and two glasses."

"Certainly, madam, right away."

He bustled off and they went into the little compartment. Archie
said, "A drop of malt whisky's more my mark, but . . ." He shrugged,
smiling.

The beds were made, one above the other, and she whispered in his
ear, "This is a special occasion, darling. Tell him we're tired and are
going to sleep soon, and do not want to be disturbed."

She sat down on the lower berth, waiting, looking idly around. The
little room was panelled in mahogany, inlaid with rosewood. The mon-
ogram of the Midland Railway was sandblasted into the ornately
framed mirror on the forward partition, and red velvet curtains swayed
across the closed window. At the head of each berth was a hook and a
circle of green baize for gentlemen to hang their watches on retiring.
The mirror was flanked by sepia photographs of Leicestershire and
Yorkshire scenes. Faintly she heard the engines labouring far away,
rushing her magic carpet northwards, rattling over bridges, rushing
over junctions. No, the magic was in his body, and until he took her
she was merely existing.

The attendant came bearing a tray, bottle, and glasses. "Open it,
sir?"

"If you would."

She sighed inwardly. More time passing and she not in his arms. She
kept her head turned, as though looking out of the blind window. She
heard Archie mumbling, and the man saying, "Very good, sir. I'll call
you at 6.30. The dining-car comes on at Carlisle. Change at Kilmarnock at 8.22. Good night, sir. Good night, madam." She did not turn
her head. The door shut, a bolt slid.

She tore off her hat, threw it onto the top berth, and opened her
arms. Archie came toward her, filled glasses in hand, "We'll not waste
this, though. It's cold, cold as a Sassenach's heart."

She said, "Let's drink it quickly . . . oh darling, at last!"

They stood, facing each other, swaying with the motion of the train.
The shrill call of an engine whistle was blown past on the hurrying
wind. They emptied the glasses. "Another," he said, "and another."

"Not for me."

"I'll finish it. We've six hours, woman!"

"And then ninety-six hours at Dalmellie. Oh darling, do hurry. I'm
. . . melting!"

"Go on then. Undress. I'll watch you."

She began to undress, taking off her clothes with lascivious movements and poses, and at last lay back naked on the lower berth, her arms out to him, all the floor and upper berth littered with coat, skirt, blouse, corset, bust bodice, petticoat, camisole, underdrawers. By then he had his coat and shirt off and she could admire the muscles sliding silkily under the smooth hairless skin of his body. Thirty-six years old, four years younger than herself; barely a touch of grey in the thick dark hair. There was the scar near his right nipple, where a Malay girl had ripped a five-inch gash across his chest in Singapore . . . the nose broken in Rio de Janeiro. And his eyes, probing her, aware of her as a person, as Fiona, understanding her. Her arms ached, tears blurred her eyes, as she cried, "My own darling . . . come to me." Through the tears she saw that he too was naked, and ready, and hungry.

She had been lying awake for half an hour, on the lower berth, staring at the bottom of the berth above in the dim blue light. He had fed her, but she was not assuaged, needing him to pass more of the wild honey of his seed into her. Her swollen lips ached and longed. One day he would make a baby in her: then bliss without boundaries would lap her. But perhaps he could not, for they had been lovers nine years now, and although it was only infrequently that they could consummate their love, surely if he were fertile, she would have become pregnant in those hundred or so matings? Guy and Virginia proved that the barrenness was not in her . . . but it was disloyal and ridiculous to think that Archie Campbell, the most wonderful man that God ever created, could have been denied the gift of fertility . . .

She said, "Darling?"

No answer. The train rocked, the wheels clickety-clacked on the rail joints, a station passed in a blur of closer, louder sound, suddenly falling back.

"Darling . . . what time is it?"

He couldn't be asleep. He must have heard her. She lifted her leg and pushed her foot up against the bottom of the upper berth—"Darling!"

"Eh? What is it? Are you all right?"

"What time is it, darling?"

"Why do you want to know? Och, you don't want to know at all, you just want another cup of tea, and it's no' a bad idea, at that."

She saw his legs drape dimly over the edge of the upper berth, then he landed soundless and in perfect balance on the floor. She reached out, spread her thighs and pulled him down.

Afterwards they lay side by side, squeezed in very close. Archie said,

"You've as lickerish a tail as the Mexican dancer who near bit my ear off in Vera Cruz. Why doesn't Quentin light the fire, tell me that? You never have."

She tried consciously to think without letting this passion, this touch of his flesh on hers, the soaking heat in her loins, distort her thoughts. She said, "When I married, I was a virgin, of course. And a McLeod . . ."

"The fire's there in all McLeods, just waiting."

"Just waiting, that's right. I was ready, willing, longing, even. But Quentin never saw that. He's ashamed of having to make love, I think. He never looked at me the way you do . . . you did, from the beginning. I've never seen that tenderness in his face, nor the strength . . . except toward the men, his soldiers . . . brutal, foul-mouthed private soldiers."

"But he's not a pouf, surely? I've met him, what, just three times and he seemed normal to me. But only women really know about poufs."

"He's normal," she said, "too normal. Dull. He doesn't like paintings, except of horses. He doesn't read books, except about soldiers. His idea of a perfect meal is roast beef, roast potatoes, and India Pale Ale. He's got two wonderful children, but he doesn't care anything for them, hardly spends a moment with them."

"Only seems not to care, perhaps, Fiona. There's many a man born without the gift of the gab . . . or any other way to show what he feels."

She gathered herself and burst out—"Archie, why don't I leave him, and come to live with you? I'm a good cook, and I can sew and darn—and I'll learn to wash clothes."

"There's the McLeod blood," he said softly, "wild as the Cuillins. Reckless. A McLeod never cares what anyone else thinks. What about your mother?"

"She'll understand. She wasn't happy with my father, either."

"Quentin's family, then? They're a decent lot, I understand."

"I don't care what any of them think!"

"Guy and Virginia, then?"

She felt the tears coming and buried her face in his shoulder, and mumbled, he hardly able to make out the words, "Oh God, I wish the Sinn Feiners would murder him, or there'd be a war and he would be blown up. Then we could get married and live together the rest of our lives."

She felt his arm moving, a hand stroking her hair, then his voice, low and soft and with the Glasgow burr accentuated. "Ye like art, Fiona, but you're no' an artist, or ye'd understan' yer husband better.

But I'm thinking ye only understan' yersel'. That ye can express, an' make plain . . . while he understands you, but canna make it plain . . . And you may be getting your war sooner than you think."

She stirred, raising herself on one elbow. The train was climbing, the engines working hard, the rhythm of the wheels slowed over the rail joints. "What do you mean?"

He spoke carefully, seriously—"I have a German friend, an artist, Helmuth. I think you met him at the flat once . . . or at the Academy, was it? . . . He's been staying with me, only went back to Germany yesterday. His uncle's in the German General Staff, a colonel, he said, and this uncle's talking about the need to attack France before France attacks them."

"But why would France attack Germany?"

"Revenge for 1871 . . . and the best moment for France would be when Germany is threatened, or actually attacked, by Russia."

"But . . ."

"Look, lass, Helmuth doesn't think the way his uncle does, and no more do I, but it's soldiers that have the power, not painters, in Germany at least . . . Russia is Serbia's protector, you might say. And the Austrians are threatening Serbia because of the murder of the Austrian Archduke in Serbia last month, but if the Austrians attack the Serbs, the Russians will come in to help the Serbs . . . and then the Germans to help the Austrians . . . and that'll be the moment for France to go for Germany by the back door, d'ye see, while they're facing the Russians."

"But . . ."

"That's enough of this talk, at such an hour. I'm going back to sleep."

She put her hand on his penis and scrotum, and fondled them. He kissed her ear and said, "When the man wakes us, eh? Before breakfast."

Unwillingly she let go, and he kissed her again, climbed easily up into his berth, and was soon snoring rhythmically and musically, while she lay on her back, her hands between her thighs, thinking of him.

The seventh hole at Dalmellie is a par 4, 415 yards, a difficult hole, usually played across a fierce wind off the Firth of Clyde, the bent grass bowing low to the sandy soil, the air full of salt and a smell of seaweed. Archie had only taken up golf since meeting Fiona. She had taught him; with the help of a good eye, the power of concentration and, according to himself, an inborn ability to play the game shared by all Scots, he had made himself a fair player, with a handicap of 14. Fiona's handicap was 4, playing off the women's tees, and she hit a long ball. At this hole she gave him a stroke.

Archie watched her tee up and give her driver a couple of practise wiggles. They were playing even so far, two holes apiece and two halved. Unless either of them foozled, they'd probably halve this one, too.

She addressed the ball with greater concentration, her grey-streaked blond hair blowing free in the morning wind, her face turned down, the grey eyes hidden, the long legs spread under the McLeod tartan kilt, the heavy nailed shoes biting firmly into the short turf. She swung, and he followed the flight of the ball down the fairway. It was a clean drive, nearly two hundred yards, and a long roll, right in the centre of the fairway.

He addressed his own ball and swung. The wind took it farther right than he had intended, and the ball ended up in the edge of the rough, a little short of Fiona's. This might be her hole, after all.

They shouldered their own clubs—it was she who had refused to take a caddie, saying that she had so little time with him that she did not want to share any of it with a golf caddie.

They trod off together. Archie said, "How are Guy and Virginia?"

"All right. They're both still at school, of course."

"Didn't I see that Guy was going to be asked to turn out for Kent?"

She nodded. "He doesn't seem very keen on it. He told me at Henley that he's a good schoolboy bowler, but doesn't think he's good enough—strong enough, was his word—to hide his something-or-other from grown-up professionals. What would that be?"

"Heaven knows. They didn't play much cricket round the slag heaps when I was growing up . . . but that boy's got his head screwed on the right way, Fiona. And Virginia—does she still hate school?"

"I suppose so. That's the impression I get from her letters, though she doesn't write about it much. She knows she's got to get an education whether she likes it or not. Quentin would never take her out of Cheltenham Ladies College—even if she had any idea what she wants to do instead, which she doesn't, and nor do we."

"Not many girls really know what they want out of life at fifteen. Or boys, come to that. Is Guy still set on being an aeroplane pilot?"

"And designer—yes."

"When will they be home?"

"Wellington breaks up on the 21st, but Guy will spend a few days with a school friend in London. Tom—you know, my naval brother— asked him and another friend, a boy called Yeoman, to stay with him in his flat but Guy had already accepted the other people's invitation, so he'll go there and the Yeoman boy will stay with Tom, whose flat is quite close, I believe. They'll all see plenty of each other . . . Virginia will go straight home on the 28th. Mrs Orr will look after her."

"You won't be back from your mother's?"

"Not till August 2nd."

They reached their balls and Archie swore—"What a stinking lie! I think I'd better take the niblick."

Fiona said, "Do you carry a mashie-niblick? You'd get a bit more distance."

"No. It'll have to be the niblick."

He made a good recovery and the ball rolled sixty yards up the course, resting in the middle of the fairway well past Fiona's drive ball. Fiona looked at the green, and felt the wind on her cheek. A good brassie shot would put her on in two, and the seventh wasn't a difficult green as far as she could remember. And she could remember well, for this Dalmellie was the course on which she'd reached the semi-finals in the Women's Championship in 1906, the year after she'd met Archie.

She waggled the club gently, twice, adjusted her stance, checked the wind once more, and swung. The ball sang down the course, low and fast, curling gently to the nudging of the wind, to land on the near edge of the green, roll up the gentle slope and stop within five feet of the hole. A gruff voice from behind her cried, "Beautiful shot, madam . . . gorrgeous!"

Fiona started in astonishment, and turned. She had been concentrating so much that she had not realised that an old man pushing a bicycle had arrived beside the fairway on the narrow sandy path which skirted the links, between the brown grass and the unquiet, grey-green white-capped sea.

The old man, wearing a tam o'shanter, tweed breeks and jacket, and a large scarf, said in a strong Lowland accent—"I hope I didna alarrrm ye, madam. It's Mrs Rowland, isn't it? Fiona McLeod that was? That backswing, so sweet and easy and without pushing, yet the ba' flies two hundred yards, like a bird directed to the very centre of the green. I saw that swing so often, eight, ten years back on this very course, that I'd recognise it anywhere. And this is Mr Rowland, nae doot."

Archie took off his cap with a slightly exaggerated bow—"Major Quentin Rowland, at your service, sir." He spoke as though with a pebble in his mouth but the Glasgow burr could not be altogether hidden. Fiona turned away to hide an incipient giggle.

The old man said, "Your wife's a credit to Scotland, and to the great game, sir. But I'll not be interrupting ye further. Good day, sir. Good day, madam."

He climbed onto his bicycle and wobbled on along the path, pedalling hard in the light sand that covered it.

Archie said, "Pheeew! So I'm Quentin now. And you're better known even than I thought."

"It doesn't matter."

He shook his head—"Better hurry up. That foursome behind us is on the sixth green."

He struck his third, which rolled near the hole, and they walked faster down the fairway. She said, "Archie . . . I'll get a divorce and we'll be married."

Archie said nothing for a while. He loved Fiona in many ways, but she was not the only woman in his life. His models, other painters' wives, chorus girls, every now and then a sex-starved lady client whose house or garden he was painting—his specialty was landscape, but he was a good artist in all fields in his medium, oils—all shared his bed from time to time, for longer or shorter periods. He did not think that he was yet ready to become a respectable monogamist; and if he was, he doubted very much whether Fiona Rowland would be the mate he'd choose. He was in a way more a physician to her than a lover; and that was the way it should remain.

He said, "You'll get no divorce from the courts without committing public adultery . . . which won't be good for Guy and Virginia. And you canna be certain that Quentin will institute proceedings even then. He might be sure you'll go back to him after you get over your infatuation."

They came up to their balls and Fiona stopped, staring—"You've stymied me!" she exclaimed in vexation.

She putted to the lip of the hole, the ball rolling close past the left side of Archie's, which blocked a direct shot at the hole for her. Archie putted, and missed, the ball rolling well past to leave him with a six foot return.

Fiona said, "Guy's nearly grown up. I can't go on living in misery just for his sake when he's going to be a man, on his own, in two years."

Archie missed his return putt and swore aloud.

Fiona said, "Louise—John's wife—can look after Virginia. She thinks I'm a bad mother, anyway, and . . ."

"Hush, woman!"

Archie sank his next putt, then, for a six: Fiona holed out for a four.

"I give you one here," she said. "Still mine, by one . . . Virginia will be married soon enough."

"Not so easily, with her mother known to be living in sin with a low-class Scots painter . . . Come on, Fiona. Let's play gowf, and leave the talking till the evening."

A hand on his shoulder awakened him, and her voice in his ear, "Darling . . . darling?"

He half turned, for he had been lying on his side with his back to her in the wide bed. "What is it?"

"It's Tuesday morning—our last day."

"What time is it?"

"I don't know. About four o'clock." A clock in the corridor chimed four, in confirmation.

He rolled over, slid his hand down her belly into her pubic hair, and began the process of making love, gradually coming awake and absorbed as she responded.

Afterwards they slept a little, then he got up, drew back the curtains —for he loved the early light—then climbed back into bed, and she curled up against his side. He felt her soft weeping and tried wordlessly to soothe her. The sobbing stopped and when she spoke her voice was almost steady—"None of the Rowland men are any good to their women. Richard can't give Susan children, and I know she wants them desperately. I like John the best, but he's so dull that it's hard to imagine him exciting Louise—even if she thought it proper . . . He's religious, too, inside himself, and I think that comes between him and his real nature . . . I've never seen Tom with a woman of his own—only dancing at parties and so on. I think he's afraid of us. The Governor's probably the best of them. I've always felt that Mother—Mrs Rowland —was as happy sexually as a woman can be. He's old now, of course, and so's she—and not too well either, I'm afraid."

"And Quentin. Is he still making love to you?"

"No. He knows I don't want it, from him."

"Why did you marry him?"

She moved sharply in the bed. "I wish I knew. It was what one was supposed to do. He was a good-looking subaltern in a good regiment, with some money. My mother was doubtful, because he was English. She didn't want a McLeod to marry a Sassenach. To tell the truth, I wanted to get away from home—not from Skye, but from being under mother's control . . . And he was very young and eager—only twenty-two. His colonel was furious—they nearly made him leave the regiment

—the Wealds don't like officers to marry until they're captains. They say, 'Subalterns may not marry. Captains may marry. Majors should marry. Colonels will marry.' But Quentin was determined . . ."

Archie cut in, "Sounds as though he does have a fire in him, somewhere."

"He did, for me, for a time . . . And I did want to be on my own. All girls feel like that. Or ought to. I can't understand why Alice hasn't left home ages ago. There's no need for her to look after her parents. They can afford servants or companions."

"Perhaps it's love," Archie said.

Her hand was at his loins again, squeezing, caressing. He thought, what had he done, what did he have, that had lit this unquenchable flame in her? She didn't look anything like a sultan's houri, or one of those women whose life is men. She looked like a McLeod of Skye, yet she was his mind, body, and soul. He shivered involuntarily, understanding suddenly that he was also hers. He had seldom had any trouble ending a liaison with other women—the models and typists and hungry rich—but what if he wanted to cut away from Fiona? Would he be able to? She was strong and God knew she was determined.

A picture came to him, unasked, of his widowed mother alone in her little house in the Gorbals . . . what would she think if she knew that her son was lying in a bedroom like a bloody palace with a McLeod all over him, begging for more? Fiona awed him now; but he wasn't ready for her again.

He said, "Did you see the papers yesterday, where all the chancelleries of Europe are in a dither about Serbia and Austria? What we were talking about in the train?"

She kept her hand where it was, but said, "No, I didn't see that."

"Well, some military correspondent was pointing out that once any of the big countries mobilised, war would be inevitable and that applied especially to France and Germany."

"I don't really understand, Archie, and what could it have to do with us?"

"Helmuth said his uncle hinted that Germany might invade Belgium as part of their plan to attack France."

"And so . . . ?"

"Britain has guaranteed Belgium's frontiers. We'd have to go to war —or break our promise."

"It's ridiculous," she said, "I can't believe there'll be a war, and as for us being in it . . ." She sat up suddenly. "You wouldn't go, would you? Volunteer?"

He laughed, "Me? *Ah'm* no' crazy, lass! Let the soldiers fight. They get paid for it . . . But I tell ye, there'll be dancing in the streets if we do get into it. The times are strange. The people won't care whether it's the French or the Germans we go against. There's something rising in the blood in these islands . . . they're spoiling for a fight. I don't like it, but I sometimes wish they'd get it, and more than they bargained for."

He slid out of bed, went to the window, and looked out. The sun was well up. Beyond the links, Arran, wreathed in scudding cloud, rose out of the grey Firth, the smoke from a black steamer drawn across it by the wind. The sea was rougher than it had been recently, waves driving up from the south-west to break in a line of spray along the sandy shore. Foam was being blown along the outer dunes, where the gorse and heather bushes thrashed in the wind. A sunlit shower rode slowly up the near fairway, and the flag in the centre of the hotel's circular drive stood out straight from its pole.

The Dalmellie Hotel was built directly opposite the sixteenth green of the famous course. Guests in any of the front rooms could look straight down on the green and in addition had a good view of the approach from the 16th tee, the 17th tee, and the fairway to the 17th green.

Looking down, Archie thought there was something strange about the 16th green—a large green tilted slightly to the south, and kidney-shaped—a brute to putt on when the ground was hard. He stared down, his eyes puckering. Then he said aloud, "My God! You'd better come and look at what your sisters have been doing in the night."

"What is it?" Fiona cried. "What's the matter?"

She got out of bed, naked, and hurried to him. He pointed, wordless. She stared down—"I don't see . . ." Then she saw, and read aloud what had been carved in the holy turf of the 16th green at Dalmellie, each letter six inches wide and three feet high—VOTES FOR WOMEN above the hole: and, below it, NO VOTES, NO GOLF.

"They've gone mad!" she said. "The suffragists have gone mad!"

She stood at Archie's side in the floor-length window, he in pyjama coat only, she altogether naked, her arm round his waist. An elderly gentleman in ulster and deerstalker stood in the driveway, staring up at them, jaw dropped. Fiona did not notice because Archie was at her side; nothing else mattered, except, to a lesser extent, the sacrilege that had been committed below. Archie did not notice because the certainty struck him that, like those suffragist women, Fiona was, in one respect, mad. They would stop at nothing to get their votes, and nothing could stop them. With Fiona it was not votes, but him, Archie Campbell. He headed back for the bed, feeling suddenly glad that his train left for Kilmarnock and London in three hours.

Daily Telegraph, Friday, July 17, 1914

ACTRESS'S MARRIAGE
BARRISTER'S PETITION
STORIES OF SUPPER PARTIES

In opening the case for Mr Whelan, Mr Campbell said there was here not only the tragedy of a child wife but the fate and future of Mr Whelan. Personally he (counsel) has never had the pleasure of hearing the co-respondent, but he was well known on the stage and had a rate of remuneration which even Mr Marshall Hall might envy. (Laughter). Did they expect that Mrs Hussey would have taken Mr Whelan home and introduced him to her husband if she had been engaged in a guilty intrigue with him? They knew the amount of freedom which was allowed to young married women and girls today was much greater than it used to be. He was old enough to remember when the favourite motto was, "There's no place like home". Now it was, "There's no place like the supper-room." Things had changed. The world had gone ahead, and the jury and himself were getting old-fashioned. The theatrical profession claimed and enjoyed a far greater amount of freedom than ordinary people and it was inevitable owing to their calling. Were they going to sit in judgment on the respondent because she was young and fond of life and society?

Mr Marshall Hall called the witness who earlier in the day had been taken ill. He said that during the week in August when both respondent and co-respondent were staying at the hotel, they breakfasted together at least three times. When he was getting ready the breakfast the co-respondent would be playing the piano and the respondent singing. They breakfasted alone. Mr Campbell suggested to the witness that his visit to the hospital that morning had interfered with his memory.

WITNESS: Oh, no; it was only my leg. (Laughter).

MR CAMPBELL: I suppose someone has been pulling it. (Laughter).

Cate read the whole long piece with interest. It was not quite as sordid a tale as most such proceedings were; and the fact that the petitioner was a barrister and the other two were in the theatre added a spice to the whole. George Robey had been mentioned several times, beside other well-known names.

Mrs Hussey had acted rather imprudently, but how were women supposed to act, in these times? Were they not usually helpless victims of their place in society? A couple of months ago, when he was in Hedlington late in the evening, a woman had offered him her body and, when he shook his head, had offered him her daughter, "Only twelve, sir . . ." She'd been better dressed and better spoken than most women of the street, face painted, but sad. What had brought her to that pass? He remembered, in the '90s, you could buy an hour with a guaranteed virgin for under five guineas in London; and you didn't have to search, either—they were thrust at you. But the fault was the men's, surely, for demanding such services?

Women were in a strange position these days. Millions of them worked in sweat shops and cotton mills and no one worried about them there; but with machines replacing manual physical strength in so many occupations, why shouldn't women drive lorries, steam rollers, make cars, pour steel? There were many nurses, but few women doctors, veterinary surgeons, professors; or directors of companies—and no judges, bishops, barristers, or Members of Parliament, although in these latter cases there was nothing inherently unfeminine about the work. Were women then tempcramentally unfit to hold such positions— which many of them surely aspired to—or was it merely traditional male prejudice? And, stemming from that, lack of facilities for women to learn the skills that would fit them for the positions?

He could not believe that women were congenitally unfit. He could think of a dozen girls, hardly released from day nurseries and the care of governesses, married off after one season and at eighteen or twenty suddenly chatelaines of eighty-room palaces and mistresses of fifty servants, and expected to house, feed, and entertain cabinet ministers, archdukes, international bankers and their wives—or mistresses. And they'd all done it, with aplomb. No one was going to tell him such women could not learn anything, manage anything, if given the chance, and proper training. Nor could he believe it was only the upper-class women who were so gifted—again, it was a matter of education, and opportunity.

He picked up the paper, but slowly laid it down again. It was a matter of waste, really—not justice or anything else so abstract. Lady Barbara and Lady Helen were being wasted, so was Alice Rowland, so was Carol Adams in Beighton . . . a dozen other names and faces sprang to mind, including his own daughter Stella; and if he could think of a dozen in a minute, how much waste of women must there be in the whole Kingdom? And was it only sexual? Were men and women not being wasted in great houses doing menial work which was sometimes unnecessary, and sometimes was or soon would be replaceable by machine?

England could afford such waste now, apparently—but what if there were an economic revolution, and national production had to be greatly increased? Then, he thought, there would also be a social revolution, and a sexual revolution . . .

Waste . . . would a woman be wasted if she were to marry his brother-in-law Tom Rowland? Tom was a bachelor, and dedicated to his Service, but Cate did not recall his name ever being linked with that of any woman. Nor did he seem to need them . . . as he himself did, he thought ruefully.

Good heavens, things had come to a pretty pass if for a woman to become a wife could be regarded as a waste . . . but he knew that he wasn't thinking of the woman—he was thinking of Tom.

London: Saturday, July 25, 1914

7 They sat in the front row of the dress circle, all three in white tie and tails. It was only a music hall in the Strand, but Tom had taken the two boys to an early dinner in the Savoy dining-room, and there evening dress was, of course, compulsory. Besides, Commander Tom Rowland, R.N., did not like to go to the theatre—any theatre—in a smoking jacket, still less in a daytime suit. It was not done, certainly not by a naval officer, though increasingly large numbers of people who one would have thought knew better were in fact doing it.

He sat in the centre, his nephew Guy on his right and Guy's friend Dick Yeoman on his left. On stage George Robey and an unknown actress were acting out a skit of scatological and sexual innuendo so raw that he was amazed that the Lord Chamberlain had not long since closed the theatre. He glanced surreptitiously at the boys, wondering whether they understood all the allusions, and what their mothers would say when they heard he had taken them to such a performance. Guy was laughing frankly and unashamedly, and certainly seemed to be aware of all that was being said or hinted at. Dick was a little flushed, often looking down at his hands, not at ease.

The woman said, "When I feels I needs to be alone, I squats among the cabbages and peas."

The audience guffawed and slapped its collective thigh. Smoke from two hundred pipes and cigars and a few of the new-fangled cigarettes rose in a blue haze, filling the high theatre, and smarting in the eyes and nostrils. From the dress circle bar behind them there was the crash of broken glass and voices raised in drunken song.

Guy leaned over to him and whispered, "When this show opened, that line was 'When I feels the need to be alone, I squats among the artichokes and leeks.' The Lord Chamberlain's office said she had to change it so she did!"

The skit went on. George Robey was a darling of the people, especially of Londoners, and the crowd in the gods loved him. He had only to raise those great dense eyebrows for a storm of laughter to rock the old building; the actress, lifted to his level by their partnership, had only to throw away a quite innocent remark for the people to see in it all the caustic innuendo, usually sexual, of Cockaigne. Dick Yeoman was loosening up, and laughing with Guy, albeit not as freely, as though ashamed to be enjoying such filth. Tom saw the humour that made the crowd laugh, but himself felt no sense of fun. He did not want to laugh, but he made himself do it, as he had taught himself to do many things, since childhood, that were done.

The skit ended, the curtain dropped, and a juggler entertained the audience for ten minutes, not very well. They shifted restively in their seats and from the gods, almost as invisible in the tobacco smoke as the ancient Greek gods in their Olympic clouds, some began to boo. A raucous voice yelled, "Pack it up, myte, and go 'ome to yer trouble and strife!" The juggler gallantly finished his act and vanished, bowing and visibly sweating. The management wasted no time in getting on the next act. The curtain dropped and, while a performing dog danced on its hind legs, caught sticks and balls, and turned somersaults in front of it, thuds and scraping sounds from behind it showed that scenery was being moved into place.

Guy looked at his programme. "'Erin go bragh: Russell Wharton and Edith Fanshawe.'"

Erin go bragh: Tom thought—Ireland for ever. Ireland was a touchy subject these days, with the Ulstermen threatening open rebellion against Home Rule, the government unwilling to enforce it, the army dangerously near mutiny on the subject, and the ordinary Englishman getting very hot under the collar on one side or other of the argument. He was surprised that the theatre management had put the skit or whatever it was into the programme in the first place, and more surprised that fights and riots in the audience had not caused it to be taken out since then. But the crowd was clapping as the curtain rose, to reveal two figures on stage, separated by twenty feet, each isolated in the glare of a separate spotlight, against the backdrop of a city street. The man, on the prompt side, was wearing a labourer's costume and a battered billycock hat, complete with inverted pipe stuck through the band, of the sort shown in cartoons of Irishmen, and carrying a big shillelagh—none of which served to disguise his sharp good looks and neat citified movements. Waving the shillelagh jauntily he began to sing—

> *Up to mighty London came an Irishman one day,*
> *As the streets are paved with gold, sure everyone was gay*
> *Singing songs of Piccadilly, Strand, and Leicester Square*
> *Till Paddy got excited, then he shouted to them there:*

As he sang, figures moved out of the wings on both sides, and walked to and fro, upstage from the principals, pretending to talk, new lights showing them up.

The singer swung into the chorus, joined at once by the woman and most of the audience:

> *It's a long way to Tipperary, it's a long way to go.*
> *It's a long way to Tipperary, and the sweetest girl I know.*
> *Goodbye Piccadilly, farewell Leicester Square,*
> *It's a long, long way to Tipperary, and my heart's right there!*

The lights went off the walkers behind, though they could still be dimly seen, and Wharton began the second verse:

> *Paddy wrote a letter to his Irish Molly O'*
> *Say should you not receive it, write and let me know.*

Guy whispered to his uncle, "Do you know this song?"

Tom said, "I don't think I've ever heard it."

"It's very popular. We have it on our dormitory gramophone." The chorus was being sung again, and now Guy and Dick were both humming, while the rest of the audience sang. Tom stared at Wharton. He was not tall, slightly built with blond hair which showed when he waved his billycock—and which Tom thought must be dyed.

The woman sang alone, in a palpably false Irish accent:

> *Molly wrote a neat reply to Irish Paddy O'*
> *Saying Mike Maloney wants to marry me*
> *And so leave the Strand and Piccadilly or you'll be to blame*
> *For love has fairly drove me silly, hoping you're the same.*

Everyone was singing, Guy and Dick, too—*It's a long way to Tipperary, it's a long way to go.* Tom hummed with them, having by now got a vague idea of the tune. He marveled again at the extraordinary solidarity and comradeship of the lower classes. Like their representatives in the navy, the lower deck matloes whom he commanded, they were always ready to quarrel, sing, fight, drink, weep over some sentimental trash, or blow dagoes, wops, froggies, and niggers out of the water . . . always all together, spiritually linked, as was every man and woman in the theatre.

Guy muttered, "Russell Wharton's got a good voice, hasn't he?"

Tom said, "Yes. I don't think much of Miss Fanshawe, though."

Guy said, "Wharton's supposed to have the same tendencies as Oscar Wilde."

Tom stared at the man on the stage, his arms now outflung to embrace the whole audience, the woman standing beside him. So he was one of those, and apparently admitted it, and had learned to live with it. He felt a chill of ice move down his spine, as Wharton seemed to catch his eye, and hold it. Wharton was smiling now, the lips parted, the blue eyes sparkling, looking straight into his own.

It must be imagination, a trick of the stage lighting. He wrenched his head round—"Where did you hear that?"

"There's a boy in dormitory whose father writes plays. He's full of gossip about everything in the theatre."

"That's a pretty scandalous thing to say about anyone, isn't it?" Tom said.

"I don't know, Uncle. Does it matter, really?"

Does it, Tom thought? Perhaps not, if you're an actor. For others, it mattered greatly; so much so that for many it was quite impossible to admit the fact in the first place, let alone deal with it once one had.

The curtain swung slowly down, to tremendous applause. The house lights went up, announcing an intermission. "I think I could do with a brandy and soda," Tom said. "Do you fellows want something?"

"My father lets me have a glass of sherry now and then," Dick said.

Guy said briefly, "I'm in training."

In the street after the performance, the Strand seemed to be one mass of humanity, all moving slowly, though in different directions, along the pavements and in the roadway itself. "What a lot of people," Dick Yeoman gasped. "I'm certainly glad I live in Lyme Regis, not London."

"It's not like this always, nor everywhere," Tom said. "London's full of lonely, quiet places, if you know where to look. But the Strand on a Saturday night, just when all the theatres are coming out, is not one of them."

Guy laughed and at that moment three pert girls came up from behind and, swinging into step beside them, stuck their arms through the men's, one to each. The girls were all giggling loudly and one said,

"Now, you're an 'andsome set of toffs. Wot abaht buying us a little drink?"

She was small and dark haired, with snapping dark eyes. Her clothes were thin and sleazy, pitifully decorated with glass baubles, and a coloured necklace dangled round her neck. Her head was bare—as were all three's—to the glare of the street lamps. They all wore high-heeled shoes of thin patent leather.

Tom did not know what to do or say, and he felt a flush rising in his neck. Encounters such as this were rare, thank God, but a man could not totally avoid them; for himself, they acutely embarrassed him. The boys were looking at him, Guy smiling, Dick Yeoman with an expression which he thought must be exactly matched by his own.

"C'mon, guvnor," the spokeswoman said, "*we* don't want no votes, we just want a drink . . . p'raps a little slap and tickle after, eh? We're not ugly, are we?" She let go Guy's arm, and swung round shaking her behind in the mauve dress, that reached barely to her mid-calf.

Guy said, "What's your name, miss? Mine's Guy."

"Aow, wot a luverly nime! I'm Rosie."

"Same as my grandmother," Guy said.

"We'd better be getting on home," Tom said nervously. Oh God, why couldn't he deal with women—any women—with the easy grace that Guy was showing? The girl was already less cocky: in a few minutes he'd have her eating out of his hand, and being servilely polite. As it was they were attracting amused glances and *sotto voce* advice from the passers-by. "Go on home, girls," Tom said. He felt in his pocket, found a coin and held it out—"Buy a drink and leave these boys alone. They're only schoolboys."

The dark girl swung on him, hands on hips, "And you're a poncing nance, ain't he, girls? Wot's wrong wiv us? *You* like us, don't you, Mister Guy?" She seized Guy's elbow. "Wouldn't you like to come along wiv us?"

"I think you're very attractive, Rosie," Guy said, smiling down at her, "but I think I'll have to stay with my uncle, to protect him."

"There, you old pouf! 'Ear what the young gentleman said? Come along, girls, let's find some *men!*" She stuck out her tongue at Tom, blew a kiss to Guy and then the three of them swung away and walked back east along the Strand, their bottoms wiggling.

Tom said, "Shop girls, factory girls on the spree . . . They have no morals at all, no shame . . ." They walked on westward, passing Charing Cross station. Propped against Queen Eleanor's Cross in the forecourt, a newspaper poster read, SINN FEIN BOMB IN WEST END; and another—CARSON'S VOLUNTEERS SWEAR TO FIGHT.

Tom said, "Look at those! I sometimes wonder what we're coming to."

Guy said, "Grandma thinks Carson ought to be shot. So does Aunt Margaret."

Tom thought, this is deep water, and Dick Yeoman's here; but it was a subject that would take the boys' minds off those girls, and his own inglorious role in that encounter. He said, "Well, you know that your grandmother is descended from kings of Ireland—that's my mother, Dick, she was born Rose McCormack but when she married my father she gave up her religion—she was raised a Roman Catholic, of course— and really gave up being Irish, as much as she could, for love of my father. She raised all of us to know a lot more about Ireland than most English children ever do, but we really stayed as English as our father —except my sister Margaret, who married Christopher Cate later. For some reason Ireland 'took' with Margaret, like an inoculation. She didn't go back to being a Catholic, but in everything else, she's Irish, Southern Irish. She thinks Carson's a traitor to Ireland for trying to prevent the country from becoming wholly independent of England. Carson's Irish, of course, but Northern Irish—an Ulsterman, and a Protestant—but the way he defies Parliament one might just as easily call him a traitor to England. He's quite sure that he's doing what he's doing for the good of England as well as of Ulster, and that makes it difficult. It's hard to act strongly against someone who so passionately wants to be on your side, to remain English."

Dick Yeoman had been listening, nodding his head from time to time. He said, "I agree, sir. I'm glad I'm not in the army. I wouldn't know what was the right thing to do."

Guy said, "My father took part in the mutiny at the Curragh—you know, when a lot of officers said they'd refuse to march against the Ulstermen. Granny and Aunt Margaret were furious at him, but I suppose he had thought out what was right and what was wrong, for him."

Tom said, "Your father's very level headed, Guy . . . I only hope they don't use the navy against the Ulstermen. I don't think we'd have another mutiny—if that's the right word for what happened at the Curragh—but it would not be good for the Service. We've got nearly as many Irish ratings, from north and south, as the army has soldiers."

They were crossing Trafalgar Square now, the fountains playing and hundreds of people sitting on the edges of the basins, or smoking on the plinths of Landseer's lions, lights glowing along the dark front of the National Gallery and under the pillared portico of St Martin's-in-the-Fields. A moment later they passed up Cockspur Street and walked faster, through thinning crowds, toward Tom's flat in Half Moon Street.

"What are the chances of war, Uncle?"

Guy asked the question directly, the blue eye and the brown eye level, one cold and piercing, one warm and affectionate. He sat with a glass of fresh-pressed lemonade in his hand, Dick Yeoman in another chair beyond the fireplace, Tom standing in the centre, his back to the empty grate.

Tom said, "It's more likely than it was a week ago, I'm afraid."

"Will we be in it?"

"I don't know. Today the Serbians accepted the Austrian ultimatum, but with some reservations. Whether Austria will take that as good enough, nobody knows. If they don't, and attack Serbia . . ." he shrugged, ". . . most of continental Europe will be dragged in."

"But we aren't allied to anyone, formally, are we?"

"There's the Triple Entente between us, Russia, and France, but it wouldn't compel us to enter *any* war between France and Germany, as far as I know. I'm just a simple sailor. I fight whomever their Lordships of the Admiralty tell me to fight. If this crisis had blown up a week earlier we would have had all our three home fleets in being. This year's naval exercise was a practise mobilisation of the fleets, including the call-up of the reservists, instead of the usual manoeuvres at sea. But the fleets dispersed the day before yesterday. We couldn't afford to keep them waiting any longer, even though the situation looks anything but settled."

"If war is declared," Guy said, "the Navy's mobilisation will probably be easier, though, won't it? Because they've just done it . . . I think Germany does mean to fight, sooner or later. Why else should she have widened the Kiel Canal, so she can move her biggest battleships through?"

"Ah, you read about that, did you? It's suspicious, I agree, but they could be preparing for anything . . . we might attack them, for instance. Or that's what they'll say."

"*The Riddle of the Sands* coming true," Dick Yeoman said in a dreamy voice, a glass of sweet sherry in hand. "I wish I could have been Carruthers . . . sailing a converted lifeboat among the shoals, finding out the German invasion plan. That's my favourite book. Have you read it, sir?"

"Of course I have," Tom said, smiling down at the boy. He was really pretty rather than handsome in the face, only the strength of his neck and jaw saving him from femininity. "Sailing is my favourite sport, when I get a chance. But I don't have a boat at the moment. I've just done three years on the China Station, and I sold my old boat before I went out."

Guy said, "I'll have to be getting back to the Hovings now, Uncle. Mrs Hoving wanted me in by midnight."

"When are you going home?"

"Tuesday. Virginia gets back from Cheltenham that day, and I'll go down, too."

"I may not see you again, then. After I've put Dick on the train tomorrow, I'm going down to Wiltshire for the last week of my leave . . . unless my friend Charlie Arbuthnot at the Admiralty calls up with an emergency posting for me."

"The Hovings are taking me to watch aeroplanes at Farnborough. I hope to meet some of the pilots who'll be coming down to Hedlington for our airshow on August 5th."

Tom showed his nephew to the door, where Guy paused, hand on the doorknob—"See you at school on September 21st, Dick. Have a good summer. Thanks for everything, Uncle."

Tom said, "Mind you don't fall in with any more factory girls, young man. Though you seem able to defend yourself more than adequately."

"If I want to," Guy said, with an oblique grin, and was gone.

Tom returned to the fireplace. "Sit down, Dick, the night is yet young, and you're going home tomorrow. What time's your train?"

"The eleven o'clock from Waterloo, sir. It's not too full on Sundays—most people are already at the seaside by then, or have started to come back."

Tom said, "Yes, Lyme's a bit far for the day-tripper crowd." He poured himself a whisky, weak with plenty of soda, and eyed the young man lolling in the easy chair. He moved gracefully, whatever he did—more gracefully than Guy even, though you could tell that Guy was an athlete. There was always a hint of danger in Guy's movements, a message that limbs and brain were equally capable of sudden actions, violent changes, unexpected decisions . . . not with Dick. The boy's eyelashes were his most remarkable feature . . . women must hate him for those long, long silky lashes, that were a full shade darker than his curly blond hair. Seventeen years and a bit, the same as Guy. Tom had learned in these last few days that the two boys had gone to Wellington in the same term, though not the same dormitory, for Guy was in the Beresford and Dick had said he was in something called the Lynedoch.

Dick said, "Guy's a tophole chap, you know, sir."

Tom said, "I'm glad to hear you think so."

"It isn't that he's so good at games. I'm sure he'll be fly half for the XV this winter, and of course this year was his third in the XI . . . it's him. He'll be a school prefect next term, everyone's positive, though they already have two in the Beresford—and it's very rare for a dormitory to have three . . . I wish he liked sailing, then he might come down to Lyme and stay with us."

"What sort of a boat do you have?" Tom asked.

"A Bristol Channel pilot cutter. It's Dad's, well, the family's really. Mummy likes to sail, too, and so do my sisters—I have three. Terrible girls! And my brother, of course, the one who was rowing for First Trinity at Henley . . . She's not a fast boat, so we don't go in for racing, much—just cruising."

"Those Bristol Channel pilots are wonderful sea boats, though."

"You need one to sail off Lyme," the boy said, his eagerness growing, "It's all right inside West Bay, but to get round Portland Bill you have to make Portland Race, and that's . . ."

"I know it," Tom said, smiling, "I nearly lost a destroyer in Portland Race on a really bad night."

"Is St Alban's Race as bad, sir?"

"It can be worse."

"Westward there are no races, but the farther down channel you get, the more you are facing the open Atlantic, and . . . but it's very stupid of me to try and tell *you* about all this, sir."

Tom said, "Don't call me 'sir,' Dick. It makes me feel about ninety-five. If you were to join the navy and come as a snotty into my ship, then it would have to be 'sir,' but now . . . Tom."

The youth smiled up. "Thank you . . . Tom."

Tom looked down. "I wish we could go sailing together."

His heart began to pound, his head was a little light, and he felt queasy under the breast bone. The boy had been four days in his flat and this longing for him had been growing all the time. But growing toward what? Tom closed his mind to the question. He did not know, he did not want to know, he did not dare to know. Four nights the boy and he had spent alone in the flat. This was the fifth, and last, night.

He forced himself to keep his voice steady—"I told you, I have no boat now. I used to keep my little ketch down at Buckler's Hard . . . so if I go sailing, it has to be as crew with someone else."

Dick jumped to his feet. "Oh, I wish you could come down to Lyme, sir . . . Tom. My people would love it! Dad's awfully keen on the navy. He wanted to be a sailor himself but his eyes are dud . . . Do you think you could come down this summer?"

Tom looked down into the eager eyes, under those taunting, flaunting eyelashes, the eyes blinking now in the intensity of the boy's emotion. His trousers were tight, and Tom could clearly see the bulge of his genitals. What would the boy do if he reached out and put his hand on that bulge, gently undid the buttons? The thought caused a spasm which made him turn round quickly, take a box of matches off the mantelpiece and fumble with his pipe. He was being swept forward by the nameless flood, the curse that had been laid on him. Could he live through this night without disgracing himself, and ruining this young man's life?

A bead of sweat ran down the side of his face and he wiped it off with a handkerchief, "Phew, it's hot in here . . . terrible summer we're having."

"It's wonderful sailing weather, though," Dick said. "And swimming. Do you like swimming, Tom?"

Tom met the boy's eyes. He found it hard to breathe, as a strong erection grew inside his trousers. The boy's eyes were down, looking at it, and he seemed to be holding his breath. Dick took a step toward him. As if by accident, but it was no accident, Dick Yeoman did what Tom had just held himself back from doing a few moments ago—his hand brushed Tom's fly, and rested, the palm opening.

The telephone rang. The pipe fell from Tom's mouth and he started violently. He muttered, "God!" and stooped to pick up the pipe. Dick Yeoman sank into a chair, his face flushed, his hand trembling on the arm of the chair.

Tom went to the telephone and lifted the receiver off its hook. "Rowland," he said.

"Tom! Charlie Arbuthnot here. You are posted to *Monmouth*, as commander. Come to the Admiralty at once, to take delivery of some secret documents for the captain—who is Brandt, by the way."

"I thought *Monmouth* was refitting."

"She was. She's ready. The job was finished in a hurry and she sails very soon. We haven't sent out the war-readiness signal yet, but it's likely at any time now. See you in half an hour . . . And bring your gear with you. We'll be sending you straight down by the newspaper train."

Tom returned the receiver to its hook and walked back to the fireplace. The flood had abated, desire vanished. The boy knew it. Tom said, "I have to go—now. Jones will be here at the usual time to make your breakfast and see that you get a cab to Waterloo . . . Why don't you go to bed? It's been a long day."

"Couldn't I help you pack?"

"Not really, Dick. Thanks all the same." He put out his hand and they shook, formally.

Daily Telegraph, Saturday, July 25, 1914

ULSTER PREPARED FOR A BLOCKADE
PROVISION FOR A YEAR

From Our Special Correspondent. BELFAST, Friday night. Anyone who has watched the progress made by the head-quarters staff appreciates that very little has been left undone to make complete the preparations for a grave emergency. We may be sure that the subject of the food supply has not been forgotten, and if it should be the in-tention of the Government to blockade Ulster ports when a Provisional Government is in being, they will find that the attempt to force the loyal province to surrender will be a much longer process than they imagine. . . . The potato crop promises to be a record in yield and of ex-ceedingly good quality. The export of meat is also an im-portant part of Ulster's trade. The meat supply certainly will not fail. . . . There will be no difficulty with regard to the milk, butter, and egg supply.

THE WOMEN AND CHILDREN.

The following have been selected vice-presidents of the 'Help the Ulster Women and Children' Council:

Sir Edward Carson	Mr Rudyard Kipling
Earl Roberts	Dr Bruce Poeler
Mr Walter Long	The Duchess of Somerset
Viscount Milner	Lady Greenall
Earl Curzon	Mr Harold Smith, M.P.
The Duke of Portland	

The object of the Council is to provide hospitality for loy-alist refugees who may be driven out of their homes by civil war or disturbance . . .

The Ulster news was depressing, as always, Cate thought; but the bra-vado and the threats seemed less important today—because their shadow was being swallowed by another, larger, blacker shadow falling over the whole of Europe, perhaps the world. It looked like war now, which the continentals seemed to want, for one reason here, another there. But England had everything she wanted. Why should she go to war? One did not make war without serious cause, imminent and mortal danger . . . or a promise. An Englishman keeps his word, he'd told Laurence and Stella a hundred times, since they were little children. And England had promised to protect the neutrality of Belgium. But that was all. If the Germans and French kept away from Belgium, all would be well. And surely they would. Surely neither the Kaiser nor the French president—never could remember his name—were so stupid as deliberately to bring out against them the richest country in the world, the biggest fleet? They must understand what sea power could do to them . . . what bulldogs the English were. Once they got their teeth in, they'd never let go . . .

He shook the paper irritably. He was thinking like a Tory politician making a Boer War recruiting speech. What was the truth of the matter? The British Empire was huge, but just what was its power, for war? Canada, South Africa, New Zealand, Australia, and Newfoundland could be relied on to send their men; but there weren't many, when reckoned against the German or French armies. They would also send wheat, meat, wool, and raw materials of all kinds as long as the seas were open to them. India could send many men . . . but did England really want native troops fighting a white man's war, in Europe? It might lead to a great deal of trouble later. The Indian Empire had great resources in minerals, too, and some foodstuffs—rice, wheat, tea, he thought, and jute: but the country also required many soldiers to keep the peace so it wasn't all a credit. The rest of the Empire—Fiji, Samoa, Rhodesia, Jamaica, and the Antilles, the Gold Coast, Gambia, Nigeria, Kenya, Mauritius, the Seychelles, Ceylon, the Anglo-Egyptian Sudan, Egypt itself—under British protection—Sierra Leone, the Solomon Islands, British Honduras, the Gilbert and Ellice Islands . . . much of it produced raw materials—hard woods, copra, tea, coffee, sugar—but all of it needed governing, policing, and protecting. Sea power was the link that kept these colonies under British rule; but the mighty navy would be hard put to it to keep the many chains unbroken against an enemy strong at sea, and at the same time protect the heart of the Empire, the British Isles, against invasion.

Cate got up with a jerk, throwing the paper down. He felt a premonition that war was indeed coming; and he could suddenly see, as vividly as he could see the lawn and trees outside, the actuality of the sacrifices and the changes—the sale of all those farms and mines, and railways and investments, to buy munitions of war; the undermining and eventual disappearance of manor and castle, pub and farmhouse, stable ānd kennel, a whole wonderful way of life; the lives or livings of hundreds of thousands, perhaps millions, of those people, the Garrods and Gorses, Cates and Rowlands and Strattons, the people you could rely on, and trust . . .

Tuesday and Wednesday,
August 4 and 5, 1914

8 On July 27th, 1914, after four weeks of threats, counterthreats, entreaties, offers, negotiations, denials, warnings and ultimatums, Austria declared war on Serbia. On July 30th Russia ordered general mobilisation. On July 31st Austria and Germany followed suit. On August 1st Germany declared war on Russia, and demanded to know from France what France's attitude would be in the Russo-German war. France replied that she would act in her best interests; and, the same day, ordered general mobilisation. On August 2nd, Germany demanded passage through Belgium for her armies, since this was the route laid down in her Schlieffen Plan for a war on two fronts. Belgium refused the demand. On August 3rd Germany declared war on France, and her armies entered Belgium, whose frontiers and independence she and others had guaranteed. Among those others was Great Britain, who now required Germany to withdraw her troops from Belgium at once. If Germany did not agree to do so by midnight of August 4th, German time, a state of war would exist between Great Britain and Germany. The British fleet was ready: the warning that war was imminent had gone out to all warships on July 28th. The army's mobilisation plans were complete.

As the hour for the expiration of the ultimatum—11.00 p.m. Greenwich Mean Time—approached, the people filled the streets of Britain's cities. In London, dense crowds waited outside Buckingham Palace. King George, Queen Mary, the Prince of Wales and Princess Mary appeared on the balcony. The crowd was silent, expectant. It was sixty years since Britain had taken part in a European war—the Crimean War against Russia.

At eleven o'clock the crowds everywhere released their held-back emotions in a long hour of frenzied cheering and shouting. Patriotic songs welled the summer night. Outside the Palace they sang *God Save the King*, and *Rule, Britannia*. Nearly everyone was filled, drunk, with heady enthusiasm. Now God be thanked, for the stale, flat years of peace were washed into history, and forgotten. The Great War had begun.

In the Foreign Office, Sir Edward Grey, the bird watcher of Fallodon, His Majesty's Principal Secretary of State for Foreign Affairs, stood looking out of his window at the lights in St James's Park, a private secretary at his side.

The private secretary said, "Some of the lamps are going out, sir. Is it in case the Germans send over Zeppelins to drop bombs?"

Grey, worn and weary, said slowly, "Henry, the lamps are going out all over Europe. We shall not see them lit again in our lifetime."

Guy flung his bicycle down at the edge of the airfield and ran forward. The sun was not yet risen, its presence a bright glow below the eastern horizon. It was a hot, still morning. The B.E. 2(c) sat at the edge of the field, its engine turning, the four-bladed propeller whirling slowly. The pilot was sitting in the rear cockpit, and Guy's friend, Ginger Keble Palmer, standing beside him, his flying helmet on, his goggles lifted to his forehead. The two were talking, their heads close.

Ginger noticed Guy first and waved a gloved hand. As Guy came up he shouted, "We have to cancel the show, Guy . . . flying back to Farnborough at once . . . war . . ."

Guy tried to control himself. He had been looking forward to this day, and the first flight he had been promised, ever since the airshow had been planned two months ago. But the newspaper headlines had been so threatening that he could not sleep last night, for a premonition of what might happen, and had got up long before dawn to come to the airfield.

The thin-faced pilot looked at him a long time through his goggles and Guy turned away, for a tear was forming in his eye and he did not want the others to see it. He heard Ginger shouting, "This is Guy Rowland, Geoffrey. The one who is going to be a test pilot for us."

Then he heard the pilot—"Ten minutes won't lose us the war . . . Hey, I'm Geoffrey de Havilland." Guy turned. The other's gloved hand was out, stretched over the side of the cockpit. "Jump in."

Guy gasped, "Honestly, sir?" Then, unable to speak another word, he found the slots in the plane's fabric side and clambered into the front cockpit. The engine roared into louder life, and Ginger backed away. De Havilland shouted, "You'll get a little windblown . . . Fasten that strap round your waist . . . You really want to be a test pilot?"

"Yes, sir," Guy shouted, "if I don't find myself in the R.F.C."

The nose swung and the machine gathered speed. The engine roar increased still more and Guy settled back. He was going to fly, for the first time in his life, with England's greatest young aircraft designer, in the Royal Flying Corps' newest aircraft, de Havilland's B.E. 2(c). He knew its characteristics by heart—8 cylinders in V, aircooled, 90 horsepower, 2,150 lbs at take off, maximum speed of just over 72 miles an hour at 6,000 feet . . . could carry a machine gun and 225 lbs of bombs—though this particular machine, equipped with dual controls for tests and training, carried neither, nor yet even the roundels of the R.F.C. The engine was encased in a riveted shell of some shiny metal, steel or aluminium; the lower wing was well staggered back from the upper; two struts on each side gave structural strength to both wings; and two vertical metal pipes, one from each bank of cylinders, carried the exhaust gases straight up and over the middle of the upper wing.

August 5, 1914 . . . the date would live in his mind till the day he died . . . the date and all that happened on it. The windsock at the hangar drooped in the still air, the sun was just rising above the long, level line of the North Downs. The tail lifted, the ground rushed by faster and faster . . . it had gone, it was no longer touching, holding the aeroplane down, it was sliding past, mysteriously slower and slower. The laws of gravitation and inertia were suspended, the aircraft and its passengers sliding into a new dimension. The B.E. 2(c) arrowed into the yellow ball of the sun.

Guy closed his eyes for a moment of pure ecstasy. One day he had done the hat trick against the numbers 2, 3, and 4 of the Winchester batting order. Another, he had taken 7 for 38 against an I Zingari side containing four county and two England players . . . but never had he felt anything like this before. The wind rushed against his closed eyelids, slowly growing colder. His hair tugged at his scalp, and his skin was fretted by the air's rough embrace. The eight cylinders purred in harmony close ahead, and a smell of petrol and engine oil mixed subtly with the summer air.

He opened his eyes. The machine tilted to the right, a steady slow wheel across the sky . . . steadied . . . tilted to the left . . . steadied . . . climbed again, the sun now behind.

"Like it?" The firm pitch of de Havilland's voice cut through the rushing roar of wind and engine.

"It's . . . the top!" Guy flung back.

"See that stick between your knees? Take it, and put your feet on the pedals, gently. Now feel what they do."

Guy felt the stick move a little to the right. One pedal depressed and the other rose against his foot. The plane's right wing dipped and it began to turn. As it settled into the turn the stick moved to its central position, then a little back, then left past central. The wings levelled. The stick centred.

"Now you try it."

Guy took the stick more firmly and gently pressed one pedal down, just as he had felt. The voice behind was encouraging—"Good . . . now the other way . . . stick a little back, or you'll lose altitude . . ."

"We're steady on 2,100 feet," Guy said.

"We were at 2,300 when you took over . . . Complete the circle without losing height . . . Good . . . Now line up at the airfield . . . there it is . . . stick forward gently . . . use the pedals to keep her on line . . . throttle back a bit, toward you, easy . . . altitude should be dropping . . . good . . . good . . ."

The sun was a golden ball in the morning haze, the B.E. 2(c) flying into the heart of it. Guy half closed his eyes against the glow . . . de Havilland was drunk, or mad . . . he was letting him land the plane, his first time in the air . . . No, it was natural. The air was his element. The ground was a place where he had to eat and sleep and go to the bathroom. His life, his heart, his brains, were here.

He eased the stick forward . . . right rudder . . . left . . . nose down a bit more . . . air speed ought to be close to forty when he landed . . . but there was no dial to show him . . . no wind . . . he could guess. The grass rushed up to meet him, and silently, without a bump or a graze, he flew the craft onto the grass, tail high.

He felt the stick move back, and the throttle close. The tail sank. The plane stopped, the dust whirling around them as the propeller circled, the engine sputtering.

De Havilland's voice sounded a hundred miles away. "Not exactly a three-point landing . . . but very smooth. I had my hands on the controls all the time but never had to override you. Sure you've never flown before?"

"In dreams, sir. Many times."

At the head of the table Lieutenant Colonel Pitchford said, "There are three changes in the mobilisation details for today. A Company will hand in bayonets for sharpening and sandblasting at 10.23 a.m., not 10.50 as in the order. No difficulties there, Major Rowland?"

Quentin Rowland said, "No, sir."

The Commanding Officer of the 1st Battalion, the Weald Light Infantry continued, "C Company will draw war scales of ball ammunition at 4.58 p.m. instead of 11.02 a.m. as at present ordered. Major Wylie?"

"We're down to be issuing first field dressings at that time, sir."

"Talk to the quartermaster about fitting that in somewhere else . . . A Company's rehearsal of train loading will take place at 3 p.m. at the station, today, instead of tomorrow. Major Rowland?"

"It will be a bit of a rush, but we can get it done, sir."

"Now, any questions about personnel? Do any of you foresee any problems with the people you now have? Are they all fit for war, in one rank higher than they now hold? Officers first."

Quentin thought of his officers—Irwin, his second in command: Hedges, Eden, Tate, and McDonald the subalterns. McDonald was over thirty-six and in many regiments would have had his captaincy long ago; but promotion had always been very slow in the Wealds, as secondment and applications for the Staff College were severely discouraged. Perhaps he should recommend that McDonald be left behind in the depot at Hedlington to train the recruits who would presumably be flooding in. But where was his replacement to come from? And what about himself? He knew he was a competent officer, and had proved it in South Africa and on the Indian frontier . . . but this was going to be a bigger war. And the colonel had said, 'one rank higher.' Could he command the battalion? He didn't know, and couldn't know, until he had tried; and by then it would be too late; and the men would suffer from his incompetence. But surely the colonel would not expect him to judge of his own fitness? He said nothing. Nor did anyone else.

"Warrant officers? . . . N.C.O.s? . . . I won't ask about the men. If you haven't trained your private soldiers, you're not fit to command companies—and it will soon show . . . That's all, gentlemen. Next mobilisation meeting tomorrow, here, same time."

The company commanders saluted and filed out. Major Bergeron, the battalion second-in-command, Lieutenants Burke-Grebe and Corbett, the adjutant and quartermaster respectively, stayed behind with Colonel Pitchford. Quentin headed slowly across the barrack square toward A Company office, his head bent, thinking—war at last. France, Russia and now England against Germany and Austro-Hungary. Everyone knew the Austrians were no good. It would be over in a few weeks, then they could all go back to normal peacetime life. Meaning life with

Fiona, as it had been these past nine or ten years? That wasn't normal. Perhaps he should wish for the war to go on a long, long time. Perhaps he could at last find a way to show Fiona that he loved her, and always would, even if she no longer loved him. If only she needed him, as the men did, he could show her. But she didn't.

"War!" Harry Rowland muttered, looking out of the window into the garden. The high wall that shut in Laburnum Lodge kept out most sounds of the town. He wondered whether the people were gathering outside the Town Hall this morning. Perhaps he should be there, instead of at home, guarding a cold he'd picked up a day or two earlier. Summer colds were always the most annoying. He blew his nose again, gently, for the septum and nostrils were sore, and turned back into the room.

"What shall we do?" he asked his wife. Rose was sitting in her accustomed high-backed chair, a piece of sewing in her lap.

"Do about what, my dear?" she said, keeping her head bent as she adjusted the spectacles on her nose. She always wore spectacles for sewing now.

"About the war. I was supposed to retire at the end of this month, and we were to go round the world. That's out of the question now."

"Going round the world is, I agree."

"What about retiring, then?"

"I don't see why you shouldn't retire, Harry. Richard is ready to take your place, and eager to do so. He has waited a long time. He is full of ideas and enthusiasm."

Harry began to pace the Wilton carpet. "But . . . the war alters everything. There'll be all sorts of changes at the factory. We'll get military orders and have to re-design or at least modify the Sapphire to suit. We may have to increase production greatly. Or we may be ordered to make munitions—guns—anything. For Richard to take over now would be like changing horses in midstream."

She put down her sewing with a sigh, took off her glasses and put them on the sewing table beside her. "Harry," she said, "you never wanted to retire and now you're using the war as an excuse to go back on your promise to Richard. Without that promise he would have left Rowland's years ago. By now he'd probably be head of Daimler's, or Mr Ford's British factory, or even have a firm of his own, like Mr Austin."

Harry scowled at the floor. What she said was literally true, but the war changed all the previous conditions. It wiped the slate clean. Promises given in peace, for peacetime, did not hold.

His wife continued, "If it's keeping yourself occupied that's worrying

you, we should start an organisation here in Hedlington to look after
the people who stay . . . the women whose men are volunteering even
now . . . the wounded, when they come back . . . the widows.
There'll be widows, you know."

"It won't last a month!" he exclaimed.

"So much the better," she said, "but if it does, there will be great
suffering here. We can do something to alleviate it. Or you could go
into politics."

"I'm no politician."

"You could be, now that you'll have the time."

He stopped his pacing, and said, "Rose, I am going to stay on running Rowland's, my own firm, for the duration of the war . . . and
that's that."

"Very well, Harry. You're making a mistake, a cruel mistake."

Bob Stratton, standing in a partitioned-off, comparatively quiet corner
of the machine shop devoted to assembling rims, hubs, and graduated
lengths of thick wire into wire wheels for the Rowland Sapphire, listened intently as Collis, the head tuner, set to work on another wheel.
In front of Collis on the bench was a row of half a dozen pitch pipes; a
hollow steel tube was clamped at one end to one of the wires, at the
hub, the other end of the pipe resting in Collis's right ear. As Collis
plucked that wire with a fingernail of his right hand he blew into one
of the pitch pipes, which he was holding in his left hand. Head cocked
at the same angle as Collis's, Bob Stratton listened, bowler hat pushed
to the back of his head.

After half a dozen wire spokes had been tested, he thought that his
suspicion was justified; after another two complete wheels had been
done, he knew. He moved round close behind Collis and, as he was setting up a third wheel, said in a normal speaking voice, "How old are
you, Collis?"

The man did not answer. Bob raised his voice and repeated the question. Still no answer. Bob went out into the clamour of the chassis erection shop, bowler hat now set squarely on his head, and watched two
men setting up the chassis side members of a Sapphire, the Order Book
number of that particular car already wired to the right side member.
Bob watched, knowing that his eyes would see anything sloppily or im-
properly done, while he allowed his mind to wander . . . Collis had
worked at Rowland's for thirty years, the last sixteen, ever since Rowland started using wire wheels, in his present job. It was skilled work,
and he was one of the highest paid men in the factory. Now . . . he
shook his head involuntarily, and one of the two men setting the sec-

ond side member down on the wooden trestle where it would be built up, said in alarm, "Have we done summat wrong, Mr Stratton?"

"No," he growled. "Just handle the cross members a bit more easy when you get to them."

He walked on. Mr Harry had been in a rare state yesterday when war only seemed certain. A real bad temper, he'd been in, which was unusual for him. And now that war had actually come, what would he be like?

"Morning, Dad." He looked up and met his eldest son's eye. Frank was dressed in blue overalls, and wearing a greasy cloth cap, like most of the men. He said to his father, "You'd best take a look at the generator, Dad. Tanner says he's going to have to shut it down for twenty-four hours to change the main shaft bearings."

"He can do it Sunday," Bob snapped. A memory of the Reverend Mr Hunnicutt's favourite sermon tweaked at his conscience; but this was for the Rowland Motor Car Company, and to enable the four hundred men to work when they should be working. The Good Lord would understand.

Frank said, "He says they may not last till then."

"Tell him they must . . . and, Frank, I'm moving Collis to the paint shop."

"Collis? But he's . . ."

"Deaf. Gone deaf."

"Well, we should retire him. He's not worth his money in the paint shop."

"I can't. I only found out because some work he did for me on the wheels for Victoria weren't right. 'Twouldn't be fair to sack a man on account of something I'd never 'a found out about otherwise."

Frank said, "He must be tuning them by instinct, or something. The testers haven't found anything wrong with the wheels, have they?"

"Just one percent, the normal . . . I'll move him, and explain to Mr Harry. You tell Mr Richard if he tries to move him back."

He started to walk away, nodding briefly at his son, when he saw Harry Rowland's young houseman hurrying down the cluttered floor, past the row of chassis, under the gantry arm, an envelope in his hand. He said, "What is it, Brace?"

"Mr Harry told me to give you this note." Bob took the envelope, opened it, and read—"*Bob—have decided to stay on for the duration of the war. Will you stay on with me? If so, tell no one, except Frank, and he must not talk either until I have had an opportunity to speak with Mr Richard, who's in Manchester, as you know. H.R.*"

Bob took one of the pencils protruding from the breast pocket of his blue suit, and scrawled—*"Mr Rowland—Yes—Bob Stratton."* He handed the envelope back, and Brace hurried away down the clangorous shop.

Bob turned back to his son. "Frank, Mr Harry's staying on, because of the war. So am I. You're not to tell anyone about Mr Harry, yet."

Frank Stratton looked up, and stopped humming. His cheerful smile had vanished, the wide mouth was firmly closed. He gazed directly at his father as he said, "You stay, Dad, and I go."

"Where, Frank, where can you go?"

"To join up, of course."

"You're thirty-six, man."

"And as fit as any of the lads that'll be in the recruiting offices. And I've been thinking, ever since we heard about the war, that I ought to go, in any case." He began to take off his work gloves.

Richard Rowland sat in his hotel room, his notes spread on the table before him. His visit to Mr Ford's plant at Trafford Park had been a revelation. It didn't make him feel less eager to visit Detroit, but more so, for his eyes had been opened to a new vision. Hearing talk, or reading about what was being done at Trafford Park was very different from seeing it in operation . . . the moving assembly line, with the chassis moving forward not on their own wheels, which in the early stages weren't even fitted, but carried on a jointed steel frame which was pulled forward on its own track . . . the overhead channel with its line of assembled wheels, tyres already fitted, rolling down by gravity over the assembly line, as they were wanted . . . the second assembly line of completed bodies coming in at right-angles from their own shop to join the line of chassis . . . The man who'd shown him round, the famous Mr Lea Perry in person, had explained that at Highland Park, in Detroit, the bodies were brought in overhead, and lowered directly onto the chassis—but what he had seen was amazing enough . . .

Men's involvement Richard noted on his pad. The Ford system was so new that the labour force was still in general wonderstruck at it, and to an extent proud to be part of it. But he had detected something while going round that he had never seen at Rowland's—a listlessness, even though the work was being done efficiently. It would be difficult to keep men's interest in doing the same small job repetitively, minute after minute, hour after hour, day after day.

One model, one colour he noted. "You can have it any colour you like as long as it's black," Mr Perry had told him that Mr Ford had said; and all the cars he'd seen at Trafford Park were Model Ts and all were black . . . but could Rowland's do the same, at the price they were asking? But he was going to put the price down, when he took over . . . and the quality? What about quantity? Trafford Park was geared to make 6,000 cars a year, and had done so last year, 1913. But Rowland's made a maximum of 2,000, and that working at full stretch. The whole line-assembly system would have to be carefully reviewed as to its suitability for a small production base, and he'd get the accountants onto costing. Meantime, he'd talk to a production line expert. Another side where Ford's organisation was infinitely stronger than Rowland's was the sales department. At Rowland's you made the best car you could for the price, let the world know in an unobtrusive manner what you had done, and waited for gentlemen to come and order the car they wanted . . . Ford's salesmen went out and grabbed people by the throat, persuaded them they couldn't live without a Model T, and didn't leave till they'd got a deposit on one. Well, the Governor wouldn't like it, but times were changing, and if Rowland's was not to go under, it would have to change too.

He spread out the blueprint of the main assembly room floor that Mr Perry had lent him, and began to study it intensely, jotting down notes on his pad all the while. It showed, in a kind of bird's eye view, drawings to scale of all the machinery and the conveyors, and a maze of fine lines and arrows indicating the route each part had to follow on its way to becoming part of a car. It even showed where the men had to stand, for a major part of the Ford philosophy was that work must be taken to the men—not men to the work.

A strange noise intruded on his concentration. For a time he tried to ignore it, then could not. He got up, went to the window, and leaned out. The street below was full of people, mostly men. The noise was cheering. Someone on a horse was moving slowly through the crowd, someone in khaki uniform, touching his hand to his gold braided cap . . . a general, obviously. They were cheering a general—Lancashire workmen who'd probably never seen a general before, and if they had, would as like as not have jeered him down the street, or thrown tomatoes and filth at him. Now they were beginning to sing, *On Ilkla Moor 'baht 'at*, surely? He strained his ears to catch a tune in the half-formed booming below . . . *Rule, Britannia*, by God!

He returned to his table, adjusted his thick spectacles and stared at his notebook. He'd forgotten about the war. But who could know what would happen? He himself would never get into a service, with these eyes. He might be needed in some sort of war production, if it went on long enough. But he was committed to Rowland's. And what would, or might, happen to Rowland's? He was about to take a ship out on stormy and uncharted seas.

Anne Stratton, bent over the zinc tub in her kitchen, was washing babies' nappies. She poured more hot water from the big kettle on the stove, and began to scrub harder. Agnes, four, played loudly on the floor in the hallway, and Lily the two-year-old stamped and shouted in her crib. Anne's belly felt enormous and this time she was sure it was going to be a boy. Frank had always wanted a boy, and she had felt dreadful when they'd told her the second baby was another girl. She smiled, wiping a strand of brown hair from her eye, leaving a smear of soap in its place. Dear Frank . . . no woman would ever have a better husband, and soon now he'd be Works foreman, and there'd be more money coming in. Perhaps she could have a girl in all day to help, not just four hours every afternoon. But Frank had said last night that if there was a war, it would be hard to find girls for service, because they'd be taking the place of the men in the factories. Fancy that! Who'd have thought that women could work those big oily machines, even if they wanted to!

She heard the front door open and looked at the clock. Who would be calling at this hour, and not even knocking? The war had only been going on a few hours, and already people were acting strange. She called out, "Who's there?" wiping her hands on her apron.

"It's me." She recognised her husband's voice, and ran through to the front hall, crying, "What's the matter, Frank? Have you took sick?"

"Daddy, Daddy," Agnes cried, running after her.

"Da, Da, Da!" Lily called, throwing a wooden toy out of the crib and beginning to cry because she could not reach it.

"I've left Rowland's," Frank said, "and I had a couple of pints on the way home. No, I'm not drunk, woman."

"You've left Rowland's? What . . . what? I don't understand." She sank into a chair, feeling faint. This dratted baby in her was kicking, and sometimes made her feel that she was in two places at once, and not recognising either.

"Dad's staying on, so I left. I'm going to enlist."

She leaped up—"Frank!" Her voice rose in a shriek. "You can't!"

He said grimly, "I can, and I must. I won't stay on at Rowland's because Dad's broken his promise. And even if he hadn't, I know I ought to volunteer."

She stared at the familiar, beloved, sandy-haired man with the big ears. But this was not the man she knew, her man, for whom she waited with a permanent passion and love—in bed, in the house, everywhere, longing for his touch. He was not smiling, or humming. The mouth was straight and eyes serious. He said gently, "I have to go, Anne. I couldn't live with myself if I didn't."

She knew it was hopeless even then, but muttered, "And leaving me with the baby, your son, due in two months . . . Couldn't you wait till then?"

He said, "I can't wait, love."

She began to cry. How long would he be gone? What would happen to her? She had always liked men, but once married to Frank she had been able to channel all her sexuality, all the secret longings and desires, into matings with him, her husband. How would she be, without him?

"They're saying it'll be over in a month," he said comfortingly. "Don't cry."

She didn't look up. "Do you believe that?"

After a long time he said, "No."

War, war, war . . . the single syllable throbbed in Fiona Rowland's head like a bass drum, beating close in dense jungle, and she trapped in the same jungle, not knowing how to get out, nor how to reach the drum and stop its incessant throb.

She heard Guy and Virginia talking in the kitchen with the maid, and for a moment tried to listen to what they were saying, but soon gave that up.

War, war, war . . . Quentin would be going to the war with the battalion. He was a company commander, and would be in danger, because he would do his duty faithfully, whether it was boring or frightening, just his duty—beyond that he could not go, or see.

Her sister-in-law's voice echoed inside her head, "He's a nice man . . . his class doesn't matter . . . your marriage does."

Archie was worth everything, everybody. What would he do now? She answered her own question: he would do something quixotic, when he'd had a drink too many. He'd said he wouldn't volunteer, but how could she be sure, with the crowds singing *Land of Hope and Glory* in the streets, and everyone drunk with patriotic fervor? Archie would join up, and be sent to fight, and die leading some heroic attack, and in the same paper that they published his name and the fact of his death, on another page there'd be an account of the death of Major Rowland. She gave an involuntary howl of anguish and wrung her hands together.

Guy and Virginia poked their heads round the door. "What was that, Mummy?" Virginia asked.

"What? That noise? Oh, I twisted my ankle, but it's all right." She made up her mind. "Listen, Guy, I have to go to London. I've got some things I must arrange . . . the war, you know. Mrs Orr will see that you get fed."

"When will you be back?" Guy asked.

"Tonight, if I can get the business done. If not, I'll telephone." She kissed them both quickly and hurried out of the room and upstairs.

John and Louise Rowland stood side by side in the cow barn of High Staining, watching the men milk the herd. The farm foreman, Fred Stratton, was himself milking, because one of the labourers had not turned up—gone to join the army, Fred said. Louise turned to her husband. "What are you going to do about replacing Hillman?"

"And Foden," John said glumly. "He says he'll go as soon as he's saved enough money to buy coal for his wife through the winter. That'll take him two months, if he's careful."

"He's not, is he?"

"No."

"So he'll take longer . . . and stay all winter, perhaps?"

John shook his head. "I don't think so. That's not like Foden. He'll get tired of it, and go."

"So, what are you going to do?"

"I don't know." He turned away and started walking back toward the house. Fred was touchy about being watched. Fred was touchy about a lot of things; and he didn't really like farming, so why didn't he dismiss him, as Cate suggested?

Louise said, "Have you thought of employing a woman—or women?"

He stopped and stared down at her. He was not quite as tall as most of the Rowland men, but burlier, with bigger hands, and a heavy face that would have fitted him better if he had become a parson, as he had once hoped, rather than a gentleman farmer. She was short and plump and birdlike, and still carried a trace of her native Yorkshire in her accent, and did not think women should have the vote, but did think there should be more women doctors, and dentists, and such.

He wondered, why didn't I think of that? It would never have crossed his mind . . . nor Quentin's . . . his other two brothers, Richard and Tom, might have thought of it, and both the sisters, Margaret and Alice, would have; but not he, nor good old Quentin.

He answered her question, "No." They were standing now at the black-painted front door of High Staining, the sixteenth-century farmhouse that stood on the hill over Walstone, looking down on church and village and, across the meandering Scarrow, at the vast pile of Walstone Park. Above, the thatch creaked with the heat and starlings flew in and out of their nests in it, feeding their young.

She said, "I know a young woman who would like to work on a farm—Carol Adams."

He started. "The Vicar of Beighton's daughter? That big horsey girl? She certainly looks strong enough. But how would a Roedean girl really like cleaning out stalls, spreading muck, drenching cows? We couldn't afford to give her only the light, clean work."

"She'll do it all. I know. She talked to me about it the day before yesterday."

"It's an idea . . . a good idea."

"She'll be an excellent worker. And she won't get drunk. Only one thing worries me about her."

"What?"

"She's twenty-four, and single. It doesn't bother some girls—most girls, thank heaven—but Carol Adams needs to be married. Parsons' daughters often do. Like some cows need the bull more than others. You know. You can recognise it."

John shook his head wonderingly. "I can't."

"Other men can," she said, "and we'll be responsible for her."

"H'mm," John said. "I'll think about it . . . Where are Naomi and Rachel?"

"Shopping in Hedlington. They're looking for good luck charms for Tom and Quentin. They'll be back by tea time."

"Are they going to get more gold swastikas, like Naomi gave Boy when he went out to India?"

"Oh, they couldn't afford that. Besides, the swastika is Mr Kipling's badge or trademark, so Naomi thought it was just right for India. They'll probably buy enameled black cats or something like that."

Probyn Gorse sat in his gaol cell on the tiny stool provided, his hand held out. A brown rat sat up in a corner, five feet from him, cleaning its whiskers. Probyn had seen that it was a female rat and adjusted his tactics accordingly. You could afford to be a little bolder with the female animals than with the males, for they were not so afraid of being challenged.

The rat came forward a foot, its nose twitching, smelling the crushed breadcrumbs in Probyn's hand. It backed off again, six inches.

Probyn watched it lazily, from the corner of his eye. It would take about another hour probably. Tomorrow, much less time. Soon after that she'd come straight to him, just exercising enough caution not to be taken quite off guard if he should suddenly hit out at her. Watching the rat, his thoughts left the cell, and the bleak walls of Hedlington Gaol. August 5 . . . the Walstone coverts would be very dry this summer. The rabbits in the big burrows along the Scarrow would be better off than the rabbits in the higher warrens, for the river water would hold the grass and weeds green for them. Swanwick's keepers would be keeping a close eye on the young pheasants in Ten Acre and Stonehale copses, and they should all be flying well by the time the season started. But the poults might have suffered from the extreme dryness of the summer. Everyone knew that too much rain was bad for pheasant poults, but they didn't do so well without enough water, either. But water wouldn't do to bait them. A little feeding in some corner well away from the rearing field . . . a few paper pokes in holes in the ground, with grain to be picked—and the pokes birdlimed to make blindfolds for those too-eager poults struggling about in the brush . . . and easily found by his dog afterwards . . . drat it, he didn't have a dog . . . have to do something about that soon's he came out . . .

Skagg was no fool, almost wise enough to be a good poacher; but he wasn't wise enough to stop Probyn Gorse taking the pheasants that were his due: and spitting in Swanwick's eye in the process.

He felt a small tickling, moved his eyes, and saw that the rat was eating the crumbs out of his hand.

Fletcher Gorse sat at one side of the battered table in Probyn's cottage, by the river. His brow was furrowed, and he was breathing stertorously, a worn pencil stub in his hand and a sheet of paper spread before him.

Florinda said, "You're making more noise than if you was pulling a cart."

He looked up. "Everything's in my head, Florrie, except the words . . . I told Mr Cate, remember. I always listened in school, especially when teacher was reading poetry, but I didn't see the words. I mean, when she read about kings and battles, I saw the king and the battle . . ."

"That's fine for listening to poetry, Fletcher, but for writing it, you've got to have the words, eh?"

She was sitting on the other side of the table, cleaning her nails with a splinter of wood. A few moments later, the beautification done, she turned her head to Probyn's Woman, stirring a pot on the stove. "What do you think of this war? Do you think it'll make any difference to the likes of us?"

"It will be like having an angel in the house," the woman said, "the Angel of Death." She said nothing more.

Florinda said, "And you, young man, are you going to join up? It's the thing to do, doncher know . . . the only thing, really!"

Her accent and tone were amazingly accurate reproductions of those of the upper class, not an imitation of any one person, but a perfectly extracted and blended *mélange* of what all three of them had heard all their lives from the Swanwicks, the Rowlands, the Cates, the lords and gentry of their land.

Fletcher said, without looking up—"You ought to go on the stage, Florrie." Carefully he wrote down half a dozen words.

Florinda said in her normal voice, "What's Dad going to do?"

"About the war?" Fletcher answered. "Nothing. Why should he?"

Florinda, slender in the waist, full breasted, as lovely an animal as her brother, both lively of eye, said, "He bicycled down here Sunday, you know. He was all for war then, but he never said he'd be joining up if there was one."

From the stove Probyn's Woman said, "They won't take him, even if he tries. He's simple."

Florinda thought, that's true, in a way: Willum Gorse, her father, seemed to like the idea of the war, but couldn't associate it with his own life. That was where he was simple . . . or wise?

At the Rowland Motor Car Company Bert Gorse found his half-brother cleaning up the floor of the machine shop, sweeping the swarf and filings into pans with a steel brush, carrying them to bins by the entrance, and dropping them in.

Bert said, "What the hell are you still working for, Willum? The dinner whistle went ten minutes ago."

Willum looked up, smiling, "Got to get the job finished afore eating, Bert. You remember the day Dad got sent to gaol?"

"Course I do. What of it?"

" 'Twas in the afternoon, eh? But Mr Bob give me the whole day off! So in the morning I saw Colin Blythe take three wickets and Frank Woolley make forty-five not out. Then I had to go to catch the train. I told Mr Bob I wasn't *just* going to see Woolley, so I didn't. I went to Walstone, too, see?" He chuckled and slapped his thigh.

"Put them things down," Bert said angrily. "How the hell can we force decent working conditions out of the bosses if people like you work just for the fun of working . . . just to line the bosses' pockets, to tell the truth?" He lowered his voice. "One of these days you'll be joining the union—the U.S.E.—and then you'll work to the rules, and no more."

"You be careful, Bert," Willum said anxiously, "Mr Harry doesn't like the union, no more does Mr Bob. You'll get the sack, and then where . . . ?"

Bert said, "Just keep your mouth shut, same as I do, and some others in this factory, I can tell you. When there's enough of us—we'll *strike* . . . Where's your dinner?"

"In my pail, out in the coat room."

"Well, let's get it. Mine's there, too." They walked out of the empty shop together, found their lunch pails and sat down at a deserted bench in the wheel room.

Bert munched angrily on a hunk of bread and cheese he'd put in this morning. A man needed a wife, or he near starved himself to death; but he didn't have any time to go courting . . . nor know any woman worth the trouble. He said, "So now they've got their bloody war."

"Who, Bert?"

"The bosses—Harry Rowland and the rest of them."

"Mr Harry didn't want the war," Willum said defensively. "He told us only Friday he hoped it wouldn't come, but if it did, we'd win it, he said, and we'd all help, he said. I 'spect you'll be going back, eh?"

"Back where?" Bert said, lowering his piece of bread and glaring at Willum.

"Why, the army, Bert. The Weald Light Infantry. I remember you joining up, and how proud I was to walk into a pub, you in your red coat."

"But you don't remember me being courtmartialled, sent to the Glass House, and discharged undesirable? I only went in 'cos I was bloody well starving, and I swear I'd shoot myself before I'd go back. The only time I liked in the army was when I conked that sergeant with a bottle. Go back? You're daft! You're not thinking of joining up, are you?"

"Me?" Willum's brow creased. "I couldn't join up, Bert. Why would they want me? My work is sweeping the plant floors, isn't it?"

Bert patted him on the arm and said, "Yes, it is. And don't you forget it." He ate more bread and cheese, then with his mouth full said dreamily, "Perhaps it's for the good. This war's going to destroy everything it touches, Willum. Capitalism, the landed gentry, the bosses, the bankers . . . There'll be a revolution."

"Not here," Willum said, apprehensively. "That would be wrong."

"There'll be revolution all over the world—revolution!" Bert repeated. "I can feel it coming. I can smell it in the air."

Willum took another bite out of his cold meat pie. "Bert," he said, "perhaps you're right, but . . ." he hesitated, "are you sure it will be the revolution you want?"

"What one's that, for God's sake, Willum?"

"One that's good for all of us, of course. For Mr Harry and Mr Stratton, and you and me, and Dad, and Lord Swanwick and Squire Cate in Walstone, and . . ."

Bert shook his head in despair, and ate faster.

Niccolo Fagioletti stood against the restaurant door, watching. They were getting rowdy and it looked as though there might be a fight before long. This was not a very high class restaurant and it didn't serve very good food—just plenty of it, and plenty of cheap Chianti and, of course, beer and spirits. The English always drank too much when they got excited and when they drank too much, first they sang, then they fought, then they vomited, then they gave him a tip, and then they went home, arms round each others' shoulders. He wished for the hundredth time that his friend Giorgio would get that long-promised job at the Savoy for him. The Savoy would be good at any time, even though he'd have to shave more carefully and Ethel would have to keep his shirts and dress clothes spotless—but after working a year in this place it would be heaven. It would be worth any sacrifice to . . .

"Hi, you . . . you with the stubble on your chin!"

A red-faced man at a big table was beckoning. He went over. "Did you want something, sir?"

"Yes, I did. I want another bottle of wine. This one's empty." He thrust an empty Chianti bottle into Niccolo's hand.

Niccolo kept his face unmoved. Stinking English drunks. He got another bottle, noted it on the bill, took it to the table and began to open it.

One of the other men at the table said, "You're an Italian, aren't you?"

"No, sir."

They all stared at him. "What are you, then? Spanish, Portuguese?"

"English, sir, by naturalisation."

"Oh, I knew you weren't English . . . What are you going to do now?"

"I don't quite understand, sir," Niccolo tried to keep his patience. He had had plenty of practise; but this had been a bad day, and these were particularly loud people and, as he had seen, drunk.

"I mean," the Englishman said in a slurred voice, " 'bout the war? Italy's a member of the Triple Alliance. That means she'll fight on the Huns' side."

"I don't think Italy will fight at all," Niccolo said, "and, as I said, I am English."

He knew he was getting red in the face and under the collar. His English was good, but not perfect and of course these people recognised his accent.

"Then you'll join up, eh? Tell you wha', you come and join up with us. We're going to Scotland Yard as soon as we've finished lunch, and we're going to join up in the Royal Fusiliers. You come with us, eh?"

Niccolo poured the wine. "I'd like to, sir," he said, "but my wife wouldn't let me."

"And the Royal Fusiliers wouldn't have him," another man said. "Who'd want to fight alongside a pack of dago waiters? Good God, they'd run all the way back to Italy the first shot they heard."

"Is that all, sir? Thank you, sir," Niccolo retreated to his place, white napkin over his arm. Better try to wipe these insulting pigs from his mind. Think of Ethel's big breasts, seeming even bigger because her body was so slight—but Ethel wasn't giving him a baby, and the other Italians would soon be laughing at him because he wasn't a man, couldn't fill a woman's belly. He'd have to show them the four-year-old he'd fathered on that snivelling little shop girl in Fulham . . . Think of Carlotta. Her breasts were just as big as Ethel's and she was a Sicilian, passionate, and she bit him all over when they made love. She understood men. Perhaps he could get rid of Ethel and marry her. She'd give him a baby, for sure. Perhaps he could divorce Ethel. Or have the marriage annulled. But she was still a Wesleyan, and her parents hadn't let her promise to have any children raised as Roman Catholics, so they'd been married in the Wesleyan chapel in Hedlington . . . so was he really married at all? He'd speak to Father Giacomo about it, pretending he was asking on someone else's behalf . . . A man would be mad to go to war, with the world full of willing women, good food, wine . . . and he still young, his loins throbbing readily at the sight of every shapely leg, and one saw plenty these days. The St Leger would be coming up soon. Five bob each way on Kennymore would be a sure thing. He'd had a hot tip on Black Jester, an outsider . . . but better play safe, and split ten bob between Kennymore and Peter the Hermit. He half closed his eyes, swaying on the balls of his feet.

Ruth Hoggin watched as her husband devoured an enormous plate of stewed tripe and onions, washing it down with two large bottles of Bass. She brought him more potatoes, and when he had finished took the plate away and served him a large helping of suet pudding and treacle. The sweat ran down his fat jowls, and damp black hair stuck out of the shirt collar, the stud undone. She looked at him lovingly. He was her man, and a man for men. His baby was growing inside her.

Less than six months to go now, and thank goodness the days of morning sickness were over.

He pushed back his chair and belched heartily. She said, "Bill, I wish you wouldn't do that."

"Why the 'ell not?"

"It's not nice."

"My mum says, 'Let the wind go free wherever you be,' and she means farts, too." He lifted one cheek of his rump off the chair and farted. "War!" he said, his little eyes gleaming. "War, at last!"

"It's wonderful," she said. "Those Germans have needed teaching a lesson for ages. Building a navy like ours, how dare they!"

"It'll be a great war," he said dreamily, belching again. "Millions of men, trillions of shells, hundreds of ships . . . and everything they make blown up as soon as it gets made. So they'll have to make more to replace 'em, whatever they are . . . shells, guns, motor bikes, blankets, boots, buttons. An' food, 'specially food. A man can't miss, unless 'e's blind, dumb, deaf . . . and stupid. Oh, what a lovely war!"

"You're going to join up?" she said. It would be dangerous, but that wouldn't stop her Bill. And the war wouldn't last long. And everyone was saying it—men ought to join up.

Bill sat up roaring, "Join up and get my balls shot off by some fucking 'Un? I'm not bloody mad, you silly cunt!"

"Don't use that language," she said automatically, and then, "You're not going to join up?"

"No!" he roared, "I'm going to make a million . . . pounds! At-fucking-least! Listen, I've been running a barrow in Hedlington, right? Selling tinned goods wot's lost their labels, at special prices, so I can say, 'P'raps these are mixed peaches, fruit salad, pears, all Fancy quality, ma'am, a few carrots and tomatoes, ma'am, only a few, it's just your luck what you gets, ma'am,' only I know all except one or two are tinned carrots, 'cos I tore the bleeding labels off myself!"

Ruth said, "That doesn't seem fair."

"Fair?" he roared. "I'm a business man! Only two weeks ago I reckoned this war was coming, and I took out all the money I've saved—five hundred quid."

"Bill! What did you do with it?"

"I went to the bank and I mortgaged this 'ouse, and everything else an' I got fifteen 'undred more quid out of the stingy bastards. Then I went to London—remember?—to Eastcheap, and I bought twenty thousand cases of California tinned peaches, seconds, at two bob . . . two thousand quid, and I paid cash on the nail. No one wanted that stuff, it'll be terrible. They all thought I was barmy, 'cept one old Jew, who guessed I was betting on the war coming, and wanted to come in with me, for half—he knew I'd strapped myself to get the cash . . . but I said not bloody likely . . . The stuff's due next month, and I've already been offered six bob a case—that's a profit of four thousand quid, woman!"

"Four thousand pounds! Bill, I—I—"

"But I didn't take it, see? I'll sell in a couple of days, when the stories about food shortages coming have put the wind up everyone. I'll clear another two thousand, you'll see. And I'll use that to do it again, jobbing in Eastcheap. Soon, I'll be getting the canners in California to print my own label on the stuff . . . and in Italy, too, for the Naples Plum Peeled Tomatoes—I've got my eye on a good buy there."

"You'll be living in London?"

"Most of the week. I'll be back as often as I can, Ruthie. Can't do wivaht me greens, can I?"

She stared at him wonderingly. London seemed so huge, and so far away, though it was barely thirty-five miles: and here Bill was, carelessly going off to conquer it.

Bill said, "There's a lot of tricks to this trade, and I know 'em all, 'cos I've been keeping my eyes and ears open, while I've been waiting for the right opportunity. I'm a wide boy, I am! Oh, what a lovely fucking war! I 'ope it goes on for ever . . ." His voice softened. "I do love you, Ruthie, and I'll miss you when I'm in the Smoke. Give me a kiss. There!" He kissed her gently. "Now, I've a train to catch, so up them stairs and down with them drawers."

"Oh, Bill!"

Lieutenant Charles John Christopher Rowland, known as 'Boy' Rowland since childhood, frowned into his champagne glass. He was tall, with dark hair, brilliant blue eyes, and a longer face than most of the Rowlands. There was very small resemblance between him and his father, John Rowland; still less with his mother, Louise. The young man sprawled opposite him in another easy chair said, "Why so glum, Boy? We're at war!"

Boy shrugged. "I was thinking of my father. He studied to be a parson when he was young, but gave it up . . . I know he'll be unhappy about this."

The other said, "I suppose so. Can't be helped, though. *We're* happy. So cheer up."

Boy said, "And when I'm not thinking about my father, I think about those damned *pakhals*. The Court of Inquiry found it was my fault, and I have to pay."

"How much?"

"Two pakhals at thirty-two rupees seven annas two pies each—sixty-four rupees fourteen annas four pies altogether. That's a lot of money."

"I suppose so. But the C.O. has to approve the findings, then it goes to Brigade. Why, you won't be docked till Christmas."

"Christmas is a great time to lose nearly half your month's pay, I don't think."

"Don't cry before you're hurt. You may be dead by then . . . Waiter! Another bottle of champagne."

"Very good, sir."

The white-jacketed white-gloved mess waiter backed away a pace, then turned and walked out of the crowded anteroom. Each of the two young men wore the twin stars of a lieutenant, in gold thread, on each epaulette of his white hot-weather mess jacket, a deep green silk cummerbund round his waist, and tight white overalls strapped under his mess Wellingtons. Boy's companion raised his glass, "While he's bringing the next one, let's finally kill this one. What toast shall we drink to now, Boy?"

"Victory," said Boy. He felt a little muzzy, and with reason, for he had drunk a lot of champagne at dinner, and half a bottle since, plus a couple of brandies. The fans creaking dustily overhead, pulled by the punkah boys outside, did nothing to lessen the oppressive damp heat of early August in the plains of India.

"We've drunk to that already . . . I know. A *slow* victory, otherwise we won't get there in time."

"All right. To a slow victory!"

They drank. The other subaltern said, "Now what?"

"Another toast?"

"I'd be falling on my face. We need some exercise. Tell you what, Boy, let's go and mob that rotter Terrell's room. I found him reading a book yesterday."

Boy felt uncomfortable. His companion was a jolly good sport, but there were one or two good sports who read books, too. Still, the unwritten rule in this battalion, he knew, was that an officer should read nothing more serious than the *Sporting Times*.

He said, "Well, perhaps it was Field Service Regulations. Let's let him off this time, eh? I'll warn him tomorrow."

"All right. Boy, you're a good sport . . . The 1st Battalion will be in action in a week or two, lucky dogs."

"My uncle commands a company in it. I think it's A."

"Never met him. Heard of him . . . open it, waiter. Here, gimme!"

He got up unsteadily, worked the cork with his thumbs, and when it began to move, swung the neck of the bottle round, like a weapon, finding a target in a bald head showing over the back of a deep leather chair six feet away. Pop went the cork, flying through the air to strike the bald head in the middle, accompanied by a squirt of champagne. Champagne splashed over the old copies of the *Illustrated London News* and the *Pink 'Un* laid out on the mess table against the wall. The bald head leaped up and turned, revealing the scarlet face of Major Roberts. He bounded forward, spurs jingling, shouting "Young devil!" He seized the bottle from the laughing young man's hands, shook it vigorously and squirted it into his face.

"Spurs off!" cried the adjutant, George Clifford, "over the roof! Waiter, clear all bottles and glasses off the main route. Champagne all round by the last man over. Line up outside!"

The young and middle-aged men herded out into the star-filled night, breathing of hot flowers, water tinkling in the shallow channels to irrigate the mess garden of the 2nd Battalion, the Weald Light Infantry, now stationed in Lucknow, India. Soon the anteroom was empty, but at the dining-room table Colonel Gould still sat, port glass in hand, head bent in discussion with his quartermaster, old Lieutenant Fry, and his second-in-command, Major Trotter. The mess sergeant stood close, South African and Indian Frontier medals on his white coat, three chevrons in Light Infantry green on a scarlet background stitched to his right sleeve. Down the polished rosewood table, long enough to seat sixteen a side in comfort, paraded a regiment of gold and silver cups, mugs, bowls, figures, model ships, towered pillars, and animals—trophies and gifts of the officers of the Regiment since its raising in 1727 by Roger Durand-Beaulieu, 3rd Viscount Cantley and 1st Earl of Swanwick; he had earned his earldom, it was said, by teaching the Hanoverian King George I to speak passable English. On the far wall hung the Colours, encased and crossed, bearing all the battle honours won by the battalions of the Regiment since 1727.

The three grey-haired men conferred, nodding, listening. The roof rang to the crash of boots, cries, oaths, laughter, and yells. Dust fell from the ceiling cloth in a shower. The mess sergeant, seeing that no one was looking at him, permitted a smile to crease his leathery face.

Roger Mortimer Christian Durand-Beaulieu, 9th Earl of Swanwick, leaned back in his chair in the small room off his library—perhaps originally used by a librarian—where he often discussed family problems with his wife, the countess, or his children. "It's no good," he said gloomily, pouring himself another glass of port from the decanter set on the table, "some people are going to make money out of the war, but we're not. We'll be taxed more heavily than ever. That swine Lloyd George will see to that. The hunt's going to cost more—if we can find huntsmen to look after the hounds. Every day Vickers tells me of something that's going to cost more—or bring in less. This damned barrack will cost more, and it needs a new roof now."

"We can't possibly afford that," Lady Swanwick said firmly.

"But Vickers says it's leaking in the servants' quarters. He's obtained an estimate . . . two thousand six hundred pounds."

"Out of the question!"

The earl nodded. "Obviously. Why can't we marry Cantley off to some Yankee heiress?"

"Because such people are not so common in England as they used to be, and they'll vanish altogether now that war is declared. And I don't think he will allow us to pick him a wife, however rich. Besides, I think he likes being a bachelor."

"Working for those bloody Jews," the earl muttered, "and spending all his money on . . . daubs! I can't make head or tail of that stuff. Picasso, Matisse, Braque, all dago and frog trash."

"It was you who suggested he join Toledano's bank," she said patiently, "so that he could make enough money to save the family fortunes."

The earl grunted angrily, and said, "Helen should . . ."

The countess interrupted him. "Now don't start on Helen and Barbara, Roger. They've been through a London season, and no one wanted to marry them, and that's that. I won't have them sent out husband hunting. They're nice girls and they have a right to live at home as long as they want to."

"As long as they *have* a home, you mean," he growled.

Neither said anything for a while, then the countess said hesitantly, "Do you think they'll volunteer?"

"Who?" the earl said; but she knew by his manner that he had had the same thought as herself. "Cantley and Arthur," she said.

The earl said, "Arthur won't . . . can't . . . it would be idiotic for him to go into the army when he has a safe seat, and he's only a step away from a cabinet post. And he's a married man. Cantley could, I suppose, though he hates soldiers. Artists and writer johnnies and long-haired poets are more his line. But he knows he's got to make money."

"Remind him, dear," his wife said, "otherwise he might think it's his duty to go. *Noblesse oblige.*"

"So it does, I suppose," the earl said. "Wish *I* could go back. Those five years in the Coldstream were the happiest in my life."

"You were a bachelor then," the countess reminded him, "and very rich, when London society really was rather splendid."

"Don't think I have not been happy with you, Flora," the earl said hastily, "but just recently everything seems to have been going wrong with the money. We've accepted Amersham's invitation for the twelfth this year, but I'm damned if we'll be able to afford to go next year."

"If Lord Amersham's grouse—and gamekeepers—haven't gone to war by then."

"Ours, too, perhaps. My father was a hunting man, as you know, and you might say he preserved foxes. I'd prefer to preserve pheasants and get rid of the hunt, but I can't. I'm the earl."

"You moved the kennels away from the Park, at least."

"The truth is that you can't really hunt and shoot pheasants over the same ground . . . You're right, though. I'll see that Cantley thoroughly appreciates that unless he gets rich—very rich—we're all sunk." He drank some port and seemed to cheer up a little. After a while he said, "Well, we've got that devil Gorse in gaol, anyway."

"He'll be out again soon," she said.

"And I'll see that he gets put right back in again. An earl still has some power in this country, thank God!"

The Honourable Arthur Durand-Beaulieu walked down a corridor of Chelsea Barracks, escorted by a khaki-uniformed guardsman. His frock coat was impeccable, his top hat shiny and set at precisely the right angle on his head, an ivory topped cane swinging in his hand. He followed the guardsman through a door marked ADJUTANT. The guardsman came to a halt with a tremendous stamping of boots.

"Mr Arthur Durand-Beaulieu, sir!"

The officer behind the desk said, "Thank you. That will be all."

"Sir!" The guardsman saluted, turned about, and stamped out. The adjutant of the 3rd Battalion the Coldstream Guards waved a hand at his cluttered desk, "Do make it short, please, Arthur. This frightful mobilisation, you know. . . . And I thought you were in Italy."

"I was. Came back just in time. George, will you take me into the regiment?"

"Oh, I expect so. I'll tell the Regimental Adjutant, and he'll ask the Regimental Lieutenant Colonel. I should imagine he'll be happy to accept you, unless he knows of some secret vice of yours which no one else does. But won't the government collapse without you?"

Arthur laughed. "Not the government. My dear father might. Give me a tinkle, then? Mayfair 4569. By the way, who's your tailor?"

The adjutant scribbled on a piece of paper and said, "Johnson, Pegg, 2 Clifford Street . . . Dorothy in good health, I trust?"

"All right, considering. Had a miscarriage last week. No son and heir to the overdraft this time round. She'll go back to nursing as soon as I go overseas."

"Sorry about the miscarriage. Find your own way out, Arthur, there's a good fellow. I must deal with these confounded papers. By the time I get through them the war will be over."

Christopher Hengist Cate, squire of Walstone, master of Walstone Manor, walked slowly in the water meadows by the Scarrow, above his village. His son Laurence and daughter Stella walked beside him in the heat of the afternoon. The Scarrow was low, he noted. It had been a long hot summer, and the heat showed no sign of abating.

"How long do you think the war will last?" his son asked.

"I don't know," Christopher said, thinking, surely it can not go on long enough to catch Laurence in its clutches.

"Oh, it's so exciting!" Stella said. "If millions of men volunteer, where will they all go?"

"They'll set up tented camps as they did in the Boer War," he said.

"Here?"

"Everywhere."

"Soldiers in Walstone!" she said, and her father heard the thrill in her voice. She was eighteen, and very susceptible. He recognised it, but what was a father to do or say to her? It was her mother's job, and duty; and Margaret had gone to Ireland. He couldn't say he missed her as a wife. Blyth and Mrs Abell ran the house just as well in her absence as when she was present; and of course there'd been no sexual intercourse for years; but he and the children missed her as a mother.

A young woman came toward them through the fields, dressed in a bright green cotton dress many times patched, auburn hair flying. "Hullo, Mr Cate," she called. "Isn't it exciting, about the war? All the lads of the village are going to join the army, they say."

"Then who'll milk the cows and help with the ploughing?" he said, smiling at her.

"Oh, Fletcher and I'll come any time you want us. Good afternoon, Miss Stella, that's a lovely dress . . . Good afternoon, Master Laurence. I saw a strange bird in the Upper Bohun wood yesterday. It was on a tree, pecking and twisting its head all ways."

"Quite small?" Laurence said excitedly.

"Yes. Brown and grey . . . very pretty marked, it was."

"A wryneck!" Laurence cried. "They're rare! Thank you, Florinda, I'll look for it tomorrow, first thing."

Florinda's mobile face sobered. She said, "What do you really think about the war, squire? It'll change things, won't it?"

Christopher said, "It will . . . Florinda, I've never been to war, but I've thought about it a bit. I see war as a being of its own . . . not created by man, only released by man as from a cave. Men think they direct it, but really it grows, and feeds, and guides itself, for its own purposes."

The girl's face was intent, her lips a little parted. Watching her, Christopher thought with a now familiar pang at his loins that she was beautiful, aware, and charged with sexuality. He said, "Well, goodbye, Florinda." He tipped his straw hat with its silk band in the Winchester colours. Florinda did a half curtsey, and ran on.

Stella said, "She's awfully pretty, isn't she, Daddy? Don't you think so, Laurence?"

Laurence said shortly, "I wasn't thinking about her, only of what a swizz it will be if the war's over before I'm old enough." But as he spoke the surly words his heart was tight, and there was a constriction at his throat. At eleven last night, all the family and servants sitting up in the Manor for peace to die, fear had gripped him that he would have to go.

His sister's emotions were exactly opposite. The unknown had always drawn her, and she felt now that she was living at a higher level than ever before. What would there be for women to do in this war? Would she be called upon to fire guns, drive cars, cook for hundreds of men, nurse the wounded and dying . . . women did other things, for men, she knew . . . bad women, it was said: but if the men were sent off in hundreds of thousands, who would look after them? What would *they* do, deprived of all women? Perhaps she . . .

She felt herself flushing, and stooped, pretending to fasten her shoe lace, while her father and brother waited for her, talking quietly.

Margaret Cate sat in a back room of a house in a respectable residential neighborhood of Dublin. Round the dining-room table, now bare of white cloth and silver, but littered with newspapers and ashtrays, sat six men and one other woman.

One of the men said, "Redmond's going to go with the English, for the war."

"What about implementing the Home Rule bill?" another asked.

"They won't do it, not a chance. They'll suspend the bill till the end of the war, and then they'll declare it null and void and start all over again."

Margaret cut in, "But then there'll be the war behind them, and us— a hundred thousand Irish will have fought for them, and heaven knows how many died."

"Not if we can help it," a man muttered in a brogue deeper and softer than the others.

"We can't," Margaret said with determination. "Our people are going to join the British regiments and fight, whether we like it or not, even if it's only for the money to pay the rent and keep the children from starving . . . but afterwards we'll be able to say, we did our part, now we have deserved independence."

The man who had spoken first, and who seemed to be the leader, laughed shortly and said, "It will make no difference, Maggie. And Sinn Fein can not afford to sit back and let the English keep the initiative. We will attack as soon as the Home Rule bill is suspended. We will declare war—against Redmond and his lackeys, and against the English, simultaneously."

They were all silent in the face of the speaker's obviously suppressed rage. He continued—"We shall look for help from our own friends, in America, or wherever we can find them. And from England's enemies— Germany, Austria. And we shall strike not only in Ireland, but in England. Several score of our members live and work in England, and we have their names and addresses. I want someone to go over and organise them, work out a plan to commit acts of sabotage in England, to make the English people realise we are still here, and fighting."

"Like the suffragists," a man said.

"Not like them. They've given up the fight for the duration; we're just beginning . . . Who'll go to England for us, at once? Someone not well known here, and not known at all in England?"

The man next to Margaret said, "I will." He was tall, with dark hair and pale blue eyes, and the classic Irish long upper lip beloved of cartoonists.

The leader said, "Very well, Dermot. I was hoping you'd speak up, because you're the best man for it. Maggie, will you give him what help you can—but don't get caught. We may need you, too."

"I will," she said.

Archie Campbell stood back from his easel and looked at the painting set on it, brush in hand, palette balanced on the other arm. It was a harbour scene, a steamer being pulled by tugs out of a narrow dock, a full rigged ship spreading its sails in the estuary beyond—the water black and filmed with oil and iridescent coal dust, chimney stacks, a grey sky, patches of orange undercoat all over the tramp's hull—an industrial seascape, the sort he'd grown up near, in Glasgow, and lived in during his years at sea. Staring at the painting, which was nearly done, he wondered suddenly how that Spaniard, Picasso, would have dealt with the same subject. Some of his fellow painters dismissed Picasso as a charlatan, but he was far from that. His line, in the drawings Archie had seen, was incredible . . . but he must have double vision, or at least a gift of sight that was different from other people's, for he saw objects from two or three aspects at the same time, and synthesised what he saw into something that, while difficult to understand at first, was obviously and clearly what it was, distortions or no. That painting *Nude Descending a Staircase* was another example of the same sort of experimentation, only this time the aspect was the same, but time advanced—like a section of cinema film, with motion frozen. It was extremely interesting, but . . . not for him.

He stepped forward, and applied a broad brush stroke to the water. There, that was nearly it . . . and now what? Take a couple of days off, and play golf down at Sandwich? Start the portrait of Malcolm Campbell, the racing motorist, which Campbell had commissioned from him, on the strength of their sharing the same clan name? But Campbell, being what he was, had probably joined the Argylls by now, or the Flying Corps . . . the country had gone collectively mad, as he had prophesied to Fiona: but, by God, this madness was dangerously infectious. He had felt a stirring himself, knowing all the time it was lunacy, when a detachment of the London Scottish had marched past him one day in the street, hodden grey kilts swinging, piper skirling ahead.

The telephone rang in his living-room, next door to the studio. He put down palette and brush, went through and took the receiver off its hook. A tinny voice, which he nevertheless at once recognised, said, "Archie? I'm in town."

He pursed his lips and sighed quietly, "What's the matter?"

"Nothing . . . I was worried about you, in case you were joining up."

"I told you I wouldn't."

"You're sure?"

"Of course I'm sure, woman."

"What are you doing?"

"Painting."

"What?"

"A nekked woman. The model's lying on the couch. She has a bonnie ginger bush."

Pause: and then, "Don't tease me, Archie. I love you so much."

More gently he said, "But I do paint nekked women, Fiona. Often. And will continue to do so."

"Can I come and spend the night? I feel frightened . . . because of the war. I've seen dreadful things in dreams, Archie . . . earth torn to shreds, white faces staring up, like a carpet of dead daisies on it. And Quentin, all bloody."

"Come on," he said, "I'll stop your nightmares for the night—but you must go home tomorrow. Aren't Guy and Virginia at home?"

"Yes."

"They'll maybe need you more than you need me."

In 23 Greeley Crescent, Hedlington, all was quiet. Mrs Rowland had telephoned from London that she could not come back till the following day and was spending the night with a friend. Ivy the maid had asked for permission to go out for the evening, and Guy had given it. Mrs Orr had reported all cleared up, and everything ready for breakfast, and had gone home. Guy and Virginia were in the drawing-room, both drinking ginger beer. The windows were open, the night full of stars, a light wind in the plane trees along the crescent, the occasional sound of horses' hooves, once the racket of a car engine.

"Where do you think Mummy's staying?" Virginia asked. She was lying sprawled on the floor, looking up at her brother. She was fifteen years old, still with her hair in pigtails, and looked very much like a female version of her father Quentin, except for the pale eyes, and the breasts shaping out her white blouse.

"I have no idea," Guy said briefly. Virginia didn't like their mother, and Guy did not want to get into an argument with her. Mother probably had problems on her mind that they could not understand. His sister was looking downcast at the rebuff; he softened it quickly, for Virginia had worshipped him since she was three. He said, "She'd tell us if it mattered, sis. She doesn't seem to be happy, and I don't know how we can help unless she talks to us."

"She won't," Virginia said. Then, after a pause—"What are you going to do, Guy?"

The blue eye and the brown moved to meet hers, but apparently independently, like guns in the turret of a battleship. He said, smiling, "About what?"

"The war, silly! Lord Kitchener is calling for volunteers. Your King and Country need *you!*" She pointed a finger at him, trying to set her plump young face into a stern expression. "Are you going to run away and join up?"

He said decisively, "No, I'm not. I've agreed to play for the county, but really I don't think my body is quite ready for first class cricket, and nor is my mind. It's the same with flying—battle flying—only more so. I'm going to finish my time at Wellington, making myself ready, body and soul and mind. On New Year's Day, 1916, I'll be eighteen and three quarters. On that day I'll take a commission in the Royal Flying Corps."

"Oh, Guy," she whispered, adoring. She jumped up. "But suppose the war's over by then?"

"If it's over, it's over. I won't be hurried again. But it won't be. And you?"

"As soon as I've worked out what to do, I'm going to run away. I'm not going to moulder away in that stinky Cheltenham Ladies College while I could be helping to win the war!"

The four of them sat in the low-ceilinged drawing-room of High Staining, the curtains still back, for the sun had only just set. Smoke rose from the chimneys of Walstone below, and even inside the house they could hear the fitful bellowing of Splendid XV, the bull, from his pen.

Naomi said, "I wonder if Girton will close down."

"Why should it?" her mother asked.

"I don't know," Naomi said, "but surely no one will want to be sitting studying when there's a war on."

"War is not women's work," Louise Rowland said.

"Oh, Mummy, there'll be all sorts of things we can do—and must. We'll be lorry drivers, conductors on buses and tubes, nurses, of course, and much, much more . . . May Frobisher said women would take over nearly all office work, if there was a war and it lasted a long time. The suffragist movement was exciting enough and I'm sorry it's been stopped, in a way . . . but this will really mean more for women. It's thrilling!"

Her father said sombrely, "It's a curse laid on all mankind. In the end, no one will have gained. Only, we will have lost many of our young, who could have contributed so much to the country and the world—poets, painters, priests, even manufacturers, inventors, scientists, scholars . . ."

"It is very sad," Rachel Cowan said. The big dark eyes were damp with suppressed tears—"Already people are saying that Germans eat babies, rape women . . . I am sorry, Mrs Rowland, but that's what they're saying . . . that they toss Belgian babies up in the air, catch them on

their bayonet points and then toast them over fires . . . and to nuns
. . ." She shivered and her voice rose, emphasising the cockney in her
accent—"It's not true. They're ordinary people, like us. I know because
I have relatives in Germany. I told you. They are Germans. They are
. . ." she paused, seemed to gather herself, and ended, "they are German Jews. My father's real name is Cohen . . . but, of course, you
have already guessed that, haven't you, Naomi?"

Naomi said, "No." She was puzzled. Rachel was small, her nose was
straight, and Jews were supposed to have great hooked noses: also
Rachel was generous and kind, and really sympathetic to anyone's
unhappiness.

Rachel said, "Now English Jews will be killing German Jews . . .
and everyone will be murdering the truth."

John Rowland said, "We have no choice. We made a promise and we
must keep it, whatever the cost." The young woman's intensity made
him feel uncomfortable. It was not British but, of course, she was a Jew
. . . but Jews could be British, like Disraeli, surely? He gave up.

Rachel said, "Everyone will suffer, but those will suffer most who always suffer most—the poor, the working people."

"I think you'll find that the young men of our class will sacrifice a
great deal, too," John said, "but I hope they won't make a fuss about
it."

Rachel said, "I didn't mean . . . I'm sorry, Mr Rowland, I spoke
foolishly. Your son will be in the war, I suppose?"

Louise said, "We don't know where they'll send Boy's battalion. If
the war is over quickly enough, it may not leave India."

Rachel said, "I do pray that he will be safe."

"So do we, Rachel."

Stephen Merritt put down *The New York Times* and said, "So they
have their war." Outside the windows, the Hudson sparkled under the
summer sun, a paddle steamer thrashing its wide waters.

His son Johnny said, "The Germans have, you mean, Dad."

His daughter said, "Another egg, Dad? There's time."

Merritt shook his head. "I'm fat enough already, Betty. I just hope
and pray that we shan't get involved in this madness."

Johnny said, "But, Dad, the Germans invaded Belgium, which
they'd promised not to do. I think we should join in, at once. Germany
would probably make peace then."

Stephen said, "It isn't quite as simple as that, Johnny."

Betty said, "We all know why you think England can do no wrong,

Johnny. How could the divine Miss Cate belong to a country that isn't perfect in every respect?"

He said, "Oh, shut up, Betty. Leaving England out for the moment, Dad, isn't it true that the Germans picked the quarrel, because they think they're ready and the others aren't?"

Stephen said, "There's something in that. But they also feel themselves encircled."

Johnny said, "I think we ought to fight. It's the only honourable thing to do."

His father sighed. "Honour is a hard word to translate into action, where a hundred million people are concerned . . . a hundred million lives and livelihoods. Come, Johnny, or we'll miss our train, and then what would happen to the banking system of the United States? Oh, listen, both of you . . . I'm cancelling our trip to New Mexico and Arizona this year. I can't leave Wall Street with things the way they are in Europe."

Betty said, "I knew something would happen to prevent me getting that squash blossom necklace for my birthday. Oh, well . . ."

In the First Lord's room at the Admiralty, Winston Churchill was closeted with his principal naval adviser, Admiral Prince Louis of Battenberg, the First Sea Lord. Winston strode up and down, a cigar in his mouth, occasionally stabbing a stubby forefinger at one of the maps on the wall. "The first priority is to defend these islands against attack by the German High Seas fleet," he said.

"I agree," the admiral said, stroking his pointed beard.

"That is the task of the Grand Fleet, and thank God, because of the naval review last week, the Fleet is already concentrated and on its way to Scapa Flow . . . which must be properly defended against all weapons as soon as possible, including Zeppelins and submarines, admiral."

"We are doing all we can. We do not think the Zeppelin threat is very serious. They can not carry big enough bombs, nor do they have proper devices for aiming at a comparatively small target, such as a battleship's deck. Submarines are more dangerous."

"Very well. Next, we have to destroy the German outlying squadrons so that they present no threat to our trade, or to ships bringing troops from the Dominions and Colonies. The most important seems to be the German East Asia Squadron, based at Tsingtau. What does it consist of?"

"Two armoured cruisers—*Scharnhorst* and *Gneisenau*—and three light cruisers—*Emden, Leipzig,* and *Nürnberg*—all under Vice Admiral

Graf von Spee. He is a most capable and resourceful officer, sir. And his squadron won the gunnery prize for the whole German fleet this year. Also, *Dresden* may join them from the Atlantic. She's another light cruiser."

"How do you propose to deal with von Spee?"

The First Sea Lord hid a smile. His political master did not like to give any foreigner the idea his language was worth pronouncing properly; so had called the German admiral 'von Spee' to rhyme with 'spree,' though Battenberg had just pronounced it correctly, 'von Spay.' He answered the First Lord's question—"Concentrate our American squadron under Rear Admiral Cradock . . . the battleship *Canopus* is very old and slow, but she is a battleship . . . the armoured cruisers *Monmouth* and *Good Hope,* and the light cruisers *Kent, Cornwall, Glasgow,* and *Penrith.*"

"Not much margin of superiority there. And none if *Canopus* can't keep up."

"It's the best we can do, sir . . . unless we send down two battle cruisers."

"We can not spare any, can we? And they would be wasting their time until we have located this von Spee." An impish smile flitted across the First Lord's plump face as he again lispingly mispronounced the name.

"I think we have made the best arrangements possible," Battenberg said.

"So do I. Now, admiral, pray let us consider the matter of protecting the B.E.F. on its way to France. Then—Amsterdam: what can we achieve by sending a force there? Then—Friesia: what are the possibilities of landing marines there? Then—the safe-guarding of our naval oil supplies. Then . . ."

Daily Telegraph, Tuesday, August 4, 1914

VIOLATED TREATIES

There seems to be no limits to the mad haste with which Germany pursues her intemperate course—the independence of Luxemburg has been ruthlessly set aside. Next it became the turn of Belgium. A curiously cynical ultimatum preceded the military measures—long since prepared —by which Belgian neutrality was violated . . . an equally cynical offer (was) made, as we learnt yesterday, to the British Government, promising that if we condoned Ger-

man proceedings we should have the satisfaction of knowing that after the war was over some compensation for any
breach of regularity should be made to the violated kingdom. It is needless to say that in both cases an indignant
refusal was returned. But we can hardly have a better or
more significant example of that high-handed insolence
which we are learning to associate with the Teutonic character . . . Germany would seem to have learned to considerable purpose the teachings of NIETZSCHE, together
with his contempt for the 'slave-morality' of Chris-
tianity . . .

To us in this country the neutrality of Belgium is a vital
matter, quite apart from the sacredness of the treaty by
which it was first guaranteed. The conquering nation
which occupies Belgium and the Low Countries threatens
our shores from extremely close quarters, and holds, as
has been picturesquely said, a pistol at the heart of England. She will not easily submit to such an insult. Already
she is calling up all the reserves and embodying the Territorial regiments. The entire navy was completely mobilised early yesterday morning. England sees the necessity
forced on her of declaring war. Strong in the consciousness of the enthusiastic support of the whole Empire, persuaded also of the justice of her cause, she will know how
to take all appropriate measures for her own protection
and the dignity of her name.

Cate rested the paper on his lap. He wished the press would not use
such provocative words as 'cynical,' 'insolent,' 'sacredness,' and the rest.
Hatred and scorn of Germany might be popular, but they should not
be necessary, and could be very unwise. Such emotionalism was deliberately used by press and politicians to save the trouble of explaining to
the people the inner necessities of events. It was an insult to the common people, to the ordinary Englishman, who in his heart knew well
that every nation had to protect its own vital interests, or it would soon
cease to exist. Today's enemy might of necessity become tomorrow's
friend . . . it had happened often enough even in his own lifetime:
France had been the enemy, and Germany generally regarded as a
friend and counterweight to French pretensions. Then the Germans
started their colonial programme, which meant building a fleet . . . and
the Kaiser had rattled the sabre, and Edward VII had won over the
French—whose press and people had been bitterly, furiously, anti-

British at the time of the Boer War, to the extent of the grossest personal insults against the Queen's person . . . So now France was one of England's allies; and another was the last country Britain had fought against in Europe—Russia; so it was vain and silly to hate the Germans; and foolish in the extreme to despise them. But were they behind their leaders, heart and mind? Were the Russians willing to fight for the sort of lives they led? How firm was the French endurance against hardship and sacrifice? How well would Britain marshal not only her manpower, but her collective brainpower?

It would take time, he thought, but in the long run, we'll show them.

Hedlington: Thursday, August 13, 1914

9 Susan Rowland sat at her husband's side on the front seat of the Rowland Sapphire. Stafford, the young chauffeur, sat in the back. Richard nearly always drove the car himself, though Stafford, who had started as a stable boy, would dearly have liked to have driven it, sitting high and alone in a peaked cap, a long dust coat over his green uniform, bowling through the hop fields toward Hedlington on another of that summer's endless procession of burning days. Susan scanned the fields as they passed to see if she could tell, just from looking, that her husband's country—and, for sixteen years now, her own—was at war. Not yet, she thought. It would come. There would be changes, great changes, but for the moment the English seemed to be pretending that war with the mightiest military power in the world was somehow not a fact but a thing only imagined. The hops hung heavy on the poles, the cows grazed unhurriedly in the fields, the wheat stood ready for the scythe, indeed here and there the harvest had started, and men were advancing against the golden ranks in slow rhythm, blades sweeping, flashing.

"Has Quentin's regiment left for France yet, do you think?" she asked her husband.

Richard said, "I believe not, but they will be going soon, I'm sure. Tom sailed on H.M.S. *Monmouth* just before war was declared."

"What sort of a boat is that?"

"I asked old Commander Quigley—he said it is an armoured cruiser."

"I don't suppose we'll hear from him, or about him, for ages. I can't think how battleships get any mail, or send it off, if they're always at sea . . . Do you think Margaret will have seen Quentin?"

Richard's voice was grim, "I very much doubt it. Margaret's interest in Ireland is in direct opposition to Quentin's. He is—or was—there to keep the peace; she's there to start a revolution, if I know her."

"Poor Christopher!"

She was silent, thinking of Christopher Cate, the withdrawn English gentleman, musician, scholar, lover of all wild life, farmer, squire, friend and more to his tenants . . . Margaret needed a very different man if she was to be managed: but was she?

Richard took his foot off the accelerator and the Rowland slowed. They had driven via Walstone, and were now close to the southernmost houses of Hedlington, passing the fairgrounds and the Scarrowford county cricket ground. The fields gave way to rows of small brick houses and those to shops, taller stuccoed buildings, Tudor half timbering, Georgian houses and banks, the pillared Town Hall, built in 1810, the South Eastern Railway station.

"What's happening?" Susan asked, wondering, for crowds lined both sides of the street, and seemed to be waiting expectantly. Horse-drawn drays, a few hansoms, and small delivery vans clip-clopped up and down between them, as though too intent on their own business to be aware of the crowd. Then she heard music, a fast drum beat and bugles shrilling over all.

A policeman at the side of the road, a tall burly man with a walrus moustache, raised one hand majestically, and Richard stopped the car. The policeman said, "Stop here, at the side, if you don't mind, sir. They're coming now."

Richard took off his driving glasses and blinked at the policeman. "Who's coming, constable?"

"Why, the reservists, sir. The Regiment's reservists. Marching to the station with the Depot band."

"Where are they going to? France?"

The policeman, who wore the Queen's and King's South African war ribbons, and two others that Richard did not recognise, on his left breast, looked at them pityingly. "They're going to join the 1st Battalion in Ireland, sir, and then the battalion will sail for France."

"That's Quentin's battalion," Richard said. "Thank you, constable."

Susan leaned forward, not knowing quite what to expect. She had been married to Richard Rowland for sixteen years now. For the first few of those years they had lived here in Hedlington, the rest in Beighton, a dozen miles away. All that time, although Richard's younger brother Quentin had been an officer of the Weald Light Infantry, she did not remember ever having seen him in uniform; to tell the truth, she had not seen much of him or Fiona at all, for Richard and Quentin were not close. But for all that time, too, Minden Barracks, the depot of the regiment, had squatted on the lower slopes of Busby Down, at the western edge of the town, an ugly pile of blackened yellow brick . . . and she had never been inside it, or known anyone but Quentin who had. She had seen a few soldiers in the streets at night, sometimes drunk outside pubs in their scarlet coats, sometimes picking up a harlot behind the Town Hall; but as far as it had affected her life, the army might not have existed. The army wasn't really a part of English life—as it wasn't in America; here the navy was, yes, but not the army. And now the army was going to absorb almost everything else in the country. It was a strange and frightening thought. She realised that she had no idea of what was to come—neither to the country, nor, now, this instant, up the street. Would it be a phalanx of men in red tailcoats, shakos, and white cross belts, like the pictures in the Californian school books of the hated enemy of the Revolution? Men with tall bearskins and measured tread, as she had seen once when Richard had taken her to see the changing of the Guard outside Buckingham Palace a few weeks before the old queen's death? Or . . .

They came round the corner, a small band first, perhaps thirty men in all, of whom eight or nine were buglers, then ranks of men in khaki uniforms, many ill-fitting, peaked caps awry, marching not well in step, some already limping. She said, "Are *these* Quentin's men?"

The constable was still close by, and heard her. "These are reservists, madam. Some of 'em ain't put on a pair of ammunition boots for five years. Some of 'em only arrived in yesterday. And a few of 'em's been at the beer, too. But they'll fight, madam, they'll teach old Kaiser Bill to laugh on the other side of his ugly mug."

All the men, bandsmen and reservists alike, were wearing a big red rose stuck in the chinstrap of their caps, on the right side. The step was short, the drums beating a light fast rhythm so that the reservists had difficulty making their booted feet move quickly enough. They carried rifles at the full length of the right arm, parallel to the ground, held at the point of balance.

She said, "Why are they wearing roses?"

The constable said, "In honour of the battle of Minden, madam. August 1st, it was. Six regiments of British infantry got the wrong orders, and marched straight at heaven knows how many French cavalry protected by hundreds of guns. They went through fields and orchards on the way, and picked roses, and put them in their hats. And then they marched right through the Frenchies, out the other side, turned round, and marched back through 'em again. Ever since, in every Minden regiment—that's what they're called, madam—every officer and man wears a rose in his hat on August 1st, every year. We learned all that as recruits, before we was allowed off the square."

"But it's August 13th, constable."

The policeman scratched his ear and said, "So it is . . . well, I don't know for sure, madam, but I suppose the colonel up at the depot thought it would be a good idea to have the reservists wear the rose, show off to the townspeople, sort of an advertisement, like."

"And the quick marching?"

The constable opened his mouth, but Richard answered first. "I know that, Susan. They're Light Infantry. Light Infantry and Rifles were originally used to get out in front of the rest of the army as scouts when advancing, and catch up from behind in retreat, so they had to be able to march faster. My brother commands a company in the 1st Battalion, constable—Major Quentin Rowland." He raised his voice to be heard above the band, which was now passing them.

"I was 2nd Battalion, sir, but of course I know the name. You're Mr Harry Rowland's son. I thought I recognised you, but I've only been on the force here for a few months. Moved from Canterbury in January . . . my wife died and I couldn't bear to stay there."

At the tail of the parade marched half a dozen sergeants wearing the same bugle and prancing horse cap badge, and the red rose, but also a red sash and, at the left side of their caps, a bunch of coloured silk ribbons. They stopped, waited till the sound of the band was fainter, then one shouted, "Who's for the King's shilling? Your King and Country need You!" All the sergeants pointed, each one picking a particular young man in the crowd to point at . . . "Step up, lad! Join your regiment, our regiment, the Weald Light Infantry, and fight the Kaiser. Step up, step up!"

Men, young and not so young, drifted out of the crowd, looking embarrassed. A woman cried in a loud voice, "No, you don't, Charlie Smith! You stay here and work on the allotment!"

"I've a right mind to go back myself," the constable said. "I'm only forty-five. No wife, children grown up . . ."

"We're going to need police at home as well as soldiers in France," Richard said. "May I move on now?"

"Certainly, Mr Rowland. Police Constable Waygood, sir." He saluted and Richard engaged gear.

The three women sat round the table in the morning-room, looking out over the lawn. Alice had set out the croquet hoops, for her father had told her that he'd play a game with her as soon as he'd had his talk with Richard. It would not be as long a conference as it might have been, she thought now, for her mother had told them the secret. So there'd be no trip round the world for her parents, which was a shame; but the effect on Richard would be much more important. Richard would not be happy, at all. Her eldest brother did not readily show his inner feelings; but from nursery days she had known him well, and she knew that he would be hurt, and probably obstinate—as obstinate as their father.

Rose Rowland said, "I see in the newspaper that the Germans are advancing on Brussels. The German general's name there is von Kluck."

Alice Rowland said, "And it seems that the French advance into Alsace has been stopped . . . and Liege fell nearly a week ago, we now learn."

Rose said, "The news is not good, I fear, so far."

Susan Rowland cut through the war talk to get to the subject that was uppermost in all their minds. She said, "I wonder what Richard will do." There were tears in the corners of her violet eyes.

Rose said, "You think he will not want to stay on?"

Susan said, "We've never discussed it, mother—why should we? He was promised the management, it was all arranged, the date was fixed a year ago, was it not? But he has been talking a great deal of what he intends to do when Rowland's is under his control. I don't think he could bear not to have that power and responsibility."

"I agree," Alice said, re-threading her needle.

"I hope they don't quarrel," Rose said.

"If they do, *we* must not," Alice said. "Families need unity among themselves in this war, just as Britain does."

She put down her sewing and reached out to pat the dachshund bitch at her feet. "Be quiet, Freda!" She pulled the long silky ears. "What *is* the matter?" The bitch was standing up now, looking toward the door, a low growl faint in her throat. The two male dachshunds, Max, Freda's mate, and Bismarck, their son, snored in the sunlight by the window.

The door opened as Freda gave a short sharp bark. A tall man dressed in brown, with pale eyes, a long upper lip and big ears was standing in the door, closing it behind him. "Mrs Rowland?" he asked. "Is one of you ladies Mrs Rowland?" He had a strong Irish brogue.

Rose put down her sewing. "I am Mrs Harry Rowland, and this is Mrs Richard Rowland. But who are you, and how did you get in? Did you not ring? Or ask to see the butler?"

"No, ma'am," the man said. "A lady in Ireland gave me this address, in case I was in trouble."

"Who was the lady in Ireland?"

"I don't want to speak her name, except to you, ma'am."

Rose signalled briefly to her daughter. "Alice, go upstairs and give Carrie immediate work to do on the third floor. Make any excuse you like. In two minutes I will take this man to the QT room."

Alice went out without a word. Rose waited, counting the seconds silently. Freda watched, head cocked to one side, Max and Bismarck snored, Susan kept her eyes on the tall stranger, wondering.

Rose said, "Come with me," and led out of the room, down the hall and up the wide front stairs. On the first landing she walked past Alice's bedroom, on the left, past Harry's and hers on the right, then on the left the one that had been used by the elder boys, Richard and John—since called the RJ room—and then, beyond Harry's dressing room, to the bedroom that had been Quentin and Tom's—the QT room —now never used except when the house was full of guests, and that had not been for fifteen years, that she could remember. The key was at her waist, now in her hand. She opened the door, and went in, followed by the man. She closed the door behind her, and the man said, "'Twas Mrs Cate, ma'am. I left Ireland three days ago, but someone must have given me away. The police were on my trail as soon as I arrived in Holyhead. I gave them the slip, but they would have had me soon enough. Can you hide me for a while, a short while?"

"I can hide you here for forty-eight hours," Rose said briefly, "then, at night, I'll let you out and you must go . . . No, I don't want to know what you are doing or have done."

"The other ladies downstairs . . . ?"

"They will say nothing to anyone," Rose said. She made sure there was a chamberpot under the bed and said, "You must use that, and the basin. I will get some paper before I go downstairs. I will clean up after you have gone."

"I don't know how . . ."

"Not a sound, day or night. No movement. If I can bring food, I . . ."

"My pocket's full of bread, ma'am. 'Tis enough."

"Money?"

"I have plenty."

Rose nodded and went out, locking the door behind her. After getting a spare roll of toilet paper from the W.C. at the end of the floor, and giving it to the Irishman, she started downstairs. Alice joined her on the landing, coming down from above. She said, "Carrie will be busy for another ten minutes. She said she had nothing more to do on this floor."

Rose said, "The QT room's not due to be dusted again till the end of the month . . . Tell Susan to say nothing to anyone, not even Richard."

"Very well, mother."

Richard sat in the easy chair to the left of the fireplace in the study, a large well-lit room looking out on the side garden, the high walls lined with leather-bound books, an oil painting of foxhounds over the mantelpiece, and another, a portrait of his father's father in clerical dress, by the door. The room smelled of cigar smoke. It had smelled of cigar smoke ever since he could remember; and ever since he could remember, whenever he came in, his father had been sitting in the chair on the other side of the grate. He was there now, a cigar between his lips. Sunlight shone through his dense curly white hair and bronzed his already bronzed skin, marked by fine lines. The blue eyes were clear and sharp. Richard waited. His father didn't like to be asked questions. He had summoned Richard to this meeting last night by telephone, soon after Richard's return from his week-long visit to Manchester. It must be to do with the handing over of control of Rowland's; or perhaps what he and mother had decided about their trip round the world. That obviously could not take place now: but Britannia ruled the waves, and after a few weeks, when the navy had had time to clean up the last German commerce raiders at sea, there was no reason why they shouldn't visit America. Susan's parents would be very disappointed if they didn't get at least that far.

Harry Rowland said, "Richard, I've been thinking what is the best thing for me to do."

Richard said, "Wait a month or two, father, and then take your trip. Or some of it."

His father was frowning and looking into the fireplace. He said, "Your mother and I are not going to take any trip, Richard. I'm going to stay on at Rowland's."

Richard did not speak for a long time, for he felt as though he had run into a wall in a black night, sensing nothing till he was brought up short, winded, a pain in his chest. To gain time he took off his spectacles, polished them with his handkerchief and replaced them. At last he said, "You promised that I should take over on September 1st this year."

"I know, but the war's changed everything, don't you see?"

"No, father, I don't. If I could join up, it might be different, but nobody will want a forty-four-year-old man with bad eyesight." He took off his spectacles again, to emphasise what his father already knew perfectly well. His father was now barely more than a shape in dull grey, the colour of the suit he was wearing.

He heard his father's voice saying, "I'm sorry, Richard. We are entering upon a time of great difficulty. Private motor car manufacture may be shut down, and our factory ordered to make munitions or other war material. On the other hand, if we play our cards right we may be able to obtain substantial government orders for ambulances, motor cars for staff officers, and the like. Lord Kitchener is talking about an army of seventy divisions—and I understand that we now have five. Seventy! Heaven alone knows how many motor cars such an army would need— These are stormy and dangerous waters, Richard, and I believe I am best fitted to steer our ship safely—and profitably—through them."

"I agree that times are going to be difficult," Richard said, striving to keep his voice steady. "The problems will be entirely new, whether we make motor cars for the military, or are ordered to turn to something else. It will need a flexible mind to overcome the difficulties, find solutions—perhaps in areas entirely new to all of us. It will be a great strain, day and night. Would you not agree that it is a task for a younger man?"

"No, Richard, I think that it's no time to be changing horses in midstream."

Richard got up suddenly and stood in front of the fireplace. "Father, I am forty-four. I have been preparing to take over from you for nineteen years, since I entered as an apprentice in '95. I'm ready."

"I'm sorry, Richard."

The old man's obstinate, Richard thought. Kindly, most of the time, but he liked his own way, and all his life he'd had it. His father went on. "Bob Stratton has agreed to stay on, too."

Ah, Richard thought, that explains why Frank Stratton had suddenly gone off and joined up as a private soldier. He had meant to enquire more deeply into that, but had not yet had time. He said, "Lucky for Frank that he can join up. Though I am bound to say that I think you have done a great injustice to him, as well as to me, by forcing him to do so."

"You are being unreasonable."

"I could say the same, father, but I won't . . . I am resigning from the firm."

Now it was his father's turn to look as though he had walked into a wall. "Resign? You can't do that, my boy! What are you talking about?"

"I mean what I say. I shall not work in Rowland's unless I am given the position I was promised, that is, managing director, in full control."

"But . . . but . . . what will you do?"

Richard's mind had been racing, since he had said that he would resign. He had only just made the announcement; but he recognised that he must have been thinking about this problem before he knew it would exist. Something the American Stephen Merritt had said at Henley had been fermenting in his brain, almost unnoticed, and unacknowledged, but now bubbling out . . . commercial road vehicles! There was a manufacture eminently suited to Mr Ford's mass production methods, much more so than the passenger-car field; more suited to wartime conditions, too, for if the army would require x ambulances, they would certainly require a hundred times x load-carrying lorries; vehicles that could distribute soldiers and all their requirements from railheads forward in any war zone of the world; and, where there were no railways, from the ports all the way to the fighting line, far faster than horse-drawn transport.

He said, "I shall make commercial vehicles. Lorries."

"Where?"

"Here in Hedlington. I know the labour, the craftsmen, the banks . . ."

"You know the banks, but which one of them's going to lend you the money to start such an enterprise?"

Richard said, "I don't know . . . I shall get advice from Stephen Merritt. He offered to give it."

"Merritt? Merritt? . . . Do you mean the American?"

"Yes."

"And what if he is not interested in your proposal?"

"I don't know, father, but I shall succeed. After Mr Merritt, I shall probably go to Lord Cantley at Toledano's. He's known me all his life. He knows what I have done . . . and what I could do, on my own."

His father got up stiffly. "I am sorry that you should desert me at this time. And even more sorry that you should plan to set up in Hedlington in competition with me for the available workmen—who will become scarce as more men go to the war—and for materials. Perhaps, if we were to enter into some sort of partnership, we . . ."

"I'm sorry, father. It's too late. You have forced me to consider something which I now realise I have wanted to do for many years. My mind is made up."

They were driving out of Hedlington, heading east on the direct road to Beighton, Beighton Down rising in short sere grass to its long clean skyline on their left, sun-parched fields to the right, the spire of Hedlington Church piercing the golden bowl of late morning behind them.

"Will Toledano's take the risk?" Susan said. "I'm sure Lord Cantley will recommend it, but he's not in charge, is he?"

"No, old Isaac is still alive and very much in charge, I believe. But I know his son David quite well—and if I can get David to speak for me, the old man will agree. There's a very strong attachment between Jewish fathers and sons. A Jew would never have done what father did to me. Or Bob Stratton to Frank."

"Frank's left, too? I've heard nothing, while you were away. No one came near me. I didn't notice it at the time, but I suppose they knew, or some did."

"Frank joined up. My first hope for financing is not Toledano's, but Mr Merritt. I told father I'd start my business in Hedlington, but I was very angry then. I'll start it where we can, and depending on what advice Mr Merritt gives, or what conditions he puts on providing the money. There might be some sort of partnership . . . but he'll probably suggest the formation of a private limited company in England, with his bank holding a majority of the common stock, and the rest of the shares distributed between me, as managing director, and a British merchant bank—I'd recommend Toledano's."

"How are you going to approach him?"

"I must find out where he is first. I believe he and the son went home about ten days after Henley. Stella said something about being invited to a ball in London but being unable to go, and they were sailing two days later . . . I'll send a cable to him at his bank in New York. I really think he will respond favourably. I believe he recognised, at Henley, that he and I think the same way, follow the same principles, about manufacturing motor vehicles, or as he would say, automobiles."

She said, "What are you going to call your lorries?"

He had thought about that desultorily, since the meeting with his father, to no result. He thought of the town—Hedlington? A set of initials such as R.A.C., for Rowland Automotive Company? He was going to make big, powerful vehicles to carry scores of men, tons of equipment, shells, food . . . Vulcan? It was already used.

"Jupiter," he said, "the Jupiter Motor Company."

He repeated the name to himself: Jupiter . . . Richard Rowland's Jupiter lorries, the best. No, that was not to be his aim: Jupiter lorries, simple and economical to build, drive, maintain, and repair . . . stand-

ardised designs and interchangeable parts . . . parts available anywhere in the country . . . the world . . .

He'd need a Works foreman, and it would be a good idea to find his
man before he started building, or altering an existing factory, as the
case might be. Frank Stratton would be the perfect man for the job,
but Frank was in the clutches of the army, who would certainly not let
him go easily. He'd try, though—visit the depot and, on the strength of
his family connections with the regiment, see the officer commanding
and try to get Frank out.

Or Bert Gorse, perhaps, Willum's half-brother? Behind his hostile attitude, Bert was a very capable man. He had the one quality that a
foreman must have and the majority of workmen did not—the ability to
think for himself. But could he be converted from his socialist ways?
How would he do, working with American methods—production lines,
time and motion studies, the rest?

"Begging your pardon, sir," the young chauffeur said from the back
seat. "We should turn here, if we're going home."

Richard awoke from his daydream. "Thank you, Stafford."

They were sitting in the drawing-room after dinner, Harry, Rose and
Alice, Bismarck and Max in their baskets to one side of the fireplace,
Freda's basket empty. The French windows to the garden stood open,
and Rose said, "It's getting a little chilly, Alice. And we'll be going to
bed soon."

Harry was reading, or pretending to, his daughter thought. He had
been quiet and grim all day, since the interview with Richard. He had
not liked doing what he did, but he felt he must. Alice wondered who
was right. Perhaps, in the end, Richard would be grateful for what father had forced him to do—go out on his own.

She put down her book, *The Old Wives' Tale* by Mr Arnold Bennett, went to the window and stepped onto the narrow terrace. "Freda!"
she called, "come here, you naughty dog!" Rustlings in the laurels
along the wall. "Freda!"

A small shadow detached itself from the bushes near the path round
to the front door, and waddled toward her in the starlight. On the terrace the bitch sidled past her, hurried into the room, jumped into her
basket and curled up with one eye open, pretending she had just been
awakened from innocent sleep.

"You're a bad dog," Alice snapped, pointing. "Bad dog! Why do you
wander so?" She closed and bolted the French windows, sat down, and
picked up her book. Mr Bennett was rather a gloomy writer, at times;
but one must persevere. She began to read again.

Bismarck leaped out of his basket and simultaneously there was a crash somewhere in the passage. Harry put down his book. Rose was on her feet, her hand to her heart. "What's that?" she cried.

Alice caught her mother's eye. The same thought was in both their minds—the Irishman in the QT room, upstairs. They hurried to the door and out into the lower hall. Men's voices were raised at the front. "This is the house. Up the stairs! You, Jones, don't let anyone out."

Alice switched on the hall electric light. The front door was open and three policemen were in the house, one portly older fellow at the door, two pounding toward the stairs. Parrish the butler appeared from below, crying, "Here, here, what do you think you're . . . ?"

"You be quiet," the police sergeant said. " 'Oo's 'ouse is this?"

"Mr Harry Rowland's," Parrish said. "And there he is, wanting to know what you burst in 'ere for, I daresay."

Harry went forward, "What's the matter, sergeant? I don't understand . . . Why didn't you knock at the door, or ring the bell?"

Rose stared at the sergeant, her heart pounding. They had no right to come in without a search warrant. She should demand to see it; and obviously they didn't have one. Then they'd have to leave, and before they came back she could get the Irishman out of the house . . . perhaps. For they would leave someone on watch in the street. If they were indeed after the Irishman. She had better wait . . .

The sergeant had not realised that this was the house of Mr Harry Rowland, of the Rowland Motor Car Company. His tone altered. "Sorry, I'm sure, sir. But we 'ad a report about something suspicious going on 'ere. Lights in an upper window, flashing on and off."

Rose kept her face still—but what were they talking about? The Irishman wouldn't be such a fool as even to use the light in the QT room surely, let alone flash it on and off? But they were getting dangerously close. She could not afford to wait any longer. She stiffened herself, ready to speak. Alice took her elbow and held it tight, whispering, "Wait."

The sergeant said, "Come 'ere, you." A fourth man sidled forward. He was a little fellow in a celluloid collar and black four-in-hand tie. "This man saw lights flashing from upstairs. He pointed it out. There was a light, going on and off like, he says."

"Right at the top?" Rose said.

"Yes'm. That's what you said, didn't you?"

"Yes, sergeant."

Harry said, "Well, let's go upstairs and find out. Though I can assure you there are no spies in this house, and very likely none closer than Chatham." He led the way up the stairs, followed by everyone else, except the portly constable guarding the front door.

As they passed the first floor landing Rose suppressed a surge of relief. If they didn't find what they were looking for higher up, they would want to search this floor, too, perhaps the whole house: but for the moment the matter looked less dangerous.

On the second floor landing a green baize door barred the entrance to the servants' rooms, to the left; to the right, a short corridor was flanked by a storeroom on one side and another guest room on the other.

The little man said, "I think it was this way, sergeant." He pointed at the baize door.

Harry said, "Who's in, Parrish?"

The butler said, "Martha and Carrie went out together; they are to be back by eleven, sir. Judith's visiting her aunt in Ashford, and won't be back till the last train. Mrs Stallings is still in the kitchen, making a pâté, she said. Laura's in her room, or should be."

Harry said, "Laura's the kitchen maid, sergeant. Which is her room, Parrish?"

"This one," Rose said. "One moment, sergeant. Step back a little, please." She knocked on the door and a young woman's voice said, " 'Oo's there? I'm busy."

"Mrs Rowland," Rose said, "and several men. Are you properly dressed?"

"Oh yes, m'm," the voice answered. The door was opened from inside and Laura the kitchen maid stood in the doorway blinking in astonishment at the crowded corridor. "Why, madam . . . sir . . . what's the matter?"

Rose walked into the room, saying, "Excuse me, Laura." She looked at the window, and saw material hanging from the curtain rod, and more of the same on the bed. She said, "Have you been making curtains, Laura?"

"Yes'm. I 'ope it's all right. I mean it was my money, and . . ."

"Perfectly all right, Laura. You had sewn the curtains today, perhaps, and now you were trying to hang them up?"

"Yes'm. I'd get them up, and then the wind would blow them a little open, and I'd try to take them down 'cos I thought perhaps they ought to be 'eavier. And twice I fell off the chair. It's a bit rickety, m'm."

Harry said, "There's your spy signalling with lights to the Germans, sergeant . . . Laura hanging up curtains!"

Alice, standing at the back of the others, felt an intense desire to laugh. The change from imminent danger to farce was too much. She tried to stifle it but after a few moments of vain struggling she exploded in a tremendous guffaw. She bent her head and turned the laugh into a cough.

Her father said, "Are you all right, Alice?"

She nodded, red in the face. Bismarck barked twice and started back along the passage, to wait by the baize door.

The sergeant said, "I 'ope we didn't inconvenience you, sir. We didn't 'ave time to get a warrant, and if it 'ad been a spy, and it might 'ave been . . . then we'd all 'ave been in trouble, wouldn't we, sir?"

"Don't you worry, sergeant. I won't report it. We all have our duty to do."

"Thank you, sir. Thank you, ma'am. Come on now, you two. Good night, sir, good night, ma'am, good night, miss."

When they had all gone, and Parrish had closed and this time locked the front door behind them, and the Rowlands had returned to the drawing-room, Harry said, "Searching for spies! In Hedlington! Who'd have believed it possible?"

"And entering without a warrant," Rose said.

"It's the war, my dear," Harry said. "It's only been going on nine days and already people are acting strangely. Even Alice, laughing then. It wasn't really a laughing matter."

Alice said, "I suppose not, father, but if we don't keep a sense of humour, this war's going to be impossible to bear, before very long."

Daily Telegraph, Thursday, August 13, 1914

. . . by piecing together all available information some idea can now be formed of the military situation. Naturally one cannot disclose what one may know or deduce concerning the whereabouts and movements of—(excision by censor)—but the proceedings of the enemy are to some extent, at any rate, known. A group of German army corps are probably assembled in and around the fortress area of Metz . . . Another group of perhaps rather greater strength stretches across Belgian Luxemburg and Namur province. Its right flank rests on the Meuse in the neighborhood of Huy. Three army corps, of about six divisions, with a powerful corps of cavalry, have established themselves on the left bank. This army threatens to attack Brussels, or, alternatively, to invade France in the direction of Mons.

A division in each of the contending armies numbers

twelve battalions, each of a thousand infantry. It has also 2,500 artillerymen, with detachments of cavalry and the auxiliary services, including a total personnel of about 17,000 men.

Christopher Cate got up and looked at the war map hung in front of one of the bookcases. In the stationers they sold little coloured flags on pins you could stick into these maps, and so pretend that you were an expert on the General Staff. All that he himself could see was there must soon be a clash on the French-German border. In another part of the paper it had been stated that the Germans had comparatively few troops on the Russian front, and obviously planned to deal France a knockout blow before turning to deal with the Russians. Quentin had once explained to him that what happened before opposing forces met was called strategy, and was the affair of generals and staffs; what happened afterwards was called tactics, and was the affair of subalterns and soldiers. The time of strategy must be nearly over, and the decisions soon to be left in the hands of the fighting men.

The other news in the *Telegraph* was just as important, though not as exciting. The Bank of England was prepared to discount, at the request of holders, all approved bills of exchange accepted before August 4th . . . the great Cunard liner *Lusitania* had arrived safely from New York, though it was believed that a German-armed merchant cruiser had been lying in wait for her in the Atlantic . . . the King had offered Balmoral Castle as a hospital for wounded sailors and soldiers should the need arise . . . the Admiralty was reassuring neutrals that it was quite safe to send their cargoes to Britain over every ocean and sea . . . except the North Sea, where the Germans were scattering mines indiscriminately . . . Field Marshal Sir John French had had an audience of the King . . .

But Sir John was the Commander-in-Chief of the British Expeditionary Force, so he was obviously saying goodbye before going over to France. Quentin might be there already, but probably not just yet. There were still a few days left, a week or two at the most, before the paper would be printing accounts of battles actually fought rather than speculations on battles that might be fought; and listing the names of those killed and wounded, not in some remote tribal skirmish, but on England's doorstep.

London: Sunday, August 23, 1914

10 The train burst out of the Swanley tunnel into ardent light and Harry Rowland again raised his newspaper. It was an hour and a half's journey from Hedlington to Victoria on the South Eastern, which gave him good time to digest most of the news out of the *Observer* before the rumbling of the carriage on Battersea Bridge warned him that they'd be in Victoria in four minutes.

He found he could not concentrate, and soon lowered the paper. The first-class compartment was empty except for himself. It was a slack time of day, on Sundays. If travelers were going to London, they'd have gone earlier; if they were returning from the country, they'd come later . . . Ellis had given him no inkling of what he wanted of him. A Member of Parliament became both more and less important in wartime. The fate of the country obviously depended, in the last analysis, on every M.P.'s wisdom and courage; but the day-to-day running of the war was being done by Lord Kitchener, Prince Louis and presumably Asquith, the Prime Minister, Lloyd George, Churchill, and one or two others. Prince Louis of Battenberg . . . he had heard some gossip about him, and dismissed it from his mind. Something about him being not to be trusted, because he was a German by birth. He might get Richard to ask old Commander Quigley what he thought; but he had not seen his eldest son since the day of the unpleasant interview. He sighed, wondering—was I right, or wrong, really? How could anyone know, for sure? He had simply felt that with Germany at his country's throat, it would be wrong to change the management of an important firm. Richard should not have taken it so personally. He should have considered only what was best for England, not for himself . . . but he was comparatively young still, and the young had their dreams and visions. He tried to remember what it was like being in his forties, what was the difference then from now. After a time he gave up, and looked out of the window, unseeing.

The train puffed on through the late summer, past Ravensbourne and Bellingham, Nunhead and Peckham Rye, into the city now, Brixton, Clapham, Wandsworth Road . . . many other lines below, then the familiar deep rumble, the Thames swirling past, an ebb tide carrying the brown water fast to the sea, a tug struggling against it towing two barges. When he was young, and coming to town on this line on business, he used to stand up here and start collecting his papers, hat, and umbrella from the rack. Now he remained seated until the train came to a full stop. It was not so easy to keep your balance in the case of a sharp stop as it used to be; and the consequences of a fall could be a great deal more serious.

The train glided to a halt, and he stood up. A few minutes later he was in a taxicab moving fast up the almost deserted reaches of the Buckingham Palace Road. At five minutes to eleven he walked slowly up the nine steps to the portico of the Reform Club and turned to the porter's desk. He had been in here many times in his life but, although he was a Liberal by political persuasion, and this was *the* Liberal club, he was not now a member. His father had entered him for it and he had in fact been a member until the Royal Automobile Club was founded a little farther along Pall Mall when he had, naturally, joined that.

The head porter remembered him still, though, and touched his cap as Harry approached. "Morning, Mr Rowland. Nice morning."

"Too hot for my liking, Chessman," Harry said. "We need more rain, now that most of the harvest's in . . . I have an appointment with Mr Ralph Ellis."

"Certainly, sir. He said to tell you he'd be in the Morning Room. This way, sir."

"Don't bother to come with me, Chessman. Good heavens, my memory's not that bad."

"No, sir. Thank you, sir."

Harry went up a few more steps, turned right along the panelled wall of the great Saloon, gazed idly at the ornate oil portrait of a defunct Marquess of Westminster, and entered the Morning Room. A few members were inside, talking, one with what looked like a tall glass of brandy at his elbow. A bit early for that, Harry thought. Ellis was sitting in a leather armchair the far side of the room, facing the door, newspaper across his ample belly, pipe in hand. He saw Harry and started ponderously to his feet, shedding the newspaper onto the carpet and scattering tobacco ash down the front of his worsted suit. His grey walrus moustache was yellow-stained, and when he stood upright his pot belly was even more pronounced than when the spread newspaper partly hid it. He was seventy-five years of age.

"Rowland, glad to see you, my dear fellow," he boomed, thrusting out his hand. "Sit down, sit down. What about a glass of sherry?"

"Well . . ." Harry thought, I ought to be stronger minded, but . . .

"Oh, come on. It's past eleven o'clock, and I've just been waiting for you to come to have one myself." He struck the bell on the table beside him and a club waiter glided up. "Two sherries, George. Amontillado do you, Rowland?"

"Certainly."

"All right. How have you been keeping? And Mrs Rowland? Good, good. What's Richard up to?"

Harry waited till the sherry was served, then said, "He is trying to start a new business—manufacturing lorries."

"In Hedlington, I heard."

"Yes."

"It'll be good for the town. More men at work, more money in circulation." He shot a keen glance at Harry, and Harry thought, he's going to ask why Richard left Rowland's; but Ellis said, "John still farming? Miss Alice well? And Tom at sea, I suppose."

"In H.M.S. *Monmouth*, an armoured cruiser."

"And Quentin in France, eh? The P.M. told me yesterday that Kitchener thinks the B.E.F. will meet the Huns today or tomorrow at the latest. Then we'll show them something, eh?"

"I certainly hope so."

Ellis continued, "The French are having very heavy casualties I hear. Very heavy indeed. And they're not advancing . . . Here's to your good health, Rowland . . . and all your family . . . especially Tom and Quentin." He drank half the glass and put it down. He wiped his moustache with the back of his hand, and picked the newspaper off the floor, puffing heavily. He folded the paper and put it on the sidetable, while Harry waited. At last—"You're a good Liberal, Rowland, aren't you? Always have been, eh?"

"Yes. My father was, and I have seen no reason to change my allegiance, though mind you, I didn't agree with some of the party's attitudes during the war . . . I mean the war in South Africa."

"No more did I, but that's all over and done with, and we're united again. Rowland, you are a popular man in Hedlington, and one of the biggest employers. You have a good reputation for fair dealing and honesty. You're a gentleman. You're not as young as you might be, but the P.M. likes experience . . . How would you like to replace me as Member for Mid-Scarrow?"

Harry took up his sherry glass and drained it. So this was what Ellis had wanted. He felt no particular shock, only surprise; he had not expected this. He turned the idea over in his mind . . . to become a Member of Parliament . . . to be Harry Rowland, M.P. . . . He thought, if Ellis had come to me with this proposal a month ago, I would probably have given up the factory; but now . . .

Ellis interrupted his thoughts: "You won't have to fight an election, because Asquith and Balfour have agreed on a truce for the duration of the war. If a member dies or resigns, the only candidate—of the two main parties—will be someone of the same party. So his election will be assured."

Harry thought, that doesn't seem quite fair. How can the people express their views about anything if there are no real elections? Suppose the government was losing the war through bad management? They'd still have their permanent majority in the Commons, so they couldn't be thrown out.

"Of course, the war may be over in a few weeks," Ellis said. "Some of the soldiers think so, and a lot of the politicians, particularly the Conservatives. Then you'd have to electioneer, but, between you and me, I don't think it will be over so soon. Well, what do you say?"

Harry said, "When are you proposing to resign your seat?"

"A year from now, more or less. I don't want to fix an exact date yet, but it won't be before the end of September next year, 1915—D.V.— and it won't be later than the end of 1915."

"May I ask why you want to resign? I trust you are quite fit."

"Oh, certainly, certainly. The fact is that I don't like being in London so much. I have a nice house on Beighton Down, well, you know it, you've been there . . . and a good garden, which Janet wants to make the best rose garden in Kent, and that's where I want to spend the rest of my life. I'd resign right away only the P.M.'s put me on a committee to study war production needs—I expect he'd ask you to replace me on that, with your experience—and I want to give my successor time to nurse the constituency. Just because there's a truce, we mustn't tell the electorate, here's your next M.P., and produce some fellow they've never heard of, or thought of as their M.P., out of a hat . . ."

"What does nursing the constituency consist of?" Harry asked.

"Come with me, as much as you can, whenever I'm in Hedlington on political matters. If I make a speech down there, sit on the platform with me. Sometimes, when I'm supposed to open a bazaar or the like, I'll tell the local committee I'm busy in Parliament, and to ask you to take my place."

"I'm not much of a hand at speech making," Harry said dubiously.

"It's easy. A little practise, and you'll find it's easier than falling off a log. The central committee people tell you what they want said. You never make more than three points, make each of them three times, in different ways, praise our brave soldiers and sailors nowadays, and mention God in the last sentence. Mention Him favourably." He chuckled largely and banged the bell beside him. "Made up your mind? Two more amontillado sherries, George."

Harry said, "I can't give up Rowland's, you know."

"You won't have to. The ordinary business of M.P.s is less than it was, because so much is done by the cabinet on its own authority. If you come up to London once or twice a week, that will be ample. You ought to have some place to stay overnight if the House sits very late, or you have to be on call for a critical vote—but I doubt that we'll have any of those, with this truce . . . or you could stay at a hotel every time."

"My son Tom has a small flat, which is empty now."

"Good! Well . . . ?"

"When do you want to know?"

"I'd like to know right away because we're having lunch with the P.M. at 10 Downing Street. We are due there in—" He pulled a heavy half-hunter out of his waistcoat pocket—"twenty-five minutes."

Harry said, "I'm afraid I couldn't give you an answer until I have talked with Rose. She will be affected, and I shall take her advice. She is wiser than I, and understands what I can and should do more thoroughly than I myself do."

"Very good. I shall tell the P.M. that. Or you can tell him yourself. Well, if we finish our sherries, and pump ship, we can walk to Downing Street in good time . . . I hope I am raising my glass to the next M.P. for Mid-Scarrow."

"Don't say another word, my dear fellow," the Prime Minister said to him as they sat down to lunch. "You must discuss the matter fully with your wife. We are, after all, in no hurry."

Margot Asquith said, "You will be, if Henry Wilson's right. I hear from France that he says the German advance will run out of steam in another week, and then we will be over the Rhine by the end of September."

Harry watched her in fascination. She was tall and beak-nosed, dressed now in cream and scarlet with a sweeping hat. She was not beautiful, but wherever she was, attention concentrated naturally on her.

Ellis said, "Lord Kitchener doesn't agree, I believe."

The Prime Minister said, "Kitchener says flatly that the war will last at least three years. As you may have heard, he plans to raise no less than seventy divisions by the middle of 1916!"

"Kitchener's mind is like the revolving beacon of a lighthouse," Margot Asquith said, "most of the time it shows blank and dark, secretive, giving no information. Then the flash comes and a piercing light is thrown into some hitherto dark place."

"Very good, Margot," the other male guest said. He was a burly man, much the same shape as Ellis, but even taller and not so heavily paunched. He was the 17th Earl of Derby, who had served in the War Office earlier in the century, and also been Postmaster General, both in Conservative Governments; a great nobleman and a man of powerful influence in the country, particularly in his native Lancashire, he was much respected by politicians of both parties.

The two other ladies present were sisters, apparently old friends of Margot's, and Harry never did hear their surnames. One was called Phyllis and the other Irene. Irene now said, "Lord Derby, I thought we had a big army, but we only have these few men in France. A contemptible little army, the Kaiser called them, didn't he? Why is that?"

Lord Derby said, "The army is actually small by continental standards, because we have no conscription, as they all do. But we could put double the number of men into France now if it were not for imperial policing, particularly in India. Roughly speaking, half our regular army is always at home and half abroad at any moment. The infantry number about a hundred and twenty battalions—or did when I was at the War Office. So of those hundred and twenty, sixty are abroad—nearly fifty in India alone, the rest in Malta, Gibraltar, Hong Kong, Rangoon, and so on."

The Prime Minister said, "I asked K when he would be able to get those men back and he said, 'As soon as I can find troops to replace them' . . . I suggested the Territorials, but he has a low opinion of them. Still, we must take some risks, and many regular troops overseas are making preparations to move at this moment."

Derby said, "But I imagine we will have to be sure the outlying German cruisers have been disposed of before they can sail?"

"Certainly."

Now Margot Asquith turned to Lord Derby, and started an animated conversation with him about the character and capabilities of the commander-in-chief of the British Expeditionary Force, Field Marshal Sir John French. Asquith looked tired and grey, and his usually sharp eyes seemed to be unfocussed, as though he was not really here in Number Ten, but miles away—perhaps in France with the B.E.F., perhaps on another planet.

Margot said, "French is too emotional. Good heavens, I've seen him crying like a child when someone congratulated him on what he did at the Curragh. It's the French generals who are supposed to weep and gesticulate, not ours—even if this one's name is French."

Derby laughed dutifully, "Ha-ha."

"The man we ought to have in command is Smith-Dorrien," Margot said.

"What about Haig?" Ellis asked.

"He looks beautiful, but . . ." she tapped her head, "solid bone."

"Oh, come, Mrs Asquith," Ellis said, "he has a brilliant record."

"No imagination," Margot said firmly, "*and* an intriguer. As he's a personal friend of the King, that could be very dangerous."

The Prime Minister looked up from his soup. "You really mustn't slander our generals like that, Margot. It gives me indigestion—to think you might be right."

"Oh, I am," she said cheerfully, "I am. What do *you* think Mr . . . ah, the famous motor car, of course . . . Mr Rowland?"

Harry said, "I know nothing of our generals, Mrs Asquith, I fear. But they must be good surely, or they would never have reached their high positions?"

Margot Asquith said, "You *are* an innocent . . . Herbert, Winston tells me he has got Rupert Brooke into the navy, as a sub lieutenant."

"The poet? Herbert's friend?"

"Yes. And Raymond's."

Servants came silently to remove the soup plates and Margot said, "Roast grouse. We get bombarded with them every Twelfth . . . more than we can eat."

The grouse arrived, preceded by a healthy aroma of decay, for they had been well hung.

"And now," the Prime Minister said, smiling wearily, "we are going to have to talk shop, if you ladies will excuse our rudeness. I wish I didn't have to bring the war to the dining table, but Ares consumes Cronus as fast as Cronus consumed his children . . . Derby, Kitchener has told me about recruitment, and how the recruits will be physically disposed of and housed . . . and I must say it appears that a great many men are going to pass the coming winter in tents . . . but I have not understood about the provision of uniforms, especially of boots. I dare not take up any of K's precious time by asking what he will regard as silly civilian questions—so would you be good enough to enlighten me?"

He went on eating, slowly, while Lord Derby began to answer the question with a long and careful explanation. Harry listened, feeling very much on the inside of great events—more so, really, than if they had been discussing the replacement of Field Marshal French, or the plans for a general offensive; for those would sooner or later be matters of common knowledge, while who would know how the army got its boots? Margot, Irene, and Phyllis talked among themselves, and Harry saw now why the women had all been placed at one end of the table, and the four men at the other. But they talked quietly, even Margot lowering her voice, until the explanations were over and lunch finished.

Margot was already standing up, and the men rising, when the butler entered and whispered a word in the Prime Minister's ear. He said, "Excuse me," and went out of the room. Margot said, "Makepeace, bring the coffee to the Middle Drawing Room, please."

"Yes, madam."

They followed their hostess through double doors into the Pillared Room, across that and through another pair of double doors into the Middle Drawing Room, which looked out over the garden of Number 10 and across Horse Guards Parade to the back of the Admiralty.

Margot said, "Do you have any relatives at the front, Mr Rowland?"

"One son at sea and one in France," he said.

"I have three sons," she said. "Step-sons, to be precise. I wonder how many of them will come through safely—if Lord Kitchener is right."

"Let us pray that they all will," Harry said. "Yours and ours and everyone else's."

"That's impossible," she said briefly. "It *is* a war, after all."

The door opened and the Prime Minister came in. He seemed to have shrunk since the moment when he walked out of the small State Dining Room. He said, "The British Expeditionary Force, or at least part of it, is heavily engaged at Mons, and has been since early morning. President Poincaré has just got through on the telephone to their Embassy here, and the Ambassador called me . . . It appears that Sir John has had to cancel his recent orders to advance, since our men are confronted by the German General von Kluck's First Army . . . we are outnumbered nearly six to one. I've told the King."

Derby said, "Mons? I think it's in Belgium. A mining town . . . I must be getting back to the War Office, Prime Minister."

"You'd better. Give me a telephone call as soon as you hear anything definite. K will be very busy, I imagine."

Lord Derby went out, after brief goodbyes. The butler came in with the coffee tray and Asquith sat down heavily in an easy chair. He rested his head in his hands and spoke slowly, seeming not to be aware that anyone else was present, for he did not address anyone in particular, or even the company in general, but as though soliloquising—"K has always said that the big danger is that a gap may develop between the French army and ours. Then Field Marshal French would be tempted to retire toward the Channel ports . . . and K says that must not be allowed to happen. He told me a week ago."

"Why, Prime Minister?" Harry asked.

"The French will feel that we have deserted them. And the Germans will be able to concentrate on finishing off the French, rather than have to tackle both of us at once."

"I see," Harry said, not seeing very well, but not wishing to pester the Prime Minister with further questions. Privately he was thinking, if the B.E.F. retreats toward the Channel, and the Germans don't divert troops to follow or mark them, they will be on the German flank, and that was supposed to be a good position.

Asquith finished his coffee quickly and stood up. Harry rose with him. He came over and said, "Keep this offer of ours a secret for the time being, Rowland."

"I understand."

"Except from your wife and immediate family, of course. I am sure they can be relied upon not to gossip about it."

"Certainly."

"Ellis, if Rowland accepts, let him tell you. And you do whatever is necessary to have your Liberal Association accept him. Rather, to make them think it is they who have chosen him. You understand?"

"Certainly, Prime Minister."

"I must go. Lloyd George is coming over to discuss new taxes."

Margot Asquith groaned. "What a bore . . . How long will he be staying?"

"Two or three hours, I suppose."

"Oh good, that'll give me time to get Irene and Phyllis safely out of the house before he's free."

"My dear Margot, really!"

"Herbert, don't pretend you don't know that Lloyd George can't be
alone with any woman for thirty seconds without attempting to obtain
some sort of sexual satisfaction . . . and, astonishingly, often achieving
it."

Sunday night dinner at Laburnum Lodge was always a cold collation,
to give Mrs Stallings the afternoon off. What service was necessary
was provided by Brace, the houseman, rather than Parrish. This night
the collation was Melton Mowbray pie, one of Harry's favourites, and
a salad. He tried to concentrate on the taste and satisfaction the pie was
giving him, but memories of his visit to Downing Street kept crowding
in, especially, and incongruously, a mental picture of the Chancellor of
the Exchequer upending Irene on the main stairway and hurling back
her petticoats to reveal . . . He shook his head and Rose murmured,
"Is the pie not good, Harry?"

"Very good, my dear. I was just daydreaming."

Rose looked round. The trifle was on the sideboard, plates ready. She
said, "You may go, Brace."

"Sure, ma'am? I've nothing to do."

"No. Go along. Take down the dirty dishes in the morning early.
Walk the dogs now."

"Right, ma'am. Good night, madam, good night, Miss Rowland.
Good night, sir."

"Good night, Brace."

The servant left the room and Harry said, "I have something to tell
you about my visit to London."

"As if that has not been quite obvious since your return," his wife
said calmly.

"But I'd rather wait till we are in the drawing-room," he said.

He returned to his eating. Asquith, distinguished, cautious . . . a
brilliant man. Not as strong perhaps as some of the other pillars of the
party, notably 'the Welsh wizard' as the yellow press called David
Lloyd George. It would be a great experience to work with such as
them in the highest service of the country. It was flattering that they
apparently wanted his advice on war production—but he didn't need to
be an M.P. for that. He could say whatever he had to say as an expert,
called in or co-opted with others to give advice and information to the
Parliamentary Committee. Perhaps Ellis had told them about his reputation for fair dealing with his workers. He'd never allowed a union, of
course, because, as he told the men, no employer could give them more
than he was giving them, and stay in business; and they believed him.
No trouble since January 1900, and that had only involved half a

dozen men, and was soon over, with the troublemakers dismissed and other good men hired in their room. But things were different these days—the unions were getting more powerful everywhere, socialist members of parliament supported them, and there were a great many upstart employers with no sense of responsibility toward those dependent on them. Perhaps the whole country, civilians and soldiers, employers and employees alike, should be put under military discipline, and given military rates of pay, and no more; but that was unthinkable.

The meal finally ended, he led the way to the drawing-room, port glass in hand. Alice looked into the morning-room, picked up her knitting, and then joined her parents. She put the ball of khaki wool on her lap and started knitting. "What's that?" her father asked.

"Socks for soldiers," she said, her head bent, "for Quentin's men."

Harry took his stance before the fireplace, thumbs in his waistcoat, gold watch chain across his waist. He said, "The Prime Minister has asked me to consider standing for Mid-Scarrow when Ellis retires, in about a year from now. Mr Asquith thought I could help the government in the matter of war production. I told them—Ellis was there at the lunch, also Lord Derby—that I could not give an answer until I had discussed the proposal with you, Rose. This is all in confidence, I may add, and must remain so until the Prime Minister decides to let it be known . . . that is, if I accept, of course. What do you think, Rose?"

His wife patted her grey hair absent-mindedly, and looked him straight in the eye, thoughtfully, measuringly. She said, "You could be as good a Member as Mr Ellis, there's no doubt. Better. You'd have to spend more time in London than I think you'd like."

"We are all going to have to put up with some inconvenience, indeed sacrifice, for the country's sake," Harry said.

She nodded, "Yes, but . . ."

"I want to help the country in whatever way I can. My first responsibility is to make more and better motor cars for the army, if we get the orders . . . by the way, Ellis hinted that he was doing his best to see that we did . . . but if the Prime Minister believes I can be of use as an M.P., in addition, then I do not think that I would be justified in refusing for purely selfish reasons."

"What do you think, Alice?" his wife said. "You know your father at least as well as I do."

Alice looked up, a half-smile on her broad face. "I think father's already made up his mind."

He pretended to glower at her. "What are you saying, Dormouse? That I am wasting your time?"

"You want to accept. I don't see any reason why you should not, if Mother doesn't."

His wife nodded. "I think you should accept. Perhaps you can knock some sense into their heads about Ireland. The Irish are volunteering in thousands for the war, Harry, tens of thousands! Now's the time for generosity, for England to make a big gesture. The Irish are very sentimental people, and such a gesture now would mean more than any formal measures later."

Harry said, "That's just about the only reason why I would *not* want to go into parliament, to become involved in the Irish question. I'm a manufacturer, my dear, I don't have the patience for that sort of thing."

She said, "You'll have to. And at least you can tell Mr Asquith what I think. Meanwhile, tell him you'll accept."

"All right," Harry said suddenly, "very good. I will write to Ellis tomorrow morning." He finished his port and looked round, breathing deeply with satisfaction. The tall curtains were drawn back to let the summer air breathe in off the garden, heavy with the scent of Kentish roses. It was very quiet, no sound from the town. No more quiet than usual on a Sunday evening, perhaps, he thought, but . . . He said, "Quentin may be fighting for his life at this instant, barely a hundred miles away. He may already be wounded . . . or dead."

"The battle you told us about when you came in?"

"Yes. And Tom's ship may already have been sunk by one of those beastly German submarines. Treacherous swine! You saw Richard today, did you not, Alice?"

"Yes, father. I had lunch with them. He's found a big warehouse in North Hedlington that he thinks can be converted into a factory. It's not perfect, but can serve to start with, he says."

"Has he succeeded in obtaining the capital?"

"He had an encouraging answer to a cable he sent to Mr Merritt in New York, but Mr Merritt will have to consult his board of directors, and the war situation will have to be considered."

"Clearly," Harry said. He changed the subject abruptly. "I see that Guy did not do well against Yorkshire yesterday. Two for seventy-two is not very encouraging."

"He did not seem to be depressed when I spoke to him last night on the telephone. But it's a shame that no one from the family was there to watch—except Virginia, of course."

"Everyone had other things to do," Harry said shortly. "I'm tired, Rose. I think we should retire now."

"Very well, my dear."

Daily Telegraph, Wednesday, August 26, 1914

BRITISH ARMY AT THE BATTLE OF MONS
A SPLENDID STORY

Paris, Monday (received per Courier, Tuesday) Graphic stories of how the British troops at Mons fought during the two days in which they bore the brunt of the main German advance reached Paris in the early hours of this morning when officers arriving from the front reported at the War Office and, in subsequent conversation with their closest personal friends, told of the wonderful coolness and daring of our men . . . The shooting of our infantry on the firing line, they said, was wonderful . . . The firing was not the usual firing of nervous men, shooting without aiming and sometimes without rhyme or reason, as is so often the case in warfare. It was rather the calm, calculated riflemanship of the men one sees on the Stickledown range . . . There was no excitement, no nervousness; just cool methodical efficiency. If the British lost heavily heaven only knows what the Germans must have lost because, as one of their wounded officers (whom the British took prisoner) remarked, "We had never expected anything like it; it was staggering."

Cate read to the end of the report with pulse beating fast. So it had come, and Britannia had no cause to hang her head. Field Marshal French could not yet give the exact number of casualties, still less any names, but he estimated that the army had suffered about two thousand . . . two thousand, in two days! That fitted with Lord Kitchener's first speech in the House of Lords, reported on the same page where, among other things, K had said, "European fighting causes greater casualties than the campaigns in which we are generally engaged in other parts of the world." The only saving grace of the situation was that no war could last for long at such a scale. People had been talking about the war being over in a few weeks; and he had not believed them; but perhaps they were right, not from foolish optimism, but from a better understanding than he of the destructiveness of modern war. He read on:

FIGHT FOR CIVILISATION

Paris, Wednesday (1.25 a.m.) An official communiqué issued at midnight says: "Our army, calm and resolute, will continue today its magnificent effort. It knows the reward of this effort. It is fighting for civilisation and the whole of France is watching. She also is calm and strong, knowing that her sons, with the heroic Belgian army, and with the vigorous British army, support the burden of a conflict unprecedented both as to the joint bloodshed and its duration. The Russians are marching on the roads of Eastern Prussia, and Germany is invaded."—REUTER.

A tear fell from Cate's eye, and fell on the page, followed soon by another.

Le Cateau, France: Wednesday, August 26, 1914

11 Two o'clock in the morning, and the candles guttering low. General Sir Horace Smith-Dorrien, commanding II Corps of the British Expeditionary Force, turned to Major General Hamilton, commanding the 3rd Infantry Division. "How soon can your troops move off?"

"To continue the retreat, sir?"

Smith-Dorrien nodded.

"Not before nine a.m. at the earliest," Hamilton answered emphatically. "They've been marching all night. We could cover the movement of the other divisions from our present positions, perhaps."

Smith-Dorrien shook his head. "The 4th Division is even more scattered than yours. Also it is part of III Corps, as you know . . . though whether General Snow has any contact with his Corps headquarters, I have no notion." He turned to the bull-like figure of Allenby, commanding the B.E.F.'s Cavalry Division. "What is your situation?"

"We're all tired, sir. Men and horses. The Germans are very close. In my opinion, unless we can break clean now," he emphasised the word, repeating it—"*now*, we shall be forced to fight at daylight. What is the situation of I Corps, sir?"

"Apparently they were attacked yesterday at Landrecies, and are continuing the retreat . . ."

"You have no contact with them?"

"No. I've sent signals and despatch riders, in the hope that I can persuade General Haig to co-operate with me, and he may do so yet, but it is possible that a gap is developing between the two Corps . . . which would make it still more imperative that we continue our retreat, as the Chief has ordered."

No one said anything. A candle flared momentarily, lighting up Smith-Dorrien's long, pensive face as he leaned over the farmhouse table, looking down at the spread map. After two minutes he stood upright. "Allenby, will you take orders from me, and act as part of this corps?"

Allenby said, "Yes, sir."

Smith-Dorrien said, "Very well, gentlemen, we will fight and I will ask General Snow to act under me as well."

The officers in the room breathed a collective sigh of relief. After seventy-two hours with its backs to the enemy, the B.E.F. would now turn, at bay.

Quentin Rowland plodded wearily on down the gravelled road, its surface gleaming faintly white under the starlight, the young moon long since set. The night was full of sounds—the creak and thud of his men's boots behind him, the same from battalion headquarters in front, the sigh of the wind in the hedgerows and through the heavy branches of the poplars, reaching up on either side to cut shapes out of the sky. It was not the regular swing of British infantry on parade but a more staccato beat, for A Company, 1st Battalion, the Weald Light Infantry was not keeping step as well as on a Minden Day parade. Nor were they marching with the Light Infantry crack and snap, but trudging, under heavy packs, full ammunition pouches, rifles, bayonets, all the paraphernalia of field service marching order. The last time Company Sergeant Major Pierce had got reports from the platoon commanders, the company strength had been 84 out of the 126 of all ranks who, three days earlier, had scrabbled for cover in the smoking slag heaps south of the Mons-Condé canal, and there played their part in holding up the advance of three German divisions.

How far had they marched since then? Fifty miles, sixty? Quentin tried to remember: the 23rd—fighting—no rations: night of the 23rd—marching all night: 24th—marching most of the day: night of the 24th—outpost duty, no rations: 25th—rear party of the division . . . A long way, a long time, always the field grey masses following, relentless. His men were falling asleep on their feet, stumbling along in their ranks, being supported by comrades, cursed by corporals as weary as they, some falling over unnoticed, to lie in a dead sleep at the dark verge of the road. When morning came, those men would find themselves staring down the muzzles of German rifles, to spend the rest of the war in prisoner-of-war camps. How long would that be? There seemed to be an incredibly large number of Germans. They had marched down to the Mons canal like a football crowd, and like a football crowd had melted away under the concentrated rapid fire of the British riflemen. But half an hour later, another such mass had followed, their field guns whip-cracking fire over the makeshift British trenches. The second mass had withered away, like the first . . . and the third, which had tried to advance by creeping and crawling through the piled corpses of their predecessors . . . and again . . . and again. In one advance platoon of his company, the wooden stocks of half the men's rifles had charred from the heat of the barrels beneath. One of the battalion's two machine guns, placed in his company's area, had seized up, the water in its water jacket boiled away, so that it became useless. In its place they had used an East Surreys' gun, found in an angle of the canal bank, its crew dead around it.

If only they could turn and face the enemy . . . just for a day, perhaps. The men were not yet downhearted, but their mood was more sullen than Quentin liked. He knew he was not a brilliant officer, and had no thought that he would ever reach any command higher than that of a battalion of his regiment. But that was all he wanted, and he wanted it because he understood the cockneys and Men of Kent and Kentish Men who formed it. Irish, too, for a large proportion of the British Infantry line had always been composed of Irishmen, especially since the potato famines of the mid-nineteenth century. He felt for the soldiers, and with them, by processes deeper than thinking or imagining; and they understood him. He understood them and loved them the way a man was supposed to love and understand his wife . . . in his own case, much better. Fiona was quite incomprehensible to him.

His feet were sore and he had worn huge holes in both his socks. His batman had repaired them with cobbling work that made him feel he was marching barefoot on a coarse rope mesh. His pipe, that he had been smoking off and on all through the night's march, was burned out and tasted bitter on his tongue. He wondered what his brother John was doing now. Well, that was a stupid thought, for at 4 a.m. John would be asleep in his double bed, Louise lying beside him. John had no more imagination than he himself had, yet he seemed to have made a success of his marriage. Perhaps John and Louise were no longer passionate lovers—if they ever had been—but he was sure they still shared an intimate personal life; whereas his own . . .

" 'Ere, 'ere! *Roko! Tum kaun ho?*" His Company Sergeant Major darted forward in the gloom, shouting Hindustani imprecations. Most regular soldiers had served many years in India, and believed that anyone who wasn't British must be a native, and therefore would understand Hindustani. A voice answered in French, shouting something coarse, in which Quentin could only understand the word 'Merde'—shit! Horses loomed huge ahead, crossing from left to right. Quentin saw that they had reached a crossroads. He said to the men beside him, "Halt here," and went forward, ash plant swinging.

Peering up against the stars, he made out the long lances, horsehair plumes, and brass helmets of French dragoons, and called up "Qui êtes vous?"

"Va te foutre," a gruff voice answered.

"Je suis un commandant anglais. Combien êtes vous?"

Another voice answered him, "Deux cents, mon commandant. Nous passerons vite."

He leaned wearily on his stick. Two hundred dragoons, he thought, crossing their line of march in the dusty, pre-dawn hour, and cutting in between his own battalion headquarters and the rest of the battalion. The C.O. would not be pleased. Still, there was nothing to be done about it until they had passed, and that wouldn't be long.

He called, "Sar'nt Major! Put out four men, with a sergeant, to block this crossroads, both sides, when the French have passed, until the rest of the battalion can get past. Then they can catch up."

"Sir!"

The C.S.M. bustled off, calling out. Men stumbled forward, fixing bayonets. The last of the dragoons disappeared into the dark and the British column trudged on again. The soldiers at the head of A Company's leading platoon were talking. "Where did those Froggies come from?"

"God knows, Ginger."

"Where were they going?"

"Not even God knows that, mate."

A chuckle. A voice said, "They're going to 'ave tea with von Fuck."

"Or wipe the snow off the focking Roosians' boots what was supposed to be in this foight with us."

The platoon officer said, "Mind the language there, Murphy."

"Sorry, sorr."

Quentin nodded in agreement and felt a little better. Hedges was right not to permit foul language in his hearing; but the fact that the men were joking was a good sign.

A soldier spoke to the subaltern, "Is it true that von Fu—von Kluck called us a 'contemptible little army,' sir? Even after wot we did to them at Mons?"

Hedges said, "I don't think it was von Kluck, Wickilam."

Quentin turned his head and spoke over his shoulder. "It was the Kaiser, in a general order to von Kluck. And it was before Mons."

The C.S.M. said, "Someone 'alted ahead, sir."

The group of figures took dim shape. The earliest light was beginning to tinge the eastern darkness to their left, as they marched almost due south. A voice spoke harshly, "Who's there?"

Quentin recognised his C.O.'s voice and said, "A Company, sir."

"Rowland? Where in the name of God have you been? We've been waiting here ten minutes."

"French cavalry cut across us, sir."

The colonel swore under his breath. "Those . . . ! They've done it twenty times if they've done it once, wandering about the countryside like lost baboons . . . Pull your company off into that field there, Quentin. The rest of the battalion will follow you. The men can have an hour's nap where they lie. As soon as they're in the field, you come back here for orders. We're going to stand and fight."

"Fight, sir?" Quentin's stolid determination was lit by a flare of enthusiasm.

"Yes, fight." Behind him Quentin heard the word repeated down the ranks as the company trudged past into the field . . . fight . . . fight . . . we're going to fight. A ragged cheer rose, quickly suppressed by C.S.M. Pierce's acid—"First, sleep! You lot couldn't fight a girls' school now."

"Where are we, sir?" Quentin asked.

"There's a little town to our right front called Le Cateau. The Corps is going to fight on a generally east-west line through it. Our brigade headquarters has lost touch with the East Surreys, and our job is to hold this flank until touch is regained with them, and then we will all rejoin the rest of the brigade south-west of Le Cateau."

"Yes, sir."

"I'll tell you more when I give out orders. Oh, one more thing you can tell your men later—do you know what today is, Quentin?"

Quentin wrinkled his brow and thought again of the days and nights that had passed. "I think it's the 26th," he said aloud.

"Quite right," Colonel Pitchford said with a touch of impatience. "The anniversary of Crecy. The 568th anniversary, to be exact. And we are going to make the anniversary just as glorious as the bowmen did that day."

"I'm sure we will, sir," Quentin said stolidly. Lieutenant Colonel Pitchford was a good soldier, he thought, but somewhat unpredictable.

"You have no imagination," Pitchford said, but he was smiling in the faintness of a misty dawn.

"Nearly six o'clock, sir," C.S.M. Pierce said, "and we've brewed some char." He handed over a mug of hot tea. Smoke rose from the corner of a building at the edge of Le Cateau, where Quentin's own batman, and that of his second-in-command, Captain Irwin, were burning pieces of old lumber to make a fire. The mist was rising from the valley of the Selle, the stream that flowed northwards through Le Cateau. Behind them the land rose, already clear of mist, to low rolling hills.

"Any news from the forward platoons?" he said.

Irwin, standing beside him, mug in hand, said, "Nothing, sir. They had trenches a couple of feet deep when I went round, about twenty minutes ago. It's good soil to dig in."

Quentin gulped down a mouthful of tea. "Think I'll take another look round . . . something ought to be happening soon."

The bell in the Town Hall struck six. Then sharper sounds exploded overhead and behind with sharp cracks. The batmen looked up from the fire as four more cracks followed the first.

"Well, their guns are in action," Irwin said. "Their infantry will be close. Or cavalry."

Rapid rifle fire broke out from ahead, where two of the company's platoons were lying in their hastily dug trenches in an orchard. The distinctive rattle of a German machine gun filled the air with a continuous clatter, and ricochets whined off the walls and showered them with brick dust, to blend with the yellow powder that already covered them from days and nights of continuous marching and fighting.

The shelling increased.

"What are our guns doing?" Quentin muttered worriedly.

"Trying to work out their bloody sums," his second-in-command said from close by, standing against the wall of a little house.

"Begging your pardon, sir," Pierce said, "I don't think we've got any guns supporting us now. Fifty-two Field Battery went back to its brigade."

"So it did. The colonel told us. Well, we . . ."

A lieutenant of artillery cantered up on a sweating magnificent bay, followed by a trumpeter. The rumble of gun wheels echoed from the cobbled street behind. The subaltern reined in, saluting, "Number 2 section, D Battery, R.H.A., sir! . . . We got separated from the battery. Where are the enemy?"

"Straight ahead, by the sound of them," Quentin said. "Look, I can see horses."

The artillery officer swung round in his saddle, bawling, "Take post! Cavalry advancing, front!"

The teams cantered out into the open and wheeled so that the gun muzzles now faced the enemy. The crews leaped off their horses, and took post by the 13-pounders, while the horseholders trotted their horses back into Le Cateau. The officer was shouting, "Eight hundred! Corrector 130! Gunfire, gun control, fire!" The guns barked and bounced, smoke jetting from their muzzles.

"There's the Germans!" Quentin's batman breathed in excited awe. "Uhlans!"

"All German cavalry aren't Uhlans, Stubbersfield," Quentin snapped. "Uhlans have flat-topped hats."

The 13-pounders were firing fast, the explosive barks very close. The artillery subaltern stayed on his horse, his binoculars to his eyes. German shells began to burst over and among them. A gunner beside the breech of a gun doubled over and lay still; another crawled away, dragging a shattered leg.

The subaltern said, "Oh, I should have told you earlier. The East Surreys, or part of them, are to your right. We passed through them."

Quentin said, "Thanks. That's giving them something to think about!"

From in front a soldier, bent double, ran toward them, rifle at the trail. He pulled up panting beside Quentin and knelt. "Germans getting past us, sir. Mr Hedges said to ask you if he can retire to the barns there."

Quentin said, "Tell Mr Hedges, no. To hold the position. Tell him I'm going to push the enemy back with the reserve platoon." The runner said, "Yes, sir," turned, and ran back the way he had come. Quentin said, "C.S.M., where's Mr Tate?"

"I'm here, sir."

"Your platoon ready?"

"Yes, sir."

"Work along the northern edge of Le Cateau, the houses and fields, that way, for three hundred yards from here. There are Germans in there. Probably cavalry. Drive them back, then return."

"All right, sir."

The young officer blew a whistle and in a moment he and his twenty men moved off through hedges and toolsheds, rifles at the high port, bayonets fixed. Almost at once firing broke out from the direction they had gone, and bullets began to fly round the house where Quentin had set up his company headquarters. A runner arrived from battalion, with a written message: "We have linked up with E Surreys AAA Germans heavily infiltrating B Company position, also East Surreys AAA Prepare to retreat to high ground south-east of your present position, on my order only AAA Acknowledge."

C.S.M. Pierce was already scribbling the acknowledgement on a message pad. Quentin scrawled his signature. Men staggered out of the mist, bleeding, arms hanging shattered. "Mr Hedges is dead," one mumbled. The C.S.M. said, "Go on back, you—that way. 'Ere, put a field dressing on that one, or he'll bleed to death."

Quentin said, "Irwin?"

"Yes, sir?"

"Take a couple of men and go back in the direction we've been ordered to retire. I expect Major Bergeron will be there, co-ordinating. If he isn't, choose a good position for us. We'll find you, or you'll find us, by the firing, if the Germans follow up."

The shelling had died down, but the main sound of firing had circled round from north-east to north and now to north-west and even west.

The Horse Artillery officer said, "If you're going to withdraw soon, I'd better get the guns back a bit, so we can cover you."

Quentin said, "Right. Do it now, as fast as you can, while there seems to be a bit of a lull."

The subaltern shouted to his sergeant and the teams galloped out of Le Cateau, limbered up, and took the guns to the rear. The subaltern said, "I'd better go back with them, sir. I'll get a good position on the slope so that we can shoot at whatever we see coming at you."

"Good man!"

"Wish we had some 18-pounders. They do a lot more damage than we can . . . Well, good luck, sir." He saluted, jammed his cap down on his head and spurred the bay into a full gallop, followed by his trumpeter.

A soldier ran up, and leaned against the inner wall. His pale eyes shone like beacons through the three-day layer of sweat and coal dust and brick dust. "Mr Eden's dead, sir. A shell burst near took his head off. Sergeant O'Leary sent me back to ask whether he could retire now."

"Not yet," Quentin said, "hold hard. Make the Germans pay for every yard."

The man ran. Quentin turned away. It was time he found another reserve, if Tate didn't come back soon . . . but here they were, slipping through the mist in twos and threes, heads up, and seeming not to expect anyone to be following. Tate appeared, limping on his stick. "Gave 'em a bit of a bloody nose, sir," he said cheerfully. "We reached a big hedge, and there was a squadron of cavalry right in front of us. They weren't Uhlans. They were trotting across our front in close order. Couldn't believe my eyes! Gave 'em ten rounds rapid from the whole platoon, and then charged. They bolted—what was left of them. But I saw an awful lot more coming on behind—infantry."

"And you?"

"Bullet grazed the calf, sir. Nothing broken. It hurts a bit but I'm all right." He lowered his voice, "I've lost Foster, sir."

"Your platoon sergeant?"

"Yes, sir. Can't think what happened to him. One moment he was there, then he wasn't. Suppose he got hit and fell into the bushes some-where, and no one saw him. Should I go back and look for him?"

"No," Quentin said decisively. He had always had his doubts about Sergeant Foster; it was very possible that the fellow had not been killed. He set his jaw. "Well done, Tate. Get your men back to where you were just now. If we get the order to withdraw, you will cover the rest of us."

Another runner arrived from battalion with another written message: "Carry out retreat orders as my P.9 AAA 2-i-c co-ordinating new defen-sive position."

Good, Quentin thought. Bergeron was up there. Irwin would have found him, and there'd be a good position to fall back on.

He turned to the C.S.M. "Runners to the forward platoons, Sar'nt Major. Withdraw south-east as ordered, at—" he looked at his watch "—seven-twenty a.m. Number 3 platoon will cover from present position of Company Headquarters."

He filled his pipe with French tobacco. An old lady had given him the tobacco out of her little shop in the early light of dawn, when the sound of men digging and cursing and giving orders in a strange lan-guage had awakened her and she had found, to her astonishment, that the war had come to Le Cateau in the shape of a battalion of British in-fantry. The tobacco would probably taste vile, thought Quentin, who had a deep distrust of everything foreign, but it would be better than nothing, and he had five minutes to wait before the withdrawal began. He checked that the machine gun, just come back from a forward posi-tion, was in place, and ordered Tate to be sure to provide a couple of men to help carry it back when No. 3 platoon, too, withdrew. Those Vickers guns, which many people, himself included, had derided as me-chanical toys not worthy of British soldiers, had proved themselves in-valuable complements to the skilled riflemen's fire at Mons, and it looked as though they would do the same here.

The crack of 13-pounder shrapnel fired from behind Le Cateau showed that the Horse Artillery section was in action again. Quentin thought, good. But back there, Bergeron would give them other tasks: A Company would no longer have its own private artillery support.

The sun was beginning to paint the houses of Le Cateau and reveal, as a drawn blanket reveals a sleeping nude, the village of Bazuel a mile down the road to the east. From overhead Quentin heard the buzzing of aeroplane engines, and thought, they haven't been much use so far . . . strange, to think that war would ever be waged from those moth-like machines, wheeling about in the huge sky.

German machine-gun fire, in volume, began to tattoo the houses to his left, breaking windows and knocking off slates. Shrapnel burst over-head in irregular rapid whipcracks, the cottonwool bursts in air rein-forced by the loud booms of high explosive shells from heavy howitzers. Fountains of earth rose and dropped back, clouds of choking yellow-black smoke drifted low over the grass, through the orchards, and among the houses. On the British side, at least one 60-pounder battery was in action from somewhere across the Selle, the shells bursting three or four miles down the Roman road to the north-east of Le Cateau, to judge by the sound.

The Germans would attack any moment . . . not the original formless infiltration, but a planned, lined-up assault. That was good. Infiltration was more dangerous, because you never knew where the strength of it would develop; it was like water trickling, finding a path through the defenders' fire. But when they lined up and attacked in mass, not even heavy artillery support could douse the rifle and ma-chine-gun fire that would burn them away, like chaff along the edge of a wheatfield.

Seven-twenty. The rifle fire forward increased, then died down. He was standing beside Tate, houses behind, fields ahead. "Be ready now," he muttered. Figures appeared, some running, some walking steadily, a few being supported. They passed, and Quentin called out, "Well done! Well done, Sergeant. Back up the hill there! Captain Irwin will give you orders."

"We killed a hundred of the buggers at least," an older man mut-tered, a reservist . . . Quentin remembered his face from Bareilly; or was it Lahore?—but could not recall his name.

"Well done, well done!" Sergeant Miller passed. "That's all, sir. No one left, except the dead, and a couple of men too bad to move."

"Good. Stand by, Tate." He puffed on his pipe. He ought to be afraid, but he was not. Tate knew fear, but was visibly conquering it. The men close by, lying prone, rifles ready, were looking at him out of the corners of their eyes. He felt nothing. Tate was the brave one, and these private soldiers facing death, and worse, just because—they were afraid not to.

"Here they come," Quentin said quietly.

The grey men took form among the scattered trees, spiked helmets covered with grey cloth—a mass, such as Quentin had seen across the Mons Canal, and fired into again and again with a rifle taken from a dead soldier. Officers in front, swords drawn, the soldiers in the foremost rank firing from the hip. A private near Quentin grunted, staggered to his feet and fell, coughing blood over Quentin's boots.

He said, "Let them have it!"

Tate dropped to one knee, bellowing, "Number Three Platoon! Two hundred!" Every man's left thumb slid his backsight down—"Front! Enemy advancing! Ten rounds . . ." each man pushed his safety catch off with his right thumb: "rapid, *fire!*"

The platoon opened the devastating fire which had held the canal at Mons—at least fifteen aimed rounds a minute, and many of the men capable of twenty-five rounds—the rifle steady as a rock in the tripod support of left elbow, right elbow, and right shoulder, head steady, nothing moving between each shot except the right wrist, flicking the bolt back and forward.

A storm of shrapnel from the Horse Artillery's 13-pounders burst over the reeling Germans. The Vickers machine gun opened fire with a full belt in a long, swinging, traverse. The enemy, half a battalion in mass, wilted, turned and ran, stumbling, falling, dying. By 7.30, there were no enemy on their feet within three hundred yards. Quentin said shortly, "Retire, Tate."

He turned and trudged back as the platoon rose, spread out, passed the last hovels of Le Cateau, crossed the railway in a deep cutting, and climbed the hill. A few shells from German 77-mm guns cracked over-head, but from the ground there was no fire, only silence, and grey and brown corpses strewn in the orchard and at the edge of the town, and men groaning with many wounds, writhing in their own blood.

The hours passed relentlessly. At nine, the clock in the bell tower of the Town Hall played a cheerful carillon before striking the hour. At eleven the Weald Light Infantry retreated another thousand yards to the south-west, with the East Surreys on their right as they faced the enemy. The sun continued its steady circling of the southern horizon and everyone's tongue was swollen and mouth parched, except for the lucky ones whose post or path was by the Selle. The mist of dawn had been replaced by the fog of war, for the higher commanders, at least. To the Weald Light Infantry and the East Surreys, on the high ground south and south-west of Le Cateau, the situation had been becoming clearer all day: large numbers of Germans were between them and the rest of their brigade, and the original plan of rejoining them was out of the question. The two battalions were making a slow fighting retreat, with Germans coming at them continually, sometimes head on, more often passing across their front up the valley of the Selle in an apparent attempt to find the right flank of the main British line, and turn it. This they were beginning to do, to judge from the sound of the firing, and the actual sight across the valley of grey figures swarming up the opposite slope. The Wealds had been, if not ignored, then at least treated with disdain for the past few hours, as though the Germans were aware that there were not enough British on their left flank, but isolated east of the Selle, to stop their incessant slow forward trickle. The Germans paid heavily for their disdain—the battalion's two machine guns, and the concentrated fire of the riflemen, all shooting in enfilade, had done murderous damage as the Germans passed across their front; but von Kluck's corps commanders had long purses, or acted as though they had.

Before noon Quentin had been mystified by the sight of smoke rising from many chimneys in Le Cateau—until he realised that the housewives were preparing the midday meal for their men. The war had come, yes, but men had to eat, too. Now a denser, more evil smoke was rising from part of the town, as houses burned; and south-west of it, on the slope across the Selle from his position, the 18-pounder guns of a British Field Artillery battery were in action, as they had been for the past few hours from the same exposed and forward position. Earlier the guns had been firing toward Le Cateau and west of it; now, with Germans infiltrated round their flank, they were pointing almost directly at the Wealds' positions. The shrapnel burst white over the valley bottom directly below. The gunflashes were bright even in the sunlight, and from time to time an empty shrapnel shell case would ricochet and hurtle over head, wailing like a banshee. The grey flow of German infantry crept on, not regularly, or fast, but without cease.

Quentin put his pipe away. Time to visit his platoons again—check how many fresh casualties they had suffered, whether they had been taken to the rear, check the ammunition situation, see the men, be seen . . .

A soldier appeared, hurrying laboriously up the back slope of the hill. He tapped the sling of his shouldered rifle in salute and said, "Post, sir."

"Post? Post what?" Quentin growled.

"Post's up, sir." He fished in his haversack and dredged up a bundle of letters and a few small parcels.

C.S.M. Pierce took the string-tied package and shook his head as the man saluted again and ran back the way he had come. "No post since we left the Curragh, and now it comes right in the middle of a battle!"

Quentin said, "Don't distribute it now, Sar'nt Major."

Pierce said, "Begging your pardon, sir, I'd like to try. I was round the company half an hour ago and some of the young 'uns are getting jumpy, seeing the 'Uns passing by in front and 'earing firing from behind as well. Sergeant Tilehurst had to stick his bayonet a couple of inches into one young fellow's backside, who was sort of sneaking off, easy like."

"You're right. There seems to be a lull . . . but get a move on. Some sort of orders must be coming soon now."

"One for you, sir," the C.S.M. said, handing over a letter. "And another." For a moment, seeing a blue envelope, Quentin thought it was from Fiona. But that was not her handwriting. It was his mother's. He opened the envelope.

It was dated August 24th, the day after Mons. Father had heard of the battle when lunching with the Prime Minister the day before. The letter had really come quickly then. They all hope he is well and unhurt. Guy played for Kent against Yorkshire and took two wickets for seventy-two runs, which is really very good for a schoolboy, isn't it? Fiona will give you the news, of course (but Fiona will do no such thing, of course). Richard is proposing to start a factory to make lorries, and has asked for a loan from a Mr Stephen Merritt, an American banker, whom we met at Henley. Tom is on H.M.S. *Monmouth*, but no one knows where. Father and Alice are fit and well, and she herself is as well as can be expected (what does that mean?) . . .

The other letter was from Guy, written on the Sunday, August 23rd. Virginia is well, so is Mother, but busy. He played for Kent against Yorkshire and after the Tykes had taken a few overs to make sure he was no more than he seemed, they flogged his bowling all over the field . . . but he had got Rhodes out. Well, one lives and learns. Lots of love . . .

He put down the letters and stared westward across the valley, unsighted. Fiona would not be writing . . . he saw her as he had last seen her, on a brief leave from Ireland . . . cursory, perfunctory, as though her mind was somewhere else. His wife? Technically, but in reality? A housekeeper, and not very efficient. Nor a good mother, as was obvious even to him. What could he do to make her believe in, and return, his love?

"Major! Major Rowland!"

He started, turning. The C.S.M. was there with a message form. "Orders, sir. We are to retire, all of us, at 3 p.m."

Quentin wrenched his mind back to reality and the present, and glanced at the form. Times, lines of withdrawal, rendezvous . . . He looked at the valley. It would be a close thing, another forty-five minutes to go, and the Germans already so far forward. If only some reserve force could come now and hit them in the flank, they'd be sent reeling back in such disarray that they might not recover for days. But the only force available, General Haig's I Corps, was miles to the east, as far as he knew, and probably continuing its retreat.

He sat back, beginning to think what orders he would have to give, saying, "Send for Captain Irwin, please."

"Sir!"

He had three platoons in arrowhead forward, and one to the left of company headquarters, in reserve, but able to fire into and across the Selle. One of the battalion's machine guns was with his left forward platoon. B Company was echeloned back on A's right, and had to conform with A's movements. The C.S.M. broke in—"Look, sir!"

He looked up, at the same time becoming aware of the thin, now familiar drone of an aircraft engine. The machine's wings glinted in the sun, turning. The Germans were firing at it, and now he saw the roundels of the Royal Flying Corps plain under the wings, and the heads of pilot and observer seen through the struts and wires. Lower, lower it came. He stood up. He shouted at the C.S.M., "Get ready to rescue them, Pierce, if he crashes. Take all the H.Q. runners."

"Sir!"

Pierce bustled off, yelling orders. German rifle fire directed at the aeroplane cracked lower and heavier overhead. The machine glided over Quentin's head no more than twenty feet up, its engine sputtering and banging. It hit the stubble barely a hundred yards away, bounced twice and rolled to a stop. The C.S.M. was already running out toward it, followed by four soldiers with rifles.

Quentin watched as the pilot climbed out of his seat, jumped to the ground, and hurried toward the C.S.M.'s party. They met, arms waved for a moment, then two of the soldiers took up sentry posts over the machine as it stood throbbing on the turf, the propellor turning idly. The observer stayed in the aircraft, the others turned and ran toward Quentin. The German fire had ceased, for as the machine was landing it had passed over a fold in the crest, hiding it from their sight.

The pilot came up, tearing off his flying helmet and goggles. He looked about nineteen, Quentin thought, and was a 2nd Lieutenant. "I have a message from II Corps that I'm supposed to drop on the forward brigade headquarters this side of the Selle. But I can't find any brigade headquarters over here. Could you pass it on, if I give it to you?"

Quentin said, "There isn't any brigade headquarters this side the

Selle—just us and the East Surreys. But I'll send it to my battalion headquarters, and the C.O. will know what to do when he reads it."

He scribbled briefly on a message pad, and gave the note and the airman's message to his C.S.M. "Deal with this." To the airman he said, "Won't that machine start flying, if no one's holding it? The observer can't do anything, can he?"

The pilot said, "No, sir. The friction of the tail skid's enough to hold it except on tarmacadam, and we don't see any of that in France."

"Will you need any help to get off again?"

"No, sir. These old B.E. 2 a's can take off from a hearthrug . . . How's it going here?"

"All right. I've had twenty-nine killed and wounded in my company, and I imagine the others are the same. More Germans than we expected, but we're giving them a bloody nose."

"Not more than *we* expected," the young man said heatedly, dragging a gold cigarette case from his pocket and lighting a cigarette. "We've been reporting the exact strength, and direction, and speed of the German columns since before Mons. None of those old fogeys at G.H.Q. believes us. I myself told General Wilson what I'd seen with my own eyes. He told me I must be mistaken—his maps showed otherwise. Can you believe it?"

"I think Field Marshal French and General Wilson know what they're doing at least as well as you do," Quentin said stiffly. The young man should have asked his permission before lighting up one of those damned cigarettes that were the latest fashion. The R.F.C. seemed to think that because they knew how to fly these smelly machines the rules of military discipline did not apply to them: but the truth surely was that they applied even more strongly because they could not be enforced in the normal ways.

The pilot's childlike face was haggard with strain, and his eyes bloodshot and deep sunk. He made a last attempt to make Quentin understand. "Sir, we look right down on them all day long. They can't hide themselves, and so far haven't made any attempt to do so. Nor have our own people. We can count them, too, and often have to— because G.H.Q. never really knows where our own troops are. We tell them, and they believe us. But when we count the Germans, in just the same way, they don't believe us . . . because they don't understand the air war. And *you* suffer . . ."

Quentin felt a grudging compassion for the worn boy, suddenly seeing in him the face of his own son Guy: but the war would be over before Guy could be in it, in any capacity. He said gruffly, "You look tired. Like a drop of whisky? I have some."

"No, thank you, sir. It helps for a few minutes, then, no *bon*. And I'll be flying till dark, and after. And I'm afraid my plugs are oiling up."

He saluted and ran for his machine. Quentin found his C.S.M. at his elbow. "Message gone, sir."

Quentin looked at his watch. Two-forty. "Where's Captain Irwin? I sent . . ."

"Here, sir. I was trying to get the machine gun unjammed."

"Did you? We'll need it badly soon."

"Yes, sir."

"Well done, Steve. Sar'nt Major, get headquarters ready to pull back in ten minutes. Steve, I want you and the platoon sergeants here in five minutes, for orders. The platoon commanders to stay with their platoons." He sat down on the bank once more, his chin cupped in his hands. He'd be leaving twelve dead on the field, with the seventeen wounded, that came to over a third of the strength that had marched into Le Cateau before this day's dawn. And the day was not finished yet. A sudden increase of firing across the valley, both German and British, both artillery and small arms, made him raise his head. On the angle of the hill across the Selle, the British 18-pounders that he had seen earlier were firing faster, at targets in the valley below. The German artillery was firing concentrations of shrapnel at them, and at the barely discernible khaki-clad infantry close by in shallow trenches and behind the thin hedges. Brown and white and black puffs of smoke increased in number and density, the smoke drifting slowly across the hill, now obscuring, now revealing the scene. But there was little to see except the smoke, for the German infantry was all but invisible, and if it moved at all, moved slowly and in dispersed units—no longer the heavy masses of Mons and this morning.

Suddenly there was movement, to the left, the south—violent movement. Teams of horses, riders bent low over their backs, charged down the slopes, bursting through the tattered hedges, dust flying behind the racing hoofs and rolling wheels of the towed limbers. Quentin pulled his binoculars out of their leather case and put them to his eyes. Withdrawal must have been ordered for the other brigades of the division across the Selle there; but first they had to extricate the guns: and the guns had been placed far forward, the teams sent back into cover—because the 18-pounders could not engage targets over the convex slope of the hill from any farther back. Now, in a storm of shell and rifle fire the gun teams were coming up, full gallop, the limbers bouncing and crashing in air, to take back the guns. In the circle of the lenses he saw a pair of horses go down, bringing the rest of the team in ruin on top of them, legs, bodies of the drivers flying, the limber upended, another separated from its team, the leathers cut, the limber flying down the slope, turning over. Two of the teams reached the guns, the crews were dragging them out by hand, limbering up . . . one crew down, reaped by a scythe of machine-gun fire . . . another team galloping away, gun and all . . .

"Sir!" someone shouted in his ear. "Platoon sergeants here!"

"Shut up! Look!"

He waited, breathless, sweat running down his nose under the binoculars, fatigue and thirst forgotten. Three guns were limbered up and going back. Little figures were struggling with two more . . . taking out the breech blocks . . . one last team fought its way down, one horse short, its traces cut, the animal dead . . . a triple burst of artillery fire exploded on it; neither man nor animal moved again. Scattered lumps and humps broke the clean line of the slope. Three abandoned guns and the skyward pointing trail of another stood silhouetted against the blue sky.

He put the binoculars away and faced the waiting men—Irwin, Pierce, Sergeant Tilehurst and three corporals. He frowned at them, on the point of asking why the platoon sergeants had not come, as ordered: then remembered that Hedges and Eden were dead, and Sergeant Foster had disappeared, so the senior corporals in those platoons were now acting as platoon sergeants.

As he began to speak, a shell burst immediately overhead. Captain Irwin was hurled forward and sideways to land groaning five feet away on his face. Blood was seeping through the khaki of his left trouser leg in two places, and the white bone showing in another.

"Stretcher-bearers!" the C.S.M. called. " 'Ere, 'urry up, man."

Quentin kneeled quickly beside his second-in-command. The face was twisted in pain, the eyes wide with shock, the mouth distorted. He took his hand and said, "You'll be all right, Steve." Then the stretcher-bearers came, doubled low, for the Germans had suddenly turned their whole attention to the two or three hundred men of the Weald Light Infantry and the East Surrey Regiment who were holding the high ground east of the Selle. It was getting hot and would soon get a great deal hotter.

Quentin began to give out his orders for the withdrawal, his voice rising so that he could be heard above the crack of the bullets and the explosions of the shells.

The sun rose slowly, burning away another morning of mist across the fields of Picardy. The 1st Battalion of the Weald Light Infantry marched steadily southward, as they had all afternoon and all night after the battle. They were marching away from the enemy, and the ranks of every company were thin, for they had not reached the brigade rendezvous at Busigny without losing a few more men to straggling, exhaustion, and the oncoming darkness. The Germans had not interfered at all, and once contact had been broken on the forward slopes, there had been no pursuit—only the endless tramp tramp through the burning afternoon, the heavy twilight, the hot darkness.

Soon after dawn they had passed through a village where there was enough water for every man to refill his water bottle, and take three mouthfuls in his hands, no more, under the strict eyes of the watching officers. There was plenty more water—but no more time.

It was here that C.S.M. Pierce, glancing idly up at a window, had seen a face peering behind half-drawn curtains and shouted, "Foster! What the 'ell . . . ?" He ran into the house and came out a moment later with Sergeant Foster, uniformed, carrying his rifle. Quentin said, "Why did you leave your platoon, Sergeant Foster?"

The sergeant looked right and left, as though seeking a way of escape. At last—"Nothing to say, sir."

Quentin said, "You're a damned disgrace to your uniform. You're under arrest. Leave him his rifle, Sar'nt Major. Have him march with headquarters, and you be his escort until a court martial can be convened."

Then the march continued. The strength of the battalion grew as they began to pick up stragglers, men lost from other battalions, brigades, and divisions in the confusion of the battle and retreat. Most of them swore they were the sole survivors of such and such a battalion, and Quentin answered all such stories with threats of court martial, until his C.S.M. said softly, "You know, sir, I'm afraid other officers are 'earing stories just like that from blokes wearing our cap badge . . . sole survivors."

Quentin realised that Pierce was right. The Wealds had not lost many men to that cause: but then they had not suffered any catastrophe such as those he had heard of in the rumour mills of the long night, meeting other officers, hearing reports of messages sent and received . . . the King's Own Royal Regiment had been ambushed by massed artillery and machine guns and lost 400 men in two minutes . . . the Gordons and Royal Scots had been left to defend the front line to the last, to enable the rest of their division to get clear; and had finally vanished without trace under the German hordes . . . the King's Own Yorkshire Light Infantry—another Minden Regiment—had lost a company in a minute on the open flank over the Selle . . . the artillery had lost over thirty guns, and saved as many from impossibly exposed forward positions, some with German infantry less than two hundred yards away.

The II Corps had faced the enemy, and were retreating. So they had been defeated, albeit by greatly superior numbers. But Quentin knew his men well, and the feeling in the thinned ranks was not of defeat. It was of victory. They were obeying the orders to retreat, but it was with mounting impatience. His company wanted to turn round and give the Germans another, bigger bash on the nose, next time with the numbers a little more even.

Dust rose from a passing battery of 4.5-inch howitzers, followed by a battery of 18-pounders at the trot. Quentin realised that in the excitement over the capture of Sergeant Foster he had forgotten to fill his own water bottle, and he did not know when there would be another chance. He coughed in the dust and swore silently.

The company passed a cottage, a woman bending over low in the patch of front garden, her rear to the passing troops, the raised short skirt revealing the backs of plump white thighs. A voice from the ranks called, "*Bus* with your *pichi,* mum, let's 'ave a *dekko* at the *dusra chiz.*"

Subdued chuckles and Sergeant Tilehurst's sharp voice . . . "You *chuprow,* Smithers."

Silence for a few minutes, tramping in the dust, then, " 'Oo wouldn't be in the navy?"

Pierce this time—"You might as well be, Tompkins, for all the good you are as a soldier."

Quentin trudged on. Tom was probably having a pink gin served to him in the wardroom of H.M.S. *Monmouth* by a white-jacketed Maltese steward. In a few minutes he'd go to his cabin, have a hot shower, and then be served a good dinner—sherry, roast beef, wine, port . . . Compare that with this! Private Tompkins was right!

The C.S.M. was at his elbow. "We'll have to promote at least one corporal to sergeant, sir."

Quentin said, "I was thinking of Conklin, if Mr McDonald agrees."

"Oh no, sir! Begging your pardon, sir, that Corporal Conklin's like my sister Bets—wipes his arse before he shits, begging your pardon, sir. Corporal Walton's the best of our two-stripers now."

Quentin said, "I'll speak to Mr Hedges . . . I mean, Sergeant Jones. I think we did pretty well yesterday, considering."

"We was all right, sir," the C.S.M. said, "remembering only a few of these blokes ever 'eard ball ammunition being fired before Mons. Not

many was in South Africa with us, and since then, there's been, what—
five-minutes scrap one day up by Fort Sandeman in '06, and that's the
lot. They did all right, sir."

Somewhere back in the rear files of the company ahead—C in today's
order of march—the men began humming a tune. After a time Quentin
recognised it: *It's a long way to Tipperary.* His own men took it up,
and the humming condensed, deepened, and throbbed like the sound
of an immense swarm of bees. Ahead of him a lance-corporal stooped to
the grassy verge of the pavé, plucked a poppy and stuck it behind his
chinstrap, shouting to his comrades at large, "Roses for Minden, pop-
pies for Le Cateau, eh, mates?"

The humming grew louder, and behind Quentin a pleasant high
tenor rose with the words—

> *It's a long way to Tipperary, it's a long way to go,*
> *It's a long way to Tipperary, to the sweetest girl I know.*
> *Good bye Piccadilly, farewell Leicester Square,*
> *It's a long, long way to Tipperary, but my heart's right there!*

Daily Telegraph, Friday, August 28, 1914

GERMANS FLEEING FROM RUSSIAN INVADERS
"RUNNING LIKE HARES"
"SCENES OF PANIC"

**From Our Own Correspondent. NEW YORK. Thursday.
Despatches printed here today describe a state of affairs
in East Prussia just as thrilling in detail and as significant
in portent as that which has prevailed in Belgium, but in
this case "the boot is on the other foot." It is agreed on
all sides that the Russian advance proceeded with the
steadiness, the precision, and the giant pressure of a great
steam roller, and the effect upon the Germans, military
and civilian alike, has been awe-inspiring.**

**Thus it happens that the Russians almost everywhere
advanced without much difficulty, rounding up Germans
and chasing them like packs of frightened animals toward
the Vistula. "The Cossacks are coming" is a cry in East
Prussia today sufficient to stampede an entire village, albeit, so far as one can judge from despatches printed here,
the Cossacks are positively lamblike when compared with
certain Uhlans operating in Belgium.**

Cate read the piece again. It was odd that information about the Russians advancing should have to come via New York. One would have thought that the *Telegraph* would have had Our Own Correspondent in St. Petersburg, if not closer to the front. And the tone of the report made him uneasy. He could understand German civilians running like hares from a Russian army, but German soldiers? A German army? It seemed unlikely, unless they were very much outnumbered—which they were, of course. In the very early days of the war, the newspaper strategists had carefully explained that the Germans would leave their eastern borders as thinly defended as possible, and use the troops so saved to knock out France. So what was happening in East Prussia, when you took out the emotional language, was that the campaign was going according to plan—the German plan.

He returned to the paper. A French General de Lacroix had given his estimate of the military situation in the *Temps.* He said,

"*Germany is in danger. She has brought the greater part of her force against us and attacks us with extreme violence because it is imperative for her to remove a portion of her forces which we are fighting and to send them against the Russians. Our northern army must not be content with resistance. It must, even after a retreat, return to the attack. It is only by the offensive that we shall learn when the Germans reduce their forces on their west front.*"

Easier said than done, Cate thought; but the general was probably right. It would be a subtle matter of timing, wherein a day or two might make the difference. It would certainly be a long and hard war if the Germans did manage to knock France out of action within the next week or so, as they obviously intended to. Whether they succeeded would depend finally on General Joffre and the French soldiers . . . and Quentin and his men, too, of course. The Kaiser would live to regret having called them a "contemptible little army."

New York: Friday, August 28, 1914

12 The board of directors of Fairfax, Gottlieb was meeting in the airy board room on the 27th floor of the building on Lower Broadway. Sitting beside his father, his chair a little drawn back so that he would not appear to be at the table itself, Johnny Merritt waited, note pad and pencil in his lap, for the present discussion to end. His father, as chairman of the board, was listening to a final explanation from the director with the most experience in the subject: Johnny, as his private secretary, would record what his father had recommended, and other points of interest; the secretary to the board, sitting at the far end from his father, would make the official record of the meeting, the voting, and the decisions.

The speaker finished and Stephen Merritt waited a moment, stroking his chin, before making his recommendation. The directors accepted it unanimously. Johnny made his note.

Then Stephen said, "The next item is the proposal to go into the manufacture of commercial—freight carrying—road vehicles in England. As you will see in the notes to the agenda, it is proposed to form a limited liability company with Mr Richard Rowland, of Hedlington, England. We would own the majority and controlling equity interest. The rest of the common stock would be distributed between Mr Rowland and a British merchant bank, in proportions to be agreed . . . As you know, for some time now we have been seeking a suitable opportunity to invest in the automobile business. We have discussed what we are looking for—good management, plentiful skilled labour, an existing network of good roads. Britain meets all those requirements, and I believe Mr Rowland to be at least a competent manager—though, if we approve the agreement in principle, I would propose to go over to England and thoroughly investigate Mr Rowland's production plans and ideas, before proceeding further. Let's have some discussion on the general idea, though. Morgan?"

Morgan L. Fairfax II, president of the bank, said, "I'd like to hear some other opinions first."

"George?"

George Neidorf, a railroad president by profession, said, "I have been for the idea of investing in automobile manufacture all along . . . and in Europe. But is this the time?"

"You mean the war?"

Neidorf nodded. "Yes. We are looking for a country with a growing economy, where increasing prosperity will enable a higher proportion of small business men to buy the vehicles we will make. But the war is going to bankrupt all the nations in Europe if it goes on for more than a month or two."

"It won't," another director said. "The Germans will be in Paris in another three days. By this time next week, it will all be over."

"That I doubt," said a third, "and England may fight on, in any case."

"What with? Their army will be killed or captured en masse as soon as the French surrender, and then what can they do, however many battleships they have?"

Johnny longed to speak up: England would not be defeated, would not give up—he knew it in his deepest being; but he said nothing, only making a note on his pad.

Neidorf said, "At least we must all agree, Stephen, that the situation looks grim for Britain. Is this the moment to consider investing in *anything* there?"

"No," said two directors simultaneously.

Then no one spoke for a time until Stephen Merritt said, "I am, in principle, for the proposal. I do not myself believe that France will fall so quickly . . . nor Britain. If the war continues, there will be a great demand for commercial vehicles to carry munitions and supplies to the fighting fronts. Roads can not be put out of commission so easily as railroads. Yet I agree that the risks are severe, at this moment."

One of the directors said, "I think we should definitely keep out of Europe until the war's over."

Stephen said, "The situation is so fluid that perhaps we would be unwise to make a firm decision now. I move that we reconsider this proposal at the next board meeting a month from now. By then we should have a much clearer notion of the future course of events."

"Second," George Neidorf said.

The motion was carried 7–2.

Later, in his father's large office overlooking Upper New York Bay, the Statue of Liberty greenish on her island, Staten Island ferry boats dragging steam trails across the dancing waves, Johnny said, "I think the board is making a mistake."

Stephen said, "I'm not sure. We are really in the dark, but there was no alternative. If I hadn't suggested the postponement, the motion would have been to drop the whole idea, and it would have carried handily . . . We can afford to wait and it is the wisest thing to do."

"They're fighting and dying over there," Johnny said, "while we sell them munitions, and make money out of their misery."

"Their folly, too, Johnny. It's not our war, and pray God it never becomes so."

Johnny said nothing. During the war's twenty-eight days he had come to think that it was every civilised country's war, particularly America's, to help defeat the jackbooted Huns and their power-mad Kaiser; but he knew it was pointless to say so. His father had heard his views, many times.

The Heskeths' house in Nyack was barely two hundred yards downstream from the Merritts', on the river front. The Heskeths were giving the dinner and dance, and they had invited Carol Ruttledge, of course. She was on Johnny's arm now, as they strolled slowly across the grass below the big house. The moon was half full, the Hudson gurgling softly at the pilings by the boathouse. A dozen other couples were walking the lawn, washed by the ragtime music and electric light streaming down from the open windows and doors of the house. Carol spoke little, just enjoying the evening, and his company. She was a nice girl. He only wished everyone would not assume that because he often danced with her, and had known her since grade school, he was madly in love with her, and therefore push them into each other's company at every opportunity. He liked her; she was a good dancer, pretty, shapely, kind, and reasonably intelligent; and her parents were very rich. He just did not love her.

The lights and the water and the music reminded him of Henley and the Phyllis Court Ball. That had been another night like this, even though that English river was so quiet and small, hardly more than a creek, the music different, the trees so heavy, the grass so green, and everywhere, intangible, a pervasive sense of history. And Stella.

Some of her family would be in the war already—the navy commander who'd been walking the towpath with the boys—and Stella had told him that another uncle was a major in the army. Perhaps the major had been at Mons, or that other battle two or three days ago, at Le Cateau. Perhaps the commander had been in the sea fight off Heligoland, which was in this evening's papers. Perhaps one or both of them was already dead.

Carol Ruttledge said, "What are you thinking of, Johnny?"

"The war," he said briefly. "Let's go inside. I have to dance this one with my sister."

"Don't sound so gloomy about it," she said, laughing. "Lots of young men would jump at the chance to dance with Betty."

"I know, but she's my sister."

He straightened his white tie, patted his stiff shirt front into place and, having left Carol with her mother, went to find Betty. She was in one of the front rooms, sitting with two young men, a glass of white wine cupped in her hand.

"My dance," Johnny said, holding out his hand. He heard the jazz band strike up a ragtime twostep.

"You don't really want to dance with me. Sit down and have a rest. You look as if Carol wore you out."

Johnny poured himself a glass and sat in an easy chair opposite the two young men, his sister at his side.

One of the young men said, "We were talking about the war. Betty says you're all for us going in."

Johnny knew them both slightly. The speaker was Carl Zinnemann, the other Floyd Botsford. Zinnemann was a senior at Princeton, Botsford two years out of Columbia.

He said, "Yes, I do. We have special ties with England—and Scotland and Ireland—the roots of our country are there, our constitution, law, history . . ."

"Not my roots," Zinnemann said.

"It's a war for civilisation," Johnny said.

Zinnemann said, "I think the Germans have as much civilisation as the British . . . Beethoven, Goethe, Wagner, Liszt, Schiller—"

"Attila, the Kaiser's hero, Bismarck . . ."

Zinnemann flushed. "Bismarck was a sight greater statesman than any Britisher. If he were still alive and in power the war would have been over already. As it is, it won't last another week."

"It wouldn't be over in a week if we went in."

"Why not? What can we do?" Zinnemann sneered. "It would take us at least a year to get a big enough army raised and trained. People like you could go off individually and fight for the Limeys, but how many of you are there? Not more than there are of us, who'd go and join the German army tomorrow, if we thought we could get over there in time."

Johnny felt his neck getting red. His fists were doubled. He said, "I knew you had German ancestry, Zinnemann, but I didn't know you admired the baby-killing nun-raping Huns who are waging this war."

Zinnemann was on his feet. "You take that back . . ."

Betty jumped up and grabbed his arm. "Sit down, Carl! And you apologise, Johnny!"

Johnny said, "I will not apologise. I will be at the boathouse for the next quarter of an hour if your German friend wants to tackle someone stronger than a Belgian nun." He stalked out.

They parked the Cadillac at the Erie railroad station in Tuxedo and set out on the trail that led north-east out of the village and up the slopes of Pine Hill. It was a hot day and soon they were both perspiring freely as they climbed through the oak and rhododendron forests, Johnny wearing knickerbockers, knee stockings, stout woodsman's boots, a cotton shirt open at the neck, and a light jacket. His sister wore a grey skirt several inches shorter than was customary for a young woman of her age, a white blouse, and also woodsman's boots. After an hour and a half's hard going, saying little, they crossed Black Ash Swamp and reached the summit of Tom Jones Mountain. They flung themselves down on the exposed glacier-scored rock, Betty fanning herself with her straw hat.

She said, "Next time we come here, Johnny, I'm going to wear breeches, like you. I swear it."

"They'll throw you in the stocks in Tuxedo," he said.

"A girl I know at Smith went mountain climbing in Switzerland last summer with her parents. She told me the women climbers there—the good ones—wear breeches and stockings, and a long skirt over them. Then, as soon as they're out of sight of the village, they take off the skirt, leave it hidden under a rock, and put it on again on their way back."

Johnny laughed. He'd seen one or two musical comedies where actresses appeared as dashing hussars or the like, and very attractive they looked too, in a rather indecent way. But ordinary women, in trousers . . . he couldn't get used to the idea. Next thing, someone would say that men ought to wear skirts . . . well, Highlanders did, of a sort.

The Kanawauke Lakes spread out below, the water glistening slate blue in the shade of the densely leaved trees round the banks. Little

Long Pond lay directly under them, Lake Sebago farther south. The ridges of the Ramapos undulated blue green in the heat haze to the west, the isolated hump of High Tor blocked out the Westchester Hills to the east.

Johnny said, "It was good of you to come with me today, Bet. I desperately needed to get out, and have a good sweat, but if I'd come alone, I might have jumped off a cliff."

She said, "You haven't said a word about what happened last night. You don't look as though you had a fight."

"We didn't," he said. "Zinnemann turned up at the boathouse ten minutes later, but by then I realised I shouldn't have said what I did, so I said I'd fight if he wanted to, but first I would say I was sorry. He seemed glad . . . I'm bigger than he is! Let's get on."

She held out her hand and he pulled her to her feet. His own hair was dark brown, hers much lighter, her eyes dark blue, the skin of her face marked with a few fading tomboy freckles. She was five-foot-six, lithe and slim, small bosomed. She had a lovely smile, and he had always been very fond of her; in fact, now that she was nineteen and would soon be someone's wife, he knew he would feel jealous of her husband—for a time at least. And if the husband mistreated her, there'd be trouble.

She walked in front of him along the rocky trail leading northwards over the grey rock of the Hudson Highlands. She threw back over her shoulder, "Do you really think the British and French are so much better than the Germans and Austrians, Johnny?"

He did not answer until he had time to collect his thoughts. Then he said, "None of the countries is perfect, including us. But I really think Germany wanted the war. She already has the most powerful army in the world, and she means to have the most powerful navy, and then she'd be master of the world . . . including us."

Betty said, "Could they beat us?"

He said, "I don't know. But if they came on at once, after beating the French, we would be nowhere near ready."

"But . . . would the British let them?"

"I don't think so. But then we'd depend for our existence, eventually, on the British navy. If we go in now, we'll be playing our proper part."

She said, "Did you see in the morning paper that the Germans have won a big battle over the Russians somewhere in the east?"

"Yes. And in the west the Germans are only thirty miles from Paris. I hardly slept all night, Betty. I was thinking . . ." He stopped.

After a few minutes Betty said, "About what?" They had started up Hogencamp Mountain, and the trail was not easy to find in places.

He said, "What I ought to do . . . I've thought a lot about this war and I really do believe it's a war for civilisation, as I said to Zinnemann. If that's true, we should get into it, or give up any pretence of being civilised."

Another long pause: then she said, "But we aren't in it. And Mr Wilson's swearing we never will be."

"Then it's up to each of us as individuals. I'm thinking of going to England, to join the British army."

She stopped so suddenly that he ran into her, treading on the heel of her boot—"Johnny! You're going to run away to the war?"

He said, "Go on, Betty!" They started forward. "It's not running away. I'm over twenty-one, and no one can stop me. I've been working in Dad's bank for a month now, and I suppose it's interesting . . . or could be when I learn more about it—but Great Scot, I can't keep my attention on bonds and debentures and percentages when men are dying so that we can live in comfort, and hold our elections, and bring up our children the way we want."

"Are any of the Cates in it yet?" she asked.

She was not teasing him, and he answered the question as seriously as it had been put. "None that I know. Her uncle Tom Rowland, the navy man, will be. I had a letter from Stella yesterday. She's joined something called the Voluntary Aid Detachments, and is going to do work in hospitals. You know what I think of her, but what I feel about the war has nothing to do with that."

"I know," she said, still serious.

"I'm not thinking of going just for her sake. It would be kind of silly, wouldn't it, to get myself killed for her, personally, when I want to marry her."

"You really do? You've never said it right out before."

"I do. I must see her again, and spend more time with her, so that we can get to know each other better—but I'm certain. Dad said I'd soon forget her—there are many other girls in the world, he said . . . and I suppose that's why everyone's been throwing Carol Ruttledge at my head . . . but, heavens, Betty, Stella has just possessed me. I dream of her, of being with her, talking to her, dancing with her. I can't think of anyone else."

"Poor Johnny," she said; and then, a little later, "Lucky Stella."

They relapsed into a close silence; crossed Hogencamp, went down through the Lemon Squeezer and rested and ate sandwiches by Island Pond. They knew the pond well. In fall they had seen it circled by the

flames of maple and dogwood, in winter by snow and ice and the white
columns of the birch; and this day they saw two beavers at work on
their house in the centre of it; and three deer—two does and a fawn—
drinking at the edge; and as they watched the deer Betty said softly,
"I'm not questioning you, Johnny, but don't you feel that this . . . all
this, all over our country . . . is worth preserving too, as it is . . . untouched by war, its young men here to enjoy it, and later, their children?"

Johnny found his voice hoarse, as he answered her: and he was on
the edge of tears—"Of course, I do. But—at the price of other young
men's lives? Foreigners' lives? If we are to keep this, it's up to *us* to do
it. It's a matter of honour."

She took his hand and squeezed it, kissed him on the cheek, and
whispered, "Johnny, Johnny, why can't I be a man, and come with
you?"

Then they strode quickly down to Arden, long familiar to their family, and Averell himself drove them back to their car at Tuxedo.

As they started off, Harriman waving to them from the station yard,
Betty said, "When are you going to tell Dad?"

Johnny said, "Tonight."

The house was built into the slope, so the basement den and games
room had windows and doors opening out onto the lawn. The three of
them were in there now, the windows open, moths fluttering against
the screens, katydids noisily warning of early frost, the moon high over
the Hudson. Johnny's father paced up and down, hands behind his
back. Betty sat in a big chair, her feet curled up under her, a magazine
face down on her lap. Johnny stood by the fireplace, resting his elbow
on the mantel: his Harvard oar slanted across the brick wall above the
fireplace behind him.

Stephen Merritt said, "While you were hiking, I telephoned Sarnoff,
the cable man, in New York. The battle in East Germany seems to be
over, disastrously for the Russians."

"That's what the Germans say, I suppose," Johnny said. "Has there
been any news from the Russians?"

"I don't know. But think what it might mean! If the Russians have
indeed been heavily defeated, and the Germans do reach Paris within
the week . . . the war will be over! What point will there then be in
you going to England?"

Johnny said, "I don't think the British will give up. And it takes
more than one defeat to knock the Russians out. Napoleon learned
that. They'll just keep on retreating until they are ready to turn again.

And the British will always be at the Germans' back, starving them of all supplies from overseas. And I think there ought to be at least one American over there to show the Britishers that we don't all think of nothing but our profits."

Betty noted her brother's tight jaw; he was obstinate—always had been, and sometimes hot tempered; but usually very sensible. Their father obviously didn't think so now.

"I am not thinking of profits," Stephen said, flushing, "I am trying to use common sense—which you seem to have thrown out of the window."

He walked back and forth a few more times across the pine floor, scattered here and there with Navajo rugs. He stopped, facing his son. "Look, Johnny, take a month. It's August 30th today. If I'm right . . . if all the news is pointing the right way . . . the war will be over within two weeks. If I'm wrong . . . if some miracle saves the British and French before the end of September—then go by all means. In fact, well . . ." he stopped and ended, "How about it?"

Johnny looked at his sister. She said, "I think Dad's right, Johnny. However soon you go, you will never get to France soon enough to help in *this* battle . . . but if the British and French do survive, they'll need all the help they can get, afterwards."

"All right," Johnny said suddenly, "I'll wait till September 30th."

Stephen said, "Good man!" He shook his son's hand warmly. Betty jumped up and threw her arms round his neck, the magazine fluttering to the floor. "Oh, I'm so pleased!" She stood back. "And when you do go to England, I'm coming with you. Life's too exciting these days to moulder away in Northampton."

"You'll do no such thing!" Stephen said indignantly.

She pouted. "I want to meet this Guy Rowland Johnny has been talking about. He has one blue eye and one brown, is very good at cricket, and has his nerve. And he has a face like a hawk."

Johnny said, "He's only a schoolboy, Bet. Isn't that called cradle robbing?"

Stephen said, "You're going to finish your four years at Smith, young lady. This country needs educated women just as much as educated men."

She tossed her head. "I could learn more useful things in England. They are going to need women for all sorts of positions they've never been in before—if they survive this next month."

Stephen paced up and down his spacious office as, a month ago, he had paced up and down the big den in Nyack, trying to persuade Johnny not to rush off to England. Now Johnny sat at the desk, making notes as Stephen talked. It was September 25th, and the board meeting was due to start in an hour.

Stephen said, "Gentlemen, last time we met there was a big battle taking place on the Russian front. We now know that it was the Battle of Tannenberg, a disastrous defeat for the Russians. They had 30,000 killed and 92,000 captured. The Russian army commander, Samsonov, committed suicide. But . . ."

"How many did the Germans lose, Dad? Shouldn't you say that, too?"

"Right . . . something over 10,000 killed and wounded. But the Russian threat had seemed large enough, before the battle, for the Germans to remove two army corps from the Western Front and ship them by train to reinforce their general in the east—Hindenburg. Those two corps did not arrive in time for the battle of Tannenberg, and they were not, of course, present to fight on the Western Front. Their absence was one of the factors that resulted in what the French are now calling the Miracle of the Marne, and . . ."

"A little slower, Dad. I'm not Miss Levinson, you know. All right."

Stephen said, "From the outbreak of the war until September 5th, the British, Belgians, and French either retreated, tried unsuccessfully to advance, or, as at Le Cateau and several other places, fought brief delaying actions. But in Berlin the Chief of the German General Staff, Moltke, kept receiving reports of huge German victories, which were in fact imaginary, or at least exaggerated."

"Dad, what about putting in here what *The New York Times* correspondent in Berlin wrote—that the more sober Germans were asking, 'Where are the captured guns?' There were some, he said, but not enough to justify the talk of smashing victories."

"Good idea. Ready? The Allies were indeed in the process of being overwhelmed—but it had not happened yet, and Moltke made the fatal mistake of thinking that it had. Confident that final victory was close at hand, he sent the two army corps to the east. He also weakened von Kluck's First Army, the outer end of the greet wheeling movement that was to encircle Paris; so much so that von Kluck turned inward across the front of Paris, instead of sweeping behind it."

He walked to the war map hung on the wall, and pointed—"The army next to his, von Bülow's Second, also swung farther inward. These movements left a gap between the German First and Second Armies, and they exposed von Kluck's right to attack from the garrison of Paris, and from a new French army—the Sixth—recently formed to the west."

"I'll take this map through to the Board Room," Johnny said. "There isn't one in there."

"Right. Slowly the opportunities were seen, and the movements necessary to take advantage of the situation were ordered. The French Sixth Army attacked von Kluck in flank. General Gallieni sent out the Paris troops, some of them in a fleet of a thousand commandeered taxicabs. The British, moving cautiously at first for fear of walking into a giant trap, turned and advanced into the gap between von Kluck and von Bülow. Farther east two more French Armies advanced . . . crossed the Morins, reached the Marne—here—and crossed it."

"Paris was saved," Johnny murmured.

"And a long war assured. Russia has been severely wounded, but not killed. The German strategic plan has failed. The French casualties have been staggering—nearly a million so far. There can be no quick, final victory, anywhere."

They sat round the same board table, high above Broadway and the Upper Bay. They sat in the same places. Stephen Merritt faced the directors, all swivelled round in their chairs to look at him and the map, and ended his summary: "There can be no quick, final victory, anywhere." He sat down, and after taking a drink of water, said, "Now, we must take up the business we postponed at our last meeting—the question of investing in the production of commercial automobiles in Great Britain, specifically with Mr Richard Rowland . . . What's your position now, Morgan?"

Morgan Fairfax said, "I don't know how the Germans managed to throw away their opportunity, but it seems obvious that they have. Now the battle lines have almost reached the sea. There's war from Switzerland to the North Sea!"

Another director said, "I agree with you, Stephen. I see no chance of quick victory for either side now . . . though of course I do not pretend to be a military man."

Neidorf said, "The longer it lasts, the more need there will be for commercial vehicles. As a railroad man I hate them—they'll be the death of us one day—but they're here to stay and they're profitable. I think we should go ahead."

One after another the other directors agreed. Stephen said, "Good. You'll be glad to know, I imagine, that your decision will have the approval of Mr Morgan and Mr Mellon. I spoke to both of them yesterday on this matter. They are confident that the Allies will defeat the Central Powers, though it will take a long time, unless Germany quickly sees the light, and gets what terms she can, while she still has a huge army. I believe that that is what Mr Wilson is even now urging them to do, while simultaneously pressing the British and French to accept any reasonable terms for ending the conflict. I shall word this motion so that we are committed to investigate the possibility of producing commercial automobiles in Great Britain, working through a British company to be formed there. I propose to go over myself . . . but how much are we willing to put into this—maximum—if we eventually go ahead?"

Fairfax said, "That will depend in part on what you recommend, Stephen. But a couple of years ago Studebaker bought E.M.F. for five million, and that was a successful, profitable company. I suggest you should be thinking in terms of three million dollars or so to get this company started—from us, that is—and perhaps two million more from the British bankers. Later, we could, of course, put more in."

Neidorf said, "I agree. We're not actually committing money if we say we're thinking in terms of three million—we're giving Stephen information he's going to need."

Stephen said, "I propose to get the General Motors people to give me a production expert, to come with me. One of the men they stole from Ford, who knows production-line technique. G.M. owes us a favour—they'll do it."

The directors agreed, and so it was carried.

Half an hour later, in the office of the Chairman of the Board, Johnny burst out, "Is the President really trying to get the British and French to go easy on the Germans, if they ask for peace?"

"I believe so," his father answered.

"I hope they don't go for it," Johnny said. "After all the suffering the Germans have caused, they've got to be made to pay."

His father sat down heavily, looking up at him. "With young men's lives, Johnny? Women's happiness, children's futures? Cities, churches, factories? All these must be weighed in the balance. What have you decided to do?"

"I still want to go over and join the British army."

"You're not cut out to be a soldier, Johnny, especially not a British soldier. Oh, I know you have the belly for it. You want to help the British, right? They have plenty of young men of the right sort to officer their armies. And, of course, their navy. But they don't produce enough automobiles . . . trucks. So come over with me, and learn something of the business. I can only stay a month or so, but then I'll leave you behind, with the production man, as our representatives with Rowland . . . if we decide to go ahead, that is."

After a long silence Johnny said, "It seems pretty tame when I've been talking big about going off to fight."

His father said seriously, "If this war goes on as long as I think, and now fear, that it will—you too may be fighting, in time. If not from choice, from necessity. Let the war come to you, Johnny, if you can, rather than going out to find it. You'll be close to Stella, and that's what you really want, isn't it?"

"Yes," Johnny said slowly, "up to a point. But I also want to keep my self-respect. I'll go with you, and work with you for a time, but if after a few months over there, living among a people at war, I feel that I have to fight with them, I'll join up."

"Good enough, Johnny," his father said, holding out his hand.

The New York Times, Friday, October 9, 1914

THE DOOR OF OPPORTUNITY

In the long periods of trade dullness and slow recuperation that follow upon the world's wars, the talk of bankers and financial writers about repairing the wastes of war has a doleful sound in the ears of the great and small captains of industry. According to all economic experience the period of trade arrest and depression following upon this war will be unusually prolonged, it will be a severe trial of the patience and the stability of the world's men of business. We shall suffer with the rest, for neutrals as well as belligerents must join in the task of repair. But there are very good reasons for the belief that, if we will, we can materially lighten the burden upon our industries and can put ourselves in the fortunate position of enjoying a good deal of prosperity at a time when the European nations will be straining at the hard task the war will impose upon them. It depends upon ourselves whether we occupy this exceptional position or take our place at the treadmill with the rest.

Our opportunity is further pointed out by Mr Schwab's order for $5,000,000 worth of motor trucks for the Allies; by the figures of the enormous decrease in England's exportation of cotton manufactures, by reports from Louisiana that the sugar planters are again cheerful because of the demand for their product due to the cutting off of the supplies of German beet sugar. It is unnecessary to multiply instances.

It depends upon ourselves. There is nothing under-handed, there is nothing unfair or ungenerous in reach-ing out to possess ourselves of a larger share of the trade world. There will be great needs to be supplied and for a long time our commercial competitors across the Atlantic will be unable to supply them. It is our opportunity, it is the open door for the United States.

It is a question of courage and capacity. If we have lost both the outlook is gloomy indeed. If we prove that we are self-reliant and resourceful we can beyond doubt take a greater place in the world's markets than we ever before filled and profit generously by the venture.

Johnny Merritt looked up at his father. "Have you seen the editorial, Dad?"

Stephen nodded, continuing to read his own copy of the newspaper.

Johnny said, "That's the most transparent exhortation to make money out of other people's misfortunes that I've ever read. We really ought to be ashamed of ourselves."

His father lowered his paper. "Not ashamed, I think, Johnny . . . sad, perhaps, that these are the hard facts of economics. Are you sug-gesting that we should *not* sell the Allies motor trucks? Refuse to take Uruguay's wool crops for processing—which used to go to England? Re-fuse to sell cane sugar to replace the beet sugar?"

"We'd have some moral justification if we were also doing our share of fighting," Johnny said. "As it is, I feel that any money we make, any prosperity we enjoy, will be tainted with blood—the blood of people who are fighting our battle."

His father stood up, folding his paper. "We sail in a week, Johnny. It may look different from the other side, to both of us. Meantime, whom do you think will take the World Series? It starts today, re-member."

"The Athletics," Johnny said, brightening in spite of himself. "The Braves don't believe they can beat them, so they won't."

At sea: Monday, September 14, 1914

13   "Bear off forra'rd!" the midshipman in command of the pinnace called. "Full ahead!" The boat chugged out of the lee of *Monmouth*'s wall-like steel side, and into the open water off Santa Catherina. Tom Rowland, sitting in the sternsheets, did not look back. The formalities had been observed. Captain Brandt had stood nearby when he went over the side, between the quartermaster, boatswain, and sideboys. He had saluted the captain, and been saluted in turn by the man who was taking his place. Brandt had acknowledged his salute, and as soon as Tom was safely over the side, turned back to pacing the quarterdeck. He was a good sailor, a good captain, and an easier disciplinarian than many post captains, Tom thought. It was a pity that he did not like Tom. They had served together once before, and during that battleship commission of ten years ago Brandt had developed a deep dislike to Tom, founded on what, Tom had no idea. It was just something a man had to live with—all men, in all walks of life; but in the navy, when in the normal course of events the two were likely to be thrown together again, at any time, to spend three or four years cramped against each other in the steel hull of a warship—it was hard.

He breathed deeply. He was free. His two suitcases were at his feet . . . thin smoke from *Monmouth*'s funnels drifted away on the trade wind, the sun shone, the pinnace plunged and lurched, for the waves were high even in this sheltered anchorage. And there, four cables ahead, *Penrith* heaved and jerked at her anchor. He had known her previous commander only by name. He was sorry that the man had been attacked by cerebral malaria; sorrier for the sake of his family that he had died a week ago. But it was pure good luck that her next senior officer was a junior lieutenant commander, not yet in the zone for promotion; and that *Monmouth* had a lieutenant commander well inside the zone, and a favourite of Brandt's; and that *Penrith's* Captain Leach was a friend of Tom's . . . The exchange had been authorised, and here was his new ship—not his, but John Leach's, and Leach was a good man, cheerful and wise, beloved of the lower deck. Any ship of John Leach's was a taut ship, and a happy one—a combination not always easy to achieve. She was a Guzz ship, the crew half West Countrymen, the other half the ubiquitous cockneys, Scots, and Irish.

There she tossed, a light cruiser of the old Grey Funnel Line, built in 1911—long, low, 25 knots designed maximum speed, no armour but some protective plating, a narrow knifelike bow, a turret mounting two 6-inch guns on the foredeck, then a marked step down under the bridge to the after deck, five turrets on each side, each mounting one 4-inch gun . . . four tall, raked funnels, the middle two with three white stripes painted round near the top. The 6-inch guns could hit at 11,200 yards, the 4-inch at 9,800 . . . but in a seaway the turrets on the main deck were liable to be flooded if the ship rolled more than a few degrees. She carried 375 men and displaced 4,800 tons.

He could see the officer of the watch on the quarterdeck now, telescope under his arm. Now another officer was appearing from below. He counted four gold stripes on his sleeve . . . good old John, coming out himself to greet his new commander!

"Slow ahead!" the midshipman commanded. The pinnace came round slowly, its heavy motion easing as it came under *Penrith's* lee. A sideboy was on the gangway, and the boat's coxswain handed him Tom's gear. The midshipman saluted, and Tom said, "Thanks. Good luck." He stepped lightly across the small rising, falling gap onto the gangway's platform. Behind him he heard the midshipman order, "Bear off! Full ahead."

He was up the gangway, at the top, saluting the quarterdeck. The Officer of the Watch was formally reporting his arrival to the captain, but John Leach was coming forward, hand outstretched. "Tom! Welcome aboard. I am really delighted to see you . . . and have you as commander."

"Thank you, sir. So am I."

September 28
The wind whistled through and round and over and under the thin bridge plating as though it had not existed. Wind was the predominant

impression Tom had of Punta Arenas, the small Chilean town and
port on the west shore of the Magellan Strait—the southernmost town
in the world. The wind had been blowing when they arrived in the
morning, hot in pursuit of the elusive German cruiser *Dresden*, rumoured to be in the South Atlantic. It had blown all day, while boats
scurried to and fro—taking officers ashore to receive and send despatches from the Admiralty via the local British consul, for wireless
could not yet reach London from ships anywhere at sea, nor vice versa.
From London, signals went by cable to the consuls, thence by land line
to such wireless stations as were in British hands, or were permitted by
their governments to accept messages in cipher—messages arranging for
coaling, collection of mail, buying stores and hardware to replace sea
damage . . . Then, at dusk, when Captain Leach came back from the
conference on board H.M.S. *Good Hope*, the armoured cruiser which
wore the flag of Rear Admiral Sir Christopher Cradock, commanding
all British naval forces in the South American region, he had immediately summoned Tom and the navigating officer, Lieutenant de Saumarez, to his day cabin. As soon as they were seated round the big table
Captain Leach had said, "You remember on the 25th—three days ago—
we met the liner *Ortega?*"

"Carrying French reservists from Oceania back to France, wasn't
she, sir?" Tom said.

"Yes. Her captain told the admiral that on the 18th—ten days ago—
he'd met *Dresden* in the Pacific, but managed to escape by entering
neutral waters. We didn't know where *Dresden* had gone after that,
but probably to join von Spee in the Pacific, so we set off after her."

"And didn't catch a glimpse," Tom said.

"Not unnaturally," the captain said, "because she's been sighted
since in Orange Bay. The consul told the admiral this morning. How
far is Orange Bay, pilot?"

"Over three hundred miles, by the channels, south-east," de Saumarez answered without hesitation. "It's one of the bigger bays north
of Horn Island . . . but there are hundreds of them—bays, sounds,
channels, inlets . . ."

"The admiral has ordered our squadron to sail for Orange Bay at
0300, local time, in the order *Flag—Glasgow—Penrith—Monmouth—
Otranto*. No sound, especially from the anchor cables. No lights whatever until *Flag* puts on her station-keeping lights, then all ships follow
suit. Moonrise is at 0307. Speed, 16 knots, which will bring us to the
mouth of the Magdalena Channel at first light."

"Thank heaven for that, sir," de Saumarez muttered. "The channels are a nightmare to navigate at night. Doing it gave me grey hairs, four years ago."

"The admiral is well aware of that, pilot," Leach said a little testily. His eyes were red-rimmed, and underscored by dark circles. The ship had been running in heavy seas for a week before reaching Punta Arenas, the crew at readiness all day and with all guns manned at night. The captain had spent twenty hours a day on the bridge, for ten days in succession . . .

At 3 a.m., the light of the crescent moon thrown faintly up from under the horizon onto the scudding cloud patches, the squadron sailed—dark, silent, the sea a whitish blur, capped by whiter patches, shimmering, moving. The departure had not been seen or heard by any of the many German sympathisers living in the town. Half an hour after sailing, the flagship lit her dim station lights, and the others followed suit. Leach and Tom were on the bridge with de Saumarez. Tom said quietly, "Why don't you have a kip, sir, until we reach the Magdalena? This is easy . . . comparatively."

Leach hesitated, muttering to himself, "The Strait's wide enough. The guns are manned. God, I'm tired, Tom. All right. Pilot, you too, two hours' shut-eye. Tom, you have the ship until the Magdalena. I'll be in my sea cabin."

"Aye, aye, sir."

The captain disappeared, followed unwillingly by the navigator. Tom knew how they felt; they were doing a brave thing, especially John Leach, for a captain could never pass on or share his responsibility, and the Magellan Strait, though wide, was not an easy waterway even in the best of conditions—which, according to all the sea lore Tom had ever heard, never existed. But it was also a wise thing, for ahead lay 'the channels,' 140 nautical miles of twisting waterways, strewn with islets, reefs, and rocks, unlighted, shaken by sudden waves and cyclonic wulliwas. Both captain and pilot would need all their skill for that stretch, before they could relax again in the wider passage of the Beagle Channel.

It began to snow. Tom huddled deeper into his greatcoat, and pulled the thick wool scarf a little higher round his neck. Under the greatcoat he was wearing his cold weather serge uniform and two thick sweaters. His hands were encased in two pairs of wool gloves, and his feet in two pairs of thick socks.

He rocked back and forth on his feet to the roll of the ship, watching the moonlit bulk of *Glasgow* ahead. He gauged the apparent size of her and the relative positions of the station lights, for those were the only ways he had of judging her distance ahead, and hence whether *Penrith* was keeping station.

It was a relief to be working with a trained and practised crew. Three-quarters of *Monmouth's* lower deck hands had been reservists, posted into the ship after her hurried refit. The flagship was in even worse state, with over 90 percent reservists—but *Penrith* and *Glasgow* were in the middle of commissions started long ago, in peace time; and both had been on foreign stations at the outbreak of war, where reservists could not easily be sent; so neither carried more than a handful of them.

Glasgow seemed to be a fraction smaller than she should be, and he said, "Up ten revs."

Sub-lieutenant Mountjoy, the officer of the watch, standing the other side of the quartermaster at the wheel, repeated the order, then leaned forward and spoke down the voicepipe to the engine room. "Up ten revolutions."

The tinny voice from the engine room came back, reconfirming. Mountjoy said, "*Glasgow's* turning to starboard, sir."

"I see it, Sub." He waited, his eyelids half closed against the stinging snow, until *Penrith* had reached the same position at which *Glasgow* had made her turn, then ordered, "Port ten."

"Port ten, sir."

"Ten degrees of port helm on, sir."

Tom waited till the turn was nearly completed, and then ordered, "Starboard five!"

"Starboard five, sir!"

"Five degrees of starboard helm on, sir!"

"Midships!"

"Midships, sir."

"Steady!"

"Steady, sir . . . Course north 160 west."

Penrith steadied on the new course. The wind slashed deeper through all Tom's clothes. The six men on the bridge were frozen into their duties, their positions. At the after end two seamen messengers were shrunk into themselves for warmth, far apart, one on the port and one on the starboard side. Tom glanced back, as he did every few minutes in a long-learned reflex, to check the ship astern . . . no undue sparks from the funnel, nothing amiss with the outline of masts and boats and guns, nothing unusual about the way the sea ran along the barely seen flanks of the ship.

Glasgow was closer. "Down ten revs!"

The order was passed in the prescribed ritual sequence. No one moved.

"Port five . . . Midships . . . Up ten revs! . . . You're wandering all over the channel, quartermaster! Watch your steering, man! Port five! Midships!"

A wardroom steward came up with a mug of hot cocoa for Tom and another for Mountjoy. With Tom's permission, the boatswain's mate sent one of the messengers to the galley for cocoa for all the bridge watchkeepers. The quartermaster was relieved and went below, yawning and rubbing his eyes. An hour passed, the quartermaster was relieved again, and also the officer of the watch. Tom stood at his post, his lids grown heavy and his eyes beginning to smart. His feet were aching with cold. Every now and then spray hurled across the bridge as *Penrith* plunged into an unusually big wave. The wind blew from the south-west at 30 to 35 knots, without cease. Snow draped the whole forecastle and the 6-inch turret almost directly below the bridge.

He had received a letter from Dick Yeoman while at Santa Catherina, just before transferring to *Penrith*. The letter had been written early in August. Dick hoped he was well, told of a good day's sail in West Bay, and regretted that Tom would not be able to join them this summer—unless the Huns caved in very quickly: did Tom think they would? It was an innocent letter, but it had made Tom uneasy. Was young Yeoman of the same persuasion that Guy said Russell Wharton was? Or was he just innocent? Could he, Tom, have imagined what he was sure had happened in the flat? He wrenched his mind away . . . but it would not go far. What show was Wharton in now? Something better than that second rate collection of music hall clichés he'd taken the boys to, he hoped. The very night he'd been ordered to join *Monmouth*. Wharton had looked perfectly normal, not like what they said he was. But what *were* they supposed to look like? Oscar Wilde had been a big, powerful man, and . . .

"Sir! Commander!"

He looked up and realised at once what Skyring, the officer of the watch, had been about to say: *Glasgow* was closer than she should be.

"Down ten revs!" he snapped.

The moon was dim, and *Glasgow* no more than a faint blur. He eyed the shape closely. *Penrith* had only been half a cable out of station, and slowing fast now: no danger of a collision.

Skyring went back to his post. Tom said nothing. In this sort of situation you couldn't take your attention off the ship for a moment—your whole attention.

And dawn was close. De Saumarez came up onto the bridge, saluted, and said, "I had a good kip, sir. Cape Froward bears 272. We're twenty minutes from the mouth of the Magdalena Channel."

Tom looked at the eastern sky, and stooped over one of the brass-throated pipes arrayed in a row along the front of the bridge screen—"Captain, sir."

The voice answered at once, "Yes?"

"Bridge, sir . . . First light. Twenty minutes to the Magdalena."

"Thanks, Tom. I'll wash, and shave, and be up in ten minutes. Send for a cup of kai for me, will you?"

"Aye, aye, sir."

He swam slowly up out of sleep, thinking of someone. Dick Yeoman? No, someone older . . . The Engineer Commander, who had begun to show the same reasonless hostility toward him that Captain Brandt had? Perhaps that was it . . . It was unpleasant, and would become more so, for the cramped wardroom was not a place where enemies could avoid each other. But what could he do? He thought of Quentin. He had received no letters from the family, and did not know whether Quentin had been at Mons and Le Cateau, the Marne, the Aisne, or at Ypres but he thought he probably had, for an English language newspaper brought aboard in Montevideo had mentioned the gallant stand of the Weald Light Infantry at Le Cateau. On land, all movement, forward or backward, seemed to have stopped, though not the killing. Strange sort of war . . .

He considered where *Penrith* was—in the maze of channels and islands between the southern tip of the American continent and Cape Horn: and what she was doing—hunting for the German light cruiser S.M.S. *Dresden*. *Dresden* had been in the Atlantic when the war began, but had promptly vanished from British ken. It seemed clear that her best hope was to join von Spee's powerful squadron, which had left China weeks ago. Von Spee had tried to coal at Tahiti on September 22nd, but been driven off; so was in all probability heading for this same area—the southern tip of South America—with the intention of rounding the Horn and making his way to the focal points of the Allied shipping lanes between Montevideo and the West Coast of Africa. So while it was *Dresden* they were looking for, it was quite possible they might come upon von Spee's whole squadron, with or without *Dresden*.

He remembered meeting Admiral von Spee earlier that year in Tsingtau, when his ship had visited the German base on a courtesy call . . . a big man with wide shoulders, a short greying torpedo beard and remarkable eyes, that were somehow like his nephew Guy's, except that the German admiral could combine the hardness of Guy's blue and the softness of his brown in the one colour, sky blue. And his squadron proved his drive and the power of his personality: it was a beautifully trained machine, and showed it at sea as well as in port. To overcome that squadron now would not be an easy fight, even if weather and all other circumstances conspired to help the British.

Still no one had called him. He yawned, thinking the commander is a sort of spare part, really. He was surplus until the ship was in action when, as damage control officer, he had a great deal to do. Otherwise, he was responsible for the discipline of the crew, and was President of the Wardroom Mess, while the captain dined alone in his own cabin: he was not a watchkeeping officer, so he had no responsibility for the bridge unless specifically sent for: he was not the navigator, the First Lieutenant, the gunnery officer, the chief engineer, the wireless officer, the surgeon lieutenant-commander, the paymaster lieutenant . . . all had their specific resonsibilities. His were all, under the captain—and none.

He got up, shaved, dressed, went to the wardroom, and was given bacon and eggs by the steward, while the youngest sub-lieutenant sprawled asleep on a sofa and the surgeon played backgammon with an engineer lieutenant at the far end of the mahogany table.

He went up on deck, and to the bridge, saluting the captain. It was still snowing, but the wind, or perhaps a vagrant hour of sun, had cleared the ship of the previous snow; the new snow was falling on bare steel. He could see *Good Hope* and *Glasgow* ahead, and *Monmouth* astern, the taller bulk of the armed merchant cruiser *Otranto* bringing up the rear. They were still doing 16 knots—*Otranto*'s maximum in a seaway—and the navigating officer was calling a continuous series of orders to the quartermaster and engine room as the squadron plunged on through low cloud, snow, and sleet. Rocks and low islands appeared and disappeared on either side, the bow waves of the leading ships washing over them. Sea birds swooped and circled, settled on the gun turrets and mastheads, and flew off. Six seals swam in *Penrith*'s wake for a time, then sheered away. The captain stood close to the binnacle, watching, but did not interfere with de Saumarez's running of the ship.

After a time he said without turning his head, " 'Morning, Tom. Had a good sleep?"

"Plenty, sir."

"We're just about to leave the Cockburn Passage."

They were facing the Southern Ocean. The waves rolled in twenty feet high, wind-whipped foam along their crests blending into the driven snow above. *Penrith* plunged deeper at each wave, water bursting upwards and outwards in giant green-white explosions, to be driven back—the wind now dead ahead—to drench fo'c's'le and bridge and everyone on them. Below, the skeleton crew huddled in A Turret, arms wrapped round the stanchions and gun levers. On the wings of the bridge the lookouts peered forward and to the sides, gloved hands dark and wet, eyes rimmed with snow.

"Starboard fifteen," de Saumarez called.

"Starboard fifteen . . ."

Glasglow was turning again, broadside on now. Now *Penrith*. The huge waves were smashing into *Glasgow* as though she were a wall of rock, pouring over upper decks in solid masses. Now it was *Penrith's* turn. She heeled over under the blows, now coming from the starboard side as the squadron turned into Brecknock Channel.

"Past Aguirre Island, sir," de Saumarez said to the captain.

"How far to the entrance to the Murray Channel, pilot?"

"A hundred and sixty two miles, sir."

"Ten hours, and dark. That's according to plan . . . Tom, take a look round. See how much water we shipped, what state we're in below decks. That was a bad half-hour off Aguirre."

A young sailor at the back of the bridge eased forward to follow Tom. Tom stared at him a moment, then said, "Ah, you're my new messenger, aren't you? Bennett?"

He remembered that he had posted his previous messenger, a veteran sailor, to one of the 4-inch guns, where he was needed, and asked the Chief Boatswain to replace him with an inexperienced OD. This must be the man, but he didn't remember seeing him before. He was a young fellow of about twenty, medium height, a rounded jaw, curly light brown hair—what could be seen of it—grey eyes, and a marked dimple. He wasn't as sturdily built as Dick Yeoman but, apart from that, there was a resemblance . . . the eyelashes for one, Bennett's paler than Dick's but just as long, and as disturbing.

He felt a compulsion to speak, and threw over his shoulder, "Why haven't I see you before?"

"Had a beard when you come aboard, sir. Took it off two days ago. I looked a proper daft brush . . . The Division Officer gave me permission, sir," he added hastily.

The sailor's accent was markedly Geordie, and Tom said, "You're from Newcastle?"

"Dipton, sir. County Durham."

Tom nodded, but said no more. He felt that the wide eyes were boring into his back: wide, and innocent looking—but so were Dick Yeoman's.

October 2

Three days later *Penrith* steamed back into Puntā Arenās, with *Monmouth* and *Otranto*. The squadron had found nothing in Orange Bay, and all the ships needed coaling. These three vessels were anchored off the town, each with coal lighters to port and starboard, the lighters hired by the British consul and placed in readiness in response to Admiral Cradock's signal from Orange Bay. Cradock had taken *Good Hope* and *Glasgow* to the Falkland Islands for the same purpose.

Penrith was an anthill of crawling humanity. Every officer and man at work was wearing his dirtiest and oldest clothes. Every hatch and crevice that could be sealed up, by whatever means, was sealed against the all-pervasive coal dust. Only the captain, the commander, some cooks, and half a dozen sentries, wireless operators and lookout, were not engaged in the work, under the general supervision of Jimmy the One, the First Lieutenant, Lieutenant-Commander the Honourable William Mainprice-King. Half a dozen gangplanks spanned the space between the cruiser and the lighters alongside. Hundreds of men walked endlessly up and down those planks, backs bent under 50-lb sacks of coal. As they reached the coal bunker hatches, each man stooped forward, emptied the sack over his shoulder into the hatch, then turned away lefthanded, and headed back to the lighter, while the man hard on his heels emptied his sack, turned . . . then the next . . . and the next. The ship boomed like a metal gong to the rumble of the falling coal. In the lighters scores of men worked with shovels, sweating in the cold damp air, to load the sacks. Every now and then a sailor staggered and fell, to pick himself up under the oaths of the petty officers. Twice a sailor managed to fall overboard. Captain Leach had allowed shore leave in batches since arriving at 4 p.m. yesterday, and half the crew had fearful *pisco* hangovers. Others were still drunk, the cheap liquor not yet having drained out of their systems. On the quarterdeck, three sailors, always excused by their skills from the almost weekly punishment of coaling, sat on a life raft and played popular tunes to a fiddle, mouth organ, and penny whistle. The sweating, bowed sailors hummed and cursed, cursed and hummed to the tunes as they worked.

Captain Leach sat with Tom in his day cabin in the stern, the scuttles screwed tight shut and further blocked with wet towels round the rims. Those scuttles could keep out a heavy sea, but some water always trickled in, and where water could trickle, coal dust could seep. Bottles of Guinness provided by the British consul sat on the table between them, half a case more at their feet.

John Leach said, "We'll be sailing as soon as we've coaled, Tom . . .
west. Rendezvous at the Chonos Archipelago."

"So we're definitely headed for the Pacific?"

The captain nodded. "And I don't like it. The Admiralty hasn't understood this war yet—imagine having three armoured cruisers like
Aboukir, Hogue, and *Cressy* on slow patrol in the Channel! And allowing each of them to try to rescue the others' crews when they were torpedoed. Three cruisers sunk in a row—what a triumph for that U-boat
commander! And what a sock in the eye for us! And if the Admiralty's
tactics are out of date, their strategy's worse. They're trying to command this squadron from seven thousand miles away just because they
have wireless and *can* get orders to us—even though it usually takes a
week. And if we have to ask any questions about the orders in a hurry
it means giving ourselves away—not our exact positions, of course, but
the fact that some warship of ours is in the general area . . . What
they ought to do is simply dispose of the available ships according to the
priorities of the navy's tasks. What Churchill is doing—oh, I'm sure he's
behind it—is giving detailed instructions to the admirals, often without
giving the admirals the means of carrying them out. Now, if they'd give
Admiral Cradock a couple of battle cruisers, from the squadrons of them
sitting at anchor in the Firth of Forth, tell him to get on with destroying von Spee, and after that just pass on whatever information they
can get, he'd have the job done safely, soundly . . . and soon."

"Where is von Spee, sir?" Tom asked.

"Not heard of since he was at Tahiti on September 22nd. He could
be anywhere. Good God, he could be steaming up the Strait . . . and
we couldn't do much, even if our whole squadron was here."

"*Canopus* . . ." Tom interjected, more to hear his captain's views
than from any belief that the old battleship allotted to Admiral Cradock could be of real use. Leach drank deep of the stout. "*Canopus* is a
battleship, yes, but so slow that she couldn't catch a rowing boat . . .
and her guns are so old that von Spee's cruisers out-range her! Her engines are museum pieces. The Admiralty seems to think that by sending us *Canopus* they've given us superiority over von Spee, but even
with *Canopus* we're inferior. Especially if we meet them in a heavy
sea, because half our guns are on the main decks, and will be flooded
out. Theirs are all centre-line mounted, on the upper deck. The light
cruisers are about equal . . . but if our armoured ships get put out of
action, we can do nothing. If we try to close, *Scharnhorst* and *Gneisenau* will sink us without allowing us to get in range."

Tom said, "I thought the Admiralty were going to send us a modern
armoured cruiser—*Defence,* wasn't it?"

"It was," Leach growled, "then they cancelled the order. They think we're strong enough as we are. We're alone, Tom. If I go, you're the captain. The navy doesn't recognise posthumous orders, but listen—I have a feeling we're going to meet von Spee soon. God grant that we can do our job—which is to damage him at least, because he can't even get repairs done, while we can . . . but if we run into bad luck, and the admiral goes with the armoured cruisers, don't sacrifice the ship and the crew without cause."

"I won't, sir," Tom said, "but if we think there's any chance—the slightest—of inflicting damage on the enemy, it's our duty to try, at whatever cost, surely?"

"Quite right," Leach said. "You needn't fear that I won't do what I can, but if that is *nothing* . . ." He didn't finish the sentence, but emptied his glass and stood up, stretching. "What would the admiral say if he found me drinking stout at ten a.m.? Well, Kit Cradock would probably join us. He's a good man, Tom. Brave as a lion, too." He shook his head admiringly and said, "I'm going to get into something suitable and join the crew. They'll appreciate the Old Man getting dirty with them—until I'm so dirty they won't know me from any OD."

Tom said, "Don't you think there might be a danger, sir, of some matlo taking out a grudge on you, because he'll be able to pretend he didn't know who you were?"

"Not in this ship," Leach said confidently. "You have the ship, Tom. Make all preparations to sail at midnight. The orders are in the chart-house. The coaling won't be so bad, but I'll have to listen to *Tipperary* for the five-thousandth time."

On the bridge of *Penrith* Tom Rowland looked at his watch. Two p.m., Chilean time, November 1st, 1914. Four days since they had heard German warships using their wireless; one day since they had entered the port of Coronel to deliver despatches from Admiral Cradock to the British consul, and from him pick up messages from the Admiralty; three hours since they had sailed from Coronel, to rendezvous with the rest of the squadron 50 miles to the westward, in the South Pacific; with some of the squadron, to be exact, for old *Canopus,* true to her recent form, was still in the secret harbour of the Chonos Archipelago, 400 miles south, attempting to repair her engines.

The other ships were all here now—*Good Hope, Monmouth, Glasgow, Otranto, Penrith.* The time was five minutes past two in the afternoon. The yeoman of signals had his telescope to his eye—"From flag, sir . . . take station on a line of bearing north-east by east from flag in order *Monmouth Otranto Glasgow Penrith* . . . distance apart of ships fifteen miles . . . course north 34 degrees west, speed 20 knots . . . enemy closing stop . . . execute!"

The officer of the watch began giving course and speed directions. The captain said, "Make sure everyone's had a meal, Number One."

The First Lieutenant said, "Aye, aye, sir! Action stations?"

"Not yet. I'll take the ship. Stay here, Tom, for the time being."

The ship heeled far over as it changed course in the heavy sea, the great waves running endlessly up from the south, the funnel smoke blowing away to port as *Penrith* gathered speed to take up her position at the end of the line. To the east the crestline of the Andes gleamed brilliant white above a lower violet murk that obscured the foothills.

Tom leaned back. The orders were given, the ship and her 375 men obeyed. For the moment he was little more than a passenger: soon, it might be different.

3.57 p.m.: Skyring's voice from the foretop was excited—"Bridge! Smoke, bearing green nine-oh!"

At 4.17 p.m. from the bridge of *Penrith*, with the telescope, Tom could observe the German squadron, off to the east—the armoured cruisers *Scharnhorst*, *Gneisenau*, and the light cruisers *Dresden* and *Leipzig*. . . . Another light cruiser was probably somewhere in the neighbourhood—*Nürnberg*. She might be close enough to join in the battle. The smoke poured from the funnels of the four German ships, as they plunged on, intervals perfect between the ships, guns already trained round to starboard. He had seen them once before, at about this distance, in the South China Sea, but that time they had exchanged salutes only, the ensigns dipping and jerking up again, the good luck signals fluttering at the masthead and, together, whipping down.

"Action stations, please," Leach said quietly. "And hoist battle ensigns."

The alarm buzzers screeched through the ship. Men ran up and down steel ladders. Tom set off round the bowels of the ship, seeing to it that all watertight doors were closed and the ship secure. The captain's Maltese steward came to the bridge with a teapot, milk jug, hot water jug, sugar bowl, teacup, and saucer on a silver tray. He said, "Will you take your tea before or after the battle, sir?"

Leach laughed. "Oh now, Fiorino."

The steward poured expertly, while balancing the tray, and the captain sipped, his eyes always on the enemy squadron.

The signals from the flagship were few . . . *assume close order* . . . *course east*. Time passed: message from the forward turrets on the main deck, starboard, which was now the weather side—*seas almost washing the crews out of the turrets.* Answer: *remain at action stations.*

Course east-south-east, 12 knots.

"The admiral's trying to close," Leach said quietly. "He wants to engage before dark."

"The Hun's running away," Sub-lieutenant Mountjoy said scornfully.

"We'll see," the captain said. "One thing's sure, whatever he's doing, he has the legs of us, as a squadron."

The sun settled lower toward the turbulent sea. The wind swept the foam off the wave tops, as with strokes of an open razor, each time they heaved up, so that to look southward, the present course of both squadrons, was to peer into the hard driven spume. The bridge was coated with salt, water ran free along the steel decks, the bows plunged, submerged, rose. Northward, the wind chased the foam for miles across the sea, not allowing it to settle. A dull pinkish tinge began to appear in the sharp southern light.

Tom thought, we haven't been able to get von Spee within range while the sun was shining in his gun layers' eyes. Now it's sinking into the western sea directly behind us; we will be silhouetted in black against it.

6.20 p.m., sunset. From the foretop—"Bridge! Enemy has opened fire." Orange and scarlet flashes rippled along the side of the leading German ship.

"Bridge, range one-one-two."

Extreme range of our 6-inch, Tom thought. The German flagship was aiming at the British flagship—*Good Hope.* The British were now steaming south in line ahead, in the order *Good Hope, Monmouth, Glasgow, Penrith, Otranto.*

"Engage *Leipzig.*"

"We can't get in touch with the flagship, sir, by visual or W/T."

"Range decreasing!"

"He's turned toward us, at full speed," Captain Leach muttered.

"Range—eight thousand."

"My God, he's hit *Good Hope* . . . she's on fire amidships!"

6.53 p.m. Range six thousand, six hundred, all guns firing that can. Tom said, "I'll take a look round, sir."

"All right."

Tom ran down the bridge ladder, Bennett at his heels, and started aft along the upper deck. *Leipzig,* at the rear of the German line, was engaging *Penrith,* ignoring *Otranto,* which was helping *Penrith:* but her 4.7s would not be much use. Shells screamed close overhead, to burst in the water with tremendous splashes, water rising in columns, hovering, slowly sinking back. The acrid smell of cordite, blown into every crevice of the ship by the wind, made him cough and his eyes smart. Dense brown smoke drifted northward, in low, intermittent clouds.

This was Tom's first time under fire, and he was surprised to find that he was not afraid, though he felt a vague sense of unease, a foreboding that something unpleasant was about to happen: to whom, or how, he did not know. None of the crew had seen action either, and among them, as they crouched at their guns, seas sweeping over them, or stoked the insatiable furnaces, he saw strain and expectation, exaltation and fear, sometimes on the same face.

A heavy clang echoed through the ship and he thought he heard a scream. It came from below forward, and he ran down a ladder, Bennett following. A sailor came staggering out of B forward turret, on the main deck. The man's left arm was almost severed at the elbow, and pouring blood. A sailor from the ship's disengaged side came over and supported him up the ladder toward the upper deck. Once the ship's watertight doors were closed there was no other way to get him to the wardroom which, in action, became the surgeon's operating theatre.

Tom eased through a narrow entrance to the turret. One man was working the gun, single-handed. A jagged hole ten inches across had been torn in the outer steel casing, and the walls of the confined space were plastered with brains, flesh, eyeballs, splintered bones, and swaths of bloody serge. The gun's breech and mount were deep scored, but it was being fired, by the one man, whose right knee was a pulp. Bennett whispered, "My china was in this turret." His voice trailed away and Tom said shortly, "Bad luck. Find the gun control officer and ask him if he needs any help."

"Aye, aye, sir!"

The young sailor's face was pale in the glare of the electric light. He darted off. "Well done, Simpkins," Tom said quietly to the Leading Seaman at the gun, "we'll have relief for you right away."

"I'm all righ' . . ." the killick murmured, in the same moment sliding slowly sideways to the steel deck, unconscious.

Tom went to the gun control position, motioned the gun control officer aside, and lifted the navyphone. "Bridge!"

"Tom?"

"B.2 gun crew knocked out, sir. The gun seems all right. A.3's crew are taking over. Four dead, two severely wounded. The gun's firing again now, sir."

"Good. Come up."

7.10 p.m. *Good Hope* lay stopped in the water to the south, burning with a dense black smoke that mingled with the brown clouds from the warring guns. *Monmouth* was slowing, glowing all along her length. Out of the eastern gloom the German guns flashed, brilliant and regular. The shells pounded into the two mortally stricken armoured cruisers.

7.20 p.m. "My God!" Leach whispered. A glow of flame crept along *Good Hope*'s deck line, then limned the funnels and masts, like St Elmo's fire. A strong scarlet light, black shot, illuminated the ocean, the waves, the hastening ships. *Good Hope* blew up, vanished.

"*Monmouth*'s ceased fire," Mountjoy said. His voice was unsteady.

"Still think von Spee's running, sub?" Leach said. The sub was very subdued. "No, sir. I apologise."

Tom thought of *Monmouth*. He had had a good six weeks in her, in spite of Brandt's coolness. The curse that had been laid on him had not troubled him, for some reason. In the West Indies, one evening, he had almost fallen in love with a woman. Perhaps perpetually being careful with Brandt, always keeping a close watch on himself, had helped. Now they were all gone, Brandt, and seven hundred others . . . for no one could help *Monmouth* now. Even if she surrendered, the Germans would have a hard time rescuing anyone in this sea, if she, too, didn't blow up.

The bridge was silent. Tom knew what was in Leach's mind. Who was the senior captain? And he knew the answer: Luce, of *Glasgow*. What signal or order would Luce give now that the two armoured cruisers were gone—one sunk and one helpless?

From the foretop Skyring called, "Bridge! *Scharnhorst* seems to be engaging *Glasgow* . . . *Gneisenau*, us . . ."

"Range nine-oh . . . eight-oh."

The fight was now between two apparently undamaged German armoured cruisers, with six inches of armour round the vital belt of each ship, protecting the magazines, ammunition hoists, and engines; seven inches of armour on the turrets; each ship carrying eight 8.2-inch guns; and protected by two light cruisers, each capable of an equal one to one fight with the three British survivors: and the three British—*Glasgow*, *Penrith*, and the armed liner *Otranto*.

The yeoman said, "*Glasgow*'s sending a message, sir." They all stared into the darkness, eyes fixed on the little light winking and flashing and stuttering to the south. Tom could read one word in five, so fast was the morse message being sent, and turned away, resting his eyes.

The yeoman said, "Scatter . . . proceed at best speed to rendezvous Evangelistas . . . good luck. That's all, sir."

Eight heavy shells straddled *Penrith*. Her own guns kept firing. Sea water drenched the bridge and everyone on it, but they were all soaked already and had been since before the battle began.

Leach said, "Engine room, revolutions for maximum speed. Give us all you've got, Chief. We should only need it for an hour or two . . . port twenty!" The ship heeled over on her beam ends in the savage turn. Another salvo of shells burst where she had just been, the water ghostly white to port.

"Course, north-west."

"North-west, sir!"

Leach spoke half aside, softly, to Tom. "We're running, Tom. Let's hope von Spee doesn't head straight for the Evangelistas, too. See that everyone knows what's happened. We'll stay at action stations for another two hours, at least, until I'm sure we're clear. *Nürnberg*'s about somewhere, don't forget."

Another salvo burst to port. But there was no ship in the German squadron that could catch *Glasgow* or *Penrith*, by a full knot. In the darkness behind them Tom counted seventy-five flashes, then silence. *Monmouth* had gone.

A long while later Leach said in a dry harsh voice, "We've been well and truly thrashed, Tom. For the first time in . . . what? A hundred and fifty years?"

"It was the Admiralty's fault, sir."

"Perhaps. But the British people won't excuse us, Tom. This is the Royal Navy. We're supposed to win, always, whatever the odds . . ."

He stood in the darkness of the bridge, his face barely seen by the light of the binnacle. The effulgent moon was rising above pale clouds, the ship shuddering to her speed and the pounding of the waves on her flank, spray and water flying.

"I'd better go round now, sir," Tom said awkwardly.

Captain Leach nodded, without speaking. Tom turned away, Ordinary Seaman Bennett following.

Daily Telegraph, Monday, November 2, 1914

GLOVES FOR TROOPS
GRAND DUKE MICHAEL'S FUND

Over £5,000 has now been subscribed in response to the appeal made by the Grand Duke Michael for £25,000 to supply warm woollen gloves and mittens to the British troops in the trenches; and it is to be hoped that the remainder will be quickly subscribed, as every day the need for these comforts grows greater. The announcement that the Queen's fund for body belts and socks for the troops is about to be closed indicates the urgency of the appeal, and the gloves and mittens will be no less eagerly welcomed by our men who are already experiencing very severe weather at night.

Gloves and mittens should be of khaki, grey, or neutral wool, the gloves at least 8½ size and the mittens long enough to go well over the coat sleeve. Black or white colours should not be sent. All letters and parcels should be addressed to Grand Duke Michael, 39 Portland Place, W, by whom the appeal is made to the British public for the British troops, and not, as has been thought, for the Russian troops.

Cate put down the paper. The people who thought the appeal had been for Russian troops had common sense on their side. Why should a Russian prince appeal for comforts for British troops, in England? Had someone decided that our own royal family were already asking, appealing too much? Come to that, why had the unfortunate troops not been supplied, long since, by the War Office and Government? It wasn't as though gloves were an exotic or unexpected article of wear in northern Europe in winter. Perhaps no one had thought that the war would continue into the winter. Perhaps no one had thought.

He stood up, stretching. Garrod came silently into the dining-room and took away his breakfast plate. Stella was gobbling her kippers—she had a train to catch. She looked more beautiful than ever in her V.A.D. uniform. The severity of it only enhanced the lush perfection of her complexion and the full curves of her breasts. He said, "You'll give yourself indigestion, Stella," and went out, newspaper in hand.

In his study he stood a while thinking. Frank Cawthon had got his loan from Barclay's, but he hadn't used any of it yet. He was a careful man, who thought things out before he acted; but it would be a good idea to go and talk with him and find out when he did intend to buy the new stock. The winter months would do nothing to improve a poor herd. While he was out he'd ride on over to High Staining and talk with John. The rural labour problem was growing worse every week. In the cities men seemed willing to stay in the factories, if they were needed—a great many, even if they were not—but in the country the farm labourers had just upped and gone off to the war, although they were fully as essential to the war effort as the mechanics were. He'd get some information—facts and figures from all the farmers in the area, then he and John might go to Ellis, the M.P., and see what could be done about formulating a national policy. The first step, probably, would be to organise and train women into a volunteer farm army of some kind. John was ahead of most of the country in employing Carol Adams, but soon the effort would have to be national, not piecemeal, local, and haphazard. And it would have to be led by women, as soon as possible.

Hedlington: Tuesday, November 3 —Market Day

14 John Rowland pulled the old Rowland Ruby to a stop at the entrance to the Fairgrounds, and got out. A fine, cold drizzle was falling and John wore his belted mackintosh coat and a tweed cap, heavy boots, and leather leggings. The day's paper, bought in High Street where he had deposited Louise to do her shopping, was folded and tucked into the voluminous inside pocket of the raincoat. He had only seen the front page headlines. They were enough to settle his mouth into a grim downturn. More heavy fighting in Flanders, more long lists of the dead. Quentin's name had not appeared—yet—but it would be foolish to pretend that it never would. And he could not help worrying about Tom, too. They had not been very close—no one was very close to Tom, he thought, but in spite of the six years between them, they had been friends as well as brothers. He had watched Tom grow up, until the navy took him, at the age of twelve; after that he had gradually drawn farther away from all the family, without any hostility. Now, he had to all intents vanished into the globe-circling oceans, without trace.

He walked carefully through the mud down what had been the Fair's main road, toward the cattle and sheep and pig stalls and poultry pens at the market, beyond the Fair's north end. He only came into Hedlington once or twice a month, and the military take-over of the Fairgrounds, which had started last time he was here, was now almost complete. Three-quarters of the acreage had become a tented camp. Rows of tents of all sizes covered most of the space between the Scarrow and the road. Squads of men marched to and fro to the screamed commands of sergeants and corporals: but they didn't look like soldiers, for uniforms had not yet been made for them, nor did they carry rifles— there were none: they carried broomsticks. He looked at the men as he passed, wondering whether he would see Frank Stratton. He had never known Frank well, but about the time he himself was studying for the church, Frank had been visiting Laburnum Lodge quite frequently, courting a young housemaid—or pretending to. He couldn't have been much more than sixteen then.

He didn't see Frank, but thinking of him made him wonder, should I be wielding a pretend rifle, rather than doing what I am doing—trying to run a dairy herd, rather inefficiently? Would I be any better as a soldier—an officer, presumably? He'd like to go as a padre, but it was a little late to think of taking up the career he had abandoned eighteen years ago to become a farmer—a gentleman farmer. Louise would tell him he had taken leave of his senses. She'd be right; but on this day he did not feel contented with his life.

He reached the cattle pens, and walked through the maze to the far end. A large black and white bull lay peacefully in one. In another were four cows of the same breed. Frank Cawthon, of Abbas Farm, chewing a straw, was leaning over the heavy railing, looking at the bull, who was chewing the cud. Their jaws moved in rhythm.

"Morning, Frank," John said.

Cawthon glanced up. "Morning, Mr John. That were bad news in the paper this morning."

"Very."

"Young Mr Charles still in India?"

"His regiment's on its way to France, Frank. We had a letter yesterday." John wanted to change the subject. Neither he nor Louise found it easy to discuss the fact that Charles was approaching the war. He would be closer to home, of course, than he'd been in India, and able to spend his leaves at High Staining: but he'd also be closer to death. The fighting in France was becoming more violent by the week. A strange new underground war, apparently, the enemies barely seeing each other, living in mud and water and cold, while shells hurtled overhead in both directions, to pulverise the earth and tear their bodies. From what he could learn from the descriptions and photographs, and the sketches of war artists, it was not at all like any previous war; nor like anything that the generals had expected.

He said, "What do you think of this breed?"—nodding his head at the black and white cows.

"Friesians," Cawthon said shortly. "Dutch. I was looking at the Farm Journal. These here cows give a quarter again as much milk as a

Shorthorn for the same feed. And they'll last five, six lactations. The Shorthorns only go three, before you have to cull."

"I heard the milk has a lower butterfat content."

" 'Tis true. Less than three percent—a Shorthorn gives a little over three. But the extra quantity makes up for it. They're hardy . . . don't get too many diseases. And the meat's good when you want to slaughter."

"Are you thinking of changing your herd?"

Cawthon said, "I am that. It'll take some money though. And good prices for the Shorthorns, when I sell them."

"You were going to get some fresh stock, you said that day when I came to Abbas with Mr Cate."

"Aye, but I haven't started, and better than getting new Shorthorn stock might be to change to Friesians. They're nearly all imported now, but there's a British Friesian Society, I know, and they could help me a lot, starting with 'em. I'm going to talk to Farnham—he's the fellow that brought these here."

He walked off, a bent, squat figure, rain dripping off the back of his shapeless felt hat, heavy rubber boots on his bow legs, his tan coat nearly down to the ground.

John stared at the bull. He thought—should I change to Friesians, too? More milk, but less butterfat. What did the country need most? More milk, surely, in times like these. It was rather like the conflict between the Governor's ideas on making motor cars, and Richard's— quality against quantity; high volume and cheap production against low volume and expensive production. But with Jerseys and Guernseys available, a farmer could always mix some of their high butterfat milk with the Friesians', to get the right percentage . . . indeed, he'd have to, for three percent was the legal minimum of butterfat in milk to be sold to the public.

" 'Morning, Mr Rowland."

It was Howard Ashcraft, another dairy farmer from west of Walstone, down river from the village. John hoped he too would not talk about the war, and was almost relieved when Ashcraft said, "Sorry to see in the London paper about Mrs Cate being arrested."

John said, "She will probably be released again tomorrow. It read as though they had very little evidence against her."

Ashcraft was a blunt outspoken man; not many others would have brought up this subject.

The farmer said, "Well, she feels strong about Ireland. We all know that. Not that I agree with her, mind, any more than you do, belike . . . How's the young lady doing, as a labourer?"

"Miss Adams? She's a good hard worker. Fred seems to be pleased with her. He told me she's doing well."

"Can't be strong as a man, though, eh? How does she like the muck, her being the parson's daughter and all?"

"She does whatever she's told, and hasn't complained so far. She even helps in the house, though she doesn't have to."

The farmer said, "Well, I never thought I'd be looking for a woman as a cowman, but what else can I do, with all the men running off to join the army? If it gets worse, danged if I don't go myself!"

John laughed. "You'd have to lose some weight before the army would have you, Howard." He did not add—and lose a score or more of years, too; for Ashcraft was short, very paunchy, and at least sixty.

They started talking about the price of linseed cake then; and the price of beef. It ought to be going up, for the army was making great demands for bully beef—"but all that comes from Argentina, or somewhere else in South America," Matthew Fleck, another local farmer, cut in. Then they talked of the price of milk . . . and the cost of wages . . . and the difficulties of getting labour . . . and the prevalence of charlock in the wheat fields this year . . . and the price of artificial fertilizer . . . and whether the war would affect the supply of nitrate from Chile. "It will, it will," Fleck growled, " 'cos the price of sulphate of ammonia's going up at the gasworks, and that shows they think we're not going to be able to get the Chilean nitrate instead."

John pulled out his watch. Nearly twelve. He said his goodbyes and walked back between the pens. He had sold nothing—he had brought nothing to sell: and he had bought nothing—but he had been given an idea. He'd talk it over with Fred this afternoon; and then get Christopher's advice. For if Frank Cawthon was seriously thinking of changing to Friesian cattle, he would be well advised to think about it himself: Frank was a good farmer.

Men were still drilling with broomsticks in the rain, but there seemed to be fewer of them. Others were lining up, tins in hand, outside a big tent that must be the cookhouse. Bugles blew, cracked and inexpertly. A sergeant strutted by with a red sash diagonally across his chest, medal ribbons bright about his left breast pocket, a pace stick stuck importantly under his arm. As he passed John he whipped his head to the right and his right hand to the peak of his cap in salute. John thought, why on earth . . . ? Then he realised that someone else was passing the other side of him—an officer of the Weald Light Infantry, who returned the salute with a touch of his swagger cane to his cap. John thought, that was the first time he had ever seen an officer of the regiment in uniform, in Hedlington. And now he saw two, three, four, many—watching the drilling, hands clasped behind their backs; walking into a tent where a flag flew outside; talking in a small group beyond the cook tent. The war had come to Hedlington. It was still raining.

Louise was waiting for him in the downstairs sitting-room of the South Eastern Hotel, the sprawling, comfortable Victorian red brick building opposite the railway station, built by the railway company in 1851. Inside it was all dark, with mahogany panelling and deep leather chairs. The dining-room beyond was large and airy, with big windows looking down the slope toward the Scarrow and the Weald. They went in at once to lunch, for Louise had announced that she was famished, and he could have his glass of sherry at the table.

They sat down, the old waiter creaked over on flat feet and handed them a menu. It was always table d'hôte at the South Eastern, with a choice of vegetables; but the food was of excellent quality and very adequately cooked. John studied the card while Louise told him what she had bought—curtain material for Carol Adams' room; a pair of stout shoes for the winter; some flannel underclothes, ditto; writing paper, envelopes, knitting wool . . . They ordered—Brussels sprouts and roast potatoes to go with the roast saddle of lamb, mint sauce, and red currant jelly; then apple tart and cream.

"And," she went on, after ordering, "I bought some fireworks."

"Fireworks?"

"It's Guy Fawkes' Day, the day after tomorrow."

"Of course," he said. "But . . . will they let us have fireworks this year?"

"No one's said not," his wife said, "and why shouldn't we?"

He thought, it might frighten people. The Germans kept threatening to drop bombs from Zeppelins and aeroplanes. It just seemed strange to be letting off explosives for fun, when so much was being used to kill, not so far away across the Channel.

She said, "I met Mr Handforth in the street." Handforth was the Cates' solicitor. "He assured me that Margaret would be released tomorrow. But who'd ever have imagined the police would be searching Walstone Manor for treasonable documents—explosives, even, I heard."

John said, "They didn't find anything."

"That doesn't mean that Margaret didn't have anything, does it? Perhaps she had warning they were coming, and hid whatever she had."

"We mustn't hold her guilty before she is proved so."

She sniffed. "Margaret doesn't pretend to be innocent. She says it's for Ireland, and that makes anything all right." She leaned forward, "Don't look now, but the Merritts have just come in."

"Who?"

"Mr Merritt and his son. The Americans Richard and the Governor met at Henley. Richard was driving them down to Hill House a day or two ago, and dropped by High Staining, on their way to call on the Cates. You were out somewhere. They've seen me. They're coming this way."

John pushed his chair back as the two Americans walked between the white-clothed tables toward them. Louise said, "Mr Merritt, this is my husband."

"Pleased to know you, Mr Rowland. Mr John Rowland, isn't it?"

"Sorry to have missed you the other day."

"Well, we've met now. Nice to see you again, Mrs Rowland."

"I do hope you're comfortable here," John said.

"Very much so, sir. This is a very pleasant establishment with a friendly atmosphere, even for non-combatants. I trust we shall meet again, soon." Bowing, they went on their way to a table in a far corner by the window. John watched them sit down, their heads closing as they began to talk, the menu left untouched on the tablecloth.

Louise said, "Richard said that they are almost certainly going to lend him the money he needs to start his business, or form a company for him, which would come to the same thing. I don't know how much it will need."

"About a million pounds," John said, "I asked Richard."

"Goodness gracious! What a lot of money!"

"Making motor cars is an expensive business, my dear."

"Well, they can afford it, I suppose, because they're not spending it on fighting the war. They'll get richer and richer while we get poorer and poorer."

John said, "I think the Americans may be wise, dear. Wiser than we. This war's a terrible thing."

The old waiter served the first course and they began to eat. Louise spoke between mouthfuls, "You know when Mother and Alice came down last Sunday?"

"Of course."

"Alice told me privately that there is bad feeling now between Richard and the Governor. The Governor never thought he'd really do what he said he was going to do . . . or find the capital, or anything. Now it looks as though he will succeed, and your father's very upset."

John said, "The Governor likes having his own way. He always did." He thought to himself that he had been a good father, on the whole:

affectionate, reasonably flexible and understanding of his children's diverse characters and emotions.

"It's a shame, though."

John said, "It will get worse when Richard's factory starts working, and he takes mechanics and craftsmen away from Rowland's. Last week's *Courier* was full of speculation about the wages Richard's going to pay—even though it isn't certain yet he's going to get the money from the Merritts. He told me that several people have already asked him if he's going to pay American rates, like Mr Ford's."

"Five dollars a working day, I read. That's over a pound a day, isn't it? About three hundred and twenty pounds a year. I don't think Tom gets more than that as a commander. What are the Merritts doing now?"

"Talking. The son is drawing on a piece of paper. Why?"

"Christopher told me that he—the son, Johnny's his name—is very taken with Stella."

"He's a good looking young man. Stella is lucky."

"She's too young to get married . . . but she ought to."

"Why?"

"*You* know, John."

"No, I don't."

Louise dropped her voice. "You remember what I said about Carol Adams? About cows and the bull?"

"Oh yes. I suppose Stella is a bit flighty."

"Flighty is not quite the word I would use. Susceptible would be better, I think. And with Margaret really not being a mother to her . . . I mean, I can't imagine Margaret *listening* to her, if she needed help, or advice."

"Are we any better with Naomi?" John asked suddenly.

His wife stopped, her fork in midair. She lowered the fork and said quietly, "I sometimes wonder." She picked up the fork again, chewed the mouthful, swallowed, and said, "Charles will be in France soon."

"I know."

A long silence. "I can't bear to think of it," she said, her voice breaking. She dabbed at her eyes. "When he went to Sandhurst I never thought he'd be fighting Germans or French or people like that, only natives."

John said patiently, "He'll do his duty, whomever he has to fight."

She put away her handkerchief and said, "The Germans are no different from natives, really, the way they behave—raping nuns and killing babies."

John said, "I don't know whether we really ought to believe everything that we . . ."

"They cook people," Louise said flatly.

"My dear, it may not be true."

"They boil them down for soap. It's true! It was in the newspaper!"

John thought of Rachel Cowan's words the day after war was declared. The hatred that she had prophesied was already abroad in the land. He sighed, wishing again that he had persevered in his wish to become a clergyman of the Church of England. Now, surely, if ever, charity and hope were needed in the world: but he was a farmer, a gentleman farmer.

For the first twenty minutes of the drive back to High Staining, they had talked, avoiding what was closest to both of them—the imminent arrival of their son on the battlefield across the Channel. Instead they spoke of the weather (it was still raining): the poverty of the year's local hop harvest: and the price of Friesian cattle. Then they had fallen silent, each listening to his own thoughts, the hiss of the tyres on the gravelled road, and the patter of rain on the canvas hood. John drove slowly, Louise huddled up beside him, both wearing gloves and goggles, for visibility was poor, whether he tried to see through the spattered windshield or peer over the top of it into the driving rain. They passed through Walstone soon after three in the afternoon, forty-five minutes after leaving the back yard of the South Eastern Hotel, where guests other than residents left their motor cars, and took the narrow lane to High Staining.

With the house close ahead, no more than a hundred and fifty yards up the slope, the Rowland lurched to the right. This was followed immediately by a heavy thump thump thump from that side. "Puncture," John said briefly. "It'll be another horseshoe nail."

He climbed out and stood a moment in the rain, water dripping off his cap and coat, inspecting the right front tyre. It was flat.

"Can't we just drive it to the stable?" Louise asked. They still called the place where the car was kept 'the stable,' which was reasonable enough, as it still was the stable—the horses and trap and dog cart were at the far end of the same building, all presided over by Palmer the groom, who had his quarters above.

John shook his head. "It would ruin the tyre, cut it to pieces. Come on, it's not far. Leave your packages."

He helped his wife out of the car and they started up the remaining distance, hurrying through the rain. A minute after leaving the car, they passed the hay barn, where hay was stacked after it was brought in from the fields, and stored until it was needed. As they passed the half-open sliding door John distinctly heard a sound like a stifled scream. Louise heard it, too, and stopped with her hand on his arm—"What was that?" she whispered, her face paling.

"Don't know." He started toward the barn door, Louise at his heels. They went in, half-running, to stop dead a yard inside the door. In front of them, not ten feet away, Carol Adams, the Vicar of Beighton's daughter, lay on her back under a man. One arm was round his neck, pulling him down to her, her skirt and petticoat thrown back to bare her loins to his thrusting, her legs round his lower back. His trousers were off completely, thrown into the hay to one side, the great gluteal muscles of his buttocks contracting and releasing as he drove in and out of her body. Her eyes were closed when they first saw her, and she had one hand in her mouth, biting into it to stifle the animal sounds of sexual arousement that were pouring out of her. She was still making a lot of noise, though nothing now as specific as a scream; but she heard Louise's loud gasp. Her eyes opened, and she stared at them for several seconds while the man continued to thrust, but she did not seem to see them. Then recognition came, and dragged her violently back from that place of instinct rather than reason, where she had been. She cried, "Fred!"

The man paused, then obviously unable to control the oncoming orgasm, thrust finally down and held tight, groaning and jerking rhythmically.

She had closed her eyes again, and lain still, realising that she was helpless to move him for the moment. After a time she said quietly, "It's Mr Rowland, Fred . . . and Mrs Rowland."

Fred Stratton lay on her, turning his head a little to one side to breathe. He said, "You'd best go. I'll come up later."

Louise turned and went out. John said, "Come to my office," then he followed his wife; but before going to the house he went to the stable, found Palmer cleaning saddlery, and told him to go down to the Rowland, change the wheel, drive it up, repair the puncture, and bring the packages to the house. These horseshoe nails hadn't mattered when he was a boy: now, with all the cars and motor bicycles on the roads, they were becoming a real nuisance, indeed an actual danger.

Then he faced the house, and Louise. After changing his outer clothes and boots for something drier and more comfortable, he went to the office. She was waiting for him there, in front of the fireplace, his Cambridge oar slanting across most of the wall behind her.

"He's got to go," she said at once, her hands folded in front of her.

"I suppose so."

"He's been above himself ever since he came here—and not very good either, you say."

"Yes," John agreed. Fred would have to go; but he wished the whole unpleasantness could have been avoided. For one thing, whom could he get to replace Stratton? He voiced the thought.

"I don't know," Louise said, "but we'll find someone. Or you can run the farm without a foreman."

"I can try," he said doubtfully. "Christopher's suggested it more than once, but . . ."

There was a knock at the door and John said, "Come in."

It was Fred Stratton, still flushed from his exertions, rain drops pearling his coat and reddish hair. The wide-set blue eyes stared straight at John, the mouth was firm. He said, "I'll be leaving, Mr John."

John said, "I suppose you'd better."

"I didn't like the work anyway. I've been here four years, and how many days off have I had?"

John said, "Very few, I know. Farming is a demanding business."

"Not for some." Fred's voice and demeanor were surly. John thought, now he's trying to work up anger to justify his conduct. He said, "I do not wish to quarrel, Fred. If you want to go now, I agree that you should . . . What are you going to do next? I am sure my father will be happy to find a good place for you at Rowland's."

"I don't want that," Fred said, a little less angrily, "I never liked factories. I'm going into the army."

"You're going to join up?" Louise interjected, surprise apparent in her voice.

"No," Fred said curtly, "I am going to be an officer. I'm as good a man as many that are."

Louise sniffed. John said, "I am sure you are. The Wealds?"

"Why not?" Fred said belligerently, "why should I join a crowd of Welshmen or something, just because I didn't go to Eton?"

"Quite, quite," John said. "You know that my brother is a major in them."

"Major Quentin. I know. Is he all right?"—the tone was less abrasive.

"So far as we know, touch wood——" John religiously tapped the oak desk. "He knows you, from visits here, and Mr Cate will write a letter of commendation, I'm sure . . . the rector, too."

"I don't go to no church," Fred said, "don't believe in it. My dad and mum are chapel."

"My father will certainly do all he can for you. It might help, you know."

"Well, thanks," Fred said grudgingly, "that's kind of you . . . Don't blame the girl. I talked her into it."

Louise sniffed again, and John said, "Quite."

"I'll pack. Then I'll walk to the station and catch the evening train."

"I owe you a month's wages," John said.

"You don't owe me anything," Fred said. "I'm leaving. You're not sacking me. You could send my bag after me to Dad's place—85 Jervis Street. I'll be there a few days." He nodded and said, "Well, goodbye . . ."

John stood up, his hand out. He had once been a clergyman, almost. It was noble to forgive. Besides, the lusts of the flesh were hard to control in the young, and Fred was only thirty-one. After a moment of surprise, Fred took the hand, shook it, said, "Goodbye, Mrs Rowland," and walked out.

"Well!" Louise said, sinking into the hard chair opposite the desk, "Fred Stratton an officer! They'll never take him."

"I think they will," John said gently. "Lord Kitchener's armies are going to be so numerous that our class can not possibly supply officers for them all."

She said, "But . . . he might go to Charles's battalion! Or Quentin's. And eat with them in the mess, and everything."

"He might. There's nothing we can do about it, my dear. It's the war . . . and it might turn out for the best."

His wife said, "I can't see how, but—" she shrugged, and changed the subject. "Carol will have to leave, too. We can't have that sort of behaviour at High Staining."

John didn't speak for a time, his thoughts progressing in the same groove they had been moving in since he saw the girl's ecstatic face pressed back in the hay, stalks in her hair. What to do? She was twenty-four; not exactly elderly, but no longer a minor by any standards. She had committed a folly—several times by now, probably; but how many others had done, and were doing the same—even girls of her class, infected by the spreading virus of war? And the men? But what would Louise say—fearing perhaps that the next man to fall into her trap would be himself?

He said, "I'd like to keep her. If I'm going to take over the running of the farm myself, I need people with some experience—and intelligence. Carol has them."

Louise said, "What if she's pregnant?"

He said unhappily, "I don't know. We'd have to send her home. She'd have to tell her mother, I suppose."

"Well, we can only wait and see. If she starts getting morning sickness, we'll know."

"Then you don't mind her staying?"

"Not after I've had a little talk with her . . . And it'll be best if you have *only* girls on this farm, John. As to what to do if Carol is pregnant, well, we'll have to cross that bridge when we come to it."

There was a small tap on the door, and Louise said, "Here she is." John said, "Come in."

Carol Adams entered, not exactly sidling, but not walking in firmly, head high, as she used to. She stood just inside the open door, as though keeping her escape route open, her hands nervously intertwining, and said, "I'll go home, Mrs Rowland."

Louise said, "Come in, girl. Shut the door."

John said, "Fred's leaving."

"He said he would, some time ago. He . . . he wasn't really happy here. Nothing to do with—this."

"I know. Look, Carol, I am going to manage the farm myself. I need labourers. If you will promise to behave yourself here—I don't want you to leave."

She did not speak, head hanging. He said, "Will you stay?"

She said in a small voice, "If you want me. If Mrs Rowland doesn't mind."

Louise said, "You can stay, Carol, but there are some things we must talk about. John, will you tell Wood we'll be having tea in twenty-five minutes? Come with me, Carol."

The two women went out, Carol closing the door carefully behind her. John stared at the oar over the mantel, feeling a great sense of relief.

They were in bed, the high double bed that Louise had inherited from her grandmother and brought down from Yorkshire at great expense soon after their marriage. The rain hissed gently against the window panes, the electric light was on at the bedside, for John had been reading, a book he'd bought in Hedlington after lunch, on breeds of milk cattle round the world. He had been studying the Friesian breed.

When Louise finished her toilet, she climbed into bed beside him and said, "Carol is sure she's not pregnant. I asked her how she knew. She blushed scarlet then, and said Fred used those things, those rubber things you can buy. For the man."

French letters, John thought to himself. He had heard that the French had the impudence to call them *capotes anglises*. He himself had never used one, feeling that they were somehow wrong; but whether withdrawal from the woman's body—at the moment when spouses ought to be closest, physically as well as spiritually—was any better, he did not know.

Louise said, "I promised not to say anything to her mother, as long as she behaves herself. We can't have a parson's daughter demeaning herself with the local men. I don't know how she could bring herself to do it with Fred. But then, girls like Carol can hardly control themselves."

"Then her promise to behave herself is not of much value, is it?"

"You'll have to keep an eye on her . . . You'll need another labourer."

"I know, but heaven knows where I'm going to find one."

"Carol told me something. Lady Helen wants to work on a farm."

"Lady Helen Durand-Beaulieu? Swanwick's daughter?"

"How many other Lady Helens do we know? She's spoken to Carol about it several times, apparently."

"You said I ought to get all women here, but I don't know whether I want to. It's too much responsibility. What dreadful trouble we'd be in if Lady Helen went like Carol!"

"She won't," Louise said firmly. "That young woman has her head screwed on the right way. She's quite different from Carol, and with the two of them working together, each of them's going to find it harder to stray."

"I don't know whom they're going to stray with, the way the men are leaving for the war . . . unless it's to be with me."

She patted his hand beside her on the quilt. "I don't think you're the philandering kind, my dear. Do you think—" she hesitated—"Charles has been with a woman yet?"

John said, "I don't know. He's twenty-one and in the army—I suppose so."

"I hope it wasn't with some dirty native. Love is too important for that. But I don't think he would go to such a woman . . . and he's too nice for those wicked married women in India that Mr Kipling used to write about, in hill stations, wasn't it?"

It was his turn to ask a question that had been in his mind, off and on, for a year or more; but he had not thought that Louise had wished to talked about it. Now he said, "What about Naomi?"

She said, "Naomi? Why, John, you can't be suggesting that she . . ."

John felt awkward, but persevered. "Well, we've just seen that young ladies are not . . . different . . . not all of them. And do we know Naomi, really, even though she is our daughter?"

His wife spoke with a little less certainty. "She's not like Stella or Carol. She's not man mad. She doesn't flirt. In fact, she tries to make out that she despises young men. She's not 'modern' like some of the girls you hear about in London. She's not experienced enough to be one of the sort that used to be in the old King's set . . . and I hear he always treated unmarried women with great delicacy. It was the married ones they all considered fair game. And most of them delighted to be so, I understand."

"I wonder what it can be like, at Girton? I can't imagine it, somehow. A community of young women, but under discipline, involved with a wider community of men. I should think she'd be happier doing some kind of work, and having a little flat of her own."

"She's too young for that," Louise said sharply, "and I don't approve of young women of our class working in that way . . . But when she's away, I don't know what she's thinking, or feeling. Her letters don't tell us."

John said quietly, "Is it really any different when she's at home, dear?"

Louise said at last, "No. I suppose it started when she became a woman . . . you know. She built a barrier. I've heard other mothers say the same thing of their daughters. There were certainly many matters I didn't want to speak to *my* mother about. I'd rather talk about it, whatever it was, with other girls. Naomi's the same, I suppose. Only, now that I'm the mother, it hurts."

"Rachel Cowan is the one Naomi confides in, as far as I can see."

Louise sat up in bed a little and faced her husband. "I don't trust that young woman. There's something unhealthy about her. You know what I think—she has a crush on Naomi. She's in love with her."

"She's not very pretty," John said.

"That shouldn't turn her head toward another woman. Oh, there can't be anything . . . *beastly* about it, but it's unhealthy."

John said, "We started talking about Naomi at lunch, then we turned to something else. But we ought to discuss it. What is she going to do when she leaves Girton?"

Louise stirred uneasily. "I don't know . . . Most of the girls at Girton are going to be teachers, or professors. Naomi's not that kind. We'll have to discuss it with her. She has two more years, doesn't she?"

John said, "Listening to her, I get the impression that she is finding Girton rather confining, even now. When the full effects of this war have been felt by all of us, she might feel that even more strongly."

Louise said definitely, "She must finish her tripos or whatever it is. And by then we will all have decided what she is going to do."

After a while John said, "Have you told Naomi the facts of life?"

Louise said, "Living on a farm, she knows what happens, of course.

But the emotions . . . I hope she doesn't know, yet how can a girl guard herself if she doesn't know? She looked like a being from another planet, when we went into the barn, didn't she? Carol."

John nodded. Carol Adams' normally pleasant but rather large and not beautiful face had been transformed, the skin suffused and translucent, straw like a halo round and in her hair, an intense aura of emotional crisis radiating from her struggling body.

Louise said severely, "She was like an animal."

John thought privately, yes, but there was a great human affection, too, in the way she was holding Fred. He remembered her, lips parted, teeth clenched on her own hand, the moaning of the primal symphony pouring out into her lover's ear, driving him to further passion, the final rhythmic shudders.

He turned to his wife and they made love, without words, or acknowledgement of love, as always.

Daily Telegraph, Tuesday, November 3, 1914

FIGHT FOR CALAIS
HOTTEST SINCE MONS
GERMAN FORLORN HOPE

From Wm. Maxwell. In France, October 28. **The road to the coast is barred: the march on Calais has failed as the march on Paris and Warsaw failed. There is a halt in the fighting in the north. Does it mean that the enemy is exhausted or is about to change his plans? He has paid a heavy toll on the Yser, yet he gives no sign of retiring. On the contrary he clings grimly to the one footing he won a week ago south of the canal—the loop near Tervaete, midway between Dixmude and Nieuport. It is manifest that the Germans have not given up all hope of forcing this passage to the sea. Tervaete, if it remains in their possession, is to be the covering point for another assault . . .**

Yes, the German plans had been foiled, thanks to the courage and determination of the fighting men of many countries; and, obviously, to some major miscalculations on the part of the German General Staff, which was supposed to be so all-knowing. Thank heavens for human weakness, in this case! The war would go on a long time now, that was sure, unless President Wilson could persuade the warring powers to come to terms; that would be no easy task. Everyone's blood was up; all had suffered so much that all wanted more than victory now—they wanted revenge, a pound of flesh.

A long war called for more manpower and more production. America would play an important part on the Allied side. She would try to keep out of the actual fighting, of course, while selling her goods and raw materials to any who could buy them—and take delivery—at much enhanced prices; for countries with a powerful enemy at their throats are in no position to haggle over prices. The only weapon the Allies had was the Royal Navy. By blockading the Germans, and their allies—indeed the whole continent of Europe that was not directly under Allied control—the navy could reduce America's possible customers to one —the Allied side. So far, so good, but that wouldn't help unless the Allies could also refuse to accept inflated prices, and that they could not usually do without risking defeat.

But surely the biggest step Britain could take to increase her war effort was to increase her own productivity by every means possible. Lloyd George was on the right track there by trying to get the trade unions to give up many of their restrictive practises for the duration of the war. But the managerial side would have to give up something too—and learn something from the more efficient methods of the Americans and, yes, the Germans. Richard Rowland was in the forefront there, as John was by employing women. That new company Richard was hoping to form with American capital, to make lorries with American production-line techniques, was a giant step in the right direction. The soldiers in France, and the sailors at sea were every moment having to deal with new problems, work out new methods to deal with new dangers. It would be criminal folly for the business men, the trade unions—and the government—to think that at home the nation could still carry on "Business as Usual".

Hedlington: Thursday, November 5, 1914

15 A thin ground fog filled the valley of the Scarrow between Beighton Down and Busby Down, in North Hedlington. The locomotive pulling a small train of shallow goods trucks northwards toward Rochester emitted billows of white smoke in the damp air. Its whistle shrilled curtly for a level crossing, the wheels of the trucks ground over the factory siding's rail joints, the loose couplings clanked one after another as they took the forward strain. The people who passed, hunched men on bicycles, women with shawls over their heads and market baskets on their arms, wore dark, heavy clothing against the chill: it was only 45°F., but in this damp the cold penetrated to the bone.

Four men stood in the entrance of a huge warehouse set on a rail siding between the South Eastern railway running lines and the Scarrow, just above the barge terminus, the upper end of commercial navigation. The floor of the building was concrete, the metal roof supported by steel tie beams. Large sliding doors were spaced at regular intervals along the west side, where the rail spur ran past the warehouse. The main doors, where the men stood, were each thirteen and a half feet high and twelve feet wide, sliding apart to form an opening thirteen and a half by twenty-four feet.

"It looks all right," the short man with the bowler hat stuck on the back of his head said. His accent and clothes were unmistakably American, and an American would have recognised from the grating of the syllables that he came from the Middle West. He continued, "You'll have to have an engineer test that the ties will take the extra weight of the roof windows we've got to put in. The walls won't support the travelling cranes, of course. They'll have to stand independently. The floor looks O.K., but it'll have to be tested, to take a hundred pounds a square foot. And we can cut the doors out to seventeen feet overall, if we want to run overhead trolleys or cranes in through them later."

Richard Rowland eyed the floor. The assembly line which Mr Overfeld was dying to build, on the Ford model, would fit nicely into the building. Sub-assemblies could be delivered through the side doors. It might be necessary to cut more doors on the river side, too. There was at least a hundred yards of unoccupied land between the building and the river bank. They could store the sub-assemblies and lesser parts there, and feed them in by belt, perhaps. Or . . .

Stephen Merritt said, "This seems suitable, then, for the assembly plant, Mr Overfeld?"

"Yes, Mr Merritt," the man in the bowler hat said, "we'll need a body shop, probably, unless we contract out for them, too. Power plant. Lighting for winter, at least. Paint shop. And a lot of storage, so production isn't held up because a sub-contractor's men go on strike—or a ship carrying engines hits a rock."

"Or is sunk by the Germans," Richard said. "They could call motor engines war material."

Stephen Merritt said, "How soon can we fit out this building? And design and build another—for all the things you mentioned?"

Johnny Merritt waited at his father's side. They were both wearing dark grey overcoats, dark grey felt hats, with silk scarves, Johnny's white, his father's beige. Richard and Overfeld talked technicalities for a few moments, then Overfeld said, "Are you willing to pay overtime?"

"Whatever's needed," Stephen said. "Time is money, in this case."

"If we can order what we need from Detroit right away, by cable, and if they have it, and can put it on ships on the East Coast within, say, three weeks . . . another two weeks to get to Liverpool . . . that's five weeks. From then, we should be ready to roll in another six weeks, in this building. That's toward the end of January. And if Mr Rowland can get the design, and the materials, and the contractors, and the labour—here, the other building should be ready about the same time."

"Freighter space is tight, I know," Stephen Merritt said. "Perhaps we could hire a small ship just to get the assembly line equipment over, with a first shipment of engines and sub-assemblies from Armbruster's."

"Do you think you'll definitely buy Armbruster's now?" Richard asked.

Stephen said, "It looks that way."

Richard felt in two minds about the prospect. Armbruster's was a

small firm which made commercial vehicles in Columbus, Ohio. Fairfax, Gottlieb had an option to buy it, by the end of the year, at a very
low price. It was a good firm, but was having trouble competing in the
American market, and the bank's original thought, in acquiring the option, was to put in more aggressive management to make the firm more
competitive. That could still be done, but if part of Armbruster's production was shipped to the new plant in Hedlington, put together
there, with other parts sub-contracted from smaller manufacturers all
over England—Richard would be very much a small-scale version of
Ford, Reo, and other American automobile manufacturers who had set
up operations in Britain. When Richard had first talked in detail to
Stephen Merritt about his ideas, he had thought to design and make
his own vehicles, from the bottom up; but Merritt had made him see
that there was no time for that; nor would it be so efficient as assembling parts made elsewhere. The design of machine tools, dies, forges,
and presses for Richard's all-new lorry—let alone the making of the tools
—would take many months, years even; and in wartime Britain the high
grade tool steel might not be made available. At all events, the new factory could not possibly have produced a lorry within a year and a half.

Armbruster's made two models, one with a 116" wheelbase and a 24
hp 4-cylinder engine, designed for a payload of 30 cwt; and another
with a 131" wheelbase and a 45 hp 6-cylinder engine, designed for a
payload of 3 tons. In discussions with the Merritts all had agreed that if
they finally did use Armbruster's major sub-assemblies, they'd concentrate on the larger model.

And, at the beginning they'd be receiving crated sets of parts, which
wouldn't need much more than a few spanners to assemble. The crux
of the problem after that was to get sufficiently large orders quickly
enough to make the Ford-style assembly methods justifiable in terms of
capital outlay. And by then, say a year from now, they ought to be
thinking and planning in terms of a Mark II J.M.C., in which the
American components might be no more than the engine, gearbox, and
back axle—all the rest would be British made, and adapted to the original basic Armbruster's design.

Stephen turned to his son, "It's time we put up or shut up. What do
you think?"

"This is the best prospect we've seen," Johnny said. "I think we
should go ahead with the whole project, based on making the vehicles
in this building. I think we may have some difficulty getting hold of
some materials, though. And labour."

Stephen said, "Our bank has had dealings in the past with the
Chancellor of the Exchequer, Mr Lloyd George. I will see him, and ad-

vise him of our plans. He can not but welcome such an influx of American capital, at this time. And I shall cable New York this afternoon, because . . . I agree with you."

Richard said, "Well, good! I'm delighted. But when you see Mr Lloyd George, please stress the importance to us of getting some large government orders, quickly—otherwise we might get into financial trouble . . . and England would lose what's going to be a very efficient and effective plant."

They walked toward the back of the warehouse, where they had left their cars, Richard his Rowland and the Merritts their hired chauffeur-driven Rolls Royce. There they parted, after agreeing to meet again the following day with more detailed notes on design factors for the new building. Then the Americans drove away. Richard stood a moment, looking at the warehouse, soon to be the headquarters of J.M.C.— Jupiter Motor Company. The Armbruster assemblies would have American sizes of screws, bolts, nuts . . . little would be interchangeable with standard British parts. That didn't matter now, it might later; what did matter was that parts within each machine should be interchangeable, so that a bolt missing from somewhere could be replaced by another from somewhere else; and of course that the parts in one J.M.C. machine were interchangeable with those in another.

A clock in North Hedlington struck twelve and he started his car; his next appointment was at 12.15 in the White Horse, nearby.

He drove out through the open wire mesh gates of the warehouse yard, got out, closed and locked the gates behind him and was about to get back into the car when a man accosted him. "Mr Rowland." He recognised Bert Gorse, and said, "What can I do for you, Bert?"

"Got a cold. Took the day off . . . You going to make the new factory here?"

"Perhaps."

"When'll you be starting work?"

"Not for some months yet . . . two or three. We'll be building before then, though."

"There's Yankee money behind you, I hear."

Richard answered coldly, "There is American interest in the venture." He wished he could trust Gorse, wished he could make him realise that his best interests lay in using his intelligence to help the managers, the owners, rather than in trying to weld the unthinking and largely unskilled workers into an organised opposition.

"You'll be paying Yankee wages?"

"We'll pay well. I must go . . ."

"Will you give me a job, as soon's you're ready? A better job than I got now, with Mr Harry?"

Richard looked into the narrow-set green eyes. There weren't many working men as sharp as Gorse—or as skilled—or as dangerous, perhaps. But he was going to be in a terrible bind for overseers and foremen of all kinds. His father would be furious, but that couldn't be helped.

He said, "I'll take you . . . if you promise to do no union work."

"You're making a mistake," Bert said, real earnestness in his voice, "if you supported a union—the Engineers, say—they'd support you."

Richard said, "If you want a shop foreman's job, you've got to get out of the union. That's final."

He engaged gear and drove off. In the rearview mirror he saw Bert Gorse standing, legs akimbo, arms folded, cloth cap pulled down over his forehead, watching him go.

As he slowed to turn onto the main road a small boy ran alongside and shouted up at him, "Penny for the Guy, mister!"

He found a sixpence in his pocket, pressed it into the grubby palm and drove on, the treble voice chanting behind him, "Thanks, mister. Penny for the Guy! 'Oo'll give a penny for the Guy?"

Outside the White Horse in North Hedlington, the inn sign hung still in the damp windless air. It showed the prancing White Horse of Kent, a broken chain flying from its neck—the same device which, set over a stringed bugle horn, was the cap badge of the Weald Light Infantry. It was a big pub, with saloon, private and public bars, a dining-room facing over the muddy Scarrow, and a reputation as a good place for assignations. The owners, an ex-petty officer R.N. and his wife, possibly an ex-chorus girl and certainly an ex-barmaid, were honest and reasonably hard-working, and they were not inquisitive: business flourished.

Richard sat against the wall in the saloon bar, the solicitor Jim Hutton opposite, a plate of cold tongue, pickles, salad, and sliced bread and butter between them, tankards of beer at their sides. Jim had a deformed right foot, wore a club boot, and walked with a limp. Besides being a solicitor he was also the Conservative party agent in Hedlington. Richard had hardly known him until, soon after leaving his father's firm, he had also decided to leave the family solicitors, and put his affairs in Hutton's hands.

Hutton put a slice of tongue, with mustard and mustard-and-cress onto a slice of bread, and said, "Your father's nursing this constituency for the Liberals, Richard."

"No one's ever admitted it—but I've heard it rumoured."

"It's a fact. Someone in the Liberals' parliamentary office talked, and it got out. If he's nursing Mid-Scarrow for the Liberals, someone ought to be nursing it for the Conservatives."

"There's a political truce," Richard said, drinking some bitter. "Ellis is a Liberal, so if he dies or retires, the Conservatives have agreed not to oppose whomever the Liberals put up for the seat."

"The war might be over soon. Or the truce break down. Then what? They'll have a well-known candidate, and we'll have no one."

"I don't think the war'll be over soon."

"Nor do I, frankly. Rowland's got a good order for staff cars for the army last week."

"I heard."

"We ought to be able to get a big order for you . . . Jupiter, isn't it?"

"J.M.C., it will be."

". . . . in return for us keeping the truce."

"Perhaps. But we're not going to be able to turn out any machines for some months . . . six, probably." He looked round as a red-faced man with a paunch, black bowler hat, celluloid collar, and bright green tie slapped Hutton on the back, "'Ullo, Jimmy boy. Afternoon, Mr Rowland."

Hutton said, "Oh, so you know Mr Rowland."

"All of 'em," Bill Hoggin said heartily, "I married into the business, so to speak. My Ruthie's Bob Stratton's daughter. Got a little problem to speak to you about."

"Well, I'm busy all this afternoon, but . . ."

"Make it four o'clock, Jimmy boy," Hoggin said. He fished in his pocket and planked a five-pound note on the table beside Hutton's tankard, "Cash in advance, can't say that of most of your clients, can you?" He tipped his hat and moved on to the far end of the saloon.

"Coarse brute," Hutton muttered.

"It looks as if the war's bringing *him* prosperity, at least."

Hutton nodded. "He's in the food business, in Eastcheap. Don't know why he's down here in the middle of the week . . . probably has some shady deal brewing, and wants me to tell him how to get round the law. He's making a mint, though . . . until he gets caught . . ." He turned to face Richard directly, "We'd like you to nurse the constituency as the next Conservative party candidate for Mid-Scarrow. The committee has discussed it and all agree. You are young, energetic, progressive, the sort of man we want. Between you and me, the party has too many old fossils—landowners, relics from the dark ages. And it will make good publicity that you and your father are quarrelling."

"Not exactly quarrelling."

"You know what I mean."

Richard thought—why not? He could do the job as well as most, if he were elected. And it might help him get orders for J.M.C. He said, "All right. I accept."

"Good!" Hutton stuck out his hand, and they shook. "We won't make any public announcement and, of course, the truce is still in effect, but we'll be ready if it's broken, either locally or nationally. Anything I can do for you, meanwhile?"

Richard said at once, "Yes. I'd give a lot to have Frank Stratton as Works foreman. He's a marvellous mechanic and he manages men well, particularly unskilled labour, which most of ours will be. He's in the Wealds—joined up in August. He's at the depot here still, I know."

"I know the depot commander—old Colonel Bainbridge—dug out from retirement a week after war was declared. I'll telephone him this afternoon."

"I don't know whether Frank will come out, even if the army's willing to let him go. He has a strong sense of duty."

"A couple of months of army life may have cooled his ardour."

They finished the meal, talking desultorily until Hutton left for his office. Richard sat back, thinking. Soon, he should go home and start working on the problems to be discussed with Overfeld and the Merritts tomorrow; meantime, he would just spend a few moments at peace, thinking, and digesting.

One of the matters he had discussed with Hutton just now was his will. He had no children, so to whom should he leave his estate—which might become very considerable if J.M.C. prospered? After Susan, of course . . . It was unfortunate, but something vital had gone out of their sexual relations, once they knew that no child would ever come of them. For the first five or six years they had been as near perfect as was possible, but during those years they had been telling themselves, one day it will happen. They had not then accepted the fact of sterility; but afterwards, gradually, sterility came in . . . not only the physiological fact of it, but increasingly in the sex act, and to some extent in their whole marriage, even their friendship.

He finished his beer and got up . . . designs for the new building . . . see Toledano's, with Stephen Merritt about capitalizing J.M.C. . . . study blueprints of Ford's Manchester plant more closely . . . think very carefully about wise use of capital . . . He went out, put on his driving glasses, and headed the Rowland for Beighton. He'd get in three hours or so of work before he had to come back to Hedlington to pick up his sister Alice.

Hill House, Beighton, where Richard and Susan Rowland lived simply with a butler, chauffeur, cook, and two maids, was a brick house, built about 1880, on the slope of Moncton Hill, halfway between Hedlington and Walstone on the Moncton Hill road, so called to differentiate it from the river road, which ran up the Scarrow, through Cantley and Taversham, to Hedlington. Scarrow Rise, five miles to the south, hid Walstone, but on a clear day the upper floors of Walstone Park could be seen over the west end of the Rise. It was quite dark at six o'clock on this Guy Fawkes' Day, as Richard drove slowly past the kennels of the North Weald Hunt, on the outskirts of Beighton, and into the village. The hounds were giving tongue in their kennels and he wondered why until, coming round the final bend, a pair of rockets whooshed up into the clouded dark above, fiery sparks trailing in their wake. Smoke from bonfires in back gardens, and a giant one on Beighton Common, rose straight up in the still damp of the evening. Silhouetted against the fires, two boys were playing conkers, swinging the dried chestnuts fiercely in turn. Firecrackers danced down the gravelled road, Roman candles sputtered, girls screamed excitedly. At every bonfire a broomstick or pole wilted under the weight of the Guy that had been built round it—straw stuffing, a torn coat, rag doll face, a black hat.

Children danced round the fires, chanting, "Remember, remember the Fifth of November, the Gunpowder Treason and *Plot!* Remember, remember the Fifth of November, the Gunpowder Treason and *Plot!* Remember, remember . . ."

"The children do so love Guy Fawkes' Day," Alice said, at his side.

"So do a lot of grown-ups," Richard said, indicating the thirty or forty people gathered round the bonfire on the common. More rockets rose, to land God only knew where. The village constable strode ominously toward two boys in a small cottage's tiny front garden. "Now, look 'ere, you young rapscallions, you'll be setting fire to the thatches, you will! Point them things out that way, see?"

They drove on, turned up the narrow road to Hill House and soon swung round the tight circle in front of the house, and stopped. All the front windows were open; and Susan was standing in the bowed front of the drawing-room, looking out over the flying rockets and glowing bonfires below. The chauffeur bustled up, opening the door for Alice. "Evening, Miss Alice, evening, sir. Will you be wanting me to take Miss Alice back to Hedlington, as usual?"

"Yes, Stafford. About half-past nine probably."

"Very good, sir."

Stafford was twenty-three. Richard wondered how long he would be able to keep him; and whether he ought to try.

They went into the house, Susan at the front door now to hug Alice and kiss Richard; then to the drawing-room, and Summers serving sherry, the curtains still drawn back, the fires and lights below haloed by damp, smoke from the bonfires drifting slowly up the hill and into the house. In the bright light Richard noticed that his wife looked drawn, and said, "Are you feeling all right, Susan?"

She said, "Your father called, a few minutes ago. Mr Ellis heard a rumour in Parliament today, and called him. There's supposed to have been a battle at sea off Chile, in the Pacific, a few days ago. The news has only just arrived here, because two of our ships were sunk and the others had to escape as best they could. One of the ships sunk was H.M.S. *Monmouth*."

"Tom's ship!" Richard gasped.

"Yes. Mr Ellis said that the Admiralty do not intend to make any announcement until they've checked all the facts, but they probably will tomorrow."

"No one was saved?"

"Mr Ellis said that there were no survivors from either ship. And that we didn't sink any of the German ships."

Richard stood a long moment, silent. Tom . . . floating cold and dead in the ocean, being eaten by fishes. He shivered, drank down his sherry, and said, "I don't think anyone's heard from Quentin for nearly a month."

Susan said, "The casualty lists are getting bigger every day."

"And hate growing every minute," Alice said quietly. "Yesterday in Hedlington I heard some people booing a lady down the street, and I asked a man what she had done. He said the lady was called Mrs Schmidt. When I asked some more questions it turned out that she was English, married for twenty-five years to a German who deserted her and left England five years ago. I would never have believed English people capable of such blind, stupid hatred."

Richard said, "Boy will be in France any moment now. John told me."

They were all silent. At length Susan said, "Mr Hutton called, too, while you were out. He said he spoke to Colonel Bainbridge, and to Frank Stratton. The colonel thinks it could be arranged for Frank to be released from the army, but Frank doesn't want to go. He said to give you his respects, but he would rather stay in the regiment."

Richard said, "I was afraid so . . . but thank heaven for the Frank Strattons of this world, all the same. And as for Tom and Quentin, we must keep hoping."

Then they spoke of other things, Richard mostly quiet while the two women talked in low tones. At last Richard remembered something that had been at the back of his mind for several days. He waited for a pause in the conversation, then said, "Alice, how old are you?"

"Thirty-four. And unmarried . . . that's what you are going to point out, isn't it?" She laughed lightly. "You have a suitor for my hand?"

Richard did not smile. She was his favourite sister. Being the eldest, nine years old when she was born, he had looked after her a great deal, when the nannies and governesses were enjoying their half-days off. After she came out and was presented at Court he had tried to find suitable young men for her—to no avail. Now, she came regularly to dine with them at Hill House once a month, sometimes more often.

He said, "In a few months I am going to have J.M.C. producing lorries. There will be a great deal of paper work to organise and keep track of before that is achieved—starting now. You are educated, even if the Governor wouldn't let you go away to school or university. You have taught yourself to type, I know. You have a good head for figures. And you have a good mind to read and understand things . . . such as government regulations, tax laws, and so on. We're going to need a secretary for J.M.C., someone to start and run the office. Will you accept the position?"

Alice said nothing, looking into the glowing coals of the fire.

Richard said, "It will not be easy, Dormouse. It'll be a real challenge. But I think you can do it."

Then Alice said, "My dear Lamps, I would love to—but I can't."

"Mother?" Susan said.

Alice nodded. "She's not well. I don't know what's the matter with her. She won't go to see the doctor. Perhaps it's just old age. Whatever it is, someone has to look after her. Not every minute—she's not as ill as that. But some of the time. Take the weight of running Laburnum Lodge off her. Look after the Governor when she's too tired even to talk to him."

Richard said, "You have too much talent to waste it. Oh, I know it's not a waste, to look after Mother. But there are others who can do what you're doing. The Governor can afford to get a housekeeper, and a nurse or companion perhaps. But you are capable of living your own life, a much more exciting and rewarding life."

"I'm capable of it, yes, Lamps, but I can't . . . Mother has to be looked after by someone who loves her. Same with the Governor . . . and anyway, I'm writing to a Mrs Jason Kerr in Hammersmith who's started something called a Tipperary Room there, for wives and relatives of soldiers and sailors to sew and knit and learn home nursing, and how to be good mothers, all sorts of things."

"But . . ."

"I'm going to start a Tipperary Room in Hedlington."

Richard said, "Well, it's something. But you're capable of much more than that . . ."

"Perhaps. But it's all I can do, with the other. I really am sorry, Giglamps."

The three of them sat in Stephen Merritt's suite on the second floor of the South Eastern Hotel. The sitting-room, with angled bow windows, was large and comfortably furnished; the bedroom was smaller, as it had recently been bisected and half of it turned into a private bathroom and toilet; but the wash-handstand in the bedroom had not been removed. At the same time central heating had been put in throughout the hotel, and the three radiators in the room were all gurgling quietly. It was a sound that the Americans had seldom heard since their arrival in England: but welcomed, as a sign that, here at least, they would not need to wear their overcoats indoors. The windows were shut, and the red curtains drawn to keep out the raw cold and the low fog drifting south up the Scarrow valley from Rochester and the sea. A steam engine whistled and then chuff-chuffed out of the station on the Tonbridge line, all sounds softened by the heavy curtains. It was ten o'clock.

"The British sure like to set off fireworks," Overfeld said. His bowler hat was hanging on the back of the door, revealing a shaven bullet head. "Back there around dinner time it was like the 4th of July. And why the scarecrows they were burning everywhere? Are they meant to be the Kaiser?"

"No—Guy Fawkes," Johnny said. "He and some other Roman Catholics tried to blow up the Houses of Parliament. They were caught and executed."

"When was this?"

"1605. As I'm living in England, I thought I should know."

"You don't have to tell me the day or the month. Remember, remember the Fifth of November, the Gunpowder Treason and *Plot*. That crazy ditty's been ringing in my head all evening. It still is."

Stephen coughed. "Time we wrapped it up for the day, then. Let's see where we are . . . The cable's gone, recommending that we close the deal to buy Armbruster's. Also listing the main items we want bought and shipped over here . . . and instructions on hiring sea transportation. You've worked out a rough floor plan for the new building, and you're going to go through it with us and Mr Rowland tomorrow?"

"That's right, boss," Overfeld said.

"On Monday Johnny and I and Mr Rowland will go to London to hire lawyers to arrange incorporation, and the British end of the financing. Mr Rowland is to have the managing directorship of the new firm, with a salary to be agreed on plus ten percent of the net profits, after tax. Also ten percent of the common stock will be offered to him at one fifth of par. Another director will come from the British bank—probably Toledano's. Two will be members of the Board of Fairfax, Gottlieb in New York. The fifth will be resident here, and will have the proxies of the New York directors. And that will be you, Overfeld. But you will take Johnny here into your full confidence. He's here to learn, but he can't unless he's shown, and told. He's going to send me informal reports on how things are going here—not only with the plant, but in England generally, and with the war—so don't think he's going behind your back."

"No, sir," Overfeld said vigorously. "Writing's not my game. Johnny went to Harvard."

"Quite. But you send financial statements, which must be worked out and agreed on by Mr Rowland . . . What are your plans for next week?"

"Try to find a builder capable of putting up that new building in a hurry. And make a guess at the materials he will need, so that we can ensure they will be on hand when he wants them. Cable a pal of mine in Detroit to come over as plant foreman. He works for Cadillac now."

"Docs he have tact? English workmen aren't going to like an American foreman, you know."

"Morgan's Welsh—came over as a baby with his parents. His dad worked in the coal mines. Morgan can charm the birds out of the trees. We'll have to pay him, though."

"Give him twenty percent more than he's getting now, to start with." He sat back, yawning. The room was full of cigar smoke, for both he and Overfeld smoked, Overfeld vile thin brutes of the kind called Wheeling stogies. He appeared to have brought a thousand of them over on the ship with him. Overfeld said, "What do you think of the war, boss? Are the British and French going to make it?"

Stephen said, "I think so. I hope so. We shall have thrown a few million dollars down the drain if they don't."

"That'll be true of a lot of other concerns," Overfeld said. "The British and French are buying one heck of a lot of goods from us . . . on credit."

Stephen nodded. Overfeld was a shrewd man, for all that his formal education had ended at the 12th grade. He had seen what was only just beginning to be apparent even to experts: that America might be

drawn into the war to protect her own investments. It was not a likeli-
hood—yet: and it never would be if the U.S. could sell to both sides
equally . . . but the British blockade prevented all but a tiny trickle of
sales to the Central Powers. Without firing a shot the Royal Navy was
slowly forcing her toward a position of support for the Allies, and who
could prophesy how far that support would finally have to go?

Johnny said, "I think that if we can hold Ypres, and prevent the
Germans getting round our flank—the northern flank—we'll be all
right."

"We, Johnny?" Overfeld said, "O.K., O.K., I was only having you
on."

Johnny stood up, stretching. "I'm off to bed. Any reason why I
shouldn't go down to Walstone for the weekend, Dad?"

Stephen thought. "None at all. When will you go?"

"I'll bicycle down tomorrow evening, when we're finished here. Mrs
Cate has invited me to come whenever I want to, and yesterday I got a
letter from Stella, asking if I would like to come down this weekend—
they're going cubbing on Saturday."

"What's that?" Overfeld asked.

"Killing fox cubs, with the foxhounds . . . I've read about it. Sunday I don't know what we'll do; walk on the Downs perhaps. Go to
church, I know. Mr Cate always goes. I'll be back here in time for dinner Sunday night."

"All right. One thing, Johnny. Stella's a sweet girl I'm sure, but
make sure she's not involved too closely in her mother's Irish affairs before you get too involved with *her*."

"Mrs Cate hasn't done anything wrong," Johnny said shortly.

"They have not yet been able to prove that she has," his father corrected him. "Perhaps because of items like this." He pushed a copy of
the London evening paper toward Johnny, his finger on the back page.
Johnny read: the item stated that a man found murdered yesterday in
an alley near Paddington had been identified as an Irishman, and was
rumoured to have been a Sinn Feiner who was also a police informer.

Johnny said, "Mrs Cate wouldn't know anything about that, even if
it's true."

"Perhaps not," Stephen said, "but don't forget what I said. Be careful . . . Good night, Johnny. See you at breakfast—eight o'clock sharp."

"Good night, Johnny," Overfeld said: but stood up before speaking,
to show that he knew he was talking to the boss's son.

The Rowland purred northwards out of Beighton. It was a quarter to
ten, and there were nine miles of narrow country road ahead. The acet-

ylene headlamps bored into the half-darkness, for clouds dimmed the stars and an almost-full moon. It had stopped raining, and the celebrations and re-enactments of Guy Fawkes' ghastly deed of November 5th, 1605, were over for the year. Perhaps they'd be the last for a long time, Alice thought. The explosives used could not be much, in terms of what the army was using in France, but next year they might all be going over there, to kill, rather than celebrate.

She sat beside Stafford on the front seat, huddled into her winter coat, a big scarf pulled down over her hat to frame her face and keep her ears warm, her hands in a fur muff.

She thought that Susan had looked more lonely than ever. And Richard, though so busy with the plans for the Jupiter Motor Company, was not happy. It was a tragedy when people who loved each other could not have children. So often they seemed to turn against each other in secret ways. And what did she know about that, someone might ask, seeing that she had not even known a man, as the Bible put it, let alone given birth or suckled a child? She was withering on the vine, many thought . . . unwatered, drying up. She didn't feel like that, in herself; but perhaps she seemed like it, to others. Much that she would like—such as marriage, and children, even such as the position Richard had offered her—was apparently never to be hers. So she had better think of other matters, or she would start feeling sorry for herself.

She said to Stafford, "Our men are putting up a wonderful fight at Ypres, aren't they?"

"Yes, miss. I sometimes think I ought to be there with them. I'm young."

She sighed, not wishing to answer or speak to the implied question. It was for the young men who would be killed to decide, not to women and old men safe and warm in England.

The chauffeur said, "I hope the Commander turns up, miss. So does Mr Summers and Mrs Baker and the girls. We was all so shocked when Mrs Rowland told us, in the servants' hall."

"I hope so too," she said, "and I do believe he's all right. I just can't believe that he's dead. Or Major Quentin. One day soon we'll get a telegram from the Admiralty saying that the Commander was picked up in the sea . . . perhaps by a tramp ship that didn't have wireless, so couldn't report anything till it reached port."

"I certainly hope so, miss."

Then soon they were in the outskirts of Hedlington, slowing down, for the streets were ill-lit, and liable to be full of drunken men and women, and others, not drunk, but going home from the pubs, full of beer and not as careful as they should be. They passed through the centre of the town, past the South Eastern Hotel and the station, turned off and in a few minutes came to Garston Road. Laburnum Lodge was the fourth house on the left, going up.

A lamp post stood outside the gate to the driveway. It was burning, its gaslit mantle throwing out a sphere of light to illumine the leafless trees, a patch of roadway, the open wrought iron gates to the drive, the shiny leaves of the laurel hedge—and a shape dangling from the green painted horizontal metal crossbar just below the lamp, where the town lamplighters used to prop their ladders when they lit each street lamp by hand, before the present system of pilot lights was installed, and the main gas turned on all over town from the central gas station.

"Stop," Alice said. "What's that . . . on the lamp post?"

Stafford brought the car to a stop, in the pool of darkness between that lamp and the one before it. He jumped down from the driver's seat, and Alice climbed down on her side. They walked back together, into the light, and looked up, staring into the hissing mantle.

"Oh . . . oh . . . oh!" Alice choked, unable to speak, not knowing how to swear.

"It's a dog," Stafford said. "Well, I'll be . . . someone's hanged a dog, miss. It's one of them long dogs. Oh my God, it's not . . ."

"It's a dachshund," Alice said, feeling she would burst. "And it is ours. It's Freda."

"Oh, miss . . . the swine, the dirty swine! The poor dog!"

"Don't be sorry for Freda," Alice choked. "Be sorry for the people who did this. Get a ladder from the house, please, Stafford. I'll wait here."

Daily Telegraph, Friday, November 6th, 1914

VICTORY OF THE RUSSIAN ARMY
THE GERMAN RETREAT
QUARRELS WITH AUSTRIANS

Petrograd. Thursday. **The following official communiqué from the Great Army HQ is published here today: "We continue to progress on the East Prussian front. The Germans are falling back along the whole front, only keeping a fortified position in the region of Wergboliwo. On**

the left bank of the Vistula, the Russian army is continuing its vigorous offensive, pursuing the retreating enemy. The crossing of the San by our troops continues with
success. The Austrians are retreating. In the Black Sea
region no change is reported." REUTER.

Cate read on: the Germans and Austrians were arguing over the conduct of the war, and over responsibility for the defeat—according to the
report. He remembered the triumphant communiqués of August about
the all-conquering Great Army, the snivelling dissension-torn Teutons
. . . and then, Tannenberg! War was terrible; and one of the most terrible things about it, in the long run, was the cynicism it was breeding.
The Russians seemed to be the biggest official liars—or self-deluders—
but he could not absolve his own government from some of the same
folly.

He went to the study and sat down at his desk, thinking. That had
been a good celebration of Guy Fawkes' Day in Walstone yesterday.
Young Tommy Snell had burned his hand quite badly, picking up a
firecracker on a dare; but that was about average for the occasion. P.C.
Fulcher had reported that old Mrs Watson's thatch caught fire, but he
and a few others had been able to put it out without much damage
done. Magistrate's court this afternoon . . . one motor car speeding,
and one poaching case, not Probyn, thank heaven. He hadn't seen
Probyn for quite a time . . . ought to go down and see how he was
. . . help him get a dog, perhaps . . . but that would only help him
poach the more efficaciously. What business was it of his what Probyn
did with a dog, until he'd done it? There were several sets of small puppies about in the village, he knew . . . and some of them the right
breeds, teachable as gun dogs, and for, er, silent work at dark or
dusk . . .

Frank Cawthon had made up his mind to change the Abbas herd to
Friesians. It was a bold step . . . in the forefront, just like Richard and
John Rowland, in their ways. British farmers didn't take kindly to foreign breeds of cattle, any more than they did to foreign ideas; but
Frank had showed him facts and figures, and proved his case. And the
aim was what the aim of every man, woman, and child in Britain, who
wasn't in the fighting line, should be—produce, make, save!

Farm accounts for income tax purposes . . . they could wait. He took
out a sheet of the heavy white notepaper printed in black Roman capi-
tals with the WALSTONE MANOR, KENT; and then *Tel: Walstone 1*. He
pulled the ink pot a little closer, dipped his relief nib in the blue ink,
and began to write:

November 6th, 1914.

Dear Laurence,

Thank you for your letter of last Sunday. You will have heard that the police came to arrest your mother that day, and to search the house for explosives and treasonable documents. They found nothing, and your mother will be released tomorrow, I am assured. She would send you her love if she were in a position to do so, I am sure.

We are delighted to hear that you have been tried for the Second XI. Most public schools have long since turned to Rugby, but soccer is a good game, too, with more finesse, and more opportunity for the boy (or man) who is not of great size to excell.

The Montagu's harrier I mentioned last week seems to have left. No one I've asked has seen it since. It would be rare for one to stay on in England after late October, so I suppose it has gone to the Continent. I hope none of the farmers has shot it. Cubbing has been going well, and . . .

Walstone: Saturday, November 7, 1914

16 Probyn Gorse sat at the little table, eating Irish stew off a cracked china plate with an old wooden spoon. The sheep that formed the base for the stew had been quite old when its fellows accidentally pushed it over the edge of a chalk pit on Beighton Down. The shepherd might have sold the carcass to a butcher in Hedlington, telling his master that foxes had got it, or that it had been stolen by the soldiers now manoeuvring every day all over the Down: but he never seriously considered that course. Instead, he thought of his friend of many years, Probyn Gorse, who could always be relied on to do a man a good turn when he had the chance; and he divided the carcass in two, and sent word by a passing baker's van to Probyn to come up to the Down. Probyn had come, at dusk, with an empty sack, suspecting what might befall, and this was the fifth day the family had been eating the sheep—and the last. They'd had sheep's head and brains, cooked over the open fire; and roast leg of old ewe, very tough but tasty; and cottage pie and shepherd's pie; and a Kentish form of haggis which was part of Probyn's Woman's mysterious store of cooking lore; and now, at the end, Irish stew, the potatoes, onions, and carrots provided in part by the bounty of the Cates, and in part stolen by Fletcher, or 'borrowed' by Florinda from the kitchen garden of Walstone Park.

The twins were hunched over the wood fire, Florinda reading and Fletcher writing, by the light of a candle set on the table behind them. The Woman stood motionless nearby, watching Probyn eat. Her own food was still in the pot: she would eat later. It was four o'clock and getting dark, but not raining.

Probyn had been out of prison not quite a month. He had somehow avoided going to prison before, due mainly to the good will of Squire Cate. Now he wondered whether he had been right to avoid it so assiduously. The food wasn't good, but it was edible and there was usually plenty of it. The bed there was more comfortable than the bed here: no woman to keep his back warm, but much time to think, of stars and earth, of animals and birds, of the life he lived, and of the death that would come.

He pushed his plate away, done. Fletcher heard the sound and looked up. People seldom spoke to his grandfather when he was eating. He said, "Saw the hounds today. Cubbing in Felstead Woods."

"Squire out?"

"Yes. And Stella and a young fellow who was talking funny. American, maybe. He looked sweet on Stella."

"She'd best be careful, if she can," Probyn said.

The Woman said, "I heard today that Bob Stratton only likes the ones with no hair on it."

"Where did you hear that?"

"In a pub in Hedlington. I was there this morning . . . From a woman I know. A whore, she is."

"Don't believe everything you hear from whores," Probyn said. He shook his head. "It ain't natural till it's got hair on it . . . but them poor buggers can't help themselves. He'll finish up in Dartmoor for life, likely . . . Stella was with an American?"

Fletcher nodded, adding, "And she's flirting with a wounded officer, too. She must have been to Hedlington half a dozen times, to parties and dances at the barracks, since he came out of the hospital. I don't know his name."

"Irwin," the Woman said, "Captain Irwin. Wounded in the legs. He was bad for a time, and still walks with a cane. He'll be at the barracks for another couple of months at least. Mary told me. She was selling some of her needlework, in the saloon, getting money to buy a book that'll learn Willum how to read, she hopes."

"Wonder who'll get Stella on her back first," Fletcher said. "Him, or the American?"

Probyn found his pipe on the mantelpiece, filled it from a battered tin of tobacco, and began to smoke. The Woman filled a bowl with stew, and ate it, standing, bowl in hand.

Fletcher got up with a single lithe movement, but the Woman had moved slightly and his shoulder knocked the bowl from her hand. Fletcher swore aloud, then said, "Sorry."

The Woman scraped up the mess, and took what little was left in the pot to refill her bowl. Fletcher stood frowning, staring into the fire. He said suddenly, "This place is getting smaller every day, Granddad."

Probyn did not answer. There was nothing to say. Fletcher was no longer a boy or a youth, but a man. Now everything he had known as a boy would seem to shrink. And he wanted a place of his own, to bring his girls, and write his poetry, think his thoughts. It was natural. But there was nothing he could do about it. Fletcher would have to do it himself.

Fletcher said, "I reckon I'll go and live in the woods, and write poetry."

Florinda said, without looking up from her book, "And take Sally or Jane with you, so's you won't have to lie on the ground . . . or gather wood . . . or pluck . . . or cook . . . or draw water . . . ?"

Fletcher said, "Or Mary, or Ada, or Babs down at Mortlock, it could be."

"And eat grass?" Florinda said.

"If I work at the hop picking every year, I can save enough money to buy what I need, but can't find, for all year."

"Don't be ridiculous, my dear man," Florinda said, "you know perfectly well you can't do such a thing." The other three looked up startled, for it was Florinda speaking, but the voice had been the voice of the Countess of Swanwick, perfect in tone, intonation, accent, timbre, and the words chosen. Probyn looked down again with a shake of his head. She had always been a good mimic and, in the years since she and Fletcher had come to live with him, he ought to have got used to it; but he hadn't. And now she was better than merely good, she was perfect. Florinda continued, "And I must say, Probyn, that I agree with this young man. This cottage is really too small for words . . . and it's positively indecent that I should have to sleep with a man, at my age . . . even worse, the man in question is none other than my brother."

It was quite dark outside now. Probyn listened. Still not raining. Good. The rabbits didn't like to come out too early if the grass was wet.

Fletcher said to his sister, "You got nothing to worry about. You only live here your day off. You got a great big room of your own at the big house."

"My dear fellow, have you ever seen the rooms allotted to the staff at Walstone Park? Minute, positively minute! And the roof of mine leaks directly over my bed. Every morning it appears that I have suffered an involuntary emission of urine . . . bed wetting, my good man, bed wetting . . ." Her voice changed—"Good afternoon, Mrs Gorse, good afternoon, Florinda . . . I have brought you some vegetables from our garden . . . How is Probyn? And Fletcher? Both well, I hope . . . Well, I must be getting along. Goodbye, goodbye . . ." Her voice returned to natural—"She'll be coming round again now, I suppose, now they've let her out of prison."

"Who brought the carrots and potatoes?"

"Garrod. Blyth's past seventy, and Squire's going to have to get a new butler any day—but where'll he find one?"

The Woman said, "He won't, with this war. Garrod'll do the job. She ought to know how—been at the Manor over thirty-five years now." She went out, closing the door behind her.

Fletcher said to his sister, "You never told us how you like it, at the Park."

Florinda grimaced. "Ah, it's a bore. Lady Swanwick's not a bad old dame, but the job . . . I learned it in a week, working for Lady Barbara, and it's nothing. Look after her clothes, brush her hair, tell her what to wear. Being a lady is easy work, once you've got the hang of it. How to eat nice, talk nice, walk nice, and act dirty."

"And you've learned?" Fletcher taunted.

"Yes, I have," she said slowly, not teasing or fooling; and though her voice was upper class it was not imitative—it was a voice that had suddenly become hers. "I am going to be one, soon—very soon. Things are happening."

Probyn stepped over to the fireplace and gave her a sweeping slap on the face. She made no sound but bent forward, her hand to her cheek. Probyn leaned over her, pointing—"You mind how you lead on the men at the Big House, Lady Blah! They're servants, but they're men too —some of 'em. You know better than to get your belly filled, but how'd you like to finish up under a hedge, strangled with your own stockings . . . you wear 'em now, don't you? You be careful, see?"

"All right, Granddad," she said quietly, her hand still to her cheek.

It was quite dark. Probyn said, "Tell her to set the alarm clock for five when she comes in," and went through to the bedroom he shared with the Woman.

Fletcher called after him, "Shall I come with you in the morning, Granddad?"

"No," he grunted, and closed the door behind him. In darkness he pulled off his clothes, down to his grey wool combinations, and climbed into the cold bed. He lay awhile, thinking. Time was when he didn't need to have the alarm clock wake him, but now either he didn't wake up, or he couldn't sleep, remembering what time he should get up. He

didn't have to tell the Woman he'd want a hot cup of tea before he
went out. She'd learned that the day he got her.

Outside, by the fire, the Woman had come in, and was sitting in the
chair Probyn had vacated. To his sister Fletcher said, "'Tis not one of
the servants at the Big House?"

Florinda shook her head.

The alarm rattled at five, and Probyn stirred. The Woman was already
up, no light showing in the front room, but two pieces of wood burning
in the stove, a pan on, tea stewing, milk ready in an earthenware pot to
one side, brown sugar in a jam jar. Probyn dressed carefully, slowly, in
the dark. Over the combinations he pulled on a brown flannel shirt, a
size too large for him, that Squire Cate had bought for him years ago in
a jumble sale, trousers of wide-wale corduroy, dark brown, patched in
two places, held up with frayed red braces, and also a wide leather belt;
then the moleskin waistcoat, stitched together from the skins of a dozen
moles, black, shiny, smooth as the inside of a woman's thighs; a short
jacket of the same corduroy as the trousers, the elbows patched with
leather; two pairs of socks, both thick wool, loosely woven—these the
Woman had knitted for him herself, the wool unravelled from various
pullovers and cardigans that the gentry kept giving to the poor. Probyn
had no use for cardigans, but in his profession there was nothing worse
than cold feet; and his boots—brown, hobnailed, laced with strong cord,
well soled and heeled, well greased—were as waterproof as anything
could be short of rubber.

The tea was ready and he sat in the chair by the table sipping it, for
it was too hot to drink fast. The moon was five days past full, and light
from its distorted sphere poured in through the dusty windows, onto
the table, the cup he drank from, the Woman standing ghostly pale by
the stove. He left half the tea in the cup, and went out to the outhouse,
pulled down his trousers and opened the flap of his combinations, and
sat waiting for the bowel movement. Five minutes and it was done. He
always went to the outhouse before leaving for work. In the woods it
was not good to have to shit. For one thing you were at the mercy of
anyone who happened to see you; for another, the keepers always went
out with dogs, and the dogs would pick up the smell of the shit from a
long way off on a good scenting day, and be after you . . . He wiped
himself desultorily with the paper, almost as coarse as packing paper,
that was the best the Woman could find. When he was a boy, they
used to use leaves. Now everyone used this stuff, and what the hell
good was it, besides costing money? That was what people were aiming
at—that everything should cost money, that used to be free; or that it

should cost more money. So now they made what used to be simple, complicated.

Back in the cottage he put on his cap, a tweed cap peaked fore and aft, a deerstalker of the sort that Sherlock Holmes was always shown wearing. It was raw cold outside, not raining, but blowing gustily from the north-west; but Probyn did not untie the knot that linked the earflaps on top of the cap, and pull them down to tie the knot under his chin. That would have kept his ears warm—and prevented him hearing.

He went out then and to the door of the lean-to shed built against the side of the cottage, toward the river. He slid back the bolt, and went into the semi-darkness, leaving the door open to the flooding moonlight. His eyes were quite accustomed to the quality of the light now, and he could clearly see the two hutches, set side by side on a shelf four feet off the ground, where he kept his two ferrets. They were both jills, small, and both awake, for they knew his hours, and had heard him through the wall, getting up out of bed. They were pacing their hutches, peering red-eyed through the wire mesh—padding, turning, staring, half-standing, claws in the mesh, turning . . . lithe, small, pointed nosed, dirty ivory in colour, with darker yellow at the neck. Probyn had always had jills, only. They were much smaller than the hobs, but they could kill a rabbit just as easily, and that was all he wanted of them; and when one came in heat he would borrow a hob from anywhere—there were plenty of ferret hutches and ferret fanciers within five miles of Walstone, farmers and labourers as well as poachers—and put him in with the jill, and in return for the pick of the litter, he'd have more ferrets to sell. And the jills were more manageable, and less liable to forget their training and put a pair of needle-like teeth through your hand.

He watched them for a few moments. He never made up his mind which ferret to hunt until he had taken a look and seen how they were. The one in the right hutch, Mrs Keppel, was moving more smoothly than Queen Alexandra in the left. The Queen was anxious, overeager; she might be hard to get off a rabbit . . . He opened the right hutch and gently picked up Mrs Keppel, closing his hand on her back from behind, just behind the front legs. With his other hand he picked the ferret bag off its hook on the wall, opened the mouth, lowered Mrs Keppel in, and drew the string taut. She wriggled and turned a few times, and then appeared to go to sleep. He pictured her inside there, putting out her tongue at Queen Alexandra. The two jills were not friends; they were rivals for his affections, rather like their namesakes had been for the old King's.

On another longer wooden peg were hanging a dozen nets. Some of them were purse nets, with a single draw string, and some were plain nets, about twenty inches square. On the shelf, farther along, was a pile of wooden pegs, no more than Y-shaped twigs, the thickness of a forefinger, cut to a point at one end. He stuffed a dozen nets and double that number of pegs into one coat pocket, put the ferret bag into the other, hitched an empty sack through his belt in the middle of his back, took a spade out of a corner, and went out, carefully closing the door and sliding the bolt shut behind him.

After leaving the cottage he headed westward along the lane, and in five minutes reached the Hedlington road just outside the western edge of Walstone. He stayed on it only a few minutes, then climbed a five-barred gate and walked along the edge of a field of stubble, crossed another field, this one fallow, climbed another gate, dropped onto a footpath, and settled down to a shambling easy stride that looked lazy, but covered the miles. The lane ran between high hedges of hazel mixed with blackthorn, and was little used, since country roads had been improved and more people used bicycles.

Probyn's senses told him all that a man could be told of the country that he passed, and the land that he trod—the bark of a fox, far off to the north, probably in Felstead Woods; the soughing of the wind through the bare branches of the trees that stood scattered and lonely in the moonlit fields; the almost soundless wingbeats of a barn owl, hunting over by the river which here ran close to the path; the scurry of something very small, probably a field mouse . . . but at the same time his conscious mind was reviewing his affairs as a man, a sentient human being rather than a two-legged hunting animal . . . Florinda was up to something—that he was certain of; but only seeing her Saturday afternoons and evenings wasn't enough to know her now. She, too, was growing up—and away . . . The war was going to make it harder for a man to follow this profession of his, in some ways. In others, it would be easier. Men were marching and running all over, day and night, playing at soldiers; that disturbed the game, and there'd be fewer birds and rabbits about—but the soldiers also poached, and why not? So the gamekeepers had hundreds of poachers to worry about, not just Probyn and old Simmons in Beighton, who was getting past it; and young Budden in Felstead, who didn't have the experience to be a proper match for Skagg and the rest of them . . . he thought of Fletcher. He wondered if Fletcher and Florinda fucked. They slept in the same bed—always had—so perhaps they did. The Woman thought they used to, when they were fourteen, fifteen, so they could find out what it was all about; but didn't any more, having taught each other what there was. They loved each other, that he knew.

He thought about his son Willum, the twins' father. What would happen to him if Mary died? He ought to be in an asylum, if everyone had his rights, being looked after . . . an asylum, or the army, where they told you when to wipe your arse and when to come in out of the rain . . .

So, thinking and sensing simultaneously but separately, after nearly two hours and seven miles he came to the railway embankment half-way between Cantley station and Felstead & Whitmore station. It was thirty feet high in the centre, and three hundred yards long, spanning a shallow valley where a side stream flowed into the Scarrow from the north, passing first under the Hedlington road, and then, forty yards on, through a culvert in the embankment. Probyn climbed the embankment, crossed the two pairs of lines, and went carefully down the other side. The dawn light was beginning to dim the brightness of the moon, and he set to work quickly. If he had a dog he would have set it to sniffing at the rabbit holes that pockmarked the foot of the embankment on this, the southern face, all along the bottom ten feet; but Skagg's knaves had shot his dog and he had not yet got another so he went to the west end of the embankment, where there were six or seven holes well separated from any others, probably not connected except among themselves, and began to cover each of them with a net. The purse nets he spread carefully over the holes, one for each, hammering in a single peg at the top, the draw string tied to it. He used four of these and for two others used square nets, each kept in place by three or four pegs, at the corners, depending on the shape of the hole. He sat down by the last, unnetted hole at the base of the embankment, and waited, spade resting between his knees.

The Scarrow began to show as a faint line of silver behind the willows fifty yards in front of him. This was railway property he was on, demarcated by two wire fences, one on each side of the embankment. He was poaching, but from the South Eastern & Chatham Railway Company, as it had now become, not from any private landowner. The rabbit warrens along this embankment were not well known, except to poachers, and they were hard to reach. The fields all round belonged to a hot-tempered farmer who was not above firing a twelve-bore past the ears of trespassers, so that the only safe way to reach the warrens was to walk down the railway line . . . and though the South Eastern & Chatham did not make much effort to stop poaching on their land, they objected very strongly to anyone walking on their right of way. The line was almost straight between Cantley and Felstead &

Whitmore stations, so that both stationmasters, the signalmen in their high boxes, and porters working on the platforms, could see from one to the other . . . and the would-be poacher would find an angry railway servant bicycling furiously along the cinder path after him, shaking his fist and swearing . . .

The light was strong enough. Seven-thirty, no frost, just some wind, and the damp, rain in the air, rooks beginning to awaken in the rookery across the river. Probyn got up, opened the mouth of the ferret bag, and eased Mrs Keppel out of it at the mouth of the unnetted hole. She stood, sniffed, turned round, and seemed to want to go for a walk. He picked her up gently and put her back, her nose pointing down the hole. She looked at him once as though to say, "You really want me to go into this one?"—a message so clear that he involuntarily nodded— then she walked into the darkness. As soon as she had gone, he put a square net over the hole, staked it firmly, went back to the high wire fence and leaned against it, facing the embankment, his head and eyes slowly moving to watch all the seven holes.

He waited. Below, Mrs Keppel wandered seemingly aimlessly along the black corridors of the warren. She smelled the rabbits close, trod over pellets of their dung, peered, sniffed, and went on, more like a moving wave than an animal, rippling. Close to one side she heard the sudden scut and thud of a rabbit flying off in a panic. They had smelled her. She moved on, slowly, deliberately.

A rabbit tore out of a hole directly in front of Probyn, burst into the purse, and was caught. Probyn darted forward, loosened the draw string and pulled the rabbit out. It had been kicking and struggling but, held now by the hind legs, it ceased, and hung limp, the bulging eyes staring down. Probyn hardened his right hand and chopped downward at the back of its head. Its neck broke with a crack. He dropped it to the grass, quickly reset the net, and went back to the fence.

Another rabbit burst out higher up, to be caught in one of the square nets. It was a big strong buck; the earth of the embankment was friable and Probyn had twenty yards to scramble up the bank. Before he reached it it had pulled two of the four pegs out of the earth, slipped out from under the net, and darted down the embankment, under the fence, and away. Probyn swore aloud. Prince would have got to the net in time to hold the rabbit.

He climbed back down to the fence. The light was growing stronger every minute. After five minutes he went to the warren and bent down, listening to the earth in several places. She was still moving; he did not hear her silent passage, only the thumps of the rabbits as they fled . . . another darted out, to be firmly caught and quickly despatched. A few minutes later, another . . . The three rabbits lay stiffening on the damp grass near the fence, their white scuts showing, a few pellets of excrement expelled from their bodies in their last spasmodic throes.

It was a little after eight o'clock now, and a distant engine whistled from the north. That would be the down passenger train, Probyn thought, that stopped at every station from Hedlington up the Scarrow valley, and then over to Ashford. Mrs Keppel had not come out, nor had any more rabbits. Probyn stared at one of the netted holes, his lips pursed. He should have put her on the line—the fine cord by which he could retrieve her if she got a rabbit in a dead end, killed it, and stayed down there to drink the blood: the line was in his pocket but she hadn't done this for months and he thought she was over it. She was near her heat and that might be upsetting her.

He walked slowly across the steep-sided embankment, listening, at every few steps kneeling, one ear pressed to the ground. Between two holes near the top of the warren he heard a sharp rapping sound below ground. He waited . . . a few seconds later the rap was repeated. He nodded. Mrs Keppel had a rabbit cornered in a dead end; the rapping sounds were the rabbit kicking the ferret back as she tried to get a grip. It might go on for five minutes, but sooner or later the ferret would sink its teeth in flesh and start sucking the blood; then she would go on until the rabbit was dead and she herself bloated. Then she might not come out of the warren for a day, or even two.

Probyn fetched his spade, which he had leaned against the fence and started to dig. The train whistled again, closer—that was for the level crossing at Cantley station. Probyn kept working: it was a down train and would therefore be on the other side, the line farthest from him. Neither driver nor fireman could see down the embankment on this side where he was—and even if they could it wouldn't matter: trainmen were much less officious than station staffs, though a guard sometimes shook his fist at you, if he saw you . . . but what more could he do?

The train passed, leaking steam, its connecting rods clanking, the wheels thunking over the rail joints. Probyn went on digging, more carefully, for he knew that Mrs Keppel was not far down.

Barely two feet below the surface, his spade cut into an earth corridor. Listening, he heard a chewing sound close to the right. He stuck his head into the hole he had dug and saw Mrs Keppel's tail eighteen inches into the corridor, and a brownish bulk beyond—the rabbit. It was no longer kicking, and Mrs Keppel had it by the throat. He took off his corduroy coat, wrapped his right hand in the skirt of it, reached in and gently tried to get hold of Mrs Keppel's body; but the tunnel was too tight, and all he got was her tail. He caught it and pulled firmly, expecting to feel the needles of her teeth at any moment. The corduroy would lessen the depth of the bite, but she'd easily break his skin. She did not bite, keeping her jaws buried in the throat of the rabbit, which she was pulling after her. Her greed has saved my skin, Probyn thought: it had happened before. He took his hand out of the corduroy, caught Mrs Keppel at the proper place and with his other hand pried her teeth apart and kicked the rabbit down the bank. It was not in bad condition. He could not sell it to a butcher, but it would make a good meal at the cottage.

Carrying Mrs Keppel carefully, he walked down the bank, picked up her bag, and dropped her in, moving his hand back quickly as he did so. She would be in a bad temper and full of blood lust for a little while; but she'd be all right by the time they got home.

And now to get home . . . first, back up the embankment, cross the rails, hurry down the northern side before the up passenger train passed, which it did as he reached the lane. Then, into the lane, and swing along as he had in the night, but watching now, for the sack that had been hitched through his belt now swung over his shoulder, tied to the haft of the spade, heavy with the weight of four rabbits. He was off the angry farmer's land, the path was a right of way, and then he had only a short distance of the main road to walk along before reaching the cottage . . . and even that could be avoided if he smelled danger.

He must think what to do next week. It was tempting to have a go at Swanwick's pheasants . . . but Swanwick's men had shot Prince, and put him, Probyn Gorse, in gaol. His score with Swanwick required more than a brace of pheasant to settle: it required a massacre like they had with the grouse up north, or like the new King went to in Norfolk, with the pheasants. His revenge required forethought and planning. It would be nice to give Swanwick his present at Christmas . . . but not this Christmas; it was too close. It would take time, and work, to make the keepers think he was going to do one thing, so that he would be free of them when he actually did something else, on the Day. And he would need outside help . . . old Henry Simmons perhaps? No, he needed people who weren't poachers—people Skagg and his turds would not suspect. That would take time, a little trickery, maybe—and patience. *Patience is a virtue, possess it if you can.* He remembered Willum coming back from school, repeating that over and over again: said teacher had taught him, when urging him to keep on trying to learn to read. Patience, and then . . .

He stopped. A blueish grey lurcher was coming down the footpath toward him. It limped badly, hardly letting its right front paw touch the ground. It had not seen him, or smelled him. The wind was blowing from it to him. He waited. It had no collar, looked to be about eight months old, wet, coat not brushed for a long time, hungry—you could see its ribs through the coat. He said softly, "Hullo, there . . . here." He held out his hand, half-crouching.

The dog—it was a male—stopped dead, yelped with fear, and darted sideways off the path, trying to burst through the hedge: but the hedge was too thick and it struggled back onto the path. Probyn said sharply, "Stay!" The lurcher stopped in its tracks . . . been trained, or started, at least, Probyn thought. "Heel!" he snapped.

The dog crouched lower to the ground, frightened. He thought, it's been mistreated. It crawled toward him. "Good dog," he said. When it came within reach he patted its head gently, then pulled its ears. Looked like a Pointer-Springer-Labrador cross. Apart from that yelp, it had made no sound. It rolled over on its back, tail wagging . . . been taught not to make a noise—a poacher's dog—not Budden's or Simmons's, he knew theirs . . . He took the foot and felt it, the dog whining very low. The shin bone had been fractured into the wrist joint. Perhaps it had been thrown out of a train—it had some bruises and cuts, and several patches of dried blood on its coat. But why? Some people couldn't manage dogs, that was why.

He opened the mouth of his sack and let the dog sniff inside. It leaped up and down whining louder now, saliva dripping from its jaws. "Starving," he muttered, "can't catch anything with that bad leg . . . . You come with me," he said, standing up, "and you'll get something to eat—maybe a bit of that rabbit, eh? What's your name? You don't know? Well, you're Duke, see, the Duke of Clarence. He was a bleeder, same as you've been bleeding . . . Heel!"

The Duke of Clarence obediently fell in at his left heel and, limping along without a sound, followed Probyn home.

Daily Telegraph, Saturday, November 14, 1914

TURKEY'S WAR WITH THE TRIPLE ENTENTE
FORMAL DECLARATION

Amsterdam, Friday. A telegram from Constantinople received here from Berlin states that the Porte has published an Iradé containing Turkey's declaration of war against the Allied Powers. The Iradé gives the history of the events before the war, and declares that part of the Russian fleet tried to lay mines outside the Bosphorus and committed other hostile acts against Turkey. Without

> replying to Turkey's proposal that an inquiry should be
> held into these incidents, Russia, it is asserted, recalled
> her ambassador and opened hostilities. Great Britain and
> France also recalled their ambassadors. These Powers
> declared a state of war with the Ottoman Government and
> the Sultan consequently ordered a declaration of war, con-
> fident in the help of the Almighty. The Iradé is signed by
> all the Ministers. REUTERS.

Cate found it difficult to worry about the Sublime Porte and his actions
when everyone was talking about the defeat the navy had suffered off
the coast of Chile: and he himself worrying about the fate of his
brother-in-law Tom Rowland. Tom had been in H.M.S. *Monmouth,*
reported to have been sunk with all hands . . . so he must be dead. He
did not know Tom well—no one did—but he liked him; and would not
give up hope.

But the Turkish news was connected with Coronel, in a way; for
they were both failures of the Royal Navy. When he had a moment
he'd read the report on Coronel more carefully, and also try to find out
the truth behind the Turkish declaration of war; for old Commander
Quigley had told him just yesterday that if the Turks declared war it
would be because the German cruisers *Goeben* and *Breslau* had been
allowed to escape the whole length of the Mediterranean and find ref-
uge at Constantinople, where their guns would be a powerful argument in persuading the Sultan, who had been sitting on the fence—like
the Italians—to come down on the German side.

The Commander had prophesied that admirals' heads would roll for
the escape of those two ships; and at Coronel one admiral had already
gone, apparently . . . but where did the blame really lie?

The house felt empty again, with Margaret gone—this time she'd
said, for good; or until Ireland was free. That would not happen until
after the war, perhaps not at once then. Stella was working at Lady
Blackwell's Hospital in Hedlington, Laurence at school . . . waiting,
growing . . . like the war. It was lonely here, and winter a slow time
for farmers and landowners, except for the hunting. He might go to
Godalming next weekend, watch a Charterhouse 2nd XI game, and go
to chapel on Sunday, take Laurence out to lunch and try to console
each other over the loss of their wife and mother. He might take Stella
with him . . . but no, she was going to Wellington with her Grandfather Rowland, and young Johnny Merritt, to watch Guy play rugby.

Wellington College, Berkshire:
Saturday, November 21, 1914

17 Guy Rowland stood in front of the mirror on the green painted partition in his room, brushing his hair. Five minutes to breakfast and he was feeling hungry. He always felt hungry for breakfast on the day of a match, whether it was cricket or rugby; and he ate as much as he could get. He was always hungry again by lunch, but ate little. The mirror was cracked and slightly discoloured and he stooped closer to make sure his parting was straight. To the right of the mirror, over his table, hung a reproduction of an oil painting showing a mass of white clouds, blue sky, a small gnat-like flying machine and, dim below, white cliffs: Bleriot crossing the English Channel—July 25th, 1909. Across the top of the picture was folded a silk square, blue and black striped; the square was folded so that the stripes ran vertically, to show that Guy had got his dormitory colours for cricket, first; though for two years now he had also had them for rugger. His blue-tasselled dormitory rugby cap hung from the top right corner of the picture frame, his brand-new school cap, black and gold, with a gold-thread tassel, hung from the top left corner. On the shallow peak of the cap was embroidered the figure '1914'; and above, a gold embroidered horseshoe, the crest of Guy's dormitory, the Beresford. Beyond the table, a big window occupied most of the outer wall over the window bench, giving a wide view onto the Combermere quadrangle. The time fag chanted "Twenty-six past" and booted feet scurried down the dormitory: that was the last call, the fag himself now hurrying downstairs on his way to the school dining hall.

More scurrying feet, these coming into the dormitory, stopping, coming on—a knock on his own door. "Come in," he said, and turned, ready to go.

Dick Yeoman came in, pale and wide eyed. "Hullo, Dick," Guy said, "I'm off to breakfast. What's up?"

He noticed that Dick's hands were trembling. Visits between dormitories were not allowed: and Dick was in the Lynedoch. He himself, being a dormitory prefect, should have ordered him out, perhaps reported him: but he was obviously in trouble, and that mattered more than the rule.

"What's up?" he repeated, smiling.

"I'm going to be sacked," Dick said, his voice cracking.

"What for?"

Dick stared at him, looked down, and said, "You know."

Guy thought, I don't know, but I can guess. He said, "Tell me, though."

"I was . . . tossing off in my room. With three others. Last night, after lights out. Fairway came in. He must have heard . . . or someone told him. He took us straight to tutor's who said we'd go to the Master this morning."

Guy sat down on his narrow bed, indicating the chair with a wave of his hand. He gave up any hope of breakfast. "Go on."

"We've been. The Master sacked us . . . we're not to leave till tomorrow morning, because they've got to find our shirts and socks and handkerchiefs in the Ma Hags', but we're supposed to stay in our rooms."

"Were the other boys your age?"

"Two were. One was a squealer Dickinson brought in. Second term. I never touched him."

Guy said, "Do you like girls?"

"I do, but I'm sort of afraid of them, Guy. They make me stutter . . ." His face was deep red now, and his eyes firmly fixed on the strip of carpet . . . "I have always liked this . . . I mean, with other chaps . . . a boy at my prep school taught me. Have you—had a woman?"

Guy shook his head, smiling. "No, but I've been in love—helplessly, hopelessly, with a village poacher's granddaughter—when I was eight and she was ten. I took her behind a hedge and kissed her. She showed me how!" He laughed. The breakfast bell was ringing, and he'd be absent. Oh, well . . .

Dick said, "It's my people . . . I think Mummy won't mind too much, somehow. But Daddy! I can't face him!"

Guy thought a moment, then said, "Look, I'll telephone him. I'm going out with my grandfather tonight, after the match, and I'll call him from the hotel. You have a telephone at home?"

Dick nodded . . . "Lyme Regis 43. What are you going to say?"

Guy said, "What I'm saying now . . . I don't think tossing off, even with other fellows, is so terrible. It's only a question of who gets caught. I love Wellington, but I can't pretend it's a natural life here, or at any public school. I miss Virginia, my sister . . . touching her, hearing her voice . . . my mother's even . . . the cook, the maid . . . You may find that you stop being afraid of women once you feel that you really are a man, not a boy."

"I'll join up," Dick muttered. "Perhaps that will make my father feel better about me."

Guy said, "You're only seventeen, Dick. It's not the end of the world . . . What are you doing about food?"

"They're sending us food from Hall. We're not to go down to meals."

"I'll come and see you, as soon as I can . . . after chapel, probably."

"You're a brick!" Dick said, jumping up and wringing Guy's hand. "And I haven't congratulated you on your cap. Last Monday, wasn't it?"

Guy pointed at the oblong white card, with the embossed crest and the brief handwritten legend below: *G. Rowland has been elected a member of the Wellington XV. 16th of November '14,* and signed by the captain of the school rugby team.

"Now go along," Guy said. "I'll come downstairs with you in case some officious Orange prefect tries to arrest you."

"You've missed breakfast!"

"Not yet," Guy said. "I think I'm going to have had a severe bout of diarrhea, and will beg to be fed . . . for the sake of the school, part of whose honour will be entrusted to me on Big Side this afternoon."

They started running together down the steel-edged steps, swinging fast, one-armed, round the steel stanchions at each half-landing, under the boards bearing the names of all previous Beresford school prefects, rugby caps, and cricket colours since the school's foundation, as the nation's memorial to the Iron Duke, fifty-five years before—the present disaster in no way able to affect their animal energy.

School prefects who were not members of the XV gave up their places at the High Table when a match was being played at home, so that all the members of both teams could lunch there, sitting alternately, Wellington boys and visitors. Today the opponents were from Wokingham

School, a public school rather smaller than Wellington, and a century or two older. Their team could have walked over without any undue exertion, for Wokingham's Georgian buildings were barely four miles away across the Caesar's Camp heath.

Guy found himself seated between Grant-Meikle, the Wokingham fly-half, his own opposite number, and a square-built boy of eighteen who must have weighed fourteen and a half stone, in spite of being no more than five-foot-nine; and whose build and determined but perhaps not over-intelligent look bespoke his place in the team—second row forward. They talked desultorily of their past games. Guy explained how he had regularly been tricked out of position by the fly-half of the 60th Rifles, whom they had played a few weeks ago . . . but the man had been a Cambridge blue, just joined the regiment. He ate sparingly, for he had succeeded, after some wheedling, in getting Gunn the dormitory man to serve him two helpings of eggs and bacon at breakfast. Now he ate a mouthful or two of the roast mutton and offered the rest to the Wokingham forward, who devoured it with thanks; and took a little pudding, and a glass of water, and that was all.

Then, after sitting some time at the High Table when the rest of the school had left, they went to the changing rooms, each visitor accompanying his lunch companion to the latter's dormitory changing room, for there were no separate facilities for the XV, or visiting teams. Guy chatted politely with Grant-Meikle while the latter stripped and put on the white shorts, green stockings, and green and white striped jersey of his school; and he himself the navy blue shorts, orange and black jersey, and—today for the first time—the orange and black stockings and the gold and black cap. Grant-Meikle donned his school's tasselled cap, which they wore more on the top of the head than at Wellington, where it was customary to wear ordinary dormitory caps or football caps so far back that they could not be seen by anyone standing in front of the wearer. Lastly, they both put on white woollen sweaters, Guy's with a huge Beresford horseshoe embroidered on the front; and, carrying their studded boots slung by the laces round their necks, joined other members of the two teams striding through the school cloisters, walked out of the Path of Duty gate, and past Turf and the great copper beeches, now leafless, on their way to Big Side.

A large, burly man of about forty hurried by, wearing a clerical dog collar and pince-nez . . . "Good Luck, Rowland," he said as he passed, "and don't give Grant-Meikle there a chance to kick. He's a very good drop kicker."

"Thank you, sir," Grant-Meikle said, taking off his cap as Guy negligently raised two fingers of his right hand a few inches.

The cleric strode on, smiling. Grant-Meikle said, "Is he a Master? Is that all you do to them—raise a finger?"

Guy said, "To assistant masters—we call them ushers—yes. To the Master, the headmaster, we take off our caps. That was the Reverend A. J. Fenn, who's also the assistant rugby master. His nickname's Sheddy."

The school was going down in a steady stream, boys in pairs and threes and sixes, all wearing the caps of their respective dormitories, here and there the swinging tassels of a rugby cap, mostly wearing overcoats against the raw cold of the November afternoon. The bare elms creaked to a slow west wind, and there had been a touch of frost, long gone, in the morning. The buildings of Wellington rose like a smaller Versailles out of the birch and pine of Bagshot Heath behind them. Guy began to experience a well-remembered tingling and tightening: half an hour to game time . . . punt about, practise drop kicking and passing co-ordination with the scrum-half and the three-quarters, then— battle! He remembered Rhodes's words to him in the pavilion after the Yorkshire match . . . "Tha's got to get on top, lad, right off . . . and not let go. Tha's got to want to *kill*." He must try harder to live up to that advice . . . but it was difficult. Rugger was a game, after all, not a war.

A diffident voice called him from the side of the path—"Rowland! . . . Guy!"

He turned and recognised a familiar gangling form—"Ginger" Keble Palmer, walking with another, burlier figure in an army officer's uniform, single embroidered stars on his cuffs. "Ginger!" he cried, then recognised the other as David Toledano, a rugby hero of his first year at Wellington, since capped for Oxford and tried for England. He remembered his guest and said, "This is Keble Palmer—he used to be here, and now designs aeroplanes for Mr Handley Page. I hope to go there, too, when the war's over. And David Toledano . . . 2nd Lieutenant, isn't it, sir?"

"Good heavens, don't call me 'sir,' Guy . . . Yes, 2nd Lieutenant, Royal Field Artillery . . . not bright enough up here—" he tapped his head—"for the R.F.C."

Guy introduced Grant-Meikle, then they all walked on together.

Toledano said, "I try to keep in touch with what Ginger's doing, but it's not so easy from Larkhill . . . but I'm still hoping that one day the three of us will found a firm that will make England the leader in the air as she is on the sea."

"Was," Grant-Meikle said. "Coronel was a bit of a shock."

"Someone told me you'd lost an uncle there, Guy," Toledano said. "Is that true?"

"My family thought so for a time, but when we didn't see his name in the casualty list, I got permission to telephone the Admiralty during class-room hours, and spoke to an officer I knew would know—Commander Arbuthnot. He said Uncle Tom had been transferred to H.M.S. *Penrith* weeks before the battle. We'd had no letter from Uncle Tom, so we didn't know. *Penrith* was at Coronel, but had no officer casualties, Commander Arbuthnot said."

"Good! We'd better cut along, Guy. Mind you beat those Wokingham rotters!" Smiling, he held out his hand to Grant-Meikle and finished—"Have a good match!"

Ginger Keble Palmer waved, calling, "You *must* come and see what we're doing at Handley Page, Guy . . . and what we're going to do."

"I will, in the hols."

They turned off along the gravel path toward the squash courts as Guy and Grant-Meikle headed for the freestanding wall which was the 'dressing room' at Big Side. Guy's mind was still on Ginger Keble Palmer. It was Ginger who had really been responsible for turning his energies and dreams to the air. Two years older than he, Ginger was designing aircraft, on paper, when still at Wellington; and had taught Guy the theory of aerodynamics. He had prophesied that one day, before they were old, aircraft would carry passengers across the oceans of the world . . . or bombs, Guy thought. Ginger would never fly the aeroplanes he designed—his glasses were as thick as pebbles, as thick as Uncle Richard's; but it had always been planned between them that Guy would be the test pilot, and pass what he learned by actual flying to Ginger at his drawing board . . . and to David Toledano at his desk as the financier of their dream firm.

Then they were at the wall, hung with hooks for their sweaters. They sat on the ground, separated now, Wellington to the right, the visitors to the left, and put on their rugger boots. The Big Side turf was never a bright emerald green for it was based on springy heath soil, not clay; and because of that it drained well, and a good game could be played on it after heavy rain when Wokingham's field, for instance, would have quickly turned into a quagmire. Six hundred Wellington boys, all compelled to watch, were lining up by dormitories on the duckboards along the near touch line. Many green-capped Wokingham boys had walked over too, and had been allotted a length of duckboard. Two girls' schools from Bracknell and Crowthorne were there, eighty girls in dark blue coats and hats with yellow or blue ribbons and dark blue stockings. Guy grinned, remembering the last home match here when a Wellington wing three-quarter had had his shorts torn off by a hand tackle, right in front of the girls' schools. The team had formed their usual protective zareba round the victim while another pair was obtained and thrown in—but not before the girls' schools had been given a fifteen-second view of Burton major's hairy thighs, loins, and private parts, at twenty feet range, while Burton stood bewildered, not realising among the gasps and giggles that his middle parts were as bare as a gorilla's.

The Wokingham team were punting about at the squash courts end, Wellington at the other, the three-quarters passing in a swift diagonal movement from an imaginary scrum. Guy heard a voice call—"Guy!" and he ran off toward his grandfather. They were standing a little past the end of the wall, in a group—his grandfather, Stella Cate, and a man he knew but for a moment couldn't place: then he recalled the occasion—it was the young American they had met at Henley. He hugged his grandfather, kissed Stella on the cheek, and shook Johnny Merritt's hand. "Come to learn how to play football?" he asked.

Johnny grinned . . . "This is not my game, but I daresay I could give you guys a few pointers."

"Good luck, Guy," his grandfather said. "I know you'll be busy after the match, so let's say we'll meet you at Great Gate half an hour after No Side. All right?"

"Make it an hour, please, Grandpa," Guy said: then he remembered that he had not had a chance to see Dick Yeoman again, and must do so; word was out through the school by now that Dick and two others had been sacked, and another, a squealer, given twelve by the Master. "An hour and a half. I've got to change, and then we have tea with Wokingham before seeing them off, then I have a job to do. I have an exeat till ten o'clock."

His family drifted away, waving, to be replaced by a tall dark-skinned youth wearing heavy glasses, in uniform, a 2nd Lieutenant's stars this time on his shoulders, accompanied by a smaller older man with a walrus moustache, fiercely jutting eyebrows and also wearing heavy glasses.

Guy said, "Hullo, sir. Come to see us beat Wokingham?"

"If you can," the man replied. "What do you think of John in his uniform?" He looked at the youth with an expression of immense pride.

"2nd Lieutenant, Irish Guards, I think," Guy said.

"Ensign," John Kipling said, smiling. "We don't have 2nd Lieutenants in the Foot Guards. I'm under instruction with the reserve battalion of the Coldstream at Windsor—with a lot of others from the Brigade."

"Well, you look every inch a guardee," Guy said, laughing. "Flatfoot Heavies, my father calls them."

"He's Weald Light Infantry, isn't he?" the older man cut in. "I knew them in Lahore, *consule Planco*. Good regiment! They wear the scarlet, or did then."

"They still do, Mr Kipling—but they look down on Heavy Infantry, even Guards."

Rudyard Kipling laughed loudly, his teeth shining out under the moustache, the glasses gleaming under the awning of the eyebrows. "Well, each to his own. John was going into the navy. Jackie Fisher himself promised him an appointment, but his eyes . . . I persuaded Lord Roberts to accept him into his regiment—he's Colonel of the Irish, you know."

"Bobs Bahadur," Guy said.

"Ah, *you* don't have to prove to me you read my books, you young scoundrel," Kipling said. "Run along now, and beat Wokingham. John's as keen on Wellington as if he were still here—and playing . . . good luck. Hope we'll see you again at Bateman's soon. Mrs K. has a very soft spot for you." They waved, and Guy ran out onto the sacred short turf of Big Side. A rugger ball came arching through the air toward him, tumbling end over end as it fell. He caught it on the run, pivoted, and then remembered—Wokingham was watching. That was a trick to keep for the match, not give away before it . . . a trick to use for the kill.

1st Half: Wokingham attacked continuously, since their forwards outweighed the Wellington scrum by half a stone a man, and shoved together. Wellington's only attacking movement came to naught when, there being no one left over, the Wokingham full back tackled the last man. A lack of imagination was shown here, particularly by the centres, who twice would have broken through if they had run straight instead of across the field. The pack performed excellently against their heavier opponents. The hooker often managed to get the ball against the odd head, even after McKenzie was injured and had to leave the field. Wellington were lucky the half time score was only 5–0 against them.

2nd Half: The Wellington three-quarters initiated an attacking move from the kick-off which went all the way to the right wing, then back to his centre, who scored under the posts. It was easily converted. Five minutes later a similar movement by Wokingham resulted in a similar score. Wokingham 10, Wellington 5. For the next twenty minutes play was mostly dribbling, which was to the advantage of Wellington, who thereby were able to overcome the handicaps of weight, and of playing one man short. With five minutes left, d'Arcy on Wellington's right wing received the ball five yards out on an extra long pass from his centre, slid easily past his opponent, sold the full back a perfect dummy to Rowland, who was backing up, and scored in the corner. From a difficult angle Rowland was not able to convert. The score was now 10–8 against us.

The final minutes of play were fast and furious, and it says much for the training of both teams that there were no offside calls. With a minute and a half left in a well-fought game, and the Wellington pack dribbling well, the ball bounced up into Jameson's hands. The extra Wokingham forward was there to tackle him, but Jameson swung full round and passed back to Rowland. Rowland ran forward and made to pass inside. The man covering him— Grant-Meikle—took his eye off him for a moment, and at that precise moment, Rowland, pivoting on his left foot, while still apparently going at full speed, put a drop kick through the goal posts from forty yards out. That remained the score at No Side—Wellington 12, Wokingham 10. The forwards are to be congratulated on making the result possible A.J.F.

"It's a funny game," Johnny Merritt said. "All those fellows getting down and shoving each other like bulls, or something. I could never see what they were doing—or trying to do."

"You wait till Sheddy Fenn writes it up for the paper," Guy said, laughing. "The forwards will get all the kudos. Quite right, too. We'd never get the ball without them."

"But you won it, with that drop kick. They weren't expecting that."

"No," Guy said, "they weren't." He smiled inwardly.

Johnny said, "Each half was forty minutes . . . with no time-outs, and no substitutions . . . that's hard work. And no protective padding. I don't know why you don't break every bone in your body."

"I feel a bit bashed about," Guy said. A thin line of dried blood marked a long gash on his forehead, got from a flying boot: and a dull bruise glowed under his left eye . . . "McKenzie has a broken collar bone. He played ten minutes with it before it began to hurt too much and he had to leave."

They were sitting in the lounge of the Wellington Hotel, by the railway bridge in Crowthorne, hard by the station, whose signboards read *Wellington College—alight here for Crowthorne*. It was from there that Guy went home at the end of every term, taking one train to Guildford and another to Hedlington, with a change at Tonbridge. Stella and Johnny were sitting to his right and left, facing each other; and his grandfather opposite himself. A glass of lemonade was in his hand, and a piece of plaster across the back of his right hand. In the changing room after the game Grant-Meikle had told him he was a blighter, laughing . . . *he* was supposed to be the dangerous drop-kicker.

After seeing the Wokingham team into their char-a-banc Guy had gone to see Dick Yeoman. Dick was in the dumps again, and determined now to join up. Guy did not try to dissuade him. There was a war on—John Kipling was already in the Guards, seventeen years old, and there was no reason Dick should not go. But it was a pity that Dick, believing himself to be a pansy, was going to rush into an all-male institution. It would be like school, only more so. Here, after all, there were Ma Hags, tutors' wives, and even daughters. It was such a waste, too . . . not that Dick might lose his life in the war . . . that was something all of them would face; but that he would go on believing that this incident was a sort of final disaster, that his life was ruined —and he not yet eighteen. He decided, while talking in a low voice to Dick in his room in the Lynedoch, that he must do something about it. He half made up his mind what that something must be, but he said nothing of this to Dick, only tried to cheer him up, and stress that the end of the world had not come. Then he ran down to Great Gate just as his grandfather drove up in the big Rowland Ruby . . . a word with Burgess, the Head Porter and ex-sergeant-major of Grenadiers, to remind him of his exeat . . . then out and away.

He listened to the general talk. His Aunt Margaret had left home and gone to Ireland, but no one knew where. His grandfather looked uncomfortable while Stella was telling him that—perhaps because Johnny Merritt was present—but such a thing couldn't be kept secret. Stella herself had been cubbing, on foot . . . took Johnny out last week. How had he liked it? It seemed cruel, though very colourful; why weren't the foxes shot? That was a good question. Guy liked foxhunting himself, but knew it would never be a passion with him. One day, perhaps, he would match his brain and his muscles against a snow leopard 18,000 feet above sea level in the Karakorams, one against one, as his father had done on leave, when serving in India. Perhaps hunting Germans in the air would be his passion.

Stella said, "I work in the new Auxiliary Red Cross Hospital in Hedlington now, Guy. It's in that huge house on Daneway. Lady Blackwell's lent it to the government."

"You're a nurse?"

"Oh dear no. I'm a V.A.D.—Voluntary Aid Detachment—Immobile. That means I only work in a hospital near home. I go up to Hedlington four days a week."

"What do you do?"

"Bathe the men, change dressings, serve meals . . . anything the sisters let us. Some of us are learning a little real nursing, too, by accident, so to speak. The sisters don't have time to touch us."

"Do you get paid, Stella?" Johnny Merritt asked.

"Oh no! We serve for nothing."

So she was 'Stella' to Johnny Merritt now, Guy noted. He was looking at her as though she were a beautiful *objet d'art*, but very fragile. Well, that was a fair enough description of Stella, in a way.

His grandfather said, "Have you heard anything from your father, Guy?"

"I had a letter a couple of days ago, Grandpa. He was all right then, but said that his battalion was having very heavy casualties. He couldn't say where he was, but I believe it's near Ypres."

"The casualties are terrible," his grandfather said, "but we must not lose heart. We are facing a clever and fiendish enemy. Our leaders know what they are doing, and we must back them up, to the hilt."

No one said anything for a time; then Guy said, "John Kipling was watching the match, Grandpa. With Mr Kipling. Did you see them?"

"*Rudyard* Kipling?" Johnny Merritt said with a start.

"Yes."

"He was there this afternoon?"

"Yes. His son was at Pearson's—that's a house, not a dormitory—from '11 till this February when he left to go to a crammer's."

"You know Rudyard Kipling, then?"

"Very well. He used to come up for the weekend, to take John out, sometimes with Mrs Kipling. They'd stay at the Queen's Hotel in Farnborough. Two or three times I've spent a week at Bateman's in the holidays, when John invited me. Mr Kipling loved to hear us telling stories about the school. It's very different from Westward Ho! in my day, and *Stalky's*, he said."

"Well, well," Johnny said. "Smart, football and cricket hero—and well-connected . . . what are you going to do, yourself? Join up?"

Guy said shortly, "No. I'm staying here till the end of next year. Then I'm joining the Royal Flying Corps."

A gong sounded for the start of dinner service, and Harry Rowland said, "Hungry, Guy?"

"Yes, Grandpa, but I have a trunk call to make. It's rather important. Do you mind if I have the charge put on your bill here?"

"Not a bit . . . It's not to—er—Paris, is it?"

"No. Lyme Regis."

"Run along then. We'll have another glass of sherry while he's telephoning, eh, Johnny?"

Guy walked to the hotel office and requested his call to Dick's father. It took a quarter of an hour to get through. He had already planned what he should say to Mr Yeoman, and so, while he waited, he thought of the evening with his grandfather.

Much had been said, and more would be: much had been left unsaid. Guy knew that his uncle Richard was planning to oppose his grandfather for a seat in Parliament—and Johnny was working for Uncle Richard; but that was not mentioned: only the factory to make lorries, with money from Johnny Merritt's father's bank. The hanging of poor Freda had been discussed a lot—but his grandfather, though admitting it was cruel and senseless, had become so rabid against the Germans that even he obviously felt, deep inside, that there was some justification for hanging dachshunds. The older that men were, Guy had noticed, the more fierce they were against all Germans, as Huns, and bestial barbarians . . . Stella had told them of Probyn Gorse's sworn determination to get his own back on Lord Swanwick, not so much for having him sent to gaol, as because his keepers had killed his old dog, Prince. Now he had a new one, a lurcher he'd named Duke of Clarence, Stella said: and everyone in the village was busy guessing what Probyn would do to avenge the old dog. Guy thought, I must go and talk to Probyn and see if I can help. It will put some excitement into the hols . . . just over a month to Christmas. It would be fun to talk to the twins in the little cottage, and kiss Florinda, pretending they were still kids kissing among the hazel bushes, and then having peeing competitions into the Scarrow—competitions which he always won.

His telephone call came through, and he put the receiver to his ear.

Guy walked out of the Path of Duty gate an hour before Sunday morning chapel, and crossed the gravel to the front door of the Master's Lodge. It was a foggy, damp morning, the tops of the trees like ghostly fingers barely seen through the thick air, moisture congealed on every blade of grass, the South Front disappearing into it, the chapel unseen.

A maid came to the door at his ring and he said, "I'm Rowland, miss. Beresford. Please tell the Master I would like to see him."

"Very good, sir. Come in." She led him down the passage and into the Master's large book-lined study. She went out and Guy waited expectantly, standing. The Master had his little whims, which most of the school knew about. Sure enough, a section of bookcase swung suddenly back and there he was, materialised like a large and rather untidy genie —Mr William Vaughan, M.V.O., M.A., Master of Wellington. Boys wore their dormitory caps indoors at Wellington, and Guy now took his off in salute. "Good morning, Master," he said.

The Master sat down behind his desk. He was as big as Sheddy Fenn, with mild eyes, a vaguely harried expression, and a large moustache. He was wearing a dark grey suit of heavy serge. He said, "I was just going to send for you, Rowland . . . but you must have come on some other matter, heh?"

"It's about Yeoman, sir," Guy said. He had felt a little nervous while crossing the South Quad and walking down the Path of Duty, but now action was joined, and he felt fine. "He told me that he has been expelled. Is that true, sir?"

Vaughan looked unhappy, then tried to be stern and said, "It is. He and others, who were caught in disgraceful conduct."

Guy said, "It's a natural thing, sir. Everyone does it, though not together. Expulsion is so serious that it will affect his whole life . . . it's not what he did, but the expulsion, that carries the disgrace, sir. I know him well. I think all he needs is to grow up, and meet girls, and . . . he'll be a normal man, like many others who have done what he and the others did, while they were here, but change as soon as they leave and go out into the world . . . Couldn't they all be beaten, sir? And perhaps put into different dormitories?"

Vaughan stroked his heavy moustache and shook his head slowly from side to side. He said, "Has anyone asked you to speak to me? Have you told your tutor that you were going to? Or Yeoman's?"

"No, sir. I just thought I *ought* to do it. I spoke to Yeoman's father yesterday on the telephone, warning him that Dick was very upset. I told him that Dick's the same boy he has always been, but I'm afraid he doesn't see it that way. Dick will be rejected at home, too."

Vaughan said, "I wish I could show mercy, Rowland . . . but we would have the most bitter protests from parents if this sort of thing was condoned. Someone would tell the press, and soon Wellington would not only have no reputation, but no boys—parents would not send them here."

"If you could have Yeoman transferred to the Beresford, sir, I promise you he would never do this again."

"I'm sure you could, Rowland . . . but there is an extra factor here which I am afraid can not be overlooked in any circumstances—the Lower School boy, who was being perverted by the others. I have administered a sound thrashing to him which I hope he will never forget, and he will not be expelled. The others must be. I am sorry."

"So am I, sir. Thank you for listening."

Vaughan said, "Wait a minute . . . you are a strange young man, Rowland. I see now why your tutor has been pressing me to do what I only decided yesterday to do . . . I was about to send for you to tell you that you are a school prefect . . . from today. There are already two in your dormitory, I know, and I was unwilling to make a third . . . but I was wrong. You are an exceptional boy." He held out his hand—"Congratulations."

"Thank you, sir."

Guy shook the Master's big hand, turned, and left. Outside the door of the Lodge, he put on his cap, from force of habit. Then he took it off, grinning to himself, and put it back in his coat pocket: school prefects were the only boys in the school who did not wear caps, except football caps and those only on games afternoons. Then he headed into the school, and ran up the Hill-Lynedoch stairs.

He went to Yeoman's room near the far end of the dormitory, knocked, and went in. Dick was sitting on his bed, his suitcases standing ready on the floor by the door. He jumped up as Guy came in. He had the look of a hunted animal; then he recognised Guy and cried, "Don't come in, Guy . . . they'll think . . . No one's spoken a word to me all day. I thought Fairway was my friend, even though he discovered us . . . I know he had to report it—but when I went to say goodbye to him and hope he gets into his father's regiment, he turned his back on me."

"Come on, Dick," Guy said, "time to start for the station, or you'll miss your train."

"Don't come with me," Yeoman pleaded, "I can carry the suitcases, and the Steward's sending on the tuck box later."

"Come on," Guy said, ignoring him. He lifted one of the cases. Unwillingly, Dick picked up the other. They went out into the dormitory hall and started the long walk down it, between the green and brown painted wooden partition walls. A small crowd of boys in the middle of the hall, standing round the mute dormitory gramophone—on Sundays it was not allowed to be played until after chapel—parted and made way as they approached: all except one, a tall fair youth with his hands in his pockets, and no cap on his head.

He stood his ground and said, "Who gave you permission to come in here, Rowland?"

"No one," Guy said, setting down the suitcase.

"It's customary to call a school prefect by his name when you speak to him."

"So it is. My name is Rowland."

Then the other saw that Guy was not wearing a cap and his scornful expression changed to anger as he snapped, "I'll beat you for this!"

"I don't think so. I am a school prefect. Now get out of the way please. We have a train to catch. After chapel I'll meet you behind the rhododendrons, if you like."

Fairway stood aside then, saying, "The farther I can get from a pervert the better. And perverts' friends are usually perverts, too, aren't they?"

Guy put the suitcase down again, as Yeoman behind him muttered desperately, "Let's get on, Guy . . . please . . . please!"

Guy said, "I toss off, Fairway. So do you. So does everyone else in this dormitory, except perhaps your newest squealer, whom you haven't taught yet . . . Don't forget the rhododendrons."

He started on again, the boys standing back, Fairway scarlet in the face, someone giggling behind his hand.

So Dick and Guy went out together, along the cloisters of North Quad, South Quad, the Path of Duty gate, past the Master's Lodge, and Turf, and the copper beeches, and Big Side, and along the footpath to the station. The mist clothed every object round them in opalescent grey.

"I'll never see any of this again," Dick said. "I've loved my time here . . . thanks to you. And congrats on being made a school prefect."

"There'll be other Wellingtons," Guy said.

"You're missing chapel."

"I know."

"But . . ."

"Don't fret about it, Dick. I'm not."

They walked on together, each weighted down with a heavy suitcase. Guy thought, it's true, what I have just said to him—that I'm not fretting about missing chapel. And it was true, as he had told Dick several times, that the world was not going to come to an end because of this unfortunate incident. But he was beginning to feel, as he read the newspapers and studied the pictures in the *Illustrated London News*, that over there in France the world that his parents had known, and that he had expected to grow up into, and take his place in, as generations before him had, would indeed come to an end if the fighting continued for long on its present scale. And he felt certain that it *would* go on longer—much longer; and, hard as it was to imagine, that it would grow bigger, much bigger, much more primal—and at the same time much more sophisticated.

Daily Telegraph, Tuesday, December 22, 1914

BATTLE OF CORONEL
VIVID STORY BY A PARTICIPANT

November 4. Have just entered the Straits at noon today, after two and a half days' run. The place where the action took place was near Coronel, about 800 or 900 miles north of here, so we've had a long run. I do hope you stick the news all right, because I'm certain that we should be reported sunk or sinking, and it will be another two or three days before we can send news from Port Stanley.

STOKERS SINGING

The ship's company have been complimented upon their coolness during action. Down below the stokers were singing "We'll all go the same way home," and "It's a long way to Tipperary," whilst other witty sayings were common, such as "Don't get dizzy," "There's another sausage for you, and English at that," as each shot went. One of our subs had his hat taken off . . . another (man) remarked, as a big shell missed him by a hair's breadth, "Humph, I thought my birthday had come" and continued unhooking 6-in. shells from the ammunition hoist. Another gunner said, "I've got a jam," to which someone replied (thinking of our rations of late), "Try marmalade."

Still, apart from all this, it was really awful.

The letter had been written by someone on board H.M.S. *Glasgow,* and presumably mailed when the ship reached some port. It was over six weeks since full reports of the battle had been published in the press, with maps and diagrams, and Cate knew just where Coronel, Punta Arenas, and the Falklands were . . . names that he had hardly heard of two months ago.

Only three days to Christmas. He must check the list of Christmas boxes and pay a visit to the bank in Hedlington to make sure he had enough cash for the purpose; and enough small silver coins for Mrs Abell to put into the Christmas pudding . . . talk to Norton about which horses to ride for the Boxing Day and New Year's Day meets . . . think of a proper present for Probyn: the old rascal would really appreciate a .22 short rifle to supplement his folding .410, but if he gave him one of those, Swanwick would have a fit . . . some weatherproof clothing would be more suitable, though such a gift would smack rather of a Lord Bountiful attitude, which was very far from his true feeling for Probyn Gorse.

He went out of the front door and stood a moment, folded newspaper in hand, looking out at the frosty garden and the spreading white-barred landscape, the spidery trees. A north-east wind moaned in the roof and shook the rimed boughs of the trees. A pair of mallards raced down the wind, and swung, wings glinting in the low sun, to circle back to the Scarrow.

". . . on earth peace, good will toward men," Cate said aloud; then swore under his breath and went back inside the manor house.

Near Wytschaete, Belgian Flanders: Wednesday, December 23, 1914

18 The big crescent of the moon sank soon after one in the morning, and Charles 'Boy' Rowland took his patrol out twenty minutes later. Before the moon set, while he waited in the primitive front line trench with the men who were to accompany him, the dim bulk of the Messines Ridge had seemed to tower over them to the east and north: as soon as the moon sank, the ridge also vanished—the land might as well have been a sea, dark clouds obscuring the stars, and only paleness from a light fall of snow during the evening making a glow along the ground at the level of the eyes.

Colonel Gould had given him the orders himself—raid the enemy trench opposite and bring back a prisoner, or a body. "Brigade wants to know who's opposite us," he'd said, "and I think it's Division pressing Brigade. For all I know, Sir John French himself may have ordered this raid, originally. So get us a Hun, Boy. Take twenty or thirty men, and Major Roberts will arrange all the support you need—but try not to let a battle develop. In and out quickly. Understand?"

Roberts was Boy's company commander, and what could be arranged had been—machine-gun fire to cover the flanks; an artillery officer in the front line trench to bring down SOS fire to right and left of the chosen section of German trench on a Very light signal; stretcher-bearers in support. Every man of the raiding party was carrying six captured German "tortoise-shell" grenades, all their faces were blackened with plenteous mud from the sodden trenches, and their ammunition pouches were full. The whole raid was timed to be over in twenty minutes from first to last: the Germans were barely seventy-five yards away.

They were lined up ready in the crowded trench—Corporal Tompkins with eight men to his left, Corporal Heseltine with eight more to his right, Sergeant Swain farther along with another eight, to follow as close reserve. Jimmy Gosnell, the platoon commander of the sector, was there to see him off. The trench was little more than a series of shell holes, loosely linked to form a straggling deep ditch. In some places sandbags rivetted the parapet and parados, in others there was only the slippery wet earth. A smell of death and human excrement, mixed with cordite and lyddite fumes seemingly absorbed into the soil, pervaded the night. It was the first taste of battle in France for all of them. One of the corporals had fought in South Africa, and Sergeant Swain had fired a few shots in anger in Upper Burma in 1892, when he was a young soldier. That was the total of the raiding party's battle experience.

Gosnell muttered, "Here they come . . ."

Two figures took shape out of the darkness close in front, worming forward like lizards, on their stomachs. They slipped head first over the edge of the trench, to be caught by the men of Boy's patrol, who lowered them awkwardly to their feet. "Our wire's cut, sir," one of them said, straightening up and scraping mud off the front of his tunic. "Straight ahead, six feet wide."

"And the gap's marked, for when we come back?" Boy asked.

"As ordered, Mr Rowland. Bits of white cloth on the ground, like arrows pointing to the gap, about ten yards farther out, on the Hun side."

"Did you hear anything?"

"Not a thing, sir . . . except some barnshoot of a machine gunner loosing off over our heads. Gawd knows where they went."

"We heard them . . . He wasn't aiming at you, you think?"

"Not a chance, sir."

"All right . . . Well, we'll be off, Jimmy. Ready, Tompkins? Heseltine? Sergeant?"

"Ready, sir."

"Good luck, Boy."

"Thanks."

His stomach a tight knot, shivering only controlled by an immense effort, he scrambled up the forward face of the trench, pushed by two men of Gosnell's platoon, and once on top began to crawl forward on hands and knees, holding rifle and fixed bayonet ready in his right hand, but keeping them out of the mud. His revolver was in its holster at his belt but he did not expect to have to use it tonight; the bayonet, or one of the grenades in his haversack, would be the more likely.

He found the gap in the British wire without difficulty, crawled through, went on another ten yards and waited. The men crawled through after him and spread out to either side, the corporals closest to him. Sergeant Swain waited at the gap in the wire. "Ready?" Boy whispered. The corporals muttered, "Yes, sir," and they all started forward again, still crawling. Boy felt a momentary pang of embarrassment—what a ridiculous thing for grown men to be doing in the middle of the night! That feeling passed, but it had settled the near panic that had gripped him just before he left the trench. The clouds were thin and fast moving. A chance clearing would bring out more stars and the danger that there would then be enough light for the German sentries to make out the moving humps in No Man's Land. The wind soughed in his ears and he gave thanks for it; the worst moment of the patrol would come soon now, when they reached the German wire, and then they would need all the help they could get. His hands were cold in the woollen gloves, his head cold under the khaki Balaclava helmet which he, like all the men, was wearing. He would have given a lot to have it start to rain, or sleet, with thunder . . . All the men were flat on their stomachs now, crawling forward in a line over the broken ground, thin snow, half-frozen half-liquid mud . . . sliding in and out of scattered shell holes . . . momentary gleam of an abandoned messtin . . . a face, bodyless . . . a clip of ammunition . . . a German rifle with bayonet fixed, clutched by a fallen body, stiff in death . . . this ground had been fought over since the beginning of October, nearly three months.

The German wire . . . the men with the wire cutters slid forward. Everyone else lay silent, stretched flat, rifles out-thrust, fingers on the triggers, safety catches off. Each corporal held a grenade ready. All eyes, except the wirecutters', were fastened into the darkness ahead where, twenty feet away, Germans were sleeping, waking . . . Half left, Boy caught the flare of a match being lit in the trench, saw the gleam of a bayonet on the parapet, and the hunched silhouette behind it. He touched Corporal Tompkins' arm and pointed, muttering in his ear—"Sentry!"

Tompkins nodded and shifted his position minutely. The wire cutters clacked once, cutting a strand of wire. Boy stiffened, sweat breaking out on his forehead. How could they not have heard? Click . . . clack . . . He was trembling again . . . but they had not heard . . . The German machine gunner in their second line trench fired again, a steady ratatata, the bullets clattering far overhead and to the left. That's marvellous, wonderful, Boy thought, breathing out heavily while he could—for the machine gun's noise hid that, and the rapid snicking of the last strands of wire. The wirecutters pulled five feet of wire aside and Boy waited. One more row of wire—not thick, as they had seen through binoculars during the afternoon—but now they were barely twelve feet from the trench . . . another breathless, sweating five minutes, no nervous machine gunner to mask the sounds this time, but again the wire was cut, and pulled aside.

The cutters crawled back to him. One whispered in his ear, "Ready, sir."

Then the cutters crawled a little aside, and waited with the reserve. Their job, under Sergeant Swain, was to guard the gap in the wire until the patrol came back through it, and then keep the Germans' heads down for a few seconds longer.

Boy started forward, crawling through the gaps, the patrol close on his heels. At the lip of the German trench he waited. The sentry they had seen was twenty feet to his left. He wanted the men to be up with him so that they could all jump into the trench together, on a wide front, rather than one behind another. But when only four men were up, a dark shape emerged from directly under Boy, stretched, turned, and found himself looking straight at Boy at three-foot range. Boy pulled the trigger of his rifle instantly and the man was blasted back, his face a blur. "Now!" Boy yelled, hurling himself into the trench. His men tumbled after him, running quickly to right and left along the trench. The sentry was the most dangerous enemy, because he was awake. Boy ran toward him, but Tompkins was there first, shouting fiercely, "Hands up!" The German jumped down, leaving his rifle on the parapet, and raised his hands. Tompkins pushed him back up the forward wall of the trench, yelling, "Look out, Nobby, it's me with an 'Un!"

To the right a head appeared out of the side wall of the trench, where there was obviously a dugout. A British soldier fired and the head snapped back. Corporal Heseltine jumped close, threw aside the blanket covering the dugout entrance, and hurled in a grenade. The explosion was followed by screams and groans. But bombs were beginning to come the other way now, from other sections of the German front line. A private was down, his right arm smashed, groaning, "Don't leave me, sir."

Boy found his whistle on its lanyard, tugged it free of the pocket and blew it three times. They had their prisoner and could start back now. Then with Heseltine's help he pushed the man with the smashed arm over the parapet and waited, shouting, "Wealds! Retire! Now!" The men came running and stumbling, firing back into the darkness, grenades bursting. Another man was down, motionless in the sudden flare of a German starshell. No chance to get him out, even if he were alive. Then they were all scrambling up the trench wall, running through the gaps in the wire. Machine guns were firing, much lower and closer than before. Boy knelt, found the Very pistol in his haversack and fired it straight up. The red flare whooshed, hissed, burst, and hung there, a radiant red glow. The patrol ran on, as two British batteries of 4.5-inch howitzers began to pour shells into the German trenches which Boy and his men had just left.

A minute later they ran through the gap in the British wire, calling, "Lucknow! Lucknow!"—that night's password—and fell into the trench . . . twenty-four of them, including three wounded, one seriously—and one German. Four men remained in the German trench—dead or wounded, no one could say for certain. Corporal Heseltine and a private set off at once for Brigade Headquarters with the prisoner, for interrogation.

Boy Rowland trudged to the rear, his men behind him. C Company was in battalion reserve—that was why they had to find men for such patrols as this. He yawned, still trying to control passing fits of shivering. He ought to be thinking of the raid—the colonel would want details . . . but he could think consecutively of nothing, images passed through his mind . . . the German's blasted face . . . the silhouetted sentry . . . Private Grogan's smashed arm, torn tunic, white bone, gushing blood . . . Some of that blood stained his own tunic, all up the sleeve above his rank badges.

He must control himself. He was an officer, and these men expected him to show them an example. All his life he had enjoyed opportunities and privileges that they had not—yet he was no better than they. He must become so, or at least give them reason to believe so. A cup of tea would settle him, laced with a little rum if he could wangle some. The Intelligence Officer first, though. In the reserve area he thanked and dismissed his men, waited while they were served tea and rum, and then plodded to battalion headquarters, close by, in a shell-shattered hovel.

The I.O. met him with a smile . . . "I've seen your prisoner, on his way back . . . 35th Württembergers, of the 25th Reserve Division. How did it go? Here, have some tea—laced." He passed over a mug.

Boy sat down on the box top and told his story. When he had finished, the I.O. said, "Good. I'll pass it on to the C.O. in the morning.

Now I've got some news for you . . . You have been posted to the 1st Battalion."

"Why?" Boy said, suddenly indignant. "Isn't the C.O. or Major Roberts satisfied with me?"

"Just the opposite, Boy. We've been ordered to send two officers and twenty N.C.O.s to the 1st Battalion. They've had very heavy casualties —and we've hardly had any yet. Your uncle's in the 1st, isn't he?"

Boy nodded. "Where are they?"

"Near Plugstreet, farther south. You are to go over tomorrow. So it looks as though you've got rid of the albatross, at last."

"What? Oh, the loss statement and charge for the *pakhals*. I hope so. Those Indian *babus* are worse than leeches."

He finished the tea, feeling it warm his belly, and started back for his company headquarters. His batman was awake, and a candle burning in the muddy dugout he shared with Terrell, the battalion's newest 2nd Lieutenant, joined a week before the battalion left Lucknow for France. Yawning, he took off his equipment and gave the rifle to the batman to return to where it belonged. His batman took off his boots while he sat on the edge of the empty crates that raised the blankets out of the mud, thus forming a bed. A newspaper lay on the packing case that was their table, and a headline in it caught his eye: MORE SINN FEIN BOMBS IN LONDON. He muttered under his breath, "Good God!"

"What's that, sorr?" Reilly asked, looking up.

"Nothing . . . Thanks. That's all till . . . what time's stand to?"

"Foive-twenty ack emma, sir. But you're excused, 'cos of the patrol, loike. An' you being posted to the 1st."

"All right. I'll try to sleep till nine. Then I'll pack up."

Private Reilly blew out the candle, and Boy lay back, fully dressed except for boots and tunic, on the bed, his greatcoat spread over all. A letter from home had told him that his Aunt Margaret, after being arrested on suspicion of being involved in Sinn Fein activities, had gone to Ireland and vanished. He wondered whether she had had anything to do with these new bombings. Poor Uncle Christopher, he thought, what can we do to help him? What is . . . ? But the next thing he knew was Reilly shaking him, and watery sunlight streaming into the dugout . . . "Wake up, sorr. Noine o'clock, and I've won some hot water from the cooks."

Boy put down the old copy of the paper with a smile. "Guy seems to have covered himself with glory . . . though you can read between the lines that Sheddy's heart is still with the forwards."

"It must have been an exciting game," his uncle Quentin said, re-lighting his pipe. They were alone in the dugout, for Quentin's second-in-command had had his supper up the line with B Company, and had not yet returned. Quentin Rowland's A Company of the 1st Battalion, Weald Light Infantry, was in battalion reserve, as Boy's C Company had been in the 2nd Battalion near Wytschaete. The dugout was not luxurious, but it was in considerably better condition than the one he had shared with Terrell. This was also more professional—articles of equipment were well-worn and had been subtly modified to suit trench conditions: belts, packs, and haversacks hung from German bayonets stuck between the sandbags: half a dozen German potato masher bombs stood in a row on a shelf, ready for emergency use. There was a bottle of red wine on the table, and the meal had been potatoes fried with onions, and a very tasty German sausage. The 1st Battalion had been at war a long time—four months now. Boy said as much to his uncle.

Quentin said, "Yes, we're experienced, Boy . . . We've paid the price for it."

"You've had very heavy casualties, I was told, sir." He had never had anything to do with his uncle in a military capacity before and thought it would be wiser not to claim the relationship even in the privacy of the dugout.

Quentin nodded. "Very." He lowered his voice as though the batman in another dugout along the trench could hear. "The British regular army's gone, Boy. We did the job we were supposed to do . . . stop the Germans outflanking us and cutting us off from the Channel ports. We were fighting four or five to one for two months on end. The Germans used reserve divisions which weren't supposed to be any good . . . but don't believe it. They fought like tigers. So did we . . . mostly. There was some panic here and there. We're regulars but no one's seen anything like this before—French, German, Russian, British, it makes no difference. Some men broke—ours, theirs—officers, too. Some regiments ran that you'd never have believed would . . . I don't have one platoon commander I came out with. Sergeant Major gone—killed the last day we were in the front line by a Boche whizzbang . . . in the ranks only one man in six or seven came out with us from the Curragh . . . the rest—" he shrugged, "—recruits, reinforcements from other regiments, some Territorials who volunteered to transfer."

His pipe was drawing well now and he picked up another paper—the *Hedlington Courier*, two weeks old. "The North Weald had a great day with the bitch pack, here." He tapped the paper. "A three-mile point. That's tremendous, in our country." He put the paper down and shook his head slowly. The pale blue eyes looked directly at Boy, the forehead wrinkling with a slight frown. "I keep trying to think of hunting . . . fishing . . . walking your father's fields with a gun under my arm and a dog at my heel . . . Guy and Virginia, your Aunt Fiona . . . the house, all the things we used to do together—when we could be together . . . Nothing comes. It's as though what used to be has vanished."

Boy felt closer to his uncle than he ever remembered. He said, "I know what you mean, sir. I feel something like that and I think it'll get worse, as time passes."

"It must come back," Quentin said. "What else is there?" His manner was puzzled but determined. Boy thought, he can't imagine that there *can* be any other life than the one they all lived before August 4th this year.

Quentin said, "Have you heard about your Aunt Margaret?"

"Yes, sir."

"A bad business."

Boy had drunk two tin mugs of the red wine and felt that he could not and should not altogether conceal his opinion, though he would have to choose his words carefully. He said, "It seems to me, sir, that Carson's Ulster Volunteers are breaking the law just as much as the Sinn Feiners . . . but we don't do anything to suppress them. Aunt Margaret always thought we were being unfair in Ireland."

"Mother taught us all that," Quentin said, "but Margaret was the only one who believed it." He looked at his watch. "You'd better be going up the line. I'll send my batman up with you to show you the way. You're going to B, aren't you?"

"Yes, sir. Captain Maclachlan."

Boy thanked his uncle, and a few minutes later, heavily laden with equipment, the batman carrying his valise, started up toward the front line. The stars were hidden behind a low white haze, and the air was cold, barely stirring. Ghostly poplars stood with arms raised all about them. The ruins of a nearby farmhouse, pounded to chaos, dull brick and white plaster and broken glass, still exuded a smell of the once-heaped dung, now scattered by shellfire over acres of country. A small brick calvary stood at what had been a crossroads.

The forward trench system began and they dropped down into it. After ten slow minutes, standing aside as men sloshed back carrying empty dixies and ammunition boxes, the mud six inches deep, the trench walls crumbling, the batman stopped and said, "Here, sir—B Company headquarters."

Boy pulled the blanket aside and went down five steps, into a candle-lit cave-like room, its roof beams taken from destroyed houses, spread with sacking and covered with earth. Water dripped from the sandbag wall, and gleamed on the floor.

Boy saluted . . . "Lieutenant Rowland, sir, reporting for duty."

Maclachlan was seated on an empty shell box, a company sergeant major beside him. The staff-sergeant saluted and Maclachlan said, "C.S.M. Davies, Rowland—a Welshman, just like our revered Chancellor of the Exchequer."

"Pleased to meet you, sir," Davies said, putting out his hand.

"Sit down, Rowland. Have you eaten?"

"Yes, sir." He sat down on another shell box.

"We're just going to take a look round the trenches. You might as well come with us, and meet your platoon . . . Except for one other, you'll be the most experienced platoon commander I have, and you've barely got your second pip, eh?"

"Yes, sir. Major Rowland was telling me about the heavy casualties."

"Ah, your uncle, of course . . . It's not only the officers, though they've had the highest proportion . . . A quarter of the men are from Newfoundland, or Chile, or Australia . . . fellows who left England for England's good, some of them cashiered, perhaps shepherds, navvies, a hobo, one said he was . . . They're mostly brave as lions, but their drill! . . . The sar'nt major has permanent apoplexy over the things they do and say. They can't march—only rode, in the outback or the prairie or veldt or somewhere . . . but they can shoot well, most of them. A few certainly are wanted for murder in Tombstone, or Woolloomooloo, or Grizzly Gulch . . . Are you ready?"

They went out into the night. It had begun to snow. Boy realised suddenly that it was Christmas Eve.

Stand to was at five-thirty. 2nd Lieutenant Beldring's batman lit the candle and the two officers, Boy and Beldring, stumbled yawning into their greatcoats, then their equipment, checked that their revolvers were loaded, and went out into the trench. The sentries were at their posts on the firestep, rifles rested beside them, their left hands on the forestock, the fixed bayonet pointing up at an angle. The soldiers were coming out of their shelters along the forward wall, sliding through the mud, muttering under their breaths, coughing. Dawn was the best time to attack, since the assaulting troops could move up in darkness, and hours of daylight would be available for consolidation of captured positions; so all front line troops and immediate reserves stood to their posts half an hour before first light, and stayed there till half an hour after it. Machine guns were manned, the Numbers 2 crouched to one side, the Numbers 1 sitting behind the gun on the special raised platform built on the forward wall of the trench so that the nose of the Vickers just stuck through a narrow gap in the sandbags, which were built up two feet higher on either side to give the gunners some flank protection.

By five-thirty everyone was in position, and Boy, standing on the firestep in the centre of his platoon's sector, waited, shifting his balance from one foot to the other, and clapping his hands gently in their khaki wool gloves. His parents would be worrying about his being killed, probably. That was a useless worry, there was nothing any of them could do about that . . . what they should all worry about was getting decent clothes, better protection against the cold, the snow, the rain, above all the mud . . . Mud! He'd only been in the line a few days and already mud was becoming, in his mind, an enemy to be hated even more than the Germans.

The snow had stopped some time in the middle of the night, before he'd gone round his lines at 2 a.m. with Sergeant Knapp. He still didn't know what any of his men looked like, and Knapp was no more than a stocky shape with, he thought, a walrus moustache, and an Old Kent Road accent. He muttered close behind him now—"The captain's coming, sir."

Boy glanced round and saw Maclachlan and the C.S.M. splashing through the mud and snow toward him. He stepped down and saluted. "Good morning, sir."

"Anything to report?"

"No, sir. It's hard for me to be sure, though, because I haven't seen the area in daylight yet."

"You will, soon. Knapp will point out the principal features—such as there are. Plugstreet is not exactly one of Belgium's beauty spots." He passed on, talking to a man here, pausing to examine a plank revetment, climbing up on the firestep, making remarks to C.S.M. Davies, who carefully shone a torch on a notepad and made notes with a stub of a pencil.

The light gradually spread, crawling out of the soil, displaying the stunted poplars, the expanse of dirty snow, already pockmarked with black where shells had been fired during the night, gleaming water and mud, shattered trees, humped ruins, and—two hundred yards away—the German wire, three thick rows of it.

Boy got up on the firestep again, and Sergeant Knapp said, "Keep your 'ead down, sir! There's an 'Un sniper too good for our 'ealth, somewhere near that pile of bricks behind their front line . . . Got three of our men, this past week—two right through the eye'ole . . . horful mess . . . That's 'Ill 45, there . . . sort of an 'ill, anyway. The 'Uns look down on us from there—their artillery observers . . . we tried to take

'Ill 45 three times last November . . . got in, then got pushed out, each time."

Boy examined the long row of houses on Hill 45, a few seemingly intact, most demolished. Smoke rose—the enemy reserves cooking their breakfast in comfort.

"Them trees to the left is Plugstreet Wood, sir. The next-door division tried to clear it. No luck. Just a horful lot of burying parties."

Boy stayed at his place, covering the ground through binoculars until he had a clear picture of it in his head. When the battalion stood down he said to his platoon sergeant, "Do we have a really good shot in the platoon?"

"Yes, sir. Private Nichols—says 'e was a shepherd in Chile."

"See if you can win a telescopic sight for him. Tomorrow night we'll build a place, between our front and second lines, where he can lie up and get that German sniper . . . and any other German he spots."

"Very good, sir."

"I'll choose the place today. Stand down, now."

He waited till the daytime sentries were posted, then went to company headquarters to receive orders for the day.

There were no orders for the day, except to wait, and watch. Play cards. Write letters. Clean equipment. Fill in the latrine bay and dig a new one. Make sure there were no bent or damaged rounds in the ammunition clips. Mend holes in tunics. Clean and oil rifles. Dry out puttees. Stand sentry duty—by day it was two hours on and four hours off; by night sentries were doubled, always stood in pairs, and duty was one hour on and one hour off. Between the innumerable little tasks, the men dozed, curled up in greatcoats in the primitive dugouts, or at the side of the trench. Light snow drifted across No Man's Land, stopped, started again, stopped. The sun shone bleakly.

Sergeant Knapp came to Boy where he was restudying the list of his platoon's names and numbers, length of service and military skills, which Knapp had given him earlier. The sergeant stood in the entrance to the dugout and said, "Near ten o'clock, sir."

"What of it?"

"The 'Uns always 'as an 'ate at ten sharp, sir. Thought you'd like to come up and see 'oo they'll pick on today."

Boy put down the paper, buckled on his equipment, and came out, asking, "What kind of a hate is it? What are the men supposed to do? Get into the shelters?"

"Oh no, sir. The 'Uns might choose that moment to attack. Everyone 'as to be at stand-to stations. It's five minutes shelling."

Boy thought to himself that if the hate was a concentration of artillery fire, surely the best thing would be for the sentries to stay at their posts, the rest of the men to go to their shelters and dugouts. That wouldn't make much difference if they got a direct hit from a 5.9, but they'd get some protection against anything else, especially shrapnel.

He waited, looking at his watch. Ten o'clock. Nothing happened . . . A solitary field gun was firing half a mile to the north—but it was a British 18-pounder, apparently ranging. "Funny," Sergeant Knapp muttered. "P'raps their watches 'as stopped."

Five past . . . ten past . . . quarter past . . .

"You can't trust those bleeding 'Uns," Knapp said, very aggrieved. "Hevery day for three weeks, and now . . ."

"Listen!" Boy said, standing higher and holding up his hand. Knapp grabbed him and pulled him down. "The sniper, sir!"

"Oh yes. Thanks . . . but listen!"

Boy heard a strange sound he knew but had not heard for . . . how long? Since he left England to join the 2nd Battalion in Lucknow.

"Church bells," he said softly. "Church bells from Armentières, and Nieuw Kerke and—what's that village up there called?"

"Saint Yvon, sir . . . but wot are they ringing the bells for?"

Boy started laughing . . . "Christmas Day, sergeant! It's Christmas Day. Peace on earth and good will toward men! That's why the Germans omitted their daily hate . . . and perhaps why the sniper didn't fire at me just now."

He stood up tall, looking over the sandbagged parapet, his head and shoulders showing. A German opposite was doing the same. The German waved, then put his hands to his mouth and shouted. The words rang clear across the shell pocked snow—"Merry Christmas, Tommy!"

"Merry Christmas, Fritz," Boy shouted back. The German began to climb out of his trench, and Boy followed suit.

"Sir, sir!" Knapp was tugging at his tunic. "We ought to be careful!"

"No more than ten men are to come out. You stay here till I come back . . . Send a man to tell the captain what's happening."

"There won't be no need, sir. Look!" Knapp, standing beside Boy in the open now, gestured to right and left, where No Man's Land was dotted with men moving toward each other, pulling knife rests aside or cutting the wire so that they could reach each other.

Boy walked forward. The German who had shouted was close, waving his hand. The hand held a bottle. They met and Boy said, "Merry Christmas . . . I'm Lieutenant Rowland."

"Lieutenant Werner von Rackow, at your service!" He clicked his heels, bowed, and held out the bottle—"German champagne. Rather sweet, but good enough, in the circumstances."

Boy drank, hiccuped, and returned the bottle, grinning. The German was no more than twenty, perhaps less, six feet, slender, with a long head, aquiline features, big hands, a ready smile . . . very like his cousin Guy, Boy realised; except that the German was growing a tooth-brush moustache, and both his eyes were grey and his hair was blond.

"You speak English very well," he said, "and I'm afraid I don't speak any German."

"You will, after the war is over," the other said, laughing. "No offence, please . . . My mother is—was—English.

"You are—" he glanced at Boy's cap badge "—the Weald Light Infantry, I see. A very good regiment. You gave my regiment a bad time at Le Cateau. We found many of your dead on the field when we were eventually able to advance . . . We gave them proper burial," he added quickly.

"I am sure," Boy said, "I'm afraid I don't smoke. I have no cigarettes . . ." He felt in his tunic pockets, found something hard, and pulled it out. It was a piece of German sausage that his uncle had given him last night, to take up as a snack. Von Rackow laughed. "Thanks, but I have plenty of that."

Boy thought frantically. I must give him something, but what? He remembered the good luck charm his sister Naomi had given him when he went out to India. It was in the shape of Mr Kipling's swastika colophon, made of gold, and inscribed on the front C.J.C. ROWLAND, and on the back, along the crooked arms, *To Boy, with love, from Naomi*. He undid his top tunic and shirt buttons, and took off the charm, which lay on his chest with his identity discs on its own gold chain, and gave it to the German.

"We're enemies," he said awkwardly, "but there's no need for us to behave like animals . . . Take this, for good luck. We'll beat you, but I hope *you* come through."

Von Rackow looked at it a moment, then unbuttoned his own high-collared tunic and pulled out a locket that had been hanging round his neck, next to the skin. He gave it to Boy, saying simply, "My mother, the English lady." Boy saw a handsome oval face, the woman about forty, fair hair piled on top of her head. The back of the locket was inscribed with von Rackow's name, rank, army number, and regiment. Boy hung it round his neck, where the swastika had hung, and said, "Thank you."

Von Rackow did the same; and, as he was rebuttoning his tunic, asked, "Has the war hit your family badly yet?"

Boy shook his head, "We thought for a time that an uncle had been killed at Coronel, but he wasn't."

"An uncle of mine went down at the Falkland Islands," von Rackow said. "Do you realise, Mr Rowland, that when those squadrons met off Coronel that day, four out of five of the men present were to die within a few weeks? The English that night, ours a month later?"

Boy shook his head, not speaking. The disaster at Coronel had been such a blow to England's naval prestige that when, a month later, all von Spee's ships but one were sunk off the Falkland Islands by a superior British fleet, almost without loss, he, like most Englishmen, had had no feeling but of relief, and revenge: the slate had been wiped clean.

All up and down No Man's Land officers and men were exchanging gifts—cap badges, cigarettes, loaves of bread, tobacco, photos, wine. A British staff captain was stumbling along shouting, "No photographs of other ranks permitted! Only officers may be photographed fraternising!"

The German said, "I won't be in the trenches much longer. I've applied for the air arm."

"I'm terrified of those things," Boy said, "but I suppose they're going to become more and more important. Look now!"

He pointed up—a German plane, the black crosses clear under the wing, was circling low over the battlefield, the pilot leaning far out to observe the strange goings on below.

Whistles began to shrill. The staff captain was shouting, "Everyone back! . . . Back! Hostilities will recommence in twenty minutes!"

Von Rackow put out his hand. "Good luck to you too, Mr Rowland. I wish we could meet in other circumstances."

"So do I."

"Perhaps we will."

They saluted each other, the German formally, but with a smile, Boy awkwardly, feeling a fool, yet warm. He trudged back toward the British line, where he could see Sergeant Knapp's moonface peering anxiously over the parapet.

He jumped down and in, almost the last to do so. Ten minutes later a series of heavy thuds sounded from the east, followed by the whistling sighs of a score of shells. They burst in salvoes on the support area a quarter of a mile to the rear. Knapp sighed with relief, "That's the 'ate, sir. Not on us today."

Boy said, "Well, everyone back to business . . . Let's reconnoitre a place for that sniper."

"Right, sir . . . Two men come up from the rear, just now, sir, posted to us. Privates Maloney and Stratton, sir . . . They're 'ere, now . . . Attention!" The two soldiers standing in the trench, each bowed under greatcoat, entrenching tool, full pack, bulging ammunition pouches, full water bottle, rolled blanket, rifle and bayonet, stood to attention and stared straight ahead.

Boy said, "Where are you from, Maloney?"

"County Cork, sorr . . . I was in the navy two years, but got seasick every time we went to sea, so they let me join the army."

"And you, Stratton?"

"Kent, sir. Hedlington."

Boy stared more closely. The man was in his mid-thirties—stocky, sandy, with big ears and wide set eyes. He said, "Didn't you work at my grandfather's plant, Rowland's?"

"Yes, sir," Frank Stratton said, grinning broadly. "I remember when you were born, sir, in Hedlington, before Mr John moved out to the farm. And then Mr John would invite my dad and mum and us down to picnic during the summer."

Boy said, "Well, I'm delighted you've joined us . . . If you haven't detailed a batman to me yet, sergeant, I'd like to have Stratton. Suit you, Stratton?"

"Yes, sir."

"Good idea, sir. Then 'e won't 'ave quite so much 'ard labour as the others. No chicken, are you, Stratton?"

"Thirty-six, sergeant."

"'Ow did you get out 'ere so soon? Can't 'ave joined up before August, can you?"

"That recruit training was pretty easy, sergeant, and I kept pestering the officers, till they sent me out to get rid of me."

Boy said, "You're married, aren't you? Your wife's called—wait a minute . . . Anne."

"That's right, sir. Two girls, and a little nipper, born October 4th this year." His left hand wandered toward his breast pocket and Sergeant Knapp said hastily, "That's all, there! Dismiss!"

Boy walked off, overhearing Knapp's muttered comment—"Some folk is off their blooming rockers—thank Gawd!"

Two days later Boy was in the company headquarters dugout, listening to Captain Maclachlan finish his orders for a wiring party, to be commanded by Boy: "Normal messages by field telephone from the front line trench: emergency—red over red Very lights, for general stand to, if you suspect an enemy attack is imminent. Any questions?"

Boy looked at his notes and after a moment said, "Can I draw the wire earlier, sir? I'd like to have time to check it. Sergeant Knapp has told me that it's often tangled on the spools."

Maclachlan said, "Yes. Fix that direct with the R.S.M. Anything else?"

"I don't think so, sir."

"Well, run along then and get some sleep—all of you—before dark." Boy saluted and turned to go but C.S.M. Davies cut in—"Excuse me, sir, we've had a Form 905 for you." He handed it over. Boy read, not understanding—Lieutenant C.J.C. Rowland, 2nd Bn Weald Light Infantry, stationed at Lucknow . . . It was an Indian Army form. The ordnance authorities at Lucknow were stating that he owed them 64 rupees, 14 annas, 4 pies in connection with the loss of two *pakhals*, on April 8th, 1914. Payment must be made immediately by cheque or money order to the District Ordnance Depot, citing the number of this document.

"How on earth did this get here?" he asked the C.S.M.

"Sent on from the 2nd Battalion," he said, "with a note to say it arrived just after you were transferred. But, look you, sir, we can lose it, easily!"

Captain Maclachlan cut in—"Yes, lose it, Sar'nt Major. Although whether anyone can escape from the clutches of an Indian Ordnance Depot that easily, I am not sure."

Daily Telegraph, Wednesday, December 23, 1914

KING'S MESSAGE TO EAST COAST MAYORS
DEEP SYMPATHY WITH BEREAVED FAMILIES

His Majesty yesterday sent to the Lord Lieutenants of Durham and the North Riding of Yorkshire a gracious expression of his sympathy with the bereaved families in the bombarded towns on the East Coast, to be forwarded to the Mayors of these towns. Identical messages were received by the Mayors of Hartlepool and of West Hartlepool in these terms:—

I have felt keenly for the people of Hartlepool during the past week, and heartily sympathize with the bereaved families. Please inquire as to the progress of the wounded. I wish them all speedy recovery. GEORGE R.I.

"The Germans had a cheek to bombard Hartlepool," Laurence said, buttering a piece of toast and spreading it with Oxford marmalade, "but why didn't the navy stop them? Or sink the ships that did it?"

Christopher Cate said, "Cheek isn't the word to apply to operations of war, Laurence. The Germans took the risks involved in order to make our civilian population realise that they are not immune from the dangers of war just because we are surrounded by sea. They want us to lose confidence in the navy, and in our leaders. For the same reason they will shortly be dropping explosives from Zeppelins and aeroplanes, I am convinced."

"But what are the risks, for the Germans?" Laurence demanded. "They knew Hartlepool and those places aren't defended. And the Grand Fleet sits up at Scapa, hundreds of miles away, doing nothing."

"They aren't doing nothing," his father said. "Admiral Jellicoe occasionally orders some of the heavy ships to make a sweep south and east along our coasts, and toward Germany, in the hope of catching a German squadron on just such an operation as this coastal bombardment. So far, luck has been against us . . . and by the time the Grand Fleet itself can leave harbour to cut off the raiders, it is too late—they have a much shorter distance to go."

Laurence ate some toast; and then, unwilling to let the Germans off lightly, said, "They're dirty dogs, though, to bombard civilians, aren't they?"

Cate said, "Yes, they are." He hesitated, but decided Laurence was old enough to think more deeply into these things. He said, "The Germans say that we are attacking their women and children by our blockade. Starving them. To an extent, it is true . . . War is an unpleasant business, Laurence."

Again Laurence was busy eating for a time, then he said, "Will Uncle Quentin be home for Christmas, do you think?"

"I very much doubt it. It's only the day after tomorrow, and though he might turn up at any moment for a few days' leave, it is against the odds. After all, every man in France would like to spend Christmas at home, with his family, if he could."

"I hope at least that he has a big Christmas pudding."

"That he should," Christopher said. "Mrs Abell made him a big one last week—and another for Uncle Tom—and we sent them both off while you were still at school. Uncle Tom won't get his in time, I fear . . . but we may be seeing him soon. In yesterday's paper the naval correspondent was speculating that most of the cruisers that have been scattered all over the world can now come home—to join the Grand Fleet, or the blockading forces."

"Or get the *Goeben* and *Breslau* out of Constantinople," Laurence said. "A fleet could sail up the Dardanelles and into the Bosphorus and just blow them out of the water. They're Germans even if the rotten Turks have fitted out the crews with fezzes and pretended they're all in *their* navy now . . . rotters!"

Walstone Park: Friday, January 1, 1915

19 Johnny Merritt had a vile cold and his head felt like a boiled owl's. "This English climate!" he had muttered to himself a hundred times since the cold had started three days ago . . . "and the way they heat their rooms, or rather, don't." His father had told him he was a fool not to cry off from his New Year's visit to the Cates, in his condition, but he had been determined to go. Stella would be there; and he was beginning to feel unsure about her. When they had first met, that marvellous day at Henley, she had seemed totally absorbed in him. That remained true the first few times they had been together since his return to England; but recently he had felt her attention was wandering . . . she wasn't always available to be given tea at the South Eastern, even when he knew she was in Hedlington, but not actually at work in Lady Blackwell's hospital. She wasn't even always ready to spend all her hours with him at Walstone—though it was she who had, through her father, invited him down. Yet he loved her more than ever. The plain fact was, he acknowledged to himself, that he was jealous . . . but of whom? He answered himself—of anyone who looked at her, or took up a moment of her time. Oh well, he'd have her to himself nearly all day tomorrow, when he took her to Canterbury.

He was striding along a lane on the outskirts of Walstone with two Mrs Rowlands—Mrs John and Mrs Quentin—Mrs Quentin's daughter Virginia, and Naomi's friend Rachel Cowan. The older ladies wore sensible tweed skirts and coats, thick stockings, boots and dark grey spats; he himself wore knickerbockers and a thick Norfolk jacket, a tweed cap, and long woollen scarf. Old Mr Harry Rowland was driving down from Hedlington, with his wife and Alice. Richard and Susan were not interested in foxhunting, and were not coming—perhaps also, he thought, Richard preferred to keep away from his father. Mrs Cate had vanished in Ireland. The rest of the Rowland clan—Christopher Cate, Laurence, and Stella; John Rowland and his daughter Naomi, down from Cambridge for the Christmas holidays; and Guy—were all mounted and riding separately to the New Year's Day meet of the North Weald foxhounds, held this year as every year at Walstone Park, seat of the Earls of Swanwick.

The country looked starkly beautiful, a recent snowfall mantling the north side of hedge and copse and lying in patches in the shade of great trees. The trees themselves were bare, clean arms flung out against the pale sky, the sun a warming touch on the cheek. Frost sparkled in the grass along the Scarrow and spears of ice hung from gutters and eaves.

They crossed the Scarrow on an ancient humpbacked bridge of stone, and Johnny glanced upstream. There was Walstone Park, half a mile away, an immense grey mass, windows sparkling golden in the morning sun, lawns sweeping down toward the river, small figures in scarlet and black, horses, the glint of steel.

"What a beautiful sight!" he exclaimed, "someone ought to paint that."

"People have, several times," Louise Rowland said. Virginia added, "The roof leaks, though . . ."

A little past the bridge, on the right, the wrought iron gates to the Park, adorned with gold-painted coronet and coat of arms, were open, the liveried gatekeeper standing outside the gatehouse.

"Good morning, Furr," Louise Rowland called. The gatekeeper touched his cockaded top hat, murmuring, "Morning, ma'am. Morning, miss. Morning, sir."

"Have hounds arrived yet?"

"Just passed, two minutes ago, ma'am. The bitch pack."

Virginia said to Johnny, "The kennels used to be at the back of the big house, but Lord Swanwick—this one—moved them to Beighton. Daddy says one cannot hunt and preserve pheasants on the same land."

Johnny nodded in acknowledgement. She was a nice kid, about fifteen, he thought, big breasted, but pudgy and awkward; in a couple of years, if she acquired anything of her brother Guy's poise and carriage, and thinned down a bit, she'd be a good looker.

They started walking up the drive, through scattered trees among grazing fallow deer. The great house slowly appeared round a curve of the grassy slope, to be seen again much as Johnny had seen it from the old bridge, but now more fully frontal, as the drive swept round and headed straight for the building. The hounds were a short distance ahead, trotting up the drive, a man on horseback behind them and another in front, both wearing faded scarlet coats and dark blue velvet peaked caps, and swinging whips loosely beside them. The kennel huntsman, wearing a tweed coat, cord breeches, and canvas leggings, bumped along on a shaggy pony in rear. He had a bag slung round his shoulders and a short spade strapped to the side of his saddle. A fox terrier's small, alert face peered out from the top of the bag, examining everything and everyone as it passed. One of the horsemen swung his whip and cracked it like a pistol over the head of a hound that was straying off onto the grass, attracted by some seductive scent. "Garaway boick, Antic!" he snapped. The whip cracked again, and Antic slunk back into the pack.

Johnny counted and said, "Twenty-five hounds."

Virginia corrected him. "Twelve and a half couple. Like grouse, or pheasants, only you count *them* in braces." She giggled, and said, "That sounds silly, doesn't it? I mean, brace."

They reached the expanse of gravel in front of the main entrance, and stood to one side, on the edge of the grass. Johnny blew his nose, wished he had an aspirin, and listened to Virginia . . . "That's Lord Swanwick . . . no, on foot, with the left arm a little withered and the hunting horn stuck into his coat . . . The two men he's talking to are his sons. The one in uniform is Arthur Durand-Beaulieu—the *Honourable* Arthur—and the other, in pink with white buckskin breeches and mahogany-topped black boots, is the heir, Lord Cantley."

"I saw them at Henley," Johnny said, "but not to speak to."

"The man riding up on the piebald cob, in the black stock and low-crowned topper, is the rector, Mr Kirby . . . he's a hard man to hounds, Uncle Christopher says . . . That's Lady Barbara Durand-Beaulieu, riding round from the stables. She looks very dashing in her habit and topper and veil now, but an hour ago she was mucking out the stables and grooming her own horse. All the Park grooms but one have joined up, and now she does the work of about three of them. You've met her sister at Uncle John's . . . Lady Helen, who's working as a farm girl for them now, since . . . well, I can't tell you about *that* . . . That's Arthur's wife, in nurse's uniform, on the steps. She was a nurse at St Mary's Hospital in London before they were married . . . The man she's talking to is Old Eaves, the secretary of the Hunt."

"Is that Lady Swanwick, coming out now?"

"Yes."

"Who's the girl beside her? The very pretty one with auburn hair, in a black dress."

Louise Rowland laughed—"That's her new lady's maid, Florinda Gorse. Her grandfather's the village poacher . . . and doesn't mind serving for a few other villages, too. We passed her brother Fletcher on the way . . . Remember the young man who said the scent wouldn't be very good in some places, with this snow?"

"I remember . . . Here comes Stella."

They were coming up the drive in a bunch, having met outside the Green Man in Walstone to ride the last mile together to the meet— Squire Cate, John Rowland, and Naomi in front, Laurence and Guy and Stella behind—John in pink, with immaculate breeches and boots, Cate in black, both silk hatted; Stella, Naomi, and the boys in grey and brown, with bowler hats, and leather or canvas leggings.

Rachel Cowan muttered something under her breath and Johnny, not hearing clearly, turned to her, "I beg your pardon, Miss Cowan?"

She hesitated, then said, "It's barbarous . . . but beautiful."

"Barbarous?" Louise Rowland said. "What do you mean?"

"Not barbarous, Mrs Rowland . . . that's the wrong word . . . extraordinary . . . when men are being killed by the thousands in Flanders . . . and not five miles away, children have to walk barefooted, and go to bed hungry."

The two older women turned away, not precisely in rebuke but clearly not wishing to discuss the matter any further. This was the New Year's Day meet of the North Weald hounds, their backs seemed to say: look at the farmers on their sturdy horses, come to the local nobleman's estate, to share the hunt with him: look at the villagers on foot, come to see the splendour, standing respectfully back on the grass, allowed on this day and on the earl's birthday to come and go freely in the Park; look at the earl himself, being helped up into the saddle now by a groom. This is what the men in Flanders are fighting *for* . . . so let us not discuss anything except the hunt, please.

"Here's the Governor," John said, reining in his big bay beside them. He raised his silk hat as his father and mother got slowly down from the Rowland, helped by Wright. Alice followed, and there was a flurry of greeting all round. Horses and riders were packing in more tightly on the gravel. Servants were coming out of the main entrance of the big house, and down the steps in a steady stream, each carrying a silver tray loaded with glasses.

A manservant came up to them. "Stirrup cup, sir? Mrs Rowland?"

"What is it? It's Edwards, isn't it?"

"Yes, madam. Sloe gin on this side, cherry brandy the other."

They all took a drink, even Virginia being allowed a sloe gin by her mother.

Then, as they were handing back their glasses, a hunting horn blared a call, not very surely blown. Johnny saw Lord Swanwick with the horn to his mouth, his cheeks red and puffed out.

"Lord Swanwick has to hunt hounds himself," Louise Rowland said. "The huntsman left last month, to join the army."

"And he's not very good at it," Virginia added, *sotto voce*.

Lord Swanwick, Master of Foxhounds, rode slowly forward, past the pack on the edge of the grass and across the Park, heading northwest. The whippers-in cracked their whips and the bitches followed the Master, sterns waving in a little moving forest, the whippers-in behind them. Then followed the riders in a loose mass, squire and rector, gentleman farmer and working farmer, tenant, lawyer, officer, doctor, magistrate, schoolboy and schoolgirl, and undergraduate.

"What a splendid sight!" Johnny murmured. This was the England he had wanted to fight for . . . and still did. He watched Stella ride past, talking to an older army officer he did not think he had seen before. They were riding close, Laurence on the officer's other side, their heads turned toward each other as their horses walked onto the turf and then, following the Master's example, broke into a trot heading for Ten Acre copse where, according to Virginia, hounds always found on New Year's Day.

They found in Ten Acre, as promised; that was not surprising, Stella Cate thought, since it was rumoured that Skagg regularly slipped a bagman there every New Year's Day, early. But the fox, viewed only briefly by a few of the field, quickly headed for the Scarrow. The water brought hounds to their noses and although they cast along the banks upstream and down they could no longer own the scent.

Assembled again on the south bank of the stream, Lord Swanwick beckoned to his whippers-in. The three sat close, their horses' heads pushing together as the men discussed what to do next. The field waited a little apart, at the foot of the forty-acre plough the fox had crossed just after leaving the Park, there unfenced, and gone to the river.

A gnome-like figure glided along the river bank, and, when it reached the three, touched a finger to its battered deerstalker. "Morning, my lord."

Swanwick looked up, frowning. The frown deepened when he recognised Probyn Gorse; but a reflex action made him answer the greeting with a grudging, "Morning."

"Looking for a fox, my lord?"

"What the hell do you think we're doing, Gorse?"

"You'll find one in Abbas Wood, my lord—a big dog . . . I saw him not half an hour ago. He'd heard the horns, but I don't expect he'll want to move."

Swanwick looked at him suspiciously. He returned to the whippers-in: "What do you think?"

The elder, Billing, said, "It's as likely as not, my lord. Probyn would know better'n me."

"Nor me," Snodgress, the other whipper-in, said.

The earl continued to frown, but suddenly made up his mind. "Well, take hounds up the side, Billing," he said. "Snodgress, you take the field to the east edge of Abbas Wood. If the fox breaks covert, hold the field till he's clean free of the wood, or he'll just double back in."

"Yes, my lord."

The horn twanged, the whips cracked. Snodgress put the field into a trot, and they headed for Abbas Wood. At Stella's side Captain Irwin said, "Let's hope we get a longer run this time."

"Oh, yes," she said, smiling at him. He was quite old, over thirty certainly, and he had a funny narrow small head and narrow shoulders . . . but he was so brave, badly wounded at Uncle Quentin's side in France. The way he looked at her made her feel warm and beautiful. And his being older meant that she could trust him, turn to him for advice in the way that she turned to her father . . . more so, really. From the corner of her eye, as the horses trotted heavily up the sloping field, mud clots flying from their hooves, she saw the family group following the hunt on foot, as best they could. Johnny Merritt was waving at her . . . she waved her crop back. Johnny was very nice; but he seemed so young in comparison with Captain Irwin, and sometimes he didn't know quite what to do, and that made *her* feel awkward, for she didn't know what to do, either. Captain Irwin always knew what to do, and always made you feel confident, because he was in charge, and he *knew*, whether it was ordering China tea at the South Eastern, walking in the Park, or helping you into a taxi, or onto a horse. He limped a little from his wound and would probably never be able to go back to France, which disappointed him terribly, he said. She was glad though, not only for his sake, because he would not be killed now, but for her own . . . she did not know where she was going with him, but she wanted to complete the journey, and that was a new and exciting emotion for her. A year ago it would have been unthinkable; now, because of the war, it wasn't. Danger and the unknown were all about. They frightened some, appalled others; she welcomed them, and went toward them.

Her brother was glancing at her strangely. Perhaps she looked strange. Laurence could see things about people most others couldn't. She smiled at him, and he looked away.

Half an hour later, in the field waiting outside Abbas Wood, everyone sat more firmly down in the saddle as the shrill music of the bitches came closer through the trees, to the distant crash of boughs as the Master and Billing brought them on. Guy jammed his bowler down on his head, John his top hat. Naomi eased the reins as her mare jiggled and danced sideways under her. Old Eaves put away a brandy flask and the rector clapped his horse's neck, crying, "Ready, Springer?"

The fox slipped out of the wood thirty yards farther along. Snodgress shouted sharply, "Hold hard, gentlemen, please!" The leading hounds burst out of the wood with a crash of music like pealing bells. The fox was a hundred yards clear, streaking across the hill to the eastward. Snodgress yelled at the top of his voice "Gone awa-way, gone awaway!" and galloped after the pack. The Master emerged from the wood at full gallop, twanging his horn as he went. Closely followed by Billing, he cleared the post-and-rail fence in a long, low arc.

"Here we go," Captain Irwin said. He jabbed his spurs into the horse and away they all went, helterskelter after the fox, the hounds, the Master, and the whippers-in.

Hounds picked up a big dog fox in Abbas Wood after noon, and ran strongly eastward. After a two-mile point past Lacey's Farm, Almshouses, and Drabblegate, there seemed to be danger that Reynard would reach Whitmore Woods or Thickthorp Spinney and go to ground in one of the many warrens there; but pedestrians and bicyclists following the hunt turned him and he ran right-handed past Gladwin's Mark, Benty Grange, and Thin Withins, and crossed the Hobsdon Brook at Lambs' Holes after another twenty minutes without a check. Then Charles James crossed the railway, indeed ran along it and disaster was narrowly averted as a passenger train nearly ran over hounds, stopping just in time.

The landowner there had masked the railway's considerable fence with a thick hedge. The bitches, running hard on a burning scent, scrambled through and down the side of the shallow cutting, then along the railway lines, the fox almost in view. The Master, swearing at the top of his voice, had followed, with Billing close on his heels. Then they saw the train, coming from the direction of Hedlington. The driver was leaning out of the cab, the whistle blowing continuously. The Master stood in his stirrups, purple in the face, waving his crop. "Stop, you blasted idiot!" he bellowed. "Can't you see hounds are on the line? Stop!"

The wheels screeched as steel ground on steel. The engine driver and fireman hung out, watching, for there was nothing more they could do. Billing cracked his whip and yelled obscenities at the hounds. A lady in immaculate black put her big grey at the hedge, cleared it with ease and slid down the bank onto the railway lines. The Master shook his fist at the engine driver, thundering, "I'll have your job for this! Stop, you bloody idiot!"

The driver took his pipe from his mouth and said, "I 'ave. An' you an' your dogs are on railway property, mister."

The earl managed to give the impression that he was dancing in the saddle with rage. The engine had indeed stopped. It was an old Stephenson inside-cylinder 0-6-0 of London, Chatham & Dover ancestry and now stood hissing and breathing deeply. Passengers' heads popped out of windows all down the train. The Master swung his horse round furiously on the lady with the big grey and yelled, "Hold hard, you miserable bitch! Your bloody horse is trampling hounds!"

"All right, Master," the lady said equably. She turned the grey's head and put him at the bank and the fence and high hedge on top.

The earl was back at the side of the engine, still yelling and shaking his crop. Billing had moved the hounds well to one side.

Guy, at the top of the bank outside the hedge, said to Stella, "It must be a strange feeling, to be on horseback and still have to look up at someone."

The driver put his engine in motion and at the same time let loose a powerful blast on the whistle. Lord Swanwick's horse gave one tremendous buck, hurling the earl off onto the grass beside the line, and then stood still. Some of the train passengers gasped, some cheered. Billing was off his horse, helping the earl to his feet. Swanwick was hurling epithets at the departing engine driver.

Guy said, "What terrible language his lordship uses. I bet you don't even know half the words, Stella."

Stella sniffed, and Captain Irwin said, "A Master of Foxhounds can say things, in the field, that would get anyone else banned from decent society."

The scent was soon picked up again at Tinker's Corner. Hounds ran strongly past Coltishall and the Whin, left-handed by Brockets, Nether Loads, and Black Horse Common. Now Reynard was tiring and hounds killed in Mr Stammer's Lower Thirty Acre at three o'clock. The Master awarded the mask to Miss Naomi Rowland, daughter of Mr and Mrs John Rowland of High Staining, Walstone; and the brush to Miss Jane Felton, daughter of Mr and Mrs Arthur Felton, of Cantley.

Stella had the fox in view for most of the last ten minutes, its strength failing as the hounds tore after it, bursting through and leaping over hedges, heads up and running to view. The lane from the railway station to Felstead ran by the edge of Mr Stammer's fields, and half a dozen followers of the hunt were there as the fox passed—Probyn and Fletcher Gorse, Rachel Cowan, Virginia Rowland, and Johnny Merritt; Louise and Fiona Rowland had earlier turned back for their homes.

The leading couple of bitches jumped at the fox simultaneously, one from each quarter, as the fox turned at bay, its hindquarters sinking to the ground. The hounds' weight brought it down, and in a moment a dozen others were on it, snarling and tearing. Others yelped and bayed and tried to burrow into the heaving mass of bodies. Then Billing was off his horse, his whip cracking as he waded into the pack—"Garaway, Arrogant, garaway, Antic! Damsel, Joyful, Shatterer, Actress—garaway boick!" His whip thong cleared a circle round the torn carcass of the fox. The Master unsteadily quavered the 'kill.' The leaders of the field were up, leaning forward to take their weights off the saddles of the foam-streaked hunters. Naomi was there, perspiring, dirty, radiant; Stella, who'd jumped the last three hedges blind, not caring in her wild excitement what lay on the other side; Irwin, who'd followed her, his heart beating fast; Guy; Christopher Cate, coming now . . . the rector, a dozen others . . . John and Laurence . . .

Billing knelt beside the fox, took a knife from a sheath at his side, under his coat, and severed the head completely from the body. As the bitches eagerly watched, he cut off the fox's brush. Then he picked up the headless, tailless corpse and held it over his head. "Tear 'im and eat 'im!" he brayed, and flung it to the hounds. The bitches quickly reduced the carcass to scraps of blood-flecked fur.

Billing picked up the mask and brush and looked inquiringly at the Master. Lord Swanwick glanced round to see who was up. "Here," he said, reaching down, took the trophies from Billing's hand, and walked his horse toward Naomi's. Then he brushed the bloody stump of the brush across her face, before giving her the mask. "Well ridden," he said. "That's a mask worth having. And perhaps it'll help you persuade your father to take the hounds."

"Thank you, Master," Naomi said. Under the streaked blood on her face she was blushing with pride. Her father was clapping her on the back, Virginia running forward to congratulate her, while the Master performed the same blooding ceremony on a girl of about fourteen mounted on a chestnut pony, who had been up at the death. After blooding her, the Master gave her the brush, which she nonchalantly stuffed between the buttons of her coat, like a horn.

In the lane twenty yards away Rachel Cowan muttered, "Incredible!"

"What is?" Johnny asked.

"Naomi—she's my best friend . . . thoroughly civilised, gentle. Look at her! Covered with an innocent animal's blood, beaming. Oscar Wilde's definition is too simple."

"What did he say?"

"He described foxhunting as the unspeakable in pursuit of the uneatable . . . only most of them are such nice people, like Naomi, and Mr Rowland. No wonder foreigners don't understand the English. Do you?"

"I'm not sure," Johnny said cautiously: though, to tell the truth, he was becoming surer every day he spent in England that he did not understand the English, even those whose background and education would seem to have been very similar to his own. He was about to tell Rachel so, when his attention was diverted by catching sight of Stella, now behind most of the field, with Captain Irwin at her side. Johnny could not see clearly through all the people and horses but he thought the captain had taken her hand briefly to his lips. No one else seemed to have seen. Perhaps they all had their backs turned. Perhaps he himself had not really seen it. He forced himself to think of something else. His father was returning to New York in a week's time. Soon after that he, Johnny would have to start writing the informal progress reports. He'd better have a uniform plan for all of them: start with the war, telling his father what he could that was not in the newspapers for him to read for himself . . . come down to the state of Britain as a whole— the spirit of the people, what was on their minds, what were their opinions . . . then Hedlington, the Jupiter Motor Company, and its employees . . . He should try to warn his father of what might be expected in the near future; it wouldn't be sensible to try to read too far ahead. He'd better make some contact with Mr Ellis, the local M.P., to hear what was going on behind the scenes at Westminster, and to press for government orders . . .

He looked up, but couldn't see Stella and Captain Irwin close by. Whips were cracking and hounds moving off, leaving a mangled piece of fur in the plough. "The Master'll try Horsa's Copse, probably," John Rowland said, "and if he draws a blank there, call it a day."

Guy fell in with his cousin Laurence Cate, well back from the leaders. "That was a good hunt, a tophole gallop—" he said "—and a gallant fox."

Laurence said, "Yes": then, after a long silence, "Did you see me?"

"No, I was too busy trying to keep on top of Jamie. He goes like the wind, but jumps like a flea—straight up and down."

"I was behind you. I saw you all clear that fence this side of the railway, about a mile back . . . You went over it like birds, one after the other . . . I funked it."

"There's no need to jump every fence in Kent," Guy said.

"Yes, but I wanted to. I meant to . . . I had Billycock ready, and he wanted to jump, and he could have. He's a better jumper than any of the nags you're riding. But five yards away I just couldn't face it, and pulled him up . . . so hard I went over his head. Lucky he didn't run home."

"Well, forget it," Guy said.

"I can't. I'll have to tell Dad."

"Why? No one else will, if you don't. I don't suppose anyone else even saw."

"No one did . . . but I have to tell Dad . . . I hate hunting, Guy. I hate seeing the fox chased, and seeing it killed, like today, makes me sick. I nearly puked back there . . . then what would the Master have said? I would have made myself a laughing stock. And Dad."

"Why do you hunt at all, Laurence?"

"Dad expects it. An awful lot of things are expected of him, because he's the squire, and he knows they'll be expected of me, in my turn. So . . ."

"I understand," Guy said slowly, "but look, you have to be yourself. Everyone knows you're an expert on birds, and that's your hobby. They may think it strange that the squire's son doesn't hunt, but they'll get used to it . . . Take me along next time you're going birdwatching in the Isle of Sheppey, will you?"

"Oh yes," the younger boy said, "I'd love it. But are you sure you won't be bored?"

"Good heavens, no! We'll bicycle down, eh? . . . Heard anything about Aunt Margaret?"

The boy said, "She wrote Dad a Christmas letter from somewhere in Ireland . . . She said she was sorry for him, and us, but she had her duty to do."

Guy thought, poor Laurence: but perhaps his Aunt Margaret was right. Even so, it was hard on Laurence, and Stella. He watched her, a few yards ahead, listening with parted lips to something Captain Irwin was saying to her in a low voice, his head bent toward her as their horses walked on side by side. The picture stirred a tremor in his loins. How to describe Stella? She looked . . . dewy, open, like a rose glistening in the early morning. Poor Johnny Merritt, he thought; and then, I wonder what it will feel like when I fall in love.

He turned to Laurence. "Why don't you walk Billycock home now? Go with Johnny Merritt. Hounds probably won't find again today, anyway."

"You don't think Dad will mind?"

"I'm sure he won't. But I'll tell him you had a headache. See you later."

Daily Telegraph, Saturday, January 2, 1915

COST OF LIVING
PRICE OF BREAD INCREASED

Today the price of the quartern loaf of bread in London is 6½d. Isolated shops may be found in highly competitive localities where the price charged is only 6d. There are indications that next week the price will be 7d in very many towns and districts . . . There is some consolation in the reflection that even at 7d a loaf, bread is cheaper and more abundant here than in the countries with which we are at war . . . It is still apparent that people of moderate means are not availing themselves as fast as they might of a range of food long regarded as available only to the affluent. Game of many kinds is as cheap as some other foods of less ambitious definition. Pheasants . . . may be picked up for 2s 6d. Woodcock and snipe, which require no side dishes, are . . . 3s 6d a brace for the former and 1s each for the latter, while golden plover are selling at from 8d to 1s 3d. Plentiful as is the supply of game it

would have been even more plentiful had the usual
amount of "guns" been engaged on the coverts. But a host
of "guns" are engaged on much more serious work now.

"Sounds rather like 'Let them eat cake,' " Johnny Merritt said, handing
back the newspaper.

Cate said, "The real problem is that city dwellers of moderate means,
as the *Telegraph* puts it, have never eaten pheasant or woodcock, still
less snipe. The women would look askance at the strange birds on the
butchers' slabs, and think they wouldn't know how to cook them, or
whether their husbands would like them. Country people would be
happy to buy them—but they aren't the problem, in England."

Stella came in, kissed him on top of the head, and went to the sideboard, saying, "Good morning, Daddy. Good morning, Johnny."

"Good morning, Stella. Are you stiff, after yesterday?"

"I am. I don't ride as much as I used to, with V.A.D. work."

"I thought you usually worked at Lady Blackwell's on Saturdays,"
Cate said, seeing that she was not in uniform.

She sat down with a plate of porridge. Garrod came in with fresh
toast and poured coffee for her, saying, "Good morning, Miss Stella.
That's a nice dress . . . very pretty."

"Thank you, Garrod . . . Johnny's taking me to lunch in Canterbury, Daddy. He wants to see the cathedral, too, and where Thomas à
Becket was murdered."

"When will you be back?"

"Oh, by tea time, won't we, Johnny?"

Garrod poured coffee into Christopher Cate's cup. Glancing at her
lined face, he saw disapproval there. She didn't think Stella should be
allowed to go off by herself to lunch with Johnny. Perhaps not. But she
went off to the hospital on other days, and undressed men, helped
bandage them in intimate parts, and probably took them to the lavatory
if they couldn't go themselves. Margaret might have put her foot down,
but somehow he doubted it. Times were changing; he must learn to
change with them, a little. And he felt that Johnny Merritt was an entirely honourable and trustworthy young man.

Hedlington: Saturday, January 16, 1915

20 Three days after the New Year's Day meet, Captain Irwin had kissed her, in a dark passage of the hospital, where he was making the last of his weekly visits to have the condition of his leg checked. Meeting her in the passage on her way to a ward, he had told her about it. She had put out her hands to him, so glad for his sake, and he had taken them and, after a quick glance up and down the passage, pulled her into an alcove and pressed his lips to hers. His moustache tickled her, the bronze buttons on his tunic bit into her breast, his tongue was sliding into her mouth; she could hardly breathe; and a flood of feeling that welled out from a source somewhere in the base of her stomach was so strong that when, after a minute, he stood back from her she had to lean against the wall to be sure she would not fall. Her knees were shaking, her hands trembling, her lower lip hanging loose, her eyes fixed on him. The passage was still empty and silent. He stepped forward, his breathing shallow, and took her in his arms again, this time thrusting his pelvis against her lower body. She felt the hardness at his loins and pulled away, as a nurse passed across the far end of the passage. Then he whispered, "Stella . . . oh Stella . . ." but she had hurried off, unable to stand any more just then.

It was obvious to her, without the necessity of putting it into words, what would happen next: and it had. Secret rendezvous, more whispers, more kisses; and now, this.

She was wearing her uniform as a V.A.D., a long blue and white striped dress with a high collar, a blue apron, a white handkerchief tied in a big bow at the neck, black shoes, a simple white cap, and a badge at the left breast. On the rack above her in the compartment was a small case, looking like a doctor's black bag; it contained a pretty skirt and blouse, hat, silk stockings, a nightdress, another pair of shoes, and a few toilet articles. She had told her father that she and some other Immobile V.A.D.s had been asked to take night duty for two nights, to help the hard-pressed nursing sisters; and that the V.A.D. authorities would house them with the Mobiles, and feed them each night they served. All that was true; but she had not volunteered for duty this night. She was going to meet Captain Stephen Irwin.

She had felt uncomfortable and nervous ever since Norton had driven her down to the station in the trap—from a combined anticipation and fear of what she was going to do; and from having lied to her father, whom she loved. Her condition was sharply aggravated when she saw her cousin Naomi Rowland on the platform, obviously waiting for the same train. Palmer, the High Staining groom, was with her, but no Rachel Cowan. Stella was surprised at that until she remembered that Rachel had gone back to her home, wherever that was, a week after the New Year's Day meet.

Naomi greeted her. "Hullo, Stella, off to tend Our Brave Boys?"

"Yes," she mumbled, "I volunteered for night duty. And you?"

"Going back to Girton," Naomi said; then the train chuffed in and they got into the same 1st class compartment, and Palmer put in Naomi's bags and waited, smiling, his hand to his cap, as the train pulled out.

They were alone, and Naomi stretched out her legs in an unladylike manner, yawned and said, "Back to the female zoo. I hate living with nothing but women all the time. I think they ought to take men into Girton . . . and of course girls into the men's colleges."

Stella relaxed. She had always liked Naomi, respected her for her brains, and admired her for the way she could handle young men without apparently feeling at all overawed or overwhelmed by them.

Naomi continued, "I wish I could find a man I could really look up to. Then I might fall in love, and do something exciting. Throw my cap over the windmill . . . You *are* in love, aren't you?"

Stella blushed furiously and Naomi laughed, and went on, "So when you're not nursing Our Brave Boys you can drink coffee in the Cadena with Johnny Merritt and let him hold your hand under the table."

Stella smiled. She felt comfortable now. She leaned a little forward. Naomi knew everything. Why didn't she ask her what it felt like, with a man? Whether there was anything special a girl should do . . . But she couldn't. Even if Naomi had done it, she wouldn't talk about it. And she probably hadn't; nice girls didn't.

She sat back, and they spoke desultorily of other matters until the train reached Hedlington, where Naomi had to change. Her train was already in its platform and she hurried over, a porter carrying her bags, waving goodbye to Stella.

Stella breathed a sigh of relief. It was close to three o'clock. She wondered whether Stephen had had to tell a lot of lies to get off duty; but the army didn't seem to do much on Saturday afternoon, even with the war on. She walked toward the Ladies' Room, feeling peculiarly detached from her body. It would lie under Stephen, as the girl had lain under the boy in the hawthorn hedge; but would it be she, Stella Cate, in that body?

She was relieved to find the Ladies' Room empty. She let herself into a cubicle with a penny and, with some difficulty in the confined space, changed from the V.A.D. uniform into the skirt and blouse and hat she had packed in the bag. When she was ready she heard another woman washing her hands in one of the basins in the main part of the room and waited till she had gone; then she came out, took a quick look at herself in a mirror, and adjusted the hat and veil to hide her face. Then, bag in hand, she went out of the station building into High Street, and turned right, walking steadily, avoiding all eyes.

No one spoke to her. Boots and shoes, men's and women's, passed her downcast gaze. A soldier whistled at her from a doorway, she kept her head low . . . The Park: she was glad to see it was fairly full. It was a cold day, but not raining, and some earlier snow had melted. Children played on the swings, old people walked together down the avenues, and women with shopping bags hurried along the cross walks, using them as short cuts from the streets on one side of the Park to those on the other.

Stephen Irwin was sitting on a bench at the corner, under the statue of Sir John Mills (benefactor of the town in 1845, to the tune of a water fountain inside and a cast iron horse trough outside the Park railings; also thrice Mayor). She sat down beside him on the bench, whispering, "Stephen!"

She had expected him to be wearing his uniform; soldiers had to wear uniforms all the time now, she thought, even officers; but he was in a tweed suit with a golfing cap and heavy shoes. He stood up at once, and said, "Let me carry that bag."

"But you're not supposed . . ." she began; meaning to remind him that officers in uniform were not permitted to carry bags of any kind in public. But he was not in uniform, and she handed the bag over. He held out his arm and she took it, squeezing it as they strolled toward the eastern exit of the Park. Passing through the opened gates he turned left. Fifty yards along the street he stopped in front of a car halted at the kerb, unoccupied. He opened the door, and held it for her.

"Is this yours?" she asked. "I didn't know you had a car."

"Borrowed it," he said briefly, as she climbed in. He went round and got in behind the wheel, and said, "Wish I'd thought of this earlier . . . we could have gone out into the country plenty of times." He squeezed her thigh. She felt safe behind the veil but wished he had a car of his own. What reason had he given his friend for wanting to borrow the car?

Stephen adjusted some levers, clambered down, went to the front and swung the starting handle a few times. Soon the engine coughed into life and he ran round and climbed back into the driver's seat. They moved off jerkily, the engine stuttering at first, then, after a few final hiccups, settling down to a steady roar.

Fifteen minutes later, having passed slowly through Hedlington by side streets, they came to North Hedlington, its factories silent and its chimneys smokeless on this Saturday afternoon. Stephen jerked his head at a narrow side street as they passed and said, "That's where they found the murdered woman a fortnight ago . . . strangled and mutilated. Horrible! And that's the White Horse Inn . . . our love nest." He drove the car round to the back of the inn, where a few bicycles were leaning against the wall, and a motor cycle and sidecar parked on the gravelled area in front of the stables. He had a little bag of his own and, picking that up as well as Stella's, led up four steps to the inn's back door. It was unlocked and they went in. "Stay here," he muttered. She listened to the murmur of voices from the rooms at the front of the inn, and waited, beginning to tremble. She saw Stephen open a door, stick his head round, and exchange a few words, but did not hear what was said; then he came back, a key in his hand, motioning to her to go before him up the back stairs. On the landing he peered right and left, then walked to a door marked with the number 5 in brass. He unlocked the door, went in, flung the two cases to the floor, and turned, his arms out to her. She was breathless and gasped, "I must go to the . . . where is it?"

"I don't know," he said. "At the end of the passage, probably."

She opened her bag with trembling hands, took out her toilet case and hurried out and along the passage. The door at the end was marked W.C. in brass lettering, and the next room BATH, in the same manner; there was also a piece of paper stuck on with a drawing pin, bearing the handwritten legend: BATH 3D NOTIFY MANAGEMENT BEFORE USING AND PAY.

She was feeling queasy and after urinating she hung a long time over the hand basin, fearing she would vomit. After a few minutes her stomach seemed to settle. She awkwardly washed her sexual parts, using her own Roger & Gallet soap, and, grimacing, dried herself on the grubby hand towel hanging from a hook behind the door, and slipped back to Number 5.

Stephen was there, his back to her, looking out of the window. It was gloomy outside, rain clouds gathering. He turned, passed her, and locked the door. Then he went back and drew the curtains; finally he turned on the gas, lit the mantle with a match, and came toward her, hands spread.

She murmured, "Stephen . . . shouldn't we . . . turn off the light?"

"Why?" he said, "I want to see you . . . all of you . . . what I've been dreaming about ever since I first met you."

She unpinned her hat and took it off. His hands were at the buttons of her blouse and she was finding it hard to breathe. The blouse came off, and she struggled with the fastenings of her bust bodice . . . that came off, too, to be dropped on the floor—then her skirt, and one of his hands was inside her drawers, sliding down, where she knew the material was soaked with her secretions. It was his turn to gasp as he muttered in her ear, "My God, Stella!" His hand was on her pubic hair, finger sliding down between her swollen lips. Her knees began to give way and, half pushing half carrying, he took her to the bed, hurled back the blankets and stretched her out on the sheet. It was ice cold and she winced to its touch along her back and buttocks. Then she looked at him, and saw that he was hurling off his clothes, the trousers flying this way, the jacket that, off with the waistcoat, shirt, woollen vest, shoes, socks . . . there was the thing she had never seen clearly except on Laurence when she was too young to remember (for the boy in the hedge had been buried in the girl)—standing out like an inflamed red pole from the thicket of dark hair at Stephen's loins. She drew in her breath as he came toward her, the thing jerking with his movements.

"Be . . ." she began, meaning to ask him to be gentle with her. But there was a tide of excitement rising in her, and she bit her lips, and said no more, for she did not want him to be gentle. She was finding the answer to the riddle she had asked herself in the train—would *she* be in the body that would lie with Stephen? The answer was No. This body, responding, heaving, dripping, was not the Stella Cate she had

lived with, and in, for eighteen years. It was somebody else, tense, lust-
ful, desiring excitement above all . . .

His voice was thick—"Knees up . . . higher . . . wider . . . back!"
He knelt on the bed between her thighs, and pushed her legs back till
her knees were at her shoulders. His eyes were fixed down at the opening of her body, his small moustache quivering and saliva dribbling
from one corner of his lips. He leaned forward and the saliva dripped
onto her belly; then his lips were fastened onto hers, his body pressing
her down. A sharp spasm of pain pierced her as she felt him thrust into
her. After a moment of pushing against her hymen, hurting her where
the tegument held, it broke with an audible crack and his whole penis
slid deep into her.

"Christ!" he cried. She half-stifled a scream. "Christ!" he cried again,
"I'm coming . . . now, now!" His body jerked wildly and then he lay
still. Her vulva hurt and she knew she was bleeding. He lay on top of
her for a time and then said, "Wait," stretched out and took the hand
towel from the wash-handstand, and gave it to her. She pushed it between her thighs. There was nothing she could do about the blood-
stained sheet. The pain in her was less sharp now, but still there.

"Sorry I was so quick," he said, "but I've been waiting a long time."
He kissed her on the cheek, and she saw that now he was trembling, in
utter exhaustion.

She put out a hand, marvelling that she had been able to reduce a
man to such a state. Apart from the pain, she felt that she had not really started, and wanted to. The woman in her body was waiting for
some fulfilment, and it had not come yet. She leaned over him where
he lay beside her, and whispered, "Thank you, Stephen . . . That was
wonderful."

"I hope I didn't hurt you too much. But you can't make an omelette
without breaking eggs."

"Only a little . . . Did I do it right?"

"Couldn't be better," he said, "and I'll be better next time."

She stretched down to stroke the long white bands of scar tissue on
his legs. "Did this hurt—when it happened?" she asked.

"Not just then, really . . . shock. Afterwards, it hurt like the devil.
The operations weren't any fun, either."

He had a small head and narrow shoulders, some hair on his chest
but not much; and the thicket where the thing grew wasn't big either,
not much bigger than her own, though differently shaped. She began
to stroke his belly, wondering if she was not being too forward. After a
while she asked him, "Where shall we have supper?"

"In here. They're sending it up at seven . . . with beer and porter.

They don't have wine here, not good wine, anyway." Her hand wandered down into the thicket and touched the limp penis. She caressed its damp slipperiness, holding her breath. Slowly it began to thicken and harden. "Go on!" Stephen gasped. "Go on, suck it!"

"What?" she said, staring at his congested face under the bright light.

"Suck it, put it in your mouth!"

A hand was on her vulva, a finger rubbing the little button at the top, where the lips parted.

She bent down, staring at the thing. Did he really mean it? Did anyone really? . . . His hand pressed down on the back of her head, but she was already bending, staring at the thing, now big and stiff, so close. She had never imagined doing this, or anything like it. She stretched her lips wide and took it into her mouth. For a moment she thought she would gag, or worse, bite convulsively . . . It felt strange, tasted stranger, like nothing she had ever put into her mouth before. She was losing the power to think, as though some drug to make her faint was emanating from it. She began to suck frantically, sliding her lips up and down the shaft.

From far away she heard him gasp, "No more! On your back!"

Hurriedly she scrambled back and spread herself, knees wide. Again he entered her, again she felt a sharp pang, overlaying the duller ache in her vagina. Her body seemed close, waiting for something greater to overcome the pain. His grip was crushing her, his face pressed on her, his loins pounding . . . groans, spasmodic final thrusts . . . She held her breath, waiting . . . a dead weight, still.

So near . . . her breath leaving her in a long sigh. The woman had not reached the core of any great secret. She, Stella Cate, felt rubbery, beaten, but nervous. Next time . . . or the next?

They were lying still again, side by side under the blankets and coverlet, for there was no fire laid in the fireplace. Stella had hoped that Stephen would make love to her again before supper came. She was still sore, but she had come here to reach the heart of the mystery of life, and had not been near it. She had made it as clear as she could, without saying so in so many words, that she was ready for him, but he had said he must be careful not to hurt her, and had spent a long time caressing her private parts with his fingers. That had felt pleasant, but it was not what she wanted, and his thing had remained limp.

Then a servant girl brought up a big tray loaded with roast beef and Yorkshire pudding, cabbage and roast potatoes, and they had eaten well; and afterwards the girl brought jam puffs and cream; and after an hour and a half's digestion, Stephen seemed to have forgotten about his concern for her sore parts, for he had again undressed her—they both had dressed for supper, not having any suitable gowns or robes, and made the bed look as respectable as possible in the circumstances . . . and again, more slowly, his thing had grown stiff and red and he had made love to her, this time from behind, bending her over the bed and taking her as the dog took the bitch. It felt strange, but perhaps better than the other way . . . and for a while she had thought the mystery would be revealed, as stirrings of sexuality began to shake her; but they had gone away, leaving her in a state of uneasy calm.

Now he was smoking a cigarette, with her permission. He said, "Where's your mother?"

"Back in Ireland." She was about to add, "for good," but kept quiet. It was a family matter.

He said, "It must have been difficult having a Sinn Feiner in the house."

"Two," she said. "Laurence pretends to be nearly as rabid as Mummy about Ireland . . . He isn't really, I think, but he wants to attract attention . . . Mummy's, especially." She stroked his chest. "You won't have to go back to the war, will you?"

"Because of the wounds? I didn't think so until a few days ago. But now I'm better than they thought I would ever be. I'm a regular officer, Stella. I couldn't stay at home unless I'm crippled. Wouldn't do at all."

"Those beastly Germans! And we have people who say they aren't so bad. I was at a dinner party at the Park—Lord Swanwick's—a fortnight ago, with my cousin Naomi Rowland and her friend Rachel Cowan. We were all talking about atrocities and Rachel said she didn't believe the stories were true. Everyone turned away from her and I heard Lord Swanwick say to another man 'What do you expect of an Ikey Mo?' "

"Is she a Jew? I can't stand Jews."

"She believes in conscription—it's the only fair way, she said."

"She's right there," Irwin said grudgingly. "We've got to get the shirkers out of their cushy jobs."

"Conscription of everyone's money, as well, she says," Stella added. "She's a socialist, and awfully brainy, Naomi says."

"I can't stand brainy women."

She kissed his cheek tentatively, and said, "You won't have to worry about me. I couldn't have got into a good girls' school even if Mummy had wanted me to go to one. Our governesses used to burst into tears over my arithmetic . . . Did you see any atrocities, yourself?"

"No, not myself . . . except some burning churches, but I was only in France two weeks, and fighting three days. But I'm sure the reports are true."

She snuggled closer to him, and he said, "I'll turn out the light now, and we'll sleep a bit. To tell the truth, I'm tired. Later, if we wake up . . ."

She realised with surprise that she was stronger than he, more sexually potent. She had never thought it could be so, always having seen men as male animals, perpetually dominant, and perpetually on the hunt for females. Now, actually in bed beside a man, having taken all his strength three times, she realised that it was she who was the predator. She thought with wonder, I must be careful; if that thing failed to answer her invitation, Stephen would be humiliated . . . She, Stella Cate, with power over men!

He got out of bed, turned off the light, and climbed back, facing her. She kissed him on the end of his nose, and said, "When we're married, there won't be any hurry, will there?"

After a long pause he said, "No." She drifted off to sleep.

She lay awake, wondering. She didn't know what time it was. No light seeped in through the curtains. She wondered whether she was very bad to have had a lover at eighteen. That young unmarried girls made love she knew from the number of times that she had seen a pregnant village girl go to the altar; and had even heard of girls who were not of that class, but of her own, in similar circumstances—though with them the marriage was usually held somewhere distant, and a long journey overseas arranged. She wondered what it would feel like when she first knew that she was to have a baby. She wondered whether she should pretend to cough to awaken Stephen, who was snoring beside her, his back now turned. She wondered whether Johnny Merritt would have made love to her differently from Stephen, if it was him she had fallen in love with. Perhaps what Stephen had done was caddish; she knew her father would think of it that way—"A gentleman doesn't take advantage of a lady," he had said, many times. But she had wanted it, asked for it, really, she recognised that now. Stephen was thirty-six . . . a gap of eighteen years between husband and wife wasn't unusual, though a bit more than with most couples. She wondered if . . . A strange sound intruded into her musings, that had moved from love to guilt, to fear, to desire, to shame, to love again. It was a sound like distant small drums, or a deep humming . . . the drumbeats now together, now gradually drifting apart so that the noise was not steady but went up and down, louder and softer. She had never heard anything like it.

Stephen still snored. The sound grew louder. Should she awaken him? But he'd think she was demanding more sex . . . and he was tired.

She stole out of bed, tiptoed to the window, and pulled back a curtain. There was no moon, stars mostly clear, some masked by hazy cloud masses. The street lights burned bright and a string of lights down river shone from Scarrow Wharf, where barges were loaded and unloaded. The noise seemed to be coming from every part of the compass, north, south, inside the room, outside . . .

She looked up, and gasped, for a huge black shape was blotting out some stars . . . moving steadily from north to south, coming directly overhead.

She ran to the bed and shook Stephen—"Stephen, wake up, wake up!"

"Wha' . . . wha's the matter?"

She dragged him to the window. They reached it just as a heavy explosion shook the building and rattled the window panes, followed by another and another and another, the explosions marching closer, apparently along this side of the Scarrow.

"What on earth . . . ?" Stephen muttered, rubbing his eyes. Then he gasped, "Bombs! . . . There must be a Zeppelin up there!"

"I saw a big shape."

He found his matches and lit the gas light, only to put it out again immediately, muttering, "They might see it." He was fumbling for his clothes, which had been more tidily folded away over the backs of chairs the last time they undressed. Stella flung the window open and listened. The sound she had heard before was louder now. "Engines," Stephen said. Then she heard a faint popping, and Stephen said, "They're firing at it from the barracks, with rifles . . . miles out of range . . . Where's my tie? For heaven's sake, Stella, where's my tie?"

She didn't know, or care. More bombs were falling, to burst down the other side of the valley. Dim against the stars the monster up there seemed to be turning. She watched it with mounting excitement. At once she realised that this exhilaration, these coursing thrills, were for her similar to those she had hoped to experience a few hours ago with Stephen . . . but these were stronger, and seemed to be leading her even closer to the unknown climax.

"I've got to go," Stephen said. He seemed to be fully dressed, as well as she could see him in the darkness of the room. Screams and shouts were coming through the window now, and the sound of running booted feet. Far to the north a searchlight bored vertically into the sky—perhaps from a warship in Chatham, she thought. The Zeppelin had made a full sweep round and was heading toward the searchlight and the naval dockyards. Perhaps there were two of them, she thought, but she could only follow the shape of one, and that dimly.

Stephen said, "They'll be standing-to in barracks, and I'm supposed to be there. I've got to try to get back in before my absence is noticed . . . Where can I drop you? For God's sake, Stella, get dressed! I don't have a moment to lose."

"Have you paid the innkeeper?" she asked.

"Yes, yes! When I arranged this I paid for everything in advance."

She was feeling for her drawers, pulling them on. She said, "You go, Stephen. I'll find my own way home."

He hesitated—"Are you sure?"

She felt calm. Stephen was frantic to get away, to avoid trouble. She understood, but she had no such desire herself. She wanted to stay here. It was exciting, and already she could see fires burning. It would get more exciting. He kissed her on the cheek, and hurried out, carrying his bag. Stella finished dressing in her V.A.D. uniform, and packed away the rest of her belongings in her bag. Stephen never really looked at the pretty clothes I had, she thought—except to tear them off. She walked down the back stairs and let herself out. Stephen's borrowed car was gone. Flames were pouring out of a house far down the street toward the north. She broke into a run, her bag in one hand, her long skirt gathered up in the other.

The dark of the night was no longer darkness, nor light, but a changing, moving blend of both. Tongues of fire, yellow and red, towered up from a house here, a warehouse there, a shop, a factory. Running past the black mouth of an alley, it was suddenly lighted for her by the headlight beams of a lorry, a man with a pipe in hand silhouetted by them. The sounds were as disjointed as the light—a wave of shrieks, dying away; the roar of a falling wall becoming silence, erupting into the splinter of breaking glass; men and women shouting, children crying—but she also passed men silent, downcast, seeming to be alone, reading their own minds. The people had fallen into the same indefinable lack of pattern—some running toward the nearest fire, others running away, yet others crossing their paths at right angles, darting out of one alley, crossing the main Rochester road, and darting into a street opposite, or into one of the dingy brick workmen's houses that here lined the road.

She reached the burning house, and found half a dozen men and women outside, their faces lit by the flames—"Everyone's out!" a man cried.

"No, they ain't," a woman yelled. "My cousin Sal's youngest . . . she ain't 'ere!" Children, huddled in the ragged clothes they had probably slept in—certainly escaped in—stood shivering at the edge of the firelight, hot in front, cold behind.

The flames were not very fierce or tall yet. The building was two-storied, and small. "Where is she?" Stella asked.

"Back, upstairs, right . . . unless she come down on her own and run away. She's five."

Stella darted forward, voices yelling meaninglessly behind her. For a moment her heart pounded, then seemed to stop, and a catch at her throat nearly took her breath. It was like the moment before Stephen had entered her the first time, but stronger, more terrible, and wonderful. She ran into the house through the open door. The fire roared loudly in the rooms to the right as she ran up the stairs. It was very hot, and the paint on the walls was peeling and charring, smelling vile. The flames below gave enough light for her to find the back rooms. She opened the door at the right. A rush of smoke met her, and forced her back. She picked up the end of her skirt, covered her face with it, and tried again. It was darker yet in the room, but some light from another fire coming in through the cracked window showed no one on the bed . . . She tripped over something, stooped, felt the small soft body, picked it up and dashed back, coughing and gasping, her skirt dropped for she needed both hands to hold the child. The flames were bursting through the lower walls and she had to take two long strides through them, her face momentarily brushed by their burning fingers, her hair singed and smelling. Then she was out, choking, but . . . she had reached the secret place, the unknown delirium, just for a few seconds. They were standing round her, crying out in admiration, until a man shouted, "Stand back, you silly buggers! Can't you see she wants air? 'Ere, you, get some water out of that 'ouse there, look sharp!"

The woman addressed ran across the street. The man who had spoken was fat, red-faced, and full of energy. Before the woman came back with the water for Stella, he had gathered half a dozen men and run off up the street to a burning shop. Stella found herself alone with the cup of water. Everyone else had gone, taking the child she had rescued with them. She felt tired, now; but when she had drunk the water she got up from the step she had been sitting on, and hurried toward the next fire.

Bells clanged insistently from the south, and with them the brazen blare of klaxons. Two fire engines of the Hedlington Fire Brigade roared up, one drawn by six horses, the other motor driven, bells ringing, brass-helmeted crews hanging on along the sides. They stopped fifty yards up the street and the men jumped to the ground. Stella arrived to hear one of the men say, "See if the mains is broke, Jim."

The fat man was there, too, and cut in, "No, they ain't. I just tested that one. 'Oook 'er up! An' don't waste no time, 'cos this shop 'ere's got an old couple living upstairs wot we can't get at, 'cos the stairs 'ave fallen in."

" 'Oo the 'ell are you, mate, to be giving me orders?"

"I'm Bill Fuckin' 'Oggin, mate, and I ain't giving you no orders, I'm telling you wot needs to be done. Some of us don't take twenty minutes to get out of bed and find a fire as big as this fucker."

The firemen were running out the hoses, and hooking them to a hydrant. Ladders were extending up to the second floor of the burning shop, where the old couple were said to be trapped. Perhaps they are dead or can't move, Stella thought, because no one has come to the windows. She looked round, yawning. It was over. There'd be another time—many.

A man came running up beside her as she walked aimlessly along the street . . . "Miss, miss! . . . My wife's time has come."

Stella looked at him, puzzled. What time? What was his wife to her? Then she realised that she was wearing the V.A.D. hospital helper's uniform. The newly familiar fears and thrill came together. She shouldn't do it—what did she know of childbirth, never having seen or helped at one? But the excitement was rising, not as strong as when she ran into the burning house, but . . . yes, stronger than anything she had yet experienced with Stephen.

Common sense took over. She said, "Have you sent for the doctor?"

The man cried, "Of course I have, miss, but he wasn't there. They're all out . . . the Zeppelin!"

She thought a moment, then said, "All right. Take me to your wife and I'll do what I can. But you must keep trying to find a doctor."

This time the thrill was not as climactic as the one in the burning house; but it was as all-pervasive of her body and spirit, and it lasted longer—two hours. The woman's labour was far advanced by the time she reached the house in a side street off the Rochester road, and hurried up the two flights of stairs. It was her second child—the other stood in a crib, alternately crying and cooing in the single room. She tried to remember what she had heard and been told . . . everyone talked about hot water, but there was none, so she sent the husband off to get some, also clean towels even if he had to steal them; and she told him, when he'd brought them, to go to where the fire brigades were, and tell the firemen that a doctor was needed—one might have come by now. "And," she called after him, "if you can't find a doctor, find a Mr Hoggin." She didn't think Mr Hoggin was a doctor, but he was a man who knew what to do, and got it done.

Meanwhile, she did her best, which was mainly to watch nature do its work; wipe the woman's sweating face and forehead; and tie a twisted sheet to the rail at the foot of the bed for her to tug on when the spasms came. Stella thought, watching her, she's experiencing the same things that I did, with Stephen, and in the fire . . . she's trying to reach something great . . . for her, the baby: for me—I only half understand, so far; perhaps, in time, I'll know better what it is.

Finally, just as a doctor bustled in, dishevelled and dusty from working on bomb casualties, the baby slid out onto the bloodied sheet between its mother's thighs. Stella picked it up and said softly, "It's a girl."

Dawn was breaking as she left the house, holding up a hand to silence the husband's thanks . . . Where was she? And now that the night was past, and the work done, hadn't she heard the name Hoggin somewhere? A marriage which she hadn't been able to go to? . . . She must find her bag, if someone hadn't taken it during the night. She'd left it on the pavement opposite that first house she'd run into. She walked faster.

When she was nearly there, hurrying through a voluble crowd, a woman seized her arm, shouting, "This is the lady, inspector."

A police inspector pushed through toward them. The woman was gabbling, "Run into the house, she did . . . right off! . . . rescued my cousin's little 'un . . . near suffocated from the smoke she was . . . another two minutes and she'd 'ave been a goner . . . flames everywhere!"

The inspector had a notebook out—"I'd like to have your name, miss, so that you can receive the proper commendation."

Over the inspector's shoulder Stella saw a high car moving through the crowd, and recognised her grandfather's Rowland; and saw him in it, with Aunt Alice. She ducked, turning her head quickly, muttering, "Sorry. I have to go."

She hurried on, found her bag untouched just where she had left it, and walked quickly away. How could she possibly have explained what she was doing, how she had got there? But grandfather would have believed whatever she told him, except the truth. German bombs falling on Hedlington from the sky at night! Men riding the darkness in throbbing monsters, like giant silver cigars! But no one would believe that Miss Stella Cate, of Walstone Manor, in the county of Kent, had spent the night with Captain Stephen Irwin in a disreputable inn in North Hedlington.

She would find a telephone—there was one at the station—and tell her father that she had not been hurt in the bombing, and was coming home. They might not have heard of the raid, except that news and gossip always travelled so fast.

She walked faster toward the station. She didn't know when the first train for Walstone left Hedlington, but it would be soon, and she could wait in the Ladies' waiting room. She realised that she might walk down the High Street naked, and no one would notice. No one was seeing or hearing anything except about the Zeppelin and the bombs. The High Street was full, even at that hour. People were talking in clusters. Hundreds were walking north, to see the effects of the bombing for themselves. Every policeman was besieged by questioners. And the shops of Weingarten, gentlemen's clothier, and Hartmann, musical instruments and sheet music, had had their plate glass shattered, and the contents dragged out into the street and burned, or smashed. The town reeked of burning cloth and paper.

Stella hurried on, thinking with a mixture of excitement and disappointment, Now I am a woman. But what kind? Am I different from other women? If so, how? Why does the unknown compel me? What is the nature of the secret that has touched me, once, for a moment, with flaming fingers?

Daily Telegraph, Monday, January 18, 1915

WAR

The official communiqué issued in Paris yesterday afternoon says:

PARIS, *Sunday (3 p.m.)* We have continued to progress in the region of Nieuport and of Lombaertzyde. Our artillery obliged the Germans to evacuate their trenches for a distance of about 200 metres on the Grande Dune and destroyed the redan to the north of that spot . . .

In the region of Ypres and in the region of La Bassée and of Lens there have been artillery combats.

At Blangy, near Arras, there was a fairly lively action. The Germans had seized the foundry at Blangy, which we took at once with an energetic counter-attack, and we maintained our position there.

Our artillery continued to demolish the enemy's trenches near La Boisselle . . .

In the Argonne, on the heights of the Meuse, and in Woevre there is nothing new to report.

> In the Bois-le-Prêtre, near Pont-à-Mousson, a German attack was repulsed.
>
> In the Vosges we won some ground west of Orbey. Snow fell heavily all day.
>
> Last night's communiqué said:
>
> PARIS, *Sunday* (*11.25 p.m.*) There is nothing to report, except that snow has fallen from the Argonne to the Vosges.

Elsewhere the *Telegraph* had devoted a full page to Saturday night's air raid, including many interviews and eye-witness stories. Bill Hoggin had been prominent in the work of rescue after the raid, apparently; or, at least, in grabbing the attention of the journalists . . . That was unfair: others confirmed that he had been a tower of strength, he and some anonymous nurse who had rescued one, two, or five children from burning buildings—stories varied. Of course the local paper, the *Courier,* had gone lyrical with excitement, and barely left room to print any other news.

Cate looked across the table at his son. Stella had already left for Hedlington and the hospital, looking extraordinarily pretty and eager, as though watching the air raid through the hospital windows had somehow filled her with energy, instead, as one might reasonably have expected, with anxiety or fear.

Laurence said, "Daddy, do you have a few minutes?"

Cate waved expansively, "All the time in the world today, Laurence. No tenant problems, no boards, courts, or meetings." He looked at his son, realising that he had spent very little time with him these holidays; and Laurence was due to return to Charterhouse for the Lent term three days hence.

Laurence said, "I was wondering . . . whether going into the Weald Light Infantry . . . would be the right thing for me . . . when the time comes."

Cate said, "You could go into the Rifle Brigade."

"Well, er, I was thinking perhaps . . . that I'm not cut out for the army."

"It doesn't matter a bit. There's always the navy. There isn't the same demand, and you're too late for the ordinary cadet entrance, but we could arrange matters, I'm sure. Why don't we go to visit Chatham some day? I know the rear admiral there quite well . . . visit a ship, look at the navy, get the feel of it."

After a short pause Laurence seemed to give up, and said, "All right, Daddy, I'd like that . . . whenever you want, but . . ."

"But what? You look worried. Can't I help?"

Laurence said, "It's about that hunter . . . you said you were going to give me for my next birthday."

"Yes. I have one in mind . . . a young gelding, got some fire in him, plenty of stomach and wind, and a good lepper. He's a little young yet, but then it's ten months to your birthday, isn't it? . . . Now I want to spend the day with you. What shall we do?"

After another pause Laurence said, "Could we go to Chatham today?"

"Why not? A great idea. I'll telephone the . . ."

Garrod came in silently. "A Mr Ellis on the telephone for you, sir."

Cate got up, pushing the paper aside. The telephone was in the front hall. He picked up the receiver and said, "Cate here."

"Ralph Ellis, Cate. I'm speaking from London, but I'm coming down to Hedlington right away to meet the mayor and the C.O. of the Wealds' Depot about some of their problems . . . billeting . . . camp sites . . . training areas . . . soldiers' dependents . . . the influx of young girls from the country, who mostly finish up as whores . . . It suddenly struck me that we ought to have someone from the country-side. After all, the training's got to be in the country . . . so have the new camps . . . and the girls come from there. Could you meet us at eleven, in the Town Hall council room?"

"Very well," Cate said, "I'll be there."

He hung up, and went back to the dining-room to tell Laurence there would be no day together today. He was sorry, but it couldn't be helped. There was a war on.

Hedlington Race Course:
Saturday, February 20, 1915

21 It had rained off and on the last three days, so the course was soggy and the footing for the spectators muddy. The middle class had come armed with umbrellas, but the lower class just turned up their coat collars, for there was no shelter except in the small grandstand on the west side of the course, facing across the oval to the Scarrow and Beighton Down, above the barge wharfs. This was the second and last day of a National Hunt meet which was one of the half-dozen occasions when Hedlington Race Course, situated actually in North Hedlington, was used. It just paid its way to its shareholders, by siphoning off enough money from the betting fraternities of Hedlington, Chatham, Rochester, and the neighbouring countryside.

Ruth Hoggin sat on a bench in the grandstand, feeling that everyone was staring at her. She had dressed as inconspicuously as possible, in spite of Bill's demands that she wear something bright, like a scarlet skirt and green blouse and purple hat. It was not by reason of her sex that she would stand out at the course; there were plenty of women here, many of a much higher class than she could claim—why, a little farther along were Mr Harry Rowland and Miss Alice. Horse racing was a respectable sport, especially in the winter when the races were over fences, hurdles, and water jumps. No, what made her feel that every eye turned toward her, estimating, was that her baby was now due in three weeks. Her mother had told her that she herself had been 55 inches round the waist just before the birth of Ethel; but Ethel had been her fourth child, and this was to be her own first. She was not so large as that, by a long chalk . . . but, because it was her first, it felt like it. Every time the baby kicked she blushed, feeling that people must see the heave of her dress. Every time someone passed, she looked away, anxious to meet no one's eye.

She wished Bill had not insisted on bringing her. To her protests he had answered that it would be good for her, and for the baby. But she wasn't really worrying about the baby: it was herself. Such as the Rowlands might approve of horse racing, but she had never been on a course before she married Bill. *Her* family did not approve of racing or betting. She was afraid of the crowds, the shouting bookies, the boys running to and fro with messages, the smell of beer and gin from the stalls behind the grandstand. One of those stalls was boarded up, its windows broken and door smashed—a casualty of last month's Zeppelin raid. Even thinking of it made her thank the good Lord once more that it had happened on a weekend, so Bill was home from London. The warmth of his place in bed had comforted her that night long after he himself had gone, jumped up and out at the first bomb crash, and not returned till broad daylight, covered with dirt, his clothes charred and bloodied.

The crowd breathed out together—"They're off!" The horses dashed away from the starter's flag, mud clots flew, men roared names, *Come on! Come on!* . . . over the hurdles, flying easily, landing, one horse down, twisted sideways over a hurdle, its jockey flying one way, the horse's legs the other . . . the jockey was up, running to catch its reins but the horse evaded him and galloped on behind the others, jumping without a rider. A black horse with a jockey in crimson and green striped silk was in front by a long way, four lengths ahead of any other. He came on, the jockey rising to stand in his stirrups as he passed the finishing post.

"Blast and damn and bugger!" Bill came storming up the aisle toward her, his face like thunder. "Blast and damn and bugger!" he growled again, sitting down beside her. "Lost again!" Bill's friend sat down beyond him, and Bill said, "Milner here, too. Ten quid each, eh?"

Milner was a cadaverous man of about forty with a waxed moustache and small blue eyes in a long pale face. He wore a blue suit and a bowler hat. Now he nodded, the corners of his mouth turned down, and said, "Thought Flying Corps was a sure thing . . . had it from the horse's mouth . . . the jockey."

"Well, no use crying over spilt milk," Bill said. "What 'ave we got in the next?"

They bent over their separate copies of the London paper, folded back at the racing page, and began to mutter names and odds. The bookies chalked figures and names on their blackboards and rubbed out others. The tictac men waved arms and raised fingers with blinding speed. The crowd along the rails was liberally sprinkled with khaki and navy blue, for Hedlington was barely three miles away, and Chatham seven. Half a dozen soldiers were trying to get into the grandstand by a nearby gate, and the attendant was turning them away, for they had not bought grandstand tickets. They had been drinking and started shouting obstreperously at the attendant. Bill Hoggin looked up from his paper and shouted, "Fuck off! I can't think for your bloody row!"

"Fuck off youself," one of the soldiers yelled, reeling, "wot the 'ell right do you 'ave to sit there 'igh and mighty? Too bloody dangerous to be in khaki, eh? And not enough money in it for you, eh?"

Bill took no notice, again bent over the paper. A policeman strode majestically up—"Now move along there! Move along! And mind your language, you."

"I wasn't swearing! 'E was! That fat sod in the brown suit!"

"Now now, there . . ."

Bill turned to Milner. "I like Rose Crown in this going."

"A filly?"

"Yes, but she's big and she's a mudder. Look at what Insider says."

"How much are you going to put on?"

Bill said, "This is a good 'un . . . 45 to 1, because she's a filly. I'll lay twenty Bradburys each way."

"Forty quid! Pheeew!"

"You can't get fairy queens for fourpence, mate," Bill said.

After a long hesitation Milner said, "All right—same for me."

Bill pulled out a thick wallet and extracted eight Bank of England five-pound notes. He gave them to Milner, saying, "Put it on for me, there's a pal."

Milner took the money and walked off down the aisle, saying, "All right. And I'll have a Bass or two before I come back. My nerves aren't what they used to be, with this sort of money on a nag's back."

"No hurry, mate."

When Milner was out of earshot, Ruth said anxiously, "Bill, are you sure that horse is going to win? Mr Milner looks very worried."

He said, "I'd be surprised out of my bloody life if it did."

"But . . ."

"I'm laying off. Hedging. I did the last race, too. I'm not making any money, but I'm not losing any either. An' I know Rose Crown's not going to win or place, because she's going to be pulled."

"But why . . . ?"

"Ruthie, just keep your mouth shut, see? . . . I wonder what Harry Rowland's betting on. He knows a thing or two about the jumpers. Maybe I'll ask him."

"Oh, don't do that, Bill."

"Why the 'ell not? Cor, that baby's jumping better than that bloody nag I bet on last race . . . But p'raps I won't ask old Harry anything. That factory 'is son's building's staring 'im in the face, there, least the foundations are. An' that's put 'im out of sorts, I can see. Bet 'e's thinking what 'e could do with that Yankee money. They've been throwing the spondulicks around like water . . . and that's the way to get things done, same 'ere as anywhere else in the world."

Bill was in a good temper. She didn't understand what he was doing, or what laying off or hedging were: but it was clear, to her immense relief, that he was not really losing the large amounts of money he seemed to be. She said, seizing the opportunity, "Can you give me ten pounds, Bill, please?"

"Wot the 'ell for?"

"I want to hire Mary Gorse to make clothes for the baby. I could make them myself, but she needs the money. She says it's getting very difficult to feed everyone."

"'Ow many kids 'ave they got?"

"Four at home, not counting the twins in Walstone, with Probyn. And she had four miscarriages between the twins and Violet."

"Someone ought to tell Willum what causes that," Bill said. "'Ere, take a fiver, and tell 'er not to spend it all on drink."

Ruth said, "Bill, you *know* Mary Gorse never touches a drop! . . . You're teasing me!"

Bill said, "'Ere comes Milner. Mum's the word, remember!"

They were waiting for the last race. Bill Hoggin and Milner had had a glass of stout each at a stall and were walking away from the grandstand, heads bent. The crowd had thinned out and no one could overhear their conversation.

"'Ow much?" Bill asked.

"Seventy-six quid today. A hundred and seventy over the two days."

"I could lend you fifty."

"Thanks, Bill," Milner shook his head and his prominent Adam's apple went up and down as he swallowed. His face was pasty in colour, with red blotches. "It's no good. I've pinched three hundred and forty out of the Christmas Club I'm treasurer of, too. Meant to pay it back from the geegees. They won't find that out till next Christmas, of course, but then . . . I'll have to get the money somehow or I'm sunk."

"Jude'll take that 'ard, mate. She likes 'er comforts, don't she? *An'* being the wife of one of His Majesty's principal Food Inspectors."

Milner groaned . . . "Don't I know it!"

They walked on another five minutes, turning back toward the grandstand. Bill took the cigar from his mouth and said, "I 'ear a lot of bad consignments are turning up at the docks."

"They are," Milner said. "Half the canning machines in South America seem to have gone kerfut. We've had to condemn thousands of cases for leakies and blowers."

Bill said, "An' all that goes to the pig farmers, eh? Cheap?"

"Very cheap."

" 'Ow about me being a pig farmer?"

Milner looked up quickly, but didn't speak. After a while he said, "You know what to do?"

"Garn, 'course I do! Bore a little 'ole, let out the gas, and seal with solder . . . under the label's the best, only it takes more time."

"Some of that meat'll be dangerous, Bill. Botulism."

"I know it, mate. But 'ow many people 'ave died of botulism since you became an Inspector? Bloody few, an' you know thousands of leakies and blowers pass through all the time, that aren't spotted. *And* this war's bloody dangerous all round—don't see why the civilians shouldn't share the risk a bit, eh?"

Milner didn't speak for a minute, then—"It'll mean forging you one of the special permits pig farmers have to get before we can sell unfit meat to them."

"Get me one. Five hundred quid for you, Milner, cash. 'Alf when I get that permit, 'alf when I get my first thousand cases an' after that, another fifty quid for you for every thousand cases."

It began to rain, a light February drizzle. Neither man took any notice. Milner said, "Done."

" 'Ow long will it take you to get the permit?"

"A week."

"Meet you in the Blind Duck, Monday week, twelve sharp, eh?"

"All right. And lend me that fifty now, to keep the wolf away till I can get the permit . . . We could both go to gaol for a long time for this, Bill."

"Can—but won't. 'Cos the people who might send us there are going to 'ave their 'ands put in the jam jar too, whether they know it or not, see?" He winked, and, at the rail of the grandstand, held an imaginary coin and tapped it on the wood, saying, "Money—the root of all evil—and all good, mate."

They started up the aisle toward Ruth, then Bill grabbed Milner's arm, crying—"Hey, see that little bastard in the mac, weaseling off with his head down? That's Honest Joe, the bookie! The bookie we have our bets on for the last race!" He raised his voice in a stentorian bellow, "Welsher! Welsher!"

All over the course men and women, soldiers and sailors, turned this way and that, yelling—"Welsher! . . . Where, where?"

"There, running! The little bastard with his head down! Honest Joe!"

Honest Joe broke into a shambling run, revealing his bookie's leather satchel which he had been attempting to conceal under the mackintosh. Slipping and sliding in the mud he headed for the railway fence. The crowd ran after him, the nearest and those who had heard Bill's original yell in front, then others streaming out behind in a fan-shaped tail, all yelling, "Stop, stop, welsher!"

The man had a fifty-yard start and would have made it on good footing, but he was no mudder, especially not with thin soles, worn smooth, to his shoes. Bill Hoggin, running hard and yelling fiercely at the same time, came closer and closer and, ten yards from the fence, gave Honest Joe a shove from behind that sent him sliding on his face and belly in the mud.

Bill pounced on him, and kneeling astride him, began to rain blows on him while Honest Joe tried to shield his head. "Take that, and that!" Bill yelled. "Bloody welshing bastard!"

"'Elp, 'elp!" the bookie gasped, sounding as though he had a bad cold, for his nose was bunged with mud, and bleeding. A dozen other men had come up and one of them said, "Let me have a go now."

Bill stood up slowly, wiping his hands. He said, "There's time to put our bets with someone else, if we 'urry. Empty 'is satchel, Milner, and give everyone money for the slips they can show."

Not everyone got paid, but most did, and those who didn't gave Honest Joe a few more punches and kicks before he was allowed to climb the fence, a dishevelled and battered figure with a bloody nose, two black eyes, and torn muddy clothing, to stumble along the railway toward North Hedlington station.

Bill and Milner returned to the grandstand. Ruth was waiting with a worried face . . . "What did you do to that poor man?"

"Bashed 'im on the conk," Bill said briefly. "Now, Milner, 'ere's ten quid. Put it on anything you fancy, an' if we win, it's 'alf an' 'alf. You can't do worse than I've been doing."

Milner ran down the aisle to place the bet before the race began. Bill rubbed his hands together and said, "It cost me a bit, but 'e's 'ooked . . . well an' truly 'ooked."

"What do you mean, Bill?"

"I mean, keep your trap shut. You'll be wearing a fur coat by this time next month."

Twenty minutes later Bill and Ruth were walking south down the Rochester road, on their way home. Ruth walked slowly, feeling that she was waddling like a duck. Bill held her hand, going slowly to keep pace with her. He was in no hurry. He was full of beer, and in excellent humour. He had been prepared to lose twice as much as he actually had to get Milner where he wanted him. It had stopped raining, and the streets were glistening in the early twilight.

"Well, 'ow are the stuck-up Strattons, Ruthie?" he asked his wife . . . " 'Aven't seen much of them since I started on Eastcheap."

"Dad and Mum are well," Ruth answered. "Frank's at the Front. They had a letter from him. He'd been in a battle but was all right. He's batman to Mr Charles Rowland, Mr John's son."

"Wot the 'ell's a batman?"

"A sort of servant, I think. He said he has to look after Mr Rowland's clothes and pistol and take messages for him in battle, too . . . Fred's here, in the barracks."

"The barracks up the hill?"

"Yes. He's a 2nd Lieutenant in the Weald Light Infantry, he told me. He goes to dinner with Dad and Mum now and then, and I went over once."

"They still trying to marry him off?"

"Mum would like him to be married. He . . , well, he has got into trouble with women, you know."

"Don't we all? And that sister, wot's always crying? The one wot's married to the dago?"

"Ethel—" Ruth began; then said, "Let me rest a bit here, Bill . . . Could we have a taxi? You can afford one, can't you?"

"Course I can! But walking's good for you, and the nipper. Sit down on that doorstep there."

"I can't sit here, with people staring," she said. She started walking again, feeling more uncomfortable in her body than ever. To take her mind off it she thought of Ethel and said, "Mind, you mustn't tell anyone . . . Promise?"

"Promise."

"Dad's sending her money on the QT, through the woman next door, so Niccolo won't know about it. Otherwise he'd take it and spend it on gambling and betting, like the rest of the money. He's got a better job now—at the Savoy Hotel in the dining-room, but he still doesn't bring home enough money for them to live on. And he still tells Ethel that he'll get rid of her if she doesn't have a baby soon."

"Sounds as if she ought to walk out, anyway. There's plenty of better fish in the sea than a bleeding dago waiter wot can't recognise a three-legged 'orse or a doctored pack of cards."

"Anne's the worst off—Frank's wife. Frank seems to be happy, battles and all, but she's miserable. I go round to see her once a week, at least, while you're in London. She looks as though she's wasting away, and miserable. She really loves him."

Bill Hoggin blew his nose with his fingers, heartily expelling the phlegm into the gutter. "She'll be finding someone else to keep her tits warm if Frank's not careful."

"Oh, Bill, Anne's not that kind of woman!"

"All women are that kind of woman, if they are lonely enough, long enough."

Ruth stopped suddenly, her hand jerking out of his. She went dead white, whispering, "Oh, oh! . . . Bill . . . it's happened!"

"Wot's 'appened?" Bill cried, alarmed. She was swaying unsteadily, and trembling.

"The waters just broke." She stood with her legs apart, bent over. Bill grabbed her hand and pulled her to a lamp post. "'Old onto that, 'old 'ard now!"

He ran into the middle of the road and waved his arm at a car sweeping up toward them. The car stopped a few feet away, brakes squealing, and he ran to the driver's side, and leaned in—"My wife's 'aving a baby. Take us to the 'ospital!"

The driver was a la-di-da sort with a little moustache and a monocle. He said, "But the hospital's miles away, my good man." He was alone in the car.

"She's going to the 'ospital, mate, an' you're taking 'er, or I'll knock your fucking block off. Stay 'ere!" He ran back to the lamp post where Ruth was swaying giddily, seized her, and bundled her into the back seat of the car.

The driver drove off without a word. Ruth began to groan almost at once, crying, "It's coming, Bill. I know it is!"

"We'll be there soon, Ruthie," he said; and to the driver, "Can't you make this tin snail go any faster, mate?"

The man did not answer. Ruth's moans grew louder. Bill was sweating heavily, and the palms of his hands were wet. They passed out of North Hedlington and entered Hedlington.

A sign caught Bill's eye—LADY BLACKWELL'S HOSPITAL—with a painted hand pointing up a wide side street. "Up there!" he cried.

The driver turned the car, saying, "It's an auxiliary hospital, for the military only."

"I don't care a fuck what it is, they 'ave doctors, don't they?"

The driver stopped his car outside the front door of the big, sprawling building. Bill leant over and pumped the klaxon so that it blared like a sick donkey. The door opened and a nurse came running out, "Battle casualty?" she cried.

"No. My wife's 'aving a baby."

"This is a . . ." the sister began; then she saw Ruth's frightened face and said, "It doesn't matter. We have some women hurt in the bombing, anyway. Get out of the car, sir, and help me with your wife . . . This is your first?"

Ruth nodded and said, "It's on the way, now."

The sister smiled, "Not so fast, the first time. Come along now. How many minutes between pains?"

About half-past one in the morning Bill Hoggin, sitting in a small downstairs room in Lady Blackwell's Hospital, thought he'd have to piss again soon. He'd been to the W.C. six times already since arriving soon after five the previous afternoon. He stifled a yawn. The beer had got to him early, and he'd felt godawful for an hour or two; then that wore off, and he'd read the paper, and thought about Milner, and how best to dispose of the tinned meat he'd be getting. Sell it direct to the military buying commission if he could. That would mean greasing some palms, which would be further protection . . . Then he thought about sugar. There'd been a Royal Commission set up to look into the sugar supply situation the month the war started, back in August. Now there were rumours there'd be an allotment . . . so much per person and factory that used sugar. Sugar was going to be worth its weight in gold. If he could get some, outside the allotment, he could resell it for two or three times the official price.

God, that woman was taking a time . . . but the hoitytoity nurse had assured him that labour of several hours was normal for a woman having her first baby. Nearly nine hours now.

Couldn't put it off any longer or he'd piss in his trousers. He struggled to his feet and went out into the brightly lit corridor. A young woman was coming along it, carrying a mop and pail. She was just over medium height, with big blue eyes, a large bosom bulging out her hospital helper's V.A.D. uniform, and a perfect peaches-and-cream complexion, the skin the texture of a rose petal, glowing softly even in the hard glare of the electric light.

He stopped, staring at her. She paused, smiling, and said, "Good morning. You must be the husband of the lady who's having a baby. All the sisters are very excited. It'll probably be the only baby ever born here."

As she spoke, her look had changed its character. He thought there was recognition now; and he thought he had seen her before, too.

"My name's Hoggin, miss," he said. "Bill Hoggin."

Then he was sure. She knew him: and the occasion had not been long ago. But she said, "You mustn't worry, Mr Hoggin."

Nodding, she moved on. He went to the W.C., did his business and returned to the little room, thinking. A lady. A young lady. He ought to have asked her name. That might have given him an idea. But . . .

The door opened and a sister came in, smiling. "Mr Hoggin?"

He leaped to his feet.

"Your wife has just given birth to a 5 lb 7 oz boy. It appears that he's about three weeks premature, but mother and child are doing well. There are no complications."

"Can I see them now?"

"In half an hour. Your wife insisted on cleaning up before she would see you."

Daily Telegraph, Saturday, February 20, 1915

HOUSEHOLD COOKING
SOME MEATLESS DISHES

Now that there are distinct signs of spring, the economical housekeeper will find that, with a little thought and care, she can serve meatless fare that is both inexpensive and nourishing. The recipes . . . include suggestions for rather uncommon, if economical Lenten dishes:

CHESTNUTS WITH SPROUTS

Slit about 1 lb of chestnuts, boil them in salted water, then drain and remove the shells and inner skins. In another saucepan cook till nearly tender in fast-boiling salted water about ½ lb of Brussels sprouts, previously washed and trimmed. Melt in a clean saucepan 1 oz of butter or dripping, put in the chestnuts and sprouts, season with salt and pepper, and toss over the fire, or let all simmer gently for a few minutes. A little stock may be added if handy. When quite hot, dish up by arranging a border of

> **chestnuts on a hot dish, and place the remainder of the chestnuts and the sprouts piled up in the centre, then serve.**

I know that dish, Cate thought. He'd eaten it many times, served with chipped potatoes and red currant jelly as an accompaniment to roast pheasant. Now, partly for Lent and partly due to war shortages of meat, it was being recommended as a dish in itself. The other suggested recipes, eggs au gratin and Irish vegetable stew, were more ordinary. Indeed, Mrs Abell had served them the latter within the past week.

He frowned at the paper, his thoughts sliding from the particular to the general. Just as there was a great inequality of sacrifice in battle, many risking and giving their lives, many others staying at home and risking nothing, so there was great inequality in this necessity of eating. A Royal Commission had looked into the matter of sugar supply last August, as soon as the war began; but sugar wasn't the only commodity which needed controlling. There was great inequality in the availability of meat, milk, eggs, and some vegetables; bread was not so bad—if you had the 8d for a loaf. It came down to money: those who had it, ate well: those who didn't, didn't . . . and many of those who didn't were the dependents of the very same men who were risking their lives in the trenches. A soldier's wife was in a much worse position than the wife of a factory worker, especially if there were small children to look after, for then the wife was for all practical purposes prevented from earning extra money on the side, and had to depend solely on her husband's allotment. Broadly defining class as wealth—not quite true, but true enough for the present situation—there was another split developing between the classes . . . not, as one might have thought, on the battlefield, where the upper class were doing their share and more; but at home, in England's green and once pleasant land . . .

Land . . . the split was not only social; it was regional, in the sense that nearly everyone who lived in the country could get the fresh food needed, especially the children—the eggs, milk, butter, and meat, not to mention rabbits, fish, and game. The scarcities and the high prices were to be found among the working class in the towns, created by real shortages, bad distribution, and the machinations of the food profiteers. And the only way to correct the situation was a system of rationing, whereby the nation's whole farm production, and all food imports, were bought by the government for the people, to be distributed on a basis of need, not of ability to pay . . . this was a strange sort of socialism he was preaching to himself! The people wouldn't stand it any more than they'd stand for conscription. Not even those who would most benefit from it would like it . . . but events, as the war progressed, might force England into it.

He went out and called up the stairs, "Stella!"

"Yes, Daddy?"

"I'm going over to Abbas to look at Frank Cawthon's new cows. Want to come?"

"No, thanks. I'm studying the *Manual of Nursing.*"

Cate found his cap and went out. Stella wasn't looking well these past few days. Ought to get out in the open air more. Still, if she was to be a good V.A.D., the more she learned, the better.

Hedlington: Saturday, March 13, 1915

22 Harry Rowland and Bob Stratton sat side by side in the grandstand of Hedlington stadium, if grandstand is not too splendid a description of the tin-roofed section of seats, perhaps twelve rows deep, on the north side of the ground. For the rest, all round the playing field spectators stood on the grass—or mud—without even the simple amenity of duckboards, unprotected from whatever rain or sleet or snow might fall. A rope kept the spectators six feet back from the touch lines, and twenty feet back from the goal lines.

It was raining lightly. It had rained off and on all morning. The crowd, almost all men, huddled further into their jackets, and pulled their cloth caps deeper over their heads, or took them off to dash the rain from them, then put them back on again. Many of the men were wearing large rosettes on their lapels, blue and white for Hedlington Rovers, red and white for Sheppey United. The rain was not heavy, and did not damp the crowd's enthusiasm. The waving of rattles and shouting of cries were almost continuous, although, as there were barely fifteen hundred spectators, the sound was soon absorbed into the dense, damp air. From the grandstand Harry was hardly aware that the people across the field were shouting at all.

When both sides were ready for the fray, the referee had not arrived. A Hedlington official was finally appointed and the game began at 2.15 p.m. The first half was keenly contested, the red and white having the balance of the play

> rather in their favour, if one is to judge by the amount of
> work the respective goalkeepers had to do, for Bell was
> frequently called upon, while Sykes had very little to oc-
> cupy his attention. One surprise shot, however, in the first
> two minutes of the game, enabled United to establish an
> early lead. It was the only goal of the first half.

Harry clapped as he watched, but his mind was not here. He was a
major supporter of the Hedlington football club, and he had given his
own Rowland's Works team, and their wives, tickets to this game; but
his mind was elsewhere—in the factory. The meeting was to be half an
hour after the end of this game . . . a little more than an hour from
now. He had rehearsed many times what he wanted to say, first in private, then with Bob. He was ready, and not nervous, but he could not
stop himself from wondering what the outcome would be. The men
were in a strange mood. The war had a lot to do with it: for one thing,
every man who went away to the war made those who stayed behind
that much more important, and that importance was being drummed
into them by the trade union organisers, and the damned socialists.

A yell went up loud enough to be clearly heard outside the stadium,
and a thousand rattles set up their distinctive corncrake sound. Hedlington's centre half had passed to the outside right, who beat his
man, dribbled fast down the touch line, and sent a high arching centre
straight in front of the goal mouth, where the centre forward had
headed the ball into the far corner of the net as Sheppey's goalie swan-
dived after it, in vain.

The blue and white striped shirts danced and hugged each other
round the goal mouth. Score 1–1.

> On the resumption four goals were registered, inside of
> ten minutes—the first by Hedlington and the last three by
> Sheppey, and that ended the scoring. The spectators, how-
> ever, saw plenty to keep them up to a pitch of excitement,
> even though the football was poor. The players frequently
> tripped and kicked at one another and on occasions they
> 'framed up' in a threatening manner. The referee was far
> too lenient, and had a player or two on each side been sent
> off it would have been no more than they deserved.

The rain fell harder, as the Sheppey supporters swung their rattles in
triumph, and the ground slowly emptied. Final score: Sheppey United
4, Hedlington Rovers 2.

They were gathered in the main assembly shop, crowded round the work benches and the cars, against a backdrop of lathes and machinery, the driving belts now motionless. The arc lights glared down from the high ceiling on the wet cloth caps, the rattles, the blue and white favours, the damp sheen of their coats and the scarves still tied round their necks. It was not warm in there, but it was dry. Harry Rowland came to the end of his speech:

"Let me sum up. The Union of Skilled Engineers is trying to persuade many of you to join it. One or two of you have done so. None of the union organisers works here except, as we have discovered, Albert Gorse. They are trying to cause dissension where none existed before, or ought to exist now. You get fair wages, as good as any in Kent. Bert Gorse has been telling you that skilled workers get thirty-five shillings for a five and a half day week in Wolverhampton and Coventry. That's quite true, because there's a lot of heavy industry there, particularly the manufacture of motor bicycles, motor cars and lorries, and there's a big demand for skilled engineering labour. But you all know, too, that in a generally rural area the standard wage for skilled workers in industry is thirty shillings a week—and I am paying you thirty-two. Some of you, egged on by Bert Gorse and his outside friends, have been threatening you won't work for less than thirty-five shillings a week—a wage we can not afford to pay here, and remain competitive . . . The union organisers are also telling you your jobs will be taken away by women . . . by unskilled labour . . . that you will all be sent into the army unless you organise and let the union protect you . . . Hundreds of thousands of our boys have volunteered for the army. Yet still more production is needed. Those men have to be replaced somehow. We, the owners and managers, are certainly not anxious to see our skilled men go into the army, though of course we are all English and we hope that everyone will carry his fair share of the burden. On the contrary, it is to our interest to see that really essential men realise that they are more valuable here than in the trenches. Otherwise, who is going to make the guns and lorries and ambulances the soldiers need? . . . Yes, there will have to be replacements—dilution, the union calls it—and some will certainly be women, though I personally hope our women will never have to undertake the heavy, dirty work that many of you do, even if they are physically capable of it. The replacements will not receive equal pay for equal work, but equal pay for equally *efficient* work. If a man is not as skilled as the man he replaces . . . if a woman can't do all that the man did, including the setting-up . . . neither will receive the same wage. That's government policy in the government factories and arsenals, and I think it's fair and right, so we'll follow it here . . .

What these outsiders are asking you to do, is to consider striking for more than twice a soldier's pay . . . although he is risking his life every hour and we, all of us, live safe and comfortable at home and go back to our wives every evening."

He paused. He knew all the men, most of them very well, though none perhaps intimately: he sometimes wondered how well he knew Bob Stratton, in fact. Their minds were not made up yet. It was Saturday night, and they needed time; he had known this would be the case, and had determined that there should be no decision at this meeting. For one thing, the wives must be given time to talk to them. He ended —"I have decided, for the sake of Rowland's, that Albert Gorse will be dismissed immediately. Any man who does not turn up for work on Monday morning need not turn up at any time. He will be dismissed from that moment. Now, Bert, it's your turn."

Bob Stratton helped Harry down from the work bench where he had been standing. Bert Gorse slowly pushed forward through the huddled men, and climbed up onto the bench. He, too, had been to the football match, Harry saw. His coat was damp and the big rosette, as big as Harry's, soggy wet on the shabby lapel. He began to speak . . . about the need for skilled men to stand together, or they were at the mercy of the employers. Mr Rowland talked as though he, Bert Gorse, had been spending all his time trying to persuade men to join the union. Yes, he thought they should—because it made the working man part of an organisation as powerful as the boss—more powerful sometimes . . . but the men would know that he hadn't always been speaking about joining the union. Once, he'd asked many of them to gather and discuss dangerous machinery. The foreman said they didn't have the right to talk about that on Mr Rowland's time . . . but he'd rather waste half an hour of production than see one man go out of here without a hand or an arm . . . Another time, he'd asked them what they thought of the state of the lavatories . . . And again, about the way Mr Rowland and Mr Stratton were putting three jobs together and making two men do them. That way they got more work out of a man for the same money . . . As to wages, they knew better than he, or Mr Rowland, what it was like to raise a family on thirty-two shillings a week, with prices going up every day . . . And let nobody listen to talk about the boys in France. The war would be over one day, though the way the government was running it now, that day would be a long way off . . . and the soldiers would come back home. To what? To lower wages than they were getting when they left? To working conditions forced on them in the pretence that it would help the men at the front? Let no one misunderstand—everything that he and the union were working for here was for the men at the front, too, so that they would come back to a better England, a better Hedlington, a better job.

He looked at Harry Rowland, and said, "I am sorry you gave me the sack, Mr Rowland. If the men believe me, likely you'll have to be taking me back." He turned once more to the men. "If you want more pay, and better conditions, don't come to work on Monday. Come to the union office on Stalford Street, instead. Thank you."

He stepped down. Somewhere at the back of the shop a man whirled his rattle briefly, a strange harsh sound in the echoing workshop; but Harry could not tell whether it was in applause or derision, or for whom. He stood up. "That's all. Beckett, close the factory, please."

The men crowded out in silence. In five minutes the great hall was empty except for Harry, Bob Stratton, and Beckett, the night watchman, holding a heavy bunch of keys. Harry turned to Bob. "I know you don't drink, Bob, but would you like to watch me have one in my office?"

Bob nodded, and they walked together down the hall, out and across the gravelled yard to the manager's wing, where the clerical work was done and the records kept, next to the design department.

Harry sat down at his desk, opened a cupboard, and poured himself a stiff whisky, with a little soda from a siphon. "How do you think it will go?" he asked.

"Hard to tell, Mr Harry . . . I wish we'd won the match this afternoon."

Harry nodded. It was a wise remark; he had certainly been right not to have a vote or a show of hands now. The men were not in a cheerful mood, partly, at least, because of the defeat in the soccer. He said, "I'm going to London on Tuesday, Bob . . . Vauxhall is getting huge orders, and our car is very similar to theirs."

"Just as good. Better."

Harry said, "Ours costs a bit more . . . Another thing I hear through Mr Ellis, is that there's a move on in Whitehall to make all manufacturers who get military contracts standardise their machines . . . have one ambulance design, one staff car design, and so on, and make everyone turn out just that design."

"Won't work," Bob said decidedly. "We make ours. Vauxhall makes theirs."

"Suppose we're pressed to have parts interchangeable at least, and nuts and bolts?"

"Wouldn't be as good as what we have now. Each part is designed for a certain job in a certain machine. If the parts are the same, but the job or the machine's different, it isn't going to be as good—stands to reason."

"We might be forced to do something about it, though. I can see the problems of replacing damaged parts in the field. If they have three different makes of staff car in use, there'd have to be three times as many spare parts . . . What will we do if a lot of men don't show up on Monday?"

"There's still some skilled men left in Hedlington . . . might have to offer more money to get them out of the jobs they're in."

"What about women?"

Bob said, "I don't like it, Mr Harry. They'd be nothing but trouble, even if they could do the jobs."

Harry sipped his whisky. He agreed with his foreman: he didn't like the idea of women in the factory, except in clerical jobs, or sewing in the upholstery section, but there were two inescapable facts to be faced: one was that the supply of men was running out, and two, that many intelligent and energetic women were eager to do just such work —anything, it seemed, to show what they could do outside the home.

He said, "We have no alternative, Bob. We'll try them anywhere, in any job here, any at all. We'll run courses of training for them . . . machinists, drivers, tally clerks, lathe operators, everything . . . And until they can prove they're as good as the men, we'll pay them less. Twenty-four shillings a week. That's half as much again as they'd have been getting six months ago."

Bob said, "They'll never be as good as the men. They'll get tired . . . or tired of the job, and go home."

"We'll see . . . I hear J.M.C. is going to hire women right from the start."

Bob nodded. "Mr Richard and that American are already running training courses for unskilled labour—they're getting mostly women. And their factory's up. They'll have the first lorry out soon."

Harry didn't want to talk about Richard. A little more chat and he'd go home. He said, "How's the new grandchild coming along? Has he been christened yet?"

"Next week."

"What's he going to be called? Bob—after you?"

Bob Stratton laughed—a short unhumorous snort—"Ruthie's going to call him Launcelot, Mr Harry. Hoggin nearly burst a blood vessel when she told him, but nothing's going to change her mind. He's going to be called Launcelot, and he's going to go to Eton School when he grows up."

Harry laughed in turn, but genuinely. He thought both ideas were funny, very funny. He'd always liked little Ruthie, at least partly because she had always had a slightly eccentric streak. If young Launcelot Hoggin won a scholarship and became Launcelot Hoggin, Colleger, that was the only way *he'd* ever become an Etonian.

He asked Bob after the rest of his family: they were all well. Frank was with Mr Charles, and hadn't been sick or wounded. Fred was still in the barracks, but getting more and more impatient to get to France.

Harry said, "Mr Ellis told me there's been very heavy fighting just these last two days. Near a place called Neuve Chapelle, he said. Severe casualties among the Indians, and their British officers."

"Ah, there's been nothing in the papers about that. They want to keep that quiet, like, I suppose."

"There hasn't been time really, Bob."

"Fred's well out of it, if you ask me. But he's impatient. He's always found Hedlington a dull place . . . How's Master Guy? Playing rugby, I suppose? He ought to be careful. He might damage his right hand, and then what would happen to his bowling?"

"He may be doing something even more dangerous than bowling for Yorkshire before another summer's out . . . And there isn't going to be any county cricket this year, more's the pity. Guy thinks he would have been ready for it. I had a long letter from him a few days ago." He shook his head, remembering. "He gave me a carefully reasoned explanation of why we should stop making motor cars and make aeroplanes instead."

"Aeroplanes? Here? Master Guy's got aeroplanes on the brain."

"His arguments were very persuasive. He thinks the demand for motor cars will go down during the war, and be controlled, while the demand for aircraft will go up—spectacularly. There will be a technical explosion, now that the war is forcing us to find solutions to problems without regard to cost. Frankly, it is an exciting prospect. But I just can't see it. Perhaps I'm too old. Both of us are."

"And too sensible, Mr Harry. Those things don't have no future."

Mr Hunnicutt had again given his sermon against labouring on the Sabbath. Dinner had been roast beef and Yorkshire pudding. The wind was blowing wet leaves about the garden and banging a small bough against the wall of the shed. Inside, Bob Stratton had just put the card with the old Rowland advertisement in the window facing out on the lane, and sat down on his high stool, staring at Victoria on her stand. The wire wheels had been balanced and tuned by Cox, who had replaced Collis in the job. The Dunlop tyres were racing type, smooth and thin. The inlet ports were smooth as glass. The engine was a side valve Blumfield twin cylinder of 998 cc. Bob had been very much tempted to bore it out to 1100 cc., but in that case the only record he could go for was the out-and-out. If he kept it under 1000 cc., he could make a 1000 cc. record at the same time as the out-and-out; and that would be worth a lot of extra money.

There were two areas where Bob believed his machine could be improved. First—the valves. Overhead valves were much better than side valves for his purpose: but they weren't reliable unless you could use really high quality steel. If you didn't, the valve head would like as not snap off under stress, and drop on top of the piston. He'd long wondered where he could get hold of the small amount of high grade steel needed . . . and Master Guy had come up with the answer, when he was home for the Christmas holidays. He said he'd get some from Handley Page, the aircraft manufacturers, through a friend of his who was a designer there. The aircraft people all used high grade steel—they had to. It had taken Guy longer than he had expected, but he had done it, and the steel had come a fortnight ago, in the form of a rod three feet long and three-eighths of an inch in diameter, which was now standing against one wall of the shed. He'd get to that in due time; it would be a matter of hammering the heads to crude shape himself, and then completing on the lathe—first of course taking down the engine and machining new castings to make the overhead valves and rockers—a long job, but worth it.

The other main matter he must deal with was the frame. Most motor cycle frames seemed to have been inherited from the days of the bicycle. Consequently, they whipped when cornering at the much greater speeds of even an ordinary motor cycle. He wouldn't be doing any cornering when he was running the flying kilometre for the out-and-out speed record—but there were other, longer distance records, which involved curves; and if he could come out of the Brooklands curve faster, he'd start even the flying kilometre faster . . . A stronger frame would enable him to do that; but he wanted rigidity without gaining weight. In fact, he wanted something like the frame Cotton had patented last year . . . straight tubes running from the steering head to the rear spindle, triangulated in two planes. He'd seen the patent diagrams, and he'd seen the mock-up the Butterfield brothers had built to Bill Cotton's order, and he thought he knew steel tubing well enough to improve on it—not much, for it was already a very good design: but not much was needed.

He took out a pencil from his pocket, pulled a pad of squared paper from the drawer in the work table, and began to draw shapes for the frame . . .

93.48 miles an hour . . . that's what he had to beat: Sidney George on a 998 cc. Indian V-twin. When he'd got the new frame and overhead valves on Victoria she should be able to do 100, or close to it; but it wouldn't do to go all out the first time. When you broke a record you got a good bonus in cash from the people who'd made your plugs, tyres, carburetors, oil, petrol, magnetos—all the accessories. The men who rode for records were a close-knit lot. Bob knew them all, and he knew that when they broke a record they did it by as small a margin as they could manage: that way, the next man would have a better chance to re-break it—and so get his bonus, too. So if it still stood at 93.48 he'd try for 95 or 96 . . . but he was going to make 100 the *next* time, whether Baldwin and Baragwanath and O'Donovan grumbled or not.

He looked at a design he had made. The top end of the tubing could be thinned down a bit as the strain of a fast curve wouldn't come there, but lower down. He bent forward, making a thinner pencil line on the paper, then erasing the old one.

And when would that be—the time for his attempt? Brooklands had been closed to the public since the end of September, because of Vickers' aeroplane factory sheds inside the track. Perhaps Master Guy could arrange it . . . he was a smart young gentleman. Or was there somewhere else he could take Victoria for the attempt, when he was ready? He knew of nowhere . . . Well, the war couldn't go on for ever. Meanwhile . . .

Someone had tapped on the back window. He sat up, slowly putting away pencil and paper. The mental pictures of frames and valves faded from his mind, as did Victoria, gleaming on her stand. He walked slowly toward the door.

Normally Bob Stratton took his dinner to the works in a tin box, strapped to the carrier of his bicycle, and ate it in his office, washing it down with a cup of tea from the woman who pushed a tea urn round the floor soon after the whistle blew for the noon break. He had his box with him, and most days would have been looking forward to eating its contents—today sausage rolls, bread, butter, and jam; but he had woken up this Monday morning with a headache, and it had not got better as he stood with Mr Harry at the main gate of the plant, waiting for the men to arrive . . . or stay away.

It had been a tense time, much more so than Bob cared to acknowledge. His stomach seemed to be tied into a hard knot, and his head throbbed, particularly behind his eyes.

But the men had come, every one of them except Bert Gorse and three others: and of those three, one's wife came pale and hurrying to swear her husband was in bed sweating with a fever and filling the chamber pot with vomit. So in the end two men, both recent union members, had supported Bert. Mr Harry greeted every one as he came in with a brief, "Good morning, Johnson . . . Morning, Knight . . . glad you came." The men seldom said a word—just a nod and sometimes a wordless grunt. Their presence said what had to be said.

Bob got through most of the morning, then at half past eleven went to Mr Harry's office, told him he was not feeling at his best, and would like permission to go home. "Of course, Bob," Mr Harry said. "Stay out tomorrow, if you still don't feel right. Would you like Wright to drive you home?"

"No, no, Mr Harry. I have the bike."

So he pedalled slowly home, the uneaten lunch still in its tin. At 85 Jervis Street he wheeled the bike up the front steps and took it into the house, leaning it against the wall at the foot of the stairs. He stooped over to take the bicycle clips off his trousers. By now Jane should surely have called from the parlour, wondering why he was home.

He stopped to pick up two letters and a postcard lying on the carpet under the letter slot in the door. The second post must have come just before he got home. Nellie the maid came running up the stairs—"Oh, Mr Stratton, you did give me a turn! I was afraid it might be the Ripper!"

"Don't be daft, girl," Bob growled. "He's only killed two women and both of them at night, with a full moon, out of doors, and not close to houses . . . Where's Mrs Stratton?"

"Out shopping, sir. She said she'd be back by noon, but of course she wasn't expecting you. Shall I . . . ?"

"I'll eat what I have," Bob said, "if I eat anything."

He went into the parlour, as Nellie hurried back down to the basement. Sitting down, he wondered whether he should take an aspirin. But he didn't hold with drugs. Better to suffer, don't let it think it's got the better of you.

He glanced at the postcard—from that friend of Jane's in Ramsgate. She'd read it aloud to him when she got home. A letter from Frank: he'd read that to her. The other letter was from a woman. He could tell that from the perfumed smell of the envelope, and its pinkish-blue colour, like a hydrangea. It was addressed to Mrs Bob Stratton in a large round hand, in purple ink. The postmark was Hedlington, Saturday 4.30 p.m.

Bob stared at it a long time. This wasn't from a lady. Why should an ordinary woman in Hedlington write a letter, instead of coming round and telling Jane whatever it was?

He felt as he felt in the shed, when he heard the tap at the window —an oppressive and fearful yet rising excitement that could not be denied. He had to do it.

He opened the letter, and read. It was very short:

"Dere Mrs Stratton Your husban as little girls and pays them money." It was signed "A Friend": undated and unaddressed.

So, it had come; he ought to accept it, and acknowledge it, as he had always told himself he would do, when the time came. But now it was here and he desperately needed to deny it, and by denial somehow wash himself clean from the stain. That was exactly how he felt, those times, too, afterwards.

His headache, which had vanished when he saw the letter and first intuitively guessed what it might contain, now returned with splitting force. The walls of the room moved in on him, and retreated; the antimacassars on the backs of chairs and couch fluttered, though there was no breeze, no air. He felt that he would suffocate if he stayed a moment longer in there.

He half walked, half ran to the door, out into the passage, and toward the back door, stumbling over a pedal of his bicycle. Wrenching the back door open he started down the back steps then stopped, frozen. He had remembered something—the letter, left on the central table in the parlour. He stood, looking up to the sky; what should he do? Let it come, as come it must sooner or later? Refuse to hide? The sin itself was a punishment of God, so what did any punishment of man matter?

So for a minute, frozen . . . then he ran back, picked up the letter, stuffed it into his coat pocket, out again, and down to the shed. There he opened both doors, half-filled Victoria's tank, lowered her off the stand, and wheeled her out into the lane. Carefully setting the spark and mixture, and turning the engine over a few times with slow pushes of his instep, he kicked hard and waited, his spread feet supporting the machine, until the engine was running sweetly. Then he opened the throttle and rode down the lane.

Twenty minutes later, riding with great care, he left the eastern outskirts of Hedlington behind him, and faced the Canterbury road. He opened the throttle a little more and watched the speedometer needle creep round to forty miles an hour . . . then fifty. Four miles out a secondary road that led to Beighton and Walstone curved off to the south. Beighton Down stretched along to his left, scattered thorn bushes, a few chalk outcrops, and a flock of grazing sheep the only things marring the pale grey-green sweep of the grass. The air was chill and damp, biting now through his serge jacket as though he was not wearing it. He should have worn his short heavy fleece-lined jacket and goggles, and leather helmet . . . but he had not come out here to be comfortable, nor to test Victoria, but to escape, from what he knew, after many years, was inescapable. A hundred times he had ridden fast along this stretch, measuring the resilience of the front fork and the rigidity of the frame, hearing and feeling the exact tuning of the engine, listening to the tyres. Not now.

The road was empty, the surface hard-packed macadam, close textured, damp from an earlier shower, but not wet, the sun hidden. He crouched forward until he was hunched like a monkey over the handlebars and then with his right thumb pushed the throttle wide. The machine bounded forward, at first with a single leap and then more gradually. Bob kept his eyes on the road, a four and a quarter mile straight, most of it gradually downhill before a final mile up. He stole glances at the speedometer . . . 58 . . . 65 . . . 75 . . . 80 . . . The wind shrieked by his ears and tore at his beard. His coat flew out behind him like a cloak . . . 83 miles an hour . . . a shade more, 85 perhaps. He bared his teeth and howled madly into the wind. She would go no faster and a vibration set up somewhere in the frame was jarring his arms through the handlebars. He howled louder, more desperately. But here was the limit. Victoria reached the foot of the rise at 85. Speed dropped slowly, with the throttle still wide, to 67 at the top of the slope. Bob leaned down, his tears falling onto the petrol tank, and throttled back. It was over.

His headache had not gone, but almost so. The other, the curse, had not gone, he knew, but for a time it would leave him alone. He turned the machine in the road and followed a private car back to Hedlington at a sedate speed . . . He'd have to look into these new countershaft gearboxes, a Juckes maybe, to replace the Sturmey Archer; and perhaps a chain final drive. He himself should be wearing a suit that fitted his body tightly. Perhaps he should talk to Master Guy about fixing some sort of metal shaping on the handlebars so that the air would flow over his head and past Victoria's sides, too. His head was empty of evil, cleared by the rush of air, the smell of hot steel and burned castor oil of the lubrication system. She was a good bike—but she wouldn't do a hundred, nor yet ninety-four, the way she was now.

Daily Telegraph, Saturday, March 13, 1915

FOOD PRICES
A LABOUR CONFERENCE

A conference called by the Workers' National Committee to consider the causes of, and suggest remedies for, recent rises in the prices of food and coal, was held yesterday at the Kingsway Hall, London.

Mr J. A. SEDDON, president of the Trade Unions' Congress, moved the following resolution:

That the most effective action the government can now take to reduce wheat prices is to intervene to remedy the deficiency in carrying ships, and that the Government should at once take steps to obtain the control of more ships, and itself bring wheat from Argentina, Canada, and elsewhere at the bare cost of transport.

That the Government should endeavour to secure control over such proportion of the Russian wheat and other supplies as may be necessary . . .

That the Government should set up a representative committee . . . to determine the prices to be paid for the home supply . . . fix prices for the resale of both the home and imported supplies at rates not to exceed 40s per quarter, any loss thus incurred to be borne by the National Exchequer.

That the Government should guarantee a fixed price . . . for the 1915 crop.

That in determining prices the payment of adequate wages to agricultural workers should be taken into consideration.

Mr Seddon said the price of wheat and flour would not have risen 54 percent since October last if the Government had not neglected its duty . . . The causes of higher prices were mainly three:

The inaction of the Government.

Speculation and gambling in the wheat markets of the world.

Robbery by a shipping ring.

Mr TURNER of the Glasgow Trades' Council, proposed as (an) amendment:

The most effective action that the Government can now

take is speedily and drastically to deal with the situation by
controlling ships, food prices, and house rents.

The price of coal was the subject of consideration at an
afternoon meeting of the conference. Mr R. SMILLIE,
president of the Miners' Federation of Great Britain,
moved:

That maximum prices for coal should be fixed by the
Government.

That railway trucks belonging both to the separate railway companies and to private traders, should be pooled
and run to their fullest economic use.

That in fixing shipping freights for coasting vessels
under their control the Government should have regard
to normal rates rather than to the excessive rates inflicted
by private shipowners.

That the Government commandeer coal supplies and
distribute to consumers through municipal or co-operative
agencies.

Mr G. LANSBURY referred to the "capitalistic class" as
the great enemy of the workers . . . He appealed to the
conference to be united in fighting off "the enemy within
the gates," and to clear out of the way "all those who stood
between the people and decent living."

Revolutionary talk from a lot of wild men, Cate thought . . . but a lot
of anger and genuine frustration, too. The miners were paying more for
everything they bought, though their wages had not gone up—if anything, they had gone down; yet the price of coal had risen abnormally.
And, as much as any comparable group in the country, the miners had
answered Kitchener's call for recruits. Yet what the talkers were proposing was that the Government should take over the country as a whole
. . . and what evidence existed to prove that the Government, any
Government, was better able to run the shipping business than the
shipping industry? The insurance business better than Lloyds? The
finances of the country better than the Bank of England?

Yet . . . yet . . . it was not right that speculators should force up the
price of wheat for their own gain. But two could play at that game. If
the British Government started buying up wheat supplies in bulk, on a
national basis, in order to keep prices down, what was to prevent the
government of Russia, or Argentina, from holding back the whole supply, on a national basis, to force prices up?

He turned back to the report of the conference:

In a few weeks the passage of the Dardanelles would be forced. There was something like 10,000,000 quarters of wheat locked up in Russia awaiting shipment. That huge supply would be placed upon the market . . .

That should help, at least temporarily, Cate thought . . . once the Dardanelles were in fact forced.

Hedlington: Tuesday, March 16, 1915

23 "The knives, forks, and spoons are set out like this. You always start with the outside ones, and move in toward the centre at each course . . ." The man speaking was the adjutant of the Weald Light Infantry Depot, a tall captain with a big black moustache and a weary drawl. The new officers were standing crowded round the officers' mess oak dining table, where one place had been set for a seven-course dinner, complete with wine glasses.

The adjutant continued, raising his voice slightly to be heard above a bugle from the quarterguard sounding 'Orderly Sergeants:' "This is a sherry glass . . . this big goblet is for red wine, this long-stemmed one for white wine, this bowl shape for champagne. Port glasses are not put on the table until after the rest have been cleared away. When wine is served, you . . ."

Fred Stratton listened with an odd emotion, half interest, half resentment. He had been dining in mess for over three months now, and knew all this about how to comport oneself as an officer and a gentleman. Some of the others might not—the fellow who'd been growing coffee in Kenya until the war broke out seemed to be a rough diamond, and he didn't like to be told, either. He was muttering now, something about what the hell good was all this bollocks in the trenches. The adjutant didn't hear him, or pretended not to. And there were two or three come up from the ranks, old sweats, regular sergeants promoted to be quartermasters of the new Kitchener battalions as they were raised; but even a quartermaster was a lieutenant, dined in mess, and so had to know how to use the cutlery. But most of the 2nd lieutenants here, now in their final weeks of training before being posted to active battalions, were public schoolboys. Glancing at some of them as they listened, Fred noted that they were displaying no signs of boredom or resentment. Well, after all, this was in the end their country, certainly their army; they were the natural heirs to it—so they would not do anything to make any part of it seem ridiculous or unnecessary.

A pair of Colours hung cased and crossed on one wall. They were the Colours of the 1st Battalion, Fred knew, deposited here for safe keeping when the battalion moved from the Curragh to France. The adjutant said, "The president sits at this end, under the Colours, always. The vice president sits at the opposite end. Normally, officers may sit anywhere they wish, including president or vice president, but for the Regimental Guest Night next Thursday, both will be appointed by the P.M.C. The Colonel of the Regiment will sit in this chair—" he laid a hand on the back of one of the rows of chairs lined up on either side of the long highly polished table—"the C.O. on his right, the 2nd-in-command opposite. The quartermaster will be on the Colonel of the Regiment's left. Toasts will be offered in the normal manner . . . and what is that, Stammers?" He turned suddenly on the man from Kenya.

"The president taps the table with his mallet," Stammers said.

"Then?"

"I can't remember."

"Well, you'd better, if you want to go to France with the next batch. We don't intend to let the battalions think we're turning out a lot of yahoos . . . Stratton?"

Fred said, "When everyone is quiet the president says, 'Mr Vice, the King.' Then the vice president says, 'Gentlemen, the King,' and everyone says 'The King,' and drinks."

"In what position?"

"All seated, sir."

"Why is that? Do all regiments sit for the loyal toast?"

"No, sir. Only a few which originally served as marines."

"What does that have to do with it, Bainbridge?"

"The beams of the ships were so low overhead that the officers would bump their heads when they stood up, and actually had to stoop, until King William IV, who had been in the navy himself, ordered naval officers to remain seated while drinking his toast."

"And of course that applied to marine officers, too . . . Good. Now let's get back to the toasting. Houston, does anyone say anything else, when the loyal toast is offered?"

"No sir . . . Only exactly what the vice president proposes . . . except that field officers may say 'God bless him,' too, if they want to."

"Jerram, why are the water glasses taken off the table before the loyal toast is drunk?"

Jerram looked baffled. Fred had no idea. No one had mentioned it, yet he recalled that in fact all water glasses were removed. The adjutant said, "Anyone?"

Churchill-Gatty, one of the eighteen-year-old public schoolboys said, "So that no one can pass his wine over the glass as he drinks the toast, which would then be to 'The King over the water.'"

"The Stuarts," the adjutant said. "Precisely. Stammers, sit down and pretend you are eating peas. How do you pick them up with the fork? But before that, remember that we shall all be having a drink on Griffin tonight. Why?"

He looked round, as everyone else stared at Griffin. Griffin, an assistant bank manager in peace time, flushed, surreptitiously felt his flies, and looked down at his tunic buttons to see if one was undone.

"Well," the adjutant said impatiently, "are you all blind? How can you be fit to inspect your platoons if you can't see a glaring piece of carelessness like this?"

Churchill-Gatty said, "His lapel badges, sir—they're on the wrong sides."

"Quite right," the adjutant said. "You're blowing the bugle horns with your arse, Griffin. Drinks all round tonight. Change them now."

Griffin shook his head in self rebuke. The officers' lapel badges were similar to the cap badge, each showing a stringed bugle horn surmounted by the prancing horse of Kent, over a scroll with the single word WEALD. But on one badge the horn curved from right to left, on the other from left to right; and the mouthpiece of the horn had to be nearest to the wearer's mouth, that is, on the inside. If the badges were worn reversed, it could be said that the bugles were being blown by the rear wind—a heinous crime.

The lesson continued. From the corner of his eye Fred watched Griffin getting his badges straight. He had a wife and child to support and another child on the way. He couldn't afford to stand everyone a drink—he didn't touch a drop himself, to save money . . . He turned his attention to the adjutant, feeling surly. He wanted to be an officer and gentleman, and this was a necessary phase, training that would be valuable after the war was over, too. But now it was a bore, and a sort of insult, too, like the way they looked at your clothes, and told you where to buy your bootlaces. He had a letter from Frank in his pocket: over there apparently, he and Charles Rowland often shared burgoo out of a mess tin, each digging in with his own spoon. Charles Rowland and Frank were closer now than he himself was to Frank, his own brother. They were at the war. Of course Charles was an officer and Frank a private, but he could see that in the trenches, suffering together what they had to, there would be a bond at least as strong as the class barriers which were at the same time holding them apart . . . Frank ought to come home, if only for a few days. He'd seen Anne in the town with another man—a civilian, an older fellow. It might be quite harmless—they'd been strolling in the park one Sunday, with the children, Agnes walking, Lily and the baby in a pram . . . but there it was. Frank had better come home. But how could he? He hadn't been out more than four months . . . Getting married was a mug's game. His mother had told him that Ethel's dago husband was going out with other women, and apparently everyone knew about it except Ethel . . . Damned if *he* was going to get caught. Why keep a cow if you can buy milk?

"That's all," the adjutant said. "See that none of you disgrace us on Thursday. Dismiss."

He touched the peak of his cap in response to their salutes and stalked out, his field boots glittering like tubes of molten brown glass, the dark green double whistle cord of the Weald Light Infantry looped round his neck under the lapels of his jacket, then dividing at the top button of his tunic, one thick strand diving into each breast pocket.

Fred headed for his quarters. It was a small room, once allotted to a single officer, now shared by three in very cramped conditions, all sleeping on camp beds, and sharing the tiny bathroom and W.C. When he got there, he took off his Sam Browne and hung it on the hook allotted to him; his batman would be along in the afternoon to give it another polish, together with his chin strap, and revolver holster. On the dressing table, as he was brushing his hair, he saw an envelope. The postmark was Walstone . . . it must have come this morning and been brought to his room by the Post Corporal. The envelope was addressed in dark blue ink on a pale blue paper—a woman's handwriting, but educated, the letters firm and easily put together, as from much practise. He opened it and looked at the signature—'Stella Cate.' It was dated yesterday. He read it:

Dear Mr Stratton, I do hope you will excuse me writing to you, but as it is rather a private matter I do not want to write to the Commanding Officer officially. You see, some time ago I made a bet with Captain Irwin (I think his name is Stephen), and now I have lost it and want to pay him what I owe. It is not much,

but he does not answer my letters, and I am wondering whether
he is all right. Could you possibly tell me? Just write to me at
Walstone Manor, Kent . . . Yours sincerely,

Stella Cate.

Stella Cate, Fred repeated. He'd seen a lot of her when he was working at High Staining—a nice girl, pretty, shy—seeming, but with bedroom eyes. Betting? With Captain Irwin? On what? Irwin had thought
he'd never be sent back to active service, but his legs had healed better
than anyone expected, and he'd gone, at least a month ago, back to the
1st Battalion. Fred hadn't liked him much—thought him typical of
what most irked him about the upper classes, curt, nose in air, rather
stupid . . . Him and Stella? He wondered. Poor girl.

He set off for the anteroom and there, at one of the writing desks,
wrote a short note on the regiment's crested paper: "Dear Miss Cate,
Captain Irwin was posted to France about a month ago. I don't think
you need worry about your bet, as I am sure he would want to forget
it . . ."

He sealed it, initialled the outside so that the mess corporal could
charge the stamp to his mess bill, and called for a sherry. Sherry in
hand he strolled over to the green baize notice board. The surface was
covered with emblazoned cards: a dance at Mrs Hackworth's, all
officers of the Weald Light Infantry cordially invited . . . a *thé dan-
sant* at Lady Mallet's, all officers of the Weald Light Infantry cordially
invited . . . lunch at the Town Hall in honour of Lord Derby, four
officers invited to represent the Regiment; and the names of the four
selected by the adjutant pencilled in: his was not one . . .

He turned back, sipping his sherry. Plenty of stuff for the officers,
but what was there for the men? He ought to feel strange, a 2nd lieutenant's single star on each sleeve, sipping sherry. Sherry! He'd never
touched the stuff in his life before he was commissioned. But he didn't
feel strange, and he wasn't going to, ever again. No one was going to
look down on him from now on. Whatever it took to achieve that,
he'd do.

But what *was* being done about the Other Ranks? And by whom?
The C.O. perhaps, with the R.S.M.? He ought to find out. These la-di-
da snobs he now lived among looked down on the O.R.s, treating them
as though they were somehow made of different flesh, different blood
. . . yet, they usually knew what the men thought, and felt, better
than he himself did.

He glanced at his newly acquired wrist watch—nearly lunch time;
then close order drill, followed by night manoeuvres.

At 6 p.m., the sun setting and a damp twilight settling over Hedlington, smoke from the evening fires curling up dense in the valley between the green curves of the downs, three hundred men marched out of Minden Barracks in full field service marching order. Fred Stratton, near the end of his training, was commanding a platoon of advanced recruits, also near their time to be sent out to the active battalions. The 2nd-in-command of the depot, a major, was in charge of the exercise, and there were two officers and half a dozen N.C.O.s, all recently recovered from wounds, acting as the director's assistants—without them it would have been an exercise in the blind leading the blind. It was all very well to have read the accounts and training memoranda that came out of France. It was something else to have been there.

Fred's platoon was near the middle of the column. As it approached the gate Fred saw that something strange was going on at the front. Looking forward past the lines of marching men he saw two or three policemen, apparently holding someone—a woman—and heard a deep booing, swelling slowly back down the ranks. "Quiet, there!" his sergeant yelled. "You're still marching at attention!"

The booing subsided in one place, to start again in another. Fred reached the gate and heard women's high voices, shouting, "Conscription of all men, conscription of all dividends! Don't go to fight unless everyone's called up! Why should you risk your lives for a shilling a day while others make fortunes out of the war? Conscription of all men, all money!" The policemen were keeping them back . . . three, four women in dark dresses, holding out pamphlets as they shouted, but the police were not letting them get near the marching troops. Fred stared, for behind the police he saw Naomi Rowland and with her that other girl, Rachel Cowan, who'd been staying at High Staining last summer. Rachel was tugging at a policeman's sleeve, shouting something Fred could not make out. The policeman let go of the woman he was holding and pushed Rachel hard, so hard that she reeled back and fell in the muddy street. The soldiers booed harder—but Fred knew that they were not booing the rozzers. A year ago, it would have been different, but now there was a war on. "Hit her again, harder," a soldier shouted.

"Give 'em a good spanking and send 'em back to the kitchen," another voice cried.

Naomi caught Fred's eyes as he passed. He tried to shrug and look sympathetic simultaneously; but the major was there, standing furious at the gate, calling, "March to attention! Take that man's name, sar'nt!"

"Got 'im, sir!"

"You're acting like a bloody rabble. Straighten your backs! Smarten the pace there! We're Light Infantry!"

All down the line the sergeants were calling the Light Infantry step, 140 paces a minute, even speeding it up. The soldiers straightened as best they could under the heavy packs, their right arms stretched down, the rifles sliding along parallel to the ground at the trail. Fred began to sweat under his collar. 150 a minute was all very well on a ceremonial parade, with only a sword to carry. Here, it was hard. All round he heard the men's laboured breathing, as the sergeants bayed and snarled up and down the column. Now they were facing the hill along the side wall of the barracks, climbing steeply to the hump of Busby Down. Sweat poured down his face. Beside him a corporal marched with gritted teeth. Except the sergeants, no one said a word, there was no sound but the smack of the nailed boots on the cobbles, and the grunt and gasp of the breathing.

At last the major in front called—"Route march step! March at ease!" The step slowed, rifles were slung on shoulders, and a huge collective sigh passed down the column, like some gigantic snake expelling air.

"Five minutes more of that an' I'd 'ave been marching on my chinstrap," a private nearby muttered.

The corporal at Fred's side threw back, "Then don't speak when you're marching at attention. 'Course you made the major angry."

"We wasn't speaking. We was booing."

"That's worse, you sounded like a bloody dying cow. Can we smoke, sir?"

Fred looked round, looking for his company commander, a senior captain transferred from a Territorial battalion. He couldn't see him, and swore silently. He was an officer and in command of the platoon; and orders had clearly said that the men could smoke until the exercise formally began, which would be an hour after they'd reached the rendezvous on Busby Down. Yet he did not like giving the permission if anyone more senior could do it for him. Power of command, that's what they called it, and he didn't have it yet, like these fellows who were born to it, or trained to it in places like Eton and Wellington.

Unwillingly at last he said, "All right. But all pipes and cigarettes will have to be out when we start the exercise."

"Very good, sir."

It was a pitch dark night now, a new moon, a few stars drifting in and out of low thin clouds, stirred by a damp south-west wind. It was not raining, he thanked God, and it was not cold, just raw. They'd all need the greatcoats rolled on top of their packs, later in the night; but, with luck, not the groundsheet capes. He wondered what would happen to Naomi Rowland and Rachel Cowan. Pushing the police was not the way young ladies were supposed to behave. Well, the Cowan girl was no lady, that was certain—a little Jewess from the East End, more like. She'd be lucky not to find herself in a police station cell . . . Miss Naomi, tóo, perhaps. He corrected himself—Naomi, or Miss Rowland—*not*, for him, now that he was an officer, Miss Naomi. The last he'd been able to see what was happening, she was helping Rachel to her feet and shouting at the peeler.

He heard a soldier in the ranks behind him say, "Corporal, what's this thing sticking out of the side of the rifle, under the bolt?"

A moment later the corporal answered, "That's the cut-off, Jenkins. You've had that rifle two weeks now, and you don't know that?"

"I know what it does—shuts off the bullets that are still in the magazine—but I forgot what it's called."

"You'll be forgetting your own name next . . . and you a school-master."

"This is all very different, corporal."

Fred sighed quietly. It certainly was different—sometimes interesting, sometimes boring, sometimes clever, sometimes stupid. This was the army.

The platoon crawled forward across the grass, spread out in a line to Fred's right and left. Another platoon was farther right, and a third a hundred yards behind him. The company commander was somewhere between the two lines, with his headquarters—the C.S.M., his batman, and two or three runners. The 'enemy' trench which they were approaching was directly in front, two hundred and fifty yards away, according to the company commander's orders, given out an hour ago behind a huge clump of gorse, its flowers glowing dull yellow even in the darkness, seemingly by some emanation of light from themselves. Fred had smiled to himself for a moment there, remembering the old riddle he'd first heard at school—'When is fucking out of season?' Answer: 'When the gorse is not in bloom' . . . because, of course, some gorse was always in bloom.

His hand pressed down on a sharp flint hidden in the grass and he swore aloud, stifling the sound instantly. They had been crawling five minutes already. Suppose the company commander had read his compass wrong, and led them to the wrong place for the start? Suppose he was reading his own compass wrong, this minute? It was hanging by a cord round his neck, swinging as he crawled. He stopped and peered at the luminous spots on it . . . he was going west . . . but map and compass reading had not been easy subjects for him: perhaps he was wrong, and it was east . . . or south-east . . . perhaps he should ask his sergeant, who was to his right, behind the right hand section.

"Oh, my heavens!" a muffled voice cried. "Help, help!"

"Shhh!" he hissed and, climbing to his feet, ran to the sound. "What's the matter?"

He was peering down into a hole, kneeling, the sergeant now beside him. Feeling down, they felt boots. They grabbed a boot each and pulled. The body came out slowly, struggling.

"Wot the 'ell are you doing down that 'ole?" the sergeant whispered fiercely, his face an inch from the other's nose. " 'Oo is it?"

"Jenkins," the man said, grievance in his voice. "I fell in."

"Shhh, you useless man! Where's your rifle? Where's your cap?"

"Down the hole."

"Well, get them, man. Don't stand there like a bloody hop pole!"

Without waiting for Private Jenkins, ex-schoolmaster at an elementary school, to act, the sergeant himself dived to his knees and felt round in the hole. " 'Ere's your rifle . . . can't find the cap."

"We've got to get on," Fred said. "The platoon's fifty yards ahead of us by now."

"We'll catch 'em up, sir. Just run, don't crawl. You too, Jenkins. And you'll be docked for that cap next pay day!"

"Sergeant, I . . ."

" 'Old your trap! Get moving!"

They stumbled forward in the darkness and Fred tripped over something, which gave out a shriek and yelled, "The Germans!"

"Shut up, man, it's me—Mr Stratton."

"Oh. I thought you was a 'Un, coming at me from be'ind, like."

Fred got down to his hands and knees, and continued crawling . . . five minutes . . . ten minutes . . . fifteen . . . The sweat was cold round his neck, inside the tunic collar. He had cut both hands on flints and thorns. He had checked his compass several times, but each time the platoon seemed to be going in a different direction. Why couldn't he and the platoon move across country the way old Probyn Gorse did? Because they were mostly town men, even here in Kent. The pavements of Hedlington and the Smoke was where they lived, not the woods and fields at night. The gentry spent more time in the country than most working men did, nowadays, so they were better soldiers . . . this sort of soldier, anyway.

He found himself staring at a shadow, that grew darker and more defined in the ensuing seconds, and finally came close, and stopped. A paler face peered, and a voice grated, "Who the hell are you?"

"Stammers? This is Stratton."

"What the hell are you doing here, man? You're half a mile out of position. Can't you read a bloody compass?"

"There's no need to swear," Fred said stiffly. "What are *you* doing here, then?"

"I'm on a diversionary raid . . . and *I'm* in the right place. I know. In Kenya we don't care about the bloody knives and forks, but we do know how to find our way about a flat plain at night."

"This is not flat. This is the North Downs!"

"Pimples! . . . That's your direction." He held Fred's arm and swivelled him round. "And stop crawling, and get on your feet, for Christ's sake, or you'll never get there before morning."

Fred passed the word to his sergeant and after five minutes of muttering, cursing, and bringing back men who were still crawling obstinately on, the platoon started on the new and, Fred hoped, right line, this time at a smart walk, standing upright. Time enough to change to a crawl when he got near the objective.

After fifteen minutes, Fred realised that he was hopelessly lost, and his platoon with him. The night was still now, the wind died almost to nothing. The clouds had thinned too, and clusters of stars peered through in glowing masses. He gathered his thirty men round him in a forlorn group, and wondered what to do . . . If this was manoeuvres, what must it be like in real war, when enemy machine guns and shells really kept you crawling? And to make a mistake like this would be fatal to you, and to most of your men?

He crouched down, unfastened the greatcoat from his pack and, with the sergeant's help, made a little tent out of it. He crouched under it, lit a match, and examined the compass. That was west, the right direction. He might be off the position where he should have been, but not by very far. The only thing to do was to march in the direction given, unless . . .

The pop and crackle of blank rifle fire sounded from quite close.

. . . march to the sound of the guns, they said.

"Follow me!" he shouted. Someone must have made contact, meaning that they had reached the recently dug trenches on the down, guarded by two aprons of barbed wire and manned by bayonet-fighting dummies and sandbags dressed to look like German soldiers. The platoon broke into a shambling run. "Spread out!" he called, "right and left, like we were before!"

He drew his revolver, feeling a surge of excitement. This felt better . . . The barbed wire showed dimly ahead. No sight of anyone else. Firing was increasing, from close to his right. "Charge!" he shouted. His men began firing blank, shooting from the hip. Now they were struggling through the barbed wire. He seemed to have struck a gap, by chance . . . Strange sounds were coming out of the trench . . . moaning, calling . . .

"Wot the 'ell?" his sergeant muttered, breathless beside him in the wire, struggling to free himself from the barbs without tearing his tunic.

"Sheep!" Fred cried. "Sheep bleating!"

An ancient voice called in a pure Man of Kent accent, "Will you soldiers take yourselves away from my sheep, in the name of God, now?"

A torch shone in Fred's eyes and a cold voice said, "Who's this? Stratton? Mr Stratton, would you kindly mind telling me why you have brought your platoon to the south side of the assault line, when it was ordered to be on the north? And half an hour late?"

"Oh, dear!" a voice cried in the dark, "I think I've bayoneted a sheep!"

"Wot? Jenkins! You again! You don't know your arse from an 'ole in the ground!"

The shepherd appeared, blinking in the light. "Thou'll be paying for the sheep, mister?"

"Of course, of course, my man . . . Take down all details, sergeant. And you, Mr Stratton, rejoin your company, which is in *that* direction, one hundred yards away. Do you think you can find them?"

"Yes, sir."

"And report to me tomorrow afternoon at three for extra compass instruction."

"Yes, sir."

It had started to rain before the column formed up for return to barracks, near 4 a.m., the stars now obscured and the night darker than at any time earlier. The men had been singing *Tipperary* at first, marching along the old cart track that was Daneway, on the Downs, and Fred had hummed with them. He liked that tune. After the rain began one of the men—there were always one or two in each platoon, who were self-appointed jokesters and cheerer-uppers—began one of the Wealds' favourite songs:

> We are Fred Karno's army,
> The ragtime infantry!

It was sung to a hymn tune, *The Church's One Foundation*, known to most before they joined the army and certainly to everyone since. The whole column quickly took it up:

> We cannot fight, we cannot shoot,
> What bloody good are we?

And when we get to Berlin,
The Kaiser he will cry,
Hoch, hoch, Mein Gott,
What a bloody fine lot
Are the ragtime infantry!

That lasted ten minutes, then they sang *Wash Me in the Water,* another favourite set to an old Salvation Army tune: then gradually the singing died away, and the men trudged on down toward the dim presence of Hedlington in the valley, the slung reversed rifles making a hump in the glistening cape behind each man's right shoulder.

While the soldiers were singing, Fred had talked with the sergeant. The routine details had been dealt with: a couple of names taken for minor military crimes; Private Jenkins noted for the loss of his cap—and what they were going to do about the bayoneted sheep, heaven knew, as Jenkins would not be getting any pay for months if he had to pay for that too. As the sheep was dead, perhaps the platoon could club together to buy it, and get the cooks to make an Irish stew out of it for them? The shepherd had apparently promised to let anyone have the corpse as long as he paid for it—fleece and all. Perhaps that would be the best solution. Fred told the sergeant to talk to the men about it, first thing after reveille. Business disposed of, he asked, "What is there for the men to do in Hedlington, when they get passes out of barracks, sergeant?"

"Drink, sir. Hedlington's got more pubs to the acre than any town in Blighty—'cept p'raps Aldershot."

"Does anyone arrange dances? Are there places where they can meet people . . . women?"

The sergeant laughed. He was an old regular with Boer War ribbons and a leathery face, sent back from the 1st Battalion as an instructor after Ypres. He said, "The civvies didn't want to 'ave anything to do with us before the war . . . and no one's told 'em that now their own brothers are in, not just blokes like us."

Fred thought, he's right: Frank and I and Dad and Mum and the girls never had anything to do with the redcoats, before the war. He said, "Something ought to be done. The men ought to have something better to do than get drunk. A lot of them are well educated—better than me, to tell the truth."

Now it was the sergeant's turn to keep tactfully quiet. He was well aware that Fred was not a gentleman, except temporarily by virtue of the stars on his sleeves. Fred broke the silence—"I'll talk to someone . . . see what I can do."

"Very good, sir . . . I'd better speak to the men about the sheep before we get in, sir. They won't be roused till near noon, and if we're going to get the sheep, we ought to get it early."

"All right. Carry on."

He trudged on, head bowed, rain dripping from his cape and seeping down his back. He'd like to meet a nice hot woman himself, like that parson's daughter . . . There was the widow, but she'd taken up with one of the town councillors, the councillor also having a wife . . . and now he was an officer, he had to mind his Ps and Qs. The town women were not for him, not even such as the widow; and the real ladies knew he was not a gentleman, and were polite, but distant. Perhaps he could find another like Carol Adams. No such luck!

The casualties in this latest battle, round Neuve Chapelle, seemed to have been very heavy. The lists were huge. Most of them were fellows who'd joined up in August and hadn't been in France long. Perhaps those women were right, and there ought to be conscription. It did seem wrong that some should stay at home and get rich while others were mown down by German machine guns, to rot in the mud over there. But no one said those fellows had to go. The King asked them, and they went, of their own free will. It wasn't English to tell people what they'd got to do. They ought to see it for themselves, and then they'd do whatever had to be done. But while that was happening, the best were going . . . but were they the best, or, like Bill Hoggin said, only the most stupid?

The sentries at the main barrack gate challenged the head of the column as it tramped up. The column halted, in the darkness—no unnecessary lights were shown anywhere at night, for fear of Zeppelin raids. The major went forward, and gave the password and identified himself. "Bloody silly," the sergeant muttered beside him. "Them buggers know we've been out on the Down."

Fred knew he should correct the man for using foul language in front of an officer, but he didn't feel like meeting the little burst of resentment a rebuke would arouse. A moment later, as the column began to move again, he acknowledged that the sergeant would be much happier if he had been put in his place; then he'd know what he was dealing with.

The company commander yelled orders and the platoons formed into close column. Fred suddenly remembered Naomi Rowland's face as she shouted at the police. She'd be in trouble at the police station, unless someone had been able to get her out. Someone probably had: her grandfather lived here, and was a big nob in the town; and her aunt, Major Quentin's wife; and High Staining was on the telephone . . .

but he knew he was only trying to evade his responsibility, as he had earlier by telling himself that *someone* must be organising recreation for the other ranks. "The subaltern's pride is the faithful, unsupervised performance of all duty, whether it is dangerous, or—as is far more often the case—it is boring, unrewarding, or unpleasant, and sometimes all three." That had been in the colonel's speech when he welcomed them into the Weald Light Infantry . . . rather more stirring than the adjutant's instructions about the regimental tailor, hatmaker, and boot-maker . . . and on *no* account to buy shirts of any shade of khaki darker, or lighter, than *this*—he had fingered his own, a medium shade with a touch of green in it, the correct khaki for Weald Light Infantry officers' shirts. One was not to be seen dead in any other.

Now there'd be rifle inspection, collection of unused blank ammuni-tion . . . it was half past five, and would be getting light soon. He ought to go up and ask the company commander for permission to leave the parade now—the sergeant was perfectly capable of doing what needed to be done; but he restrained himself. He was an officer, a very junior officer, and must remain till the end, till he had counted the rounds, handed them over, and dismissed the men to their barrack rooms.

It was the company commander who gave the final order, "C Com-pany—dismiss!" The men came to attention, turned right, snapped the rifles up to their right shoulders, slapped the slings with the flat of the left hand, at the same time whipping their heads to the left, where the company commander stood saluting them . . . pause to a count of three, then break off and trickle away in the rain, talking in low voices.

Fred marched up to the company commander. "May I have permis-sion to leave barracks for an hour or two, sir? I know two of those women who were in trouble with the police, when we marched out."

The captain was in a bad temper. "Don't they have husbands or fa-thers?"

"One's the niece of Major Quentin Rowland in the 1st Battalion, sir, and sister of Lieutenant Charles Rowland, who was 2nd Battalion, but I heard he's been transferred to the 1st, too."

The company commander said, "All right. Tell the quarterguard commander you have my permission. Report to me when you get back —no, at noon."

The police station was a mile away, down in the heart of the town, behind the Town Hall. A blue light shone over the door of the Vic-torian building, which was made of the same yellow bricks that had been used for the barracks and the gaol. A chink of light shone through the squared bow-type windows to the right of the door, as Fred went in, to enter a big bare room, furnished only by three benches and a large high desk with an electric lamp on it. A police sergeant was sitting behind the desk, a big constable standing beside him. A woman was standing in front of the desk, the cape on her shoulders still dripping rain. She turned as he came in and he recognised Miss Alice Rowland, old Mr Harry's daughter. There had been a Rowland car at the kerb outside, its chauffeur dozing over the wheel.

He saluted, and she said, "Why, it's Fred Stratton! I hope *you* aren't in trouble with the police!"

Fred said, "No, miss. I saw Miss Naomi—Naomi—at the gates yesterday evening . . . there was some trouble but I couldn't get away till now, and I came down to see if she's all right." He saw her looking at his uniform, and glanced down himself. The harsh light showed that his tunic and breeches were splashed with chalk and clay marks—"Manoeuvres on Busby Down," he said.

"Naomi and Rachel were arrested for breach of the peace, the sergeant has just told me. Those silly girls refused to give the police their names or anything—said they had done nothing wrong and would not help . . . so we knew nothing about it until a policeman telephoned—this man here, Constable Waygood. He knows the family and guessed who Naomi was, so telephoned us when he came on duty here. So I came at once. They only got home from Cambridge yesterday!"

Fred said to the sergeant, "The only breach of the peace I saw was when a policeman pushed Miss Cowan, the other young lady, off her feet. And do you realise that Miss Rowland is a granddaughter of Mr Harry Rowland?"

"She'll have to stand trial, same as anyone else," the sergeant said.

Alice cut in—"Quite. But can they not be released now, on my word? You know who I am."

"Yes, Miss Rowland. Yes, now that we know who they are, I can release them on your recognizances. Joe, let the young ladies out."

The constable left the room. Alice turned to Fred. "I am so glad for you, Fred—you deserve to be an officer and we're all sure you'll do well."

Fred said, "Thank you, Miss Rowland. I hope Mr Harry and Mrs Rose are well."

"Father's all right; mother hasn't been well for some time. I'm fit . . . so much so that I feel I ought to be doing much more for the war than I am. I run the Tipperary Lodge here, which is something."

Fred had a brainwave. He said eagerly, "Miss Rowland, the men up there—the privates and corporals—have nothing to do when they're not on parade, except get drunk in the pubs. There are no dances, no games, nothing. They can't meet nice women. Can anything be done for them?"

Alice regarded him seriously. "I should have thought of that myself, months ago. I'll talk to some other ladies, and some of our men, too . . . What's that game the soldiers play, with numbers?"

"Housey housey."

"We could have that, with our ladies serving tea and lemonade, and perhaps playing the game itself, with the men, for a few pennies. Dances . . . we'd have to think about that . . . places to sit and read magazines . . . perhaps have ladies whom they can talk to about their families. I know how lonely many of them must be."

Constable Waygood reappeared, the clump of his boots heard down the stone floor seconds before he appeared, leading Naomi and Rachel. Naomi rushed into her aunt's arms, half crying, half laughing. She didn't notice Fred, who saluted Alice Rowland's back and went out quietly.

Light was creeping like an alley cat down the streets. A newspaper had been thrust through the police station's letter box and Fred pulled it out and looked at the front page headline—DRESDEN SUNK . . . then in smaller type on the line below 'by H.M.S. *Glasgow* and *Penrith* at Robinson Crusoe Island.'

He returned the paper to the letter slot. So the navy had finally wiped the slate clean, after Coronel—four of the Hun ships at the Falklands, in December, and now the fifth and last.

He found that he was marching at Light Infantry pace, 140 paces to the minute, head up and shoulders back, and the tune that he whistled was his own regimental march, *Green Grow the Rushes O!* From barracks the quarterguard bugler was blowing *Gunfire,* the call for early morning cocoa, before first parade.

Daily Telegraph, Friday, March 19, 1915

BATTLE OF NEUVE CHAPELLE
SPLENDID STORY OF BRITISH HEROISM

The net results of the operations in this quarter on this day were that, not only had our original gain of ground been maintained against repeated counter-attacks, but that further progress had been made by us at some points, notably to the north-west of the village, and that we had captured over 600 more prisoners. By nightfall the German dead lay thick all along our front. Opposite the sector south of the village, there were more than 2,000 bodies, and in front of one battalion east of the village were stretched 500 more.

Prisoners who had been all through the war stated that they had never experienced such a bombardment as that which preluded the assault on Neuve Chapelle . . . One wounded Prussian officer of a particularly offensive and truculent type, which is not uncommon, expressed the greatest contempt for our methods. "You do not fight. You murder," he said . . . In spite of the exhaustion of many of them, their aspect on the whole said a great deal for the discipline and order prevailing in the enemy's ranks . . . They are almost universally optimistic as regards the situation. The idea prevalent still is that the Germans are going to finish with Russia first—which will not take long—and then with the whole of their forces will undertake the easy task of crushing France and Britain.

Johnny Merritt reread the whole story, frowning, tapping his front teeth with his pencil. His father would have read this, or something like it, in *The New York Times*, so there was no point in summarising it; but was it all true? Yesterday, just before noon, he'd been talking to one of the men putting in the roof windows at the plant. As he stood there on the roof, a wet March wind blowing and drops of rain slashing his face, the man had looked up from his work, and shouted against the wind, "Looks like the generals killed off another few thousand of our men, Mr Merritt." Johnny had knelt, asking, "What do you mean?"

"My son came home on leave yesterday. He was through a battle out there, a place called Noove Chapel, it was. Horrible mess up, he says it was. No one got anywhere—just a lot of dead."

"He wasn't wounded?" Johnny had asked.

The man shook his head. "He wasn't . . . no thanks to the generals, he says. But we'll read about a great victory in the papers, he says, you wait and see."

Johnny frowned at the paper, on which he was making notes for his fortnightly letter to his father. If the British were systematically lying about the situation at the Front, who knew what might really be happening? But perhaps the workman's son had been overwrought . . . a private soldier was in no position to see the whole of a battle, and was lucky to understand even what little happened right in front of and round him.

How to find out the truth?

Be there yourself, he answered himself. There's no other way . . . But even there, would he know? And what could he do with his knowledge, if letters were censored?

He made a note: Dad must be told that there was at least some doubt about the full truthfulness of British official communiqués.

He continued working: the main danger to be foreseen for war production was increasing truculence of the unions, as the war made further inroads into their membership, and as more and more productivity was demanded, at the expense of all unions' hard-won restrictive practises. In that quarter, much was wrong in Britain, and it would get worse.

As regards Hedlington, there had been a further influx of Engineering Union organisers, but they were handicapped as far as the J.M.C. went by the company's policy of training women. Until the unions recognised women and other unskilled labour as suitable candidates for union membership, rather than as 'dilution,' they couldn't do much in a plant employing such a high proportion of women as J.M.C. proposed to do.

Financial position . . . he leaned back, picked up the telephone and asked the operator for Isaac Toledano's private number at the bank in Moorgate. Toledano's had put up forty percent of the capital for the J.M.C., and Johnny kept in close touch with one of Isaac's assistants over the company's progress; but he talked regularly with old Isaac himself over the general state of the British economy; and Isaac seemed happy to spend the time . . . perhaps because he was who he was, son of the chairman of the board of Fairfax, Gottlieb.

At the end of the talk he thanked Mr Toledano, and noted: general financial position, still very sound; increasing sales of property in America certain, bringing pressure on sterling—but not serious yet.

He glanced at his watch and picked up the telephone again. "Will you get me Walstone 1, please?" He waited, making circles on the paper . . . perhaps he ought to tell Dad that the British ate kidneys for breakfast . . . but he knew that already. "Hullo, Mr Cate? This is Johnny . . . Johnny Merritt. Could I speak to Stella, please?"

The tinny voice at the other end answered, "Is it about your coming down tomorrow, Johnny?"

"Yes, sir. I wanted to ask her if I should bring riding clothes."

"She was just going to call you, Johnny. She says she has to work all weekend on her nursing manual . . . just to be an assistant, you

know, not a real nurse . . . so you'd better not come down. Next weekend, perhaps, eh?"

Johnny hung up. She was working too hard. She didn't have to be a
nurse. There were other things a young lady could do to help the war
effort that didn't involve so much studying and concentration . . . and
weren't so messy. But she was patriotic, and determined to do her bit
. . . and more. He felt warm again, thinking of her.

He glanced at his watch again. Time to go to the factory for the ceremony. He started for the door, then came back, took his newly acquired
trench coat out of the wardrobe, and set off once more, hurrying. It
would not do to be late when the presence of Earl Kitchener of Khar-
toum was hoped for, though not definitely promised.

It was raining in North Hedlington. It often rained in North Hedlington, Johnny thought, when it was raining nowhere else in Kent, perhaps nowhere else in England. The rain was not hard, but it was cold,
and the sky was obscured by drifting grey clouds, hanging so low that
the outline of the Downs faded into them to east and west, and the
smoke from a steam engine chuffing up to Hedlington hung in a dense
white trail along the railway.

The Hedlington Town Band played *Onward Christian Soldiers*,
mostly in tune, and very loud, to keep themselves warm. It was not a
very appropriate choice, Johnny thought, huddling deeper into his
trench coat. He and Richard Rowland, and Overfeld and Morgan, the
factory foreman, waited on a little dais erected to one side of the entrance to the main assembly shop, with Mr Reeves, the Mayor of
Hedlington, and a few other local dignitaries. A coloured ribbon had
been tied across the high doors, and a Union Jack flanked them on one
side, a Stars and Stripes on the other. The factory whistle had just
blown, and the men and women were streaming out of the various
shops, bareheaded, to gather opposite the dais. Everyone waited. The
rain fell. The band played *Tipperary*.

A large black saloon car swept in through the outer gates, a rain-
drenched inspector of the Hedlington police on the running board. It
stopped near the dais, and Richard Rowland and the Mayor hurriedly
jumped down. They reached the side of the car as the unmistakable
figure of the Secretary of War, Field Marshal Lord Kitchener, climbed
out, uncoiled himself, and stood to his full imposing height. The mayor
bowed and said something which Johnny could not hear; Richard did
the same. The field marshal's piercing eyes roved over the throng of
workers, rested a moment on Johnny's face, moved on. He started forward, not having said a word as far as Johnny could tell.

At the front of the dais, everyone standing, but Kitchener a pace ahead and a head above, he stared down at the workers. The rain darkened his tunic and the rows of medal ribbons, and glistened on his sweeping black moustache. Johnny felt he should take off his trench coat, as Kitchener was not deigning to wear one.

Kitchener spoke, in a loud, gruff voice, in brief verbal explosions, like shells—"This war will go on for three years . . . we will win . . . only if we give all that we have . . . do all that we can . . . brain and muscle as well as blood." He turned suddenly to Richard. "What do you do here? Asquith didn't tell me . . . just wanted me to say a few words on my way to Dover . . . What's that American flag doing here?"

"Er . . . make lorries, sir . . . American capital, mostly, and engines . . . our first lorry is coming out of the factory today."

Kitchener turned back to the workers. "Work hard . . . We need guns, shells, lorries, aeroplanes . . . no engine of war we don't need . . . for victory . . . for our lives . . . the army will be seventy divisions strong by next summer . . . Think of it." He turned to Richard again. "That's all. Let's see it."

Richard signalled but Morgan had already vanished and was inside the shop. Slowly the great doors were pushed open from inside. The band, which had been silent while K spoke, broke into *Green Grow the Rushes O*, the regimental march of the Weald Light Infantry. The coloured ribbon snapped, and the snout of the first J.M.C. 30 cwt lorry appeared. Tommy Japes from the paint shop was at the wheel, and a pretty young woman from upholstery, wearing trousered overalls, sat beside him. The lorry ground on out in low gear. It had been painted a sandy khaki, for it was the first of an order of a hundred from the War Office, for the army defending the Suez Canal. The colour, or the destination, sparked a sudden interest in the field marshal, once Sirdar of Egypt, and he raised one arm, shouting, "Three cheers . . . *Hip Hip* . . ." Then all the workers and watchers and notables joined in heartily. The factory whistle blew and blew, and everyone shouted himself hoarse.

Kitchener stepped down from the dais with a nod for Richard and another for the mayor and climbed back into his car, and drove off. The factory whistle blew again, and the men and women returned to work. The mayor and dignitaries left. Johnny stood finally in the rain, alone with Richard Rowland. "The field marshal is not a fluent speaker," Richard said.

Johnny said, "No. But I feel that we've been in the presence of a great man. And it's a great day. One lorry isn't much, but it's the first of a long line, that'll help to win the war."

"And the peace," Richard said. "Don't forget that, though it's sometimes hard to remember what peace is—or was—or will be. Come on, Johnny, let's have a little something to celebrate, in my office."

Walstone: Thursday, April 1, 1915

24 Probyn Gorse walked steadily along the Hedlington to Walstone road. His cottage was a mile ahead, on the right. The little piece of land it stood on belonged to him, given to his father by Squire Cate's father . . . about time, he thought, after they'd been paying rent on it for a thousand years, maybe. Then his leathery face wrinkled slightly as he thought, no Gorse paid rent, that anyone heard of . . . did some odd jobs at the Manor, gave the squire a rabbit or two, cured a pointer of the colic, other secret services, unacknowledged, such as what the Woman should be finishing on Stella now . . . yes: but rent, no.

He walked along the very side of the road, the Duke of Clarence limping close to heel. Walking there saved effort even in the old days, because you didn't have to move over for traps and carts; but nowadays it might save your life, too, the way these stinking motor cars tore round the corners, twenty, thirty miles an hour, he'd wager. A brown hump in the grass verge a hundred yards ahead caught his eye. The Duke had seen it, too, whined once, and was quiet. Probyn watched the object as he walked, but it did not move. After twenty paces he knew it was a hen pheasant. When he reached it, he picked it up and felt it gently with his strong subtle fingers. It had a broken breast bone and broken neck. It had been trodden, and would have laid eggs in a week. It was still warm and had certainly been killed by a motor car.

There was no traffic, the sun was low, and he had a rabbit in one side pocket, killed by the catapult in the other. The land to the left of the road belonged to the squire, leased out as part of one of his farms.

On the right, behind the hedge was Walstone Park land. From where he stood he could see the big house across the Scarrow, above the grass and scattered oaks of the Deer Park. He put the pheasant in the deep inside pocket of his jacket and went on.

. . . Other services: Miss Stella had not said who the man was—not that he or the Woman had asked her, that was none of their business: himself, he reckoned it was the older man who'd been at the barracks, the wounded officer, not the American. There might be another—she worked four days a week at the hospital in Hedlington now—but it was probably the officer. And probably her first man. The Woman would tell him, when he got home . . . Squire had no woman now, for Mrs Cate wasn't going to come back from Ireland. It was wrong for a man not to have a woman, a woman for everything—to cook and sew and make the fire and lie beside you in bed: but for a young man, especially the bed. Squire was fifty, but that counted as young, when it was women you were thinking of . . .

The two men came out of the lane on the right and turned toward him. They were wearing heather mixture suits and matching caps, and each carried a double-barrelled twelve bore under the right arm, and a canvas and leather bag slung diagonally over the right shoulder: Swanwick's gamekeepers—Skagg and young Dan. Probyn didn't change his even pace, but they stopped. As he came up, Skagg said, "Hold hard, Probyn."

Probyn strode on, but Skagg put a heavy hand on his shoulder and Dan eased the gun out from under his arm into firing position. Probyn knew it would not be loaded; but he stopped. They were two against one, and this time he had done nothing against their laws.

"Let's have a look in those pockets of yours," Skagg said. He slid his hand down Probyn's coat and pulled out first the rabbit, then the pheasant. "Oho!" he cried. "Where did you get these? Buy them at Hedlington Market?"

"Killed the rabbit on the railway embankment with my catapult. Found the pheasant dead in the road, two, three hundred yards back . . . the public road, Skagg."

"You're a liar, Probyn. And now we've got you, red-handed. You come along with me." He gripped Probyn's shoulder, and forced him forward.

"Go home, Duke," Probyn said quietly to the growling lurcher. The Duke slipped through the hedge and vanished. Probyn said, "You got no right to do this, Skagg."

"You come along and we'll have a word with Mr Vickers about that.

Or likely His Lordship will be pleased to see you in person. His Lordship has always had such a high regard for you, Probyn Gorse. You'll be able to tell him what you were doing on his land." He looked at Dan across Probyn, and said, "About a hundred yards in from the road, warn't he, Dan?"

Dan looked uncomfortable, but said, "That's right."

"And we had to show him the guns before he pulled the bird and the rabbit out of his pocket, right?"

"That's right," Dan said again.

Probyn said nothing. Not even Skagg would be fool enough to grab him on the King's highway unless he intended to doctor the truth. It was going to be two against one, and that one, himself, Probyn Gorse, the poacher.

They turned off the road, walked up a muddy lane and over the Old Bridge, Probyn between the two keepers, Skagg swinging pheasant and rabbit in one hand. No one said a word, until as they were passing the great front entrance of the big house, the door opened and Lord Swanwick hurried down the ornamental stairway, two steps at a time. He was wearing a hacking jacket, cavalry twill breeches, and riding boots. In his right hand he waved a bone-handled crop, the end shaped into a miniature fox's mask. His head was bare, his cheeks suffused a reddish purple, his greying hair blowing in the wind. He stopped in front of the trio and shook the crop in Probyn's face, shouting, "So we've got you again, eh? You scoundrel! You unmitigated scoundrel!"

Probyn said, "I done nothing wrong, my lord."

Skagg said importantly, "We apprehended him at the edge of Fuller's Spinney, my lord. At first he refused to show us what was in his coat, but when we repeated our request he produced these—" he held up the pheasant and rabbit.

"Give the rabbit to Mrs Rogers for the staff," Lord Swanwick said. "As for the pheasant, we've got you again, eh, Gorse? Assizes this time!"

Probyn had been quietly furious when the keepers seized him, but as time passed he realised that things might turn out well for him, if he played his cards right.

He said, "How am I supposed to have killed that bird, my lord? Shot it?"

Swanwick turned to Skagg. "You didn't find a gun?"

"No, my lord," Skagg said uncomfortably, "but . . ."

"Or hear a shot?" Probyn said, "and the bird still warm?"

"You hold your tongue!" Swanwick shouted. "Did he have a club?"

"We didn't see one, but he could have picked up a stick in the spinney and thrown it away when he saw us coming."

Probyn said, "Have a look at that bird's keel, my lord."

His Lordship glared at him, then at the keepers. Dan was looking at his boots. He wasn't a bad young fellow, Probyn thought; had to lie to save his job. Swanwick pulled some feathers out of the bird's breast, and felt with his fingers. His lips pursed.

Probyn said, "Could only have been done by a car, eh, my lord? Skagg's lying. I picked that bird up on the road, the public road. I killed the rabbit with my catapult on the railway embankment." He kept his eyes on Lord Swanwick. He was not a lawyer, but he knew the game laws better than most lawyers. He had learned a lot in fifty years of brushes with them. Game belonged to the owner of the land where it lived when it was alive, if it was killed on that land. If it were killed by some accident and fell on a public road, it belonged to whoever found it. The rabbit—well, the South Eastern & Chatham Railway could accuse him of poaching, with reason—if they could prove he had killed it on their land; but Swanwick couldn't.

Swanwick was tapping his boot with his crop. His lips were tight and his eyes bolting. He hurled the pheasant to the ground and stamped on it, shouting, "You don't seem to learn anything from gaol, do you? Suppose you found yourself in my woods with a broken nose and two black eyes, Gorse, how would you like that?"

"I wouldn't like it at all, your lordship . . . and nor would whoever done it, when I'd gone to law."

"Get off my land!" Swanwick shouted, "and . . . this is the last time I'll warn you, stay off!"

"I was dragged on, your lordship, against my will."

"Get off!" the earl screamed, striking the air over Probyn's head viciously with his crop.

Probyn wondered whether it would be wise to ask for his pheasant and rabbit back. It probably wasn't, he concluded, but if he didn't try, his case might not be as good in law. He said, "I'd like my pheasant and rabbit back, my lord."

But the earl had turned his back, obviously not trusting himself any further, and was stalking back up the steps toward the great front door.

Skagg said, "You'd better go, Probyn."

"Very well, Skagg," Probyn said. "I'll go now, but remember, you stole my rabbit and my pheasant, you assaulted me on the public road and dragged me up here, and then you lied. You'll hear more of this soon's I have a chance to talk to squire—you *and* Dan *and* His Lordship."

The Woman washed her hands in the basin of hot water, carefully scrubbing fingers and nails with soap and a scrubbing brush. Behind her she heard Florinda talking in a low voice to Stella. "There, take off your dress . . . drawers . . . I'll spread a blanket over the top so's you won't catch cold . . . Don't worry, miss. She's done this a hundred times if she's done it once."

Stella's voice was small—"Will it hurt much?"

"Just a bit . . . pass water now . . . piss—do it in the doorway . . . Lie down now, on the table. Knees up and wide apart as you can get them. The table's not very big, I know, but you won't fall off."

The Woman came forward with a cloth and gave it to her. "Clean yourself off carefully . . . your cunt. This is soapy water. Don't mind the water running down, we'll clean it all up after."

Stella felt tears of embarrassment coming, but gritted her teeth and, staring at the ceiling, carefully cleaned her vulva and vagina. That she was here was her own fault, because she had sought excitement. She ought to swear that it would never happen again: but it had happened, and she remembered, and could not swear such an oath, for she knew that at some times she was not her own mistress—with men, with fire, with danger. Lying in this exposed and humiliating position, she thought suddenly that marriage, for her, might not be a much-to-be-desired goal or fulfilment, but a necessity, a place of guarded safety. She looked up, fearful. Florinda was smiling at her. Her hair, and the Woman's, were tied up in big kerchiefs.

"I've washed myself," she said.

The Woman came forward, a stiff rubber tube in her hand. Stella closed her eyes and found Florinda's hand in her own. She gripped it hard as she felt the catheter slide into her. Before she had closed her eyes she had seen the pot full of soapy water, and the funnel . . . A pang shot through her from the lips of her vulva deep up inside. "Still!" the Woman said sharply. Florinda's grip returned hers. The pain increased, and she felt the soapy water passing into her, very slowly. She began to count, to balance the piercing pains . . . one two three . . . seven eight nine . . . thirty-three thirty-four thirty-five . . . seventy-six seventy-seven . . . a hundred.

"That's enough," the Woman said, as to herself. Stella felt the tube slowly withdrawn from her vagina. The sharp pains became a heavy ache, and suddenly her vulva and lower pubic hair were soaking wet. The Woman was mopping her with a warm wet cloth. The lamp was lit, though it was still daylight outside. Shadows danced across the cob-webbed ceiling beams.

Florinda gently disengaged her hand and went toward the sink.

Stella, eyes open now, watched as she washed out a cloth, rewet it, and bringing a bucket and brush began to wash something off the table from under Stella's buttocks into the bucket.

Stella said, "What was it . . . going to be?"

The Woman said curtly, "Can't tell, so soon. Lie still. It's over. Keep her clean, Florinda. She'll bleed more yet." She moved back to the stove and pushed a kettle onto the centre of the fire. Florinda went out with the bucket, returning in a few minutes to stand again beside Stella. She said, "You brought the sanitary towels?"

Stella nodded.

"She'll make you a cup of tea soon. You rest here for half an hour, while I go and tell your dad you've been taken poorly while you were down the village and he'll come to get you, or send Norton for you. But before you go, put on a towel. You'll be bleeding for a few days, but less than a period. If it's more than that, get your dad to call the doctor."

"That won't happen," the Woman said.

"It might," Florinda said, "but the bad bit's over. I'll be off now." She went out.

The Woman sat down on a stool, her face showing strain for the first time Stella ever remembered. She said, "Sometimes a woman dies, sudden like, when the soapy water's going in . . . My granny told me it was because the water got into a vein. That's why you mustn't pour in too much, or fast . . . Sometimes they bleed to death, here, or after they get home . . . nearly happened to one of mine, once. Only once . . . But if there's trouble, it's mostly later, and I know what does that —dirt, getting in there." She nodded at Stella's exposed and blood-stained vulva. "I'll make the tea now. Don't try to sit up yet. And don't cry. You'll have another."

It was nearly dark when Probyn got home. Fletcher was on the floor on his belly, reading a leather-bound book that Probyn remembered he had borrowed from the squire's library, his brows furrowed and his eyes squinting in the feeble light of the single lantern. The Woman was at the stove, Florinda sitting on a stool, pert and pretty in her black lady's maid dress, with heeled shoes that must have been at least two inches high.

Fletcher looked up. "Nothing, Granddad?"

Probyn sat down in the chair at the table. "Got a rabbit and a pheasant—found her dead in the road—but Skagg took me to the big house and Swanwick kept them."

"That's not right, is it?"

"No, it ain't . . . I'll be going to see squire tomorrow. What's to eat?"

"Cabbage, potatoes, beans . . . no meat today. None tomorrow, neither," the Woman said.

"Perhaps I'll go to squire this evening. We might get the pheasant and rabbit back tomorrow, in time for dinner. Or money, if they've eaten 'em themselves. Did Stella come?"

The Woman said, "Yes. She was about two months gone, a bit more. Florinda helped. Norton came down in the trap not twenty minutes ago to take her home . . . Florinda told them she'd been taken poorly in the village."

"She bled a bit," Florinda said; then switching to her upper class accent, "But she never made a sound. *Noblesse oblige*, you know. And afterwards, she held my hand and thanked me positively with tears in her eyes. She knew she could rely on me to keep her unhappy secret, she said. It would kill her father, if he knew."

"Squire not to home?"

"Norton said he didn't know where he was—visiting one of the farms, most like."

"What are you doing here, anyway?" Probyn growled, "it's not your afternoon off."

"Her Ladyship pressed me to take a day of rest and relaxation away from the artificial atmosphere of the Park. Why don't you spend the day—and the night—with your dear father, and his good lady. Do give him my regards. And His Lordship's, of course."

"Shut your trap!" He looked straight at his granddaughter. She looked like a . . . witch, in black—black dress, black silk stockings, black shoes. There was a gleam in her eyes which he knew meant something —something important.

"Out with it," he said. "What's happened?"

"She won't tell," Fletcher said from the floor. "I knew as soon as I come home—I been doing some hedging at High Staining—but she wouldn't tell. Waiting for you to come home, maybe."

"What is it?" Probyn said.

Florinda turned to the Woman. "Bert got the sack from Rowland's . . . afore the other lot are ready to hire him. He's raging, but can't do anything about it."

"You're going to get a thick ear if . . ."

"And Mother's working as a charwoman now. Cleans up pubs before they open."

"What does she do with the kids while she's at work?" Fletcher asked.

"Violet's eleven," Florinda said, "she can look after the little 'uns. And there's a woman next door who's home most of the time."

Probyn said, "I'll give you what for in a minute. What is it?"

"Cantley came down today," she said, negligently looking at her finger nails.

Probyn looked at her, puzzled for a moment. Then he began to get the idea. "And he's spending the night?" he said.

"Tonight and tomorrow."

"And Lady S doesn't want you in the house, eh?"

Florinda nodded. "But she's too late . . . I told you it wasn't a servant, didn't I?"

"Cantley," Probyn said, considering. "You could do worse."

"I'm leaving her Ladyship's service next Monday. Going to London. Cantley has a flat for me in Chelsea. I'll send you money."

Probyn nodded and called to the Woman, "Is that stew ready yet, Woman?"

"No," she said, "you don't want indigestion, do you?"

About an hour after Probyn had finished eating the vegetable stew, and he was dozing in his chair by the table, Florinda on a stool, Fletcher on the floor, and the Woman cleaning the surface of the stove, Probyn opened his eyes, listening. The wind had died down and he heard the footsteps clearly in the grass. The dog outside did not bark but Fletcher had heard too, and looked up from his book: and it was he who said in a low voice, "'Tis squire," and got up with a single lithe animal movement, as sinuous as some giant ferret's, went to the door, and opened it, revealing Christopher Cate, his hand raised to knock.

"'Evening, Mr Cate," Fletcher said pleasantly. "Come in."

Cate went in, blinking, for it was very dark outside. Even the single lantern burned strong against his widened pupils—wide from walking down in the moonlight, across the fields from the Manor.

Fletcher threw some rabbit skins off a chair in the corner and pulled it up, while Florinda smiled at Cate, without speaking, and the Woman did not even turn round or give any formal greeting. Cate was a frequent visitor to Probyn's cottage, and had been all his life, but he did not often come at such an hour as this.

Cate said, "It was good of you to come and get Norton, for Stella, Florinda. I'm sorry I was not there."

Florinda smiled, "How is she? I think 'twas just woman's curse."

Cate looked anxious. "D'ye think I should ask Mrs Abell to see if . . . she's all right? Or Doctor Kimball? Without her mother, it's . . ." his voice trailed into silence.

Florinda said, "Was she sleeping sound when you left?"

Cate nodded: and the Woman flung over her shoulder, "Let her be, squire. She'll be fine in the morning . . . better still in three or four days."

Cate sighed with relief, and after a while said, "Laurence will be pestering you to take him out when he comes home from school, Probyn."

"He'll take me, more like," Probyn said. "He knows all the birds by their nicknames, like, as well as the Latin ones. Makes my head swim."

"He wrote that he's practising the songs and calls you were teaching him. Some of the bloods—those are the big boys—bully him for it, I'm afraid."

"Aye, I suppose they would . . . Florinda here's better than I am at the calls. Show squire."

Florinda put her hands to her mouth, and in succession imitated the trill of a blackbird as it scurries along a hedge, the crake of a pheasant, and the scream of a falcon.

Fletcher said, "This here's a wonderful book, squire. I don't understand everything in it but, you know what I said before, I understand here—" he tapped his head "—without the words going in the right way."

"What book's that?" Cate asked. Fletcher handed it to him and Cate glanced at the spine and said, "*The Collected Works of John Milton* . . . That's not the easiest English in the world to understand, Fletcher, but it's great, I agree. Are you reading *Paradise Lost?*"

Fletcher said, "I finished it yesterday. Just now I was reading the bit again where there's war in heaven and Satan gets thrown down with all his troops . . . The words there is the best in the whole book, but I can't feel 'em proper. Because I never seen a war, maybe."

"Nor have I. We're lucky, I think . . . My brother's been killed. He was in the Rifle Brigade."

"Major Oswald?"

"You remember him? He hasn't visited us for three years . . . died of wounds received at Neuve Chapelle, three days ago. We've just heard the news from Charlotte, his wife . . . widow."

No one spoke for several minutes, Cate staring into the little flames leaping and crawling in the fireplace. It was not an awkward silence, for Cate knew that it served these people instead of formal condolences, which did not come naturally to their lips.

Fletcher broke it by saying, "I want to go to the war, but I don't want to fight. Unless I go, I won't feel this poetry, and if I fight, I won't be able to write my own, see?"

"I think you would," Cate said. "After Milton, you should try something more modern. I'll lend you Walt Whitman next—an American poet who is at the other end of the spectrum from Milton in one way, very similar to him in another . . . Probyn, Lord Swanwick has telephoned me about some trouble you are having with him—about a pheasant and a rabbit."

"Got the rabbit off the railway. Found the pheasant dead in the road —killed by a motor car. Then Skagg and Dan came along, and grabbed me, and took me up to the Big House, and told Swanwick they'd caught me at Fuller's Spinney."

"They lied to Lord Swanwick, then!" Cate exclaimed.

Probyn nodded, and said, "I made Swanwick feel her keel. He knew they were lying then, but he started yelling at me, and jumping on the pheasant. Would have liked to murder Skagg, I reckon, but couldn't do that, so let out at me."

"He didn't hit you himself, did he?"

"Took a swipe at me with his crop, he did, right in front of the Big House. Half a dozen maids and footmen and such must have been watching through the windows, the noise he was making, bellowing like a bull . . . but they won't say they seen anything. More than their job's worth. He threatened me, too. He . . ."

"Who?"

"Swanwick . . . with having Skagg and Dan bust my nose and give me black eyes, back in the woods, if they saw me again. I'll have the law on them."

Cate sighed, and said, "Lord Swanwick has a hot temper, I'm afraid . . . He has his troubles, too, you know. That arm hurts him much of the time. I believe—though this is really private between us here—that his financial position is not all it might be . . . and Mr Arthur is in France now."

"He's stole my rabbit and pheasant."

"Er, well, as to that, he is willing to send them back to you here, tomorrow morning."

"Skagg and Dan grabbed me, they did. That's assault, squire."

Cate spread his hands. "I know it is, Probyn, and if you insist, I'll see that your charge is properly laid, and that you get a lawyer . . . but believe me, it's best not to go to court for anything, anything at all, unless you have to. You may come before the magistrates again sometime, you know, and they'll remember that you sued Lord Swanwick. They'll try not to let it influence them, but I'm afraid that it will. You're going to get your rabbit and pheasant back, and a pound note, I think. Lord

Swanwick knows his keepers were in the wrong. This is his way of apologising."

Probyn stared into the fire. It was obvious that Swanwick had been advised, probably by Vickers the agent, that he was in the wrong; and that if he, Probyn, sued, he'd have to pay a big fine. It would be nice to keep him hooked, and eventually land him, and have everyone in Kent know that the Earl of Swanwick had had to pay Probyn Gorse twenty pounds, maybe fifty, for assault. That would be good money, too. It was tempting—tempting as the single pheasant that passed down the ride, feeding, when you were stalking half a dozen.

He said, "All right, squire . . . 'Tis wrong, but for your sake, I'll take it."

"Good man!" Cate said, jumping up from the chair and clapping Probyn on the back. "Now, I ought to be going . . . Are you all right? Need any food?"

"Nothing, squire," the Woman said.

Probyn stayed in his chair, staring into the fire, thinking. It was wrong that squire should have no woman. He could tell that he needed one . . . to talk to perhaps, to lose his temper with, cry with—the way squire could not before anyone else. He was a good man, was Christopher Cate.

Without looking up, he said, "Florinda, go back with squire and fetch that book he's going to be lending Fletcher."

After a momentary hesitation, Cate said, "Very well, Probyn," Florinda got up and, Cate holding the door open for her, went out with him, wrapping a shawl about her shoulders as she went. When they had been gone a few minutes, the Woman said, "What if she gets like Stella?"

"She knows better," Probyn said shortly. "And if she does, and wants to keep it, she can say it's Cantley's . . . It's happened afore with Cates and Gorses, since they first came here and that was a while ago, Woman."

His thoughts wandered. Florinda would do what she would do, and so would squire. But the war with Swanwick had been declared, and must be waged to a finish, getting him fined was not enough, not after they'd killed his old dog, and sent him to prison, and now this. His Mighty Lordship must suffer a defeat—the sort of defeat that made a man hang his head the rest of his life, the kind that, after it, a man couldn't look you in the eye. The war had to be fought on the chosen ground: Swanwick's pheasants—and against him, not just his keepers or servants, though they would all share in the defeat. It had to be big, bigger than he could manage by himself. He would be the general, and

he'd need, what did they call 'em?—staff officers? People helping, thinking . . . and he'd need more soldiers. Young Guy Rowland had come
round at Christmas, hinting he'd like to help, but then he, Probyn,
hadn't been ready. Now he was. When Guy came again he'd tell him
everything he had in mind, straight out; others, he could keep mostly
in the dark, telling 'em just what they had to know, and that not in
black and white; but with that young fellow, he'd do best to tell all—in
fact, to make him his right hand man.

It would take time. April Fool's Day today . . . It would be a big occasion, this shaming of Swanwick, so it ought to happen on a big occasion. What was the biggest occasion of the year, any year? What did
you remember, every year? Why, Christmas. Also, even gamekeepers
had other things than poachers on their minds at that season, both day
and night. Christmas Day, 1915, it would be then. He got up abruptly
and headed for the bedroom.

She sat quiet in the big chair, her hands folded demurely in her black
satin lap. All the lights were off except one, in a far corner over a music
stand; but Cate was not there, he was standing close to her, facing the
dark windows of the music room, the bow sweeping across the violin in
the second movement of the *Kreutzer Sonata*. He had told her that was
what he would play. She would remember the name, and the music: it
was the kind of thing she must know, once she was in London as Lord
Cantley's mistress. She would know, and learn, faster than they could
teach.

They had been halfway to the Manor, walking side by side across a
dark field, when he had said gently to her, "Would you come to my
bed, Florinda?"

"You want me to?" She was not surprised. For years now, men had
looked at her a certain way, spoken with a certain strange tightness in
their voice, and when it moved her to give them what they wanted, she
did; if not, not.

"Yes," he had answered, "but it is loneliness—and lust, I suppose.
You have grown into a very lovely woman."

She had respected Cate all her life, not because he was squire of
Walstone, but because he was a gentle man, and a gentleman, and had
never done any mean thing to her, or her family. It would please her to
go to him; so she answered, "I would come." She thought a tear glistened in his eye.

He said, "I will ask you, then. I am lonely, Florinda. And hungry."

"I know . . . I knew."

At the Manor she had waited a few minutes in the garden while he went in through the front door, and a little later opened the French windows of the music room to let her in. Now the book for Fletcher was in her lap, for he had got that almost first thing: then he had poured himself a brandy and soda and given her a glass of wine; and, finally he had taken his violin and, all the lights out except that one, the French windows open, the curtains drawn back so that they looked out on the pale green of the lawn, lit by a moon a day past full, he had said, very formally, "The *Kreutzer Sonata*, by Beethoven . . . for you, Florinda."

Then he began. She had heard him before, for sometimes he and her grandfather played together at the village fête—squire the violin and Probyn a battered fife he said he had learned to play in the army (but that was the only time he ever said he had been in the army) She did not know whether Cate was a good violinist, but she thought he could not be bad, because the sound seemed pure to her, and sweet. He was completely absorbed, his chin tucked under his head on the soft red wood of the instrument.

The fields smelled green and cool, and the sky seemed only a giant alcove for the moon. A fox barked distantly in the Home Copse, and she felt her body soften, and relax, preparing to share with Cate a wonder as magical as this, that he was sharing with her.

From far off, she wondered whether Miss Stella would come down. She must be used to hearing her father play at night—it was the only time he had free for it, what with the troubles of his farms and other affairs of the village always on his mind . . . but she might come down for comfort. And what would she think if she did come? She had been silly, trusting a silly man, but Florinda thought she'd understand the truth here. She was a Cate, and Cates and Gorses had always understood each other, through the necessities of the land they shared.

Eventually, time passing without her regarding it, Cate put away violin and bow and turned out the light. Florinda followed him quietly upstairs.

When she reached the cottage again, about three in the morning, a cold wind had sprung up, rustling the boughs and whipping the moon-silvered Scarrow. A hunting barn owl swooped low overhead as she went in, closing the door behind her. Fletcher moved over in the bed when she got in, wearing petticoat and bodice, having taken off the black dress, shoes, and stockings. He said nothing but patted her sleepily on the shoulder, and then they both slept soundly, back to back, until morning.

Daily Telegraph, Saturday, April 3, 1915

OFFENCES AGAINST HUMANITY

Foreign Office, April 1, 1915   The Secretary of State for Foreign Affairs presents his compliments to the United States Ambassador, and with reference to His Excellency's Note of the 20th ultimo respecting reports in the Press upon the treatment of prisoners from German submarines, has the honour to state that he learns from the Lords Commissioners of the Admiralty that the officers and men who were rescued from the German submarines U-8 and U-12 have been placed in the Naval Detention Barracks in view of the necessity of their segregation from other prisoners of war.

In these quarters they are treated with humanity, given opportunities for exercise, provided with German books, subjected to no forced labour, and are better fed and clothed than British prisoners of equal rank now in Germany.

As, however, the crews of the two German submarines in question, before they were rescued from the sea, were engaged in sinking innocent British and neutral merchant ships, and wantonly killing non-combatants, they cannot be regarded as honourable opponents, but rather as persons who at the orders of their Government have committed acts which are offences against the law of nations and contrary to common humanity.

His Majesty's Government would also bring to the notice of the United States Government that during the present war more than 1,000 officers and men of the German navy have been rescued from the sea, sometimes in spite of danger to the rescuers, and sometimes to the prejudice of British naval operations. No case has, however, occurred of any officer or man of the Royal Navy being rescued by the Germans.

"Scoundrels!" Harry Rowland said, pointing at the item. "They ought to be shot out of hand."

"Now don't get so excited," his wife said. "It's bad for your blood pressure."

Cate got up and helped himself to a pair of kippers from the sideboard. He enjoyed having his father- and mother-in-law coming down for a day or two: "A weekend in the country," Harry always said, "fresh air, green grass . . . not as green as Devonshire when I was a lad, mind!" The old man looked worried when he thought no one's eyes were on him: that would be the problems at Rowland's, Cate thought, as Richard and Johnny Merritt had explained to him. You thought Rose was looking better, until you realised how much rouge she had put on her thin cheeks.

"Don't you agree?" Harry said, turning to the room at large.

"Yes," Laurence said quickly. "Beasts, that's what they are."

"And you, Christopher?"

Cate kept his head down and spoke slowly, "They're the weaker power at sea. The reason they haven't rescued anyone is that they can't, without being sunk themselves. Think of that U-boat which sank our three cruisers. How could he come to the surface, and start rescue operations, with the sea full of other British ships—even if he could get more than a dozen men on board?"

"But . . . but . . . this sinking of innocent merchant ships without warning . . . that's inhuman, barbarous. It's just as the Kaiser said, they're Huns. He actually boasted of it!"

Cate said, "We've got to beat them, and we will . . . but we should try to understand their position, if only so that we can better counter it . . . They are starting what is in effect a submarine blockade. As the submarines can't come up and check papers, they're just sinking all merchant ships in areas round our coasts, meaning to starve us into submission . . . just as we mean to do to them."

Harry grumbled, "Swine!"

Laurence said, "They'll sink an American ship one day . . . and then the Yankees will come in on our side."

"I hope so," Cate said, "but I'm afraid that if that does happen it will be because it will be in America's best interests, not because the Germans are breaking the law of the sea—the existing laws . . . Father, Mother, would you care to come and look at the daffodils, while the dew's still on them?"

Flanders: Wednesday, April 21, 1915

"Dismiss!"

25 Captain Maclachlan stayed at the salute until the company had performed the Light Infantry dismiss drill, then slowly dropped his hand and walked away, his head bent. Boy Rowland followed for a few paces, then turned off down a side alley, his batman Private Frank Stratton at his heels. It had not been a bad spell in the line, as such spells went; three weeks, not much rain, and very little activity from the Boches—but it had been hard work, with every man labouring all day and part of the night to improve the trenches. In December, when he had arrived from India, the trenches had hardly existed. He had seen for himself that the ground over which the 1st Battle of Ypres had been fought was really open country, hill sections separating the valleys of the *beeks*; and that the 'trenches' were often little more than loosely linked shell holes, far more primitive than the sandbagged, revetted, and traversed trenches, complete with berms, parados, parapet, firesteps, and communication trenches, that were now being constructed in the Salient.

And now the 1st Battalion was back where it had been before it went up the line, back with the reserve brigade of the division, in Wieltje, a tiny hamlet on the Ypres-Poelcapelle road, three miles behind the front line. They were returning to the same billets, vacated yesterday evening by the battalion which had last night replaced them in the line. It was their third return to Wieltje since they first came in January. They knew each other—the few old Belgian farmers, shopkeepers, and women remaining in this corner of their country; and the

1st Battalion of the Weald Light Infantry, by number a regular battalion, but no longer manned by regular officers and men.

Boy looked at his watch. He'd just get rid of his pack, greatcoat, and blanket and then go round his platoon's billets, and make sure that a meal was on its way . . . then some 'study for the Staff College,' more commonly known as shut-eye, or a nap.

He reached the door of the little house where he and Beldring had been billeted all three times, and raised his hand to knock. The door flew open and Mme Baret's shining face appeared. She was about thirty, he thought, rather short, with curly brown hair, strong arms and legs and a big bosom, but surprisingly slim at the waist and hips. She always wore the same clothes—a simple blouse, a blue or black skirt well below the knees, rolled cotton stockings, an apron and, outside the house, wooden clogs. She owned a little patch of land behind the village where she grew vegetables; and in the backyard here she kept a few chickens. She was beaming now, her head downturned, so that she looked up at him from under her eyebrows, and her hands were at her skirt, holding it out, as she bobbed a curtsey. "*Ah, que le bon Dieu soit remercié,*" she cried, in a strong Flemish accent. "*Vous êtes revenu, sauf et sain!*"

Boy's French was fair—it was barely four years since he had left Wellington, where he had studied the language; and he had been in Flanders for over four months now. By the same token, she had had British troops billeted on her since October. She spoke quite a bit of English, and when Boy replied, "*Oui, madame, rien n'a passé. Un temps très ennuyant,*" she said, "Better is boring than exciting, *par là,* eh?" and held the door open for him to pass into the house. Boy looked at his muddy boots but before he could say anything she said, "Sit, Meester Boy, and I will take them off."

"I have to go, Mme Baret. Will you please take these to our room?" He slipped out of his pack and heavy equipment and laid them on the floor just inside the door. "Stratton, come back here after you've had a meal, and get everything clean and in good order—my revolver holster needs restitching, for one."

"I know, sir, I'll see to it."

Mme Baret said, " 'Ow long will you be? I 'ave a good dinner for you . . . special killing chicken." Her blue eyes were wide and anxious and after a moment's hesitation Boy said, "I'll be back in three quarters of an hour." He was supposed to be dining in the B Company officers' mess, in one of the schoolhouse's undamaged rooms; but Captain Maclachlan would excuse him, this time. He could not bear to disappoint Mme Baret.

He walked back up the street, meeting Beldring on the way. "You look like the cat which swallowed the bowl of cream," he said, for Beldring's expressive face clearly showed that he was in a high state of euphoria.

"Quite right, Boy," he said, beaming. "I've got four days' leave. I'm off now . . . hope nothing happens while I'm away . . . but Captain Mac doesn't think there's a chance. He's positive the Boches are going to spend this year trying to knock Russia out of the war and there will be nothing but holding actions on the Western Front."

"That means we'll be doing the attacking for a change," Boy said. "But not before you come back from leave. Sir John wouldn't dare."

Beldring shook his fist at him and hurried on to Mme Baret's where he shared a room with two narrow beds with Boy when they were in billets in Wieltje. Boy found his platoon sergeant, Knapp, who was billeted with half a dozen other men, including Frank Stratton, in the back of an *estaminet;* and together they satisfied themselves that every soldier of Boy Rowland's platoon was in his allotted billet, cleaning himself up ready for the dinner parade.

Frank Stratton sat in the yard in the watery sunshine, brushing mud off Boy Rowland's blanket. The smell of roasting chicken wafted by his nostrils would have made his mouth water an hour ago, but since then he had eaten a bowl of bully beef stew, in fact two, for the quarter blokes had wangled a double ration for the company—for the whole battalion, perhaps.

The kitchen window was straight in front of him, and through it he could see Mme Baret peering into pots, slicing vegetables with a huge knife, hurrying through to the little dining-room with dishes. Mr Charles would be eating well, soon . . . a dish flavored with love, he thought, grinning to himself. The Madame, as he always thought of her, was certainly sweet on him; the difference in her manner to him, and to Mr Beldring, was very noticeable. There wasn't anything the Madame wouldn't do for Mr Charles, in his opinion . . . *any*thing: but Mr Charles was too innocent to have seen. No, he wasn't innocent, he was a gentleman, and that was a fact. Frank wondered if he had ever been with a woman. Probably not, he thought.

The thought brought a picture of Anne to his mind and after a few moments more brushing he put down the blanket, found his wallet in the left breast pocket of his tunic and drew out the pictures of his wife, the two girls, and baby John. He sat a long time, looking at them. He loved them all. It was sad that he had to be here, but there was no other place for a proper Englishman these days. She must miss him as much as he missed her. She'd be lonely, there in Hedlington . . . of course, the children would keep her busy, and since he couldn't send home much money, though he saved all he could, she wouldn't be able to have the girl so often, if she could afford her at all. The King's uniform was the only coat for a self-respecting man to wear these days, but His Majesty certainly didn't put much money in the pockets. Still, other folks were giving up much more than he. Look at Mr Kellaway, O.C. 5 Platoon now—well into his thirties, and a millionaire several times over, by all accounts . . . no children, though. No women, either, just paintings and a big house in Berkeley Square, they said. Some of the blokes said he was a pouf. Well, maybe he was, but they shouldn't say things like that, unless he bothered them, and he was a good officer, even though he did speak sort of strange and always smelled of perfume.

For Anne's sake, shouldn't he find a safer billet, somewhere? Mr Charles kept telling him, he'd see that he was posted to the rear—that at his age he shouldn't have to live in the trenches with a lot of nineteen-year-olds. But he didn't want to go. He'd come here to kill Germans. Anything else, and he might just as well have stayed home—at least he'd have been able to cuddle up to Anne nights . . . But once, up in the line when he and Mr Charles spent an hour in the middle of the night with the sentries on the firestep, Mr Charles had said that he, Frank, ought to transfer to the R.E., or the R.F.C. even. He was wasted here, Mr Charles said—thinking of the water business. The water was carried in carts and then by hand all the way here from Ypres, and that took a lot of men, working all night when they might have been resting. Frank had worked out a way to have the water pumped from Ypres as far forward as the reserve battalions' lines, and Mr Charles had sent the idea to Battalion: and the Colonel had liked it and sent it up to Brigade. And a few days later, Mr Charles had read Frank the answer that had come down from on high: "Will Mr Rowland kindly remember that he is an infantry officer, not a plumber?" And that was when Mr Charles had told Frank he ought to transfer to the Sappers. But, Frank thought, I don't want to go. Maybe if Mr Charles went, he'd ask to go with him; but Mr Charles would stick with the battalion until he copped a packet or got a Blighty—and so would he.

He picked up the blanket, but it was clean now. So was everything else, except the greatcoat. Through the window he saw Boy Rowland poke his head round the door from the dining-room, and heard the Madame chirp something to him in French. He'd best tell Mr Charles he needed to take the greatcoat back to his own billet, to work on it and that everything else was done: then leave them to their roast chicken, with love.

Boy saw him through the window and a moment later came out of the back door, "Stratton, your brother's arrived with two other replacement officers."

"Fred, sir?"

"Yes. He's been posted to us . . . B Company. Captain Maclachlan's going to keep him at Company HQ until . . . he's needed. Take time off to go and see him."

"Thank you, sir. I will that, when I've done this."

Boy Rowland sprawled back in the parlour's only comfortable chair. At last he could relax. Stratton was on his way down the street, carrying his greatcoat. The platoon and their billets had been inspected; the men were fed and now were mostly sleeping. Later Sergeant Knapp would have a full equipment check to find out what equipment and clothing had been lost or damaged up the line, and would report to him in the evening. Mme Baret had taken off her apron and put a blue ribbon in her hair. On her feet were patent leather ankle boots, side-buttoned to the calf. He had never seen her in real shoes before—only bedroom slippers, and when she went out, the clogs over them.

Then she held open the door and formally said, *"Monsieur est servi."* The chicken was roasted to perfection, and she served with it a bottle of red wine, unlabelled but good, a loaf of new bread, new potatoes, and cabbage greens. At first she had stood behind him like a butler, as she did on the occasions when he and Beldring had asked her to cook their rations for them, rather than give them to the mess cook. But after a few minutes Boy put down his knife and fork and said, "I can't eat with you standing there, Madame. Please be so good as to sit here." He patted the chair to his left—"and join me. This chicken is excellent."

She sat, then, but never took her eyes off him, watching to guess what he needed, from the expression on his face, before he could say a word. Her bosom rose and fell evenly, but deeply, and from time to time a blush spread up from her neck across her face, causing her skin to glow for a minute, before it died away. They talked in desultory fashion. "Meester Beldring has gone on leave. He is lucky!"

"This bread is delicious. I thought the bakery had been destroyed by shell fire."

"I must 'ave another cock, to kill ze rat."

"May I pour you some more wine, madame?"

She drank liberally of the red wine, and when they had finished the first bottle, produced another. The flush on her face became permanent. There was no dessert. She said simply, "That is all, Meester Boy," stood up, and from behind his chair, leaned over, pressing her breasts into the back of his neck, her arms round him, reaching down toward his loins. She murmured in his ear, "Oh, Meester Boy, *je t'aime* . . . I love you . . . *je t'aime!*"

Boy sat appalled, stricken. Had he done anything to cause this, to lead her on? He had treated her with the strictest consideration, more so than Beldring, who had eyed her too freely once or twice . . . but her breasts were warm soft globs against him and in spite of himself he felt his manhood stirring. She had his hand now and was pulling. "Come up ze stairs, Meester Boy . . . to my room, *je t'aime, ah, wat ben ik toch gemeen, je t'aime!*"

He stood up with difficulty, turned round and took both her hands, resisting her pulling. "You're lonely, Madame. You love your husband. You have told me so many times."

"That is true, too! I don't know 'ow it can be . . . but 'e is not 'ere! I 'ave not 'eard from 'im for seex monce." Her English became more tangential as her excitement increased. She was not drunk, Boy thought, but the restraints that normally held her had definitely been loosened if not totally destroyed, partly by loneliness, partly by the wine.

He said, "Madame, I respect you. I respect you too much to touch you." As he spoke, his penis was throbbing in a powerful erection. He had never made love to a woman, and now was surely not the time, nor she the person: for she did not know what she was doing. He prayed that she would not notice the erection, for then heaven knew what she'd do.

She cried, "*Please*, Meester Boy . . . I *need* you!"

He wondered whether that could be true. Did men really need women, and women need men, as one needed water when one's body had been deprived of it? Or was it not more properly a lust that could be controlled and channelled to true love—love for someone with whom you had more to share than the ability to fornicate? And it was not only that such lusts *could* be controlled, they *must* be, if the standards by which decent people lived were to be upheld. What if Naomi, for instance, were to feel this need, and simply go and ask a man to satisfy her, as Madame Baret was now asking him? What would happen to society, to decency, to respect for women—and for men?

He said, "Madame Baret, I can not betray your husband."

"But 'e is dead! I know eet! Dead, blown to little bits, deesappear, so no one can say, 'ere is Caporal Baret, 'e is dead, we will tell 'is wife. 'E 'as gone!"

Boy said miserably, "I can not betray you, either. You have a good name here in Wieltje. You must not risk losing it. The war will be over soon, and we will all go back to England, but you will stay here. Wieltje is a small place. Everyone will know, always."

"Please, Meester Boy, oh please, please, please!"

She had noticed the erection now and her hands, tugged free, were stroking it through the trouser material. Boy broke free, hurried to the door, grabbed up his cap, and ran out into the street.

Boy sat in his uncle's billet, sipping from a glass of wine. Up the line the never-ending artillery fire continued, but it was slight now. Yesterday they had come out of the line; today they would rest; tomorrow would start the fatigues that made a spell in divisional reserve harder work than duty in the front line, where at least most of the work was necessary for self-preservation—such as trench improvement and sentry duty. The best place was forward reserve; there the men could not be scattered on fatigues, because they would be needed instantly in case of a German attack; nor were sentry duties so heavy, as the enemy could not get at them without passing through the front, second, and third lines. But back here, after the one day of rest, louse hunting, eating, and sleeping—it began: fifty men to carry sandbags up to the front; forty men for wiring in the brigade reserve area; twenty for carrying water; thirty to enlarge the Casualty Clearing Station a quarter of a mile across the fields in Wieltje Farm . . . and so on, and on, until the C.O. could barely count on a hundred men in hand out of the eight hundred he officially commanded.

Quentin said, "I had a letter from Guy yesterday. He came in third in the Big Kingsley. And now he's Rowland major. Some other Rowland's arrived, in the Murray . . . no relation, as far as I know. He'd also sent me a box of Bourbon biscuits, from Grubbies. And they actually arrived, by the same post!"

Boy said nothing, for any comment would have launched his uncle on a familiar tirade, about the base and rear-area scoundrels who stole parcels intended for troops in the front line: why, a Christmas pudding made for him last year by Mrs Abell at High Staining had never arrived, and . . . so on, and so on.

He wanted to ask his uncle how his Aunt Fiona was. He had always liked her, though she was strange sometimes, the way she looked at, or through you, as though she were miles away. But even before he went to Sandhurst he had realised that there was something wrong in the relationship between his uncle and aunt—they were nothing like his mother and father, to each other: so he kept quiet.

Quentin said, "I wonder if they've started in the Dardanelles yet."

"Nothing in the London papers, sir? It's three days old, isn't it?"

Quentin said, "Yes . . . I'm against it—the Dardanelles operation. This is the decisive front, and that's just a diversion—of men, guns, ammunition—which we need here. Especially the ammunition."

Boy said nothing. If the Dardanelles operation was a diversion, one might reasonably say the Russian Front was, too, yet it obviously wasn't.

Quentin said, "They should have done it with the navy alone, the first time they sailed up . . . in January, wasn't it? Just the navy and a few marines. We need all the soldiers we can get here." He put down the paper and said in a strange voice, "You know what I think, Boy?"

"No, sir," Boy said, wondering; his uncle looked conspiratorial, as though about to say something treasonable.

"I think we need conscription. Oh, I know it's never happened before. But there's never been a war like this before, for England. And it's going to get worse . . . bigger. People say we'll get men who'll make bad soldiers, men who don't want to fight, who aren't any good . . . but look what the navy had to do in the Napoleonic Wars! They press-ganged men out of the gaols, the pubs, the poorhouses, and made them the best sailors in the world . . . and some of them not even English!"

Unseen troops tramped by in the street, singing *Tipperary*. A loud voice interrupted the song—"We've had enough of that bloody song. Sing something else." It seemed to be a sentiment generally shared, for the singing died down, until two or three voices began—*I don't want to join the army!* which was taken up with glum enthusiasm. To the north-west, the shelling began to increase noticeably, so that the ground under the house shook, the building itself trembled and the remaining windows rattled.

Quentin said, "The truth is that only conscription will get us the men we are going to need. The trade unions are already protesting—before there's anything to protest about—but they'll have to lump it. We must have the men. Anyway, it's high time all the slackers are winkled out of cushy jobs back home and sent out here."

The shelling was really uncommonly heavy for a slack time. North-west, and about five miles away, Boy thought—about Bixschoote, held by French Algerian troops.

"All we need is conscription, to get the men into the army," Quentin continued, "and then one big push, here on the Western Front, we and the French together, and it will all be over."

A bugle shrilled in the street and Quentin raised his head, muttering, as the bugle continued—"Battalion call . . . stand-to . . . company commanders' orders . . . Wonder what's up?"

Boy stood up, finishing his wine. "Thank you for the wine, sir. I'd better be going."

Quentin nodded. "Come and see me again when the flap's over. It's probably just another Hun hate."

Boy ran down the village street. He breathed a sigh of thankfulness when Stratton joined him, fully dressed and equipped: he would not have to face Mme Baret alone. Last night had passed well enough. She had apologised for her behaviour, said she had taken a little too much wine, Meester Rowland would please forgive her; and had behaved with the utmost decorum thereafter; but now, the bugles were calling, the German shelling had increased to a hurricane of sound and fury, and she would again be in a high state of nervous emotion.

As they ran Stratton pulled a piece of paper out of his pocket and gave it to Boy. "Quartermaster gave me this for you, sir."

"What is it?"

"Don't know for sure, sir. Something to do with lost equipment and you have to pay."

"Sixty-four rupees, fourteen annas, four pies," Boy snarled. "Why the hell don't they take it out of my pay and have done with it?"

"I asked that, sir. Quartermaster said they couldn't without a court martial and . . ."

"Burn it, Stratton, at the first opportunity. Don't just throw it away, or it'll find its way back to me . . . Oh, and listen. I've spoken to Captain Maclachlan about you. You'll be promoted soon, perhaps into the Pioneer Section. You're much too experienced a man—and craftsman—to spend the war as my batman."

"But, sir—" Frank began anxiously; but Boy said, "You just take what's coming, Stratton."

Then they were at the house. Mme Baret was nowhere to be seen as Boy struggled into his equipment, helped by Stratton; then they both ran back up the street to the edge of the village, where B Company was gathering, scattered in groups to avoid unnecessary casualties from shell fire.

A man came running down the street, shouting. He was a Negro in Algerian French uniform, his face purple-black, eyes bolting. He had no rifle and was clutching at his throat and croaking in a choked voice, "*Asphyxiation! Sauve qui peut!*" He did not reach the end of the village, but stumbled, fell, and lay in the middle of the pavé of Wieltje, retching, and jerking. More Algerians ran past, a few Belgian civilians among them, all coughing and stumbling.

Boy felt his stomach tighten and his throat constrict. What on earth was this, now?

The Algerians seemed to have lost their way, for the French front was farther west, and as the battalion advanced up the road toward St Julien, they did not see any more. The artillery fire continued heavily to the west, now two ways, for French and some British guns had opened counter battery fire, while the Germans were firing their huge 17-inch howitzers into Ypres itself. Tall columns of smoke rose from the city, drifting away to the south.

At St Julien the battalion opened up, for light shelling was reported farther up the road, and continued its advance. Soon afterwards a halt was called, and they lay down or sprawled where they could. Orders and information gradually trickled down, until Captain Maclachlan could tell his platoon commanders, at a conference in a field off the Poelcapelle road, that after heavy bombardment of the French Algerian lines, the Germans had advanced behind a cloud of some sort of noxious gas. The Algerians had broken and fled, and the Germans had poured into the gap, heading for Ypres. All this was to the Wealds' left —west. Now British forces were going to attack the German flank. The 1st Weald Light Infantry would lead, two companies up, until resistance was encountered.

Boy returned to his platoon, and explained the situation to Sergeant Knapp and his corporals. Soon the battalion moved out neatly into open order, and advanced north-westward across country, bayonets fixed, rifles at the high port.

For a time nothing happened, and they saw no one. They were moving through what had been a rear area, for Boy could clearly see, to his right, a rudimentary trench system and rows of barbed wire. Suddenly, after fifteen minutes, shells began to fall among both leading companies, including onto Boy's platoon. For a moment he thought that they were British 18-pounders falling short but, listening carefully, he distinctly heard the boom of the guns from behind the German lines, to the north, and then the crack of the exploding shells. Machine-gun fire rattled by at the same time. A man fell here, another cried out, tumbling over. The battalion continued to advance, Boy's platoon on the extreme left of the left-hand forward company. Some of the men broke into a run, going forward.

"Walk!" Boy shouted. He had not seen a German close-to since his first trench raid, with the 2nd Battalion, and although he carried a revolver, he seldom drew it, but used a strong ash plant with a curved handle, with which he could point out objectives. He also found it useful for knocking down the stinging nettles that filled every ditch and bypath, ruined hamlet and farm in the Salient.

The firing increased and men were going down faster. He could see Germans now, about three hundred yards ahead, crouched along hedge and willow lines and outside farm buildings. The British artillery was firing fast, and shrapnel was bursting over the Germans.

The battalion had made contact, as ordered. A runner panted up from company headquarters. "Hold present line, sir!" the man gasped, out of breath.

Boy nodded, pulled out his whistle on its lanyard, blew it, and pushed his hand down in the signal "Take position!"

Everyone ran then, for a few seconds, to reach a ditch twenty yards ahead, where they threw themselves down, Sergeant Knapp and Frank Stratton at Boy's sides. Boy, lying flat on his stomach, said, "Get a sentry posted in each section, and everyone else digging, as soon as it gets dark . . . about twenty minutes . . . meanwhile keep their heads down, and keep the Germans' down, too."

The artillery firing increased for a while, as though both artillery commanders had decided that their respective enemies were going to attack; then died away. It became dark.

By first light there was no trench, only lines of holes two feet deep, unconnected. A message had come down from the high command, and finally reached Boy on a grubby message form from company HQ. He went round his platoon himself just after dawn, crawling from pit to pit and giving the men the information: "The gas the Germans used yesterday was chlorine. It is greeny yellow in colour. If you see a cloud of it coming, urinate on your handkerchief and tie it round your nose and mouth."

As he left one hole, occupied by two earth-stained and hollow-eyed soldiers, their entrenching tools lying on the loose earth outside, he heard one say to the other, "What if I can't piss, Bill?"

"Shit, mate! We'll all be able to do that."

The battalion waited and watched, unable to move, for every movement drew accurate German rifle and machine-gun fire. The German artillery fired steadily, but not heavily. The British stayed quiet, reserving their ammunition.

The wind changed, blowing in Boy's face. For a moment he enjoyed the different feel of it, then he started, and cursed himself for a fool. Early yesterday evening the wind had swung round from north to almost west. There had been no gas attack. Why? Because if the Germans released gas, it would be blown back into their own faces. Now, with the dawn, the wind was again northerly. Almost simultaneously, he saw it—a yellowish cloud, advancing silently across the fields toward him, toward all the Weald Light Infantry. The cloud stretched for ever, it seemed, to right and left—more British troops were to the right, Canadians to the left.

Frank Stratton saw it at the same instant he did, and cried, "Gas, sir!"

"Gas!" Boy shouted. "Get ready!" As though the German gunners had heard him, a storm of whizzbang and 5.9-inch howitzer fire burst along the British positions. Boy, crouched in his little hole with Stratton, found it hard to urinate. He tried, but nothing came. He had taken a leak just before first light, and the message . . . He should have waited . . . how could he have known? Now, there it was, a feeble trickle. A shell splinter passed across the upper sleeve of his tunic, cutting the material as though with a razor, but not touching his skin. Then the gas cloud reached them. Boy gasped for breath, a deadly pain at his throat, his eyes bulging and smarting. He pressed his face into the earth . . . it felt a little better, and the wet handkerchief was filtering out something of the gas . . . but some of his men were jumping out of their holes, kneeling, hurling themselves this way and that like landed fish. "Lie down!" he cried, realising they could not hear him, for the handkerchief over his face, and the thunder of the bursting shells. He whipped off the handkerchief, and bellowed again, then sank back, choking and retching. Dimly, through smarting eyes, he saw men running . . . back . . . and struggled to his feet, waving his arms. It was no use . . . they had gone. The green-yellow cloud moved past and he saw that he had only half a dozen men left.

He tried to breathe normally. The Germans must be advancing, but he could see no one. Should he go back, and try to collect his platoon? They were having it worse than he, for they were still in the moving cloud, moving with the wind.

He had been ordered to hold the position. He called to Knapp, "Are you all right, sar'nt?"

"Think so, sir . . . Gawd, that was awful! Shall I take Stratton and try to get some of those silly bastards back, sir?"

"No. The reserve companies will stop them, and send them back up soon." He coughed violently for a full minute, then choked out— "We're staying. The machine gunners . . . left their gun . . . there . . . you and Stratton . . . work it."

Quentin's A Company had been immediately behind B in that day's advance, and had been able to dig deeper trenches during the night, for two G.S. cart loads of picks and shovels had reached them about midnight. No one had slept all night, working. Quentin had visited each of his platoons half a dozen times during the hours of darkness, and himself worked an hour with a pick, thinking of Guy's letter; and another received from Virginia, written a week earlier, mostly about how she hated Cheltenham Ladies College. He wondered why there had been nothing from Fiona. His thoughts were not happy ones; but they had made him dig harder.

The dawn gas attack came before tea or food had been sent up. As his men tried to piss on their handkerchiefs, Quentin forgot that he was supposed to do the same as, binoculars to his eyes, he stood in his trench, watching the greenish cloud roll slowly over B Company. German artillery fire increased, but it was not accurate. Quentin thought that their observers' view was partially blocked by their own gas.

Figures appeared out of the gas cloud, running, and Company Sergeant Major Vickery, at Quentin's side, cried, "Here they come!"

Quentin dropped the binoculars: "They're ours! . . . Quick, get some men, spread out here—stop them any way you can—butt, fist, trip . . . shoot if they won't stop."

He jumped up, arms spread. Vickery was bellowing—"Up, up! Stop them!" The running British soldiers approached, veering, weaving, falling.

"My Gawd!" Vickery muttered: Quentin saw it at the same time: an officer, running with the others, the sleeve badges clear. Quentin knew who it was, but could not bring himself to say the name aloud, or even to himself. Then the staggering rout was on him and Quentin saw their faces close to; and knew at once that these men were not themselves. He ran to the officer, faced him, and caught him by the shoulders and yelled in his face: "Halt, you!" The lieutenant tried to struggle free, moaning and gasping. Gobs of yellow phlegm spattered Quentin's muddy tunic; for a few seconds the lieutenant fought like a madman, possessed of fearful strength in spite of his growing disability; then, without warning, he collapsed.

Vickery and a dozen other N.C.O.s and men had stopped most of the others; a few staggered on, heedless, but when Quentin saw a corporal near him raise his rifle to shoot one such in the back, he signalled wearily, "Let him go, Nunnelly . . . I'm afraid he won't go far."

Nor did he, stumbling, running forward, falling again, to fall and not move, less than fifty yards on. The gas cloud was close on A Company now, and the German shell fire, already falling over, lengthened the range and fell still further toward the rear. Quentin knelt by his trench, a long half minute, staring at the gas wall, wavering, advancing, baring holes, which soon closed again . . . that eerie monster had broken the Weald Light Infantry where Napoleon's Old Guard had not been able to, nor the Sikhs at Chillianwallah, nor fifty squadrons of French cavalry at Minden. It was a damned disgrace. That bloody gas had to be taught a lesson. He pulled out his whistle and blew it fiercely, then yelled at Vickery, "Advance! Pass the signal to all platoons!" He swept his right hand forward in the signal "Advance!"

His platoon commanders saw him, and at first thought he must have gone mad. In a few seconds they understood, and to right and left the men of A Company rose from the muddy earth, looking like second-rate actors playing brigands in a third-rate play, piss-stained handkerchiefs wrapped over nose and mouth and advanced. Through the handkerchiefs Quentin heard a ragged muffled cheer. His blood raced as it had not since he saw the Field Artillery rescuing their guns at Le Cateau. The company was attacking, attacking the infamous, filthy cloud. He wished he had a bayonet to stab it with . . . then they were in it, gasping, choking, he reeled as his eyes closed involuntarily against the smarting stab of the gas. Two more shallow breaths, then he was out. The air was clean, the denser part of the rolling cloud behind them, only stray trendrils creeping along the torn earth, clinging round their knees. The company stumbled on, but at a faster pace. Quentin knew the men, he knew they were wildly excited now, for they had attacked the gas, and beaten it. He saw holes in the ground ahead, heads and shoulders and peaked khaki caps. He saw his nephew, tore off his useless handkerchief and shouted, "Up, up, Boy! Charge!"

Boy jumped up, a handful of men with him, and joined the sweep of A Company. On the right more men in khaki were running forward. The whizzbangs were onto them, but obviously couldn't see clearly, or did not realise that the British were advancing, not retreating, for after a few accurate shell bursts, most of the rest fell far behind. As they moved forward, the ground began to be covered with corpses, here and there a body still moving. Canadians, Quentin saw. My God, they must have fought hard! When was it—yesterday, the day before, a week ago? Windrows of Canadians, facing in every direction in death, and Germans as dense over the sodden fields, the hedges, round the trunks of the willows . . . A farm building loomed ahead and then they were in it . . . grey shapes rising out of the grass, appearing from behind walls, jumping from piles of manure. His revolver was in his hand, God knew how, Vickery's rifle blazing at his ear, a German throwing up his hand, falling . . . the clack and slap of bullets loud in his ears, and then the same sound he had heard before—a ragged, gasping cheer. The Germans had gone . . . some lying where they had fallen, some crawling, some wounded to death, some with hands up, some running away across the field, among the brown and white cows, some grazing placidly, some legless, some dead.

The German artillery began bursting shrapnel over the farmhouse. A wooden wall caught fire. Smoke towered eastward in a dense column. At Quentin's shoulder his nephew said, "Wind's changed again, sir. There'll be no more gas."

Quentin nodded: he'd never have thought of that. By God, the farm yard, too, was full of dead Canadians. He and Boy looked at the corpses in silence for a time, then Quentin said, "They were the fellows who filled the hole when the Algerians first ran. God knows where we'd all be now, if it wasn't for them."

He turned away. There'd be a counter-attack, unless he could get the C.O. to bring up the rest of the battalion and force onward from where A had got to. A runner appeared with a message. Vickery read it aloud. "From the C.O., sir. Withdraw to St Julien-Wieltje road . . . same formation as for the attack, just about turn."

Quentin said, "All right."

Boy said, "Couldn't we stay, sir? They're probably expecting us to attack."

Quentin said, "No . . . Orders."

Vickery said, "Another runner, sir . . . the colonel's killed, sir. Shell fire. So's Major Bergeron. They must have been together. You're the commanding officer—this is from the adjutant. The previous orders were from brigade."

Quentin said, "Start the withdrawal at . . . nine ack emma. Write a simple message for me to send out to all companies, sar'nt major. Where's Captain McDonald?"

"With the reserve platoon, sir."

"Send for him to take over. I'm going back to battalion headquarters."

" 'Ope you can get us some more fire from them gunners, sir."

"I hope so, but they swear they're short of ammunition." He looked at his nephew closely for the first time. "Boy, you're wounded."

Boy's face was pale and strained, one sleeve torn and bloodstained. He said, "A shell splinter cut it hours ago. Then I got a bullet—very slight."

"Does it hurt?" Quentin asked. He'd never been wounded and couldn't imagine what it felt like.

Boy said, "Burns like the dickens, sir." He coughed violently, his eyes bulging.

"You'd better come back with me."

"I'll stay with the company, sir. Till we get back, at least."

"I'll look after him, sir," Private Stratton cut in anxiously.

Quentin nodded and said, "I'm going, then." He started back with his batman, heading south-eastward, the way he had come barely half an hour since. Soon the companies would be following, in retreat again, as at Le Cateau. But he knew that they were not depressed: they had overcome panic and gone to the enemy with the bayonet; and they had seen, in the harvested sheaves of the Canadians, how men could fight. He had been unfair to shout at those wretched men of B Company that they were indeed Contemptible. For one thing, they had been overcome by something more primitive than ordinary fear of death or wounds: and for another, they were not the old Contemptibles of Mons and Le Cateau and 1st Ypres. *They* had gone, for ever. This battle, 2nd Ypres, was being fought by the new armies, which meant, by civilian England.

Toward evening Boy Rowland trudged back, half a dozen men at his heels, toward Wieltje. They were the walking wounded from B Company. The retreat had lasted an hour, then there'd been seven hours of German shelling, attacking, shelling, attacking. Maclachlan was dead. Rush was dead, replaced by Fred Stratton, just arrived. Richards, who'd broken and run away, had vanished—some said dead of gas and left out in the fields, some said carried back to the C.C.S., but dying. He himself should be commanding the company, but the C.O.—his uncle—had ordered him back; so Kellaway was commanding. He had wanted to stay; in truth the arm wound was not serious and would heal of itself in a few days; but all day he had attacks of vomiting; his eyes smarted and the lids would spasmodically flutter of themselves. He had not been blinded, but for moments at a time could not see for the smarting, and the fluid draining out of his eyes. A persistent pain nagging behind his breastbone made him wonder if he had been hit there, unknowing, but he could find no trace of a wound or blow. Above all, he felt weary, to death.

The last person of the company he'd seen was his batman, Frank Stratton, who'd come back with him for half a mile, anxiously assuring him not to worry about anything he might have left in billets in Wieltje. He, Stratton, would see that it was collected. And he'd be waiting as soon as Boy came back to the battalion.

He walked on. His arm hurt badly, but it was all on the surface. He wondered how deeply and how badly the gas had affected his lungs. What swine the Boches were! Well, two could play at that, or any other game . . . and the prevailing wind here was generally from France toward Germany, not the other way.

As they entered Wieltje the little band of walking wounded were joined by others, all heading toward St Jean and Ypres, where dense smoke arose from many fires. One group of soldiers, all their eyes bandaged, walked slowly along the edge of the pavé, each man's left hand on the shoulder of the man in front. The man in the lead, a corporal of the 60th, wore a bandage round his head—but he had not been gassed; he could see. Divisional staff officers beside the road were giving directions to the wounded; and one called to Boy, "The W.W.C.P. is in St Jean, if you can get that far. Ambulances are following to pick up those who can't."

Boy nodded, too exhausted to speak. Columns of infantry tramped up the pavé toward the front. Stray shells burst in the village and in the fields. The sky was dark with smoke and loud with the thunder of artillery. The Germans had stopped attacking by the time he left: but they'd begin again tomorrow. He glanced at the shoulders of the men marching by in the other direction—Coldstream Guards. They looked good, and fairly fresh—must have come up from army reserve.

"Meester Boy, oh, oh!" Her wail was piercing. She came running out of a side alley at the south end of Wieltje, her arms extended. "Oh, you are 'urt!"

Many of the marching guardsmen turned round to look. Boy caught a smile here, a look of envy there, muttered remarks—"Local greens," "Officers' rations, mate."

"I'm all right, Madame Baret," he said in French. "Just a scratch." A fit of coughing prevented him saying more. She hurried along at his side, her hands reaching out supplicatingly toward him. He said, "Private Stratton . . . will collect . . . what I've left."

"Oh, Meester Boy . . ."

Another voice called in the gathering dusk. "Isn't that Boy Rowland?"

Boy stopped and turned, peering, Mme Baret now hanging onto his good arm, and weeping loudly. "Who's there?"

"Arthur Durand-Beaulieu."

Arthur fell out of the ranks and Boy saw the single Garter-badged stars of an ensign of Guards on his shoulders. He looked concerned as he said, "You look all in, Boy."

Boy said weakly, "Welcome to the Salient, Arthur."

Mme Baret fell away, and Boy turned to call after her, "Goodbye, Madame Baret. Thank you . . . for everything."

He realised that anyone who understood French, such as Arthur here beside him, might misunderstand that last phrase. There was nothing he could do about that.

"Good luck," he said. "I've got a touch of gas but it isn't as bad as it might be . . . if the men face it . . . attack it."

Arthur raised his hand. "Get well soon, Boy. I'll write to your people and tell them I saw you."

Then he ran forward to catch up with his platoon, as the Guards continued to swing by. Darkness fell as Boy and a thousand others staggered back toward St Jean. Boy thought that he had never felt so weak, and ill, and miserable, in his life.

Excerpts from the diary of John Charteris, General Haig's Chief of Intelligence:

APRIL 28 (1915). I paid a visit to Ypres yesterday. There was still heavy artillery fire. Officers who were through the German attack there last week, say the shelling was very bad, worse even than in October. Certainly the whole face of the area has been changed. Ypres is nothing but a collection of ruins . . . The whole character of the area immediately behind the trench area has totally changed. One no longer sees troops; the men stow themselves away in houses, barns, sheds, anywhere where there is cover. Horses seem to disappear by a Maskelyne and Cook magic. All that remain are the vast number of motor lorries, and they rest most of the day and work at night. As one drives through the area, all one sees is a few men loitering about the villages, occasionally a stray company marching up to, or back from the trench area; a few—very few—horse wagons, and motor ambulances bringing back their burden of aching humanity; long strings of motor lorries waiting until nightfall to go up with supplies.

The countryside is pretty enough. Nature is still trying to convince us that there is no war, or perhaps that war is vain. All the fields are green, the orchards covered with apple blossoms, the wild flowers just beginning to come out. The most peaceful, and therefore now the prettiest parts, are along the canals with their grass roadways on the banks, shaded by long avenues of high trees, barges, picturesque in the distance, grimy rather when nearby, still lazily rippling through the water. Often for long periods there is not a sound of war, not a shell bursting, nor an aeroplane scraping its way through the skies. You close your eyes and wonder if it has all been a bad dream.

MAY 9 (SUNDAY). The French womenfolk are a curious type: they dress in solemn black in the early Sunday morning, go to Mass looking as demure as a pack of Puritans. That duty over, they change their raiment with all celerity, and their interest with equal rapidity runs from the religious to the purely secular task of ogling everything in trousers that comes their way. It is human nature of course—all the world over—but it is strange with the guns shaking the windows, and the first wounded just beginning to arrive.

Daily Telegraph, Tuesday, April 27, 1915

BERLIN IN WAR-TIME

From a Neutral Correspondent. The difference between the reading public of England and Germany is that, however much you tell a Britisher about the war he always thinks that many things are kept back—whether rightly or wrongly is not my province to express . . . The German system is different.

The Press department of the General Staff meets three or four times a week the representatives of the Press. Apparently all the cards are laid on the table. Reverses are explained; successes described at length. The general policy is, as every journalist will be able to confirm: "We have nothing to hide, only tell the truth."

So those journalists leave the Reichstag's building, 99 out of every 100, convinced that the General Staff members have been absolutely frank and open with them; that they have learned the true state of affairs and that what they were not told they have no business to know.

The confidence of that nation is something colossal and . . . whether the Allies push them back as far as the Rhine, or even over it, the Press is so well organised, the publicity bureau of the General Staff, as are all other departments, such a perfect machine, that there is no question of the general public waking up to the real state of affairs.

. . . I believe, too, that in the majority of cases the German readers do get some truth but—there is a little nigger in the woodpile, the old saying that "half a truth is often worse than a lie."

                                          J. M. DE BEAUFORT

Shrewd fellow, Cate thought, even though he was only a foreigner. Other pages of the paper were full of the announcement of the grand Allied assault on the Dardanelles, and of course everything was going swimmingly. Nothing of importance on the Western Front, since the 'staggering success' of Neuve Chapelle . . . which, it had since been admitted, was no success at all. Britain had confidence, too, just as much as Germany; but it was built on knowledge of the good and the bad, and faith in the country, not on what one was told.

He listened with half an ear to the conversation of his daughter Stella with her cousin Virginia Rowland, visiting for a few days. Virginia was still at home for the Easter holidays from Cheltenham Ladies College, an institution that, according to her, was a cross between Holloway Gaol and a women's lunatic asylum. He was glad Stella was eating eggs and bacon hungrily, while she told Virginia about her work at Lady Blackwell's hospital. Cate was glad she had finally got over the spell when she had not looked well and had lost her appetite. He had always thought of her as young, a girl with her hair down—but the hair had been up over a year, and, listening to her with Virginia, she suddenly seemed to have grown, and matured. She'd be getting married soon, in a year or two, perhaps. That young American had been down again, and was obviously smitten, a regular pursuiter, as the girls called them nowadays; in some ways a very suitable match, and he clearly loved her. Whether she loved him with the same single-minded determination was another matter.

Stella turned to her father. "Did you know that Naomi is in the Girton Fire Brigade, and has to work the pump? Uncle John told me yesterday . . . and she wants me to ask you to get an official copy of her sentence."

"She and Rachel Cowan were bound over to keep the peace for six months," Laurence said, looking up. "How can we get a copy of that?"

"Well, it must be in writing somewhere, she says, and she wants to have it framed and put in her room."

Cate smiled then and said, "I'll telephone the Clerk of the Court in Hedlington and see what can be done."

Virginia had eaten nothing but toast and tea. Sensible girl, Cate thought; she was too fat already. She grumbled, "Naomi spends the night in gaol . . . and is in a Fire Brigade . . . you're a V.A.D. and work with nurses and doctors . . ."

". . . and with dustmen and plumbers," Stella said.

"Guy's working in the fabric shop at Handley Page's, Boy's fighting in France . . . and I moulder away at that stinky Cheltenham Ladies College!"

"You became sixteen only last month," Cate said. "You'll be able to go to gaol and wash out latrines soon enough. The time will pass quickly . . . too quickly, for your parents." He pushed back his chair and said to his son, "We'll go at ten o'clock, Laurence . . . not church clothes, but a tweed suit."

"Where to, Daddy? . . . Oh!" The youth looked down at his nearly empty plate, turning pale.

Cate said, "To call on the Mayhews, remember?"

"I remember," Laurence said, pushing his plate away, "Mr Mayhew will stink of whisky and Mrs will blub all over me. She'll make me blub, too."

"That's no disgrace, Laurence, when you're comforting a woman over the death of her eldest son."

"I didn't know that Samuel had been killed," Stella said. "He used to be an awfully naughty boy . . . Do you remember when he tied Mr Fulcher's bootlaces together while he was guarding the prize marrow at the Flower Show? And when he and Charlie Miller painted Mr England's donkey black and white and put it in with Mr Cawthon's cows and Mr Cawthon rushed down here to tell you there was a zebra escaped from the circus?"

"The Mayhews had a telegram from the War Office yesterday," Cate said. "Samuel was killed in action three days ago . . . I imagine they'd like me to ask the rector about a memorial service for him." He picked up his paper and went out, head a little bent.

England: May, 1915

26 Harry Rowland stood in front of the empty fireplace in the morning-room of Laburnum Lodge, a small sheaf of notes in his hand. His daughter Alice sat in her chair ten feet away, knitting. Harry declaimed: "The war is going well. Let the defeatists and weaklings take heed, and gather courage! Our troops have landed on the Gallipoli peninsula and opened a second front against the enemy . . ."

"A third or fourth front, surely, Father," Alice said. "After the Western and Russian fronts, and Mesopotamia."

"I suppose so," Harry said grudgingly, "though I don't know what good the Russians are to anyone . . . and between you and me, there'll be another front soon. I hear that the Italians have signed a secret treaty, and will be coming in on our side any day. And that'll keep the Austrians busy . . . Where was I?"

". . . a second front against the enemy."

"Yes . . . The country is solidly behind the government, and the government is united in its determination . . . Ellis told me privately that there's a great deal of intrigue going on, and Asquith may be out soon. Or, more likely, a coalition government will be formed, with Mr Asquith as P.M., but all parties represented . . . Everyone must do his bit, man, woman, and child, if the Huns are to be defeated. The torpedoing of the *Lusitania*, with the murder of 1,198 innocent souls, has finally shown the world what we, who have been fighting for ten months know already—the Huns are indeed just that—Huns, barbarians."

He boomed on, Alice listening. He made a good speech, she thought; rather in the style of Lloyd George, a man whom he privately detested as an upstart and a libertine. Unlike Lloyd George, whom she had heard once, her father passionately believed everything he was saying. Or believed that it was in the best interests of the Country that it should be said. That was fortunate because, from what she heard from the soldiers who came to the House Parties, and the women she listened to at the Tipperary Club, the war was not going well; and it certainly was not being run well.

*   *   *   *

. . . I'm so tired of Smith that I can hardly find words to express it. It's something to do with growing up—when I came here three years ago, I was a girl, and it was all exciting, and so large. I felt liberated, and very sophisticated. Now I'm twenty, a grown woman, and it all seems so childish—the rules and regulations, don't-do-this, mustn't-do-that. It's even more to do with the war over there. I know that because it's not only Smith that feels so boring and confining, but the U.S. of A. itself! I've been at Dad for ages to let me quit Smith, and I think he realises now that I mean it. But he asks, what are you going to do instead? And now I am going to tell him I must go to Europe, to take my part in the war. So be prepared to have me come over. And I'm not going to come just to be your housekeeper, either. I could do that at home, looking after Dad. I'm going to drive an ambulance in France . . . or make shells in England . . . wear trousers, anyway, and wear my hair short and done up in a bandanna, like the women in the photos in the newspapers . . .

Johnny folded the letter and put it away in a drawer of his desk. It would be nice to see Betty again, whatever she decided to do; and she was right in her determination to come over. The world's fate was being settled here.

He picked up a folder at the corner of the desk and re-read what he had already written in his report to his father. So far, so good, he thought, and took up his pen:

As I mentioned in my last, the Rowland Motor Car Company is not doing well. They are not getting the government orders they were counting on, partly because they won't settle for anything less than the best—which puts their cost up; and partly because their product is difficult to maintain in the field. It is a great pity (from their point of view) that old Mr Rowland did not retire when he was planning to. The company needs a new broom, a new brain, new direction.

As for the war in general—we are nearly half way through 1915 and the position has not really changed. There is a stalemate on the Western Front and some of the Allies are desperately trying to find a way round it, always hindered by the French, who regard any diversion of effort from that area as a betrayal. Most of the German colonies in Africa have been occupied, but all their soldiers have not surrendered, so fighting continues. The Dardanelles have not been forced, in spite of heavy British casualties. Another British army is invading Mesopotamia, moving up the Tigris. These are partly to seize enemy territory and partly to break (or avoid) the impasse by going round it geographically. Other ways have been tried—e.g. tactically—by the Germans in their use of poisonous gas at Ypres last month; by new methods of attack, as by the British at Neuve Chapelle in March. So far all have failed, for two reasons: lack of sufficient reserves to exploit success gained; and inability to move what reserves there were to the vital point quickly enough. It has been shown that it is possible to break into a fortified trench line—as the British did at Neuve Chapelle; but it has so far been found impossible to break through. What invariably happens is that the forces which have succeeded in breaking in are isolated by curtains of shell and machine-gun fire, and then systematically wiped out by counter-attacks.

This is not an encouraging prospect; but it seems to be a fact. We can expect further major allied attacks in the West—the French will not permit them anywhere else; and these will achieve limited success for short periods; and this will continue until some decisive means is found for breaking the tactical stalemate. (I didn't think all this up myself, Dad! I've been talking to officers and men on leave, and reading between the lines of the military 'experts'—though in this war I am beginning to doubt whether such an animal exists!)

*   *   *   *

Archie Campbell and Fiona Rowland were sitting in the Savoy dining-room, at a table in the windows that should have looked out over the Embankment, the Thames, and the sweep of Rennie's beautiful Waterloo Bridge; but the heavy curtains were drawn, black cloth sewn inside them and the overlapping join of the curtains secured by big pins, so that no light should show to guide a Zeppelin, perhaps already finding its way up the silver path of the Thames by tonight's glittering stars.

Under protest, Archie was wearing a dinner jacket and black tie, for to dine here one had to wear either evening dress or uniform. He told himself that it was ridiculous, but he could not deny that in fact he felt uncomfortable, not being in uniform. Most of the women were wearing evening dress, though one or two were in nurses' or V.A.D. uniform. That was different, Archie thought. Surely a woman who had been regimented all day in serviceable clothes would take a delight in putting on a pretty dress, baring her arms, letting the light gleam on the swell of her bosom . . . as Fiona was, sitting opposite him, her back to the curtains. He had only seen her three times, each for a weekend, since their stay at Dalmellie.

He said, "There's a Light Infantry officer, behind my left shoulder, two tables away. He might know you."

Fiona glanced in the direction indicated. "He's not Wealds . . . Shropshires, I think. I never know. Quentin spent hours when we were first married, going down the army list, showing me badges, all sorts of things. I know all the Highland regiments, of course, by their tartans."

Archie said, "I've always been surprised that you don't cut my throat instead of . . . what you do do. I'm a Campbell."

"It's the MacDonalds who have always been our enemies. The McLeods never were so bitter about Glencoe as the other clans . . . And I've told you a hundred times, I don't care who sees me with you."

The swarthy waiter brought their grilled Dover sole, with maître d'hôtel butter, and filled their long-stemmed wine glasses with a Clos Haut Peyraguey, then stood back against the wall, keeping an eye on their table and the other three for which he was responsible.

Archie said, "Ginger Jones was round to my studio three, four days back. He's dyeing his hair, and is going to enlist—said it was the only thing a decent man could do. He's sixty—and a very good painter."

"And a fool, apparently," Fiona said. "He might at least have waited until conscription comes. It will, you know . . . I feel it in my bones. And then what will *you* do?"

Archie shrugged. "What can I do? It is hard for thee to kick against the pricks."

"Not impossible, though. You're thirty-seven . . . they'll probably take men up to forty. But they won't take men in vital jobs here . . . and they won't take married men." She looked straight at Archie, waiting for him to acknowledge her unspoken offer.

He did not meet her eyes, but after a long time said, "I've talked to men who've come back from France—wounded, or on leave. They all say the same thing, that they want to get back there, because the air's clean, there's no humbug. England stifles them . . . hot air, false patriotism, hypocrisy."

Fiona said, "War is like a disease, Archie . . . a cancer, because it has a life of its own. Do you feel sick with it?"

He spoke with an accented Scots burr. "Aye, lass, perhaps it's burrning in my hearrt and liver."

"I can feel it, though I haven't *got* it, like you have. I just feel it. It makes my skin dry and uncomfortable, even in the bath. Perhaps I feel all those men dying."

"You have the gift, like your mother."

She said, looking beseechingly at him, "Archie, you're thinking you ought to enlist. Don't do it. I can't live without you."

Archie, in his turn, finished his wine: again the waiter came forward to refill the glass. Archie said, "Ah mun do what ah mun do, lass. Ah'll be joining the London Scottish before the week's oot." There, it was said, and now that it was said, he would abide by it. She was right—the war had somehow got into his bones, all uninvited. Perhaps it was a disease—he had not wanted it, or expected it, but it had come . . . If she had not spoken, he would probably have wasted another six months before doing what he ought to do, feeling more and more uncomfortable every day. Now she had made up his mind, for he could not allow her to dictate what he must do.

He said, "Now, let's go to bed. We don't have much time left."

*   *   *   *

Laurence Cate stood in his room at Charterhouse, looking down at the kestrel in his left hand. It was a tiercel, the dark brown eyes staring unwinking at him, the talons fast on the twig he had put between them when he first found the bird, under the chapel, an hour ago. He held it round the chest, its left wing in his grasp, the right free, for the right wing was broken. Very gently he moved his right hand to the wing, watching the bird's eyes, waiting for it to turn and pierce his hand with that curved sharp beak. He had gloves, but could not wear them for this—to feel with his fingers just where and how the wing was broken. He was fortunate that he had found and been able to capture the kestrel within a few minutes of its accident—he thought it must have been stooping on a mouse or small bird and flown into the chapel wall.

The broken bones moved freely under his fingers. He reached the humerus at the joint of the wing, and the kestrel's head turned slowly, looking now at his hand, a few inches from its beak. It half opened the beak; but Laurence could swear that it was not in preparation to strike, but to stifle any sound, or show of emotion at the pain it must be feeling. He felt the bone carefully . . . a simple fracture of the humerus an inch down from the elbow joint. The hawk never moved, seeming to gasp for breath, its beak wide.

Laurence took his right hand away and the hawk relaxed in his left. He had a small stick ready, for he had known roughly what to expect, and had already cut a clean handkerchief into strips an inch wide. He put the bird down on the table, whispering, "Lie still . . . don't flap." He needed both hands now, as he gently took the broken bone, aligned the stick along it, and bound the two in a splint with the strips of handkerchief. Then he folded the wing in a normal closed position and bound it to the bird's body in the sort of sling that Probyn Gorse called a brail. The hawk lay quiet under his hands, barely moving, its beak again open, its thorax heaving.

Laurence straightened his back—"There!" He opened the suitcase he kept under his bed and put the kestrel in it, pushing his dressing gown under the lid to hold it open, then slid the case back under the bed. He must find a name for him . . . he'd call him Graves after the big senior boy he'd admired so much his first term here . . . And he'd have to find raw meat for him—scraps from his plate wouldn't do. Rockwell had a mousetrap, and often caught something . . . He stooped to peer in at Graves; "Graves," he said, "good man! You'll be flying from the Manor soon, and you'll keep all the mice out of the stables, won't you? And your name's Graves, don't forget."

"What the blazes do you think you're doing, Cate?"

The voice behind him made him leap to his feet, turning as he did so. Overstreet stood in the open doorway, frowning at him. Laurence had heard nothing. Overstreet had no business to come in without knocking; but he was a Blood, a small tough member of the school football team, small but a bully.

He stooped down now, grabbed the kestrel and pulled him out of the suitcase. "What are you going to do?" Laurence gasped. He doubled his fists. He ought to hit Overstreet on the nose . . . charge him . . . he was bigger than he was . . . he ought to . . .

Overstreet said, "You're not allowed to keep birds in the room, and you know it." He threw the kestrel out of the open window. It tried wildly to flutter then fell headfirst onto the stone pavement forty feet below, and did not move.

Overstreet stood with arms akimbo in the doorway, staring at Laurence. "Well?"

Laurence said miserably, "Get out," and burst into tears.

"Cry baby," the other boy said, and went out, leaving the door open.

*   *   *   *

Guy took his run up and bowled again. The boy at bat in the net was the same age as himself, and as tall, but his skin was swarthy though his eyes were deep blue, and his hair fair. His full name covered three lines of print and included the word Stuart a couple of times; he was the Duke of Torla, a Grandee of Spain, First Class. He was a good cricketer, for he concentrated. He had detected Guy's change of pace and went far out with his right foot—he was a left hander—to smother the ball. Guy walked back . . . a machine gun firing through the propeller, the report reaching Ginger Keble-Palmer at Handley Page had said. A French aviator called Garros had invented it, or used it. But how could that be, if the propeller was not to be shot to pieces?

He ran up and delivered. Torla jumped forward and hit it clean and low. It would have gone for four, but for the net. Guy walked back . . . it might fire through the spinner, which would mean mounting it behind the engine: and hollowing out the crank shaft so that the bullets would pass right through the middle of the engine . . . that might be easier with a rotary engine than with an ordinary radial, and surely it could not be done at all with an in-line water-cooled engine?

The next ball smashed back past his foot and again would have gone for four. Guy looked at Torla, frowning. Torla said, "Your mind is not on your business, Guy. And we've had enough for today."

He walked up the pitch and began to take off his pads, still talking. "You must think like a matador, Guy. All the graceful passes count for nothing against the way you kill . . . *matar* means to *kill*, not make pretty patterns in the sand . . . If you don't think, always, of killing—the bull will kill you."

Guy said, "That's what Rhodes told me, last summer, in slightly different words. See you tomorrow, Grandy."

He put on his faded pale blue yellow-piped blazer and walked off under the towering copper beeches toward the Path of Duty gate . . . He'd write to Ginger and get more details, if they had them. A machine gun that could fire through the propeller would revolutionise air fighting. He'd have to think over what he had been studying, and look at it all in a new light.

In his room he found three letters on the table, put there by the letter fag from the day's second post. He opened them quickly—one from Boy: he was in a military hospital near Reading. He had been wounded and gassed at Ypres, but not badly. They were going to send him home for a month's convalescence soon, but meanwhile he'd like to spend a day or two watching cricket at Wellington, so would Guy tell him when there was a home school match that he could come and see. Reading was very close and there were lots of trains.

Guy folded the letter away, thinking, there's one thing that Boy didn't know when he wrote: that he had been awarded the Military Cross for gallantry near St Julien, Belgium, on April 22nd and 23rd this year. It was in today's *London Gazette*.

The second letter was from Johnny Merritt . . . progress with the factory . . . J.M.C. lorries rolling out at a great rate . . . Stella was working hard as a V.A.D. The sinking of the *Lusitania* had really upset her, so that she was ready to go out and give white feathers to any fellow she saw who wasn't in uniform. He didn't know whether he could stand being neutral much longer . . . did Guy think the R.F.C. would take him, as an American? Oh, and rumours kept flying round that Probyn Gorse was going to set a mantrap for Skagg the game-keeper, or even for Lord Swanwick . . . Guy smiled to himself; old Probyn was keeping the pot boiling, as he'd explained he would, during their long talk these last hols . . .

The third letter was from the Hedlington Flying School, confirming that Mr Guy Rowland would start a pilot's course on Monday August 2nd. The fee would be £15 for the three-weeks course, at the end of which the School guaranteed that Mr Rowland would be qualified to receive his R.A.C. pilot's licence. The aeronautical mechanic's course which Mr Rowland had asked about did not exist, but the School would be glad to attach him to their own chief mechanic, under instruction, for a small fee.

Guy put the letters away in the desk drawer, and began to sketch an aircraft engine, and how it could be arranged to accept machine-gun fire through the arc of the propeller blades, without damaging them. Suppose you put studs on the propeller shaft, diametrically opposed . . . when the shaft revolved, the studs could strike a cam, which would be connected somehow to the machine gun's firing hammer . . .

* * * *

Bert Gorse sat in his half-brother's crowded house, one of a row in the poorest section of Hedlington, and opened a bottle of beer. He was working at the Jupiter Motor Company now, and getting good money. He'd had a hard time for a month, between the time old Harry Rowland sacked him and young Mr Richard took him on, but he'd struggled through with the help of a rabbit or two from his father, some poaching on his own account closer to Hedlington, and sneaking an egg here, a tin there, a loaf somewhere else, out of the grocers' shops while the assistant wasn't looking and the owner was up on a ladder helping a customer. He wasn't a shop foreman yet, and he doubted whether he ever would be. The bosses had heard about his union activities, though they'd been kept very quiet . . . and that Yankee they'd brought over as works manager, Morgan, was a hard man to fool, for all his back slapping and Welsh blarney.

They were celebrating Willum's birthday, though how could you really celebrate with so many kids screaming and yelling, and Mary always sewing, mending, and never taking even a drop? He poured the beer into a chipped glass, as Willum, across the table, followed suit. He said, "Here's to the Yanks . . . they're paying for this."

Willum said anxiously, "You aren't going to do any union work, are you?"

Bert laughed contemptuously. "Course not . . . yet."

"That's good," Willum said "You'll only get into more trouble, and Mr Richard'll give you the sack."

Bert drank deep and wiped a little froth off his lips with the back of his hand. "I'll be a good boy . . . in a pig's eye, I will! When I'm ready I'm going to go for the women, see? The bosses think they've got us by the short hairs, 'cos they can always get more cheap labour—women. But what if the women join the union, and ask for the same wages as men, eh?"

"The union won't take 'em, I thought," Willum said, " 'cos they say they're . . . something bad."

"Diluting, Willum. But the union's wrong. We've got to get every worker in, not just the skilled ones. It'll take time to knock that into their fat heads down there . . . but I'll do it. Then, when we're ready . . . *strike!* Stop the machines!"

"But then they won't be able to make lorries for our boys in France," Willum said anxiously.

"Fuck our boys in France!" Bert said. "Sorry, Mary."

Willum shook his head . . . "I don't know what's going to happen next, any more . . . you wanting to stop the new factory, that'll be paying wages to lots of people . . . the Germans sending over gas, to poison our boys . . . thousands of people drowned in that ship, by a submarine which they couldn't even see . . . no county cricket this year, or until the war's over . . . When am I going to see Woolley bat again? Or Blythe bowl? . . . I tell you, I can't sleep sometimes, thinking about it."

Richard Rowland drove up to Hill House, his mind occupied with what he had seen and heard today . . . the six hundredth assembled J.M.C. 30 would come out of the old building tomorrow; and the new building was up, almost ready for the instalment of its machinery. It had been decided that he should try to persuade the War Office procurement people to increase the size of the first military order for J.M.C. 30s. He'd probably not succeed, since the soldiers would be chary of a firm they knew nothing of; but it was worth the try.

It was a lovely May evening, and Susan came out of the front door, yawning and stretching, as he stepped down, and Stafford ran up to take the car away.

"Let's walk a bit," she said, putting up her face for his kiss, then taking his arm. "I've been doing accounts all afternoon and I need some fresh air."

The roses were coming into bloom, and drifts of bluebells, wild sown, glowed pale blue under the elms in the wood rising behind the house. The lawn was a dense green, close knit and smooth, the croquet hoops set up.

They strolled across the grass, the sun still high but without heat. Susan said, "Alice called, on the telephone."

"Anything special?"

"They wanted to know whether we had seen about Boy's M.C. in the paper. I told her we had. She just wanted to talk, I think . . . The Governor and Bob Stratton are working on a design for an ambulance."

Richard stopped. "An ambulance? But they don't make a chassis big enough for that."

"Alice was wondering about that, too, but she said they are planning a sort of rather small, special one, that would be very comfortable, and go faster."

"An ambulance just for generals," Richard said sarcastically. He resumed his pacing, shaking his head. "If they go further with that, they'll be making a big mistake, I think. But they're getting desperate, I suppose . . . This is a very lovely evening, my dear. And can I smell chicken roasting?"

"I think Mrs Baker's just putting it in. We're going to have to eat less meat and fats, Richard. And sugar."

"Oh dear, I won't like that."

"You'll have to get used to it. All of us will. The hounds make much more noise in the kennels than they used to—they're getting hungry, too."

"It's difficult to get horsemeat."

"The last time Quentin wrote he swore that some of the bully beef

and stewed meat and potatoes they get is horsemeat. Perhaps that's
where it's going."

"At prime beef prices, of course. We can thank people like Bill Hoggin for that, I imagine. Do you know what I heard today? That he's
given five thousand pounds to the mayor for distribution among all the
clubs and groups which look after soldiers and sailors and their dependents—the Tipperary Clubs, Alice's House Parties, the sewing and knitting groups, the Salvation Army . . . Let's go back in now, dear. I need
a bath . . . Oh, I saw Stella today. She was having lunch in the South
Eastern with an older man. I think I've seen him before, and believe
he's a doctor. He was, ah, ogling her. She seemed to be basking in it."

"How was she looking?"

"Very well. She's quite recovered from whatever it was she had last
month."

"That's good. I wonder what it was."

"Some sort of flu, I suppose. There's always a lot of it about, in the
spring."

They reached the front door and Susan said, "Oh, Richard, I nearly
forgot . . . Stafford's given his notice. He's . . ."

". . . going to join the army," Richard finished for her. "It's time he
did, really. We'll have to find a girl, and teach her the mechanics of a
motor car . . . and how to drive it, of course."

*   *   *   *

Naomi Rowland walked slowly on the Girton lawn, Rachel Cowan at
her side. Bees droned in the flowers, the sun shone, the air was heavy
with the scents of early summer. The thick grass rustled under their
tennis shoes, and their skirts rustled as the rackets in their hands
brushed them as they swung.

Rachel said dreamily, "England at its most beautiful. When you've
been brought up in Stepney, you don't know that such places as this
exist. On days like this I sometimes wish I could stay at Girton for
ever."

Naomi swung her racket at a bee, sending it flying into the
flowerbeds. She said, "I don't . . . I feel I'm in a prison . . . two
prisons . . . Girton—and then even if I escape from that, my body's a
prison, because I'm a woman . . . I don't know whether I can stand
this for another year."

"Don't say that!" Rachel cried, "what would I do here without you?
You know I don't get on with most of the other girls."

Naomi turned moodily and walked back in the opposite direction.
"What's wrong here is that we can't hear the guns. The windows

ought to be rattling, and the walls shaking, the earth trembling under our feet, all the time, day and night . . . I'm not doing as much as Stella, even. And Girton's getting boring . . . worse than home."

She brightened, and added, "Except that I've met a pair of interesting young men . . . as far as any young men are interesting. At least these don't condescend . . . and they're interested in me."

Rachel said, "Where on earth did you meet them?"

"At a mixed squash at Q's the day before yesterday. One was at Clare and now works as a scientist for an optical company here, and the other was at King's and is now a 2nd Lieutenant of the 60th Rifles, at that Junior Officers' Course they're running in Jesus." She looked her friend up and down, and grinned mischievously. "Stan's about the right height for you. He's the scientist."

"Oh Naomi! He probably hates Jews."

"I'm sure he doesn't . . . Harry's six feet, and awfully good looking." She lowered her voice as though their formidable Mistress of Girton, Miss E. E. C. Jones, was lurking in the flowerbed—"They're night climbers—were when they were undergraduates, and still do it . . . and they're going to take me up."

"Whaaat?" Rachel half screamed, her sallow face paling. "Naomi, you mustn't! Think what would happen to you if you were caught!"

"I'd get sent down from Girton," Naomi said, "and I've just been saying that that no longer seems a fate worse than death to me."

"Death!" Rachel cried. "You might fall!"

"I might . . . but I've done a lot of high climbing, on trees and cliffs, with Boy, all my life. Even after I put my hair up." She laughed shortly and swung the racket viciously at another bee.

* * * *

It was dark in the bathroom, where Fiona lay in the bath, stretched out, her hands clasped behind her head. It was very warm in here, the water hot in the bath, and hot in the pipes of the towel rack, where half a dozen of the Savoy's great towels hung in regal splendour, waiting to hold her in their rough embrace.

If he was going, what was there left for her? She distinctly remembered Margaret trying to make her feel differently—free her of her infatuation, was how Margaret thought of it—that time at Henley, and again a few weeks later, at a chance meeting in Hedlington. But Margaret could not understand the nature of this love that bound her to Archie any more than Alice, for example, could understand the nature of sexual passion . . . though Alice, through her House Parties, was learning much that was perhaps a shock to her. One of the jobs she had undertaken was to read the soldiers' and sailors' letters to their sweethearts and wives, many of whom could not read. The letters, ill-written, splotched, stained, were like dumb men trying to shout poetry: "I am well, I hope you are well. There was a big hate yesterday. I did not get hurt . . ." a matter of inability to use the pen for the expression of feeling or emotion. There were other letters which, according to Alice, were blatantly sexual and blunt, using the common people's coarsest language to express the simplest and most direct desires. She had expected Alice to be horrified; but she wasn't. She had only said that she felt terribly sorry for them all, men and women alike: and that she was learning more about people, of all kinds, than she had learned in her thirty-five years so far.

Archie was going to leave her, not because of the war, really, but because of Quentin. He did not say so directly, but he felt that he could not enjoy her body, or even her company, unless he had faced the same risks that Quentin was facing. It would be impossible to persuade him of the selfishness and stupidity of what he was going to do. But he was a genius, and her lover, he must not be allowed to sacrifice himself, perhaps unknown, among the coarse, unfeeling men whom Quentin loved, the only human beings *he* understood.

He had said he would be back by seven, from his walk on the Embankment. It was close to that now. The water was getting cool, and she ran in more hot. When it was full she turned off the tap, reached out to the cork-covered stool beside the bath, and picked up the open razor she had placed there. It was bone-handled, plain, but very sharp. Archie stropped it every morning after shaving with it. When she drew the blade first across her left wrist, then her right, she felt little more than a slight, sharp, short-lived stab of pain. The blood began to well out as she dropped the razor back on the stool, dripping blood onto the bath mat, and then, holding both hands under water, lay back and closed her eyes.

*   *   *   *

It seemed an hour before she heard, drowsily, as from a thousand miles away, the turning of the key in the outer door, the click of the light switch, his voice—"Fiona?" There was a faint sensation of more warmth on her eyelids, as light from the bedroom flooded through into the bathroom. He called, "Fiona? I'm back." She heard his footsteps cross the carpet, his tap on the open door. "May I come in?" He wasn't usually so polite, but would just come in, joking, and scrub her back.

"My God . . . Fiona!"

She felt his arms under her, lifting her, and opened her eyes. The water in the bath was red, but not very—watery blood, or bloody water, not all blood, not solid or thick or dark. She was on the stool, his arm round her shoulders. He was tying a face towel round one wrist, his handkerchief round the other. They were dripping blood onto the floor. She felt faint and drowsy, and now, out of water, her wrists smarted. Otherwise she did not feel, at all.

"I'll call a doctor," he said.

She heard thumps and thuds, that sounded distant, and asked, "What is that . . . doors banging?"

"Guns," he said. "There's a Zeppelin raid . . . north London, I think . . . Here, I'll carry you to bed, then I'll telephone the reception and . . ."

She said, "I'm all right, Archie. No need for a doctor . . . only need you."

"They've stopped bleeding, nearly."

He was lifting her, carrying her, laying her on the bed, pulling up the sheet, the blanket. The thudding was faint and far, but continuous. She wished he'd pull back the curtains so that she could watch the pointing fingers of the new searchlights sweeping the sky for the Zeppelin.

Archie sat on the side of the bed, his face set, the broken nose prominent. "Why did you do that?"

He seemed to be whispering, but without the sibilance of a whisper —his normal loved voice shrunk to a tiny volume, its resonance lost. She said, "I can't live without you. I told you at dinner last night."

He met her eye. "This is blackmail, wumman."

She didn't speak, her eyes closing from the weight of the eyelids, without any volition on her part. She felt him get up from the bed and walk about the room; and dimly heard his staccato sentences, all spoken in braw Gorbals. "Ah've loved ye, so Ah'm responsible for ye, is tha' it? . . . An' p'rraps Ah am, God help me . . . Christ, Ah wish Ah could meet Quentin face to face, man tae man, an' tell him . . . Ah'm no' the marrying type, ye ken tha'? . . . Ye'll neverr be more than a painter's kept wumman, ye unnerstan'?"

She felt him sit down on the bed again. His hand touched her cheek and he said in his ordinary voice, "You're a mad McLeod, Fiona. But I *am* responsible for you, since we are what we are to each other. I'll not go for a soldier until later."

She opened her eyes wide, exhilaration sweeping like champagne through her so recently sluggish and empty veins—"We'll come here again for the Whitsun weekend, darling! And we must find some important work for you, so you won't be conscripted. You can paint in your spare time . . ."

"I'm a painter, lass," he said wearily. "It's not a little hobby for my spare time. It's my life . . . and to tell the truth that's why I'm not going to join up tomorrow. I'm frightened. How can I live without painting?"

"Then you understand—how can I live without you? Why, oh why, can't we get married?"

"You know, Fiona."

***

Daily Telegraph, Friday, May 7, 1915

GRAPHIC STORY FROM THE DARDANELLES

ARMY DISEMBARKED BY MOONLIGHT
DASHING COLONIALS

From E. Ashmead-Bartlett, Dardanelles, April 24 (via Mudros, Wednesday) . . . **The first authentic news we received came with the return of our boats. From them we learnt what had happened in those first wild moments. All the tows had almost reached the beach, when a party of Turks, entrenched almost on the shore, opened up a terrible fusillade from rifles, and also from a maxim. Fortunately, most of the bullets went high but, nevertheless, many men were hit as they sat huddled together, forty or fifty in a boat.**

It was a trying moment, but the Australian volunteers rose as a man to the occasion. They waited neither for orders or for the boats to reach the beach but, springing out into the sea, they waded ashore and, forming some sort of a rough line, rushed straight on the flashes of the enemy's rifles.

Their magazines were not even charged, so they just went in with cold steel and I believe I am right in saying that the first Ottoman Turk since the last crusade received an Anglo-Saxon bayonet in him at five minutes after five a.m. on April 25th.

Cate made an almost inaudible grunt as he put the paper down. Journalistic bombast about bayonets! And inaccurate, too, as British soldiers had been fighting Turks in Mesopotamia for months. He stood up as Garrod came in and silently cleared the table.

It was a pleasant day, sunny but not too warm, with a slight breeze, the sky fleeced with clouds. It would be a good day to visit his tenants, but he had been round to all of them yesterday. Mayhew still seemed to be holding to his determination not to touch another drop until the war was won. It had taken the death of his son to shock him into such a step; but, in itself, the decision was all to the good, for Mayhew couldn't take a pint or a glass and leave it at that—he had to go on, when he could afford it, until he was sodden. The visit to them the day after they'd had the War Office telegram had taught Laurence a useful lesson, for Mayhew had met them pale and upright, his hands shaking but the man himself sober and stern; and Mrs Mayhew had not wept, but stood at her husband's side, dry eyed, head up, only the tremor in her voice betraying her emotion as she thanked Christopher and Laurence for coming, and said, yes, they would be grateful if Mr Cate would ask Mr Kirby about a memorial service for Samuel . . .

It would be a good day to visit some other villagers . . . Miller the stationmaster, for instance; to ask what they'd heard of their son Charlie, in the Weald Light Infantry since last December, and now in France, he knew . . . a good looking boy, as mischievous as Samuel Mayhew, but not as original: cannon fodder, the cynics would say.

Then he ought to talk to Miss Macaulay, the postmistress, and somehow find a way to hint that it was more important than ever that she should refrain from reading people's postcards and gossiping to Miss Morelock, the schoolmistress, about what she had learned from them. Inquisitiveness was not a mortal sin, but in wartime people were very touchy; and there were surely adequate means of censorship to make sure that military secrets were not being leaked through the mail. She was an excellent postmistress and otherwise a most worthy woman. He wished there was some sort of award he could recommend her for, but could not think of any with lowly enough ranks.

To the rector, then, to discuss the lesson for this coming Sunday. Old Kirby had been talking of retirement before last Christmas, but now, who could replace him? So he was staying on, and enjoying it, and grumbling about the poor hunting there'd be this next season, with hounds half starved, huntsmen untrained, and the Master . . .

Then, perhaps, to Garth's cottage, to see Mary Maxwell that was, and the baby—Fletcher Gorse's baby, of course, but no one mentioned that, though everyone knew. He ought to try to do something about that cottage before winter came, or they'd have a cold time if it was a hard winter . . . but where was the money coming from, with taxes taking more of his income all the time, and prices going up?

Then, if he had time, to Ted England, to talk about shoeing the roan, and . . .

Then . . . anywhere, as long as it would take his mind away from the casualty lists, the endless names that his imagination would not cease from converting into young men, sprawled dead, distorted, and cold in the mud.

Cambridge: May, 1915

27 Ten o'clock, not yet full dark, the moon a few days past full, and they were approaching the Main Gate of St John's. Naomi was wearing beagling breeches and a man's tweed jacket, with dark wool stockings and gym shoes, her hair tucked into a workman's peaked cloth cap. She felt very conspicuous between the two men. Not that they were taller than she— Stan, on her left, was actually shorter, and Harry, on her right, only an inch or two taller; but she felt that everyone's attention must be focussed on them. Why were their feet making no sound on the pavement? What were they doing, heading for St John's College at this time of the evening? Why, if they looked closely they must surely ask, did the shortest of the three have his thick-lensed spectacles strapped to his face with darkened sticking plaster?

Naomi eyed the great ornamented gate towering up ahead. She had passed by here twice in daylight, to have a careful look, once Harry had told her where her first night climb would take place—"Facing the main gate there are three lead drain pipes on the wall to the left. The middle one is strongest; it stands away from the wall so that fingers can be got in behind it; and it has a zigzag about half way up."

Harry stopped and they gathered, pretending to be engaged in conversation. Harry muttered, "See the window by the bend in the middle pipe? You step onto the sill and then pull up to the top. A college porter lives in the window to the right. Don't wake him."

He looked up and down the street and said, "I'm off." He headed for the pipe, seizing it high and pulling himself up, the rubber soles of his gym shoes giving him good friction on the wall to either side of the pipe.

When he was twelve feet up, with Stan and Naomi pushed back into the shadows below him, Naomi saw two figures approaching from the south. They were still fifty yards away but there was something she didn't like about the way they walked, about the dimly seen silhouette of them. She nudged Stan, who looked and at once whispered sharply, "Prog and bulldog!" Harry hesitated a second before calling down, "Go away. I'll get up this pitch."

Stan and Naomi turned and walked off, forty yards ahead of the proctor. Behind them Naomi heard a brief grunt as Harry forced himself faster up the drain pipe. He should be on the battlements, lying down out of sight, before the 'enemy' passed. They'd have no reason to look up, and if they did they would see nothing . . . but the porter might be in his room . . . might be looking out of his window . . . It was no use worrying about all the ifs and buts, if you were to be a night climber. They walked briskly round a corner and turned sharp right into a narrow alley. "Face the wall," Stan muttered. "They probably won't even look in."

Naomi faced the wall, resigned to whatever might befall. It was fun, doing this foolish and foolhardy thing with Harry and Stan, and she was glad she had met them, glad that she had persuaded them she was a good enough climber to join them in their rooftop expeditions—the only woman among the small band of Nightclimbers of Cambridge, as far as she knew. But, since neither of them was still an undergraduate, a member of the university *in statu pupillari*, they weren't really risking much—except life and limb, of course; and that seemed the least they could do, considering what the soldiers were facing in France. Naomi, on the other hand, risked certain expulsion—not from the university, because she was not a member of it, for Cambridge did not accept women as members—but from Girton College. A few days ago she had told Rachel she didn't care whether she was sent down or not, and sometimes she still felt like that; at other times, she thought she would care, very much. So why was she facing these physical and other dangers when half the time she felt that she was doing no more than play with naughty little boys?

"They passed," Stan muttered, "we'd better go back and see what Harry's doing."

They walked out of the alley and back the way they had come, toward the Main Gate of St John's. Under the gate, looking up, they saw a dim blur on the battlements, and made out the hand signal "Come on!"

Stan said, "You next."

Naomi reached up the pipe as high as she could, when Stan ejaculated, "Good God, they're coming back!"

Naomi let go and with Stan walked off eastward along the outer wall of St John's. Once again, after a couple of minutes of purposeful walking, they turned off this time down three steps into a small area. Once more the proctor and his tophatted bulldog passed, the proctor's mortarboard tipped forward on his head, his long gown flowing. Once more Naomi and Stan headed for the Main Gate.

"Someone else might be climbing here tonight," Stan muttered, "and the progs got wind of it."

When they reached the base of the drainpipe they found Harry waiting for them. "This is no good," he said. "The court's full of porters, crossing and recrossing. So I shinned down. My old gyp just came out and told me someone's left a note at the Master's, that he would cross the Bridge of Sighs this week. Let's move off."

A few yards along the street he said, "If the university is preoccupied with St John's, tonight'll be a good time for us to tackle Trinity."

Stan said, "What climb?"

"Great Gate and Hall to the Lantern."

Stan whistled softly, "That's a bit stiff for Naomi, isn't it?"

"I can do it," Naomi said, feeling queasy at her stomach. Trinity lantern tower had always seemed to her to be unclimbable, though Harry had told her it had actually been done. "Let's get on with it," she added. "Don't forget I have a two mile walk when we're finished."

"We'll be coming with you, of course," Harry said.

Twenty minutes later, having reached the roof of the Great Gate of Trinity College, they started along the battlements, heading southward, stooping low to pass gabled windows where lights burned which would cast their silhouettes into the court below. After two minutes careful progress, Harry, in the lead, muttered, "Queen Elizabeth's Tower . . . look, put one foot here." Naomi stretched her left foot up onto a sloping tile. "Now spring and reach for the ledge . . . There!" The ledge was in her hand, and from there it was easy to the top of the Tower.

Stan joined them and Harry pointed into Trinity Lane, about fifty feet below. He said, "Some climbers always bring a couple of boxes of matches up here to throw at people in Trinity Lane. They can never imagine where the matches have come from. No one there now, though. Come on."

At the next corner, Naomi had to stretch to her fullest to reach the ledge and scramble up. Then the three padded silently left past the end of Hall, looked down into Nevile's Court, and faced the climb of Hall itself.

Harry said, "The slightly raised coping which edges either end provides the key. Holding its square edges with both hands and placing the feet on the narrow lead gutter—there—the climber pulls up hand over hand, the tension of the arms keeping the feet from slipping. The stone plaster on the summit is generally embraced with panting satisfaction."

"Is that from the Guide?" Naomi muttered.

"Yes. I know the whole book by heart, just about. But it's not as bad a climb as he makes it sound. It's a dry night, so our gym shoes will give a good grip—just lean well forward and walk up. You can hold the coping if you feel the need . . . All ready? Here we go."

He went up fast, a dim shape in the gloom. Naomi and Stan waited a few seconds, then followed. Now they were on top of the ridge of the great Hall, and rested briefly, all breathing hard after their exertion. After a moment Harry began to recite—"The distant towers of the Great, New and Nevile's Courts, looming against the dark sky, lit by the flickering lights far below; the gradations of light and shadow, marked by an occasional moving black speck, seemingly from another world; the sheer wall descending into darkness at his side; the almost invisible barrier that the battlements from which he started seem to make to his terminating in the Court if his arm slips—all contribute to making this esteemed, deservedly, the finest viewpoint in the college alps . . . Absolutely true, as you can see, except that we have a moon tonight, and no street lights. Do you really want to do the Lantern?"

Naomi peered left, at the thin tower of the Trinity Lantern, lead and glass and stone, about twenty-five feet high, rising from the middle of the Hall Ridge. She felt a sharp spasm of nervous fear, but quelled it. She said, "Yes."

Stan said, "Are you sure? We don't want to damage the glass—it's irreplaceable."

"I'm sure," Naomi snapped, feeling quite the opposite.

They edged along the ridge, the tiled roof falling away steeply on either side. Naomi kept her eyes on the Lantern until she reached it. There Harry stretched far up, took a grip, and muttered to her, "This is not hard for tall people—like a lot of the Cambridge climbs." He pulled up, swung his left leg out to the side, and continued with long easy fluid movements. After a few moments Naomi knew he was there, and moving, but could not see exactly what he was doing. The lantern was usually lit at night, but had been left dark since the first Zeppelin raids on England earlier in the year.

Naomi followed, reaching far and high. The stone was firm, the footholds wide. She realised that it was what she had seen from the ground that had frightened her. Trinity Lantern stood up there on top of the Great Hall like a thin pinnacle, seemingly without holds, spectacular, unclimbable. Here, in the dark, no sense of height in her as she kept her eyes upwards, she felt only the strength in her arms and legs sweeping her on, as she saw the holds, reached, thrust, reached again.

Harry's hand was stretched out for her. "Good girl! I can't swear to it, but personally I'll take fifty to one, in quid, that you're the first woman ever to sit on top of Trinity Hall Lantern . . ."

"There'll be more," she gasped. "Stan's not coming up. No room, he said. He's right."

She waited till her breath was again even. Cambridge was spread out like some dark tumbledown fortress below—far more exciting even than the Guide's description, and that had been written in 1901, she knew. Water gleamed in the Cam, far to the west. King's mighty chapel soared up to the south.

"Let's go down," she said.

It was not a difficult climb or a long climb up the drainpipe in the angle of the Girton wall to May Frobisher's window. May was tall, attractive, brilliant without effort, and her parents were rich; and it was easy to climb in through her window from the pipe, if the window was left open. That was the way Naomi had gone out, and now she returned the same way. May was asleep, a dark shape in the bed and Naomi did not awaken her but opened the door, looked up and down the passage and slipped out. She was glad that May was rich; she was risking her Girton career by letting Naomi use her room for this purpose; but if anything happened, and they were both sent down, which would certainly be Naomi's punishment, and probably May's too—well, it wouldn't be as bad as if it involved Rachel. For Rachel, Girton meant everything: for May, it was an interlude in a life that was going to be beautiful and pleasant, whether she stayed at Girton to graduation or not.

Naomi slipped into her own sitting room, closing the door carefully behind her, and leaned back against it, yawning and stretching. It was done, and she was home safe and undiscovered. She felt a strong surge of relief, a lightening in herself. She must have been tenser than she thought, walking back along the Huntingdon Road with Harry and Stan, trying to stride like a man. The absence of lights had helped, she knew: for a patrolling police constable had come suddenly upon them out of a side street, but in the gloom he had not detected anything amiss.

She walked through to her bedroom, and began to draw the curtains, then paused, listening to a nightingale trilling and soaring in Yew Tree Walk. After a minute, yawning again, she finished drawing the curtains, lit the paraffin lamp, and undressed. Wearing only her nightdress she began to wash her hands and face at the wash-handstand, in cold water from the jug.

The outer door to the passage opened and in the mirror over the basin she saw Rachel Cowan slip in, also wearing only her nightdress, a white cotton one with a pattern of small red flowers. "Thank heavens you're back!" she whispered, coming into the bedroom. "J-B was round an hour ago, and I was terrified you'd just be coming in."

"What was she doing?"

"Just making a round. She saw my light under the door, she said, and came in . . . told me I mustn't damage my eyes by reading too much at night. I'm sure she didn't come in here. I would have heard."

Naomi sat down and began to brush her hair. Rachel said, "You mustn't do it again, Naomi. If you're caught, they'll send you down. And it's so dangerous . . . Here, let me do that."

She stood behind Naomi, took the brush, and began long sweeping strokes. Naomi closed her eyes. The room felt warm and comfortable. Rachel talked in a low tone as she brushed—"Goodness, how black the water is! You must have been filthy!"

Naomi mumbled, "The roofs of Cambridge are picturesque, and also very dirty."

"Where did you go?"

"Trinity. Great Gate, Hall . . . and the Lantern."

"You shouldn't, you really shouldn't. It makes me sick just to think of it."

"Harry's going to France in a fortnight."

"Poor man."

"He's nice. So's Stan, in a quieter way."

"You're not in love with either of them, are you?"

Naomi opened her eyes—"Good gracious, no! They seem—very young. As though they were still undergraduates . . . much younger than me, anyway."

"Men always seem younger than women, I think. They are childish. If they weren't, they wouldn't go to war."

"But, Rachel, we couldn't help it. There was the treaty we'd signed, guaranteeing Belgium's neutrality."

Rachel said, "I know about that—but the war could have been avoided, if men had really wanted to. Now, it's so much worse than anyone imagined. It would stop soon enough if the men refused to go— all men, Germans, Austrians, Russians, French, British . . ."

"But Rachel, you were in favour of conscription. You said it was the only fair way."

"I was . . . but I was wrong. The only fair way is to stop the war. No one should go, especially working men. The aristocrats and capitalists can go, if they want to. We'll be better off without them."

"Do you count my father as an aristocrat? Or Uncle Christopher?"

"I know them, and like them . . . but, yes, they're aristocrats, parasites, really, if you look at it from the socialist point of view."

"Well, I don't know . . . I only know that if Lord Kitchener's right, and the war goes on for another two years, there won't be any men left."

"Would that be so terrible? If there are no men, women will have to take over everything—banks, industry, commerce, insurance, teaching, government . . . You ought to read *Das Kapital*."

"I can't read German."

"It's been translated, of course. I think women will make our society socialist more easily and completely than men could ever bring themselves to."

Naomi yawned, "That's enough, Rachel. Thank you . . . I'm going to bed." The rhythmical brushing went on, becoming more slow. Rachel's voice was lower, hoarser, close to her ear, uncertain. "Naomi, you are beautiful . . . beautiful . . ." Hands were under her armpits, helping her up, now round her waist, guiding her. She fell back on the bed, on top of the bedclothes, warm in the May night. In the new silence she heard the nightingale again, muffled by the curtains, but plain and strong and lovely. The light went out . . . a body slid down beside her on the bed. She felt no horror or aversion but waited, lying relaxed, to know what would follow, to learn who and what she was.

Naomi lay awake in her bed, the room bathed in morning light. When Rachel left her she thought she would not be able to go to sleep for hours, wondering, working out . . . but no, she had fallen sound asleep within five minutes, remembering only Rachel's last words, "I love you, more than any man could." And the last kiss, planted on her lips, to which she had tried to respond; but had not.

She had enjoyed the act, she could not deny it. It might happen again—probably would. Was she then, like Sappho, a lesbian, sapphic? She had heard it whispered that two of the other girls here were . . .

and two of the dons as well. When she had first fully understood what such a relationship implied, she had thought it unnatural, and unclean. Now she was experiencing it herself, and it didn't seem unclean at all, but rather warm and lovely . . . a new sort of trust and something shared, that she had not thought could be shared by women. Yet, try as she would, she could not see her relationship with Rachel growing. It was the first shared sexual act of her life, and it ought to be important, as the loss of her virginity would be: but it wasn't. There was no place here for expansion of love—only the needs of the moment, when her body would demand it and it would take place.

Rachel had told her, as they lay there together in each other's arms, that she had always had crushes on other girls, though she had never before brought them to consummation. Naomi had wondered whether that was because she was afraid of being rebuffed by boys. Was Rachel, then, truly sapphic? She had asked her. Rachel had not replied for a time, then whispered, "I don't know. If I could fall in love with a man, perhaps I'd find out, but men are so . . . such . . . bullies. They're like the worst sort of stupid aristocrat. They think everything belongs to them, including us, just because they're men."

Naomi got out of bed and stood in the window, looking out. Girton was a sanctuary . . . from men . . . from the university even, being two miles out of Cambridge, and isolated from all contacts with the rest of the university's life . . . from the world. She knew she was in a state of betwixt and between . . . not girl, not woman: not lesbian, not wife nor lover: not suffragist, not meek traditional woman . . . waiting, waiting . . .

She was wrong, in thinking just now that she was not a woman. She was. If there were no war, perhaps she would still be a girl, but the war was changing everything, for all women, especially her. Spring was gone, summer upon her. Girton was not the place to wait, in a woman's early summer, in wartime. Nor were Hedlington or High Staining, arguing with her parents over her future, making petty gestures of dissent, getting locked up for the night, being bound over for committing a breach of the peace—events which would once have seemed of enormous consequence, but now—nothing. What, then, was the place for her?

There were women in France—nurses. But she was not a nurse and the war would be over before she could learn. What skills did she have? And she didn't mean book learning or things that were done in offices with paper and typewriters. She needed to go out into the world . . . She could drive a car, and she knew more than a little about the mechanics of motor cars—learned while growing up as a Rowland, even as a girl. There'd be places for women to drive cars perhaps in France, and working with men, she hoped, not in isolated groups of women, such as Girton . . . She must go out into the world to find the true Naomi Rowland—not a student moulded by the discipline of the cloister, but a woman moulded by the discipline of her work, and self respect.

She put on her dressing gown and went along to the earth closet. By the time she'd finished the gyps would have brought up hot water, and a jug. Then she'd have to tell Rachel.

After an early breakfast she knocked on Rachel's door. Rachel called, "Come in . . . Oh, Naomi, you look so serious." She shut the door and held out both hands. Naomi took them, and said, "I'm leaving Girton. At once."

Rachel's hands dropped, her jaw dropped, her protruding eyes swelled. "What? You can't mean it! . . . You mean it? Before the Tripos exam next week?"

Naomi said, "I must go out and be myself, not a member of the college, the university, even my family."

Rachel sat down heavily. "What are you going to do?" she muttered.

"Find out more about the women's services," Naomi said, "then join the one that offers the most opportunities for me." She saw that Rachel was crying, tears slowly filling her eyes and trickling down her cheeks onto her blouse. "Don't cry," she said, sitting down on the arm of the chair and stroking Rachel's hair. "We're not going to lose each other."

"Is this . . . because of . . . what happened last night?" Rachel asked in a choked voice.

Naomi searched carefully for words, because she had to tell the truth, but she did not want to hurt her friend. She said, "In a way . . . that was a sort of symptom of what I'm suffering from, not the thing itself. It's frustration, I suppose . . . and I'm not the only one. Johnny Merritt told me his sister feels just the same at that women's university she's at in America . . . Smith, I think it's called. I've tried being a suffragette . . . protesting against injustice, for conscription . . . forgetting about politics and enjoying being what my family would like me to be, a fox hunter, a county girl . . . roof climbing, that's silly, really, what we did last night . . . You said you loved me. I love you, too, but not in the way you do, and I don't see how I ever will. I mean, I'll fall in love with a man one day, I suppose, and it won't make any difference to the way I love you . . . I'm frustrated, Rachel, and I've got to get out, and . . . be what I ought to be."

Rachel continued to cry, whispering, "I can't stay on without you. I told you, no one here likes me, except you."

"You must get your degree," Naomi said.

Rachel said, "They want me to be a teacher, and finish up as headmistress of a girls' school, and I used to want that, too, but every day it seems more useless . . . Secretly, I've been thinking the same as you, finding the university more childish, more remote from the reality of the world . . . something I ought to be free of, to do what I want to do."

"What's that?"

"Politics," Rachel said. "I want to go into the socialist movement, in politics."

"Then why don't you? You don't need a degree for that."

Rachel stood up, staring at Naomi. "Why not? They want organisers everywhere. The party is young. I'll go wherever they send me. But I'll try to get to Hedlington, to be close to you."

Naomi said briefly, "That will be lovely, Rachel . . . but remember, I have no idea where I'll be going, eventually. I'm going to telephone my father now, and leave by the first train, as soon as I can get packed, probably after lunch. I'll have to tell Miss Jones or J-B first."

"I'll stay till the end of the term," Rachel said, "and wait to hear from you, where you are. Oh Naomi, how exciting! I could never have broken out by myself."

She rushed into Naomi's arms, hugging and kissing. Naomi, nearly nine inches taller, held her friend's head to her breast and looked over her, out of the window, at the world.

Daily Telegraph, Tuesday, May 18, 1915

SUNDAY'S BATTLE
GREAT BOMBARDMENT

British Headquarters, FRANCE, Sunday. **In the Festu-bert region of the La Bassée line the British troops made assaults today, in the morning, and again later in the after-noon, and reports to hand show that material progress has been made.**

From a coign of vantage only some three miles distant from the British trenches, I was enabled this afternoon to follow the operations in this sector of the line . . . Away to the left over Festubert hung a dark pall of smoke that seemed to grow in intensity as I watched. Shells were burst-

ing the whole time—a dazzling flash, a cloud of smoke, and then a dull boom. The green fumes of the lyddite mingled with the black cloud produced by the 'Jack Johnsons,' and over all screamed the shrapnel, leaving a little speck of white as it burst . . . The guns never ceased, and now and again a reddish glare, ascending to the sky, showed where a 'grandmamma,' as the heavy shells have been fancifully nicknamed, had started a conflagration in some ruined building. An occasional shell was dropped into La Bassée, but our fire was concentrated on Festubert, where the Germans have organised some strong redoubts, fortified with machine guns.

Back in the town, only a few miles away from the firing line, everything was going on as usual. Only the passing of a few Red Cross cars laden with wounded showed that an engagement was proceeding so near.

The sight of a convoy of a hundred German prisoners marching through the street under strong escort was a token of our successful advance . . . Beside the keen, well-cut faces of their bronzed guard, they showed up in very poor contrast and the picture would have convinced even the most pronounced pessimist of the immense superiority of the Tommy over the German private.

Christopher Cate leafed through the paper again: attacks near Arras . . . short German withdrawal to their main positions in the Ypres sector . . . Allied aviators destroy an artillery park with their bombs . . . a Zeppelin drops bombs on the coastal town of Ramsgate and injures three people: the townsfolk are concerned lest the incident affect their summer season. The Germans and Austrians are advancing fast and far against the Russians, and it is possible that Russia will soon be knocked out of the war . . . but not, Cate thought, probable: there was still plenty of Russian territory to fall back on.

Something made him glance up and look out of the window, and he saw his nephew Boy Rowland walking across the grass to the front door. Cate hurried out and was there before Boy reached it. Cate held out his hand and they shook, warmly, Cate saying, "I thought you were still in hospital. You look well, considering. And congratulations on your M.C."

"They sent me home yesterday, Uncle. Thought I'd stroll over and tell you I was at home. I have to exercise every day, anyway." He took a deep breath. He was pale, with only spots of colour on his cheeks, and now coughed drily into his handkerchief. When the fit was over he said, "I can't believe it . . . no guns . . . no mud . . . no snipers."

"Have you had breakfast, Boy?"

"I'm not hungry, thanks, Uncle . . . just want to walk in the fresh air . . . in England . . ."

"Your father and mother all right? I haven't spoken to them or seen them in a week or more . . . been very busy."

"They're fine, thanks. High Staining's full of women, though. It feels funny . . . Lady Helen, Carol Adams, the girl from London, don't know her name yet."

"Surely you don't object to a little femininity after your bachelor life in the trenches?"

Boy laughed, and coughed again. Then he said, "No, I like it. It's just strange. I'll get used to it . . . I'll go on now, Uncle . . . walk up to Beighton later, perhaps."

"Wait a minute, Boy. I'll come with you. Wait till I get my cap and stick and Jack and Jill."

A few minutes later they walked together down the lane toward Walstone, the cocker spaniels at heel. Cate said, "What is it really like out there, Boy? I can't imagine it, and what I read in the papers doesn't help, somehow. In fact, it seems to make it even harder for the mind to picture."

Boy did not answer for such a long time that Cate, stricken with guilt, cried, "Please don't answer if you don't like to think about it, Boy. How inconsiderate of me, when all you want to do is forget!"

Boy said slowly, "I do want to forget, Uncle, while I'm here, yes . . . but I'll never be able to . . . ever. And I also want to try to define what I really feel . . . It's dangerous out there, most of the time. Sometimes it's very dangerous. You don't sleep well, or eat well, or breathe well . . . You see friends dying before your eyes, and can not help. You're afraid half the time, and bored the other half . . . But what's worst, for me, is the smell. The war smells, Uncle . . . smells foul . . . not like a farmyard or a pigsty, like a huge pile of human shit . . . sorry, excrement . . . in which there are bloated and blackened corpses rotting . . . Before I was gassed and sent home, I used to think of what I'd do on leave . . . dance with a pretty girl in London . . . play cricket for the village on a June afternoon . . . drink English beer . . . Do you know what's the only thing I want to do? Breathe air that doesn't have that smell." His voice was trembling.

Hampstead Heath: Whit Monday, May 24, 1915

28 The six of them walked slowly up Heath Street from Hampstead tube station, taking their pace from the rest of the crowd surging up the steep between the old houses, the bow windows, the brass door knockers, the lace curtains—Niccolo Fagioletti, Bill Hoggin, and Frank Stratton in front, and Ethel, Ruth, and Anne behind, Ruth carrying baby Launcelot in her arms. The sun shone, the pubs were all open, and malty gusts of beer and porter wafted out as they passed under each swinging, brightly painted sign. It was Whit Monday, the cockneys' special holiday of the year; and they were on their way to the cockneys' favourite meeting ground for the day—Hampstead Heath.

Bill Hoggin threw back over his shoulder, " 'Ow old's the little 'un now, Ruth? Buggered if I can remember."

"Three months and three days," Ruth answered, giving Launcelot a proud little shake to which he made no response: he was a good baby, and fast asleep.

They trudged on up, their faces darkening with the exertion and the rising strength of the sun. The distinctive lilt and thud of steam organ music came strongly down the hill and Frank said, "Remember that roundabout at the Sheep Fair, Bill?"

"I bloody do. Fair mess, that was."

"I seen worse. We said we never would, remember?"

Hoggin jerked his head down New End. " 'Ere, let's drop in on the Duke and 'ave one. This 'ill's bloody steep."

"You had one at the Horse and Groom," Ruth said reproachfully, but the men pushed into the Duke of Hamilton's crowded public bar, Bill shouting over the heads of the crowd at the bar, "Three pints of bitter! Anything for you ladies? Orright, you'd only 'ave to go pissing be'ind the bushes and chances are you'd find 'alf a dozen other women there already. What ho, Frank! What ho, Nick! An' you can drink to your brave boys, eh, now that Italy's come into the war."

Niccolo said, "They're not my boys no more. I'm British."

"Well, you'd better not go an' visit your ma and pa back 'ome, 'cos they'll put you into uniform quicker'n you can say O *sole Mio*. You was born in Italy, wasn't you?"

"Yes," Niccolo said briefly. He raised his tankard and drank. He didn't really like beer, especially not English beer, but thought it best not to make himself act 'foreign,' particularly with the Strattons—and this Bill Hoggin, his brother-in-law. He had not met Hoggin often, and hoped he never would, for he was afraid of him. He had known some men like that in Italy when he was very young—unpredictable, powerful brutes—and he had been afraid of them, too. Hoggin was even less predictable, because he was Anglo-Saxon.

They finished the beer and, wiping their mouths with the backs of their hands, struggled back into the street and on up the hill. Niccolo took off his jacket and slung it over his shoulder, after Bill had done it first. "Go on, take your coat off," Hoggin said to Frank. "It's 'ot as 'ell."

"Can't," Frank said. "I'm in uniform."

"What the 'ell does that matter?"

"They'd see a man of the Weald Light Infantry looking like a tramp."

"Garn, you mean they wouldn't see that lance-corporal's stripe. 'Ow long 'ave you 'ad that?"

"The day before I started on leave. I was Mr Charles's batman but when he was gassed they put me in the Pioneer Section and gave me a stripe. The Pioneers are the best soldiers in the whole push, and that means in the whole British army!"

"You've only been in the army—'ow long?—ten months, and you're talking like a bleeding recruiting sergeant. What's got into you?"

They passed the Horse Pond, the sound of the merry-go-round louder with every step, and hearing now the shouts and cries of the men at the booths, the giggling screams of girls on the swings and at the coconut shies.

"I'm a soldier," Frank said briefly.

"Plenty of soldiers are bloody fed up. An' they're telling them sods in Parliament about it."

"Not us," Frank said. "We do our job."

"And get your heads blown off, for nothing. Wait till you cop a packet and see 'ow you feel then."

"Don't talk like that, Bill," Ruth said anxiously.

Frank stopped, hands on hips, "Here we are . . . want a ride on the roundabout, Annie?"

"No, you go, Frank. I'm frightened of them, especially after that accident at the Sheep Fair . . . Oh look, look! Give me sixpence, Frank."

Frank followed the direction of her pointing finger and saw a tent with a sign reading: GYPSY ENGLAND, PALMIST & CLAIRVOYANT, SCIENTIFIC PALMIST KNOWN THE WORLD OVER. THE ONLY GYPSY ENGLAND LEFT. THIS LADY LEADS WHERE OTHERS FOLLOW: then in smaller lettering, READS ON HEALTH, HAPPINESS, MARRIAGE, EASES & COMFORTS YOUR MIND. DON'T STOP OUTSIDE STEP INSIDE.

Frank sighed and gave her a silver sixpence. He called after her, "We'll be at the shooting gallery, over there."

It was dark inside the tent and smelled of smoke—scented smoke: a large dried lizard hung from the ridge pole, together with a stuffed owl. The earth floor was covered with a dark red carpet, and a patterned red cloth covered the rickety table, where a crystal ball absorbed and refracted the light of a candle. Gypsy England was seated on the far side of the table, wearing a black dress, a silvery bandanna binding her hair, her eyes apparently closed, her lined face dark in repose. Anne sat down and Gypsy England held out her hand, palm up. Anne put the sixpence into it and the gypsy put the money away with her other hand, holding Anne's wrist. She peered at the palm, pressing down. The table wobbled and the crystal ball shook. Gypsy England spoke in a deep voice and a strong accent, rolling her Rs—"You are married. You have children."

"Oh, yes! Three," Anne said.

"You will have a long life . . . you will have one more child. You will be rich and your name famous . . . A tall dark man will come into your life . . ."

A tall dark man, Anne thought, trembling a little. Mr Protheroe was tall, but not dark. Mr Chambers was sort of tall and sort of dark, but not really either. How could the gypsy woman have known about them, when she hardly dared to admit even to herself that she was seeing them . . . not that they had come into her life, really, yet.

The gypsy intoned, "Have you any questions you want to ask?"

Anne hesitated. She wanted to ask how she could keep away from men like Mr Protheroe and Mr Chambers, when Frank was at the war: how not to feel so miserably alone and lonely: how to keep her faith, Frank's trust.

She spoke slowly, fearful of what answer she might receive. "Will my husband come back safe to me?"

Gypsy England leaned forward, peering into the crystal ball, her face illuminated. After a long, slow-breathing pause she said, "Yes."

"When?"

"When it's all over. That's all, love, if you want me to read the leaves that'll be another tanner."

Anne got up and hurried out, her head swimming.

They were settled on a sloping bank above a little stream, its bank of soft yellow earth. A rhododendron bush in early flower made a pink and blue tapestry behind them, the thousand candles of a giant horse chestnut tree glowed bright above them. They were looking across the stream and up the opposite hill toward the coconut shies, the merry-go-round, the rows of tents and stalls, the cockney vendors in full pearly costume, shouting their wares. From afar the steam organ was playing *There's a long, long trail a-winding*, and Frank sang softly in time, for it had become a favourite in the regiment:

There's a long long trail a-winding, Into the land of my dreams,
Where the nightingales are singing, And a white moon beams,
There's a long long night of waiting, Until my dreams all come true,
Till the day when I'll be going down, That long long trail with you.

Three girls in white dresses, with red, white, and blue sashes draped across their bosoms, tripped up, each carrying a bunch of small Union Jacks on pins.

The leader stooped over Bill Hoggin. "Take a Union Jack, mister. Join our brave boys in France."

"Fuck off," Hoggin said equably.

"Mind your language," the girl retorted. "You ought to be in uniform. 'Ere, take a flag, put it onto your shirt, to show you're going to join."

"Fuck off, I said," Hoggin repeated.

Frank said sharply, "Don't swear in front of the young ladies, Bill."

"Young ladies, my arse! Look at the lipstick on 'em—tarts more like," Hoggin said, as one of the girls gave Niccolo a flag, which he pinned to his shirt.

The leading girl bent down and kissed Frank on the cheek, saying, "You don't mind, dearie?" to Anne. "He deserves it." The other two kissed Frank in turn; then they tripped on, calling, "Who'll take a Union Jack for King and Country?"

"Why did you take one of their plurry flags?" Hoggin asked Niccolo.

Niccolo shrugged expressively, spreading his hands, "It costs nothing. And they went away. What good would it be to talk to them about how foolish it is for men to fight wars, when they can eat, drink, sleep with women, make money? And have babies. That is what life is for, I think." He looked meaningly at Ethel, his childless wife.

"We didn't start the war," Frank said, "and I like drinking and all those things just as much as you do, but first we've got to beat the Germans. And to do that we need more shells. The last three scraps I was in, our artillery had to stop firing half way through—ran out of ammunition."

Anne said, "They're going to pass a law about that—closing the pubs in the afternoons, so the workmen can't get drunk."

"I don't know as I hold with that," Frank said, "but if it's necessary to get more shells, then we ought to grin and bear it. And there ought to be conscription, that's the truth. Out there, schoolmasters and engineers and professors and scientists are being killed off as infantry privates. It's a waste, and we can't afford it."

"Then why the 'ell are you in the footslogging infantry? You're an expert mechanic, aren't you? Why aren't you in the engineers, at least? Or in a factory, back 'ere, making the guns for the rest to shoot each other with?"

"That's what I thought, once," Frank said, "but you wouldn't understand. You haven't been there."

Somehow he had got through Hoggin's thick skin and Hoggin retaliated. "Surprised you're *here*, come to that."

Frank looked up. "What do you mean?"

"I'd 'ave thought you'd be at 'ome, looking after them two little girls, instead of leaving them with your mum and dad. He's not the man to leave them with, from what I 'ear, even if they are 'is own flesh and blood."

"Bill!" Ruth cried in anguish, "you mustn't say things like that!"

"You keep your mouth shut about our dad," Frank said. "He's a better man than you'll ever be." He ought to put his fist in Hoggin's face, he thought; but that sort of fighting seemed so childish, now, after France. He hoped that Hoggin's hint was unfounded, for his mother's sake; but after a few months in the trenches you thought differently about a lot of things. Anything could be true, of anybody—self-sacrifice to make you cry, cowardice to make you ashamed for the human race, vices creeping out into the open like diseased rats, bravery shining like a diamond in a dung pile.

"Let's not quarrel," Ruth said nervously. "It's Bank Holiday, and we're all together, for the first time in ages."

"Except for Fred," Frank said. "He's down by Arras. Here, let's go up to Jack Straw's Castle and eat our dinner on the grass, and we'll bring out beer and lemonade from the bar."

They lay on the grass, shaded by oaks and beeches. Launcelot had been crying, but a sip of beer, given over Ruth's protests, had calmed him. Ruth's breasts ached, for she had omitted the ten o'clock feed. She'd have to feed him at two, but where could she find a private place in this crowd? She was not a working woman, to feed her baby in public, careless who saw her bare bosom.

Hoggin lolled on his side, a full tankard in one hand, a chicken drumstick in the other. "It's getting more bloody dangerous 'ere than in France," he said to Frank. "The *Lusitania,* the *Princess Irene* blowing up at Shereness the other day . . . near four 'undred killed there. I went down and saw that, day after. Bodies half a mile away, there was."

"And the railway crash at Gretna Green," Ethel said, "how many killed there?"

"Two hundred and twenty-seven," Frank said. "Mostly soldiers, too. The worst railway accident we've ever had in this country."

Niccolo had had enough beer long since, and had bought some cheap red wine from Jack Straw's Castle saloon bar, and was drinking it from the bottle. He leaned forward from his squatting position and said, "Ethel tells me you all know Lord Swanwick, eh?"

"The Earl of Swanwick, of Walstone Park," Ruth said. "We have all seen him, Niccolo. He comes to Hedlington often, for political meetings. He's a great lord."

Niccolo winked, "I know. I know something else, too . . . He is broke, running out of money."

Hoggin pricked up his ears. "Eh? 'Ow do you know that?"

"I heard it, at the Savoy, where I am a waiter in the dining-room for four months now, you know? The head waiter told me who he was when he brought him to one of my tables. He was with his son . . . another Lord."

"Lord Cantley," Ruth said. "That's a courtesy title. He does not sit in the House of Lords."

"Well, this Lord Cantley is a banker, I hear, and his father was telling him that he needs money, a lot of money, and asking how can they get it."

"Come into the food business with me," Hoggin said, guffawing. "If I'd 'ave two lords in with me. Which is not bloody likely!" He stopped laughing and looked hard at Niccolo. "You 'ear a lot as a waiter?"

"A lot, yes. They all talk, in the Savoy. And they are all rich, important people—Members of Parliament, Cabinet Ministers, lawyers, gentlemen from Fleet Street, and the Stock Exchange. There are signs everywhere, about the Germans listening, but they talk. Not much of it is about the war, though."

"I don't want to know about the bloody war. I want to know about money—who needs it, who's got it . . . and about dirty linen, specially about important people's dirty linen. The more I know, the more I can get. Look 'ere, Niccolo, I'll pay you something for anything you tell me, that I don't know already."

"How much?" Niccolo said, drinking copiously from the bottle.

"It'll depend . . . but I'm not going to give you a ruddy tanner for telling me that Lord Pimplefart wipes his arse with a goose's neck. Tell you what, I'll pay you five bob a week, just not to tell anyone else, see. A retainer, they call it. An' then more, for what you can find out. 'Ere, 'ere's your first five bob—now you're an employee of Hoggin, Hoggin & Hoggin."

Niccolo pocketed the coins, and drank again, emptying the bottle. Frank thought, if he isn't drunk, he has a harder head than I think he has; but he looks drunk, swarthy, flushed, dribbling a little from the corners of his full lips, perspiring, his thick curly hair dark and dank.

He said suddenly to his wife, "Why you give me no babies?"

Ruth held Launcelot tighter to her, Anne cast her eyes down. Hoggin drank beer noisily from a bottle.

"Why you no give me babies? It's not my fault."

Ethel began to cry softly, her head bent, the tears dripping onto the grass. The steam organ was playing *Tipperary,* hoarsely strident on the hot summer air. Bees hummed and buzzed in the flowers along the verge of the Spaniards Road, cars growled past, carriages rolled by, the horses' hooves clipclopping on the gravel.

Niccolo said, "I do what a man should, often enough."

"Too much," Ethel said, suddenly looking up. Her face was mottled red, and Frank remembered that she had had both wine and beer in the last hour. She was not used to either, the way they'd been brought up. Ethel turned to her brother. "He makes me bleed . . . and hurts . . . I'll never have a baby and I want a baby." She collapsed onto Anne's shoulder, moaning, "I want a baby!"

Niccolo shouted, "I will divorce you. You are no good to me, my friends laugh at me!"

"You can't divorce me," Ethel cried, "I've done nothing wrong! Why don't you go and see a doctor, like mother said? You might have a disease. You've been with other women often enough."

Niccolo lashed out at her with the flat of his right hand, striking her a resounding smack across the cheek.

"Here!" Anne cried. "Stop that!"

Frank jumped to his feet, his belly in a tight knot, the way it was when he went over the top near St Julien, three days after Mr Charles had been evacuated. He grabbed Fagioletti by the collar and pulled him to his feet.

"Put up your hands!" he shouted.

Niccolo waved his arms in the air, staggered half a pace right, half a pace left, "I'm going—divorce her," he mumbled.

"She's my sister," Frank said, "and I'm not going to have her hurt by any dirty dago. Here—" he lashed out with his right fist, landing smartly on Niccolo's large nose. Niccolo collapsed on the grass, blood spurting like a geyser.

Ethel was on her feet, shouting, "You ought to be ashamed of yourself, Frank Stratton! Can't you see he's had too much to drink? Hitting a man who can't defend himself!"

Hoggin belched long and reverberatingly, and loud. "Look, it's 'ot. I'm going off to snooze be'ind a bush with Ruthie. Why don't we all push off, and come back 'ere in an hour, eh?"

Frank said curtly to Anne, "Come on."

Anne said anxiously, "What about Niccolo's nose? It's bleeding terribly."

"He won't bleed to death," Frank said briefly. "Come on."

She got up obediently and followed him down the grass slope away from the road. They did not speak for a long time, and Anne kept a little apart from him. This man was not the husband she had known, and the difference was something far deeper than the khaki uniform and the shining bugle horn and prancing horse of Kent on his cap badge. At last she sneaked her hand into his, and said, "Do you think he'll really divorce her?"

"I don't think he can," Frank said, "not just for not having a baby. If she's been going with other blokes, that's different."

"Ethel? Never!" Anne said. "But . . . she might say she had, if Niccolo told her to. She'd do anything for him."

Frank said, "More's the pity."

They walked on, along narrow footpaths through beech and oak and chestnut, out onto high open grass, London spread out to the south, and then stopped on the hills, hands locked.

"What did the fortune teller say?" he asked.

"Gypsy England? She said I'd meet a tall dark man."

"Who's that? Do you know any tall dark men?"

"No. But I might meet one, I suppose."

"You're a ninny to believe those gypsies. All they do is take your money off you and tell you what you want to hear."

"She said we'd have another baby," Anne said softly.

He tightened his grip on her hand, squeezing, and for the first time since they had left the others, turned and smiled into her eyes, saying, "Not surprising, after what we did last night, eh?"

"Oh, Frank," she whispered.

"That was the best night we've ever had, eh? And we've had some good ones."

She usually blushed and said something about not to talk like that whenever Frank commented on their love making, but now she said simply, "You're my husband, and I love you. I felt like a . . . like the most beautiful woman in the world."

"You were, last night . . . And listen, don't you ever go out alone at night, away from houses."

"Oh, I wouldn't," Anne cried, "not with anyone. I'm your wife."

Frank said, "I'm thinking about that mad Ripper everyone's talking about. If you *have* to go out at night, you get someone to go with you, a man."

"But . . ."

"Specially if it's a full moon, or near it. See?"

"Yes," she said. Then, after a while, she burst out—"Oh, Frank, I can't bear it without you. I don't do the right things with the girls . . . It'll be worse when Johnny gets bigger . . . I'm bad tempered, nervy . . . I snap at them, everyone . . . sit at home feeling sorry for myself. I'm afraid that . . ." she stopped.

He did not take up the unfinished sentence, but said stubbornly, "I've got a job to do, and I'm going to do it, till it's finished."

"You're an expert mechanic. Couldn't you . . . ?"

"No, love. It doesn't matter what Hoggin and Fagioletti do. Personally, I wouldn't want *either* of them in the Wealds. We're a good push, we are, because we have our self respect. Goodness, Anne, I'm afraid, all the time. My knees will be knocking when I get onto that train to go back . . . but I've got to be on it. Until then, I'll try to make every night as good as last night. And every day, too."

She wiped her eyes. Thursday next, at 10 p.m., at Waterloo Station, Platform 9, his five days' leave would be up; and by midnight she'd be wondering when she'd next see Mr Protheroe or Mr Chambers.

Ethel and Niccolo had not moved. The others went, so they stayed. Ethel was still crying, but not passionately. Now it was more like summer dew filling her eyes. She stroked her husband's head where he lay on the grass beside her, face down, a handkerchief pressed to his nose. She said, "You don't mean it, Niccolo. Tell me you don't mean it."

"I do," he said sullenly, the words muffled and distorted by the handkerchief and the swollen nose.

"What shall I do?"

"Go home to your mother and father. They never liked me, because I'm an Italian . . . because I *was* an Italian," he corrected himself.

"But I love you. I want to give you a baby. But . . . please see a doctor, Niccolo."

He rolled over and appeared to be thinking, rubbing the black stubble on his chin with his hand. He said suddenly, "You will tell me you have made love with Giorgio, my friend. And I will say, go home to your mother and father, I don't want you. And I will start to divorce you. And if you don't say what I tell you, that you have fucked with Giorgio, then I shall hit you, every night, until you do."

Ethel kept on crying, softly, helplessly.

Bill and Ruth Hoggin sat in the depths of a wood. It was not cool, but it was cooler than almost anywhere else on the Heath that afternoon. Bill had his back against an elm, his shirt collar loose, a bottle of warm beer half empty in his hand. Ruth sat opposite, her knees tucked under her, her blouse unbuttoned, feeding Launcelot. Launcelot grunted and snorted and kneaded her swollen breast, milk spilling out from the corners of his mouth and running down his chin onto her breast below the nipple. She had a folded handkerchief pressed onto the other nipple, which was also dripping profusely.

"Cooeee, cooeee," Bill said, offering the baby a fat finger.

Launcelot took no notice. Bill said, "Wheee, wheee! 'Ere, 'andsome, 'ave some of this!" He poured a little beer onto his finger and held it out. Launcelot pounded away at the breast.

"'Ere, I'm your dad," Bill said, leaning forward. "Take some bloody notice when I speaks to yer."

"He's busy," Ruth said lovingly. "He's strong . . . Oh, he almost hurts sometimes, but it's like . . . the other thing, too . . . I feel warm inside, all the way."

"'Ere, Launcelot . . . Launcelot! I can't say it! It's a bloody silly name! What in 'ell made you so bloody keen on that?"

"I like it," she said, "it's the name of King Arthur's best knight."

"If I'd 'a been called Launcelot in Southwark when I was a nipper, I'd never 'a grown up, I can tell yer." He broke into a falsetto. "'Ere, Lancie Lottie! Wot the 'ell can we call 'im for short?"

"Nothing. His name is Launcelot and we'll call him that."

"Launcelot Hoggin . . . Well, 'e's not going to grow up in South-wark, so p'raps it won't matter. P'raps 'e'll be a real knight when 'e grows up. There's worse things 'appen at sea."

He lolled back, finished his beer and threw the bottle into the bushes. "That Anne is looking real rosy today. Frank's doing right by 'er, now that 'e's 'ome, I can tell. All she's seeing is the ceiling."

"Don't be coarse, Bill. They are in love with each other, still."

"P'raps. But she's in love with the prick, too. Mind you, there's nothing wrong with that. I love you, but I wouldn't give a tinker's curse for you if you didn't 'ave a cunt, now would I? . . . You 'adn't 'eard about your dad?"

"No, and I don't believe a word of it," Ruth said energetically. Bill was right about almost everything, always: except about her family. There, she had to stand up to him.

Bill said, "Well, the bloke 'oo told me is a bloody liar 'alf the time, but 'e *did* say the old man plays round with bloody little frippets."

"It's a lie."

Bill said sagely, "You're probably right, Ruthie. On the other 'and, don't believe it *couldn't* be so just because 'e's an 'igh and mighty Stratton. I reckon even the 'igh and mighty Rowlands wouldn't be no different, if we could look under their blankets the way we do each others'."

Ruth looked down lovingly at her baby, and said, "Bill, you must learn to speak nice. I'm not going to have Launcelot ashamed of his dad, when he grows up. And what are the other boys at Eton College going to think, when they hear you?"

Bill said nothing for a while and she looked up at him, surprised; she had expected an outburst. He said, "P'raps you're right, Ruthie. Not because of Launcelot or the fucking little lords at Eton . . . but I'm meeting an 'igher class of people in my business, now that I'm making big money. They don't want to ask me to their restaurants, or clubs, or even their favourite pubs . . . and that means some other bastard makes the money I might 'ave. But 'ow——?"

"An elocution teacher," Ruth said firmly. "Miss Joan Plummer. An hour every Saturday and an hour every Sunday, when you're at home."

"Thought it all out, 'aven't you? An' fixed the fee an' all, I dare say?" Ruth nodded, and Bill cried, " 'Ere, that little bugger's going to burst if you let 'im 'ave any more!"

They were walking up the path toward the south entrance and Heath Street, on their way to the tube, and home. Niccolo was on duty in the dining-room of the Savoy in three hours' time; Ruth wanted to be back in Hedlington when Launcelot was due for his next feed; and Anne was anxious to take her children off her parents' hands. Launcelot was asleep, flopped like a sack over Ruth's shoulder. Frank had offered to carry him, but Ruth didn't want to let him go. Niccolo was sobering up, which made him surly and silent.

A dense crowd filled the slope of the heath just inside the gate. Half a dozen policemen watched, sweating visibly inside their high-collared tunics. Someone was speaking from an improvised platform, where several placards proclaimed HORATIO BOTTOMLEY, THE PEOPLE'S TRIBUNE.

"Here, let's stop a minute," Frank said. "I want to hear what Bumley has to say."

"Not for long, I can't," Niccolo said.

"Only a couple of minutes. All the blokes read *John Bull* and some write to the *Tommy & Jack* column. Mr Charles said it was against orders, but the blokes do it, and sometimes Bumley gets things done that the colonel and the Regimental haven't been able to. And he sends out packets to the trenches, with Woodbines and chocolate and mouth organs, and pays for it all himself."

"Garn!" Hoggin said. "The makers give 'im the stuff, in return for 'is mentioning their names in the paper."

They had stopped and were listening. Mr Bottomley was in his mid-fifties, heavily built with a considerable paunch and an ingratiatingly direct manner: "It is you who pay," he boomed in an echoing voice, with silvery aftertones, "you, the people! Our leaders fumble and fidget —Mr Wait and See waits, but doesn't see . . ." (pause for titters) "Who pays for the mistakes? You, the people! England needs new blood, new leaders . . . leaders dedicated to serve the people, not their own ambitions. Service is my motto, my aim, my life! As I have repeatedly said in *John Bull*, we need a government of business men, who will carry the war not only to Germany in Germany, but to the enemy within our gates."

He raised his fist to heaven and boomed, "All German property must be confiscated. I mean the property of those Germhuns who are still, to our shame, living amongst us . . . All Germhuns must be locked up. Those swine cunning enough to have taken out British naturalisation papers must be made to wear a distinctive badge . . . perhaps a picture of a bayoneted baby would be appropriate. They must be indoors by dark . . . their children must not be allowed to attend any school, public or private!"

Frank muttered, "He's coming it a bit steep. The Germans are good soldiers, and brave men, I'll tell you that."

"Not 'ere they ain't," Hoggin said.

"That's why I'm going back to France," Frank said.

Bottomley continued: "The ending of the war—as it assuredly will end—in a smashing victory for us and our noble Allies, will not end the degradations we shall impose on the Huns. If by chance you should discover one day in a restaurant that you are being served by a German waiter, you will throw the soup in his foul face. If you find yourself sitting at the side of a German clerk, you will spill the inkpot over his vile head. If . . ."

"Come on," Frank said, "*Tommy & Jack* or no, he's making me feel sick."

"Old 'ard," Hoggin said, raising one hand. A thick voice, the owner obviously drunk, was shouting from the crowd—"Wot abaht con—con—conscription?"

Bottomley raised a plump hand. "I am against it . . . the people's rights must not be infringed . . . An Englishman's home is his castle. How can we fight German militarism if we are introducing it at home?"

"Thassastuff to give 'em," the voice cried. "No bloody conscription!"

A ragged cheer rose. Frank said, "Let's get on." He walked away, frowning. Hoggin said, "If Bumley's against conscription, I'm for Bumley. What the 'ell would I do in France? Or Niccolo 'ere?"

Frank said shortly, "Everyone ought to serve, equal like. But there's not room for everyone in France, even if you wanted to come. But I'm telling you, there's something there that isn't here. When this is all over, there'll be two Englands, and it won't be the rich and the poor, or the upper classes and the lower classes, it'll be those who were in the trenches, and those who weren't, like these ruddy striking tramway men. And they won't have anything to say to each other, 'cos they won't speak the same language any more."

"Take a Union Jack, mister . . . Take a Union Jack, join our brave boys in France."

The flag girls were wilted now but still trying hard, their red, white, and blue sashes soiled and their hair falling down. Lipstick was smeared all round their mouths: they appeared to have been selling kisses in return for promises to enlist; and somewhere during the day they had acquired a box of white chicken's feathers.

Niccolo's Union Jack was still pinned to his shirt. The girls turned on Hoggin. "Take a Union Jack, sir. Join our boys . . ."

"Fuck off!" Hoggin said.

The girls stepped close, and one took a white feather out of the box and pushed it through the top buttonhole of Hoggin's sweat-stained shirt. "That's *your* badge," she said scornfully, "the badge of a bleeding coward! You oughter be ashamed of yerself!"

"I am!" Hoggin shouted. "Oh dear, I am . . . but . . ." he burst into loud song:

> "*I don't want to join the army,*
> *I don't want to go to war,*
> *I'd rather hang around Piccadilly Underground,*
> *Living on the earnings of an 'ighborn lady.*
> I don't *want a bayonet up my arse'ole,*
> *I don't want my bollocks shot away,*
> *I'd rather live in England, in Merry Merry England,*
> And Roger All My Bloody Life Away!"

"Hey!" Frank said, grinning in spite of himself, "we sing that in the regiment, over there."

Hoggin poked him in the chest. "Yus, Frankie boy, I bet you do. The difference is, *I* fucking mean every word of it. You don't want to be anywhere else but in the army, in France. And that's the God's truth, ain't it?"

Daily Telegraph, Monday, May 24, 1915

STRIKERS AND THE ARMY
L.C.C.'S SURPRISE MOVE

On Saturday the London County Council issued the following notice:

L.C.C. TRAMWAYS—NOTICE
All men on strike who are eligible for military or naval service are instructed to forthwith return their uniforms and badges to the tramway depots. The London County Council are inviting men above military age to make application at once for positions as motor-men and conductors for the period of the war.

**(Signed)   A.L.C. FELL
CHIEF OFFICER, L.C.C. TRAMWAYS.**

Asked his opinion of the London County Council's notice . . . a (strikers') representative said, "There is nothing in it. It is just a bit of bluff to try and stampede the men. Possibly a hundred have gone back. But they make no dif-

**ference. The great body of the men stand firm. There are
fully 6,000 men out on strike."**

**The tramwaymen had advertised a mass meeting to be
held in Trafalgar Square yesterday afternoon . . . The
crowd was far from sympathetic, and suggested to recruiting sergeants present that they should mount the
platform and invite those of military age to enlist.**

Cate put the paper away without a word. Summer was upon him and
he had much to do. And so, when they were scything the hay in his
fields, German forces in south-west Africa surrendered to Botha,
Mackensen advanced northwards between the Bug and the Vistula,
and British troops occupied Kut-el-Amara, on the Tigris. As the wheat
was harvested, the Germans stormed Warsaw, the Italian cruiser *Giuseppe Garibaldi* was sunk by an Austrian submarine, and forty French
aeroplanes bombarded Saarbrucken; and as the cockney hop pickers,
nearly all women and girls now, came down from London, singing in
their special trains, Bulgaria mobilised to join the German side, the
French mounted an offensive in Champagne and the British another,
farther north, near Loos.

The forcing of the Dardanelles was as far from accomplishment as
ever. Russia was knocked back on her heels. The Mesopotamian campaign was bogging down, as was the Italian campaign along their
northern, alpine border. A massive German thrust against Serbia was
almost ready. The autumn rains began to fall.

Near Loos, France: Saturday, September 25, 1915

29 General Sir Douglas Haig, commanding the British First Army, stood in front of the map spread on the wall of the château's main dining-room, now converted into his headquarters' operations room. The air rumbled and the thick walls shook with the reverberations of the continuous artillery fire. Brigadier General Butler, Haig's Chief of Staff, conferred in a corner with an artillery colonel. Charteris, the Chief of Intelligence, stood a few paces to one side, talking in a low voice to a massive figure in civilian clothes—the 17th Earl of Derby. Haig stood alone, his magnificent leonine head bent forward, studying. A red-tabbed young officer passed quickly in front of the army commander with a muttered apology and started sticking coloured flags on pins into the map, and moving others. Outside, it was mid-morning, with light rain falling.

Lord Derby inclined his bullet head downward the better to hear what Charteris was saying. "Things are going very well, so far, on most of the front, which is 8,000 yards wide. The wind changed on the extreme left and blew our own gas back on the 2nd Division. That flank is held up . . . We didn't want to fight this battle at all, but were forced to do so."

Derby said, "Kitchener told me it was imperative that we and the French do something to take pressure off the Russians, or there'd be a total collapse over there. He said we must accept very heavy losses to prevent that."

"That's true," Charteris said grudgingly. "General Haig agreed that we do have to mount a major offensive. But we didn't want to do it here—the Aubers Ridge, farther north, would be a much better strategic and tactical objective."

"Then why . . . ?"

"Because Joffre and the French insisted that our attack should be practically shoulder to shoulder with theirs. So we've been forced to attack here—this Lens-Loos-La Bassée area . . . terrible country; ruined miners' houses, pitheads, mine works, all made into fortified redoubts and bristling with machine guns. Still, it looks as though General Haig's plan will achieve success at relatively moderate cost. There was heavy and accurate artillery preparation, as you know. Then we went in with all six divisions of I and IV Corps up . . . they are in the process now of breaking through to the Germans' second line of defence. Then the General will throw in the reserves to complete the break through—and break out."

Derby asked, "What reserves does he have?"

Charteris hesitated, then said, "He doesn't have any, under his own hand, at the moment. But the Chief—Sir John French—has promised to release XI Corps—three divisions—to him the moment the attack is launched . . . and behind them are the two Cavalry Corps, the Indian and British."

"XI Corps is New Army, isn't it?" Derby said, fixing his little eyes on Charteris, "all raw troops, and dug-out former battalion commanders and brigadiers?"

Charteris again hesitated, then said, "It is . . . but it's what we have been given . . . Whatever the issue of the battle the casualty list will be huge. That is the sad part of it."

Derby lowered his voice, "Do you know what I heard this morning? That the German troops have been shouting across No Man's Land 'We'll mow you down on the 25th' . . . and they've been doing that for the past three or four days. They must have known all about the attack, somehow."

Charteris muttered, "It's the French. G.Q.G. is like a sieve."

They both looked up as Haig raised his voice, speaking to the young staff officer, "Wait a minute—is that confirmed—the 15th Division on Hill 70?"

"On the slopes, sir."

"And the 1st Division into Chalk Pit?"

"Near it, sir . . . I've marked them three hundred yards short."

Butler and Charteris went forward and stood at Haig's shoulder. Butler said, "We've already had confirmation that 47 Division is in Loos Cemetery—very hard hand-to-hand fighting there . . . And the left brigade of 1st Division is in Hulluch. They are being heavily shelled . . . and so is 1st Corps Headquarters."

"It's that damned Tower Bridge," Charteris said. "You can see it from here. From the forward brigades, it must seem to be standing right over you."

"How high is it?" Haig asked.

"Three hundred feet, sir. And strongly built. We've tried shelling it, even having the R.F.C. drop bombs on it, but to no effect, as you know." Haig glanced at a group of aerial photographs covering another wall of the great room. The centre photo clearly showed the monstrous two-tiered iron structure, connected with the mining works of the area, which stood halfway between La Bassée and the Vimy ridge. Its main platform gave perfect observation over all the extensive battlefield to German artillery observers, snipers, and machine gunners. It vaguely resembled Tower Bridge in London, and had been so named by the British soldiers.

Butler said, "2nd Division reports they're having a very difficult time by Fosse 8. All the houses have cellars, and the Germans have had a long time to dig them deeper, even fortify them. They're fighting in the ruins of the miners' houses, and the slag heaps."

"Like Mons," Charteris said, but said no more. D.H.—as he always thought of his chief—had not been at Mons, which had been fought by his rival Smith-Dorrien, since manoeuvred out of his command and sent to East Africa.

Haig said, "Any news from the French?"

Butler said, "They report progress of between one and four kilometres in this section—between Auberive and Ville-sur-Tourbes." He went forward to a smaller scale map, pointing—"Particularly north of Souvain toward Tahure."

"Good . . . Has the Chief given me XI Corps yet? Or moved the cavalry?"

"No, sir."

"They ought to be moving," Haig said. "If we obtain success, it will be soon, and troops must be ready to exploit it."

The young staff officer came again and moved another flag and Butler cried exultantly, "1st Division has cleared Hulluch, sir . . . and it's still raining. The Germans can't have been able to see very well from Tower Bridge."

Haig said, "We're through the German first line, then, and through the second line in places. Now's the time to exploit our success, to hit harder still . . . here." He reached out with a leather-covered cane and touched the map. "Eastward, from Lens through Hill 70 and Hulluch.

I must have XI Corps at once. Get me the Commander-in-Chief on the telephone, please."

Boy Rowland, the white-purple-white ribbon of the Military Cross already faded on his tunic, sat in the tiny cellar of the house in Noeux-les-Mines which he shared with Beldring, now a full lieutenant. They had only arrived the previous dawn, after marching down by night from the Ypres Salient, in great secrecy, with the rest of the division. Obviously a big push was being readied—but when, where, and what would be their part in it, they had not then known. Now they knew, at least, that the attack would be in the Loos area, for shelling had been heavy all day there. Here, three miles behind what had been the front lines, they had been receiving occasional salvoes of heavy artillery fire as the Germans sought out gun positions and reserves. For the rest— rumour, counter rumour, a tremendous unceasing noise, the unsleeping eyes on Tower Bridge peering at them across the low humps and hills and slag heaps, a continuous stream of wounded men, walking or being carried to fill the ambulances that came this far forward.

Boy did not want to talk about the coming battle. They'd be in it soon enough. He would not normally have liked to discuss women, either, particularly with Beldring, whose ideas were different from his; but it was better than discussing the rumours, looking out into the dark at the staggering bandaged men, listening to the groans inside the ambulances, that were never quite drowned by the roar of their engines.

Beldring said, "Why should a man go to a tart, pay money, and risk getting clap or pox, when perfectly nice ordinary girls will do it for nothing?"

"I don't think they will," Boy said. He poured some red wine out of the bottle on the table into a cracked teacup, that was part of the 'furniture' in the abandoned house. "If they will, they can't be nice, can they?" He lifted the cup, noticing that his hand trembled slightly. The last few weeks in the Salient had been pretty unpleasant—patrols, wiring, bayonet fights on raids, continuous harassing fire at night; but that was no excuse. He must take a pull at himself.

Beldring drank, too; Boy thought he was already tipsy. Beldring waved a hand expansively. "But that's not true, Boy! Women have just the same desires as we do . . . stands to reason, otherwise there wouldn't be any children born . . . I mean, we're all animals, and the female animal is just as strongly sexed as the male. In most animals, more so. It's not the male that announces he wants to fornicate—it's the female. And women are no different."

"We're not animals," Boy said. "At least, we have to suppress all that is beastly and animal in us."

"What about this war, then? Don't tell me we're suppressing our animal nature here!"

"That's different. We're talking about ladies."

"*I'm* talking about women! And I think that ladies are just the same as other women . . . The colonel's lady and Judy O'Grady are sisters under the skin."

Boy said, "I don't believe they are. Ladies have been taught to control their emotions and desires—lusts—even if they have them the same as men do, which I do not believe, whatever you say."

"I had a couple of ladies while I was on leave in April. No trouble at all . . . one married, one a virgin. Women are beginning to *show* that they have the same desires as men. Mind, they've always felt like that, but now they're not going to pretend they don't."

"That's the war," Boy said, "but it's our duty, as gentlemen, to protect women in every way . . . from their own weaknesses and improper desires, if they have any. How do you think that married woman felt, when your leave was up, having betrayed her husband and her children, just for a momentary pleasure . . . or perhaps only because she was sorry for you, having to serve in the trenches?"

"She felt well poked," Beldring said, with a self-satisfied leer. "Five times, to be precise. She hadn't seen her husband since he joined up, in September, 1914."

Boy thought, I'd like to go on leave again, but feeling fit next time, not convalescing from gas poisoning. But women hardly entered his thoughts as he put his longings into mental pictures . . . the hunting field, himself in a pink coat and top hat; no, he'd be in uniform, on Dasher, if Dad still had him . . . at Twickenham, cheering for England in the Calcutta Cup . . . at the County Ground, a lazy summer afternoon, watching Colin Blythe apologetically spin out a side . . . walking the North Downs, Viking at heel, the Weald stretching away to the south, the Thames estuary and Isle of Sheppey dim in the haze to the north-east . . .

"Mr Rowland . . . Mr Rowland, sir?"

Boy said, "Here. Come down."

A private clattered down the steps and saluted. "Colonel's compliments, sir, and please report to him at once. Bring your kit, sir. I've told your batman, sir."

Boy got up. "You can finish the wine for me, Beldring."

"With pleasure."

Boy followed the runner down the battered village street. Shells whistled and shrieked above, flying in both directions, in almost total darkness. Every few seconds there was a crash of falling masonry, the dull thump of a shell bursting deep in the black soil, or into the side of a slag heap. Eastward, where full dark had cloaked the uneven horizon, it looked like the day of judgment. Star shells soared and burst high, casting an eerie light over the houses and mine cages and towers. Vivid flashes lit the whole horizon, with irregular orange and yellow glares reflected in the low cloud base above. Rain hissed down in the night. The tremendous noise redoubled itself by bouncing back and forth between the ground and the cloud layer.

The runner said, "Here, sir," and Boy went in through the unhinged door of what had once been a rural post office. Blankets were drawn over the glassless windows, where his uncle, now Lieutenant Colonel Quentin Rowland, commanding officer of the 1st Bn the Weald Light Infantry, was sitting astride a backless wooden chair. Boy saluted and Quentin said, "Sit down, Boy." He waved a hand at another chair. "Major Nesbitt was run over by an ammunition lorry half an hour ago. Killed instantly. I don't know whose fault it was . . . don't have time to find out . . . but I've put Burke-Greve to command his company. You'll take over as adjutant."

Boy felt stunned. Transferring from the 2nd Battalion to the 1st last Christmas had been shock enough: but moving from the intimacy of a company, living in your own little world, of your own platoon, to battalion headquarters, was worse. He said, "Sir, I'd rather not leave my platoon."

"I daresay you wouldn't," Quentin said wearily, "but you must. The new officers are good in the field, but they haven't had time to learn anything about administration, and they don't know how to write orders. Read the messages on that board there, then you'll be up to date . . . Have some wine."

"Thank you, sir," Boy said automatically. Quentin handed him a tin mug full of red wine, which tasted sharp and acid as he drank some. He read the messages—all from brigade headquarters. All battalions were to rest in billets, but prepared to move at thirty minutes' notice. That was timed 9.47 this morning. Be prepared to move—12.34 . . . ah! that was the false alarm, cancelled a quarter of an hour later, but meanwhile the men had been awakened from their sleep and had had a hard time getting back to rest, the first edge taken off their march-weariness, and the noise of the battle growing louder to the eastward . . . Issue of maps to take place at 4 p.m. at Noeux-les-Mines School. That must have been done, but the new maps hadn't reached the platoons yet. He asked, "Have the maps gone out to companies yet, sir?"

"Yes, an hour ago. Look, there's a spare set."

Boy read on. Message about artillery observers—5.09 p.m. Information about the advance of the forward divisions . . . they seemed to be going well. Perhaps there'd be a breakthrough at last. Message about . . . Good God, the Quartermaster had sworn blind that he'd get that damned thing killed, once and for all, but here it was—Lieutenant C.J.C. Rowland, the lost *pakhals,* and the demand for 64 rupees 14 annas 4 pies.

"What are you swearing about, Boy?" his uncle asked.

"Nothing, sir," he said, taking the message off the file and putting it in his pocket.

"Well, sit down. Heard anything from home?"

"Daddy and Mummy are well, sir. Naomi's in the Women's Volunteer Motor Drivers, and . . ."

"I know."

". . . but she wants to get out to France, and the only way she can get here is to transfer to the F.A.N.Y.s—if they'd have her . . . and even then our army won't use them, so she'd be working with the French or Belgians."

"Wouldn't let any daughter of mine work with *them,* I can tell you," Quentin growled. "Wouldn't let any Englishwomen come to France at all. This is no place for them." His angry wave embraced the murderous night, the howling skies, the shattered house in which they sat. Boy said nothing, thinking privately that women like his sister Naomi were capable of doing much more than cook and sew, and should be encouraged and helped to do so.

His uncle said, "Your Aunt Fiona's well, as far as I know . . . Guy's in the Upper Ten this term—it's his last. You know that he got his pilot's licence in the summer holidays? And learned to be his own mechanic. Now he says he's going to learn wireless engineering or mechanics or whatever it's called. Virginia swears she's not going back to Cheltenham next year, whatever we say. I've written her a strong letter, telling her that her mother and I know what's best for her."

Boy said cautiously, "I think it's very difficult for boys and girls, nowadays, to live as their parents did, or even as I did, when the world is like this—" he made the same all-inclusive gesture as his uncle had. "I talked to Virginia, Guy, Laurence, Stella, Naomi—all of them, while I was convalescing, and they were all, well, unsettled—even Guy, in his own way."

"Perhaps you're right," Quentin said grudgingly, "but we can't have Virginia running round the streets by herself at her age, can we?" He drank from his mug and wiped his toothbrush moustache. "Your grandfather will be an M.P. any time now. It's been an open secret that he's been nursing the constituency until Ellis was ready to retire."

"I heard that when I was on leave, sir."

"Well, Ellis is retiring next month. The election will be in November—they haven't fixed a date yet, but there'll be no opposition . . . unless a Labour fellow stands, and he won't have a chance."

"Any news of Aunt Margaret, sir?"

Quentin shook his head. Boy said, "I suppose she thinks Ireland's more important than, well, family."

"Nothing is," Quentin said heavily, "and don't you forget it, Boy . . . I'd like to be back in Hedlington. I can't imagine what it's like now. Alice writes and tells me what's been happening, how Mother and the Governor are . . . where they've put up more tents, about women marching up and down High Street in khaki uniforms . . . pubs closed all afternoon . . . Richard's factory turning out twenty lorries a day, already . . . that fellow Hoggin who married Ruth Stratton, fellow without an H to his name, on the way to being a millionaire—" he pointed to a shelf where, among tins of condensed milk and bully beef, one tin was labelled HOGGIN's, and in small letters *Plum Jam* . . . "The men use Hoggin's as the name of any jam, like Maconochie for any meat. No, Hedlington isn't real. This is real, this . . ." Unable to find the words, he again substituted the wide, repelled gesture.

"Message from brigade, sir."

Boy recalled with a start that he was the adjutant. He took the message from the runner at the door and read it aloud—"All battalions prepare to move immediately. C.O.s to Brigade HQ 8.10 pip emma for orders." He looked at his wrist watch. "It's 7.45, sir. I'll send out the message to the companies. Whom do you take for orders? I'm afraid I don't know."

"Adjutant, Quartermaster, or R.Q.M.S., depending on who's up, signals sergeant, two battalion runners . . . Send for Major Wylie, please."

"Yes, sir."

Lance Corporal Frank Stratton plodded steadily eastward down a narrow country road at the rear of the twelve men of the battalion's Pioneer Section. He had not wanted to leave Mr Charles four months ago, and he still felt somehow guilty about it; but to tell the truth this was a more interesting job for a skilled man. Being a batman, you heard some gup before the other fellows did, and you got to see the brigadier general now and then—even, once, at a distance, the divisional commander; but that wasn't much; whereas here he could use his hands. It was only

a little welding, a little carpentry, improving the colonel's dugout, putting a roof on the doctor's emergency room at the billets, things like
that—but it was something, something different from firing your rifle.
The rifle was the soldier's best friend, the sergeants kept telling you,
and he supposed it was. At all events, he kept his own bright clean and
slightly oiled at all times, whatever the circumstances: his bayonet
sharp as a razor, the blade well blackened so as not to reflect light: all
his ammunition clean, and no cartridge the least bit bent or damaged in
the clips: the magazine spring clean and slightly oiled . . . but after all
this, which was no more than any workman should do for his tools, he
didn't like the weapon. It was too simple, too direct. With that in your
hands, and aimed, you realised you were going to kill not 'someone,'
but that man, that one with the short legs, moustache and open mouth.
That didn't feel good.

The column stopped, and a few moments later Frank found himself
pushed aside by men coming back the other way. "Here, here, what's
this?" he said.

"York and Lancs," a voice answered curtly, "going into reserve."

"We're Wealds, coming up from reserve."

The two columns became hopelessly entangled in the lane, men cursing, grunting, and gasping to pass, the loads on their backs making
them bulkier than pregnant women. A heavy shell burst in the fields a
hundred yards to the right, its brilliant momentary flash of light searing
the pale unshaven faces, the gas masks hung on their chests, here and
there the shining inverted bowls of the new steel helmets.

On at last . . . half an hour, perhaps a mile: then stop again. The
pioneer sergeant came back and said, "Stratton? You there?"

"I'm here, sergeant."

"Any men dropped out?"

"None of the Pioneers. Don't know about the rest of the battalion.
There's been people going every which way."

"I've seen better at Epsom on Derby Day," the sergeant said. "This
is worse than the retreat from Mons. The only people who kept running into us then was Frog cavalry and who the hell can keep *them*
where they're supposed to be? These are ours."

"What's up now?"

"Damned if I know, but the R.S.M. says it's a division coming down
from Bethune, what's crossing our road."

Frank said nothing. Organising an army was a difficult job, stood to
reason, when you had to move a hundred thousand men, or more, left
and right and up and down, and the enemy shelling, wounded coming
back, ammunition going up, and not too many roads to do it on; but

there'd been wars a long time, and this was the army's job, its profession, like. Mr Harry would have someone's scalp if anything like this happened at Rowland's; and from what he'd heard about Mr Richard's new factory, everything went like clockwork there. Here, the more mistakes the high-ups made, the more they got promoted . . . and the ordinary blokes paid for it. Some regiments would have been getting sullen by now, and maybe worse, but this was the Wealds, and they were a good push, any way you looked at them. They grumbled, but they'd do what had to be done, whoever made a balls of *his* part.

A column of infantry passed, some limping, some with bandaged heads dimly seen in the light of the star shells, some with arms in improvised slings, some dripping blood from their hands, some with gas masks slung, some still wearing them. "Look oot for gas, mates," one cried in the darkness, in a strong Scots accent. "Oors!"

"*Our* gas?" Frank exclaimed. "What do you mean, Jock?"

"Mean? I mean oor bluidy artillery fired gas shells in front of us, but the wind was blowing from the Gairrmans to us, see? The Jerries were laughing their heads off, while we . . . we was choking to death." He ended in a spasm of coughing. Frank settled his pack on his back, and trudged on, shoulders bowed. Another balls-up. It began to rain again.

Frank lay below the lip of a shell hole at the edge of a quarry in front of Hulluch. A sandy stubble covered his chin and cheeks, and he was coated from cap to boots in mud, some white and chalky in texture, some black from the coal-bearing seams they had fought over and in. It was near noon, September 27th, and the 1st Wealds had not been rested since leaving Noeux-les-Mines near 9 p.m. on the 25th. They had marched for six hours—to cover four miles; and fought for thirty-four hours, the men now and then dozing where they were, whether in a captured German frontline trench, or in the open, in one of the pock-marked shell holes, or against the brick rubble of miners' crushed cottages. It was still raining, though not hard, and the morning ground mist was dispersing. Tower Bridge peered down on them like monstrous Siamese-twin storks made of black metal. Shells burst continuously all around, but it was not a planned barrage, such as they had experienced twice, once when they passed through the leading brigade of the 1st Division yesterday afternoon, thrusting farther into Hulluch; once early this morning when a powerful German counter-attack had pushed them out of Hulluch again. Over the whole battlefield aircraft of both warring nations flew in lazy arcs, or swooped and circled round each other—always in silence, everything but an occasional thin rattle from their machine guns drowned in the enormous din of the artillery.

The ground all around was covered with corpses. Peering out from the rim of the quarry, Frank thought that over half of them were Jocks —their kilts spread over them like shrouds, their bare wet backsides turned up in obscene taunting gestures at the clouds. Fifteen dead Germans lay in the quarry itself, most apparently blasted by a single shell, two bayoneted in the face and stomach by the Wealds' C Company and Pioneers when they stormed the quarry yesterday . . . to be driven out later . . . to retake it an hour ago . . .

Communication seemed to have broken down. Frank had not seen any officer since dawn. He didn't know whether anyone in the battalion knew the Pioneers were here, with about ten men of C Company. For the moment the shelling was too heavy to send someone to find out. They'd suffered heavily—five men gone from the Pioneers alone, out of the dozen who'd left Noeux-les-Mines . . . Shells, shells, shells! This was becoming an artillery war. Back at Ypres, there'd been shelling all right, and plenty of it, but there'd been some movement, a lot of rifle and machine-gun fire aimed at people—something personal. Here, it was the guns, the everlasting bloody guns, that had been pounding at his eardrums for two days now, and mangling flesh and blood from ten miles away . . . And he'd been thinking, a while back, that he didn't like the rifle! The truth was . . .

"Someone coming, sergeant," a soldier called from the rear of the quarry, "it's the adjutant."

"Captain Burke-Greve?" the sergeant shouted.

"No, the new one—Mr Rowland."

Frank turned in time to see Boy Rowland tumble into the quarry, followed by a burst of machine-gun fire that clattered and splattered on the rock wall of the quarry and knocked more bricks out of a ruined store shed twenty yards away.

"Keep a sharp watch forward, Jones," he said to the private beside him, and slid down the slope to join the sergeant and Boy Rowland.

Boy said, "Hullo, Stratton, glad to see you here . . . Sergeant, we're going to attack at . . . in ten minutes. A Company's on your right and the rest of C on your left. You'll command what you've got here . . . The C.O.s coming up through this quarry as soon as the attack begins, with battalion headquarters. Don't move till he gets here, then advance with us. I'll wait here till he comes."

"Very good, sir . . . Do we get any artillery support?"

"Yes, H.E. and gas . . . Everyone got his mask? The wind's right."

"What's our objective, sir?"

"The road running north-east to south-west through the centre of Hulluch . . . the Seaforths are on the battalion's right, objective the crossroads between Hulluch and Chalk Pit Wood—you can't see it from here . . . We're all supporting an attack by the Guards Division on the line Lens to Chalk Pit Wood, including Hill 70."

He sat down, breathing wearily. Frank and the sergeant waited, thinking their own thoughts. "Have a little rum, sir," the sergeant said after a time—"I always keep some in my flask—the other flask."

Boy shook his head. "Thanks . . . my throat's dry enough already. What I'd like is a hot bath. I feel filthy."

There's an officer for you, Frank thought: worrying about being dirty when he looked starving, and dog tired, and must be a little scared, too, though he wasn't showing it. Folks like the Rowlands lived different before the war, so they thought different. As for himself, he'd like a good cup of tea, with Agnes and Lily at his knees, little John on his lap, and Anne standing beside the chair ready to pour him another cup, her soft breast pressing into his shoulder. Pity Fred didn't get married. There was nothing like it.

He shook his head, wiping out the vision. "I'll go round the men, sergeant. Better check all gas masks . . . Gas masks on! Block the tube. Hand up anyone who can breathe . . . Bartlett, what's the matter?"

"I can breathe easy, corporal. Must be a hole in the mask."

"Let's have a look."

Frank examined the hood-like mask and quickly found a small hole in the material, at the back. "Lucky to be alive, you are," he said to Private Bartlett.

He opened his pack, which was lying on the slope beside his previous position, found his housewife and with a few deft strokes sewed up the tear. "That was a shell splinter did that," he said. "An inch forward and you'd have had no head. Put it on and test it again . . . All right? Everyone else all right? Gas masks tested, sergeant—all correct."

They waited. The number of shells passing overhead increased. Peering forward, Frank saw gas shells bursting in white clouds along the road on the near side of Hulluch. The wind bore the gas gliding eastward. German whizzbangs began to burst all along the tenuous and scattered British lines. Lieutenant Colonel Quentin Rowland ran down into the quarry through the shell fire, followed by the dozen men of his headquarters, running widely separated. Boy Rowland saluted his C.O. and shouted something through his gas mask, which Frank could not hear. To right and left men rose from the earth and moved forward, their heads coming to black-masked snouts. Machine guns increased their infernal chatter, men fell, tumbled, crawled.

The C.O. was signalling to the Pioneer sergeant with his hand—"Advance!"

The sergeant rose, sweeping his right hand forward. Frank jumped to his feet, carried his rifle to the high port, and walked steadily forward. Hill 70 loomed larger than it really was out of the gloom to the right. The miserable houses of Hulluch stretched across the line straight ahead, the ground between a mass of humps and lumps, and everywhere the sodden kilts.

The air chattered and sighed and moaned against the cloth sides of Frank's mask. Clods of earth rose and dashed by the eye pieces. The earth heaved. He stepped over bodies—more Scots, more bottoms and balls and hair bared to the rain—Germans, helmets smashed, brains seeping into the mud—a girl, caught trying to fly by a stray shell, face down, skirt rumpled and wet more Germans . . . a British officer, revolver drawn, face up, dead—a leg, by itself . . . A scream to his right, loud enough to be heard above the din . . . he turned his head and saw the sergeant go down, his whole stomach ripped out by a shell splinter . . . Behind him, the colonel and the rest of headquarters were coming on . . . but to the left, they were stopped. German machine guns kept up a steady giant tattoo, and more of them were in action. German soldiers appeared out of the brick rubble, charging. Frank dropped, shouting "Sights down! Half left, enemy, rapid fire!" and began to fire, the rifle propped on a dead Highlander's back. A British machine gun joined in from behind and to his left.

After five minutes the German counter-attack had withered, but so had the British attack. The Germans, from reserve trenches and strongposts in houses and ruins, poured fire across the open ground. Mortars whizzed and clacked, their bombs arching down out of the sky to burst on Germans and British. Flashes of exploding shells stippled the slope of Hill 70 with momentary colour.

They were at grips, locked, neither side able to move. The light slowly faded from the sky as British and Germans wrestled, immobile, among the cottages, streets, quarries, pits, mine shafts, slag heaps, and towering machinery between Lens, Hulluch, Loos, and La Bassée.

The battalion was in brigade reserve between Hulluch and Vermelles. It was October 2nd, and the trenches, though not as formalised as they had become round Ypres since the second battle and the first gas attacks there, were at least deep and well revetted, and becoming more so every day. Boy Rowland sat in the Pioneer Store dugout with the new Pioneer Sergeant, Frank Stratton, and 2nd Lieutenant Fred Stratton, all drinking cocoa. Boy had come to arrange for expert work on the communication trenches, and found Fred chatting with his brother. Business done, Boy had accepted Frank's offer of cocoa. The dugout was a model of what one should be: it had started with the advantage of being an underground store room for blasting explosives for a mine. In two days Frank Stratton and his men had converted it into a subterranean ironmonger's store, gleaming with picks, shovels, entrenching tools, angle irons, crowbars; in one corner, dynamite, and in another, Frank Stratton's bed . . . three planks stretched across some ammunition boxes, full of grenades.

"I wouldn't share that bed with you, sergeant," Boy said, smiling— "even if I were your wife."

"The way I see it, sir," Frank said, "is if we're going to get a direct hit from a Jack Johnson down here, it won't make any difference if a few grenades go up, too . . . How's your new batman coming along, sir? I hear he's a wad pusher."

"Absolutely T.T.," Boy said, "but all that means is that I'll get his rum ration as well as my own . . . though I'm beginning to wonder whether I should have a batman at all. After you left I had Johnson, who was wounded at Plugstreet, then O'Hara, who was killed the other day."

Frank said, "Wish I could come back, sir, in a way. You begin to feel as though you're not with the battalion, even as far back as this."

"You were far enough forward at Hulluch."

"Yes, sir . . . We need six men to get up to strength, sir."

"I'll get the C.O.'s permission to have two posted from each company."

Fred cut in. "It would be better if the C.O. would let Sergeant Stratton speak privately to the sergeant-majors, Boy. He has to have men who can use their hands. Otherwise, the company commanders send men they want to get rid of, and everyone suffers when the Pioneers come to do a job for a company. I've seen that, already."

"That's a good idea, sir," Frank said, thinking, Fred's growing a little toothbrush moustache, and his accent is changing. He doesn't talk just like Mr Charles, and never will, but he doesn't talk just like me, either. He's betwixt and between . . . and that was never too comfortable a place in this world.

He sipped the cocoa, very sweet and strong. In the communication trench a few yards away some soldiers were cleaning rifles and singing to a mournful tune:

> *If you want to find the sergeant-major*
> *I know where he is, I know where he is,*

If you want to find the sergeant-major,
I know where he is—
He's boozing up the privates' rum,
I've seen him, I've seen him,
Boozing up the privates' rum,
I've seen him,
Boozing up the privates' rum.

Fred said, "What do you make of Gallipoli, Boy?"

Boy said, "I don't know . . . I sometimes wonder if we're being told everything. It doesn't sound very good to me, reading between the lines. We should have been in Constantinople long ago, if we've really been succeeding. Once you're held up, in this war, it seems you can't get going again."

"That's what happened to the Germans in 1914," Fred said, "and now to us, at Ypres and here."

Boy nodded. "It's a rum war all right . . . We'd be better off in the navy. A lot more comfortable, anyway."

"Until you find yourself going in for the long distance swimming championship of the world, sir," Frank said. "And I wouldn't win that —can't swim . . . We lost a lot of officers the other day, didn't we, sir?"

"Five killed, five wounded," Boy said. "Nearly two hundred men, and we went in only five hundred and twenty strong."

He felt vaguely uneasy, talking so freely in front of an Other Rank. Frank Stratton was an older man, and exceptionally level headed; and he was a sergeant now . . . but all the same, perhaps he shouldn't be discussing the obvious stalemate in Gallipoli, or the heavy casualties. "Thanks for the cocoa," he said, rising.

Frank leaped to his feet, his hand at a rigid salute. "Thank you, sir. Everything will be ready at six pip emma."

Boy nodded, walking out. Frank sat down again beside his brother. Fred said, "As I was telling you when Boy came in, Fagioletti got his decree *nisi* from Ethel last week, and now he's applying to the judge to make it final right away, so's he can marry again before he joins up and fights for his adopted country."

"Fagioletti, join up?" Frank said incredulously, a part of him wishing that Fred would not refer to Mr Charles as 'Boy' in front of him. He knew it was his nickname, of course; everyone did, but that did not mean that an officer should so speak of him to a sergeant.

Fred said, "Of course not! He's got another woman in London he wants to fuck. But if he does that before the divorce is final, and the King's Proctor finds out, then the whole divorce would be off."

"Ethel was a ninny to sign that paper he wanted, about her going with other men," Frank said.

"Of course she was, but Mum and Dad couldn't stop her. She's been at home since mid June . . . sort of walking out with a bloke at the plant—Rowland's—who wants to marry her, Mum says . . . but she keeps praying Fagioletti will change his mind. Not a bloody hope in hell!"

Frank wished Fred would not use foul language in front of him. Officers did not do that, except under great stress, as in battle.

"I went over and talked to the Irish Guards C.O.," Quentin said. "Arthur's definitely gone—killed by machine-gun fire on the 27th, when he was acting as Staff Captain to the brigade. So we've lost one of the most brilliant young men of your generation, slaughtered by some sausage-guzzling Bavarian swine . . . John Kipling's missing in action near Chalk Pit Wood. He was with the 2nd Irish Guards."

"He can't have been eighteen," Boy exclaimed. "He came to Wellington my last term, and I'm . . ."

"He was a few weeks past his eighteenth birthday. You know he was a close friend of Guy's . . . in fact Guy spent ten days of this last summer holidays at Bateman's."

"Is he believed killed?"

Quentin nodded. "A sergeant said he thought he'd seen him hit by a shell."

"Mr Kipling will take it hard, I suppose."

"He'll take it like the rest of us. Like Lord and Lady Swanwick," Quentin said. "This has been a hard battle, Boy, and the men aren't happy. I can feel it. Of course, we've had very heavy casualties. Over 60,000, I hear rumoured—but don't spread that."

"The men did their best. They were wonderful," Boy said, "but—we didn't succeed. I think they want to know why. I do, myself."

They were sitting in the C.O.'s dugout, a candle glittering on the table between them, dark outside, occasional star shells bursting over the front lines, occasional distant bursts of machine-gun fire, occasional shell bursts, murmuring of soldiers in the trench and along the line of dugouts, someone playing a mouth organ.

Quentin said, "There are rumours that the reserves were too far back. The Commander-in-Chief was holding them in his own hands and when General Haig wanted them, it took too long for them to come up . . . There was confusion on the roads—troops going up tangling with troops moving back."

"I know that's true," Boy said. "It was a disgrace. The staff make a

mess and the soldiers suffer. I'd like to have seen some of those brass
hats with us in front of Hulluch . . . Is it true that two New Army divisions ran away, en masse?"

"I believe so," Quentin said, dropping his voice, "but we daren't
admit it, or others will think they can run away, too. We've got to say
that everyone behaved well—then the new men, the New Armies, will
think there's no alternative. We must mass more men when we attack,
and mass them farther forward, so there's no delay after the enemy's
first and second lines have been taken . . . Longer artillery preparation,
more guns per yard of front, more shells per gun."

Boy said nothing. The panic and exhilaration, the disgust and fear
and determination of the time of battle were welling up in him again,
and he had a hard time preventing himself from trembling. The bombardment for Loos had been as strong as it could be; yet they had not
broken through. They had broken in, but not through—and later,
counter-attacking, the Germans had done the same—broken in, and
then been held. What *could* break that pattern? It seemed certain that
men's flesh and blood could not, nor machine guns.

Quentin said, "We have to keep a close watch on morale, Boy. No
talk of failure is to be tolerated."

"Could we try to get some more decorations for the men, sir?" Boy
asked. "We haven't put in for many, and we won't get all of those. We
never do."

"I haven't put in for more because I don't believe in giving men decorations for doing what is only their duty. We don't believe in putty
decoration in the Wealds, Boy."

"No, sir."

"We'll see that the company and platoon commanders organise
games as soon as we get out of the line. Meanwhile, offensive patrolling. We've got to show the Boches that No Man's Land belongs to
us, not to them."

"Yes, sir."

Quentin seemed to sink, to lose some weight and size. In a smaller
voice he said, "We can't afford to go on losing educated men at this
rate . . . This battle is the death of the volunteer army. Something will
have to be done, at home."

He breathed deeply, standing up. "I'm going round the companies,
to see how the revetting is coming. You hold the fort here. And remember, don't allow defeatist rumour mongering. We're winning, and
we're going to go on winning, till final victory."

"Yes, sir."

Along the trench the nearest platoon were singing another verse of the same song Boy had heard outside the Pioneer Store:

> *If you want to find the old battalion,*
> *I know where they are, I know where they are,*
> *If you want to find the old battalion,*
> *I know where they are, I know where they are.*
> *They're hanging on the old barbed wire,*
> *I've seen 'em, I've seen 'em,*
> *Hanging on the old barbed wire.*
> *I've seen them,*
> *Hanging on the old barbed wire.*

Half an hour later, reading an old copy of the *Illustrated London News* in the dugout, Boy heard the cry "Stretcher-bearers! Stretcher-bearers!" He listened, putting down the magazine. German shells were falling intermittently, at long intervals, all over the rear areas. It was dark, and raining. He went out and asked a soldier passing by, "What's happened?"

"Don't know, sir . . . Some bloke copped a packet from a Jack Johnson, most likely."

Then the stretcher-bearers came down the trench, struggling and slipping in the mud and Boy pressed back against the side wall. "Who is it?" he asked.

"The C.O., sir . . . not too bad, sir."

Boy's Uncle Quentin forced himself half upright on the stretcher and gasped, "I'm all right, Boy . . . left arm and hand bit of a mess . . . back in . . . week or two. Tell . . ."

He fell back, fainting. Boy said, "Take him easy, you men."

"We will, sir. He's had a dose of morphine, too."

Boy went back into the dugout. Where was the second-in-command?

A. Extracts from a letter dated September 29, 1915, from Sir Douglas Haig to Lord Kitchener:

> You will doubtless recollect how earnestly I pressed you to en-sure an adequate Reserve being close in rear of my attacking divisions, and under my orders . . . No Reserve was placed under me . . . the Two Reserve Divisions (under C-in-C's orders) were directed to join me as soon as the success of the First Army was known at G.H.Q. They came on as quick as they could, poor fellows, but only crossed our old trench line with their heads at 6 p.m. We had captured Loos 12 hours previously . . .

B. Excerpt from Sir Douglas Haig's diary, October 2nd, 1915:

> Sir John French returns to St Omer today. Robertson tackled
> him on the question of reserves. His reply was 'the second day
> of the battle was the correct time to put them in, not the first.'
> It seems impossible to discuss military problems with an un-
> reasoning brain of this kind. At any rate, no good result is to
> be expected of it.

C. Excerpt from the diary of John Charteris, Haig's Chief of Intelligence: October 9, 1915:

> The really maddening thing about it all is that now that we
> are really getting the German side of the show disentangled
> by examination of prisoners and captured documents, it be-
> comes clear, without any shadow of doubt, that we had in fact
> broken the German line clean as a whistle. For 4 hours there
> was a glaring gap: then it was gone.

Daily Telegraph, Tuesday, September 28, 1915

PERSECUTED ARMENIANS
AN URGENT CALL FOR HELP

**Famine, typhus, dysentery are decimating the 200,000
Armenian refugees who have succeeded in reaching the
shelter of the Russian frontier. Help available on the spot
is totally inadequate. The Armenian Red Cross and Ref-
ugee Fund, whose president is Viscountess Bryce, exists
for the purpose of affording relief to these people . . .
Some idea of the suffering of the Armenians can be gained
from the following telegram which the hon. secretary of
the fund has recently received from the Archbishop of Van
and Aram, Governor of Van. "Besides Van, the provinces
of Chatakh, Moks, Sparkert, Mamertank and Khizan are
saved, the others are ruined and devastated. Men, women,
and children have been massacred. 20,000 are homeless.
Famine and infectious disease prevail. Many volunteers
are sick and wounded."**

"The Turks are seizing the opportunity of the war to exterminate their
Armenians," Cate said.

"And there's nothing we can do about it," Johnny Merritt said,
"until the war is over, and by then it will be too late. But there is one
person who could help . . . the Kaiser."

Cate looked up, nodding. Johnny was maturing rapidly under his responsibilities at the Jupiter Motor Company. Stella, sitting across the table in a light-weight tweed skirt and jacket, was looking at him with more respect than she used to. He said, "I believe the Kaiser has in fact protested the actions of his ally. After all, the Kaiser pretends to be the Protector of all Christians in the east."

"I don't think the Turks will take any notice," Johnny said. "Not unless the Kaiser threatens to remove his military advisers and stop all financial help . . . It's been a lovely weekend, sir, and stealing that extra day was well worth it. But I'd better be getting back to Hedlington, or Overfeld will be telling Dad I've become a Limey toff, too lazy to work." He laughed, putting down his empty cup and getting up from the table.

Cate said, "One moment, Johnny . . . Living down here, I'm rather out of touch with some things. Can you tell me anything about the position of Rowland's, that I ought to know? My father-in-law does not talk about his business, but I have been hearing disquieting rumours."

Johnny remained standing, his lips pursed. At length he said, "We're not privy to all Rowland's affairs, of course, sir . . . but in our opinion —Mr Richard's, Overfeld's, and mine—they'll have to get new capital by the end of the year . . . or go under. And we don't think that any bank will put up the capital needed unless there are changes in management and policy . . . perhaps not even then. That's private, sir, between us."

"Of course. I suspected as much. Thank you for telling me."

Johnny turned to Stella. "Goodbye for the present. See you in Hedlington on Thursday, for the dance at the Officers' Mess, eh?"

"Yes," she said. "I'll come and see you off."

"Goodbye, sir," Johnny said, "and thank you again for having me."

The two went out, Johnny holding the door open for Stella. A handsome couple, Cate thought; he noticed Garrod in the passage, her hands folded, her head a little on one side, a similar approving expression on her face as the young people passed.

Hedlington: Saturday, November 6, 1915

30 Richard Rowland stood under the painted metal canopy of the bandstand in the park, wearing a dark woollen scarf round his neck, but no overcoat. It was a raw day, the watery sun bearing no heat even at noon, but few working men could afford overcoats, and it was them Richard was trying to reach. He did not wear a cloth cap, as they did—they would recognise that as affectation: he was bareheaded, though Susan had whispered to him, "You'll catch your death of cold." His audience numbered barely fifty, white faces upturned, eyes unwinking. Brown leaves were packed in soggy drifts along the railings that guarded the flower beds, and round the boles of the trees. In the front rank of the spectators stood a young man in a soldier's blue hospital uniform. He carried a white cane in one hand and wore black spectacles. He couldn't have been more than nineteen.

"I wanted to speak in High Street," Richard said, "but the police . . ."

"Speak up, mister!" a woman shouted. "You ain't in your drawing-room now."

Richard cleared his throat and tried again. He was not in the least shy of public speaking; and the speech making that had taken up much of his time since the bye-election was called would have cured him if he had been; but he had not yet learned the techniques of it. He could not project his voice the way his father somehow did naturally . . . so he had to shout louder, and grow hoarser.

"I applied for permission to speak in High Street," he bellowed against the slow west wind, "but the police refused me, because they said I would obstruct the traffic. Presumably the traffic flows right through my opponent without hindrance."

That was a mistake; no one laughed; he must learn to eschew sarcasm or irony. Just speak plainly and to the point, and repeat the point three times—that's what Hutton had drilled into him when the rumours from France had convinced him that he must do what he could to put control of the country's war effort into other hands. The blind soldier stood still as a statue.

He continued: "I am standing for this constituency as an Independent, because there is a truce between the two main parties. The retiring member is a Liberal, so the Conservatives will not put up an official candidate against the Liberal candidate, who is therefore my only opponent . . . I am a Conservative at heart, and asked for the support of the party—but they refused it . . . so it is as an Independent that I canvass your votes next Thursday. You ask what do I stand for? I answer you: I say that the whole leadership of this country must be changed, and the conduct of the war put into other hands . . . or the war must be abandoned."

A scattering of boos from the audience was almost drowned by the sturdy clapping of the four people sitting on park chairs well back behind him in the bandstand—his wife Susan, Lord Cantley, Christopher Cate, and one of the town councillors.

"The Loos despatch has now been published and the worst that was being whispered, has been confirmed. Our leaders here and in France promised a great victory . . . and what do we have? Nearly sixty thousand men killed and wounded, and no advance. It was the same at Neuve Chapelle . . . at Arras . . . at Ypres . . ."

"We're not going to let the Jerries 'ave it their way," a man called up (*scattered cheers*).

"Of course not!" Richard shouted, "but we can not afford to go on like this! The Germans are masters of the air over France, with their aircraft where the pilot can fire through the propeller. Their aces Boelcke and Immelmann and Von Rackow destroy our machines at will . . . There is open warfare between our generals and our political leaders . . . the Brass Hats and Frocks, they call each other, in contempt . . . Gallipoli is failing not because it was an unsound idea but because it was not pursued with vigour. 'Wait and see' is a policy which may suit the Prime Minister's temperament, but it does not suit the pace of this war . . . What we need is a government that will conduct the war as efficiently as a business man must conduct his business. We want a strong government, devoted to this one aim—not this weak-kneed 'wait and see' coalition. We need efficiency from top to bottom in this country—on the field of battle, on the farms, in the factories . . . above all, in the government itself. That is my platform—greater efficiency, so that the people of England do not sacrifice their labour and their lives in vain . . . as they did at Loos. Field Marshal French is clearly not equal to his responsibilities, and must be replaced. The same rigorous pruning process must go all the way down the armed forces . . . but the men who wield the axe must themselves be strong, efficient, and determined."

The crowd seemed to be with him; there were a number of women among them, he had seen, and though women could not vote, they could influence their men.

He said, "I introduce to you Lord Cantley."

Cantley was a shade over six feet. He was wearing a tweed suit and, like Richard, was bareheaded. He stepped forward as Richard stood aside, and spoke out loudly and slowly. "My brother was killed at Loos six weeks ago, together with thousands of others of all ranks from major-general to private soldier. Tomorrow I am joining the same regiment. I ask you to vote for Mr Richard Rowland—Mr *Richard* Rowland—so that I and others like me can feel that what we will be called upon to do at the front is not so much effort—and blood—wasted. Thank you."

Richard stepped forward again. It was twelve-twenty, and he should be outside one of the factories in North Hedlington in ten minutes, to make his speech again. He said, "Are there any questions?"

Bert Gorse, from the front row, spoke up. Richard had been keeping an eye on him, waiting for an interruption, but Bert had bided his time. Bert said, "Are you for conscription?"

Richard said, "I am." A storm of boos and hisses greeted the answer; but they came from a small number of men, mostly standing close to Bert Gorse. Richard continued, "Everyone had hoped that all fit young men would see their duty plain—as Lord Cantley's brother did—and join up . . ." Loud but scattered clapping from a few people: Richard could not see who they were. He went on—"Many did, but many have not, and the war has grown greater than the voluntary system can cope with. Conscription is the only way to spread the sacrifices evenly and fairly, and put the right men in the right jobs, whether it's at home or in France. It's the only efficient way."

"Efficiency!" Bert shouted. "That's what you believe in, but what about the working man? What benefit is the bosses' conscription going to be to him and his family?"

More disturbance in the crowd: Richard knew this colloquy—one could hardly call it a dialogue—by heart. The agitator shouted about the working man, meaning only the working man whose trade skill was not rare enough to protect him from being conscripted into the army, if conscription was introduced.

Bert pressed what he saw as his advantage and shouted, "You're a murderer, just like the rest of the capitalists, Mr Richard . . . dragging the working man from his factory and home, shoving him into uniform, and shipping him to France to be killed . . . so you can put scabs and women in his place—and more money in your own pocket."

Richard took off his glasses and shouted down, "Come up here and repeat that, you little swine!" He could barely see the blurred mass of the crowd below, and the tall lines of the bare tree trunks behind, but put up his fists, not knowing where or when he would be hit. There was scuffling nearby and he put his glasses back on. Johnny Merritt was there, holding Gorse, Stella beside him, wide-eyed, and a bobby strolling up ponderously. "Now, now . . . you come along with me, you. Out of the park!"

"What for? I got my rights."

"Out of the park, or you'll be in the station for breach of the peace."

Johnny Merritt let go and Gorse pushed out through the crowd, muttering, the bobby at his heels. Stella took Johnny's arm and looked up proudly into his face.

A woman's voice called, "What is your position on women—votes for women, employment of women?"

Richard said, "I do not see how we can refuse the suffrage to women, and would be in favour of granting it as soon as the details can be agreed on between the parties in Parliament. If there is much opposition, then a bill should be introduced the moment the war is ended . . . As for employment, I am in favour of an immensely greater use of women in industry . . . in every branch of our national life, and effort. It is obvious that women can not fight at the front . . . but they can do everything or nearly everything else, so they, too, should be subject to conscription, with exemptions for mothers with children and so on, of course. Women should be trained in the largest possible numbers to release men for the front. It's the only efficient way."

"Blacklegs!" a voice called.

Richard said nothing; the Western Front was a devouring monster, and the people were becoming afraid of it. They pretended to be protecting their union work rules, and the jobs of their soldier comrades when they returned to industry after the war; really, they were afraid of facing Moloch, and being sacrificed.

He said, when the noise had subsided, "I am for a more efficient conduct of the war, until we win it—with the fewest possible casualties. After the war—I want more factories, more jobs, less drudgery as we make the factories more efficient—much higher pay. As you probably know, the Jupiter Motor Company is already paying wages half as high again as any other employer in Hedlington. We want to make more goods of all kinds, which will then become cheaper . . . But first, win the war. Thank you."

He stepped down, glancing at his watch. "Well done," Cantley said, "but you ought to take another cough drop."

"I've had half a dozen already today," Richard said. "My throat's burning from them."

He watched the crowd dispersing. The blind young soldier did not move until he was standing alone, no one near him; then he turned and, tapping the ground with his cane, walked slowly out of the park. Richard watched him until he disappeared, feeling chilled and ill at ease.

Johnny Merritt came up, grinning, with Stella. Stella said, "You spoke awfully well, Uncle. 'Specially that bit about all fit young men and their duty. I clapped like mad then, to drown out the shirkers who were booing you."

Johnny looked uncomfortable for a moment, then said, "I thought you were going to punch Lord Cantley just now, Mr Rowland."

"You had your fists doubled under my nose," Cantley said, laughing. "You'd better hire Johnny here as a bodyguard."

"Wasn't he marvellous," Stella cried, "the way he grabbed that awful man?"

"Bert Gorse is the right size for me," Johnny said, "about five feet four. Can't we fire him?"

Richard said, "I'd like to, believe me. But he's a very good welding instructor . . . almost impossible to replace. And he's as free to disagree with my politics as I am to disagree with his. The men wouldn't like it if I sacked him because of that . . . whereas they'd think I had the right to do so if he works against me in the factory."

Johnny said, "Which I think he does . . . Mind if we miss your next speech or two? I'm taking Stella to lunch before she goes to the hospital."

"Not a bit. No one should have to listen to that speech more than once."

The seven of them sat in the morning-room, teacups on the small occasional tables beside each chair. Alice had poured the tea and passed round the crumpets and scones and jam and thin mustard-and-cress sandwiches. Her mother sat upright in a high-backed chair, her skin a pale yellowish tinge under the rouge, which as Alice knew, she had been applying for the last year. Quentin, in uniform, sat with his back to the windows, his left arm in a cast from shoulder to wrist, the cast supported in a khaki sling; there were two short puckered scars on the back of his left hand.

Quentin's wife Fiona sat beside him, her grey eyes unfocussed. Harry sat opposite his wife, John and Louise together between them.

John was speaking about the farm: "We only have one man left now, and he's nearly seventy. Lady Helen's our real mainstay—she's a hard worker, never tires, is never ill, always encourages the others when they are tired—Carol Adams and now two London girls of the Land Army. Never been in the country before but they're getting used to it."

"I imagine Lady Helen was upset at her brother's death," Harry said.

John nodded. "She was, Father, but all she did was work harder—I never saw her cry. And now Cantley's going, I hear. She's closer to him even than she was to Arthur, as children, I remember."

Louise said, "But we're hardly making ends meet, even though we do not get good prices for milk, being close to London."

John cleared his throat and said, "In fact, we . . . we're thinking of starting a retail milk round."

"Who'd run it—drive the carts?" Harry asked.

"We would—Louise and I," John said. No one spoke. My brother, no better than a milkman, Quentin thought: a year ago I wouldn't have believed it. Glancing at his wife, he thought she hadn't heard a word of the conversation: he wondered where she was, and with whom.

John went on, "Lady Helen could manage the farm. She studies everything the British Friesian Society puts out, attends meetings . . . and she learned a lot at that course they ran in Wiltshire in August. We're going to make High Staining pay soon, for the first time since you helped me buy it, Father."

"Wish I could say the same," Harry said. "We're turning out staff cars, but the army wouldn't buy our ambulance . . . Richard made the right guess, when he left us."

If it was a guess, John thought to himself, rather than the result of a careful estimation of future probabilities.

"He must be making twenty lorries a day . . . nearly five hundred a month. They're working in three shifts, twenty-four hours a day . . . I don't understand how he thinks he can find time to run the J.M.C. and be an Independent Member, with a plan of his own, and a lot of crusading to do. I shall find it hard enough . . . if I am elected . . .

and all I intend to do is just what I'm told to do by the whips . . . and work for, or on, the committee on war production, of course. I hear Richard spoke well in the park at noon today."

Louise said hesitantly, "I think it's a pity he's standing against you, Father, but . . . I can't help thinking that there *is* something wrong in the way our leaders are conducting the war. We've been promised so much, and what have we actually received? Only these terrifying casualty lists."

Harry said, "I agree. There'll be some changes made. Mr Asquith is perhaps too much of a gentleman to give the government the strong hand it needs in these times . . . Mr Lloyd George is coming down to my meeting tonight. His secretary telephoned an hour ago."

"Down, Bismarck, bad dog!" Alice snapped, rapping the dachshund on the head to dissuade him from trying to mate with her leg. She turned to her father. "I thought they said they were all too busy when you asked the central office for support. And that you didn't need help, as you faced no real opposition."

"They did, but someone—perhaps Ellis—has made them understand that Richard's campaign is not against me, but against them. Against their conduct of the war—and that every vote for him is a vote against them, the cabinet, the coalition, all of them."

"Is Mr Lloyd George coming to the house, Father?"

"No. Ellis is meeting him at the station, and then they'll go direct to the hall. I'll be leaving at half past five."

"I don't think I should come," John said awkwardly.

"Of course not," Harry said. "I don't want you brothers fighting among yourselves. It's bad enough that Richard and I should be at each other's throats, metaphorically speaking."

"I shouldn't sit on the platform in uniform," Quentin said, "but I'll be there, in the audience. I don't believe in changing horses in midstream. Fiona?"

Fiona said, "I'll stay at home. I've heard Father's speech three times already, and I have letters to write."

Rose said, "I wish I could come, Harry, but . . ."

"No, no, you stay here and rest."

The platform at one end of the big bare hall was hung with Union Jacks and red, white, and blue bunting. A lectern stood at front centre, with a row of chairs behind. The Minister of Munitions, the Right Honourable David Lloyd George, sat a little to the left rear of the speaker, where nearly all the audience could see him. His heavy mane of hair hung over his collar and his eyes darted round the hall without cease, noticing the way a man stood there, catching the least hints of dissent or agreement, the precise curve of a bosom, a pretty face, wide eyes. Ralph Ellis, the retired member, sat on Lloyd George's right; and to right and left were the Earl of Swanwick, the Mayor of Hedlington, Mr Bill Hoggin, and other dignitaries. A blinded young soldier sat in the front row of seats, a white cane in his hands, staring sightlessly at the platform through blackened glasses.

Harry wrenched his eyes away from the disturbing presence of the soldier, and began to speak: "It has been said that we are not doing all we can and should to win the war. I have a son and a grandson at the front, and I assure you that I never forget it. They are always in my thoughts—they and the millions like them who answered their country's call. My son tells me there was plenty of ammunition for the recent battle of Loos—we have overcome the difficulties we experienced earlier in the year, thanks to the Defence of the Realm Act, and to the great man sitting behind me—Mr David Lloyd George."

Cheers broke out, together with some subdued boos. Harry knew that Lloyd George was not popular with the trade unions or the Labour party, for his efforts to overcome union rules and increase production by any and all means available.

"My son says the army needs more machine guns—they have been ordered, and we will see that the army gets them. We are going to wage this war to victory, victory over the Huns, the barbarians who have shattered half the churches and cathedrals in northern France, who have bayoneted helpless prisoners, raped women . . . murdered our heroic Nurse Cavell . . . torpedoed the *Lusitania*, without warning, a passenger ship, unprotected, over a thousand innocent people drowned . . . trampled on the rights of small nations . . . Germany, enemy of peace, must be destroyed, and we are going to do it . . . One more big push and the bully's will will break . . . A vote for me is a vote for victory."

He sat down in an empty chair and Ralph Ellis got up. "I won't waste your time with a long introduction. I've been your member for twenty-two years, and I've done my best for you. Harry Rowland's the man to take my place, take my word for it. I tell you that, and here's the Right Honourable David Lloyd George to tell you the same."

Lloyd George grasped the front of the lectern with both hands and Harry listened intently. The grey-brown mane shook, a fist was raised. The Welsh voice, perfectly tuned and resonant, soared out like an organ over the densely packed hall. The applause came at shorter and shorter intervals. The faces down there, looking up at the platform, became more and more remote, the eyes wider. Only the blind soldier's head never moved, nor his hands. Nothing seemed able to move him, Harry thought.

He realised suddenly that he was not listening to what Lloyd George was saying; and nor was anyone else. They were all listening only to his voice, and absorbing his presence. The spellbinder, the Welsh Wizard, was living up to his name. After twenty minutes, he ended—"So I say, vote for Harry Rowland—*Harry* Rowland—and victory!"

He sat down, while the hall shook to the thunder of applause, clapping, stamping feet. Ralph Ellis stood at the lectern and when at last there was quiet, said, "Would anyone like to ask any questions of Mr Lloyd George—but I should warn you that he has a train to catch in a few minutes. When he leaves, Mr Rowland will answer other questions."

A man in the middle of the hall shouted, "Are you for conscription?"

Lloyd George strode back to the lectern and pointed a finger at the questioner. "Yes, I am," he cried in a full resonant tone, "and so would you be if you saw how men's abilities are being wasted under the present system. Men vitally needed in our factories are going off to the front. We must see that the factories are not short of skilled labour, just as we must see that the trenches are not short of skilled soldiers. That's fair play for all."

"I 'eard some shop stewards refused to meet you, in Birmingham, 'cos you're on the side of the bosses, always trying to get the men to work 'arder for less money. Wot do you say to that?"

Lloyd George turned on the questioner, the mane of hair swinging, the blunt finger stabbing out—"I say that those stewards were more interested in their own positions than in fair play, or in the men they were supposed to represent. We in the Liberal Party are for a better life for the working man, and we'll see that he gets it."

The questioner was not satisfied, and shouted, "That's a lie! They wouldn't meet you because they knew you'd sell them to the bosses!"

"If you know so well," Lloyd George snapped, "why did you ask the question?"

"To show you up for a windbag," the man shouted, and now Harry recognised Bert Gorse, Willum's fiery half-brother—"and no friend of the working man!"

Lloyd George jabbed the finger out, his face suffused with anger, "You call *me* that, *me?* Who pulled the teeth of the House of Lords? Who passed the workmen's compensation act? Who?"

"Who made a million out of Marconi shares?" Gorse yelled, but by then he was being dragged out by two policemen; and as he went, men and women rained blows on him with fists and bare hands, and shouted insults in his ears.

Lloyd George recovered his calm as quickly as he had lost it. "Now, I think that man must have had a disagreement with his wife this morning," he said, grinning mischievously at the crowd. "Any more questions?"

A woman asked hesitantly about pensions for war widows. She was dressed all in black, and Lloyd George's voice purred soothingly as he answered her. Then he raised both arms and stepped back. As the crowd cheered, he muttered to Harry, "French is going, but don't tell anyone. Defend him to the end." Then with a clap on Harry's back, he was gone. The big hall seemed smaller on the instant.

Harry walked slowly to the lectern. Those muttered words about Field Marshal French disturbed him; for relieving French was one of Richard's chief planks; and now he was being told to defend him when his masters had already decided to do what Richard was insisting must be done. Politics was a dirty business, whichever way you looked at it.

The people began to ask questions. The first was about German air superiority, a subject which he knew Richard was hammering at. He answered, "For the moment, the Germans have achieved a superiority, in some areas, it is true. We hope to change the situation very shortly, in ways which I am not free to divulge." Again, he felt uncomfortable; all he really knew was that the best brains in the British aircraft industry were working on the problems of firing machine guns through propellers; and had found a solution . . . but designing and building the right aircraft to use the new invention was a different problem, which could not be solved overnight.

He watched the blind soldier from the corner of his eye while he was answering others' questions. When would *he* get up, and ask something . . . something unanswerable? But the young man sat still, no muscle moving. Someone asked about recruiting; another about who might be exempted from military service if conscription came; a third about sugar rationing. Then a woman in the fourth row stood up and called, "Will you please tell us your policy on women's suffrage and the employment of women, Mr Rowland?"

He stared, sure he'd seen the woman before somewhere, then answered, "As to suffrage, I think we must wait till the end of the war and then decide what we should do. There has been much vocal and indeed violent agitation in favour of votes for women, but as I am sure you all realise, there is also a strong feeling against female suffrage among women themselves. At all events, it is a divisive issue. We

should therefore follow the example of the leaders of the suffrage movement, and declare a truce on the subject until the war is ended."

Loud clapping broke out, continuing for some time, most of it apparently from men, Harry thought. Women's suffrage was not a popular issue these days. He himself thought women should probably get
the vote now. He hadn't liked the idea before the war—but the war had
changed that, because women themselves seemed to be changing—and
not always for the worse, as so many seemed to think.

"About employment," he continued, "I am not opposed to young
women finding employment suited to their education and skills . . .
but not of course under any sort of compulsion. There must be no
conscription of women, of any nature. I think we must agree that
woman's natural place is in the home. Her position there must be protected by all the means in our power. It is only she, after all, who can
keep the home fires burning."

The woman called, "With respect, sir, that is nonsense. You say
women can get jobs for which they have skills. But what skills do most
women have, except cooking? We want to do more, and for that we
need training. We need a government effort to persuade employers to
accept us, train us . . . give us the same opportunities as they give to
men."

"Shut up, you bitch!" a man close to the woman said, in a loud clear
voice.

The woman turned on him, "I'm not a bitch any more than you're a
male dog. We are both human beings, and English. I am asking for
equal rights for that half of humanity who are women . . . rights to
work, rights to fair and equal treatment."

The booing became louder and louder, spreading all through the
hall. Women nearby were clawing toward the speaker, who kept on
shouting in a high shrill voice, the accent more strongly cockney as she
became more excited. The police were moving in and after a few moments of confused pushing and shoving and overturning of chairs, and
a bobby's helmet being knocked sideways, the woman was escorted to
the door.

Harry wiped his brow. "I apologise for the disturbance, ladies and
gentlemen," he said. "I have nearly finished . . . I have told you what
we are doing to win the war, and how we—the Liberal Party—undertake to do more, under the dynamic leadership of Mr Asquith, Mr
Lloyd George, and their colleagues. I ask all of you to put your shoulders to the wheel. It is we, the people, of all classes, who, with God's
blessing, must save England from the Hun menace . . . save it for

cricket, hunting, football . . . for ourselves, our wives and our children. Thank you."

He sat down. Ralph Ellis took his place, his right hand raised. "So we all say, vote for Mr *Harry* Rowland, Liberal candidate, next Thursday, November 11th. Now," he looked up at the big clock on the wall behind him, "in twenty minutes the Liberal dance will begin at the Oddfellows' Hall. Music will be by Mr Jimmy Jevons' Dance Band, whose services have been obtained for us as a gift from Mr Bill Hoggin, of Hoggin's Preserves." The blind soldier suddenly booed loudly, and it was a few moments before laudatory clapping, led by Ellis, drowned it. On the platform, Bill Hoggin stood up, bowed shortly, and sat down again. Ellis continued: "A collection will be made at the door to buy comforts for the wounded at the Dartford Convalescent Depot. I hope we shall see all of you there, enjoying yourselves in anticipation of Mr Harry Rowland's victory next Thursday, November 11th. We on this platform will all be attending the dance, with our ladies. Now, ladies and gentlemen, please join me in singing together *Keep the Home Fires Burning*."

He raised his hand and set off bravely, only slightly out of tune. The audience stood up and began raggedly to sing, but soon swung into unison:

> *Keep the home fires burning, while your hearts are yearning*
> *Though your lads are far away they dream of Home:*
> *There's a silver lining, through the dark cloud shining*
> *Turn the dark cloud inside out, till the boys come home!*

The blinded soldier got up and tapped slowly across the floor in front of the front row of singers. Harry watched him, feeling the chill of battlefield graves upon him. He hardly dared breathe until the slight figure had tapped its way out of the room, under the hearty singing, for he knew that whatever question the boy might have asked him, he could not have answered it.

Bert Gorse stood outside the door of the hall, listening to what was being said inside. It was not a cold night and the front doors had been left open for better ventilation. A bobby watched him with a neutral stare, arms folded behind him, now and then majestically bending his knees slightly, hitching his testicles to the other side of his trouser fork by a subtle torso movement, then straightening up again. When the woman questioner was pushed into the street, not gently, Bert went to her and said, "They were making such a row in there I didn't hear what you said, at the end. What was it all about?"

"Jobs and training for women," the woman said briefly. She was short and dark and full-lipped, and now high-coloured. "We're trying to make the politicians and the people, especially the women, realise that women have a right to these things."

They were wandering down the street together, the bobby watching from the hall steps. Bert said, "You want to put women into the factories, so they can send more men off to get killed?"

"Women should be able to go wherever they want to, and get any work they can do. It's nothing to do with the war. We don't want anyone to be sent to France, man or woman."

"Who's we?"

"The Socialist Party here in Hedlington."

"Ah, that's where I've seen you before. At a meeting. You may want women to be able to get jobs, but you know what really happens? The men they replace get sent to France. Look at what happened at the convalescent depot at Dartford, which that old crow Ellis was talking about just now . . . They put women in to cook instead of the soldier cooks, and the men ruined the new ovens, on purpose . . . tore out all the cooking equipment there was. Must have cost thousands to replace. The women were sending them to their deaths, see?"

"We want women to be equal in everything. Equal in being against the war, too."

Bert looked at her more closely. "'Ere," he said suddenly, "come and have a drink in the Blue Boar. I'll stand one . . . as long as it's not port and lemon. I can't afford that stuff."

"I can pay for my own drinks," she said.

He pushed open the door of the Blue Boar's public bar, then paused—"You don't mind going into the public?"

She said, "Of course not. I think there only ought to be one bar."

They were in the pub then, in a dense fog of pipe and cigarette smoke. There were half a dozen other women present, all respectable-looking working women or wives, with their husbands, drinking stout and ale and porter. Khaki and blue uniforms were evenly spaced among the civilians.

"Two pints of bitter, mate," Bert called. "Grab that chair. What's your name, anyway?"

"Rachel Cowan."

"Bert Gorse. I work at J.M.C., and in the union office, on the side."

"I'm secretary of the Hedlington Socialist Party . . . all twenty of them. Do you have a relative living in Walstone? When I was staying with a friend last winter we met an old man called Gorse, who . . ."

"Probyn. My father," Bert said. "The best poacher in Kent."

"So I heard."

"Who were you staying with?"

"Naomi Rowland. I was at Girton College, in Cambridge, with her. Her father's John Rowland, of High Staining, a farm in Walstone."

"And her grandfather's that old man up there on the platform in the Hall."

"I know . . . I didn't want you to think I knew him socially."

"But you do."

"I can't help that. I'm against what they stand for. I suppose your father is, too, if he poaches from all their preserves."

Bert drank his beer, watching her closely. Jewess, he thought, a bit la-di-da because of Cambridge; but came from Wapping or Limehouse or Stepney originally. Her family probably poor as church mice—synagogue mice. He answered her implied question, speaking slowly. "My dad's a rum bird . . . He ain't against toffs, and he ain't for them, either. He doesn't poach because he thinks the birds are his, not theirs—but because he thinks the birds don't belong to anybody, which ain't the same thing . . . He hates Lord Swanwick, that old fart on the platform, with the withered arm. He likes Cate, who's squire of Walstone. And if you want to hear about poaching, wait till Christmas. Dad's sworn to poach a dozen of Swanwick's pheasants and have them on some of the gentry's dinner tables by Christmas dinner, as presents from his lordship." He chuckled delightedly.

Rachel said, "You mean, he's told Lord Swanwick about this?"

Bert shook his head. "Not him, not directly—but he's told enough people so Swanwick's sure to have heard by now. He's got a plan, and he's not the only one in it. He's got some other blokes signed on to help. He'll do it, wait and see . . . Now tell me about this Socialist party here. I don't believe in the theory, see. I think if we are going to get a better deal for the working man, it's got to be done in the factories. What we need is a national union shop, every single man, skilled and unskilled, in every single factory belonging to a union—no union card, no job—and all the unions linked together, so if one strikes, they all strike."

"What about the farms?" she cut in.

"Ah," he hesitated, "later, maybe. It's hard to organise, farming."

"But it'll have to be done soon, if farming is ever to become more than a cottage industry in this country."

"Perhaps . . . As I was saying, I believe in strong unions . . . discipline . . . getting at the bosses and the capitalists directly, through their pockets. What do you believe in?"

Rachel Cowan drew a deep breath and began: "The Socialist party believes . . ."

Alice had listened to her father from among the audience and afterwards driven with him to the Oddfellows' Hall for the Liberal dance. Now the dance had been going on for an hour and a half, and Jimmy Jevons' Dance Band was playing somewhat raggedly; the platoon of empty and half-empty beer bottles and tankards beside their chairs explained why. Bill Hoggin was there, standing against one wall of the hall, tankard in hand and big yellow rosette on his lapel, his wife beside him. Glancing round, Alice saw that her father was in earnest conversation with the mayor, their grey heads bent together beyond the band. A hundred and fifty men and women were dancing an energetic waltz. She herself had just finished dancing with a soldier with large boots, who had twice trodden on her toes; her toes hurt and as she saw another soldier approaching, she stepped quickly toward the Hoggins. It was naughty of her to avoid the soldier, she knew; but just now she needed a little time to let her toes recover.

"Good evening, Mr Hoggin," she said. "Good evening, Ruth."

"Evening, miss," Hoggin said, waving a cigar in the air with his free hand.

"Good evening, Miss Alice," Ruth said, colouring up and half curtseying. "I do like your dress. It's ever so pretty."

"Oh, thank you, Ruth. I made it myself. It took me a long time, though, what with the Tipperary Room and the House Parties and the hospital canteen and the visits to the convalescent centres . . ."

"You do so much," Ruth said.

"Not enough. How's the baby—Launcelot?"

"Why, he's eight months, Miss Alice, nearly nine . . . eight months and fourteen days."

"And always hungry," Hoggin said. " 'E's heating us out of house and home, now that Ruthie's stopped feeding him herself. Don't have to pay for that, do you?"

"Oh, Bill!" Ruth said, blushing again.

Alice said, "I should think he'd have to eat a great deal—of caviar—to worry you, Mr Hoggin. You're doing so well, and we're so pleased for you. It was very generous of you to hire the band for us tonight."

"Thanks, miss. I'm not doing so bad. Bought a car last week. Ro, ro . . . not a Rowland. Can't remember the name."

"Rolls Royce?" Alice said.

"That's hit . . . Cost me a ruddy fortune, but they told me it would last for hever, so it's worth it. *Hand* it shines a fair treat, sitting outside the 'ouse, *house.*"

Alice smiled and nodded. Bill Hoggin had obviously been taking elocution lessons, so that his speech would better suit his new circumstances. As so often, the effort not to drop aitches resulted in putting them in, heavily aspirated, where they should not be. Ruth must have made him do it. The marvel was that he had agreed to any such thing.

"We see Hoggin's jams everywhere, in the shops," she said.

"That's right," Hoggin said, nodding, "though, mind you, most of what 'as, *h*as my label on goes to the troops in France." His eyes wandered, and he suddenly caught Alice's arm. " 'Oo's that? That girl, dancing, in the green dress?"

Ruth cut in, "Why, that's Miss Stella, Bill—Miss Cate, Miss Alice's niece. And let go of Miss Alice's arm. What will she think of you?"

"Sorry, miss." Hoggin dropped the arm, his eyes still on Stella dancing with Johnny Merritt. "Is Miss Cate a V.A.D.?"

Alice said, "Yes. In Lady Blackwell's hospital. Not every day."

"But she's not with the Fire Brigade? Or the special police?"

Alice was puzzled. "No. How could she be?"

Hoggin said, "Quite right, miss. 'Ow could she be? I must have made a mistake."

Alice opened her mouth to ask a question—her curiosity had been aroused—when a man's voice said, "Miss!" in her ear; and, then, all in a rush, "I would appreciate the honour of this dance."

She turned to face a broad shouldered petty officer of the Royal Navy. He was about her own age—mid-thirties—blue eyes, bronzed, with many fine wrinkles round his eyes and the gold-embroidered crossed flags of a chief yeoman of signals on his arm. He was swaying very slightly on his well polished shoes and looking beseechingly at her, showing a fine row of white teeth.

The band was playing a slow dance now. She didn't recognise the tune or the rhythm. It must be one of the new slow foxtrots; but she thought she could keep step to it—or whatever step the yeoman chose to do, and would perhaps not get her toes trodden on. She said, "I'd be delighted," and, smiling adieu to the Hoggins, was swept off onto the creaking floor.

The yeoman was a good partner. He might be a little drunk but it did not affect his dancing—perhaps even gave it a more fluid form. He held her close, and guided her with pressures of his body against hers, rather than with his right hand on the small of her back. It was the first time she had ever been held so close against a man, and after a minute of wondering whether it was quite decent, or proper, she surrendered to the flow and glide of the dance.

He said, " 'Tis a long time since I held a woman in my arms." She thought from his accent that he came from the same county as her sister-in-law, Louise—Yorkshire. If so, he was a long way from home.

She said, "Are you married?"

He shook his head, "Marriage and the sea don't go together . . . You dance well, miss."

Blushing, she said, "So do you."

"And you're pretty . . . right good looking."

They danced round the floor, Alice feeling her contours gradually melting into his. Her voice was unsure when she asked, "When do you go back to sea?"

"Tomorrow, miss."

"I'm so sorry," she said, thinking of the winter storms, the cold, and the death that lurked below the water.

"It's my job," he said. His grip on her suddenly tightened, and he muttered in her ear, "Oh, lass, if I could only take you with me!"

She felt a growing hardness against the lower part of her stomach, where his loins pressed against hers. Harder now, and she began to lose all power to resist; she was helpless with this man, looking hungrily, longingly into her eyes . . . and was she not looking back at him the same way, with no conscious volition on her part? She felt a tingling in her nipples and warmth between her thighs, deep in her loins. No man had ever done this to her before. Her mind whispered warnings, her body held him tighter, her hips pushed forward against his thrust.

He changed the direction of their movement, and in a moment, without Alice realising how it had happened, they were through the side door of the Hall and in the alley, the Hall towering above them on one side, a high brick wall on the other; and he was kissing her on the lips, his tongue sliding into her mouth, and now one hand was on her breast, caressing. He whispered, "Oh, lass . . . oh love . . ."

He stooped quickly and raised her long skirt, his hand was inside her drawers. She sagged against him, passionately ready to give everything that was feminine or female about her, for the first time. He was fumbling at the fastening of his trousers when a man's voice nearby called into the darkness, "Miss Rowland? . . . Miss Rowland?"

And another voice, "I saw her go out this way, with a petty officer. She looked hot. Perhaps she's been taking some fresh air."

The yeoman muttered, "Jesus! The candidate's daughter!" He wrenched free. She reached after him despairingly—she had been on the verge of knowing her womanhood wholly. But he was gone, hurrying down the alley, a shadow merging into the shadows, only the thud of his shoes echoing for a moment between the walls, then silence.

Alice's skirt had dropped, and she walked slowly, trembling, toward the Hall door. "Are you looking for me?"

"Oh, there you are . . . your father asked me to tell you he wants to go home now, Miss Rowland."

It was a minor official of the local party, whom she had met once or twice. She said, "Thank you . . . It was getting awfully hot in there."

"It was, miss."

Then she was inside the Hall, walking toward her father, her trembling under control. She thought, I am considered so much on old maid that it never even crossed anyone's mind that I might be doing something improper with the yeoman. A few minutes ago, they would have been right, but the yeoman had changed her as surely as though he had formally taken her virginity; for in her mind she was no longer a virgin. It would only be a question of time before some other man would see in her the longing to give, that the yeoman, aided by the drink, had seen or felt—and then the physical counterpart of the moral and mental change that had already taken place, would inevitably follow . . . not with the first man who tried, of course; she was not hungering for just any man, but when a man came who responded physically to her, and whom she could answer with the language of love, she would do so.

They were in the car, old Wright tucking a foot robe round her father's knees. "Guy Fawkes' Night," he said as the car moved off. "You'd never know it, though. No fireworks, no bonfires, no guys. The war . . ." His voice trailed off into silence.

She thought, yes, the war is changing more things than the celebration of Guy Fawkes' Night. She was suddenly certain that the war, acting powerfully and invisibly, had been the prime mover both in her and in the yeoman tonight.

Her father said, "There was a blind soldier in the Hall this evening . . . so young . . . I wonder where he lives. I want . . ."

He fell silent. Alice said, "You want what, father? To help him? He's probably at some hospital or convalescent home."

"I want to ask him something," her father said.

"What?"

"What I should do, if I'm elected . . . try to stop the war? . . . press it to the bitter end? . . . He's been there. He knows."

The Times, Tuesday, November 9, 1915

HOUSE OF LORDS, Monday.

The LORD CHANCELLOR took his seat on the Woolsack at a quarter past four o'clock.

CONDUCT OF THE WAR
CABINET CRITICISED

The adjourned debate on matters relating to the war was resumed. Earl LOREBURN said: I was disappointed in not observing in the course of the debate any prospect that the Government intended to change its course in dealing with these matters. No Government can prosper in this country unless it has public opinion behind it. That is what gives you recruits, and that is what enables us to get our loans subscribed, to prevail against the unrest in the industrial world, and to preserve order better than any police can do.

There is a Censorship for the Press. The Government do not inform Parliament of many things we ought to know . . . Admiral Cradock's fleet was destroyed in the Pacific. It was said that he had asked for more ships. Is that true? . . . Then there was Antwerp. To us civilians that seems a very strange adventure. Men wholly untrained, who belonged to the Naval Reserve, were sent out to Antwerp. Did the military authorities approve of that before they were sent? . . . Then there was the loss of the three cruisers in the North Sea—a very serious misadventure. Sailors tell you these cruisers ought to have been recalled beforehand. No court-martial was allowed on that loss, and yet courts-martial on such occasions are an ancient tradition of the navy.

I come to the Dardanelles expedition. We know what that has been, though we do not know to the full extent all the blunders and suffering caused by it.

What's to be said about munitions? Can anyone say where the blame lies for that? A Minister and an ex-Minister had a controversy on that subject, and one of them intimated that he might be obliged to disclose the whole truth and not merely a part of it. I suppose friends intervened and all was covered up. But this cost thousands of lives.

We are again on the brink of serious difficulties in the Balkans. A new change has taken place in Lord Kitchener's temporary absence, which I hope will be short. I asked a week ago whether the landing at Salonika was effected with the approval of the naval and military authorities . . . there was no real answer given.

Has provision been made for our forces in Mesopotamia and in East Africa and Egypt?

Nearly all the youths of Europe are under arms. I was told . . . that already 15,000,000 have been either killed or disabled for life . . . Apart from this high death rate the cost of many thousands of millions on war debt will alter the whole face of civilisation, and will cast a burden not only upon our industry but also upon the lives of our children and our children's children, and we must add to that the destruction over vast areas of industrial countries.

It is no exaggeration to say that if this conflict goes on indefinitely, revolution and anarchy may well follow. Great portions of the Continent of Europe will be little better than a wilderness peopled by old men and women and children.

Viscount MILNER: In the course of this discussion little has been said about the Censorship. Of course, we are all absolutely agreed that there must be a censorship to prevent information getting to the enemy which might be useful to the enemy . . . But the fact remains that the war news published in this country, from first to last, has been most seriously misleading. It has been constantly doctored in an optimistic sense.

I would ask any candid man to compare the first impression he derived of the Battle of Neuve Chapelle or the terrible battles of September 25th and 26th—the first impression he derived from official telegrams with the impression he subsequently gathered, and the knowledge he subsequently acquired from the furtive admissions and laboured explanations of the official world and the reports of individuals who were present at these terrific fights . . . Not once or twice, but many times, I have been pained to hear officers who have returned from the front say that on the whole the German official reports of engagements between us and them have been more trustworthy than the British.

> With whomsoever the fault lies the public remains de-
> luded as to the general course of the war and as to the
> position in which the country finds itself today.

Rose took what little breakfast she ate these days, in bed, so Harry was alone with Alice. He kept his eyes down as he read on, for he did not want his daughter to see the anxiety and doubt which, he thought, must be obvious on his face. Lords Loreburn and Milner, and many others, were openly criticising the Government's conduct of the war. Loreburn, indeed, had obliquely suggested that some accommodation ought to be sought with the Germans before civilisation destroyed itself. And there was no denying that blunders had been made, and still were.

Would they continue to be made? Would it really help to drag these mistakes up and with them berate men who were surely doing their best? Had the scale of events grown beyond the power of human beings to control?

Quentin would say that the damned rotters ought to be shot: how could a private soldier be expected to do his duty if his leaders were being pilloried all the way up the line? Christopher would worry, and philosophise, standing aloof from all theory. Richard would say . . . he *was* saying . . . that Loreburn and Milner and the rest of them were right: how could a private soldier be expected to do his duty if his leaders were incompetent fools all the way up the line?

He gritted his teeth. Once the election was over, he'd have to face this problem, and settle it, by his own conscience, once and for all. Meanwhile, win the election.

Glancing up, he saw that Alice was eating toast, while immersed in the *Morning Post*. She was looking younger, and dressing more— somehow sophisticatedly—recently . . . since her mother had become bedridden? And surely that was a touch of lipstick he detected on her lips? He was about to comment on it, when he thought, she is of age, and it makes her look . . . almost luscious. Why not?

Hedlington: Thursday, November 11, 1915

31 Harry Rowland stood on the pavement outside Jonas & Johnson's, the big new four-storied department store on High Street, that sold everything from bits and braces to ladies' underwear. It was a cold morning, dull and grey, with wind blowing down the street from the north, whirling bits of paper past the big glass windows, and farther, past the station and the façade of the South Eastern Hotel. Harry wore an overcoat, and a tweed cap on his head. The wind whistled through his grey spade beard and his hands, ungloved, ached with the cold. He thought, it isn't really very cold, a few years ago he would hardly have noticed it; it wasn't the degrees, but the years . . . He could not put on his gloves, because he was there to shake hands—with people going in and out of the store, although since most of them were women at this hour, that would not produce any direct results—and with the men going up High Street to reach any of the three polling stations stretched along it.

Ralph Ellis stood at his side, flanked with two or three assistants, men and women, all wearing the big yellow rosettes of the Liberal party. Beside Harry a sandwich-board had been set up on the pavement. The hand-painted message in red and black read: FOR OUR BOYS IN FRANCE VOTE FOR HARRY ROWLAND.

A man came up, mumbling something. "Thank you," Harry said, and shook his hand. "Thank you," to another, and another— "Remember it's Harry Rowland . . . Harry's the name . . . thank you, thank you . . . Yes, I intend to ask a question in the House about the Huns' treatment of our prisoners of war as soon as I am seated . . .

thank you . . . Harry Rowland, Harry's the name . . . I have the utmost confidence in Field Marshal French, and so do the Government . . . Thank you . . . Harry's the name, Harry Rowland . . ."

Rose should be nearing the end of the examination by now. He ought to have gone to the hospital with her; but on election day, it couldn't be done. After Lloyd George had come down in person to help his campaign, nothing on earth must be allowed to stop him appearing in person, and going to vote with the men from the newspapers there, and the magnesium flashing for the photographers, but . . . Alice could look after her and of course Wright was there to do the driving . . . he had thought Wright was getting too old for the job, even at the beginning of this year; but it was only his age and a slight rheumatic condition that prevented Wright from joining the navy—if the navy would have him. They were already oversubscribed with volunteers—because, Harry was ashamed to admit it, men thought it safer than the army.

"Harry Rowland, Harry's the name . . . Thank you, thank you . . . Why, it's Willum Gorse. How's Mary, Willum?"

"Fine, Mr Harry. She cleans pubs in the morning. And takes in washing. And makes clothes, of course."

"She's a fine woman, Willum. You're a lucky man."

Willum was shuffling from one foot to the other and Harry said, "Well, run along and vote, whoever for, or Bob Stratton will be after you for taking too much time off."

"Oh, I'll be voting for you, Mr Harry. Mary told me to."

Harry laughed. "Good! Oh, have you seen your father recently?"

"Not for a month."

"Well, when you do, tell him to be careful about his plan to poach a lot of pheasants from Lord Swanwick. Everyone in Walstone seems to know about it."

"That's what Dad says, everyone's going to know, he says."

"Including Lord Swanwick's keepers. He'll get into serious trouble, warn him."

"I'll tell him, Mr Harry, but . . . he don't listen to me."

"Nor anyone else," Harry said as Willum hurried on, tugging at his forelock.

"Harry Rowland, Harry's the name . . . thank you, thank you . . ."

Ellis said, "Your hand must be getting sore."

"Numb."

"Not much longer. We ought to be going along to vote soon. The newspapers were warned for eleven o'clock."

"Thank you, thank you . . . Yes, I think we should make Germany pay for all the damage she has done . . . yes, the whole cost of the war

. . . thank you, thank you . . . we should take away all their factories, to replace ours and the French . . . How would they pay the indemnities if they had no factories? Well, I would leave that to the economists at the time. They must certainly not be allowed to get off scot free after all the suffering they have caused, and the damage they have inflicted . . . thank you, thank you, Harry's the name, Harry Rowland . . ."

The taxi deposited him at the front door of Laburnum Lodge and Harry got out quickly, almost stumbling over his own feet. He turned to the taxi driver. "Please come back here in . . . forty five minutes, punctually!"

"Very good, sir," the man said, touching his cap, then drove off. Parrish opened the front door before Harry reached it, and moments later, helped him out of his overcoat.

"Is Mrs Rowland back, Parrish?"

"Yes, sir. With Miss Alice. They returned about ten minutes ago. They are in the morning-room."

Harry hurried along the wide passage, Bismarck and Max trotting beside him, tails wagging. The door of the morning-room was open. He half ran in, his breath short, and stopped. Rose was in her usual big chair, head bowed, hands covering her face. Alice was on her knees in front of her, holding her by the elbows, whispering something.

Harry went slowly to the two women, and knelt at his daughter's side. "My dearest," he muttered.

His wife lowered her hands. Her face was yellowish grey, the dark hollows under her eyes deeper even than this morning. "I have cancer of the uterus, Harry," she said. "They are going to operate tomorrow, but Mr Frampton can not say that that will be the end of the matter."

Harry's head felt unconscionably heavy, heavier than his neck could support. When it had been thick and strong, a young man's neck, it might have—but not now, not with the constant silent worry about Tom, and Quentin, and Boy . . . and Guy ready to go. His head sank and he found a tear rolling down the side of his nose. He searched for his handkerchief in his breast pocket, found it, and blew weakly.

Rose's hand fell on his shoulder. "I'm not afraid, Harry."

"When . . . do you go back to the hospital?"

"This afternoon, four o'clock. They have to see that I don't eat anything, and then tomorrow morning early, prepare me for the operation."

"I'll come with you."

"No, my dear, I'll come with *you* . . . After you have had your lunch, and a rest, Alice and I will go to the Town Hall, then straight to the hospital. There's nothing for you to do there."

"I'll go with Mother," Alice said, "and stay as long as they'll let me. The matron said she'd let Stella be with Mother, too, if Lady Blackwell's Hospital will release her."

"I'll come immediately after the operation," Harry said.

"No one will be allowed to see her before eleven o'clock, Mr Frampton said . . . Now, Mother, why don't you put your feet up on the sofa, while Father has his lunch?"

"I'll get Parrish to serve it in here," Harry said. Painfully he got to his feet, and helped his wife to the sofa by the tall windows, overlooking the grey November garden.

Next day, Friday, November 12, the ballot boxes were opened at eleven a.m. in the Council Chamber of the Town Hall. Now the clock on the rear wall showed three-thirty, and the last of the boxes was on the table. The Returning Officer, who was the Town Clerk of Hedlington, supervised the counting, with the tellers and the party scrutineers carefully examining each slip and agreeing on the tally. Two police constables and an inspector stood by the door, checking that all who came in had the proper pass, or other good reason to be present.

The result ought to be declared before four, Harry thought, walking up and down the floor of the Council Chamber, his hands behind his back. Campaign workers standing along the wall muttered to each other in low voices, so that Harry heard snatches of their talk as he went to and fro.

". . . over six feet, he is, the police say, with a club foot . . ."

Rose had been very pale when Harry saw her at noon, but the yellowish colour seemed to be less, though how that could be in so short a time he did not understand. She was too weak even to raise her hand to his and only her large, open eyes, and the faint pressure of her fingers when he picked her hand up off the bed showed that she was alive.

". . . always a full moon, like the last one, October 23rd, it was . . . rapes them first, then strangles them, then cuts them open . . ."

Her chest hardly moved as she breathed. Stella was there and the contrast between the two women was almost more than he had been able to bear—the radiant, flushed beauty of the nineteen-year-old, her skin like a fresh peach, glowing with youth and love, her body curved and ripe—and Rose, pinched, worn, lined, exhausted, sick.

". . . no, not their breasts, low down—(the voice lowered still more) —from the cunt to the arsehole, cuts right through there, dreadful, isn't it?"

He stopped his pacing, feeling a sudden shock. The blind young soldier had come into the room, tap tap tap slowly down the centre long floor, to stand against a wall, silent, the blackened glasses reflecting the artificial lights. How did he get in? Harry asked himself, with fear. Does the mayor know him? The police inspector? Why should he be allowed in? What does he expect to . . . ?

"Father . . ." He turned, and looked up. "Hullo John . . . Louise. It's nice of you to come."

"Alice telephoned, about Mother. We had no idea."

"Nor had I. She wouldn't go to the doctor before, though I suggested she ought to. She hasn't been well for months—years, almost."

"I know," Louise said, "I was worried, too, but when Mother has her mind made up . . ." She ended the sentence with a shrug.

"Do you have any idea how the voting has been going, Father?"

"We're leading, though Richard has done much better than was expected. There's no doubt that many people are seriously concerned about the general conduct of the war."

Bob and Jane Stratton approached, "We've just heard about Mrs Rose," Jane said. "The inspector let us in. I know him."

"It's good of you, Jane. She's very weak, but the surgeon hopes she'll be much better in a day or two. It's a serious operation, you know."

"Can I go and see her, Mr Harry?"

"Of course, Jane, but I suggest you wait till tomorrow. She will hardly recognise you if you go today. Miss Stella has been with her since she was admitted, and was still there when I went, at noon."

"She's here now, Father," John said. He nodded toward the door, where Stella was coming in, Johnny Merritt behind her. Stella was in her V.A.D. uniform, and looked tired, but somehow happy, though she was not smiling. It was being with the young man, of course, Harry thought.

Bob Stratton said, "What did the doctor say—about the operation, Mr Harry? Was it successful?"

Harry tried, in vain, to hold back the tears that came so easily these days: he, who, before this year had hardly shed a tear since the cradle. He had hoped no one would ask that question: but Bob was right. The truth must be dragged out, known, and faced. "We don't know," he said. "It was a complete hysterectomy, but cancer is such a vile thing that it may already have spread to other parts or organs or systems. We can only hope for the best, and pray."

Richard and Susan walked in, the inspector saluting them. Johnny and Stella joined them and the four came on together toward Harry, Richard's spectacles gleaming in the electric lights. He said, "How is Mother, Father?" His voice was hoarse and rough.

"As well as can be expected, Richard . . . very weak. It was cancer. We can only hope for the best now."

The Returning Officer was on his feet, ringing the handbell beside him on the big polished table. The room fell silent as he read in a high, thin voice: "Parliamentary Division of Mid Scarrow. I, the undersigned, being the acting Returning Officer for the above named constituency, hereby give notice that the total number of votes given for each candidate at the election dated November the eleventh, 1915, was as follows:

Harry Rowland— 9,774
Richard Rowland— 7,858

and the undermentioned person has been duly elected to serve as Member for the said Division—Harry Rowland. Signed, Philip Howell, Returning Officer."

He then beckoned to Harry and Richard. Campaign workers opened the French windows leading onto the balcony and there the Returning Officer proclaimed the result once more, Harry to his right and Richard to his left, standing very straight and stiff-backed. Then all three men went back into the Council Chamber, and the French windows were again closed.

Richard slumped into his more characteristic stoop, took his wife's hand, and said, "Congratulations, Father. And thank goodness that's over."

Harry put his hands on his son's shoulders. "Thank you, Richard . . . The victory's nothing but dust and ashes to me now, though."

Richard said, "Politics is not my job—production is. But, Father, the majority was really very small, considering that I had no backing from any organised political party . . . only 1,916 votes. It shows that people are really unhappy about the slaughter and apparent incompetence on the Western Front. Is there no way of getting away from it? Trying somewhere else? Trying new methods?"

Harry dabbed his eyes and blew his nose, stopping suddenly to watch the blinded soldier tap tap tap across the room, stop, speak to someone, and be guided to the mayor. There, he spoke again, and the mayor bent close to answer. Harry felt a sharp relief that the young man could speak: he had feared that the war had taken his speech and hearing, as well as his sight.

He turned back to Richard: "I wish there was. But I've talked to people at the War Office . . . Lord Derby . . . generals . . . They all say the same. The Western Front is the decisive one and sending troops elsewhere is just to squander them. We tried in Gallipoli and look what happened. It's common knowledge that we will be abandoning the whole enterprise soon. We're only in Palestine to protect the Suez Canal and in Mesopotamia to protect India. I don't like the idea of more slaughter in France any more than anyone else, but . . . *is* there an alternative?"

Richard said, wearily raising his hands, "There must be. And we've got to find it."

Quentin Rowland came slowly into the emptying room. His left arm felt light and strange in its sling. That morning, they had taken the cast off, at Lady Blackwell's; and, at lunch, Fiona had told him that she did not love him, and would leave him, and the house, as soon as Guy joined the Royal Flying Corps. He had gone on eating, carefully spearing the ready-cut pieces of food on his fork, and carrying them to his mouth. "What about Virginia?" he had asked her.

"Virginia can spend her holidays at Christopher's," Fiona had answered impatiently. "She can learn to run a house. Margaret's gone and Stella's never there these days."

He had known for a long time that she no longer loved him. But why this sudden decision? He had said, "Are you in love with someone else?"

"Yes," she said, "I have been for ten years."

He ought to ask who it was, he thought, masticating a mouthful of cabbage; but he didn't want to know. He felt sad, but not angry. It was silly to think of seeking the man out and killing or injuring him. That wouldn't change Fiona's mind; only some change in himself might. And how could he change?

She had said, suddenly soft, "I'm sorry, Quentin. I can't help it."

"I understand," he said. And she, looking a long time at him, "You've changed, Quentin. I think you really do understand."

I must go to the Town Hall, he'd said; but his thoughts, as he walked slowly across Hedlington from their flat, were farther off: he must get back to France, to his battalion. It had always been his home, now more than ever.

So it was almost with surprise that, when he walked into the Council room, he recognised his father, and brothers and niece. "How's Mother?" he said. "And who won?"

His father told him; and then he stood aside, withdrawn physically and mentally from them, and watched as his father became more and more animated, regaining an intimacy with Richard which Richard's resignation, the setting-up of the J.M.C., and now the election campaign, had overlaid with conflicts and tensions.

Harry, talking to his eldest son, felt warmth almost visibly coursing through his veins. The quarrel was over, the breach healed. Together, with Richard's support, he could be strong enough to help Rose in her hour of trial and, perhaps, death. He stopped talking, suddenly chilled as he heard the now familiar tap tap tap behind him. The mayor's voice said, "Mr Harry, this is one of our heroes——"

Quentin, from the side, stared closer. The man had joined the regiment just before the war, certainly giving a false age . . . he was really about sixteen then . . . spent a few days in Quentin's A Company before the Adjutant found out that he was a natural bugler and had him transferred . . . "Wounded, gassed, and blinded at Ypres last spring," the mayor was saying . . . What was his name? Couldn't for the life of him remember.

The soldier leaned forward and spoke to Harry and Richard. "Are you the candidates? And one of you's going to be Member of Parliament?"

Harry said, "Yes. I am the new member, and this is my son."

The soldier took off his black glasses, revealing ulcerated blue-white eyeballs, no distinction between iris and sclera. He said, "Do you know what you're doing? At all?"

The mayor blustered, "Now, look here . . . !"

The soldier said, "I'm only asking them what they must have been asking themselves, all along, if they care." He turned again to Harry. "Do you?"

He replaced the glasses and tap tapped away. The mayor spread his hands and began to apologise. Richard looked at his father and said, "Well, do we?"

Harry closed his eyes and pressed his hands over them, trying to shut out the vision of the sightless eyeballs. A few moments ago he had been feeling warm, strong, good . . . He muttered, "I must think, Richard, I must think . . . Give me a little time."

The next day, Saturday, was one of those rare autumn days in England, when it is cold but sunny, the air sharp and fresh, sky brilliant pale blue, the bare branches of the trees waving in clear outline against it, hoarfrost on the grass in the early morning. Johnny Merritt drove slowly along the road to Beighton and Walstone, conscious that it was a glorious day, and confident that it would be the most glorious of his life. The road, running eastward below the North Down, gave an extensive view over the densely peopled and long-settled Weald of Kent. The slanting cowls of oast houses stood like giant monks amid the hop fields, bare and sere now, the tall poles an army of men without banners. The car purred, and he was wearing a suit of brown heather tweed woven in the Island of Lewis, in the Hebrides—a suit with knickers and a Norfolk jacket. He had ordered the suit in Savile Row early in September, but the pressure of making officers' uniforms had delayed its completion until two weeks ago, when he had had his first fitting. His second and final fitting had been on Monday, and now he had the suit; and it was perfect; and so were his greenish woollen stockings, and his plain dark woollen tie; and so was the day.

He slowed, hearing the shrill cry of a hunting horn from close ahead. Then he saw the hunt streaming across a field to his right, heading for the road. The hounds led, in full cry, sterns waving like a hurrying brown and black and white forest. He recognised Lord Swanwick, pounding along on the same great bay he had ridden for the New Year's Day meet . . . then the whippers-in . . . then the field.

Suddenly the fox crossed the road close in front of him, its tongue lolling, but running fast, and apparently easily. It disappeared through the far hedge. Three minutes later hounds came—the dog pack today, all baying and whining with excitement. Now came the Master and the whippers-in, sailing over the hedge in long curves of scarlet and white and blue and buff and black . . . foam blowing back from the green-stained bits, red nostrils flared. Another car, coming the other way, had also stopped to let the hunt pass. Many of the riders were cantering along the edge of the field, looking for a gate. Half a dozen had jumped both hedges and were in the open again, heading up the slope of the Down. The fox had vanished.

Johnny looked after them, his hands on the steering wheel, the sound of the motor loud in his ears. Ten months ago everything he had seen at the New Year's Day meet had seemed strange—beautiful and romantic, perhaps, but foreign. Now, it was not; it had become a part of him, in reality, not only in the legacy of a shared history.

The sound of the horn faded. He drove on. It was half past eleven.

At half past twelve he was standing very straight by the empty hearth in the music room of Walstone Manor, a tankard of Elephant ale in his hand, facing Christopher Cate, squire of Walstone. Cate was sitting in a high-backed wooden chair, his long legs sprawling, ale on the desk beside him.

"I have come to tell you I love your daughter, sir, and to ask your permission to marry her."

Christopher said, "Have you, by Jove? . . . Well, I'm not really surprised. We've seen a lot of you since you came over from America—how long ago?"

"Over a year, sir."

Christopher whistled. "As long as that? How time flies . . . Does your father know of this? Your mother is dead, is she not?"

"Yes, sir. I wrote to my father two weeks ago. Today he cabled me." He fished in his pocket, and handed the squire a cable. Christopher read, "*Delighted with news. Suggest you obtain Stella's parents' permission to pay your court but delay formal engagement until Betty and I arrive second week in December.*"

"Betty? Oh, your sister . . . Well, that sounds very sensible to me. You know that Stella's mother is not here to give her approval?"

"I know, sir. I'm sorry."

"I'm sure she would approve . . . except perhaps that you are not of Irish descent."

"If you want to ask me any questions about my financial position and prospects, sir . . ."

Christopher waved his pewter tankard. "That can wait till your father arrives. They must be our guests, when they come, for as long as they wish. Will you inform them? No, I'll write myself, telling him how glad we will all be if this . . . comes off. Do you have some reason to believe that Stella will agree to marry you?"

"Yes, sir. We've seen quite a bit of each other in Hedlington, sir," Johnny hastened to add, "always chaperoned or in public places, sir. I wouldn't harm her reputation for the world . . . especially as I hope that it will soon be linked to mine."

"She's here now. Did you know?"

"Yes, sir. She told me yesterday, at the Town Hall, that she'd come down by the early train this morning."

"She'll be in the drawing-room, reading, if she's not walking the dogs. Bring her here, if she's in."

Johnny left the room and Christopher Cate went to the wine cupboard and took out a bottle of amontillado and three glasses. It was a pity that Margaret wasn't here; Laurence too; but Margaret would hear about it somehow, presumably—once he'd put an announcement in *The Times* and *Telegraph*. Laurence would be home over Christmas, of course. With Johnny's father and sister here too it would be quite a jolly Christmas, happier than he had expected, with the war going the way it was.

Johnny and Stella came in and he handed them each a glass of sherry and took the third for himself. "Stella," he said, "do you know this young man?"

"Of course I do, Daddy," she said, smiling up at Johnny.

"He claims he wants to marry you. And, I suppose, take you back to America some day. What do you say to that?"

She was blushing now, then her hand went out and took Johnny's. "I think I'd like that."

"You know he doesn't speak any known language?"

"I can understand him, Daddy."

"Well, I propose that we follow the suggestion made by Johnny's father—that you should delay a formal engagement until after he arrives next month. Do you have any objection?"

Stella hesitated a bit and said, "It wouldn't have to be a long engagement, would it, Daddy?"

Johnny said, "I hope not, sir. It doesn't seem sensible to me to have an engagement at all, if it's going to be a long one."

"I agree. We'll be seeing Mr Merritt, say, about the middle of December. I hope we can plan a marriage for early February if he agrees. I'll have to get your Aunt Louise to act as hostess here and help me with the arrangements . . . though she's so busy with the farm."

"Why not Aunt Fiona?" Stella said. "She's not doing anything."

"That's a better idea. Well, here's to you both . . . your happiness . . . and from now until you are married, you may loosen the bonds of custom as far as you think good. Some old ducks will quack, but you're both sensible people and, as Johnny has said, your reputation is as important to him, now, as it is to you. You must get to know each other as well as possible before you take this step . . . the most important in your lives . . . You'll spend the day with us, of course, Johnny?"

"Love to, sir."

"And the night, too, why not? Tomorrow's Sunday."

"Thank you, sir."

"Lunch must be nearly ready . . . Oh dear, does Mrs Abell know Johnny's here?"

"I told her, early, that he was coming," Stella said, blushing.

The big sports Sunbeam rolled fast toward Hedlington in the flat light of late afternoon. Stella, sitting up straight on the seat beside Johnny, wished she could curl up closer to him, partly for warmth, and partly because it would be, somehow, more proper for what she felt. Her father was right when he said that they must get to know each other as well as possible in the next few weeks; and this brief day and night at the Manor had been a good beginning. He had stayed before, many times, and it was during those brief visits that she had felt she was really in love with him. In the intervals, when she did not see him, she sometimes had to think hard to recreate his face in her mind's eye, and certainly the timbre of his voice in her ear. But there was no one else . . . the old doctor who had flirted with her, and actually kissed her, no longer worked at Lady Blackwell's; Stephen Irwin was gone completely from her—from the world, too, for he had been killed during the summer. She had read his name in the casualty lists, and had sat still a long time, waiting to learn what she would feel at the death of her first lover, the man who had taken her virginity and taught her lust . . . no, showed her how humans express it. She had felt nothing: only a memory of the pain in Probyn's cottage, Florinda's hand holding hers, the Woman's eyes intense on her, the smell of smoke . . .

They'd walked there yesterday afternoon, she and Johnny, and talked for an hour with Probyn. Johnny had asked him about his great poaching plans and Probyn had pretended to give details, but really he'd said nothing. Florinda was still in London. She had been Lord Cantley's kept woman all summer: a thing like that could not be concealed from the village. But now Cantley had joined the army and what would happen to Florinda? Would she come back to Walstone? Lady Swanwick certainly wouldn't have her back as lady's maid, after she had been her son's mistress. And she wouldn't want to live in the cottage, after what she had known in London . . . or would she?

No one had mentioned her, not Probyn, nor Fletcher, nor the Woman. And of course, no one had mentioned what the Woman had done for Stella nearly eight months ago.

And in the evening she and her father and Johnny had sat by the fire and played Old Maid for a time; and after dinner her father had played the violin for them. She had sat, listening, her hand in Johnny's. When it was over, Johnny had leaned over and, with her father standing over them, bow in hand, had kissed her gently on the lips, and said, "I'm happier than I have ever been in my life, Stella . . . and thank you, sir."

Johnny brought up the subject now, as he slowed the big car to pass through the crooked street of Beighton. "I felt strange last night, when your father was playing for us. I didn't know then what it was. I couldn't identify it. I tried all night, and most of today."

"You've been absent-minded," she said, laughing. "You've called me Betty twice. Is she very pretty?"

"I suppose so. Yes, she is. You'll see for yourself soon enough . . . But I think I've found out why the music—the room, the evening, you, your father—all worked together to make me feel so strange. And perhaps that's the reason I called you Betty . . . I am realising—the music brought it out—that this is where I came from—England, a house like your manor . . . this earth——" he freed one hand from the wheel and waved it at the fields and the rising curve of the Downs . . . "I first felt something at Henley, but that was superficial—I was having a sort of American tourist's romantic dream. There was the Thames, Runnymede just down the river, Magna Carta, Hampton Court, Oxford . . . dreaming spires, lords, ladies, Leander . . . It was wonderful, but I was outside it. Last night I realised that I am inside it."

The car slowed again and Stella's heart beat faster. A narrow lane led off to the right toward the foot of the Down. Was Johnny going to take the car up there, where no one would come, and . . . ? He drove into the lane a few yards and stopped. The car blocked the lane from tall hedge to hedge, but it was in full view of the main road passing behind. He took both her hands, and, leaning over, kissed her. She relaxed, breathing evenly. She could feel the lack of urgency in him; there was just his gentleness, and consideration of her, his lips soft and undemanding. She felt pleasantly comforted, and her heart returned to its normal beat.

Johnny said, "I've been wrestling in my mind with what I ought to do. I was so eager to fight the Germans when I came over. I still am, but in the meantime I've learned how to run a factory. Your Uncle Richard's taught me, and it's gotten into my blood. He's a really brilliant executive. Mr Overfeld's told me so a dozen times, and he doesn't throw bouquets around much. Morgan's an excellent plant foreman, and between the three of them there's little I can do. I feel useless."

"What are you going to do, then?" she asked. If Johnny was not going to make cars at the J.M.C. she wondered where they would go, what his work could possibly be. She realised, for the first time, that they might not live in England after they were married. How could that thought never have crossed her mind before?

"I'm going to fight," he said slowly, "it's the right thing to do . . . you made me see that again, when I was losing sight of it in my absorption with the J.M.C."

"*Johnny!* I made you see that?"

"Yes. You have been so scornful of fit young men who don't volunteer. Quite rightly."

"But I meant Englishmen! You're an American!"

"I am, and always will be. But I feel . . . have always felt . . . that this is America's war, too."

She said, bewildered, "But what . . . what will become of me?" She had imagined days of peace and calm somewhere in Kent, a nice small old house close to Walstone and Hedlington, herself waiting for Johnny to come home every evening, to fly into his arms, and then . . . then surely passion would overwhelm her, more than it had with Captain Irwin? Night after night, for ever, to be held safe by that desire from all others . . . to be cradled in that excitement, needing no other.

She remembered the old doctor's kiss and blushed: her body had softened in that moment, her mind leaped in anticipation.

Johnny said, "The question is, do you want us to get married as soon as we can, or would it be better to wait till the war's over, in case something happens to me?"

She looked into his face. He was terribly serious, frowning at her. She did not know how to answer him, for the question had come at her out of nowhere, and it seemed an impossible question to answer. For months now he had been preparing her for the idea of marriage. Slowly, she had come to accept it. She would be his wife and they would make love every night and she would bear his children. What else was marriage? She felt suddenly frightened, and lost. What would become of her?

He said, "I would give anything to be able just to trot off to work every morning, come back to you every evening . . . but I can't. We'll be no worse off than all the other people who love each other, whether they're young, like us, or whether they're old, and have loved each other for years. They know, and I know, that Lovelace was right—'*I could not love thee, dear, so much, lov'd I not honour more.*'"

She said slowly, "I don't want to wait . . ." She thought, I'll stay at home with Daddy, and be the lady of the house . . . Laurence will be back for his school holidays, and we can spend our days on the Downs or along the river . . . I can give up my work at the hospital, then I won't have to go into Hedlington, and meet so many other people.

Johnny cried, "You want us to get married? Oh, my darling, how I hoped you'd say that! . . . And, you know, they won't be sending me to France at once. I'll go to some sort of training camp, but I'll be in England for several weeks, at least, and I'm not going to join up until after we're married, and have had a honeymoon."

"What are you going to join?" she asked, feeling that she was watching herself and him, and listening to the two of them talking, from a long way above, dissociated.

"The Royal Flying Corps. Guy talked a lot about it during the summer. He's quite a salesman."

Daily Telegraph, Monday, November 8, 1915

THE ALLIES AND ENEMY COMMERCE
AMERICAN PROTEST

A further Note from the United States Government with reference to the measures adopted by the Allies to prevent

goods reaching or leaving Germany has been presented to
Sir Edward Grey by Dr Hines Page, the American Ambassador in London.

It consists of a lengthy and technical argument on the
law of blockade and contraband . . . Throughout the Note
the measures of the Allies are referred to as 'the so-called
blockade,' and the American arguments are summarised
by Dr Page in the following words:

"1. The methods sought to be employed by Great Britain to obtain and use evidence of enemy destination
   of cargoes bound for neutral ports and to impose a
   contraband character upon such cargoes are without
   justification.

2. The blockade, upon which such methods are partly
   founded, is ineffective, illegal, and indefensible.

3. The judicial procedure offered as a means of repara-
   tion for an international injury is inherently defec-
   tive for the purpose.

4. In many cases jurisdiction is asserted in violation
   of the law of nations."

The Note proceeds:

"The United States, therefore, cannot submit to the cur-
tailment of its neutral rights by the measures which are
admittedly retaliatory, and therefore illegal, in conception
and in nature, and intended to punish the enemies of
Great Britain for alleged illegalities on their part.

"The Government of the United States desires, therefore, to impress most earnestly upon His Majesty's Government that it must insist that the relations between it and
His Majesty's Government be governed, not by a policy of
expediency, but by those established rules of international
conduct upon which Great Britain in the past has held the
United States to account when the latter nation was a bel-
ligerent engaged in a struggle for national existence. It is
of the highest importance to neutrals not only of the present day but of the future that the principles of international right be maintained unimpaired.

"The task of championing the integrity of neutral
rights, which have received the sanction of the civilised
world, against the lawless conduct of belligerents arising
out of the bitterness of the great conflict which is now

wasting the countries of Europe, the United States unhesitatingly assumes . . ."

Such are the general contentions of the United States Government . . . The Note does not comment on the remarkable figures quoted by Sir Edward Grey as to the increase of American trade since the beginning of the war, but proceeds to discuss the detention of American vessels and cargoes . . . (and) the complaint, to which all the others are more or less subsidiary:

"The further contention that the greatly increased imports of neutral countries adjoining Great Britain's enemies raise a presumption that certain commodities, such as cotton, rubber, and others more or less useful for military purposes, though destined for those countries, are intended for re-exportation to the belligerents, who cannot import them directly, and that this fact justifies the detention for the purpose of examination of all vessels bound for the ports of those neutral countries . . . cannot be accepted as laying down a just or legal rule of evidence . . ."

Christopher Cate put the paper down—it was four days old, and he had been keeping it in his study, waiting for an opportunity to study it more carefully; for it was a complicated subject, but obviously an important one. He did not think he could have made head or tail of it without the benefit of the evening his brother-in-law Tom had spent here, in June, when on six days' leave while his ship, *Penrith*, was having sea damage repaired before joining the blockading squadron in the North Atlantic.

"To be legal under international law," Tom had said, "a blockade has to be effective—all ships of all nations to be stopped and seized. Our blockade of Germany is not totally effective because we can't station ships in the Baltic, so there is a free two-way trade between Germany and Sweden, Denmark, and Norway . . .": that was one point the Americans were making now, Christopher noted. Tom had added, "And because of submarines and aircraft we can't blockade ports as closely as we used to. Distant Blockade can't be as effective as Close Blockade . . . but I don't think the Americans will press that argument. During their Civil War the North—the United States—declared a blockade of the South. It was not effective, but we recognised it because some day, somewhere, we might need the Americans to recognise one of ours. We'll draw on that note, if we have to.

"But this isn't really a blockade any more. In a blockade, ships and goods trying to run it are seized and confiscated. After the Germans started submarine piracy—that's what we call it, anyway—the Prime Minister said we were going to prevent goods of any kind from reaching or leaving the German Empire, but without risk to neutral ships or crews. We were going to do that by stopping ships at sea that might be carrying goods of presumed enemy final destination, ownership, or origin."

And now the Americans were saying there was no legal basis for that action, Christopher thought.

Tom had explained: "There used to be a distinction between absolute contraband—shells, guns, and so on—and conditional contraband—food, fuel, clothing. You could seize absolute contraband even though it was manifested to a neutral nation, as long as you had reason to believe that it was in fact going on to your enemy . . . the doctrine of continuous voyage. But that doctrine did not apply to conditional contraband. Now just about everything is absolute contraband."

Christopher closed his eyes, still hearing Tom's voice: "In America our consuls will give shippers Letters of Assurance, if they prove that none of the cargo is going to the enemy, either directly or indirectly. Those Letters will pass them through the patrol lines at sea . . . We have established how much of all commodities the neutral countries bordering Germany imported in each year before the war, and we're not letting them have any more now. In late 1914, for instance, Denmark was importing three times the total quantity of goods each month that she was before August that year . . . We can stop many ships moving by Bunker Control—we own most of the coal and coaling facilities for ships all round the world.

"It's a tricky business, though . . . wish I were back in the South Pacific, hunting for von Spee. That was clean hard fighting. This will be . . . well, it's dirty work. They're torpedoing our merchant seamen, and trying to starve our women and children. So are we . . .

"And it's hard on neutrals, whatever way you look at it. If any of them had a navy strong enough to bother us, we'd have to go more carefully . . . but there's only one neutral in that position, and that's America. They fought us in 1812, while we were dealing with Napoleon, largely over contraband, blockade, and other naval matters. They didn't matter much then, but now they're a big country and a strong one, and we can't afford to make them feel they must fight against us for the sake of their trade . . . They talk about the rights of neutrals, but that's eyewash. If they do come in on our side, they'll be wringing the little neutrals' necks even harder than we do . . . but you have to be careful . . . *we* have to be careful, the fellows that actually man the blockade, where all this theory and law we've been talking about is put into practice . . ."

North Atlantic: Thursday, December 2, 1915

32 Standing in the wing of the bridge, the hood of his duffel coat raised, the spray protectors of his binoculars extended, his back hunched against a steel bridge stanchion, Tom Rowland waited for the light to strengthen. A few feet to his left the officer of the watch leaned over a voice pipe, "Captain, sir . . . first light in ten minutes."

Tom shifted his feet, aching in the cold, and yawned widely. When the brief light came, he knew what he would see—a heaving waste of grey water, wind torn, a grey lowering sky that blended into the surface of the water, *Penrith's* narrow bow plunging into the long-crested rollers as they marched east toward Norway, the wildly swaying mast behind him, the reeling funnels, torrents of water rushing over the fo'c's'le, half submerging the 6-inch gun turret . . . It had been the same yesterday, and the day before that, and the day before that, ever since they had left Scapa in the Orkneys, after their last coaling.

On patrol in the North Atlantic, between Iceland and Norway . . . it was hard to say whether it was worse here than in the Southern Ocean. The seas were bigger down there, but when *Penrith* had been in those waters there had been a real hunt on, two pitched battles, and the dramatic last curtain at Robinson Crusoe's Island. Those had been days of excitement, of purpose. This patrolling had a purpose, too, of course—to enforce the blockade of Germany and its allies, and to a lesser extent to protect British shipping against German attack. Lesser, because there was not much a lone cruiser could do against marauding submarines; and there were very few German surface raiders left—and what there were, were all disguised merchant ships, flying false neutral colors. Germany's outlying warships had all been disposed of—*Emden* by H.M.A.S. *Sydney* on Cocos Island a year ago, *Königsberg* up the Rufigi river, four of von Spee's ships last December off the Falklands, and the fifth, *Dresden*, at Robinson Crusoe's Island off Chile this March. Unless or until the German High Seas Fleet came out of harbour, this would be the Royal Navy's task: combing the seas for contraband, in all weathers—searching, seizing, inspecting, escorting to port; trying to let nothing suspicious through while at the same time doing everything possible not to interfere with the legitimatè trade of neutral countries. He remembered a quote from the American writer Mahan about the navy during the Napoleonic Wars: "The world has never seen a more impressive demonstration of the influence of sea power upon its history. Those far distant storm beaten ships, upon which the Grand Army never looked, stood between it and the dominion of the world."

Still, it was better here than being with the Grand Fleet, cooped up in Scapa Flow, fearful of attack by submarines, Zeppelins, Gothas, or some other as yet unheard of product of Hun ingenuity—a chemical that would instantly rust the battle fleet's steel walls, perhaps. Here he was at least at sea. He yawned again, quickly stifling it and stiffening in a salute as Captain Leach came up onto the bridge.

"Morning, Tom. Morning, Johnson."

"Good morning, sir."

The light was spreading, and all was coming into existence, just as Tom had envisioned it . . . the sea, the waves, the spray, the plunging fo'c's'le, the wash of water over the turret.

"What speed, Johnson?"

"As ordered, sir—ten knots."

"She pitches like an old cow at this speed," the captain muttered, "go and see the Chief, Tom, and ask him whether I can safely do thirteen, and leave enough fuel for emergencies."

"Aye, aye, sir."

"And then get your head down. You look weary."

"Just bored, sir. Wish we'd sight a tramp . . . a trawler . . . a Liverpool bumboat . . . anything."

He slid down the bridge ladder, his hands on the railings, and worked his way down to the engine room, the domain of Engineer Commander Warner. Tom's feeling that Warner did not like him had become a certainty in the year since Coronel, and, as with Captain Brandt, Tom had not been able to find an overt reason for it. Warner never spoke to him except professionally, and seemed to draw imagi-

nary skirts a little aside whenever in Tom's presence. Tom prayed that
John Leach would not be forced to take official notice of it . . . but it
was not in Tom's hands; he had nothing against Warner and would
have liked to be a friend. *That* was never going to be.

Warner explained the coal situation with frigid precision, answered
Tom's few questions, and turned his back. Tom spoke to the captain on
the navyphone to the bridge, then scrambled up the steel ladders out of
the engine room as fast as he could. It was warm down there: but not
the kind of warmth he needed. Before going to his own cabin he took a
look round the mess deck, feeling the engines increase speed as he did
so. The crew's quarters were half-flooded, as they had been when he
last saw them at evening rounds with the captain yesterday.

"Pretty uncomfortable, I'm afraid," he said to a seaman standing to attention in four inches of water beside his hammock, the water surging
and sloshing back and forth as the ship pitched.

"It's fine, sir," the seaman answered lugubriously, "for ducks."

Tom laughed. "We'll be back in Scapa soon. Everything else all
right?"

"Wish we could see something . . . something to shoot at."

"So do we all. Get back into your hammock."

He went up to his own cabin off the quarterdeck, took off his coat
and scarf, unfastened his tie, took off his sea boots, and stretched out on
the bunk, otherwise fully dressed, two blankets spread loosely over him.
The ship pitched with a long slow motion, each downward lurch ending in a metallic thunk and a longdrawn shudder as the shifting buoy-
ancy of the sea lifted first the bow, then the stern, exerting tremendous
pressure on the cruiser's steel plates and keel. Her present course was
north forty-five degrees west—so that *Penrith* was heading across the
seas. That would continue for another couple of hours when, unless
something had to be investigated, she would alter course to due west
and continue on that heading until 3 p.m., when she was due to meet
another cruiser at the ends of their respective patrol 'beats.' Then back
. . . all the rest of the short day, all night, until tomorrow morning she
should sight the Norwegian coast, and turn again.

Tom swore softly. He had been weary enough on the bridge, yawning his head off. Now that he had nothing to do but rest, sleep would
not come. He reached out his hand, lit a cigarette, lifted the nose cone
of a 4.7-inch shell that was acting as a paperweight, and riffled through
the letters below. He'd received them in Scapa on their last coaling,
and had read them two or three times each since . . . one from the
Governor about Mother's operation. That must be a serious business,
reading between the lines; it was clear that the surgeon could not guar-

antee that the cancer would not return in some other part of her body. Tom liked and respected his mother, but had never felt very close to her. She had been a rather remote figure to him as a small boy, often upholding standards he felt he could never attain, and so, unwittingly, making him feel inadequate . . . and now, perhaps they were going to lose her. He tried to feel that it would make a difference to him, in his emotions, but could not. And the Governor had been elected to Parliament; but he'd known that the day after the election, when the Admiralty had sent the ship a signal about it.

Letter from Richard, about losing the same election. He didn't seem to be a bit sorry. That might be sour grapes, but Richard had always been a straightforward fellow. And he was certainly right in wanting the management of the war improved. The navy seemed to be doing its job—the job hadn't changed, and the navy had done it before; but the army was something quite different in this war from what it had ever been, and it was obvious that neither the politicians nor the generals knew how to control or use it. Some local gossip and news: John had resigned from the Hunt; it was a symbolic action, really, Richard thought, meant to emphasise that High Staining was now going to be a working farm, and John a working farmer. Of course, many ordinary farmers were keen followers of the Hunt, Tom thought; apparently they could both farm and hunt: John obviously couldn't . . . Hoggin had visited Lord Swanwick at Walstone Park, not once but twice; no one knew what it was about. Hoggin had also offered to put some money into Rowland's, an offer which had been refused. The Governor hadn't mentioned *that* in his letter . . . The man variously called the Walstone Ripper or the Full Moon Strangler was on everybody's mind, but the police were no closer to capturing him than they had ever been. A strange and horrible compulsion, Tom thought, but a compulsion . . . like his own? He picked up the last page quickly: here was the postscript and, pinned to it, the short newspaper clipping about the shooting attack on a pair of off-duty policemen in Dublin. A man and a woman had been involved: the man—picture alongside—had been killed; he had been identified as Dermot Daugherty, a notorious Sinn Fein leader; the woman, thought to have been Mrs Margaret Cate, had been wounded, but had escaped . . . My poor sister, Tom thought. For her sake, he hoped the wound was not painful. He hoped, too, that it would persuade Margaret to give up her traitorous activities . . . but of course to her they were not traitorous, they were patriotic.

He picked up the next letter. It was from Guy—a member of the Upper Ten this, his last, term. Not captain of the XV but doing reasonably well, he said. Engaged in some kind of a plot with Probyn

Gorse, which he was not at liberty to say anything more about, except that a Very Prominent Person had promised to help. And his friend John Kipling was missing in action at Loos, believed killed, and—Tom acknowledged to himself that he was looking through the letters just to re-read these next lines—"You will be sorry to hear that Dick Yeoman was also killed at Loos. I do not know whether you knew that he left Wellington over a year ago to join up. He was a private in the Sherwood Foresters when he was killed."

The sense of guilt returned to him, as palpable as the blankets. He knew that young Yeoman had not volunteered in the heroic way that Guy's letter implied, for one of the subs in *Penrith* had a younger brother at Wellington; and had long ago received a gossipy letter in which was mentioned the expulsion of Dick Yeoman for . . . that.

. . . *a private* . . . *when he was killed.* He felt cold and tired and oppressed. Surely he had killed the boy. Surely he would kill others, through the fatal flaw in him. Surely he would bring not only death, but disgrace, to his family and the Service. He saw Dick's face clearly before him, but—he stifled a groan—it was changing to Bennett's . . . Ordinary Seaman Charlie Bennett's . . . as had happened before, with increasing frequency during the past year. He had tried to wipe Bennett from his mind . . . tried to hate the young man . . . tried everything; to no avail. Bennett's image now stood in front of him, smiling, trembling, as Dick had done, that last night.

This was what Warner had smelled out in him, and turned away from in disgust. Oh God, he needed comfort, to be told what to do, how to rid himself of this curse—but there was no one to turn to, for fear; except perhaps a woman, and there were none here.

The voicepipe over his head spoke eerily, "Commander, Captain's compliments—to the bridge, sir."

Tom threw off the blankets, shoved his stockinged feet into the sea boots, shrugged into his duffel coat and hurried toward the bridge. As he went the alarm buzzers were screeching through the ship for action stations.

On the bridge Leach handed him a telescope. "What do you make of that?" and pointed.

Dim in the poor light to the west, off the port bow, the circle of the lens showed a single-funnelled merchant ship of about 5,000 tons. She was deep in the water, and making heavy weather, heading to cross *Penrith's* bows. From the foretop the gunnery officer's voice came down the voicepipe, "Target's range oh-nine-oh, sir, speed 8 knots, course north 45 east."

The yeoman of signals, swaying to the motion of the cruiser, one arm

braced round a steel stay, telescope fast to his eye, said, "No flag, sir
. . . She's hoisting one now . . . American."

"Looks like a bulk cargo ship to me, sir," Tom said. "A Yank taking
wheat to Bergen, perhaps."

The captain said, "Signal to her by lamp to report name, registry,
destination, and cargo."

The yeoman went to the signal lamp. The shutter clacked in Morse,
at first rapidly, then more slowly, as the merchantman asked for re-
peats. "By the time we get the answer," Leach muttered, "the range
will be down to 6,000 or less."

"All positions closed up at action stations, sir," the First Lieutenant
said, bounding onto the bridge.

"Guns, bring all guns to bear on her that can. Quartermaster, steer
parallel to her, until she answers."

"Aye, aye, sir."

"Revolutions for 8 knots . . . Guns, stand by to open fire if her sides
drop or she makes any other hostile movement—but only on my order.
When the Yanks stop being too proud to fight, it's the Huns we want
them to light into, not us."

The ships continued on parallel courses, heading north-east. The seas
were surging up over the port quarter of both vessels now, the sterns
lifting, and both were rolling severely.

The yeoman said, "Answering, sir . . . *Susquehanna* . . . Phila-
delphia registry . . . Baltimore to Rotterdam . . . iron ore . . . has Letter of Assurance."

Leach stared fixedly at the merchant ship for a full minute, then
snapped, "Signal her to heave to. Fifteen knots. Close the range to five
hundred yards."

"Aye, aye, sir."

Twenty minutes later, both ships stopped in the water, Leach said,
"Number One, take the cutter over and check her. Take a signalman
and half a dozen armed seamen as well."

"Aye, aye, sir! . . . Away cutter's crew!"

"Keep the guns on her, Guns. If she's going to do anything silly, it
will be in the next few minutes."

The cruiser wallowed in the waves while the davits swung out and
the cutter, its crew seated in it, was lowered into the water. The rolling
was severe and the boat was twice lowered into the sea, and twice
raised out by the high lurch of the cruiser before the falls could be
slipped and the cutter released to float away clear, as the First Lieutenant gave the order, "Give way together!" and the crew began pulling.

"Slow ahead," Leach ordered. "Keep us circling slowly, quarter-master, at this range. I want to get a good look all round her."

The cutter rose on the towering crests, sank out of sight, rose again, as the stiff, choppy navy stroke carried it toward the merchantman. After ten minutes it reached the other's lee side, and through the tele-scope Tom saw the First Lieutenant and the armed seamen swing up the Jacob's Ladder that had been lowered for them, while the boat crew remained in the cutter.

The cruiser swung on round. It had made a full circle now and was back in its original position, its 6-inch guns turning as the ship turned, always pointed at the merchantman.

Fifteen minutes passed and Leach muttered, "Why doesn't he tell us something?"

The yeoman said, "They're on the bridge, now, sir." A lamp started flashing, much faster than before, and the yeoman began to read aloud. "Name, registry, cargo verified . . . suspect Letter of Assurance forged."

"Iron ore's unconditional contraband," Leach muttered, "but if that Letter of Assurance is genuine, we'll be in trouble. Blast those damned Yanks!"

"There are a lot of Germans in America, sir. German descent, I mean," Tom said.

Leach took a turn along the bridge and back, then—"Yeoman, signal the First Lieutenant—remain on board with boarding party. Proceed to Scapa, return cutter . . . Pilot, make out a signal to the admiral. You can reach Scapa, can't you?"

"Just, sir. But they may not be able to reach the flagship."

"I know . . . Show it to me before ciphering."

"Aye, aye, sir."

The cutter was already on its way back. Tom watched it through the glass, shaking his head in admiration of the crew's boat work. They were mostly Newfoundlanders, 'Newfies' as the matlos called them—men who had left their Grand Banks trawlers and bleak farms on the outbreak of war and rushed to the Mother Country. They were un-surpassed small boat men and handled the heavy cutter in this sea as though it were a skiff in a flat calm. *Penrith* had received a score of them when she'd passed from the South Atlantic to this northern patrol work, to replace regular seamen posted to newly built ships.

Half an hour later the cutter was back at the davit-heads, well se-cured against the cruiser's rolling. "Port five," Leach said. "Course north 45 west, revolutions for 13 knots . . . Secure from action stations. You have the ship, Johnson. I'm going to get something to eat."

Tom was checking men's records of service in his cabin, early the following morning, when he heard Leach call from the quarterdeck outside, "Ship's boat sighted, Tom."

Tom dropped his pen and ran forward after the captain, feeling the ship alter course as he went. The seas had not abated during the night, and here, at the eastern end of their patrol line, the Norwegian mountains could be clearly seen ahead, their snowy flanks catching the first stabbings of the sun. Ragged clouds raced fast and low overhead. The wind had backed a little, into the south-west.

The lifeboat was nearly a mile away, dead ahead now, rising and falling on the great waves. No oars were manned, but several huddled forms could be made out.

"Sea anchor's out," Leach said, binoculars to his eyes. "Keeping head to sea nicely . . . How many men can you make out, Yeoman?"

"Six, sir . . . One's standing up. He's waving."

"Stop both engines! Away seaboat's crew! . . . Number One . . . oh, he's on the Yank, isn't he?"

"I'll go, sir," Tom said.

"Good man. Looks as though you'd better transfer them into the whaler."

Tom hurried down from the bridge. The whaler was already lowered level with the deck, and ratings jumping into it. He followed, and sat in the stern sheets, staring at the approaching lifeboat. The name on the bow was *Chanteclere, Liverpool.* A British ship. Three of the men in it were on their feet now, their mouths wide, probably cheering, but the sounds were blown away on the wind. There was something strange about the head shape of one sitting in the stern sheets next to the man at the tiller, who must be the captain, or at least the senior officer in the lifeboat. Two more were propped up in the well, heads rolling—either unconscious or nearly so.

"The one next to the tiller's a woman, sir," Bennett cried excitedly.

On the bridge Leach manoeuvred the cruiser, now almost stopped, so that her bulk sheltered the lifeboat from the wind and the worst of the spray from the surface waves, though nothing could protect either of them from the heave and thrust of the underlying rollers. At a cable's distance, he ordered the whaler to be slipped. Tom barked his orders and the whaler pulled toward the lifeboat. When they were close he ordered, "Way 'nough!" while a seaman in the bow stood ready with a boathook.

Tom called across, "We'll take you all in here!"

The man at the tiller stood up, and said, "Captain Woodcock, Master of the *Chanteclere*."

"Glad to meet you, captain," Tom said. This was no time or place for formalities, he thought; but the old merchant skipper, a small man of sixty or more, was now introducing his wife. Tom said, "Glad to meet you, Mrs Woodcock . . . Here, give the lady a hand across, Bennett."

The woman got up, swaying easily to the motion, and barked in a strong Lancashire accent, "Me? Ah was dancing across the gunnels of whalers at sea afore you was born, yoong man." She stepped easily across, carrying a small bundle of belongings, and a tortoise-shell cat.

Then the crews got the sick men across into the whaler, followed by the rest. Finally the skipper shouted, "You'll be wanting the boat sunk?"

"Please," Tom said, for that was standard procedure; abandoned life-boats could not be allowed to drift about the seas, a menace in themselves and always liable to waste the time and attention of warship captains.

The skipper undid the bilge screw and, as the green Atlantic rushed in, stepped up onto a thwart and thence into the whaler. At once Tom called, "Ready? . . . Give way together!"

At *Penrith*'s side the falls hung close to the heaving sea and it was the work of a few seconds only to hook the whaler onto them. At once the watch on deck, manning the falls, hoisted the whaler with all its crew and passengers back on board. Many hands helped the merchant seamen down to the deck.

A surge of power shuddered through the cruiser and she resumed speed and course. Three minutes later Captain Leach appeared, his hand out, "Welcome aboard."

The Master shook the hand slowly. "Mr Woodcock, captain. You know the name of my ship. We were sunk by a Hun raider."

Leach said, "Were you, by God? Are you feeling strong enough to come to the charthouse with me for a few minutes?"

"I am that."

"Bo'sun, see that Mrs Woodcock is taken to my cabin and made comfortable. And the men to the messdeck . . . these two to the sick bay . . . Tom, you come with us."

In the charthouse behind the bridge Leach put one hand on the charts spread on the big table. Lieutenant de Saumarez was already there, standing to one side. Leach said, "Show us where we are now, Pilot."

De Saumarez made a small pencilled cross on the chart—"Here, sir."

"Where were you when you were set adrift, skipper?"

Mr Woodcock bent over the chart, his stubby forefinger moving—

" 'Twas the day before yesterday . . . eleven in the morning. We hadn't taken the noon sight . . . there, within twenty miles."

"The *Chanteclere* was sunk there?"

"Yes. They gave us time to launch our two boats . . . we lost touch with the other one during the first night. It was heavy weather."

"It was. We had a rough time even in this tub. Can you describe the raider?"

"Single funnel, about six thousand tons, general cargo derricks, wells fore and aft, midships bridge structure, black hull, white upperworks, rusty . . . some timber lashed on the foredeck, name *Oslofjord, Stavanger* . . . That was false, of course."

"Of course."

"The wells are hidden by dropsides. Behind them there's a 4.7, or about that, in each well . . . We were passing each other, close, and she just dropped her sides and opened fire at once, without warning, and put a shell in our engine room first shot."

"Did you have wireless?"

"The Gemmell and Hudson Line give their ships wireless? Too tightfisted for that by a long chalk, captain."

"So there's been no report about this . . . unless someone picked up your other boat?"

The master shook his head slowly, "I'm afraid that's not likely. The Good Lord may have saved them, but I doubt it. We were very lucky to get through that first night. God's hand was on us, captain."

"Yes. Which way did the raider go when she left you?"

"She boarded us after three shots, when we were stopped. They opened the sea cocks. Their skipper didn't want to waste any ammunition, the officer who boarded us told me . . . Then we were ordered to leave, with nothing but our clothes, and a chart. Each lifeboat already had a compass stowed on board . . . We watched my ship sink—she went down stern first . . . while the raider headed north-west. She was doing about twelve knots. But just before we lost sight of her, I think she changed course to south-west . . . the wind was blowing the smoke so hard, I couldn't tell for sure."

"Work that out, Pilot," Leach said.

De Saumarez, poring over the chart, began manipulating his slide rule and in a few minutes drew a circle on the chart, "He can't be far outside this, sir. It's a pretty big area, though."

"Nearly to the Shetlands. And he might have doubled back, and be quite close," Leach said thoughtfully. "Prepare a signal to the admiral with all the information we have. Tom, take the ship for a bit. We'll head west at twenty-three knots for three hours, or until we get instructions from Flag."

"Aye, aye, sir."

"I'm going to move into my sea cabin, so the skipper and his wife can have mine."

Orders from the Rear Admiral commanding the 10th Cruiser Squadron, which was the force carrying out the northern blockade, came two hours later, as *Penrith* plunged westward at near her full speed; and Warner reported that at this speed, she'd have to head for Scapa after another thirty-six hours. The orders instructed *Penrith*, the only real warship of the squadron, together with the next ship to the westward in the patrol line, which was the armed merchant cruiser *Almanzor*, once of the Royal Mail Steam Packet Company, to search southward from their present positions until dusk of the following day. Two destroyers from Scapa had been ordered to proceed to the north-westward with all despatch. If the raider was in the search area there was a good chance of one of the four ships intercepting her during the next thirty-six hours.

Tom and Leach shared control of the ship, with officers of the watch also on the bridge, in rotation. The crew were not kept at action stations, but Leach doubled the look-outs. Seas broke heavily over the cruiser without cease, bursting like bombs against a cliff in giant bursts of spray on the starboard bow, hurling tons of salt water at the forward turret, and soaking everyone on the bridge. She was taking a beating, shuddering under the ceaseless blows, shaking her screws in the air, vibrating wildly. They saw nothing all day. Or through the long night, when all guns were manned except those on the lower deck, which could not be, for they were often under water.

Coronel again, Tom thought . . . these bloody ships are badly designed . . . but there was no German fleet anywhere at sea.

As dawn broke over the same endless tossing, heaving sea, Leach said, "All right, Tom. Time you had a kip . . . we'll get plenty of warning now."

Tom saluted and went below to his cabin, flung himself on his bunk, without taking off even his sea boots, and instantly fell asleep.

He awoke two hours later, refreshed, feeling less tired than he had since the patrol began. The scuttle and its steel deadlight were screwed down, so he switched on the electric light. He ought to go up . . . but in daylight the Old Man could leave the bridge to the officer of the watch . . . he ought to get a bite of breakfast . . . but he wasn't hungry.

He kicked off his sea boots, opened his duffel coat, and lay back again on the bunk, his hands clasped behind his head. After a while he found himself thinking of Dick Yeoman. He could see his face now, and his sturdy boy's body, by the mantelpiece in the flat that evening . . . the same evening they'd seen Russell Wharton, and Guy had said that he was one of . . . them . . . us? Yeoman had changed now to Bennett, and Tom felt an erection growing inside his trousers. It was no use pretending otherwise—it was caused by thinking of Bennett, a sailor in his own ship, his messenger, the man who'd dogged his feet on duty for thirteen or fourteen months now and, gradually, slowly, taken possession of his mind. He clenched his teeth and pressed his finger-nails fiercely into the palms. A low groan escaped him.

Ordinary Seaman Bennett came in, a message in one hand, and said, "Commander, sir . . ." He stopped, looking into Tom's eyes, the eyes meeting. His lips parted. He had a new black eye, the colour just coming. His hand went out slowly, with the message. The back of his hand just brushed the outside of Tom's trousers. Tom whispered, "Where did you get the black eye?" his voice shaking, his heart pounding.

Bennett said, "The fellows rag me because of my eyelashes. Dusty Miller called me a nance. I punched his nose, he gave me one in the eye . . . Sometimes I don't think life's worth living." His voice was as low as Tom's, and throbbing, his eyes damp. His hand rested on Tom's trousers.

Tom whispered, "Go away, Charlie . . . for God's sake."

At twelve noon, Tom and the captain both being on the bridge, *Penrith* steaming south at eighteen knots, the sea much abated, visibility less than three miles on account of driving rain and low cloud, the navy-phone in front of the captain boomed. "Signal from *Almanzor*, sir—suspicious vessel in sight, investigating."

Almost immediately the yeoman of signals said suddenly, "Gunfire, sir!"

"Where?" Leach said. "I don't hear anything."

"Listen, sir!" The yeoman swung his head this way and that. The wind whistled through the signal halyards, seas rolled noisily down the steel length of the ship, metal clanged against metal.

"I hear it, sir," the officer of the watch said. "Several guns firing—from green four five, I think."

Leach said, "I've got it now . . . more a thudding than a real sound. It's coming down wind so we might hear it from thirty miles or more . . . Course north 130 west, Skyring . . . Chief, give her all you can. We hear firing."

From the engine room Tom heard Warner's tinny voice, "You'll get it, sir."

The yeoman said, "Signal from *Almanzor*, sir . . . Am engaging enemy raider, course north . . . and his position."

"Give it to the Navigating Officer, and tell him to plot it."

Tom stood back in the leeward corner of the bridge. He did not want to see anyone, or be seen. He had buried his head as far back into the hood of the duffel coat as it would go. The events of the morning kept running through his head like a film in one of those moving picture houses, but the projecting machine was running the same pictures backwards and forwards, forwards and backwards . . . He had crossed a boundary—the frontier he had come so close to with Dick Yeoman, when Charlie Arbuthnot had called from the admiralty. He and Bennett were caught in the same web. They were both miserable—the one mocked by the lower deck, the other sneered at by such as Warner and Brandt. They had no one to turn to for understanding and affection, except each other. But Bennett was an O.D. and he himself a commander. They were jammed into a warship with hundreds of others— no privacy, no place . . . and no sympathy.

He could meet Bennett ashore . . . work it so that they both got leave at the same time. He groaned aloud. It was madness, vile madness. But it was there. What would Leach think, if he learned—one of the nicest men in the navy, besides being a first-rate captain? To gratify this . . . disease, Tom would betray his friends, shame his family, disgrace his parents. His knuckles ached inside his pockets. He knew he looked pale and ill, but no one was looking at him, and everyone was pale from the long patrol, the endless seas, the endless staring into the dull northern light.

"Bridge," the voicepipe from the foretop called, "Lifeboat adrift bearing green three-oh. There are people in it."

"Thank you," Leach said. "Maintain course and speed, sub. Pilot, plot its exact position, speed, drift, and wind."

"Aye, aye, sir."

No one said anything more. They knew why the skipper was not changing course. There was a fight going on over the horizon and this was a warship of the Royal Navy. No excuse would be accepted, and no mercy shown to a captain who did not head for the sound of the guns at full speed. Tom saw the lifeboat a few minutes later, a small helpless thing, tossing on the waves. They had rigged a small jury mast and sail in it, and were scudding down wind. The man at the tiller waved as *Penrith* approached.

"Signal 'Will return,' in the international code," Leach snapped. "They can hear the guns. They'll understand."

"Aye, aye, sir," the yeoman shouted across the bridge. The flags whipped up to the peak. The cruiser plunged on, dead into the seas now. The lifeboat became smaller astern.

The captain walked back and forth across the bridge, head down. After a few turns he stopped by Tom, and without looking at him, said, "What a bloody business."

"It can't be helped, sir," Tom said.

"I know. But that doesn't make it any less bloody."

"They looked in good shape."

Leach nodded and returned to his pacing.

Ten minutes later the yeoman said with a broad grin, "Signal from *Almanzor*, sir . . . Raider on fire and sinking. Am rescuing survivors."

"Great!" Leach cried. "Port twenty, course reciprocal! Foretop, keep a sharp lookout for that lifeboat."

Penrith heeled far over into the turn and everyone on the bridge held onto the forward rail for support.

Leach shouted cheerfully at Tom, "Ready to do your rescue act again, Tom?"

"Yes, sir," Tom said. He tried to answer the captain's grin, but the smile was frozen in him. He was making a decision even as Leach spoke: and by the time he had answered, it was made.

He had on his heavy sea boots. The duffel coat would keep him afloat for only a few seconds before it got waterlogged—but those few would matter. He ought to have something heavy.

The lifeboat became visible, and *Penrith* slowed. Tom left the bridge and hurried aft to his cabin. He took off the duffel coat, stuffed his service revolver into one pocket of his reefer jacket and the nose cone paperweight into the other. It wasn't much but it would have to do . . . that and his determination to go down.

The cruiser's frame shuddered as the engines went into reverse. He hurried up the ladders and onto the deck. The same men were there, including Bennett, but Tom did not dare meet his eyes.

A bridge messenger ran up and said, "Captain says not to launch a seaboat, sir. He's seen they're all fit in the boat. He's putting a scrambling net over."

Tom nodded and a leading seaman beside him said cheerfully, "Reckon we'll have enough ladies on board for a concert soon, sir. There's one in this 'un, too. Skipper's wife, I suppose."

"Belay that chatter," Tom snapped.

The killick assumed a serious face, obviously thinking that the Bloke must have had a blast from the Old Man, otherwise why would he be in a bad temper at a moment like this—a Jerry raider sunk and another merchant crew to be rescued?

The cruiser was very close to the lifeboat now. The scrambling net was in place. There were sixteen people in the lifeboat—the whole crew, probably. They were cheering and shouting. British. The woman was young and tall, her husband much older and wearing a pointed grey beard. Tom went over the side and half way down the scrambling net. A sailor in the lifeboat was reaching out for the net with a boathook. Judging the distance carefully, Tom expelled the air from his lungs, let go, and stepped off into a thousand fathoms of water a foot short of the lifeboat's side, between it and *Penrith*'s flank.

He gulped water, sinking fast, stiff and unmoving. It must be over soon. His head was thick, dark, everything cold as though his blood had been frozen in a single instant of time. His lungs were cracking, his thoughts going, going . . .

Hands grasped his hair, tugging, slowing the speed of his descent. He struggled, striking out at the person, dimly seen through the water, now facing him . . . There were two, one at each side. Oh God, they'd got him and he was too weak, almost unconscious, to fight . . . He was staring at Charlie Bennett at a few inches range. The other man had him by the neck, both dragging him upwards. All light went, and with it all strength.

He lay in his bunk, the captain sitting in a chair beside him. Leach was talking—"We've pumped a few gallons of water out of you, but Sawbones says you don't appear to have any other damage. I was afraid you'd be crushed between us and the boat. Those lifeboats are damnably heavy."

"I'm all right, sir. I apologise for all the trouble I caused, through my own stupidity."

"It could happen to anyone, in a swell like that," Leach said. "The two ships must each have lurched the wrong way just as you dropped. Bennett went right in after you and Bailward a moment later. The skipper held off the lifeboat till they'd got you up. They were lucky to get you, though. What on earth were you carrying your revolver for? And this thing?" He tapped the nose cone, now set back on the table with Tom's revolver.

Tom said, "I often carry the revolver, on boarding, sir. You never know . . . That—I don't know. I must have picked it up for some reason, put it in my pocket, and . . . I can't remember."

Leach nodded, though there was still a hint of a question in his eyes. He stood up. "You get back to sleep. And stay off duty till we're back in Scapa . . . You remember that convoy idea we were talking about a couple of days ago?"

"Yes, sir."

"Well, think about it in more detail. Work out some simple mean-course zigzagging formulas that merchant skippers could understand and adhere to, and I'll present them to the admiral. Convoys are going to have to come, sooner or later. It's damned nonsense that raiders—surface or submarine—should be able to approach any merchant ship— even the *Mauretania*—without risk, unless they're unlucky enough to pick on a Q ship. We'll talk about it when you're feeling better."

The door closed behind him and Tom closed his eyes. He felt immensely weary and immensely sad. All his adult life he had tried not to recognise himself for what he was. Gradually the tensions created had surfaced, as the truth thrust itself deeper into every part of his life. Today, unable to face the future's prospect, he had tried to end a life which could only lead to shame and degradation for his Service and everyone he loved. He had failed. The failure was a verdict: there is no escape. You must live with what you are.

So be it.

Seaman Bennett's face appeared round the edge of the door with a little knock. "The doctor said I could see you, sir," he said in a soft voice.

Tom slowly reached out his hand. A part of him was saying, 'Don't, it's disgusting,'—another part, 'Go on, touch, feel.' Charlie took the hand. Tom found that he was squeezing. The other squeezed back. "Thank you," Tom said.

"I love you, sir."

Tom looked into the young man's soft eyes, now brimming with tears, one rimmed by the purpling bruise. He thought, oh God, I wish I could say it out loud, but I can't. Not yet.

The seaman slipped his hand free and went out of the cabin. Tom closed his eyes, thinking that he would never sleep again, but in a few minutes sleep came.

Daily Telegraph, Friday, December 3, 1915

2ND YEAR OF THE WAR—18TH WEEK, 3RD DAY

The Germans are surrounding their movements in the Western zone with the utmost secrecy and, according to our Rotterdam correspondent, there is much speculation as to the cause. A French military critic hazards the conjecture that the enemy is preparing another violent offensive, but there is no present sign of this developing.

Another spy has been executed as the sequel to the verdict of a court-martial in London.

Down to a late hour of Wednesday the heroic little Serbian force was still holding out at Monastir, and Colonel Vassitch is stated to be receiving reinforcements.

From the rest of the Serbian and Macedonian front there is no definite news. The Germans claim to have captured some small towns in the northern corner of Montenegro.

In the Italian Chamber on Wednesday Baron Sonnino, the Italian Foreign Minister, announced that Italy has signed the compact of September 5th, 1914—to which Japan later also became a party—by which Great Britain, France, and Russia pledged themselves not to make peace except in agreement with one another.

He also declared that there was every hope of a satisfactory settlement of the questions at issue between Greece and the Allies.

That the Italians expect the fall of Gorizia shortly is indicated by a report that civil officials have been sent to the front to organise the administration as soon as the town capitulates. Meanwhile the general position on the Italian front shows no particular change.

Cate looked at the opposite page—in the West, mining, counter-mining, and artillery, otherwise, "There is nothing to report from the rest of this front."

Rain drove against the windows, shaking them in their ancient sashes. The fields were waterlogged, but it would do no harm to the crop at this season. The dead leaves lay dark in the spinneys, the wind unable to stir their sodden drifts.

The year was drawing to a close . . . the year 1915, not the second year of the war: as the *Telegraph* pointed out, that was only in its 18th

week, 3rd day . . . Africa was cleared of the enemy, all but the indomi-
table von Lettow Forbeck and his will o' the wisp native forces. Palestine . . . quiet, the Canal safe; Italy . . . no change, but no triumph;
Salonika, the same: Rumania, Russia, Serbia, Montenegro—all in trouble . . . At sea, quiet, the Grand Fleet waiting patiently at Scapa for
the German High Seas Fleet to come out . . . but it was wrong to call
it 'quiet,' for the Germans were waging a new and very effective war
under the sea, instead of on it, trying to starve Britain . . . Taxes,
prices, interest rates, all going up, but England not bankrupt yet, by a
long chalk.

And now, another great offensive brewing on the Western Front, according to some of the experts . . . he couldn't help putting that last
word in mental inverted commas now, whenever it referred to the war.

Would the blow fall on the British? More probably on the French.
They had been at war longer, and they were losing their first fire, he
heard . . . not surprising, considering the tremendous casualties they
had had, especially among officers. He thought of the map in his study,
which he had studied so often, and of Quentin standing in front of it,
his arm still in a sling, saying heavily, "When we attack, there's little
that the Germans *must* defend . . . They are so far forward of their
frontiers—industrial areas, coal mines, rail centres—that they can fall
back anywhere, move reserves not to shore up a break-through, but to
counter-attack . . . somewhere far away even, perhaps. But on our side,
there are areas which we *have* to defend. A break-through in them
would be disastrous . . . in the far north, for example, to cut us off
from the Channel. We'd have to throw in everything we have to prevent it . . . fighting on German terms."

Cate remembered asking, "What about the French? Is there any sector that's vital to them in the same way?"

"I don't know, really," Quentin had answered after a while, scratch-
ing his ear thoughtfully with his free hand, "but Verdun, probably
would be. Yes, Verdun."

Stella said, "Daddy, how many sets of cutlery would we want?"

Cate said, "Eh?" then recalled where he was: in rain-swept Kent,
with a daughter about to be married. He said, "I'd better send you up
to your Aunt Fiona's for the weekend, and she can help you work it all
out. And you'll be in Hedlington, close to Johnny, won't you?"

Walstone: Friday, December 17, 1915

33 Probyn Gorse stood in the doorway of his cottage in the early twilight, about four o'clock in the afternoon. Smoke curled away from the chimney toward the north-east, a fact which he was aware of without specifically noticing it: Probyn always knew where the wind was coming from, and where it was going to. His Woman was inside, washing the dish from his supper. He would have liked at this hour to go to the Beaulieu Arms and have a pint or two. And when he came out the moon would be up, four days from full, casting its golden gleam over bare trees and moving clouds and the rippling Scarrow. But since that dratted D.O.R.A., the pubs couldn't open when they wanted to, only for so many hours a day: the Arms wouldn't be open till six o'clock, and he had to be on his way by then.

He stood a full fifteen minutes, barely moving a muscle. What he had to do, and what others had to do, ran slowly through his mind, was severely examined, checked, and put back in its place. The night would be partly overcast, with this slight breeze, warmish for the time of the year, a moonglow even when clouds obscured the moon's face.

All was as well as could be expected. The planning had been thorough, and there Guy Rowland had helped a lot. Now came the doing, and he knew that he, at least, would not fail. Nor would young Rowland—he would have made a good poacher himself, if he'd chosen that line of life . . . Florinda and Fletcher and Bert—they'd do their parts, even though they were not really important.

Without a word, when clouds covered the moon, he started off.

There'd be light enough for the peeping eyes behind the curtain of the second cottage along the lane. The man was an idle labourer, and Probyn was certain that Skagg was paying him a few pence to report at once if he, Probyn, headed toward the Park after he had left his cottage: then the man would slip out of his back door and hurry to Skagg's cottage close by the main gate, and pass the word—Probyn's out.

Probyn did not look toward the curtain, but passed by at his rapid bent-knee gait, and into the village. The street was empty, except for a few women back from late shopping in Hedlington, walking up from the station. Probyn walked on through and into the country along the Taversham road, heading east, away from Walstone Park. A mile beyond Taversham, round a sharp corner in the road, he dived suddenly into the hedge, eased back, and waited.

No one came, except a motor car, its acetylene headlights hissing as it passed, the rubber tyres crunching the gravelled road, the engine very quiet seeming.

After fifteen minutes, Probyn slid on through the hedge into the field behind and in the moonglow headed south, crossing the railway, then the Scarrow once more—he had crossed it on the road bridge just short of Taversham—and walked west. The slope of Bohun Hill lay across the sky ahead of him as he skirted the buildings of Lower Bohun Farm, a dog barking once, then along the edges of wheat stubble on the south slope of the shallow hill, round Abbas, keeping well away from the lighted farmhouse, flitting silently along blackthorn hedges, through elm copses, so to the southern limit of Walstone Park. There, outside the four-foot wall which marked the Park boundary, he sat down and looked at the moon. About quarter to seven. He could afford to have a few minutes' rest.

He leaned back, his eyes closed, his ears attuned to pick up any untoward sound . . . The old earl, not this one nor his father, nor grandfather, but his great-grandfather, had had the wall built all round the estate except on the Scarrow side, not to keep people out but to mark the exact line inside which his keepers could handle trespassers as roughly as they wished. It was also to keep in the fallow deer, and to force fox hunters to tackle a stiffish jump, rather than burst through a hedge. There was only one gate on this side of the Park. There used to be a gatekeeper on that, too, but since the old Queen died, the gate had been kept locked, and Dan, the youngest keeper, lived in the lodge, with his wife and baby.

Seven o'clock. He rose to his feet, took an electric torch from his pocket and switched it on, keeping the light down. After shining the light along the bottom of the wall for a few moments he found what he was looking for—a spade, thinly covered with earth and grass. He took it up, measured off four paces away from the wall, and began to dig, fast. In a few minutes he had uncovered a package wrapped in oiled silk. He unfastened the silk and put it in his pocket, leaned the folding .410 shotgun against the wall, put some cartridges in his pockets, filled in the hole, and rehid the spade.

He was ready: and at that instant, he heard the sound he was expecting to hear, faintly at first, then clearly, coming and going in the clouds.

Guy Rowland sat in the rear cockpit of the Caudron, the joystick in his right hand, watching the wanderings of the compass needle with half an eye, but keeping his course by following the windings of the Scarrow as it meandered up from the south. The moon, piercing through holes in the clouds, shone here and there on the water, painting it a reflective silver: there was Hedlington, unmistakable, the rectangular bulk of the gaol under Beighton Down and the barracks under Busby Down clear in the moonlight. There was the county cricket ground where he had battled with Rhodes and Hirst and the rest of the doughty Yorkshiremen seventeen months ago—no more county cricket for the duration, though . . . The engine purred, the wind whistled past his flying helmet and goggles, and he felt as he had every time he'd mounted in the air, since he had first flown solo, this past summer —as though he were not a human being but some new creation, filled with higher powers, higher hopes and dreams, and subject to new dangers, unheard of down there. Though he knew that people were stirring below, the moonlight and darkness made it seem as though the whole earth slept, while he himself felt never more awake, never more alert and tuned for action. I am brooding, he thought, over a sleeping earth, and a sleeping people: I am no longer quite human: if I ever become afraid in the air, it will be different from a groundling's fear, just as his exhilaration now was an exhilaration none could know who had not flown a bird as light and docile, yet as powerful as this.

There was the bend of the Scarrow by Cantley . . . about ten miles now to the Park. He passed over Felstead & Whitmore station at a thousand feet, and began to descend, throttling back the engine slightly. The stick was firm but sensitive in his hand . . . You had to pretend there was an egg between your hand and the control column, the joystick . . . gently firmly forward . . . gently firmly back . . . Yet in battle you obviously couldn't afford to treat it like that; then you'd have to throw the machine about in the air, as the enemy dodged, and victory or death would depend as much on the machine's strength of construction as on your skill . . . and your desire to kill, to *matar* . . . Was he a *matador*, or just a maker of patterns in the sky?

There was the Big House . . . car lights moving up the drive—perfect timing. He was below all clouds, down to two hundred feet above the ground. In this light, it was not safe to go any lower, and he levelled off. The sweeping lights on the long drive had stopped in front of the main entrance to the house.

He banked carefully on to a west heading, edging the Caudron round and watching the primitive prototype gyro direction indicator that he was testing—the *raison d'être* for this night flight. It was ill-lit by a single instrument light and he had to strain his eyes to read it, so . . . carefully . . . delicately he banked, keeping the altitude constant, turning by the new instrument. On course, he flew west for two minutes, banked, flew north for two minutes, east for two minutes . . . south . . . west . . . jerky at first, gradually steadying and stabilizing the aircraft as he learned the responses. Thank heaven it was a calm night.

Gradually his grip on the controls relaxed, became gentle and confident. He had time to look at the Big House below.

People had got out of the car, a charabanc in fact, and were standing in a half-circle, lit by headlights. Guy repeated his pattern, flying never more than two miles from the Big House. The charabanc and the people went away. After an hour he changed to figures of eight, sweeping in lazy curves all over the Park. His hands and feet were cold and his face frozen to an icy mask, but inside he was warmed by the glow of a fierce content: he was flying—in battle, his first. Perhaps he'd do a victory roll, to celebrate . . . He put the thought firmly from him: he'd never kill any Germans if he killed himself first by doing stunts, at night, in a Caudron.

At nine o'clock precisely, the moon bursting out from the clouds, he headed back for the airfield on the downs east of Hedlington, where he had learned to fly, and where, after much soft soap, he had persuaded the chief instructor to let him try a night flight to test the new instrument. Guy was doing it for Probyn, but to him the tests were also real, for he was sure that the Royal Flying Corps would soon be flying by night as a matter of course, and that would include night raids and air fights.

A few paraffin flares had been put out in a line along the airfield and at 9.23 p.m. Guy lined up with them, a mile downwind at 500 feet. He throttled back the engine, swallowed once, and forced himself into a relaxed calm. Slowly the line of lights swam toward him . . . seemed too foreshortened so that hastily—too hastily—he opened the throttle again . . . readjusted it . . . lazily the lights came nearer . . . suddenly the first of them was under his wing. He checked the glide, held the nose in the landing attitude . . . the aircraft hung in the darkness for a second or two that seemed like minutes . . . a jerk and a rumble, the bite of the tailskid. He had a perfect three-point landing.

The chief instructor was waiting for him when he taxied up to the hangars. "Looked good, Guy."

"I was a bit rough with the throttle when I lined up."

"Anything to report?"

"The gyro's fine, as far as it goes. Needs a stronger light . . . And we're going to need some way of knowing where the horizon is, if we can't see it, or the ground. I was in clouds for a bit, now and then, and I really didn't know whether the nose was up, level, down, or tilted."

"We've talked about that before. Where did you go?"

"Oh, round and about. I'll be back Tuesday, same time. Good night."

Chapman came to the door of the drawing-room and said, "There's a party of waits outside, m'lord. Furr let them in, in accordance with your standing instructions for the Christmas season. They came in a charabanc, m'lord."

"A charabanc?" Lord Swanwick growled. "Where the hell from?"

A droning sound filled the room and the earl said, "What's that?"

"I have no idea, my lord."

"It sounds like an aeroplane," Lady Swanwick said. Lady Barbara, reading *Jorrocks' Jaunts and Jollities* the other side of the fireplace, said, "It *is* an aeroplane."

"Impossible!" Lord Swanwick said. "It's dark."

He got up, left the room and strode along the passage to the front door. The lights over the door were on and below he could see a charabanc, its headlights shining on a dozen men grouped in a semicircle, their hands behind their backs. As soon as he appeared, they began to sing *The First Nowell*. He could barely hear them above the racket of the aeroplane, except when it flew farther away. He shouted at the butler, "Who are they?"

"A group collecting for the fund for Disabled Soldiers and Sailors, m'lord."

"They're awful!" Swanwick shouted.

The name of a livery firm in Brighton was painted in an ornate scroll on the side of the charabanc. Brighton? These men had come nearly fifty miles! Impossible! He held up his hand and bellowed, "Stop!"

Raggedly the singing ceased. "You've come here from Brighton?" he asked suspiciously.

"Yes, sir . . . my lord," the leader said. He was a big man with a red nose and a woollen scarf wrapped round his neck.

"Just to sing carols here?"

"Oh no, my lord, we've sung in three places already."

"Where?"

"I don't remember the names, my lord. Big houses, they was . . . and when we're done here we're going on to Hedlington . . . been asked to sing in High Street, outside the pubs . . . till midnight."

"Here," Swanwick said, finding a Treasury pound note in his pocket. "Take this, but don't sing any more. Confound that aeroplane!"

The aeroplane passed directly overhead, its sound very loud. The waits were saying thankee my lord, thankee, and climbing back into the charabanc. Skagg was there, coming up, a shotgun under his arm. Reaching Lord Swanwick's side he muttered, "Don't like the looks of these, m'lord. They're just the sort to slip out of the charry and into the woods after a bird or even a deer. I'll follow them till they're out of the gate."

"All right. Put a blast over their heads if they try anything."

Skagg went off. The charabanc moved away. Watching from the steps, Swanwick thought that the moving lights slowed half way to the gatehouse. Skagg had been right . . . but he could deal with the blighters. As he was turning into the house he thought he heard a gunshot . . . but the infernal aeroplane was still there, circling, roaring, the blue flame from its exhausts clearly visible and, against the moon, the silhouetted head of the pilot.

Lady Barbara came out to stand beside him, "Do you think he's in trouble, Father? Lost?"

"I don't know, and I don't care. Blasted row . . . He can't go on for ever."

"I wonder why he keeps circling," his daughter said. "You'd think he'd either try to land, or go somewhere else. There's a new airfield on the Canterbury road, which he could almost see from up there."

"I'd ring up the R.F.C., but they'd only tell me there's a war on."

He led back indoors and Chapman closed the door behind him. The inside of the big house reverberated to the aircraft's engines, and Swanwick swore under his breath. Bloody stinking machines, turning gentlemen into mechanics . . .

Dan hurried from Midland Road station through the darkened streets of Bedford toward his parents' house. They lived about a mile from the station and he was perspiring even in the winter cool by the time he reached it. He ran up the steps and raised his hand to bang the knocker energetically, but paused. She might be sleeping. He tried the door and it opened—they never did lock the door; no need to, except perhaps now with so many soldiers about . . . Some girl had given him a white feather in London, right outside St Pancras station. A bloody nerve, she had. How did she know he wasn't in a vital industry? He'd thrown it in the gutter and run for his train. All the same, it made you think. Keeping Probyn Gorse away from His Lordship's pheasants wasn't exactly important to beating the Germans . . . but how could he think of leaving Ivy and baby George?

He went into the house. In the passage he heard no sound, and there was no light. God, had they taken her to hospital? Or was she already . . . ? It was near ten, and they usually went to bed at half past nine. He crept up the stairs and to their bedroom door. Stooping down he put his ear to the keyhole and listened. He heard breathing . . . snoring. That was Dad. He couldn't hear Mother. Ah, there, that was her, saying, "You're snoring, Dad."

She sounded sleepy like, but otherwise the same as usual. He straightened and knocked gently on the door. "Mum, Dad. It's me, Dan."

It took a moment or two to sink in, then his father called, "Dan? Is that you?"

"Yes, Dad. How's Mum?"

"How's Mum? How are you, Mum?"

"I'm fine . . . Come in, Dan. Dad, light the light."

Dan went in, and waited, holding his cap in his hands, while his father found the matches and lit the gas mantle. Brilliant white light shone out, blinding him, and he put his cap over his eyes. When he lowered it, his mother was sitting up in bed, a shawl thrown round her ample shoulders.

He stared at her, "You really all right, Mum?"

"Of course I am. Why shouldn't I be?"

"You're not serious ill?"

"Do I look like it?" she said.

"Are you all right, Dan?" his father said, getting out of bed, and taking Dan's shoulder paternally. "You look funny."

"I feel funny."

"Sit down, there's a good lad. Your Mum'll make you a nice cup of tea. "

"I don't want no tea."

"Have you been given the sack, Dan? Is that it? That Skagg never did like you, you said."

Dan sat down on the bed. "This afternoon . . . evening, about six . . . I got a telegram saying Mum was serious, come at once. Here . . ." He pulled the crumpled slip from his pocket and handed it over. His father found his gold-rimmed spectacles on the chest of drawers, put them on, and read aloud: "'MUM SERIOUS ILL COME AT ONCE DAD.' I never sent that, Dan. But it's from Bedford. See?"

Dan said, "I haven't been sacked. This is a practical joke, like. I bet it's one of those men I caught with His Lordship's rabbits the other day. Making me spend a lot of money for nothing."

"Lucky it wasn't a bang on the head some dark night, Dan," his father said. "Gamekeepers don't get many love letters, you know. Come down, and we'll all have a nice cup of tea."

They went down the stairs one after the other, Dan saying, "Might as well . . . and sleep in my old room. Can't get back to Walstone tonight."

His mother said, "I'll make up the bed, and you'll have a good breakfast in the morning, just as good as Ivy can make for you in that nasty little lodge house you showed us. Surprised you don't catch your death in that. His Lordship ought to be ashamed of himself, making an Englishman live in that place."

"The Big House isn't in much better shape, I can tell you," Dan said, laughing at last. He felt better, and dismissed the hoax from his mind. It would be nice to chat with Mum and Dad and hear the latest news about Dick and Mary and Peter, who'd gone for a soldier, and Janice who'd got into trouble from a Canadian, and . . .

Probyn Gorse reached the railway line at nine-thirty. The aeroplane had gone and the sky was quiet once more. He was nearly two miles from the Big House, and the .410 had been reburied in its oiled silk wrapping in the hole he'd dug outside the Park wall three months ago. The two sacks, each containing six dead pheasants—four cocks and eight hens in all—were heavy on his back as he walked carefully by vagrant moonlight toward the railway embankment. He had met Fletcher at the corner of Ten Acre copse at the agreed time and they'd entered the wood immediately. Fletcher held the electric torch for him and found the roosting birds, and he had shot them down, killing each with a single No. 5 cartridge. As soon as the work was done, Fletcher had gone to join the men from the charabanc, who were roaming the Park the far side of the Big House, two miles from where he had been firing. Some of them might get caught, but they had no weapons on them, and would have no birds, and it was unlikely that Skagg would be able to hold more than one, with Dan away, and the extra keepers, to be brought in against Probyn's promised raid, not to be hired until tomorrow. Meanwhile, here were the birds, and young Rowland had done his work so well that Probyn doubted whether anyone had heard the shots—certainly not Skagg, chasing the waits. But . . . safety first. He covered the two sacks with dead leaves, moved a hundred yards off, curled up against the foot of the embankment and went to sleep.

He awoke at four and lay quiet, his hands behind his head. It had been a good night for weather . . . for everything else, too, as far as he knew. He'd spent many, many hours in much worse straits in His Lordship's park, nights of sleet and howling wind, soaked through, Skagg on watch somewhere close: nights of black frost, cold gnawing at his marrow; nights of snow, or fog, when he could not see a yard in front of his face: nights of summer, when every mosquito in Kent seemed to have decided to settle on him, and suck his blood . . . This had been easy, and good. He closed his eyes and waited till the moon sank.

In the short dark between then and dawn, he got up, walked back along the fence and into the wood, and picked up the heavy sacks. The land rose gradually, climbing to the level of the rails, the line here being neither banked nor cut. In a few minutes he made out the white shape in the darkness ahead, and moved silently toward it.

"All right, Granddad?" Florinda asked.

"All right," he answered. "Twelve. Good big birds, too."

The faint starlight showed that she was wearing a red blouse over a white skirt. "Don't wait too long to get out of the way," he said. "Those little lamps don't throw much light, and they won't see you till they're on top of you."

She said, "I have an electric torch." She clicked it on, and a circle of light illuminated Probyn's feet.

"All right, turn it off, girl," he said. Then they parted, for both knew what to do.

Probyn waited, lying down in the grass along the fence, twenty feet from the rails, and a little below the level of the ballast. Florinda had disappeared into the darkness, walking along the railway toward Walstone station. The early morning milk train from Hedlington to Ashford was due at Felstead & Whitmore station at 5.32 a.m.; Walstone at 5.43, Taversham at 5.49.

The down distant signal for Walstone was almost over Probyn's head and he started involuntarily as it suddenly clanged down, the light changing from yellow to green. Almost at once he heard the distant muffled long continued clangour of the engine and train passing over the Scarrow bridge. Then he saw the little white light in front of the chimney. The rails sang, and he waited. The engine passed, though he did not see it for he kept his head down, pressed into the earth and damp grass. As soon as it had gone by he jumped up and ran to the side of the passing wagons. Looking ahead he saw Florinda's dim white and red shape by the rails, the waving beam of the torch. At once the brakes went on on the engine, so hard that he could hear the squeal from fifty yards back. The buffers of the wagons banged into each other all down the short train, *bang bang bang bang bang*. In half a minute the train had stopped. He stepped quickly between two wagons and, climbing up on the buffer beam, swung the sacks with a grunt, one after the other, into the shallow open wagon and, more carefully, followed them.

He heard the guard pass, his boots crunching on the cinders, walking toward the engine to find out the cause of the stop. Five minutes later he walked back again. The train started.

It stopped at Walstone ten minutes late, and at Taversham the same. A mile past Taversham, it being still dark, by a group of dense willows where the Scarrow curved away from the line for the last time, Probyn threw the two sacks off the train on the left side. Near six-twenty, still dark, as the train crawled through Ashford yards, he climbed down the outside steps, dropped to the cinders, and started a walk of twenty-one miles to Walstone, arriving in time for a late dinner to be shared with Florinda and Fletcher.

"They're hung safe," Fletcher said. "The Duke's there, with plenty of food, to guard 'em. And Skagg never caught any of those Brighton men. He was near one when I come . . . but then I got him to chase me, not knowing who I was, of course. When I thought the others had got free, I dodged off."

Florinda said, "The engine driver didn't believe me when I told him about the big rock I'd seen on the line, but the train was stopped by then, so I ran away. They didn't chase me."

"You did well."

"Thanks, Grandpa . . . I feel sorry for Dan, though."

"Dan's a gamekeeper."

"Guy Rowland was marvellous, wasn't he? Just tophole."

"Don't speak la-di-da, or I'll give you a bash on the kisser . . . And we're not done yet, are we?"

By Givenchy, it was raining, a bitter slanting rain. The trench was crowded, most of the men now wearing the inverted steel bowl helmets, glistening in the rain. Fred Stratton leaned against the front wall, soaked through, as was everyone else, shivering in the cold, waiting. The stars were hidden behind the clouds, and the soldiers pressed together were a presence of breathing men, smells of damp wool, sweat, urine, fear. Colonel Rowland muttered, "Stratton?"

"Yes, sir?"

"Ready now? Three minutes to go."

"We're ready, sir."

He counted . . . a hundred seconds . . . a hundred and fifty . . . seventy . . . seventy-five, seventy-six, seventy-seven. He heaved himself up on the firestep, feeling the presence of his platoon following hard on his heels, others to right and left. Count of twenty . . . three star shells fired by the British artillery burst overhead in blinding light. A hoarse cry rose from all round him and he began to run, his revolver outthrust. Almost at once he was on the new German wire, cutting frantically, but A Company's patrol had done their work well, and there were only a few thin strands left. He burst through and fell into the trench, his sergeant at his heels. Grenades whistled past, and burst over the first traverse.

He knew the trench well, every angle and hole and crumbling dugout; for it had been the British front line until the day before yesterday, and had twice been his platoon's sector until the Germans had attacked unexpectedly on a narrow front, and taken it. The acting C.O. had done nothing, but when Colonel Rowland came back from England this morning he'd been very angry—'proper put out,' Fred's sergeant had said—and had ordered an immediate night attack to get the hundred and fifty yards back; and Fred found himself selected for the honour of leading the attack because of his local knowledge.

The Germans seemed to be lying very low . . . not much fire coming his way, no grenades . . . Ah, the German artillery was firing now, heavy shrapnel on the trench line. They would be hitting their own men . . . if there were any. He gasped to his sergeant, "Seen any Huns?"

"No, sir," the sergeant shouted back. "Ah, there's some!" In the new light of more star shells two German soldiers slid down from the newcut firestep, which had been the British parados, their hands up. Fred saw the gleam of telephone cable leading back across No Man's Land.

"No one here, except a few sentries, with telephones and Very pistols," he shouted under the din of the shrapnel. "Send a runner back to the C.O.—we have the objective."

"Very good, sir."

Cunning bastards, he thought. Now the troops who are going to man the trench will have to come in under this shrapnel . . . and H.E., he noted, hearing the heavy bursts of German 5.9s and feeling wet earth fountain over him.

He stumbled along the trench, disposing of his men, facing them toward the Germans across No Man's Land, setting some to recut the old firestep and berm that had been altered during the Germans' short occupation, and others to clear the mouth of what had been, and now was again, the communication trench from the rear, which the Germans had blocked with earth and barbed wire.

The shelling increased. His sergeant came up. "Nasty stuff this, sir . . . Can the men take cover until it slacks off, like?"

Fred hesitated. The Germans would not attack while they were shelling the trench so heavily . . . but his orders were definite. He said curtly, "No, hold the parapet."

He stood, leaning on the muddy slope, peering into the dark. No Very lights . . . now, yes, three, four star shells from the German side . . . by their light he saw the platoon that was to relieve him struggling forward from the old second line trench, laden with wooden posts, wire, angle irons. Frank would be with that lot, with his Pioneers, to get some of this trench properly revetted and reinforced.

German machine guns swept No Man's Land and the rear area where the British relief was advancing. Men fell, others stumbled on. A man of Fred's platoon jerked forward, torn into three pieces by splinters and blasted into the mud.

"Hang on," Fred cried. "It won't be long now."

The relieving force slid and jumped down. Others trickled in up the communication trench, over the piled earth, through the barbed wire.

Lieutenant Beldring fell in almost on top of Fred, followed by a dozen men, then Colonel Quentin Rowland and the Adjutant, Boy Rowland. "Well done," the colonel said to Fred. "You've become a very useful officer. Take over now, Beldring. Hurry, man."

Beldring's men moved on, and Fred's began to return to him. "The Germans meant us to retake it . . . and then give us hell," Boy muttered. A shell hit something close with a fearful clang and roar, followed by a powerful smell of human excrement.

"Hit the shit bucket," Fred's sergeant said nonchalantly. "We're all covered with it . . . but the rain will wash it off."

"Oh God!" Boy muttered. He began to light a cigarette, his hand trembling. Boy's nerves are going, Fred thought; too thin-skinned for this stuff.

His brother Frank appeared. The colonel swung round. "Sergeant Stratton, is that you?"

"Yes, sir."

"Ready? You know what to do?"

"Yes, sir."

"Get on with it, then."

Frank Stratton turned to the men behind him, with the Pioneers' tools and bags of cement, and said, "Follow me." He led on down the trench.

The crowd began to thin, as Fred's sergeant took his men back down the communication trench. Fred made ready to follow, when several 5.9s fell along the trench and in the open on both sides of it. He himself was blasted against the front wall. He picked himself up, wiped off the mud, and felt himself, but found no broken bones or bleeding flesh. The colonel, close behind him, said, "That was close."

A man came slipping, sliding up the trench, his face pale and wet in the light of fading star shells. "Sergeant's been hit, bad, sir."

"Which sergeant?"

"Stratton, sir."

Fred pushed through the huddled figures along the trench, suddenly conscious again of the rain, for the Germans had stopped shelling. It was quiet, except for the patter of the rain on the steel helmets. He found Frank lying in six inches of mud in the bottom of the trench, two Pioneers bent over him. He knelt and shone his flashlight down. His brother's face was ash grey, blood seeping through his tunic at the waist and chest, the tunic torn in three or four places.

"Can you hear me?" he said, holding his brother's shoulder. The rain glistened in the full sandy beard that Frank had grown since being appointed Pioneer Sergeant—Pioneer Sergeants were the only men in the army permitted to wear beards, and Frank was very proud of his privilege.

Frank did not move, but his voice was clear, though slow, and gasping, "I hear you . . . Fred, isn't it? . . . They've got me . . . in the belly, Fred . . . but I'll be back . . . You tell the C.O. . . . I'll be back."

Fred squeezed the shoulder gently . . . poor Frank . . . 'a very useful officer,' old Rowley had said . . . wonder if he'll pull through . . . Rowley didn't give praise readily . . . Frank looked bad, real bad . . .

Harry Rowland sat where he always sat, beyond the grate, where a small coal fire now burned. The foxhounds still chased their quarry over the mantelpiece, the Reverend Joshua Rowland still gazed down benignly from by the door, the room still smelled of cigar smoke; but the blue of Harry's eyes was not as sharp as it used to be, not as sharp as Richard remembered it, quite distinctly, the last time he and his father had faced each other across this fireplace—a few days after the declaration of war. His father was a chastened man.

Harry said, "The day of the election results, Richard, you remember, I asked for a little time . . . I've had it, and I know what to do. I knew what was right even before the announcement that Field Marshal Sir John French has retired, which means, has been dismissed. General Haig may be a more capable general, but the point is that we were all being deceived, hoodwinked. Our people deserve better than that. No wonder they are discontented—and showed it in the numbers who voted for you. The blind young soldier made me think, and . . ."

"Me, too," Richard said quietly.

". . . Your mother did the same. I had to confess to myself that I did *not* know what I was doing. I did care, but that is not enough for people who seek, and acquire, positions of responsibility. I have taken up the seat I won in Parliament, as you know. But I mean to use it to *think* what we are doing, what we should be doing. Whatever I do, however I vote, I shall always have that blind young man in mind. He didn't say to us, stop the war. He didn't say, victory at all costs . . . He only expected us to think, when we make the decisions affecting him and the millions like him, in other words, England . . . So . . . I am going to be a whole-time Member of Parliament . . . a Liberal, when the Liberals have thought what they are doing . . . a supporter of Mr Asquith's coalition government, when Mr Asquith and the others have thought what they are doing. That will take up all my time."

Richard waited. He knew that his father had to make some decision about the Rowland Motor Car Company; what it would be, he could not guess, and had been too involved in his own work to speculate.

Harry said, "I am handing over total control of Rowland's to you. Your mother and I can look after ourselves, financially. If you can put the company back on its feet, and make it profitable, you will decide what financial arrangements to make with your brothers and sisters. But the company is yours."

Richard's brain began to work, smoothly. He admitted to himself that he must have been expecting this, or acknowledging it as a possibility, for he was not hesitating. He said, "What is the outstanding debt, Father?"

"We owe Lloyds Bank nearly three-quarters of a million pounds. That's all. We've been using that to keep the slate clean otherwise—all suppliers, subcontractors, and workmen are paid up."

"What orders?"

"None from the Government. Orders for the Ruby are decreasing.

People have less money to spend, and what they have, they feel they ought to put into War Loans, or the like. Of course, the company will not need to close. With this enormous expansion of war production, it is impossible to imagine that there is *nothing* we can do . . . We can convert to making shells, artillery pieces, machine-gun parts . . . anything. But I hope that somehow you will find a way to keep the firm what it has always been . . . in the business of making motor cars. I have failed, and I must beg your pardon for what I did to you in August last year. I was wrong. You were right. I was too old to envision this war and what it would call for."

"None of us could do that," Richard said.

"If I had given you control when war broke out, heaven knows where we might be now."

Richard's mind was moving faster and faster: where were the drawings of the airfield protection car he had worked out with Guy last summer? A plain wooden chassis, a fixed mount for a Vickers machine gun in the centre, a low rail all round for the crew to hang on to, racks for the machine-gun belt boxes . . . simple, manoeuvrable, fast, mobile . . . for protection of airfields close to the front line, or headquarters . . . the gun could be fired on the ground, or up in the air, at marauding aircraft. He'd bet his bottom dollar . . . he was talking like Overfeld, from long association . . . that he could sell *that* to the War Office.

He stood up, and held out his hand. "Thank you, Father. We are going to have to make some changes . . . but I don't believe the time has come when we will have to be content with making shell cases."

On the 20th, about the same hour of the day that Probyn had set out past the peeping neighbour's on the 17th, he was heading home down the footpath along Scarrowside, from the direction of Whitmore. He'd spent an hour talking to a man there, a farm labourer and part-time poacher, but no friend. He had enlisted the man's help in his great plan to rob pheasants from His Lordship, and even given him some details of the plan—where he would go first, and at what time. The Whitmore man was to make a diversion to attract the keepers' attention, and his reward would be a brace of pheasants.

Probyn shuffled along fast, calculating that the information would reach Skagg's ear in about an hour and a half, that is, well after dark. Then there'd be a great scurrying to and fro and Skagg and Dan and Amos and the three men just taken on as reinforcements would spend a long and probably chilly night on Christmas Eve—it had turned cold, with sharp frosts and clear skies—for he had whispered to the Whitmore man that he planned to make his great raid at three a.m. on Christmas morning. The keepers wouldn't be stumbling back into their beds till six or seven on Christmas morning. Probyn hoped it would snow all that night.

He checked his step, seeing movement ahead in the twilight: then he went on. It was the squire, walking slowly toward him by the river. They met under a willow that leant over the sliding water and the trailing weeds just below the surface.

"Evening, squire," Probyn said, stopping and touching his forelock.

"I heard you'd gone to Whitmore," Cate said. "Florinda told me. She's looking very beautiful . . . her clothes are in such good taste, too."

Probyn nodded without speaking. With the squire's wife still hiding away somewhere in Ireland, he might be hinting that he'd like Florinda to come up to the Manor again: but if he'd just seen her, they could settle that between themselves. No call for him to interfere.

Cate said, "Give up your plan, Probyn."

" 'Tis my right," Probyn said.

"Perhaps, but give it up . . . certainly for a couple of weeks, at least. You know Lord Swanwick has hired extra keepers. There are people in the village willing to watch your every move and tell Skagg, for a few pence. Skagg's angry because you've made a fool of him before. Lord Swanwick's told them he'll back them to the hilt if they get into the courts for manhandling you . . . or worse."

Probyn listened appraisingly. Squire was talking well tonight, full of feeling; and everything he said was true as true.

Cate continued, "They all carry guns, as you know. There'll be an accident and you'll get hurt . . . or killed."

Probyn said, "That wouldn't stop our men in France, would it, squire?"

"No." He took Probyn's elbow and shook it gently. "That's different, and you know it is."

Probyn said, "Don't you be worrying about me, squire. I can look after myself." He spoke firmly and Cate gave up with a shake of his head, releasing Probyn's arm. The two walked along side by side until, at Probyn's cottage, Probyn turned away with another touch of his hand to his forehead. Christopher Cate walked on, thinking of Probyn; of his wife Margaret and what she was doing at this moment; of Stella, whom he was about to lose . . . of Johnny Merritt, a well brought-up clean cut young man—Stella should be very happy with him; of his son Laurence, growing every day closer to manhood, closer to the war; of

Walstone, changing before his eyes, and in its spirit, as he was sure it had never changed in all the years it had been his family's home.

Betty Merritt sat in the arm chair closest to the fireplace in her brother's sitting-room, part of the two-room suite at the South Eastern Hotel in Hedlington where he had been living for a year now. She was wearing a thick woollen dress and a topcoat, and still shivering.

"Don't the British ever keep anything warm?" she asked.

"Oh, you'll get used to it. Wear thicker clothes."

"I am," she said indignantly, "and I'm still cold. Is it going to be like this down at Walstone Manor? Or have they kept the Roman hot water system, as well as the Roman tiles, that you've been telling us about?"

"Put some more coal on the fire, Johnny," their father said, standing up and holding out his hands to the low flames. While Johnny did as he was bid, Stephen said, "Well, let's have a look. You aren't going to keep it a secret until the presentation, are you?"

Johnny put on another two lumps from the brass coal scuttle and then went to the writing desk, opened a drawer, and came back with a small dark blue jewel box, the inscription *Goldsmiths and Silversmiths Company* on the lid in gold. He opened it and held it out for them to look.

"It's beautiful," Betty cried. "Diamonds and sapphires."

"To match her eyes."

"You must have been eating bread and cheese for six months to be able to afford that," his father said.

"Oh no, Dad. I just embezzled some of the company's money. And don't forget I'm getting a percentage of the profits. The J.M.C. is doing well."

"So we have seen from the financial statements. The board is delighted with Mr Rowland, and very pleased with you and Overfeld and Morgan, as I told you when we arrived."

"Overfeld's good, Dad."

Stephen said, "He's an excellent practical engineer." He changed the subject abruptly, speaking in a different tone. "You've bought this beautiful and expensive ring, Johnny. You are sure you are in love with Miss Cate, and that she is in love with you. But it's not too late to . . . back off a bit. Get back from the edge of the cliff and make sure you want to jump over. Many young people go through with a project in which they have really lost enthusiasm, because they think they must . . . because they don't know how to back out . . . because they've bought the ring, arranged the honeymoon . . . But nothing matters compared with making the right decision, finally. The ring can be sent back, the honeymoon reservations cancelled. Mr Cate does not want his daughter to be unhappy any more than I want you to be—and that is what will come about, if you are in fact making a mistake . . . So, before we make the formal announcement of the engagement, and fix a date, are you sure?"

"Thanks for thinking about it, Dad, but . . . I'm sure. I've known Stella for over a year now. It's enough. She's an angel and I love her. I want to make the engagement official on Christmas Day, when we're at the Manor—and give her the ring. We'll fix a date then."

"Make it soon," Betty said from her chair. "Girls don't like to wait. A girl at Smith got engaged two years ago. She still is, and when I saw her last month, she looked about forty."

"That brings up another matter," Stephen said. "That first night, after we got off the ship in Liverpool, you told us that you had made up your mind to join the British services . . . the Royal Flying Corps, I think you said. We have all been very busy since, and I have not wanted to bring it up until we have time to discuss all the implications. As they are obviously going to affect everything else in your life, including your proposed marriage, we had better do it now . . . You know that we would like you to stay on with J.M.C. for a time, say a year, and then return to New York to gain experience in the headquarters of the bank?"

"I know, Dad, but . . . I can't. British and French are dying over there for us—to protect the sort of world I want to live in, and I can't stay on here any longer. *I'm* not too proud to fight . . . It isn't as though I was really needed here. I'm not."

Stephen Merritt said slowly, "So be it then. When will you wish to be married?"

"As soon as it can all be fixed up," Johnny said. "And we don't want a fancy wedding."

"How do you know?" Betty cut in. "I'll ask Stella. I bet she wants a white dress, bridesmaids, everything."

"Mr Cate will not permit any extravagance, when England's in such need."

"Who'll be the bride's 'mother,' if Mrs Cate's still in hiding?"

Johnny said, "Mrs Rowland, I believe—Guy's mother."

"Ah, the fabulous Guy! When am I going to be allowed to meet him?"

"Boxing Day—the family go down to watch the meet of the foxhounds, which is always at Beighton that day. They hunt hill foxes on the Downs."

"When's Boxing Day?"

"The day after Christmas, when the servants and postmen and people like that are given their Christmas boxes . . . tips."

"Do we hunt?"

"I don't. And you don't have the clothes."

"Will Guy?"

"Probably. It'll be almost his last time out, before he joins the R.F.C. We'll follow the hounds on foot."

"You follow the hounds. I'll follow Guy."

"All right, sis, but you'll never catch him. I'm warning you."

"I have plenty of time."

"Three weeks? With Guy in some R.F.C. training camp on Salisbury Plain, probably?"

"Ah, but I'm not going home with Dad."

So she's won her battle to get out of Smith, Johnny thought. "What are you going to do?" he asked.

"I don't know yet," she said. "There'll be something. I feel . . . ready, somehow. It must be the war atmosphere, that you breathe here."

Johnny thought, we've got the domestic details out of the way; now's the time. He put away the little jewel box and turned to face his father and sister. "Now I have some news . . . a surprise."

Betty said, "Out with it . . . I knew you had something on your mind."

Johnny said, "Mr Harry Rowland has given control of the Rowland Motor Car Company to Mr Richard . . . to do what he likes with it. He told me an hour ago."

Stephen started up, "What? What's he going to do? Will he leave the J.M.C.?"

Johnny said, "He doesn't want to. He is thinking of turning Rowland's to the manufacture of a small motor vehicle for carrying a machine gun and three or four men, for the protection of airfields and headquarters."

"Sounds a good idea," Stephen said, "but what's the management relationship going to be, the financial arrangements?"

"He said he wanted to offer you—us—a 24 percent interest in Rowland's, in return for capital . . . and the same to Toledano's."

Stephen rubbed his chin thoughtfully, and after a while said, "It could work. Rowland's and the J.M.C. don't compete with each other. They could share some things . . . offices, draughting, billing, accounting—paint shop perhaps. We'd have to look into the money involved. Rowland's is in the red, obviously, but I don't know how much."

Johnny said, "We must have a conference, Dad. I've been thinking, ever since Mr Rowland called. I have an idea. I want to put it to you, and him, and Overfeld . . . Morgan, too."

"Tomorrow?"

"I need a little more time, Dad. The morning of the 23rd, perhaps—early, before we go down to Walstone."

"Very well. I'll see Richard and get some financial information from him before then."

Daily Telegraph, Thursday, December 23, 1915

ALL-NIGHT SITTING OF THE COMMONS

THE ADDITIONAL MILLION
RADICAL DEMONSTRATION

Before four o'clock on Tuesday afternoon the House of Commons went into Committee upon the vote to add an additional one million men to the army. It was not until half past five yesterday morning that the vote was agreed to. As a measure of precaution the Government had suspended the eleven o'clock rule and, till after midnight, the proceedings may be said to have followed customary lines. But it then became apparent that a group of Radicals below the gangway and a few Nationalists were determined to secure, if they could, the adjournment of the debate, the result of which would have been to reduce to confusion the Government arrangements for the final meetings of the session—those of yesterday and today.

What they had ultimately in view was not clearly stated. It was obvious from the outset that they would not be bold enough to vote against the establishment of the army being increased to 4,000,000 officers and men, though, like a double thread, there ran through nearly all the speeches hostility to compulsion for single men and vaguely defined charges of incapacity and inefficiency levelled against the War Office and Army Staff. Several times it was repeated that the lives of another million men should not be entrusted to the 'blunderers' in charge.

Johnny Merritt sat facing his father, the opened newspaper spread on the table between them. Johnny was speaking—"It's been a bad year for the Allies, Dad. As far as England's concerned it's been mainly a matter of disappointments, rather than defeats. So much was expected of battles like Neuve Chapelle, Arras, Loos, the Dardanelles, that when success was nil, or small, disappointment was as unreasonable as the hopes had been in the first place. But the Germans have had severe disappointments, too. They wanted to knock Russia out of the war—they haven't done it. They wanted to capture Paris within a few weeks—they didn't do it. They tried hard to get round the Allies' northern flank at the end of last year—they didn't succeed. They hoped to make a decisive breakthrough when they used gas at Ypres in April this year —they didn't . . ."

"It's the higher direction of the war that seems to be inefficient, on the Allied side," Stephen said.

Johnny said, "Field Marshal French was too emotional for his job . . . that's what the colonel I talk to at the War Office says. The soldiers would probably have liked General Smith-Dorrien to replace him, but he was manoeuvred out, and General Haig appointed. My colonel says he's not very popular, but highly regarded as a planner . . . and *if* he is emotional, which I believe he is not, he doesn't let that control his thoughts or decisions."

"It's the civilian side that worries me more than the military," Stephen said.

Johnny said, "The Germans have had a working General Staff for a long time, and an effective system of co-ordination between the General Staff and the civilian leaders of the country. The British army's General Staff is fairly new, and the navy's even newer—and despised by many senior admirals—and there's been no tradition of planning or co-ordination between the Government and the General Staffs. But I do think that in 1916 there'll be a big improvement. There'll have to be another change in the Government . . . Asquith's carrying the blame for Loos and the other disappointments, and he'll go. Someone stronger will replace him . . . Curzon, Lloyd George, Balfour, even Churchill, perhaps. There'll be a small War Cabinet. There'll be conscription. There'll be enough munitions of all kinds . . . Lloyd George will see to that. He's done wonders already."

"The Admiralty will have to find a way to beat the U-boats, or England could be in serious trouble . . . Do you think the German fleet will come out?"

Johnny hesitated before saying, "I doubt it. Why should it? As long as it sits in its harbours, the British must keep a huge force ready to fight it. If it comes out and is destroyed, the navy can turn all its energies to fighting the U-boats."

"But what if the Germans win the sea battle?"

"Ah! . . . My colonel at the War Office says Admiral Jellicoe—he's the commander-in-chief of the Grand Fleet—is the only man on either side who can lose the war in an afternoon, because if the British fleet were knocked out, the Germans could invade. Quite a small invading force would be enough to make the British bring all their troops back from France—if they could—leaving the French in the lurch. The French would give up, for sure. Their morale is not very good, after all their disappointments and losses since the war began . . . and, from all I hear, the main German land campaign next year will be against them."

"Will the French hold?"

"All experience of the war so far says they will. No one has yet broken an organised defence line . . . but England may have to help . . . There'll be a big expansion of the war in the air . . . The Russians may hold on, they may not . . . Heaven knows what will happen in Africa, Palestine, Mesopotamia, Serbia, Salonika, et cetera. I don't think any of those places matter, or can affect the final outcome . . . What do the people at home feel about the war, Dad?"

Stephen stroked his chin, considering. Johnny had matured a great deal in this last year. His written reports had been illuminating and cogent, but they had not prepared Stephen for this new incisiveness of his son's personality. Finally he said, "People are of two minds . . . at least. The British blockade and high-handedness at sea have caused much anger and resentment. If it weren't for German political ineptitude—and the Kaiser's genius for putting his foot in his mouth—it is conceivable that we would enter the war on the German side." Johnny made to protest, but Stephen held up his hand and continued: "But that's not likely as long as the Germans keep sinking *Lusitania*s and shooting Nurse Cavells . . . Again, people say, 'Why should we salvage the British Empire?' The British would get more support if they publicly undertook to free India and Ireland, for a start, at the end of the war . . . and also the German colonies they have occupied . . . People believe they're going to grab those for themselves, permanently . . . On the other hand the war is making us prosperous, very. Our trade is increasing by leaps and bounds. Many Americans are making a great deal of money out of the war, so it is popular. That doesn't mean those same people think we should join in, on either side . . . But I am afraid that we will be forced to, in the end, to protect our investments, which have been mostly on the Allied side. And I am sure that the Germans will give us the necessary provocation, sooner or later . . . What's your prognostication?"

"It's hard to say, Dad. If the British were all like Guy Rowland, the war would be over in no time . . . If they were all like his father, Colo-

nel Rowland, they'd go down butting their heads against a brick wall
. . . If they were like Mr Cate, they wouldn't have gotten into the position of having to fight in the first place . . . If they were Frank Strattons—you don't know him—they'd invent something that machine guns
and barbed wire couldn't stop . . . If they were all Bert Gorses, they'd
murder their officers and statesmen and declare a radical republic . . .
But they're all those mixed together, and the result is Mr John and Mrs
Louise, Bob and Mrs Stratton, Willum and Mary Gorse, Commander
Tom, Mr Richard, Naomi, Stella, Laurence, Virginia—even Mrs Fiona
—they all have something of Guy, something of Bert Gorse, something
of Mr Cate, something of Colonel Quentin . . . I think the dominant
fact is that the British are determined, as a people. They are so determined that they will somehow set their house in order even if their
leaders don't want to, or don't know how to. I won't say the war's still
popular—though it was, generally, until Loos—but the people don't believe there's any alternative way of dealing with Germany, except by
beating them. The British aren't all heroes. There'll be more industrial
trouble after conscription comes in—a great deal of it. There'll be more
bitterness, about those who go and those who weasel out of going . . .
but England is still financially sound, and there are still plenty of men,
to fight. The war will be waged, at whatever cost."

"And what a cost it will be," Stephen murmured.

"Yes, but we'll win, in the end."

Christmastide: 1915

34 In the last week before Christmas the waits sang all over Britain, in the evenings. This night the sky was of infinite depth, the moon huge and yellow, the stars brilliant points of scattered light. The air was still and cold, and all who went out of doors went bundled in coats and scarves, gloves and hats.

No carollers were singing outside No. 23 Greeley Crescent in Hedlington, but there was a group farther down the street. Inside No. 23 Fiona Rowland was speaking, "I can't understand why she won't tell us where she is."

"She explained in her letter, Mummy," Guy said patiently. "She said she'd let us know where she is as soon as you promise not to have her brought back, and put a notice in *The Times*."

"I ought to go to the police," Fiona said. "She may be in trouble. She may be lost."

Guy said, "She's nearly seventeen. I think she's probably joined one of the women's service groups—the Women's Legion, perhaps. She talked about them in the summer hols, and she really hated Cheltenham."

"Daddy said she had to finish there . . . the term ended four days ago, and she's vanished. I'll have to write to Daddy and tell him." She got up crossly. "It's very inconsiderate of her. When are you joining the Royal Flying Corps?"

"January 3rd," he said. "I want to hunt on Boxing Day and New

Year's Day . . . and see this sister of Johnny Merritt's he tells me is so beautiful. The 2nd's a Sunday, so I can't join till the 3rd."

His mother stood up suddenly, looking down on him where he sat by the fire. The flames touched points of orange in her grey eyes, and emphasised the fine wrinkles at the corners of them. She said, "I was going to wait to tell you till Virginia went back to school, but if she's not coming . . . Guy, I'm going to leave your father. I'm not in love with him—haven't been for years. I . . ."

"He is with you," Guy said. He and his sister had known for a long time that their parents' marriage was not the warm affectionate thing it might have been—as that between their Uncle John and Aunt Louise was, for instance; nevertheless this was a painful wound that his mother was giving him.

She said, "For years I have wanted to marry another man, a painter. Now that you're leaving home, and there would only have been Virginia, I am going to him. Virginia can live with Uncle Christopher— she'll be happier in the country anyway, and of course you can both come and visit us whenever you want to."

"Are you going to marry this man?" Guy asked.

"I want to, but . . ." she looked away, and he saw tears in her eyes, "I don't know whether he wants to tie himself . . . or feel responsible for me."

"Daddy does."

"Oh, darling, I know, I know, but . . . I'm a woman. When you deal with women remember that we need more than housing and keeping, like a horse or a motor car. We need understanding . . . we have our needs of the spirit, and they have to be taken notice of. Your father never understood me . . . or I him, I suppose. I love Archie, and he *does* understand me. We laugh and play when we're together. We have other things binding us than a house, children, meals, budgets . . . I'll go as soon as you've left. When I'm settled in London—Archie has a studio flat in the King's Road in Chelsea—I'll give up this place. The Post Office will forward any letters, if Virginia writes . . ."

"Have you told Daddy about this?" Guy asked unhappily.

"I told him when he was home wounded that I would leave him, yes."

"Hadn't you better write and ask him if he wants to keep the flat on? He may not want to have to find a new place. Or he may want to remarry."

She looked at him in astonishment. "Why, why, I suppose he might. I'd never thought of that. Yes, I'll write to him." She spoke suddenly harshly. "But I'm going to Archie, and that's that. We only have one

life to live, and time is passing . . . I'm sorry, Guy, but I'll die if I don't.
I don't care what anyone thinks or says, any more—not the Governor,
Mother Rowland, not my own mother . . . not even you. There's a war
on!" She sat down, reaching across the fire to touch her son's slowly
outstretched fingers. "How long will it continue, Guy? I pray that
Archie will never go to it, but every month it lasts makes it harder for
a man like him to stay at home . . . and everyone talks about conscription."

"It'll go on for a long time yet," he answered her slowly. "I've been
thinking about it a lot. When the war began it was 'over there'—something foreign which we were going to, as though we were going to
Paris for a weekend, or visiting Monte Carlo. Now, I can almost see it
as an animal, or a snake, crawling across the Channel and into England, into all the houses simultaneously . . . and not only into the
houses, into the people . . . It hasn't got into me yet, but it will. I
won't come back the same as I went, I know."

"Your father has changed," she said. "I felt it, when he was home."

Guy said, "I felt it, too, when he came down to Wellington. So will
Boy change, and Frank and Fred Stratton. Everyone will change, even
those who stay at home." His mother was crying silently, her face immobile, tears running down her cheeks. He had never seen her cry, before this night, that he could remember, and he knelt quickly beside
her. "Don't worry, Mummy. I understand, and I'm sure Virginia
would, if she were here. Perhaps Daddy does, even. Virginia's all right,
I'm sure. Just put that notice in *The Times*, that she wants you to. Let
her do what *she* wants to, *needs* to."

Fiona said, "And you're leaving the nest, my eaglet, going to fly."

"I have to," he said, "I *need* to. That's why I understand about you
and Archie, I suppose. I'm going to fly! Every day, all day! All over the
sky, which is one sky, no boundaries or frontiers between land and sea,
or between England and France, Germany and America—one great
sky! . . . Listen, isn't that the waits outside?"

Half a dozen members of the Walstone church choir were singing in
the frosty night outside High Staining. John and Louise, Naomi, Rachel Cowan, Carol Adams, Lady Helen Durand-Beaulieu and the two
London girls of the Land Army, Frances Enright and Joan Pitman,
stood in the doorway, huddled up, listening. After the third carol, John
said, "Very good! Come inside now for a little something to warm you
all up."

"Oh, we couldn't, thank you, John," the rector said heartily. "Christopher gave us all a glass of sherry just now, and others before that. Miss Hightower here's quite tipsy, I do declare."

"Oh, Mr Kirby!" Miss Hightower simpered.

They trooped off down the drive, the rector waving and shouting over his shoulder, "See you in church, and at the Boxing Day meet, eh?" He stopped, turning, "Oh dear, I keep forgetting that you've resigned from the Hunt . . . but that won't stop you from going to the meet, will it?"

"No, but work will," John said.

The rector went on down the drive, his old head shaking. The family turned into the house, closing the door behind them. John said, "Well, even if they don't want a glass of sherry, what about us?"

A Christmas tree was set up in the back of the drawing-room, and presents lay arranged under it, to be opened at noon the next day, after the family's return from church. John passed round sherry to the five women and raised his own glass—"Here's to those who can not be with us tonight. May they all come back safe and sound one day soon."

"Amen," Lady Helen said.

John sat down, "We've been lucky in this family, so far. Let us pray the war ends soon—"

"Amen," Rachel Cowan said to that.

John added, "—in victory."

Louise sipped her sherry, her eyes on the younger women. The London girls were in their high twenties, plain and friendly of face. Lady Helen was not a beauty, but she had one of the sweetest expressions Louise had ever seen; and the expression did not lie. She was completely open and honest, and also intelligent. She worked hard, never shirked, never gave up. She would make some man a wonderful wife soon . . . Better soon than late—she was, what, Charles's age? No, a year older, nearly twenty-four now. Naomi was home for a brief leave from her group of the Women's Volunteer Motor Drivers, which drove staff cars for senior officers of the War Office; she was living with the rest of the group in a large house in Belgravia, converted into a sort of homey barracks, its mews into their garage and workshop. She had worn uniform all the time she'd been at home, and had insisted she would wear it to church tomorrow; but, at her father's begging, had agreed to wear a silk dress tonight . . . She was looking at Rachel now, bending forward, talking to her . . . probably about women's rights, socialism, the suffrage. The two young women's lives had grown apart since they left Girton and, Louise thought, so had they themselves. They were not as close as they used to be. Louise had once thought that Rachel was a bad, even unhealthy, influence on her daughter; but Naomi was now a person of her own, not easily influenced by anyone, certainly not by a girl her own age. It was time she got married, but all the men were away at the war, certainly the best of them: and when it was over, there would be fewer, many fewer.

John said, "We ought to wait till New Year's Eve, I suppose, but let's drink a toast to 1916 . . . peace, victory . . . all our people safe home."

"And the best herd of Friesians in England," Lady Helen said, smiling.

She was the head cowman now, almost the manager, and among other things she took the cows to the bull, now Leeuwarden Rex, a Friesian, and supervised the mating. Not at all a proper thing for an unmarried young lady to be doing, Louise thought; but what *was*, these days? It didn't seem to have made any difference to Lady Helen. She was pleasant and comfortable with men of all ages—but on the surface. What lay below, she had not revealed.

Bill Hoggin sat by the dining-room table in their little house, dandling Launcelot on his knee with one hand and holding a flagon of beer in the other. He felt good, because it had been a good year for him; and, just a few days ago, he had found out who the mysterious V.A.D. of the bombing night was—none other than Miss Stella Cate, of Walstone Manor. No other V.A.D.s had been out that night until much later, in daylight, in an organised body, with doctors and nurses, so . . . what had *she* been doing in North Hedlington? It was not important to know, but it might be useful . . . as Fagioletti's little bits of overheard gossip might be.

"What a sad Christmas this is, really," Ruth said, "so many poor men in the trenches."

"The best Christmas of my life," Bill said energetically, "the best *so far* . . . 'cos 1916's going to be better. Much better! This war's going on for bleeding ever, hand hevery day it goes on I make a thousand pounds . . . at least! Near half a million this year, and I didn't really get started till I bought those California plum and apple jam futures cheap, in June."

"Half a million!" Ruth breathed, wide eyed, "I can't believe it!"

"You'd better, 'cos now that I'm 'obnobbing with the likes of Lord Swanwick—and I am, I am, I got milord ready to eat out of my 'and— we're moving into a bigger house. Got my eye on one, in Garston Road."

"Why, that's where Mr Harry lives."

"This house is next but one to Laburnum Lodge . . . We'll have to hire some staff for it . . . The banks are falling over themselves to lend me money. You can 'ave anything you like, Ruthie, fur coats, Rolls Royce cars, diamond rings . . . as long as it doesn't cost more than a fiver." He laughed uproariously at his own joke. " 'Ere, we got the bloody waits houtside. They must think I'm made of money, to come here."

Ruth said seriously, "I don't want a big house, or a lot of servants. I want you not to use bad language, Bill . . . and not blow your nose on your fingers. You're setting Launcelot a bad example. *I* know how nice you are, but other people don't. They think you're a . . ."

"Hog," he said, "Hoggish Hoggin. All the Strattons think that, eh? Well, they know what they can do with it."

The waits outside were singing or shouting *Good King Wenceslas* at the tops of their voices.

Ruth raised her own voice to be heard, "I don't want Launcelot to be ashamed of his father when he goes to Eton College." Bill was speaking better, but still used dirty words, and didn't behave himself proper. Still, he was trying, and she'd have to be patient, but firm. For Launcelot's sake, it would be no trouble.

Bill jumped up, depositing the baby in her lap, took half a dozen sixpences and threepences out of his pocket, put them on the coal shovel and placed the shovel on the burning coals in the grate. The singers began another carol, Bill muttering under his breath, "Fucking beggars!"

"Bill! Launcelot will learn!"

Bill said, "Open the window, love."

She opened the window. Bill put on a glove and dropped the hot coins onto it. Leaning out of the window he shouted, "Here y'are! Merry Christmas!" and threw the coins out onto the pavement. The singing broke off in a ragged wail as the waits dived for the coins, to rise again in shrieks and howls as they burned their fingers. Bill Hoggin slammed the window down, roaring with laughter.

"That wasn't very kind," Ruth said.

" 'Oo said anything about being kind? I said Merry Christmas, and I'm merry, ain't I? What's for dinner?"

"Roast beef and Yorkshire pudding."

"Pud?"

"Mince pies."

"I'll 'ave a dozen . . . and some more beer, love."

The front room of Willum Gorse's little house in the row up the hill toward the gaol was crowded—Willum and Mary, their four younger children, and Willum's half-brother, Bert. No one was singing carols in this mean street, the houses made of yellow brick, long since blackened with soot from Hedlington's coal fires and its few factories. The smell of stewing mutton, onion, and vegetables permeated the room from the kitchen behind, where Mary had a large pot on the coal stove. It would be ready in an hour. Meanwhile, the younger kids lay on the floor, playing with hand-made wooden animals, wooden bricks and a tin trumpet Betty had found on a rubbish heap; Violet, the eleven-year-old, was darning one of her own long black cotton stockings. Budding breasts swelled her thin, patched blouse. Mary watched her with troubled eyes—she had been caught stealing, but that was nothing to what would come, when she became a woman . . . on the edge of it now, ready to fly, out of childhood, out of others' control, out of this cramped little house and family. She wished she could talk to Willum about it.

The two men each had a glass of beer in hand, as they sat on opposite sides of the table. A crate of Bass stood in the corner, three of its bottles empty.

Willum's brow was furrowed by worry, "I don't like it, I tell 'ee, Bert. Dad will come to a mischief."

Bert said with exasperation, "I told you ten times if I told you once, that he's already done it. Three, four days ago. I didn't go to work that day, I went to Bedford and sent a telegram—but I didn't tell you about it, because if I'd 'a told you earlier, you'd 'a told everyone else, wouldn't you? You couldn't keep a secret if you got paid for it . . . Don't worry, Dad's not going out on Christmas Eve, I tell you."

"But you said he promised he would and . . ."

Mary spoke without looking up from her sewing. "Don't try to explain any more, Bert . . . You're staying for supper, aren't you?"

"If you asks me, I am. What about me putting a bob into the kitty?"

She shook her head. "There's no need, Bert. We got enough, and when Dad sends up a rabbit, we eat like earls."

Willum lifted his face out of his beer glass and said, "Everyone'll eat like an earl soon, eh? When the war's over. That's what we're fighting for, eh?"

"We're fighting so that the rich can get richer," Bert said angrily, "I've told you a hundred times. We're not fighting the Germans, we're fighting our own people—the poor. The soldiers ought to turn round and shoot their own officers, everywhere, then come home and shoot all the politicians . . . *Then* we'd be better off, I can tell you."

"But you're a union leader," Willum said slowly.

"I am, and proud of it," Bert said, "proud enough to throw their dirty money back in their faces."

"What do you mean?"

"I mean that Morgan, the Works Manager, offered me a job as shop foreman. Pay would have been double—more. But the union would 'a thrown me out. So I refused . . . We got near sixty members of the union at J.M.C. now—secret members. When we're ready, we'll *strike*. And we *can*."

Willum repeated what he had said a minute earlier. "But you're a union leader."

"I just said so, even though it is in secret."

"Then you're sort of an officer, and they'd have to shoot you. I wouldn't like that."

"You don't understand the war or anything else," Bert exclaimed, "an' you never will."

"I ought to go to the war," Willum said, frowning. "Lord Kitchener says so, in them posters. An' if I went, I'd understand it, wouldn't I? Stands to reason, eh?"

Mary said, "You're not going to the war, Willum Gorse, so don't think about it. It's a long way away, and it won't come for you, and you won't go to it. It's not for you . . . Don't talk about such things, Bert. He can't understand it and it upsets him . . . Are you still going out with that young Miss Cowan?"

Bert said, "She talks too much . . . We can't have five minutes without her gabbing about women's rights, the theory of socialism, and heaven knows what else . . . Wish she were a man, though, and she'd be a great shop steward."

"Do you really wish she were a man?" Mary said. "Last time I saw you with her you were looking right into her eyes, sort of soft like. I never seen a man look at another man like that."

"Don't be daft, Mary! Me, soft on that Jew girl? For one thing, she hates men. Only talks to me because she wants to learn about unions."

Mary said, "Why didn't you bring her here for supper? We've plenty."

" 'Cos she's gone to Walstone, to spend Christmas at High Staining. She was at Cambridge with the daughter."

"Miss Naomi," Mary said, "she looks ever so handsome in her uniform. Saw her in High Street yesterday. She'll be married soon, mark my words."

No one spoke for a time, until Bert muttered under his breath, "Me, soft on Rachel Cowan, for Christ's sake!"

Guy Rowland bicycled west along the upland road toward Hedlington, the moonlight bright on the pale surface of the road ahead, the hedges thick and dark on each side. It was half past nine and he had just completed another two hours of testing the gyro direction indicator in the Caudron. That had gone well, and so had his landing. One more night test, planned for the 27th, and then . . . his next flight would be in uniform, probably in a Bleriot Experimental 2C. A sharp wind blowing past his ears made him wish he was still wearing his flying helmet and goggles. He felt depressed because his mother was leaving his father, and because, in the morning's newspaper, he had seen the name of Lieutenant Grant-Meikle, Seaforth Highlanders, under the heading "Killed in Action." He could see his face before him now, not in uniform, not dead, but at the moment he'd been tricked out of position, enabling Guy to make that winning drop kick.

The bicycle's acetylene lamp went out. Guy swore, then stopped, dismounted, and bent over to see what was the matter. There was no acetylene hissing out of the carbide can, but the can was half full. He shook the lamp: no gurgle of water—empty: there must be a leak somewhere. Well, he could see clearly enough with this moon, and in any case he could have bicycled this road in pitch darkness, he knew it so well. Remounting, he continued westward.

A few minutes later, no sound but the wind in the trees and the purr of the thin tyres on the gravel, he heard a sharp high pitched shriek from a spinney on his right. He jammed on the brakes and the bicycle was skidding to a halt even as he thought—it might be a courting couple, and then I'll get a black eye . . . but though he had heard that women uttered all sorts of gasps and groans when making love, this had had a desperate pitch to it. He lowered the bicycle into the ditch at the edge of the road and hurried into the spinney by a low tunnel-like passage through the hedge. The moonlight, barred from the tall interlocked branches above, shone on scattered bushes, the boles of the elms, and a struggle five yards ahead of him—a dark shape above, white legs outspread below, kicking, thrashing, the near back and buttocks thrusting, hands at the other's neck. A large pointed kitchen knife glinted on the bare earth six feet beyond. Guy ran round, stooped and grabbed it up. As he grabbed, the struggle resolved and the man jumped to his feet, arms outstretched, mouthing something, trousers open at the fly, penis out and erect. Guy crouched, the knife held low and forward, and circled slowly, carefully, to his right. The man crouched and circled, too. He had a heavy club boot on his left foot, but the leg seemed of normal length. His penis was going limp as he moved, heavily stooped, arms out, staring at Guy over the woman. She lay between them, gasping, her hands to her own throat, her skirt thrown up over her breasts. The man had a big pale slab face . . . over six feet . . . eyes narrow, small, vacant . . . fourteen stone or more

. . . heavy panting breathing . . . clumsy, even without the club foot
. . . and Guy had the knife. He felt cold and his heart beat steady and
slow, his eyes fixed now on the man's. Two more steps, to get him clear
of the woman . . . make sure no roots in the way, then step in and
strike. The man turned and crashed away through the bushes toward
the hedge and the road. Guy knelt a moment beside the woman. She
began to shriek—she was young, plump, not pretty, a farm girl, the
dense triangle of her pubic hair black in the moonlight at the base of
her belly. She was all right. Guy darted after the man. The hunt was
up, a horn shrilling silently in his head.

He saw the quarry in the road, on a bicycle, pedalling fast toward
Hedlington, and no more than twenty feet away. He picked up his
own bicycle, jumped on, and followed. This must be the Hedlington
Ripper. Mad, of course. Driven by God knew what to do what he did.
Not responsible for his actions. Unarmed, with a club boot. Unfit. The
shape of the road ahead ran through his mind . . . nothing for a mile
then, near the edge of the Down, the road took a sweeping curve to the
left, then back to the right, to make an easier gradient down toward
Hedlington. Where the first curve began, a footpath cut straight down
between tall hedges. That was the place.

Guy prayed the man would not know of the path, or not think of it
. . . better press him. He crouched and pedalled harder, the knife in
his right hand. Warmth and anticipation flooded through him, and he
understood what Rhodes and Grandy had spoken of. He was going to
kill.

Twenty yards from the beginning of the curve, his front wheel was
barely a foot behind the other's rear wheel, and a yard to the left. The
curve began, the man pedalled furiously on down the road, Guy dived
into the footpath.

At the far end he threw down his bicycle and waited, crouched beside the road in the shadow of a tree. The first street lights were two
hundred yards on. The man came, pedalling more slowly; he had seen,
and heard, that his pursuer had given up.

When he was eight or nine feet away Guy stepped out, his left arm
raised to strike at the man's face. The man jerked up his arm on that
side, his right, to ward off the blow. Guy struck in hard under his ribs
with the knife point, blade up. It went in easily all the way. He let go
of the handle as the moving body and bicycle passed, falling sideways,
crashing, the man sliding on the gravel, face down. Guy walked forward, turned him over, and pulled out the knife, its handle now slippery with blood. He wiped the knife blade and the handle, and his

own hands, on the man's coat. He was dead, eyes open and staring at the moon, gravel scrapes down the pale face.

Guy stood, the knife in hand, looking down. He had done it well, and had enjoyed it.

There had been no need to kill the wretched madman. He could have followed him, calling for the police . . . or stopped him, and held him at knife point . . . but he hadn't. He had not made pretty patterns in the sand: he had killed, with fervour and compulsion. In the end, cricket and rugby were only games to him: but this was not, and here he was a matador, after all. And that, he would have to live with, the rest of his life.

He began to tremble, shaking and shivering uncontrollably, and knelt to vomit at the side of the road as the lights of a car came up the hill.

They sat round the table in Stephen Merritt's suite, five men—Stephen, Johnny, Richard Rowland, Overfeld, and Morgan. Betty was out, doing some last minute Christmas shopping with Richard's wife, Susan. Richard finished explaining his plan, which was, in brief, to run both Rowland's and the J.M.C. as linked enterprises, with himself as managing director of both, Overfeld his deputy, more particularly responsible for day-to-day supervision of the J.M.C. The J.M.C. would continue to make trucks, but Rowland's would convert to something else, preferably the mobile machine-gun vehicle, which Richard intended to explain to the War Office, and solicit orders for, immediately after Christmas; and his father Harry, as M.P., would see that he got a hearing from the military. Finances had already been discussed, and Fairfax, Gottlieb and Toledano's had both agreed in principle to put up the necessary capital. As time passed it was his intention to weld the two companies much closer, so that all used the same parts, even engines, perhaps.

When Richard finished talking, Stephen said, "I've been burning up the cables to New York the past two days, and the board have given me a great deal of discretion to act on their behalf. As Mr Rowland has said, we have in principle agreed to provide the money asked for. Now we have to work out the details, including making and selling the protection vehicle. As to practical engineering, do you have anything to say, Overfeld?"

Overfeld shook his head, "Nothing, boss. Except, I'd like to have a look at the plans for the machine-gun vehicle . . . Why don't we call it the Rowland Mobile Protection Vehicle . . . MPV . . . to see what's the best way to put it together."

"Me, too, boss," Morgan said.

"You'd better call in Bob Stratton, when you're doing that," Johnny said, speaking for almost the first time, "if he stays on."

"Might he not?"

"He was supposed to retire when Mr Harry was, in September, 1914 . . . and now Mr Harry's gone, he might want to go, too."

"I wish we could get Frank," Richard said, "but that's out of the question."

Stephen waited a few moments, then said, "Johnny, you wanted to say something, I know."

Johnny drew a deep breath, waited a second or two to steady his voice, then said, "I think we're aiming too low . . . thinking too small. The number of MPVs we can make and sell will never be large. At the end of the war Rowland's will be back where it was in 1914—selling a few good cars to a few rich people—only it'll be outsold and outshone by Crossley, for instance, who've had such large war orders . . . We should abandon Rowland's as it now stands—sell it to the government or anyone else who can use it to make shells, or guns, or war material.

"The future's up in the air . . . now, and after the war. We should start a new company to make aeroplanes. The demand will be insatiable until the war's over and then, well, if we always think ahead and use the best brains, we'll stay ahead, and afloat, in the sky."

There was a long silence. At length his father said slowly, "Have you any suggestion as to what sort of aeroplanes we should build?"

"Yes," Johnny said eagerly. "Guy tells me the R.F.C. and the R.N.A.S. are both turning toward pure bombing aeroplanes. He put me in touch with a man who designs them . . . George Keble Palmer, who's been designing for Handley Page for the past four years. I've spent a lot of time on the telephone with him. He has a design ready—his own, nothing to do with Handley Page—for a twin-engined heavy bomber."

"Where would we build these bombers?" Stephen asked, his eyes fixed on his son.

"We would have to build them at an airfield, so that they can be flown away when completed. I have confirmed that there is land available, cheap, abutting on Hedlington Airfield, four miles out of town. I calculate that we'll need roughly a million pounds to get started. We could share the capitalisation with Toledano's."

Mr Morgan whistled long and low. Richard stared at Johnny, his brain running fast. The young man had astonished him. This was a different person from the fellow who mooned over Stella like a lovesick calf.

Stephen turned to him, "What do you think?"

Richard said, "We can't make a final decision here and now, obviously. We must talk to Keble Palmer, face to face, look at his designs . . . but Johnny's right. I was thinking too small, and my vision was restricted to the ground. I say that we should work out what it will cost in money and time to start the sort of firm that Johnny has in mind . . . Can we keep Rowland's going, too? I don't know much about aircraft manufacture, but I do know there's a great deal of wood and fabric working, chemical doping, and so on. We'll have no jobs for many of Rowland's men at the aircraft factory."

Stephen said, "I think Johnny's right there, too. We should convert Rowland's to making shells. It'll be profitable, so we don't want to sell it. Who'd run it?"

"I could keep an eye on it," Richard said, "but the day to day supervision would have to be done by Bob Stratton. He's capable of it . . . if he's willing to stay."

"Then we have to find a plant foreman for the aircraft factory. We should look in the body shops, I suppose."

"I wish more than ever that we could get Frank Stratton out of the army," Richard said. "If there's conscription, I suppose he could be ordered out of uniform, just as legally as other people would be ordered in."

"We'll try again, once we agree on the whole idea, in principle," Stephen said. "But there's one small matter that we have not settled. Who's going to supervise the aircraft factory—let's call it the Hedlington Aircraft Company?"

"Well, I suppose I'd be the overall director," Richard said.

"Yes, but who's going to be the man on the spot?"

Morgan looked at Overfeld; Overfeld looked at Richard; Stephen looked at his son. Slowly the others did, too. Stephen said, "You've talked yourself out of the R.F.C., Johnny."

Johnny said, "But Dad . . . I've promised . . . I've said . . ."

"Yes, and then you have come up with an idea that we ought to have thought of for ourselves. This is your baby . . . and you must raise it. You'll have Mr Rowland here to turn to. We'll find you a good works foreman, somehow." He stood up, and held out his hand, "And, Johnny, don't tell me you really want to go to war. Mr Overfeld's been telling me how keen you have become and how good. You're a business executive, now, Johnny, and you're going to carry a heavy load of responsibility, for a great deal of money, and men's jobs, and soon, men's lives . . . Deputy Managing Director of the new firm . . . Congratulations!"

"Home, please, Kathleen," Richard said, settling back in the seat beside his wife. It was funny how one called most of the female staff by their Christian names, and the men by their surnames. He had never dreamed of calling Stafford anything but that . . . hadn't known what his Christian name was, to be truthful. In this particular case it might be something to do with class. Females qualified to be chauffeurs were all ladies, as yet, and rather adventurous ones at that.

"So," Susan said, "you're going to get another factory."

"I think so," he said, "though it can't be decided for a few weeks yet. We have a great deal of work to do on facts and figures."

"That'll make three," she said, "Rowland's, the J.M.C., and the one for aircraft . . . shells, lorries, and aeroplanes. Your babies."

He glanced at her, for there had been an odd intonation in her voice. She said, "They *are* your children, you know, and always have been. To you they mean what they would to anyone else, and also what the children we haven't had would have meant."

"Well, I don't think . . ." he began. She went on, as though he had not spoken, "I need children, Richard. I'm going to adopt two."

He stared at her, dumbfounded. "Adopt . . . two children . . . babies?"

"Not babies, children . . . about six or seven, I should think. War orphans. We can afford it."

"Of course, but . . ."

She put her hand over his on the seat. "I need them, Richard. Believe me."

He was silent then; there was nothing to say. He had neglected her for his work, he could not deny it. And she was right, that the plants he had supervised and the cars or trucks that they had turned out had been his beloved children, fruit of his brain rather than his loins.

"Very well," he said; and, a long while later, "Good."

The earl said, "So Hoggin's going to get the roof done for us. He knows a contractor who'll do it for half of what anyone else has quoted. And he'll lend me most of that, at low interest. Smart fellow, Hoggin."

"And unscrupulous," the countess said. "You should be very careful in any dealings with him, Roger."

"Of course I will be . . . am," the earl said. "Have to have him down for tea one day . . . or a drink. That would be more his line."

"A drink with you in the study," she said firmly, "and you will have an appointment half an hour later."

"All right, all right," the earl said. He rubbed his hands in front of the fire. His wife was sitting to one side, knitting. He said, "We're

going to get that swine Gorse tonight. Skagg has information as to just
where and when he's coming. We'll give him something to remember
us by. We'll teach him to poach my birds . . . and have the infernal
impudence to announce ahead of time when he's going to do it."

His wife said, "Roger, you are obsessed with Probyn Gorse. He has
you bewitched. You would do better to be thinking about Cantley."

"He won't be sent to France for weeks or months yet," Swanwick
said, "he has to be trained. The Coldstream don't want any raw ensigns
in the trenches."

"But he *will* be sent, sooner or later."

The door opened and two young women came in, their elder daugh-
ter, Lady Barbara Durand-Beaulieu and their widowed daughter-in-law,
Mrs Arthur, wearing the evening dress uniform of Queen Alexandra's
Imperial Military Nursing Service, which she had joined, from St
Mary's Hospital, the day after Arthur's death had been confirmed. She
was at present a ward sister in the big military hospital at Netley, on
the Solent, but spending forty-eight hours' Christmas leave with the
Swanwicks.

"Some waits are coming up the drive," Lady Barbara said cheerfully,
"led by old Commander Quigley, I think." She spent so much time in
the stables now that, however much she washed and bathed and perfumed, a slight, pleasant aura of horse manure always hung around
her.

"Oh God," the earl cried, "I heard enough carols from those
blighters from Brighton the other day—if that's where they really came
from . . . Came here just to poach a deer or two for Christmas venison,
if you ask me—gave Skagg a devil of a time. You go and listen to them.
Tell 'em I've got a cold, anything. I suppose you'll have to invite them
in for a drink afterwards."

"We always have, and always will," the countess said placidly. "Run
along, girls."

As soon as they were alone again, she said, "When the waits leave,
we must talk about that . . . girl. Florinda Gorse. Cantley must be
made to give her up before she's in a position to sue him for something."

"What use can she be to him when he's at Windsor? He may already have given her her marching orders."

"Or she's left him, because he's not rich enough. We're going to face
hard times, Roger, unless the war ends soon and Cantley can go back to
Toledano's and start making some real money, a great deal of money."

"We've faced 'em before," the earl said. "Come on, I suppose we
ought to go out and listen to those bloody waits."

Archie Campbell reached behind him, without looking, found the bottle, lifted it round, and drank. His eyes never left the painting on the easel before him. It was a landscape, half impressionist, half abstract. It had started out as an early winter scene in Hampshire. He'd done the preliminary sketches and applied the first broad brush strokes near Winchester. There'd been the steeple of a village church in the background, meadows, cows, hedges, a stream, trees along the line of it, a farm house; and one figure, a man carrying two heavy pails of milk, in the foreground, coming toward you.

He leaned forward to look more closely at the man, and stumbled into the easel, just grabbing it in time before it fell, then lurching back, to rest his buttocks against the table behind him. Must be losing his balance . . .

He was losing his balance, that's why the malt whisky was low in the bottle—not the other way round. Because the painting had changed, not overnight, but in the days he'd been working on it. The steeple had gone, painted out, flattened, you might say. The farm house was there, but it was only a ruin now, as he stared at it—and how had that happened? The rich green grass had turned dirty brown-green, and uneven. By daylight you'd swear there were holes, big holes, full of water or snow . . . The cows were lumps. That was the trouble with abstractions—*you* knew they were cows, but if you painted them in the abstract, how did anyone else know they were cows? Another viewer might see them as sheep, or bushes, or dead bodies.

And the man struggling along, with shoulders bowed under the milk pails, was . . . Christ, he had become a soldier, ammunition boxes slung from his shoulders, the square-edged shapes of full ammunition pouches across his chest, bayonet and entrenching tool at his side, the steel helmet an inverted bowl on his head, his eyes gleaming a terrible white.

It was no use trying to deny it. Perhaps he was avoiding the war, perhaps not, but it had come to him . . . come *for* him! He reached for the bottle again, and again drank, staring at the painting on the easel. It wavered, moved before his eyes, surging in and out of focus, everything in it becoming more clear to his eyes—a soldier, heavy laden, on the blasted battlefield, corpses, the soldier at the limit of his strength and endurance.

The telephone rang. Archie turned slowly, listening, staring. It rang and rang and rang. Archie carefully replaced the bottle on the table, and went out.

Ten minutes later he barged in through the doors of the Chelsea recruiting centre, fell to his knees, pulled himself up by holding onto the table in front of him, and said, "I wanna join up . . . Argylls."

Two sergeants behind the desk looked him up and down, grinning. One said, "You're right to choose a *Scotch* regiment, laddie, we can see that."

"I'm a Campbell," Archie cried, "a bluidy Campbell. So I mun go to the Argylls. If they'll take me!"

The sergeant said, "It's Christmas Eve, laddie. An' ye've had a drop or two too much. We can't pin the ribbon on you in this state. Come back in the morning . . . not tomorrow, Boxing Day, eh?"

"I wanna join the Argylls, now!" Archie said, weaving and half falling. "Take me away *now!*"

The other sergeant muttered to his comrade, "That's a good suit of clothes, Bill. He'll like as not fall down and freeze to death if he tries to walk home . . . We'd best send him home in a taxi. He'll be back on Boxing Day, if he means it."

No waits ever came to Probyn Gorse's cottage and none came this evening; but about eight o'clock Skagg the head keeper came, with a brace of rabbits, and banged on the closed door.

"Your granddad in?" Skagg asked innocently.

"I don't see him," Fletcher said.

Over the young man's shoulder Skagg saw Florinda and the Woman, at the stove. Probyn might be in the bedroom . . . but the dog hadn't barked. He was out with Probyn, on the job, that's why. But in case he was wrong, one of the new men had been watching the cottage since afternoon—just as an extra precaution: though now that he knew when and where Probyn was going to take the pheasants, it didn't really matter how he got there.

He lifted up the rabbits, "Compliments of his Lordship, for all of you. Merry Christmas."

Fletcher took the rabbits with a nod, but no word. Skagg walked off and Fletcher closed the door behind him. He threw the rabbits to the Woman, then sat down at the table and picked up the book he had been reading.

Florinda said, "I'm going back to London tomorrow, soon's Granddad gets home."

Fletcher put down the book. He knew that his sister wanted to talk to him, or she would not have interrupted his reading. He said, "Back to the same place? Cantley's leaving you there?"

"He told me he'd have to give it up by the end of January."

"So you're coming home? Don't reckon Lady S will want you back in the Big House, though."

"I'm going to get married."

The Woman stopped her stirring but said nothing, listening. Fletcher said, "To Cantley?"

"He didn't ask me. Another man did."

"Who?"

"The Marquis of Jarrow."

"We *are* high and mighty, aren't we?" Fletcher said, grinning and slapping Florinda's hand as it lay on the table beside his book. "Who the hell is he when he's at home?"

"He owns a dozen coal mines and most of Newcastle-on-Tyne."

"So he says."

"So Cantley says. He found out for me, after I told him. Cantley's a good man . . . I wish he'd asked me, but he didn't."

"And the Marquis of Jarrow is tall and handsome and strong, with wavy fair hair, an' he's the best horseman in England, and . . .'"

"He's sixty-one, about five foot nothing, and sozzled most of the time."

"And you're going to marry him?"

She shrugged. "Why not? He's not going to last more than a year or two. It's worth it. I know where I'm going."

"Good luck," he said, picking up his book once more. He read half a dozen pages from *Leaves of Grass*, the cottage instantly sinking from his consciousness as he read, to be replaced by shouting cities, waving corn, whistling axe blades . . . wind, movement . . .

"Hey!" Florinda said, "you're breathing like you've just run a mile after a girl."

"I don't run after girls," he said. "They run after me."

"Read aloud, Fletcher."

Out of the cradle endlessly rocking
Out of the mock-bird's throat, the musical shuttle,
Out of the ninth-month midnight,
Over the sterile sands, and the field beyond, where the child leaving his
    bed wander'd alone, bareheaded, barefoot,
Down from the shower'd halo,
Up from the mystic play of shadows twining and twisting as if they
    were alive,
Out from the patches of briers and blackberries,
From the memory of the bird that chanted to me,

*From your memories, sad brother, from the fitful rising and falling I
    heard,*
*From under that yellow half-moon late risen and swollen as if with
    tears,*
From those beginning notes of yearning and love there in the mist,
From the thousand responses of my heart never to cease,
From the myriad thence arous'd word,
From the word stronger and more delicious than any.

He paused, sucking in a deep breath, and said, "'Tis like a magician
. . . I don't understand, but I do. I . . ."

She interrupted him. "Are you writing anything?"

"Not since I got these—Shelley and Whitman. I'm not good
enough."

"Yes, you are! Don't be afraid. They're dead."

"I know that, you silly cunt."

"I mean, this is 1915. What you say will be different from what they
said—when was it?"

"Damned if I know."

"Well, it wasn't *now* . . . You've got to write! That's why squire lent
you those books. Not just to read them . . . that would be like putting
the bull to the cow, and nothing happening. Those books are the bull,
and you're the cow. You got it inside you. Squire expects it to come out
—poetry . . . They're saying in the village you ought to be in France."

"I don't care what the buggers are saying. Nor did you, till just
now."

She said earnestly, "Fletcher, I told you I know where *I'm* going. I
was meant to be a lady . . . rich and beautiful. That's what I have
to be, and I'm going to be. You were meant to be a poet. If you won't
be a poet, the only other thing you can be is a man . . . a fighting
man. Either write your poetry, or join the army. Otherwise you're wasting your life. I won't have it."

He did not answer but took up the book again. This time he was not
transported; for his sister's vehemence had brought his own poems back
into his mind. They were tucked away in a drawer in the bedroom. He
sat awhile, thinking, then closed the book, went to the bedroom and
brought out his poems, with his stub of pencil, and began to pore over
them, listening to the rhythms, painfully inscribing a correction here,
removing a word there; until suddenly he jumped up. "I'm going to
have a couple at the Arms."

Bob Stratton sat in the front parlour at 85 Jervis Street, reading the paper and listening with half an ear to his wife and daughter talking in low tones across the fireplace from his chair.

Jane said, "Isn't that just like Master Guy, to go and hide himself when they want to give him a medal and the key to Hedlington!"

"Where's he gone?" Ethel Fagioletti asked listlessly.

"To the Lake District. Mr Harry told your Dad—wants to walk in the mountains, alone, he said. Won't come home till New Year's Day . . . just to say goodbye to his mother before he goes into the Flying Corps . . . His picture in all the papers, and everything! What a boy he is!"

"Man now," Bob said. "He's killed someone."

"He had to! In self-defence!"

"So they say."

"And a good thing, too! That girl would be dead but for him . . . and goodness knows how many more women . . . all cut up . . . and he didn't really have a bad foot even, that was just disguise, ugh!" She shivered. "Don't let's talk about it . . . You must speak to Willum about Violet, Bob."

"Little Violet?"

"She's not so little any more, Bob. Eleven now, and can't fit into her dresses, at the top . . . She's been caught stealing—sausages, it was, from Adkin's. He caught her, and spanked her and sent her home . . . but Mr Adkin told me that if he ever catches her again, he'll have the police on her. He knows I take an interest in them."

"What can Willum say? It's Mary who has to teach the girl."

"She needs a father's hand," Jane said. "Even Willum's better than no father."

Ethel burst into tears, as though the word 'father' had opened a tap.

"Don't cry now," her mother said sharply, "you're going to be free on December 29th, and Mr Willbanks wants to marry you. You're better off than you deserve, sitting and moping over that dirty Eyetalian."

"But I love him," Ethel sobbed. "He'll come back to me when he's got over his infatuation with that woman."

"Oh no, he won't!" her mother cried, "because you won't have him! The very idea! Have you no pride? After him making you sign that paper that you'd been going with other men! *You* ought to be divorcing *him*, not the other way round, that's what! Make him pay, what's it called, alimony."

"It doesn't matter," Ethel said.

Bob lowered his paper. "If you don't want to get married you ought to get a job in an office. Or a factory even. Mr Harry's always employed some women in the fabric shop, but now we're employing them every-where, and so are all the other factories in Hedlington, just about."

Ethel shuddered, "I couldn't work in a factory, Dad."

Jane said, "That Fagioletti was the one who couldn't make the ba-bies, if you ask me . . . probably going with dirty Italian women when he was supposed to be at work, and using himself up, and getting dis-eases . . . You marry Mr Willbanks, Ethel, and then everything'll be all right. He'll give you babies."

Ethel wiped her eyes and put away her handkerchief. She said, "I saw Anne with a man, last week."

"Where?" her mother said sharply, "what were they doing? What time was it?"

"They were outside Lloyds Bank," Ethel said, "about eleven o'clock, talking."

"In the morning?"

"Oh yes. I didn't want to interrupt, so I didn't speak to Anne."

"Do you know who the man was?"

"No, Mum."

Jane turned to her husband. "I'd best speak to Anne about this, Dad. It's Ethel who needs another man. Anne's got a husband, and she'll be getting herself into trouble if she's not careful. Even if she's seen talk-ing to a man in the street. What would Frank think, if he heard about it? There's people who'd write and tell him a thing like that."

"There are," Bob said. "Interfering old cows! She must be lonely, Jane."

"Better lonely than having your husband hear that you're a loose woman," she said.

Bob got up. "I'll just go down to the shed for half an hour. There's a little job I have to do on Victoria."

"Wait a minute, Bob. I hear the waits outside—and isn't that some-one knocking at the door?"

Bob got up. Nellie was out with a young man who was sweet on her. He opened the door to face a group of carol singers in the street and, on the doorstep, Miss Alice Rowland. He stared, doubting his eyes. "Miss Alice . . . what . . . ?"

The carol singers burst into *The First Nowell.*

Alice raised her voice. "May I come in, Mr Stratton? Thank you."

He followed her through to the parlour. Jane and Ethel were on their feet, Ethel half curtseying. Alice said, "Frank's been wounded, Mrs Stratton. He's in Lady Blackwell's Hospital."

"Here? In Hedlington?" Jane cried, tears bursting from her eyes. Bob put his arm round her shoulder to support her. "How bad is he?"

"In critical condition, I'm afraid," Alice said, "but the doctor who called us up said he's conscious most of the time, and he's so fit and strong, that they're sure he'll pull through. We thought we should tell you so that you can pass it on to Anne in any way you decide . . . You can visit the hospital in normal visiting hours, though whether you'll be able to see Frank will depend on his condition at the time."

Jane sank into a chair, dabbing her eyes. "Thank you, Miss Alice," she muttered. "Give our respects to your mother and father."

"I will," Alice said. She turned and went out, followed by Bob. In the hallway she said to him in a low voice, "He's lost one kidney, has a punctured intestine, and punctured right lung. He was operated on in France. The lung's draining now, but they think they may have to operate again on the intestine as there's a blockage . . . but the doctor was very hopeful. He really was. And of course he'll never have to go back to France."

"Thank you," Bob muttered. She went out, turning suddenly at the kerb. "Oh, I nearly forgot. My father would like to talk to you, at our house, tomorrow morning, about nine."

She walked away and Bob stood, staring at the waits. They finished *The First Nowell* and began another. He found a shilling in his pocket, walked slowly down to them, and gave it to their leader, then turned and re-entered his house, head bowed.

One group of waits had been and gone from Walstone Manor. Johnny and Betty Merritt and Stella Cate were still out carolling with another group. Stephen Merritt was upstairs in his room, changing for dinner. Laurence Cate sat with his father beside the big fire leaping in the drawing-room grate.

He was seventeen now, by over a month; he had been given the beastly hunter, and every day uneasiness grew in him. Walking Beighton Down, hoping to spot one of the few carrion crows, or even rarer hen harriers . . . slowly searching the Scarrow for three miles up and down stream from Walstone for waterfowl . . . sitting in the woods, quiet, until the wrens came to feed from his hand—all these, which had been the solaces of so many earlier holidays, no longer kept him content. His voice had long since broken, and he suffered unaccustomed stirrings and inexplicable emotions when girls passed close, or touched him. He knew that he was at an in-between stage, no longer a boy, not yet a man. He'd seen Guy the day before Guy had killed the Ripper and in him the change had already taken place. He was no longer the brilliant schoolboy who had bowled for Kent last year. He was not much changed in appearance—a little taller, a little firmer, stronger seeming everywhere, but in manner he was different. Laurence had been almost afraid to call him 'Guy'; and would be even more so now, after the killing. He shivered suddenly.

After a time he spoke to his father. "Do you think they'll bring in conscription, Daddy?"

Christopher Cate rested his book on his lap. "I think so, soon."

"Do you think it's a good idea?"

Cate paused to collect his thoughts. He said, "You must remember that the army has been feared and hated in England ever since Cromwell ruled the country with it. It's an illegal organisation."

"Illegal?" Laurence said, startled. "What do you mean?"

"The Army Act is the law that enables the army to function—sets out powers of discipline and punishment, describes military crimes, and so on. But it is not effective unless Parliament passes another act, the Army *Annual* Act, every year. That gives the Army Act force—but only for one year. The reasoning is that if the army, under some modern Cromwell, tried to seize power, there would shortly be no authority for anyone to give orders, or get paid, in it. So, to impose conscription would be a very big step for England to take, but it's the only efficient way . . . and you can say that it's the only fair way . . . that everyone should serve his country, and let the experts decide in just what way, what service each should give. I can not deny all that. But I still do not like it. I do not think it is fair, though it appears to be."

"Why not?"

Christopher said, "People say it's wrong that the best should go first . . . and when they say that, they often mean the most educated, the richest—the upper class. There are as *good* men and women in every class . . . but I say that it is *right* for the upper class to go first. The ordinary people of England work hard for very little, Laurence. Many go to bed hungry every night. Many have to go barefoot . . ."

"Not here, Daddy," Laurence interjected.

"Some, sometimes . . . many, in the big city slums, in the coalpits, in the factory towns, when there is not enough work, in the mill towns, when the Americans and Japanese and Indians sell cheaper cotton goods here . . . We live in a country where there is no threat of revolution. We are secure in our possessions. Our tenants and labourers do not lie in wait to shoot us in the back from behind walls as we pass, or kill us with sickles when we go to watch the harvesting. Our servants are the best in the world, but still Englishmen, looking you straight in the eye . . . We have the pick of the world's materials to use for our own purposes—to eat, drink, make clothes, shoes, motor cars. We owe the country, and the common people something. They give us a stand-ard of living, a way of life, unequalled in history. We owe them, in re-turn, our lives, whenever we are called upon to give them. If someone falls in a lake, or the sea, it's a gentleman's duty—and privilege—to go first to rescue him. If a house catches fire, it is our privilege to go into it first, and try to save life. And when there is a war such as this—it is our privilege to go first, whether into the army, or into the enemy trenches —at whatever cost. Only so can we earn our position—and keep it."

Laurence stared into the dancing flames for a long time; then he said, "But Dad, what if no one follows—if the common people don't volun-teer?"

His father said, "If the ordinary people of England are not willing to fight to preserve the society we have built here in the past thousand years—then we have failed to make it good enough for them. We, our society, deserve to go down."

Again Laurence was silent a long time. When he spoke his voice sounded distant, even to himself. He said, "Daddy, I was wondering . . . do you think I could be a parson?"

Cate looked at him in astonishment. "A parson? A Church of Eng-land parson?"

"Yes," Laurence said, "I'd like to be rector here . . . Mr Kirby's pretty old . . . I could be his curate, and learn all about it, though I know what he does already, really."

Cate nodded his head, wondering. "Then you'd be squire and par-son. It's called squarson. We've done it before. Your great-great-great-grandfather was squarson . . . lived here, not in the Rectory, of course . . . You'd still go to the university, but you'd have to read something special, I suppose . . . classics rather than mathematics, if you were thinking of that."

Laurence's mouth felt dry and his hands were sweating. He should force himself at the jump, make the declaration from which he could not back away: but he said, "I'll ask the housemaster about becoming a parson, and then . . . well, if the war ends, soon, I'll go to Oxford, oth-erwise . . . I'll go into the Wealds when I'm eighteen, and then go to Oxford after the war. Do you think that'll be all right?"

"Of course," his father said heartily. "Do another year at Char-terhouse, and then we'll know what the situation is. Conscription will probably be in by then, and we'll have to see what its terms are. But you won't go to France till after you're eighteen and a half, at least. There's been a good deal of protest about sending children to the slaughter . . . Here come our carollers." He stood up as Johnny, Betty, and Stella trooped in. "How do you like our old English customs, Betty?"

"Oh, it was lovely," Betty Merritt cried. "The village so beautiful, the thatched houses, the people coming out to talk to us . . . the glasses of ginger wine . . . and a *gorgeous* young man, not very tall, but slender, and *so* handsome, with lazy eyes." She turned to Stella. "The young man who came out of the Beaulieu Arms and sang two or three carols with us? No one introduced him. Was that the famous Guy?"

Stella said, "That was Fletcher Gorse, our head poacher's grandson."

Stephen Merritt came in, smiling; followed closely by Blyth, the butler. "Dinner is served, sir," he said. "And I took the liberty of providing Mrs Abell with three shillings, a dozen sixpences, and half a dozen threepences to put into the Christmas pudding, as usual."

"Thank you, Blyth. Remind me to pay you back tomorrow. And tell Mrs Abell we'll be five minutes—no more, I swear."

Bob had waited all day, waited till Ethel had gone to bed. All day he waited, and thought, turning over in his mind what Mr Harry had said: what had been, and were, his own thoughts; what would be best. Only once had his thoughts changed their course—when they had visited Lady Blackwell's Hospital, with Anne. They had not seen Frank, but an old doctor had come out and told them he was in the same condition—critical, but holding his own: they should come again on Boxing Day, and might be able to see him.

He said, "Mr Harry's given control of Rowland's to Mr Richard."

Jane put down her sewing and waited. She knew that her husband had been thinking; and had waited for this moment.

"Mr Richard doesn't know for certain yet what he's going to do, but probably he'll be converting us to making shells. He and young Mr Merritt will be starting a new factory at the airfield, to make aeroplanes. He wants me to stay on as manager of Rowland's, whatever it makes in the end. I'll get double the pay, because I'll be manager, not foreman."

She waited till she was sure he had finished then said, "What do you want to do?"

He said, "I was looking forward to retiring last year, when Mr Harry asked me to stay on . . . I was going to work on Victoria . . . a little in the garden . . . take life easy . . . you know."

"I was afraid of it," she said firmly, "I didn't know what you would do with yourself, what you'd be like, with no Rowland's to go to every morning."

"I've been thinking the same thing, the last few months," he said. He fell silent, thinking now of the shed. If he had more time there, he would put up the poster more often. He saw Violet Gorse suddenly, as she looked with her skirt lifted and her drawers down . . . and closed his eyes, wincing. It would be the end of him. He must go on working . . . but making shells? It would be boring and dangerous, both; and there'd be a lot more women workers, and they'd be trouble.

He said, acting the devil's advocate, "Mr Richard would be my boss."

"You wouldn't see him unless you have some trouble you couldn't deal with," she said. "And you don't dislike Mr Richard. You're just afraid of him, because he's so modern, and you're not."

"You know what I think?" he said, his mind going off at a partial tangent. "They'd have asked me to be foreman of the new factory, but they want Frank, when he's better."

Jane said, "They didn't know about Frank in time . . . You don't know the first thing about aeroplanes, and you don't want to. That's why they didn't ask you."

Bob saw a tear in her eye and said, "He'll come through, love. God wouldn't let him die . . . I'll stay on! I'll show 'em I'm a better foreman than Frank will ever be."

She took up her sewing again, saying, "I think that's the right thing to do, Bob."

Probyn Gorse came down the hedge lines from Scarrow Rise toward Walstone at his usual pace, though the only light was that of the gibbous moon, still high in the sky, and he carried slung on his back the two heavy sacks of pheasants, each brace now labelled. He had spent two hours shaking off any possible pursuers, and now had six houses to visit, the six biggest in Walstone, excepting the Park. There he would not go, not because he was afraid to, but because the labels would not make sense there.

A week ago, when setting out from his cottage, he had reviewed the plans, and known that they were as good as could be. What remained then, beyond being always in the mercy of chance, was the execution—the doing. His helpers had done their jobs well. Mr Kipling, a famous writer Guy Rowland said, had hired the men in Brighton, just as Guy Rowland had plotted with him to do during the summer. That was before the Kipling boy was killed in France: Guy had told him that he'd written to Mr Kipling to say how sorry he was about the son and that of course the poaching plan was off as far as Mr Kipling was concerned. But Mr Kipling wrote back that he'd given his promise, and he'd do what he'd said, especially as it was the sort of prank that his son would have loved. In fact, the son had written about it from

France, just before he went missing, wishing he could be in Walstone on the great day.

Florinda had done just right. And Bert, sending the telegram—he'd given up a day's pay to do that, pretending to be sick. And Guy, of course, getting the labels written in gold writing at some posh place in London, and flying the aeroplane. What a noise those contraptions made! If flying them at night got more common, a man could let off guns all over, and the keepers wouldn't hear . . . Fletcher had been busy, too . . . first holding the torch for him; then running across the Park to distract the keepers chasing the Brighton men; then picking up the pheasants and taking them, with the Duke of Clarence, to the abandoned cottage in the fields below Scarrow Rise—where the pheasants had been hung from a burned beam, guarded by the Duke, these six days. The Duke was a hungry dog still, though Fletcher had left some meat for him, and Probyn had taken out a big chunk of beef earlier this night, when collecting the pheasants. The lurcher now trotted silently to heel. . . .

It was done. He had sworn he would make Swanwick and his keepers pay when they shot his dog, and took him for killing a pheasant that he'd found dead on the King's Highway. He'd used some tricks, but a man had to have a few up his sleeve, when he was setting himself against a lord and his armed gamekeepers. He'd have to tell squire the whole truth, one day—he'd enjoy it; but let the rest wonder how he'd done it. It wouldn't do them no harm.

He reached the outskirts of Walstone and paused, running through in his mind the order of the houses he would visit. Rectory first . . . then the Manor . . . then . . . He became aware that the motionless air was shaking, almost soundlessly—almost but not quite. His breath hung plumed in the frosty night as he stood in the moonshadow of the old Saxon church, square towered, flint built. Under his feet the earth trembled. Now he heard it plain—a heavy thudding, irregular but continuous, rising to crescendoes, falling, never dying.

A superstitious fear crept in his spine. What could be causing this unearthly movement of earth and sky? This was Walstone, this had been his land for centuries and more than centuries. He knew the feel of the earth and the touch of the air and the fall of the light—but this had never passed before. His fear mounted to a panic.

Planting his feet, he gripped the sacks more firmly and swore aloud, once. "I'll not turn back now!" he whispered, addressing the sky—for where else could the Being responsible for this reside?—and trudged rapidly up the Rectory path.

Christopher Cate was awakened by a knock on his bedroom door and the voice of Blyth from outside—"Sir!"

He had not been sleeping well and was fully awake in an instant, feeling uneasy. He switched on the bedside light and saw that it was after seven o'clock.

"What is it, Blyth?" he asked.

"May I come in, sir?"

"Come in." The door opened and the butler appeared, wearing an overcoat and scarf over his official trousers. "I hope I've done right, sir, but I've never heard of such a thing . . ."

"I'm sure you've done right. What is it?"

"I had risen, sir, and gone down to the pantry to make myself a cup of tea when I heard the front door bell ring. I went along as quickly as I could, but when I opened it, there was no one there."

"It's still dark, isn't it?"

"Oh, quite, sir . . . there was a package tied to the footscraper."

"Is it still there?"

"I thought I'd best leave it, sir, in case . . . well, I thought it might be a German bomb, you being the squire."

Christopher got out of bed, swung his feet into his bedroom slippers, and put on his dressing-gown. He still felt uneasy, but could not think why. "No one else about yet?"

"No, sir."

Christopher led downstairs and to the front door. It was cold out, the moon low, stars fading, and a green glow spreading in the east behind Scarrow Rise, the buildings of High Staining in silhouette a mile away on the shoulder of the slope. Two yellow lights in the outline showed where John Rowland and one of the land girls were preparing for the morning milk round.

The package by the footscraper was done up in thick brown paper and, as Blyth had said, firmly tied to the footscraper by a stout cord. He said, "Get me a knife, please."

While the butler was away his uneasiness crystallised. The dawn air was shaking, alive with a motion of its own, communicated now to the Queen Anne outer fabric of the Manor, shaking the medieval timbers of the inner walls, and the Roman stones of the foundations. His hand trembling slightly, but uncontrollably, he took the knife from Blyth's hand and, bending down, cut the cord and picked up the package. It was soft inside. He cut the string that held it closed and slowly pulled out a brace of pheasants, a cock and a hen. Their legs were tied together, with a white card attached, inscribed in a fine gold copper-plate hand:

*To the Squire of Walstone and Mrs Cate,
with best Christmas wishes from
The Earl and Countess of Swanwick.*

then, in smaller lettering at the bottom: *These birds have been hung
seven days.*

Cate held the birds in his hands, the gorgeous shot green and black
plumage of the cock spreading in a fan from the body. Cate saw none
of the beauty, for his inner eye was focussed, like his ears, on the foreign presence that was filling the air with menace. At last, he understood.

"The guns from France," he whispered.

"What's that, sir?"

"Listen . . . can't you hear?"

After a time, standing in silence by the door, his head cocked, the old
butler said, "I hear it, sir. What did you say it was?"

"The guns, from France."

"Goodness gracious, sir! That must be . . ."

"A hundred and forty miles away. But it's here now, here in England."

He turned into the house, carrying the birds. Blyth closed the door
behind them. "Will you be wanting breakfast now, sir, or will you go
back to bed? I do apologise for disturbing you, but I thought . . ."

"You did quite right . . . Merry Christmas!"

"Sir? Oh, yes indeed, Merry Christmas to you, sir."

"What am I to do with these birds?"

"Why, eat them, sir. Mrs Abell will be delighted to prepare them."

"You know where they came from . . . and it's not directly from His
Lordship."

A small smile crossed Blyth's cautious old face. "I may venture a
guess, sir. But I doubt that His Lordship will wish to make any in-
quiries, or see the birds back."

"The less said, the better, then? I think you're right . . . That old
scoundrel hoodwinked everyone. Take them. I'll get dressed and then
work in the library, and have breakfast at the usual time. We'll all leave
for church at a quarter to eleven. Make sure that boy Cyril has a dark
tie. The last one I saw him wearing was bright green."

"I instructed him last Tuesday to purchase a black one, sir, but he
said he had a right to wear whatever tie he chose, and he was in any
case going to leave your service in the New Year. There's a war on, he
informed me."

Christopher nodded: it was true. He said, "And you're leaving, too. This is your last Christmas with us."

"I have been thinking of that for some time, sir. It makes me very sad. But it can't be helped. I am getting too old to serve you as you deserve. Garrod will do all that I can, except perhaps in advising you on matters pertaining to the wine cellar. Women and wine were never meant to go together, except in an, ah, different context."

Christopher smiled and walked slowly away, along the empty passage, the first light now flowing in more strongly through the windows at the end, beyond the music room.

In the drawing-room he stood by a window, watching the light give life and colour, disclosing the lichen-covered sundial, the copper beech taking on its winter green, the robin landing on the windowsill beside him and tapping on the glass with its beak, demanding its right—food from the squire, food for a hard winter, food from the Men of Kent, whose companion it had been. Opening the window a little he could hear the guns still, but more faintly, as other presences in the daytime air gradually smothered them. They'd return with darkness, and thud louder and louder in men's ears, and more and more deeply shake the foundations of earth. Meanwhile it was another day, Christmas Day, a day of celebration, of worship, of prayers for strength, and of dedication for the next day . . . the next year . . . and the next . . .

The robin hopped in through the open window and cocked its head. Without taking his eyes off the little bird, Cate felt for the old biscuit tin on the windowsill beside him, opened it, and filled his hand with crumbs. Then he held it out. The robin hopped into the palm of his hand and began to peck away with great satisfaction, its red breast growing brighter every moment with the light.

"Who killed Cock Robin?" Cate murmured to it. "Not I, not I!"

AMONG THE WOUNDED
HOSPITAL FESTIVITIES PLANNED

This year, of course, peculiar interest attaches to the festivities in the hospitals, for practically every one has its quota of wounded soldiers. The wards, always bright and pleasant, are elaborately decorated. The Christmas fare will be good and plentiful, and the public has contributed in a most praiseworthy manner gifts of food and little luxuries, in addition to useful presents.

The wounded soldiers in the 1st London General Hospital at St Gabriel's College, Camberwell, will be provided with every luxury they can desire, thanks to the generosity of the public. Even the most seriously wounded can not help but catch the Christmas spirit of joy and happiness that prevails everywhere.

The wounded who have been apportioned to that wonderful building in Stamford Street which was to have been His Majesty's Stationery Office, and is now King George's Hospital for Wounded Soldiers are, under the circumstances, fortunate. Under the superintendence of the Marchioness of Ripon, who will be assisted by Coral Countess of Stafford, Mrs James, Mrs Beaumont Nesbitt, Lady Lister-Kaye, Mrs Holman Hunt and others, a splendid programme of festivities has been planned for the enjoyment of the thousand or eleven hundred men who now occupy the spacious wards.

The German artillery was plastering the British front line and reserve trenches and had been doing so since the dawn of the day before Christmas Eve. They had started firing because their High Command thought they had detected a British build-up and believed they were about to face another major assault. Their heavy batteries were concentrating on breaking up the coming attack—the targets being cross roads, villages or the remains of them, bridges, likely headquarters areas. Meanwhile, the British thought the violent artillery fire was the precursor of a German assault, and answered with their own counter-preparation fire. The lighter guns of the field artillery on both sides joined in from time to time, when alarms reached the observation posts, or the artillery officers themselves believed that the enemy were beginning the assault.

As the shells whistled through the frosty air for forty-eight hours, the infantry cowered deeper into their dugouts, or manned the firesteps, heads bent as though the protective crouch would guard them against shrieking shell splinters and the lead hail of shrapnel. Dead bodies were hit time and again, torn to pieces and scattered as manure over the frozen earth. The corpses hanging on the dense rows of rusty barbed wire were frozen in impossible angles. Dead horses lined the roads behind the front, legs extended, bellies blown up; it was cold, but they had been there a long time. In their dugouts officers took aim with pistols at the rats that owned the land, feeding on the flesh that lay everywhere, or had been stuffed into sandbags, or hung black out of the crumbling earth of a trench wall.

Where the trench lines were close a soldier shouted "Merry Christmas! *Fröhliche Weihnachten!"* and climbed out, waving a white handkerchief above his head.

Two rifle shots rang across the mutilated earth, and the soldier fell, struck by one bullet from in front and one from behind. He lay in frosty No Man's Land, moaning and moving, a long time, and died about eleven o'clock, when at home the bells were ringing for church.